The ADVENTURES
IN LITERATURE Program

ADVENTURES FOR READERS: BOOK ONE

Annotated Teacher's Edition
Teacher's Manual
Tests

ADVENTURES FOR READERS: BOOK TWO

Annotated Teacher's Edition
Teacher's Manual
Tests

ADVENTURES IN READING

Annotated Teacher's Edition
Teacher's Manual
Tests

ADVENTURES IN APPRECIATION

Annotated Teacher's Edition
Teacher's Manual
Tests

ADVENTURES IN AMERICAN LITERATURE

Annotated Teacher's Edition
Teacher's Manual
Tests

ADVENTURES IN ENGLISH LITERATURE

Annotated Teacher's Edition
Teacher's Manual
Tests

CURRICULUM AND WRITING

Fannie Safier
Secondary English Editorial Staff
Harcourt Brace Jovanovich, Publishers

Donna LeMole Saucier
Campbell Independent School
Campbell, Texas

Special Adviser
Jerome Smiley
Chairperson Elmont Memorial High School
Coordinator of English for
Sewanhaka Central High School District
New York

ADVENTURES
for Readers   Book Two

PEGASUS EDITION

Harcourt Brace Jovanovich, Publishers
Orlando   San Diego   Chicago   Dallas

ACKNOWLEDGMENTS

For permission to reprint copyrighted material, grateful acknowledgment is made to the following sources:

The Bodley Head Ltd.: "The Slaying of Humbaba" and "The Flower of Youth" from *Gilgamesh and Other Babylonian Tales* by Jennifer Westwood.

Brandt & Brandt Literary Agents, Inc.: "The Land and the Water" from *The Wind Shifting West* by Shirley Ann Grau. Copyright © 1973 by Shirley Ann Grau.

Curtis Brown (Aust.) Pty. Ltd.: "The Parachutist" from *Dadda Jumped Over Two Elephants and Other Stories* by D'Arcy Niland. Copyright © 1963 by D'Arcy Niland.

Curtis Brown Group Ltd., London: The Ugly Duckling by A. A. Milne. Copyright © 1941 by A. A. Milne.

Curtis Brown, Ltd.: "A Time of Beginnings" from *No Chinese Stranger* by Jade Snow Wong. Copyright © 1975 by Jade Snow Wong. Published by Harper & Row, Publishers, Inc.

Gerald Carson: Abridged from "The Glorious Bird" by Gerald Carson in *Natural History* Magazine, Vol. 88, No. 6, June–July 1979.

Don Congdon Associates, Inc.: "The Gift" by Ray Bradbury. Copyright © 1952 by Ray Bradbury, renewed 1980 by Ray Bradbury. "A Cap for Steve" by Morley Callaghan from *Esquire* Magazine. Copyright © 1952 by Esquire, renewed 1980 by Morley Callaghan.

Coward-McCann: "Calling in the Cat" from *Compass Rose* by Elizabeth Coatsworth. Copyright 1929 by Coward-McCann, Inc.; © renewed 1957 by Elizabeth Coatsworth.

Joan Daves: From the speech "I Have a Dream" by Martin Luther King, Jr. Copyright © 1963 by Martin Luther King, Jr.

Arthur Gordon: "The Sea Devil" by Arthur Gordon. Copyright 1983 by Arthur Gordon.

Grafton Books, a division of the Collins Publishing Group: "Antigone" in *Men and Gods* by Rex Warner.

Harcourt Brace Jovanovich, Inc.: "The Apprentice" from *Four-Square* by Dorothy Canfield. Copyright 1947 by Curtis Publishing Company, renewed 1975 by Downe Publishing, Inc. "old age sticks" from *Complete Poems 1913–1962* by E. E. Cummings. Copyright 1958 by E. E. Cummings. From "For My Sister Molly Who in the Fifties" in *Revolutionary Petunias & Other Poems* by Alice Walker. Copyright © 1972 by Alice Walker.

Harper & Row, Publishers, Inc.: From pp. 81–83 in *An American Childhood* by Annie Dillard. Copyright © 1987 by Annie Dillard. From pp. 13–16 in *Black Boy* (Retitled: "The Street") by Richard Wright. Copyright 1937, 1942, 1944, 1945 by Richard Wright.

Henry Holt and Company, Inc.: "The Road Not Taken" from *The Poetry of Robert Frost,* edited by Edward Connery Lathem. Copyright 1916, © 1969 by Holt, Rinehart and Winston; copyright 1944 by Robert Frost.

Houghton Mifflin Company: Shane by Jack Schaefer. Copyright 1949 by Jack Schaefer; © renewed 1976 by Jack Schaefer. The pronunciation key from *The American Heritage Dictionary of the English Language.* © 1981 by Houghton Mifflin Company.

Daniel Keyes and his agent, Richard Curtis Associates, Inc.: "Flowers for Algernon" by Daniel Keyes from *The Magazine of Fantasy and Science Fiction.* Copyright © 1959 by Mercury Press, Inc.

Alfred A. Knopf, Inc.: "Mother to Son" from *Selected Poems of Langston Hughes* by Langston Hughes. Copyright 1926 by Alfred A. Knopf, Inc., renewed 1954 by Langston Hughes.

Ursula K. Le Guin and her agent, Virginia Kidd: "The Rule of Names" by Ursula K. Le Guin. Copyright © 1964, 1975 by Ursula K. Le Guin.

CRITICAL READERS

CONTENTS

Part One THEMES IN LITERATURE

CHALLENGES   **9**

GENERATIONS   **77**

AMERICAN HERITAGE

Part Two FORMS OF LITERATURE

SHORT STORIES

203

DRAMA

285

NONFICTION

POETRY

Part Three LITERARY HERITAGE

WRITING ABOUT LITERATURE

ADVENTURES
for Readers   Book Two

PART I

THEMES IN LITERATURE

CLOSE READING OF A SELECTION

Developing Skills in Critical Thinking

Reading literature calls for you to follow carefully the sequence of events, to determine how one event may cause or affect a future event, and to understand the writer's purpose or the main idea of a selection. You must also *infer* or make logical guesses about characters and events when the writer doesn't tell you something directly. Reading demands action: you must question the writer's purpose, use of particular words, inclusion of some facts and omission of others. You must be aware of *what* the author is doing, *how* the author is doing it, and *why*.

In the following selection, Annie Dillard, an American writer, shows how her discovery of a book led to her realizing that a special relationship exists between a reader and an author. Use the notes alongside the selection to guide you in your reading. Then turn to the analysis on page 6.

FROM
An American Childhood
ANNIE DILLARD

The Homewood Library had graven[1] across its enormous stone facade: FREE TO THE PEO-PLE. In the evenings, neighborhood people— the men and women of Homewood— browsed in the library, and brought their children. By day, the two vaulted rooms, the adults' and children's sections, were almost empty. The kind Homewood librarians, after a trial period, had given me a card to the adult section. This was an enormous silent

Thinking Model

Why does Dillard mention the inscription?

What can we infer about Dillard from this statement?

1. **graven:** inscribed.

room with marble floors. Nonfiction was on the left.

Beside the farthest wall, and under leaded windows set ten feet from the floor, so that no human being could ever see anything from them—next to the wall, and at the farthest remove from the idle librarians at their curved wooden counter, and from the oak bench where my mother waited in her camel's-hair coat chatting with the librarians or reading—stood the last and darkest and most obscure[2] of the tall nonfiction stacks: NEGRO HISTORY and NATURAL HISTORY. It was in Natural History, in the cool darkness of a bottom shelf, that I found *The Field Book of Ponds and Streams*.

The Field Book of Ponds and Streams was a small, blue-bound book printed in fine type on thin paper, like *The Book of Common Prayer*. Its third chapter explained how to make sweep nets, plankton[3] nets, glass-bottomed buckets, and killing jars.[4] It specified how to mount slides, how to label insects on their pins, and how to set up a freshwater aquarium.

One was to go into "the field" wearing hip boots and perhaps a head net for mosquitoes. One carried in a "rucksack"[5] half a dozen corked test tubes, a smattering of screw-top baby-food jars, a white enamel tray, assorted pipettes and eyedroppers, an artillery of cheesecloth nets, a notebook, a hand lens, perhaps a map, and *The Field Book of Ponds and Streams*. This field—unlike the fields I had seen, such as the field where Walter Milligan played football—was evidently very well watered, for there one could find, and distinguish among, daphniae, planaria,

What words does she use to make the surroundings seem mysterious?

What is her purpose in listing the various devices?

Why does the "well-watered" field seem exotic or unusual?

2. **obscure:** not noticeable; indistinct.
3. **plankton:** tiny animals and plants.
4. **killing jars:** jars containing poison, used in preserving insects.
5. **rucksack:** a type of knapsack.

water pennies,[6] stonefly larvae, dragonfly nymphs,[7] salamander larvae, tadpoles, snakes, and turtles, all of which one could carry home.

That anyone had lived the fine life described in Chapter 3 astonished me. Although the title page indicated quite plainly that one Ann Haven Morgan had written *The Field Book of Ponds and Streams*, I nevertheless imagined, perhaps from the authority and freedom of it, that its author was a man. It would be good to write him and assure him that someone had found his book, in the dark near the marble floor at the Homewood Library. I would, in the same letter or in a subsequent one, ask him a question outside the scope of his book, which was where I personally might find a pond, or a stream. But I did not know how to address such a letter, of course, or how to learn if he was still alive.

I was afraid, too, that my letter would disappoint him by betraying my ignorance, which was just beginning to attract my own notice. What, for example, was this noisome-sounding substance called cheesecloth, and what do scientists do with it? What, when you really got down to it, was enamel? If candy could, notoriously, "eat through enamel," why would anyone make trays out of it? Where—short of robbing a museum—might a fifth-grade student at the Ellis School on Fifth Avenue obtain such a legendary item as a wooden bucket?

The Field Book of Ponds and Streams was a shocker from beginning to end. The greatest shock came at the end.

When you checked out a book from the Homewood Library, the librarian wrote your

What does this tell us about Dillard's attitude toward opportunities for women in the early fifties?

Reading is an active experience that invites questions and responses.

6. **daphniae . . . water pennies:** very tiny water creatures.
7. **larvae . . . nymphs:** immature stages in various insects' development.

number on the book's card and stamped the due date on a sheet glued to the book's last page. When I checked out *The Field Book of Ponds and Streams* for the second time, I noticed the book's card. It was almost full. There were numbers on both sides. My hearty author and I were not alone in the world, after all. With us, and sharing our enthusiasm for dragonfly larvae and single-celled plants, were, apparently, many Negro adults.

Reading is a shared activity.

Who were these people? Had they, in Pittsburgh's Homewood section, found ponds? Had they found streams? At home, I read the book again; I studied the drawings; I reread Chapter 3; then I settled in to study the due-date slip. People read this book in every season. Seven or eight people were reading this book every year, even during the war.[8]

Every year, I read again *The Field Book of Ponds and Streams*. Often, when I was in the library, I simply visited it. I sat on the marble floor and studied the book's card. There we all were. There was my number. There was the number of someone else who had checked it out more than once. Might I contact this person and cheer him up? For I assumed that, like me, he had found pickings pretty slim in Pittsburgh.

She couldn't find any viable streams or ponds.

The people of Homewood, some of whom lived in visible poverty, on crowded streets among burned-out houses—they dreamed of ponds and streams. They were saving to buy microscopes. In their bedrooms they fashioned plankton nets. But their hopes were even more vain than mine, for I was a child, and anything might happen; they were adults, living in Homewood. There was neither pond nor stream on the streetcar routes. The Homewood residents whom I knew had

Note the contrast between child's hopes and adults' hopes.

8. **the war:** World War II (1939–1945).

little money and little free time. The marble floor was beginning to chill me. It was not fair.

Her conclusion.

Analysis

In this excerpt from *An American Childhood*, Annie Dillard tells about her encounter with a remarkable library book: *The Field Book of Ponds and Streams*. When writers tell us about their childhood experiences, they tend to select and include only those details that will create a particular effect or serve their central purpose.

This passage by Dillard may be divided into three sections. First she describes the adult room of the library and her discovery of the field book; then she describes the field book and her reaction to it; finally she comes to realize the importance of the book for other readers.

Dillard begins by stating the motto inscribed over the library entrance: FREE TO THE PEOPLE. From this we can guess that the selection will be about receiving something, in this case—knowledge. She tells us that she has earned the trust of the librarians and is allowed to enter the adult section. (We can infer from this that, as a child, Dillard must have been an extremely good reader and mature for her age.) She describes the adult section in such a way that it seems more like a cathedral—a holy or sacred place—than a library; "an enormous silent room," "leaded windows set ten feet from the floor." And even though her mother and the librarians sit nearby, there remains something mysterious and secret about the room: "last and darkest and most obscure." In the "cool darkness of a bottom shelf," as if she is exploring a cave or feeling underwater, she discovers *The Field Book of Ponds and Streams* by the naturalist Ann Haven Morgan. She immediately compares the appearance of the field book to *The Book of Common Prayer*—the service book for the Church of England. We may infer that the field book will inspire or influence Dillard in a special way. The book reveals techniques for exploring the "field" of ponds and streams and for capturing and preserving creatures therein. In her imagination she moves beyond the barren, drab football field to an exotic, watery world of "daphniae, planaria, water pennies . . ." Dillard reads actively: she asks questions, has concerns, expresses amazement that a woman can write nonfiction with such "authority and freedom," considers the author a friend. Then she arouses our curiosity by saying: "The greatest shock came at the end."

Dillard discovers, to her delight, that reading a book is an experience that a reader shares not only with the author but also with many other readers—here, black adults from Pittsburgh's Homewood section. She imagines how the field book excites their hopes and dreams for leaving Homewood, finding a pond or stream, or buying a microscope. Then she realizes that, as a child, she still has a future opportunity to leave home and become a naturalist, but adults in Homewood have been denied that opportunity. She sums it up clearly: "It was not fair." Dillard has discovered much more about life from *The Field Book of Ponds and Streams* than its author ever intended.

With practice you can develop skill in reading and analyzing a literary work. Here are some guidelines to follow.

Guidelines for Close Reading

1. *Read for pleasure and for meaning.* Part of the enjoyment of reading good literature is thinking about it and sharing your thoughts.

2. *Read at a comfortable pace.* Gather in and appreciate details of narrative and style.

3. *Look up unfamiliar words and phrases.* Try to get the meaning of unfamiliar words and expressions from context, and then check the meaning in a dictionary.

4. *Read poetry aloud.* Your pleasure in poetry will be enhanced by listening to its sound.

5. *Take note of any interesting comparisons or unusual associations.* Be aware of language that appeals to your senses and comparisons that suggest imaginative relationships.

6. *Read actively, asking questions as you read.* Respond to clues and draw inferences from them. Dillard says that, as a child, she was allowed to check out books from the adult room. This means that she is reliable, responsible, a very good reader and probably mature for her age.

7. *Determine the author's overall purpose or the underlying meaning of the selection.* Try to phrase this idea in a sentence or two, in this fashion: *This narrative shows how Dillard discovered that great differences exist between opportunities open to a child and those available to adults.*

CHALLENGES

A challenge calls for a test of strength or skill. In this unit, "challenges" are situations where individual courage, honesty, strength, and intelligence are tested. The challenges in this unit take many forms. In one story, a man wages a life-and-death battle with a gigantic sea monster. In another story, a girl decides to protect and teach her handicapped brother. In another story, a boy faces a gang of bullies and wins pride and self-respect. All of the people in this unit are "tested" and prove themselves to be winners. You might find that some of their tests are ones that you yourself have already faced.

The No-Talent Kid

KURT VONNEGUT

Plummer was as tone-deaf as boiled cabbage. But he was determined to win a place with the A Band. All it finally took was a smart business deal—and an eight-foot bass drum.

It was autumn, and the leaves outside Lincoln High School were turning the same rusty color as the bare brick walls in the band-rehearsal room. George M. Helmholtz, head of the music department and director of the band, was ringed by folding chairs and instrument cases; and on each chair sat a very young man, nervously prepared to blow through something, or, in the case of the percussion section, to hit something, the instant Mr. Helmholtz lowered his white baton.

Mr. Helmholtz, a man of forty, who believed that his great belly was a sign of health, strength and dignity, smiled angelically, as though he were about to release the most exquisite sounds ever heard by men. Down came his baton.

"*Blooooomp!*" went the big sousaphones.

"*Blat! Blat!*" echoed the French horns, and the plodding, shrieking, querulous[1] waltz was begun.

Mr. Helmholtz's expression did not change as the brasses lost their places, as the woodwinds' nerve failed and they became inaudible rather than have their mistakes heard, as the percussion section shifted into a rhythm pattern belonging to a march they knew and liked better.

"A-a-a-a-ta-ta, a-a-a-a-a-a, ta-ta-ta-ta!" sang Mr. Helmholtz in a loud tenor, singing the first-cornet part when the first cornetist, florid and perspiring, gave up and slouched in his chair, his instrument in his lap.

"Saxophones, let me hear you," called Mr. Helmholtz. "Good!"

This was the C Band, and, for the C Band, the performance was good; it couldn't have been more polished for the fifth session of the school year. Most of the youngsters were just starting out as bandsmen, and in the years ahead of them they would acquire artistry enough to move into the B Band, which met in the next hour. And finally the best of them would gain positions in the pride of the city, the Lincoln High School Ten Square Band.

1. **querulous** (kwĕr′ə-ləs): fretful; complaining. In other words, it wasn't much like a waltz.

Violin Concerto (1971) by George Schreiber (1904–1971). Watercolor.
Courtesy of Kennedy Galleries, Inc., New York

The football team lost half its games and the basketball team lost two thirds of its, but the band, in the ten years Mr. Helmholtz had been running it, had been second to none until last June. It had been first in the state to use flag twirlers, the first to use choral as well as instrumental numbers, the first to use triple-tonguing extensively, the first to march in breathtaking double time, the first to put a light in its bass drum. Lincoln High School awarded letter sweaters to the members of the A Band, and the sweaters were deeply respected—and properly so. The band had won every statewide high school band competition in the last ten years—every one save the one in June.

As the members of the C Band dropped out of the waltz, one by one, as though mustard gas[2] were coming out of the ventilators, Mr. Helmholtz continued to smile and wave his baton for the survivors, and to brood inwardly over the defeat his band had sustained in June, when Johnstown High School had won with a secret weapon, a bass drum seven feet in diameter. The judges, who were not musicians but politicians, had had eyes and ears for nothing but this eighth wonder of the world, and since then Mr. Helmholtz had thought of little else. But the school budget was already lopsided with band expenses. When the school board had given him the last special appropriation he'd begged so desperately—money to wire the plumes of the bandsmen's hats with flashlight bulbs and batteries for night games—the board had made him swear that this was the last time.

Only two members of the C Band were playing now, a clarinetist and a snare drummer, both playing loudly, proudly, confidently, and all wrong. Mr. Helmholtz, coming out of his wistful dream of a bass drum bigger than the

one that had beaten him, administered the *coup de grâce*[3] to the waltz by clattering his stick against his music stand. "All righty, all righty," he said cheerily, and he nodded his congratulations to the two who had persevered to the bitter end.

Walter Plummer, the clarinetist, nodded back soberly, like a concert soloist receiving an ovation led by the director of a symphony orchestra. He was small, but with a thick chest developed in summers spent at the bottom of swimming pools, and he could hold a note longer than anyone in the A Band, much longer, but that was all he could do. He drew back his tired, reddened lips, showing the two large front teeth that gave him the look of a squirrel, adjusted his reed, limbered his fingers, and awaited the next challenge to his virtuosity.

This would be Plummer's third year in the C Band, Mr. Helmholtz thought, with a mixture of pity and fear. Nothing, apparently, could shake Plummer's determination to earn the right to wear one of the sacred letters of the A Band, so far, terribly far away.

Mr. Helmholtz had tried to tell Plummer how misplaced his ambitions were, to recommend other fields for his great lungs and enthusiasm, where pitch would be unimportant. But Plummer was blindly in love, not with music, but with the letter sweaters, and, being as tone-deaf as boiled cabbage, he could detect nothing in his own playing to be discouraged about.

"Remember, now," said Mr. Helmholtz to the C Band, "Friday is challenge day, so be on your toes. The chairs you have now were assigned arbitrarily.[4] On challenge day it'll be up to you to prove which chair you deserve." He avoided

2. **mustard gas:** a poisonous gas.

3. *coup de grâce* (kōo′də gräs′): finishing stroke (strictly speaking, the blow that ends suffering).
4. **arbitrarily** (är′ bə-trĕr′ə-lē): without any rules or standards.

the narrowed, confident eyes of Plummer, who had taken the first clarinetist's chair without consulting the seating plan posted on the bulletin board. Challenge day occurred every two weeks, and on that day any bandsman could challenge anyone ahead of him to a contest for his position, with Mr. Helmholtz as utterly dispassionate judge.

Plummer's hand was raised, its fingers snapping urgently.

"Yes, Plummer?" said Mr. Helmholtz, smiling bleakly. He had come to dread challenge days because of Plummer, and had come to think of it as Plummer's day. Plummer never challenged anybody in the C Band or even in the B Band, but stormed the organization at the very top, challenging, as was unfortunately the privilege of all, only members of the A Band. The waste of the A Band's time was troubling enough, but infinitely more painful for Mr. Helmholtz were Plummer's looks of stunned disbelief when he heard Mr. Helmholtz's decision that he hadn't outplayed the men he'd challenged. And Mr. Helmholtz was thus rebuked not just on challenge days, but every day, just before supper, when Plummer delivered the evening paper. "Something about challenge day, Plummer?" said Mr. Helmholtz uneasily.

"Mr. Helmholtz," said Plummer coolly, "I'd like to come to A Band session that day."

"All right—if you feel up to it." Plummer always felt up to it, and it would have been more of a surprise if Plummer had announced that he wouldn't be at the A Band session.

"I'd like to challenge Flammer."

The rustling of sheet music and clicking of instrument-case latches stopped. Flammer was the first clarinetist in the A Band, a genius that not even members of the A Band would have had the gall to challenge.

Mr. Helmholtz cleared his throat. "I admire your spirit, Plummer, but isn't that rather

ambitious for the first of the year? Perhaps you should start out with, say, challenging Ed Delaney." Delaney held down the last chair in the B Band.

"You don't understand," said Plummer patiently. "You haven't noticed I have a new clarinet."

"H'm'm? Oh—well, so you do."

Plummer stroked the satin-black barrel of the instrument as though it were like King Arthur's sword, giving magical powers to whoever possessed it. "It's as good as Flammer's," said Plummer. "Better, even."

There was a warning in his voice, telling Mr. Helmholtz that the days of discrimination were over, that nobody in his right mind would dare to hold back a man with an instrument like this.

"Um," said Mr. Helmholtz. "Well, we'll see, we'll see."

After practice, he was forced into close quarters with Plummer again in the crowded hallway. Plummer was talking darkly to a wide-eyed freshman bandsman.

"Know why the band lost to Johnstown High last June?" asked Plummer, seemingly ignorant of the fact that he was back to back with Mr. Helmholtz. "Because," said Plummer triumphantly, "they stopped running the band on the merit system. Keep your eyes open on Friday."

Mr. George Helmholtz lived in a world of music, and even the throbbing of his headaches came to him musically, if painfully, as the deep-throated boom of a cart-borne bass drum seven feet in diameter. It was late afternoon on the first challenge day of the new school year. He was sitting in his living room, his eyes covered, awaiting another sort of thump—the impact of the evening paper, hurled against the clapboard of the front of the house by Walter Plummer.

As Mr. Helmholtz was telling himself that he would rather not have his newspaper on challenge day, since Plummer came with it, the paper was delivered with a crash that would have done credit to a siege gun.

"Plummer!" he cried furiously, shaken.

"Yes, sir?" said Plummer solicitously[5] from the sidewalk.

Mr. Helmholtz shuffled to the door in his carpet slippers. "Please, my boy," he said plaintively,[6] "can't we be friends?"

"Sure—why not?" said Plummer, shrugging. "Let bygones be bygones, is what I say." He gave a bitter imitation of an amiable chuckle. "Water over the dam. It's been two hours now since the knife was stuck in me and twisted."

Mr. Helmholtz sighed. "Have you got a moment? It's time we had a talk, my boy."

Plummer kicked down the standard on his bicycle, hid his papers under shrubbery, and walked in sullenly. Mr. Helmholtz gestured at the most comfortable chair in the room, the one in which he'd been sitting, but Plummer chose instead to sit on the edge of a hard one with a straight back.

Mr. Helmholtz, forming careful sentences in his mind before speaking, opened his newspaper, and laid it open on the coffee table.

"My boy," he said at last, "God made all kinds of people: some who can run fast, some who can write wonderful stories, some who can paint pictures, some who can sell anything, some who can make beautiful music. But He didn't make anybody who could do everything well. Part of the growing-up process is finding out what we can do well and what we can't do well." He patted Plummer's shoulder gently. "The last part, finding out what we can't do, is what hurts most about growing up. But everybody has to face it, and then go in search of his true self."

Plummer's head was sinking lower and lower on his chest and Mr. Helmholtz hastily pointed out a silver lining. "For instance, Flammer could never run a business like a paper route, keeping records, getting new customers. He hasn't that kind of a mind, and couldn't do that sort of thing if his life depended on it."

"You've got a point," said Plummer, looking up suddenly with unexpected brightness. "A guy's got to be awful one-sided to be as good at one thing as Flammer is. I think it's more worthwhile to try to be better-rounded. No, Flammer beat me fair and square today, and I don't want you to think I'm a bad sport about that. It isn't that that gets me."

"That's very mature of you," said Mr. Helmholtz. "But what I was trying to point out to you was that we've all got weak points, and—"

5. **solicitously** (sə-lǐs′ə-təs-lē): with concern.
6. **plaintively**: sadly.

Plummer charitably waved him to silence. "You don't have to explain to me, Mr. Helmholtz. With a job as big as you've got, it'd be a miracle if you did the whole thing right."

"Now, hold on, Plummer!" said Mr. Helmholtz.

"All I'm asking is that you look at it from my point of view," said Plummer. "No sooner'd I come back from challenging A Band material, no sooner'd I come back from playing my heart out, than you turned those C Band kids loose on me. You and I know we were just giving 'em the feel of challenge days, and that I was all played out. But did you tell them that? Heck, no, you didn't, Mr. Helmholtz; and those kids all think they can play better than me. That's all I'm sore about, Mr. Helmholtz. They think it means something, me in the last chair of the C Band."

"Plummer," said Mr. Helmholtz evenly, "I have been trying to tell you something as kindly as possible, but apparently the only way to get it across to you is to tell it to you straight."

"Go ahead and quash[7] criticism," said Plummer, standing.

"Quash?"

"Quash," said Plummer with finality. He headed for the door. "I'm probably ruining my chances for getting into the A Band by speaking out like this, Mr. Helmholtz, but frankly, it's incidents like what happened to me today that lost you the band competition last June."

"It was a seven-foot bass drum!"

"Well, get one for Lincoln High and see how you make out then."

"I'd give my right arm for one!" said Mr. Helmholtz, forgetting the point at issue and remembering his all-consuming dream.

Plummer paused on the threshold. "One like the Knights of Kandahar use in their parades?"

"That's the ticket!" Mr. Helmholtz imagined the Knights of Kandahar's huge drum, the showpiece of every local parade. He tried to think of it with the Lincoln High School black panther painted on it. "Yes, sir!" When he returned to earth, Plummer was on his bicycle.

Mr. Helmholtz started to shout after Plummer, to bring him back and tell him bluntly that he didn't have the remotest chance of getting out of C Band ever; that he would never be able to understand that the mission of a band wasn't simply to make noises, but to make special kinds of noises. But Plummer was off and away.

Temporarily relieved until next challenge day, Mr. Helmholtz sat down to enjoy his paper, to read that the treasurer of the Knights of Kandahar, a respected citizen, had disappeared with the organization's funds, leaving behind and unpaid the Knights' bills for the past year and a half. "We'll pay a hundred cents on the dollar, if we have to sell everything but the Sacred Mace," the Sublime Chamberlain of the Inner Shrine was on record as saying.

Mr. Helmholtz didn't know any of the people involved, and he yawned and turned to the funnies. He gasped suddenly, turned to the front page again, looked up a number in the phone book, and dialed feverishly.

"Zum-zum-zum-zum," went the busy signal in his ear. He dropped the telephone clattering into its cradle. Hundreds of people, he thought, must be trying to get in touch with the Sublime Chamberlain of the Inner Shrine of the Knights of Kandahar at this moment. He looked up at his flaking ceiling in prayer. But none of them, he prayed, were after a bargain in a cart-borne bass drum.

He dialed again and again, always getting the busy signal, and walked out on his porch to relieve some of the tension building up in him. He would be the only one bidding on the drum, he told himself, and he could name his own price. If he offered fifty dollars for it, he could probably have it! He'd put up his own money, and get the school to pay him back in three years, when the plumes with the electric lights in them were paid for in full.

He lit a cigarette, and laughed like a department-store Santa Claus at this magnificent stroke of fortune. As he exhaled happily, his gaze dropped from heaven to his lawn, and he saw Plummer's undelivered newspapers lying beneath the shrubbery.

He went inside and called the Sublime Chamberlain again, with the same results. To make the time go, and to do a Christian good turn, he called Plummer's home to let him know where the papers were mislaid. But the Plummers' line was busy too.

He dialed alternately the Plummers' number and the Sublime Chamberlain's number for fifteen minutes before getting a ringing signal.

"Yes?" said Mrs. Plummer.

"This is Mr. Helmholtz, Mrs. Plummer. Is Walter there?"

"He was here a minute ago, telephoning, but he just went out of here like a shot."

"Looking for his papers? He left them under my spiraea."[8]

"He did? Heavens, I have no idea where he was going. He didn't say anything about his papers, but I thought I overheard something about selling his clarinet." She sighed and then laughed nervously. "Having money of their own makes them awfully independent. He never tells me anything."

"Well, you tell him I think maybe it's for the best, his selling his clarinet. And tell him where his papers are."

It was unexpected good news that Plummer had at last seen the light about his musical career, and Mr. Helmholtz now called the Sub-

lime Chamberlain's home again for more good news. He got through this time, but was momentarily disappointed to learn that the man had just left on some sort of lodge business.

For years Mr. Helmholtz had managed to smile and keep his wits about him in C Band practice sessions. But on the day after his fruitless efforts to find out anything about the Knights of Kandahar's bass drum, his defenses were down, and the poisonous music penetrated to the roots of his soul.

"No, no, no!" he cried in pain, and he threw his white baton against the brick wall. The springy stick bounded off the bricks and fell into an empty folding chair at the rear of the clarinet section—Plummer's empty chair.

As Mr. Helmholtz, red-faced and apologetic, retrieved the baton, he found himself unexpectedly moved by the symbol of the empty chair. No one else, he realized, no matter how untalented, could ever fill the last chair in the organization as well as Plummer had. He looked up to find many of the bandsmen contemplating the chair with him, as though they, too, sensed that something great, in a fantastic way, had disappeared, and that life would be a good bit duller on account of it.

During the ten minutes between the C Band and B Band sessions, Mr. Helmholtz hurried to his office and again tried to get in touch with the Sublime Chamberlain of the Knights of Kandahar, and was again told what he'd been told substantially several times during the night before and again in the morning.

"Lord knows where he's off to now. He was in for just a second, but went right out again. I gave him your name, so I expect he'll call you when he gets a minute. You're the drum gentleman, aren't you?"

"That's right—the drum gentleman."

The buzzers in the hall were sounding, marking the beginning of another class

8. **spiraea** (spī-rē′ə): a shrub in the rose family.

period. Mr. Helmholtz wanted to stay by the phone until he'd caught the Sublime Chamberlain and closed the deal, but the B Band was waiting—and after that it would be the A Band.

An inspiration came to him. He called Western Union, and sent a telegram to the man, offering fifty dollars for the drum, and requesting a reply collect.

But no reply came during B Band practice. Nor had one come by the halfway point of the A Band session. The bandsmen, a sensitive, high-strung lot, knew immediately that their director was on edge about something, and the rehearsal went badly. Mr. Helmholtz was growing so nervous about the drum that he stopped a march in the middle because of a small noise coming from the large double doors at one end of the room, where someone out-of-doors was apparently working on the lock.

"All right, all right, let's wait until the racket dies down so we can hear ourselves," he said.

At that moment, a student messenger handed him a telegram. Mr. Helmholtz beamed, tore open the envelope, and read:

DRUM SOLD STOP COULD YOU USE A STUFFED CAMEL ON WHEELS STOP.

The wooden doors opened with a shriek of rusty hinges, and a snappy autumn gust showered the band with leaves. Plummer stood in the great opening, winded and perspiring, harnessed to a drum on wheels that could have contained a dozen youngsters his size.

"I know this isn't challenge day," said Plummer, "but I thought you might make an exception in my case."

He walked in with splendid dignity, the huge apparatus grumbling along behind him.

Mr. Helmholtz rushed to meet him, and crushed Plummer's right hand between both of his. "Plummer, boy! You got it for us! Good boy! I'll pay you whatever you paid for it," he cried, and in his joy he added rashly, "and a nice little profit besides. Good boy!"

Plummer laughed modestly. "Sell it?" he said. "Heck fire, I'll give it to you when I graduate," he said grandly. "All I want to do is play it in the A Band while I'm here."

"But, Plummer," said Mr. Helmholtz uneasily, "you don't know anything about drums."

I'll practice hard," said Plummer reassuringly. He started to back his instrument into an aisle between the tubas and the trombones—like a man backing a trailer truck into a narrow alley—backing it toward the percussion section, where the amazed musicians were hastily making room.

"Now, just a minute," said Mr. Helmholtz, chuckling as though Plummer were joking, and knowing full well he wasn't. "There's more to drum playing than just lambasting[9] the thing whenever you take a notion to, you know. It takes years to be a drummer."

"Well," said Plummer cheerfully, "the quicker I get at it, the quicker I'll get good."

"What I meant was that I'm afraid you won't be quite ready for the A Band for a little while."

Plummer stopped his backing. "How long?" he asked suspiciously.

"Oh, sometime in your senior year, perhaps. Meanwhile, you could let the band have your drum to use until you're ready."

Mr. Helmholtz's skin began to itch all over as Plummer stared at him coldly, appraisingly. "Until hell freezes over?" Plummer said at last.

Mr. Helmholtz sighed resignedly. "I'm afraid that's about right." He shook his head sadly. "It's what I tried to tell you yesterday afternoon: nobody can do everything well, and we've all got to face up to our limitations. You're a fine boy, Plummer, but you'll never be

---

9. **lambasting** (lăm-băst'ĭng): beating or pounding.

rattle of the big drum as it followed its small master down the school's concrete driveway.

Mr. Helmholtz ran after him with a floundering, foot-slapping gait. Plummer and his drum had stopped at an intersection to wait for a light to change, and Mr. Helmholtz caught him there, and seized his arm. "We've got to have that drum," he panted. "How much do you want?"

"Smile," said Plummer. "Shrug! That's what I did." Plummer did it again. "See? So I can't get into the A Band, so you can't have the drum. Who cares? All part of the growing-up process."

"The situations aren't the same!" said Mr. Helmholtz furiously. "Not at all the same!"

"You're right," said Plummer, without a smile. "I'm growing up, and you're not."

The light changed, and Plummer left Mr. Helmholtz on the corner, stunned.

Mr. Helmholtz had to run after him again. "Plummer," he said sweetly, "you'll never be able to play it well."

"Rub it in," said Plummer, bitterly.

"But you're doing a beautiful job of pulling it, and if we got it, I don't think we'd ever be able to find anybody who could do it as well."

Plummer stopped, backed and turned the instrument on the narrow sidewalk with speed and hair-breadth precision, and headed back for Lincoln High School, skipping once to get in step with Mr. Helmholtz.

As they approached the school they both loved, they met and passed a group of youngsters from the C Band, who carried unscarred instrument cases and spoke self-consciously of music.

"Got a good bunch of kids coming up this year," said Plummer judiciously.[10] "All they need's a little seasoning."

a musician—not in a million years. The only thing to do is what we all have to do now and then: smile, shrug, and say, 'Well, that's just one of those things that's not for me.' "

Tears formed on the rims of Plummer's eyes, but went no farther. He walked slowly toward the doorway, with the drum tagging after him. He paused on the doorsill for one more wistful look at the A Band that would never have a chair for him. He smiled feebly and shrugged. "Some people have eight-foot drums," he said kindly, "and others don't, and that's just the way life is. You're a fine man, Mr. Helmholtz, but you'll never get this drum in a million years, because I'm going to give it to my mother for a coffee table."

"Plummer!" cried Mr. Helmholtz. His plaintive voice was drowned out by the rumble and

---

10. **judiciously** (jōō-dĭsh′əs-lē): wisely and carefully, like a judge.

Reading Check

1. What do the members of the A band receive?
2. Before the last competition, how many years in a row had the band won all the state contests?
3. What does Mr. Helmholtz think the band needs in order to win the next contest?
4. Why doesn't Mr. Helmholtz buy the drum that the Knights of Kandahar are selling?
5. What does Plummer say he will do with the drum if Mr. Helmholtz will not let him use it in the band?

For Study and Discussion

Analyzing and Interpreting the Story

1. In this humorous story, Mr. Helmholtz has a problem: he wants to beat Johnstown High School in the next statewide band competition. What does he think he needs in order to accomplish this?

2. Walter Plummer has a problem, too. Why does he want so much to be a member of the A Band?

3. How does Plummer plan to solve both problems?

4. Like all other comedies, this one ends with everyone happy and all problems solved. **a.** What compromise does Mr. Helmholtz finally propose? **b.** By accepting this offer, what will Plummer get?

5. Plummer may be "as tone-deaf as boiled cabbage," but he is certainly *not* a "no-talent kid." Tell what you think Plummer's talents are.

Language and Vocabulary

Using Footnotes, Glossary, and Dictionary

There are several methods you can use to find the meaning of an unfamiliar word in this book. You can check to see whether it is footnoted, as the word *querulous* is on page 11.

If an unfamiliar word isn't footnoted, it may be in the glossary in the back of this book. For example, you might not have known the meaning of the word *florid,* used on page 11 to describe the cornetist. The glossary defines *florid* in this way:

florid (flôr′ĭd) *adj.* Red-faced; ruddy.

The abbreviation *adj.* tells you that the word is an adjective. You will find a key to the pronunciations in the glossary at the back of this book.

A dictionary contains more information than either the footnotes or the glossary. A dictionary not only cites all the meanings a word has, but also tells something about the history of the word. For example, here is a complete dictionary entry for the word *florid* from *Webster's Ninth New Collegiate Dictionary.* (Like all dictionaries, this one uses its own symbols to indicate pronunciation.)

flor·id \′flȯr-əd, ′flär-\ *adj* [L *floridus* blooming, flowery, fr. *florēre*] (ca. 1656) **1 a** *obs*: covered with flowers **b** : excessively flowery in style : ORNATE **2** : tinged with red : RUDDY <a ~ complexion> **3** *archaic* : HEALTHY **4** : fully developed : manifesting a complete and typical clinical syndrome <the ~ stage of a disease> – **flor·id·i·ty** \flə-′rid-ət-ē, flȯ-\ *n* – **flor·id·ly** \′flȯr-əd-lē, ′flär-\ *adv*

From *Webster's Ninth New Collegiate Dictionary.* ©1986 by Merriam-Webster Inc., publisher of the Merriam-Webster® Dictionaries. Reprinted by permission of Merriam-Webster Inc.

The information in brackets tells the history of the word. The abbreviation *L* stands for "Latin." What Latin word does *florid* come from? What is its **obsolete** (*obs*) meaning— that is, a meaning that is no longer in use? What is its **archaic**, or old-fashioned, meaning? What other meanings for *florid* are listed in this dictionary entry?

Use the glossary to find the pronunciations and meanings of the italicized words in the following quotations from "The No-Talent Kid." Compare these definitions with what a dictionary tells you.

> . . . or, in the case of the *percussion* section, to hit something . . . .

> . . . to brood inwardly over the defeat his band had *sustained* in June . . . .

> . . . the days of *discrimination* were over. . . .

Writing About Literature

Explaining Motivation

The word **motivation** refers to some reason or cause for a person's actions. In "The No-Talent Kid," Plummer and Mr. Helmholtz both have goals and strong motivations for working toward those goals. Write a short paper in which you explain the motivation of either character. Give examples of behavior that reveals the character's motivation. Begin with a topic sentence such as this one:

> Plummer desperately wants to have a letter sweater and to be admired by the other band members.

To support your topic sentence, use specific details from the story.

For assistance in planning and writing your paper, see the section called *Writing About Literature* at the back of this textbook.

About the Author

Kurt Vonnegut (1922–)

Kurt Vonnegut tried many jobs before he finally became a writer. He studied biochemistry in college, and was a police reporter, a public-relations man, and a teacher. During World War II, when he served in the infantry, he was captured by the Germans and sheltered underground in a slaughterhouse in Dresden. He was in Dresden when that city was firebombed by the Allied forces. Vonnegut used his war experiences as the basis for *Slaughterhouse-Five*, one of his best-known novels.

Vonnegut is known for his science fiction and humorous social criticism. His science-fiction work includes *Player Piano*, his first novel, and *Cat's Cradle*. In the novels *Breakfast of Champions*, *Slapstick*, and *Jailbird*, he offers distinctive perspectives on the Nixon years and life in general.

Vonnegut's writing has won him a strong following among college students. He has written another story about Mr. Helmholtz, called "The Kid Nobody Could Handle." He has also written many science-fiction stories. One of these that you might enjoy is "EPICAC," which is about a computer that falls in love with a mathematician.

Raymond's Run

TONI CADE BAMBARA

Squeaky had a roomful of ribbons and medals and awards. But what did her brother Raymond have to call his own?

I don't have much work to do around the house like some girls. My mother does that. And I don't have to earn my pocket money. George runs errands for the big boys and sells Christmas cards. And anything else that's got to get done, my father does. All I have to do in life is mind my brother Raymond, which is enough.

Sometimes I slip and say my little brother Raymond. But as any fool can see, he's much bigger and he's older too. But a lot of people call him my little brother cause he needs looking after cause he's not quite right. And a lot of smart mouths got lots to say about that too, especially when George was minding him. But now, if anybody has anything to say to Raymond, anything to say about his big head, they have to come by me. And I don't play the dozens[1] or believe in standing around with somebody in my face doing a lot of talking. I much rather just knock you down and take my chances even if I am a little girl with skinny arms and a squeaky voice, which is how I got the name Squeaky. And if things get too rough, I run. And as anybody can tell you, I'm the fastest thing on two feet.

There is no track meet that I don't win the first-place medal. I used to win the twenty-yard dash when I was a little kid in kindergarten. Nowadays, it's the fifty-yard dash. And tomorrow I'm subject to run the quarter-meter relay all by myself and come in first, second, and third. The big kids call me Mercury[2] cause I'm the swiftest thing in the neighborhood. Everybody knows that—except two people who know better, my father and me. He can beat me to Amsterdam Avenue with me having a two-fire-hydrant head start and him running with his hands in his pockets and whistling. But that's private information. Cause can you

imagine some thirty-five-year-old man stuffing himself into PAL[3] shorts to race little kids? So as far as everyone's concerned, I'm the fastest and that goes for Gretchen, too, who has put out the tale that she is going to win the first-place medal this year. Ridiculous. In the second place, she's got short legs. In the third place, she's got freckles. In the first place, no one can beat me and that's all there is to it.

I'm standing on the corner admiring the weather and about to take a stroll down Broadway so I can practice my breathing exercises, and I've got Raymond walking on the inside close to the buildings, cause he's subject to fits of fantasy and starts thinking he's a circus performer and that the curb is a tightrope strung high in the air. And sometimes after a rain he likes to step down off his tightrope right into the gutter and slosh around getting his shoes and cuffs wet. Then I get hit when I get home. Or sometimes if you don't watch him he'll dash across traffic to the island in the middle of Broadway and give the pigeons a fit. Then I have to go behind him apologizing to all the old people sitting around trying to get some sun and getting all upset with the pigeons fluttering around them, scattering their newspapers and upsetting the wax-paper lunches in their laps. So I keep Raymond on the inside of me, and he plays like he's driving a stagecoach, which is OK by me so long as he doesn't run me over or interrupt my breathing exercises, which I have to do on account of I'm serious about my running, and I don't care who knows it.

Now some people like to act like things come easy to them, won't let on that they practice. Not me. I'll high-prance down 34th Street like a rodeo pony to keep my knees strong even if it does get my mother uptight so that she walks ahead like she's not with me, don't know me, is

---

1. **the dozens:** a game in which players trade insults. The first person who shows anger is the loser.
2. **Mercury:** the ancient Roman messenger god, known for his speed.

3. **PAL:** Police Athletic League.

all by herself on a shopping trip, and I am somebody else's crazy child. Now you take Cynthia Procter for instance. She's just the opposite. If there's a test tomorrow, she'll say something like, "Oh, I guess I'll play handball this afternoon and watch television tonight," just to let you know she ain't thinking about the test. Or like last week when she won the spelling bee for the millionth time, "A good thing you got *receive,* Squeaky, cause I would have got it wrong. I completely forgot about the spelling bee." And she'll clutch the lace on her blouse like it was a narrow escape. Oh, brother. But of course when I pass her house on my early morning trots around the block, she is practicing the scales on her piano over and over and over and over. Then in music class she always lets herself get bumped around so she falls accidentally on purpose onto the piano stool and is so surprised to find herself sitting there that she decides just for fun to try out the ole keys. And what do you know—Chopin's[4] waltzes just spring out of her fingertips and she's the most surprised thing in the world. A regular prodigy. I could kill people like that. I stay up all night studying the words for the spelling bee. And you can see me any time of day practicing running. I never walk if I can trot, and shame on Raymond if he can't keep up. But of course he does, cause if he hangs back someone's liable to walk up to him and get smart, or take his allowance from him, or ask him where he got that great big pumpkin head. People are so stupid sometimes.

So I'm strolling down Broadway breathing out and breathing in on counts of seven, which is my lucky number, and here comes Gretchen and her sidekicks: Mary Louise, who used to be a friend of mine when she first moved to Harlem from Baltimore and got beat up by everybody till I took up for her on account of her mother and my mother used to sing in the same choir when they were young girls, but people ain't grateful, so now she hangs out with the new girl Gretchen and talks about me like a dog; and Rosie, who is as fat as I am skinny and has a big mouth where Raymond is concerned and is too stupid to know that there is not a big deal of difference between herself and Raymond and that she can't afford to throw stones. So they are steady coming up Broadway and I see right away that it's going to be one of those Dodge City[5] scenes cause the street ain't that big and they're close to the buildings just as we are. First I think I'll just step into the candy store and look over the new comics and let them pass. But that's chicken and I've got a reputation to consider. So then I think I'll just walk straight on through them or even over them if necessary. But as they get to me, they slow down. I'm ready to fight, cause like I said I don't feature a whole lot of chitchat, I much prefer to just knock you down right from the jump and save everybody a lotta precious time.

"You signing up for the May Day races?" smiles Mary Louise, only it's not a smile at all. A dumb question like that doesn't deserve an answer. Besides, there's just me and Gretchen standing there really, so no use wasting my breath talking to shadows.

"I don't think you're going to win this time," says Rosie, trying to signify with her hands on her hips all salty, completely forgetting that I have whupped her many times for less salt than that.

"I always win cause I'm the best," I say straight at Gretchen, who is, as far as I'm concerned, the only one talking in this ventriloquist-dummy routine. Gretchen smiles, but it's

---

4. **Chopin** (shō′păn′): Frédéric François Chopin (1810–1849), a Polish composer and pianist.

5. **Dodge City:** the setting of the old television series "Gunsmoke," which often featured a showdown between the marshal and a gunfighter.

not a smile, and I'm thinking that girls never really smile at each other because they don't know how and don't want to know how and there's probably no one to teach us how, cause grown-up girls don't know either. Then they all look at Raymond, who has just brought his mule team to a standstill. And they're about to see what trouble they can get into through him.

"What grade you in now, Raymond?"

"You got anything to say to my brother, you say it to me, Mary Louise Williams of Raggedy Town, Baltimore."

"What are you, his mother?" sasses Rosie.

"That's right, Fatso. And the next word out of anybody and I'll be *their* mother too." So they just stand there and Gretchen shifts from one leg to the other and so do they. Then Gretchen puts her hands on her hips and is about to say something with her freckle-face self but doesn't. Then she walks around me looking me up and down but keeps walking up Broadway, and her sidekicks follow her. So me and Raymond smile at each other and he says, "Gidyap" to his team and I continue with my breathing exercises, strolling down Broadway toward the ice man on 145th with not a care in the world cause I am Miss Quicksilver herself.

I take my time getting to the park on May Day because the track meet is the last thing on the program. The biggest thing on the program is the Maypole dancing, which I can do without, thank you, even if my mother thinks it's a shame I don't take part and act like a girl for a change. You'd think my mother'd be grateful not to have to make me a white organdy dress with a big satin sash and buy me new white baby-doll shoes that can't be taken out of the box till the big day. You'd think she'd be glad her daughter ain't out there prancing around a Maypole getting the new clothes all dirty and sweaty and trying to act like a fairy or a flower or whatever you're supposed to be

when you should be trying to be yourself, whatever that is, which is, as far as I am concerned, a poor black girl who really can't afford to buy shoes and a new dress you only wear once a lifetime cause it won't fit next year.

I was once a strawberry in a Hansel and Gretel pageant when I was in nursery school and didn't have no better sense than to dance on tiptoe with my arms in a circle over my head doing umbrella steps and being a perfect fool just so my mother and father could come dressed up and clap. You'd think they'd know better than to encourage that kind of nonsense. I am not a strawberry. I do not dance on my toes. I run. That is what I am all about. So I always come late to the May Day program, just in time to get my number pinned on and lay in the grass till they announce the fifty-yard dash.

I put Raymond in the little swings, which is a tight squeeze this year and will be impossible next year. Then I look around for Mr. Pearson, who pins the numbers on. I'm really looking for Gretchen if you want to know the truth, but she's not around. The park is jam-packed. Parents in hats and corsages and breast-pocket handkerchiefs peeking up. Kids in white dresses and light-blue suits. The parkees unfolding chairs and chasing the rowdy kids from Lenox as if they had no right to be there. The big guys with their caps on backwards, leaning against the fence swirling the basketballs on the tips of their fingers, waiting for all these crazy people to clear out the park so they can play. Most of the kids in my class are carrying bass drums and glockenspiels[6] and flutes. You'd think they'd put in a few bongos or something for real like that.

Then here comes Mr. Pearson with his clipboard and his cards and pencils and whistles and safety pins and fifty million other things

6. **glockenspiels** (glŏk´ən-spēlz´): musical instruments, something like xylophones, often used in marching bands.

he's always dropping all over the place with his clumsy self. He sticks out in a crowd because he's on stilts. We used to call him Jack and the Beanstalk to get him mad. But I'm the only one that can outrun him and get away, and I'm too grown for that silliness now.

"Well, Squeaky," he says, checking my name off the list and handing me number seven and two pins. And I'm thinking he's got no right to call me Squeaky, if I can't call him Beanstalk.

"Hazel Elizabeth Deborah Parker," I correct him and tell him to write it down on his board.

"Well, Hazel Elizabeth Deborah Parker, going to give someone else a break this year?" I squint at him real hard to see if he is seriously thinking I should lose the race on purpose just to give someone else a break. "Only six girls running this time," he continues, shaking his head sadly like it's my fault all of New York didn't turn out in sneakers. "That new girl should give you a run for your money." He looks around the park for Gretchen like a periscope in a submarine movie. "Wouldn't it be a nice gesture if you were . . . to ahhh . . ."

I give him such a look he couldn't finish putting that idea into words. Grown-ups got a lot of nerve sometimes. I pin number seven to myself and stomp away, I'm so burnt. And I go straight for the track and stretch out on the grass while the band winds up with "Oh, the Monkey Wrapped His Tail Around the Flag-pole," which my teacher calls by some other name. The man on the loudspeaker is calling everyone over to the track and I'm on my back looking at the sky, trying to pretend I'm in the country, but I can't, because even the grass in the city feels as hard as sidewalk, and there's just no pretending you are anywhere but in a "concrete jungle" as my grandfather says.

The twenty-yard dash takes all of two minutes cause most of the little kids don't know no better than to run off the track or run the wrong way or run smack into the fence and fall

down and cry. One little kid, though, has got the good sense to run straight for the white ribbon up ahead so he wins. Then the second-graders line up for the thirty-yard dash and I don't even bother to turn my head to watch cause Raphael Perez always wins. He wins before he even begins by psyching the runners, telling them they're going to trip on their shoelaces and fall on their faces or lose their shorts or something, which he doesn't really have to do since he is very fast, almost as fast as I am. After that is the forty-yard dash, which I used to run when I was in first grade. Raymond is hollering from the swings cause he knows I'm about to do my thing cause the man on the loudspeaker has just announced the fifty-yard dash, although he might just as well be giving a recipe for angel food cake cause you can hardly make out what he's saying for the static. I get up and slip off my sweat pants and then I see Gretchen standing at the start-ing line, kicking her legs out like a pro. Then as I get into place I see that ole Raymond is on line on the other side of the fence, bending down with his fingers on the ground just like he knew what he was doing. I was going to yell at him but then I didn't. It burns up your energy to holler.

Every time, just before I take off in a race, I always feel like I'm in a dream, the kind of dream you have when you're sick with fever and feel all hot and weightless. I dream I'm flying over a sandy beach in the early morning sun, kissing the leaves of the trees as I fly by. And there's always the smell of apples, just like in the country when I was little and used to think I was a choo-choo train, running through the fields of corn and chugging up the hill to the orchard. And all the time I'm dreaming this, I get lighter and lighter until I'm flying over the beach again, getting blown through the sky like a feather that weighs nothing at all. But once I spread my fingers in the dirt and crouch over the Get on Your Mark, the dream goes and I am solid again and am telling myself, Squeaky you must win, you must win, you are the fastest thing in the world, you can even beat your father up Amsterdam if you really try. And then I feel my weight coming back just behind my knees then down to my feet then into the earth and the pistol shot explodes in my blood and I am off and weightless again, flying past the other runners, my arms pumping up and down and the whole world is quiet except for the crunch as I zoom over the gravel in the track. I glance to my left and there is no one. To the right, a blurred Gretchen, who's got her chin jutting out as if it would win the race all by itself. And on the other side of the fence is Raymond with his arms down to his side and the palms tucked up behind him, running in his very own style, and it's the first time I ever saw that and I almost stop to watch my brother Raymond on his first run. But the white ribbon is bouncing toward me and I tear past it, racing into the distance till my feet with a mind of their own start digging up footfuls of dirt and brake me short. Then all the kids standing on the side pile on me, banging me on the back and slapping my head with their May Day programs, for I have won again and everybody on 151st Street can walk tall for another year.

"In first place . . ." the man on the loudspeaker is clear as a bell now. But then he pauses and the loudspeaker starts to whine. Then static. And I lean down to catch my breath and here comes Gretchen walking back, for she's overshot the finish line too, huffing and puffing with her hands on her hips taking it slow, breathing in steady time like a real pro and I sort of like her a little for the first time. "In first place . . ." and then three or four voices get all mixed up on the loudspeaker and I dig my sneaker into the grass and stare at Gretchen, who's staring back, we both wonder-

ing just who did win. I can hear old Beanstalk arguing with the man on the loudspeaker and then a few others running their mouths about what the stopwatches say. Then I hear Raymond yanking at the fence to call me and I wave to shush him, but he keeps rattling the fence like a gorilla in a cage like in them gorilla movies, but then like a dancer or something he starts climbing up nice and easy but very fast.

dinner table, which drives my brother George up the wall. And I'm smiling to beat the band cause if I've lost this race, or if me and Gretchen tied, or even if I've won, I can always retire as a runner and begin a whole new career as a coach with Raymond as my champion. After all, with a little more study I can beat Cynthia and her phony self at the spelling bee. And if I bugged my mother, I could get piano lessons and become a star. And I have a big rep as the baddest thing around. And I've got a roomful of ribbons and medals and awards. But what has Raymond got to call his own?

So I stand there with my new plans, laughing out loud by this time as Raymond jumps down from the fence and runs over with his teeth showing and his arms down to the side, which no one before him has quite mastered as a running style. And by the time he comes over I'm jumping up and down so glad to see him—my brother Raymond, a great runner in the family tradition. But of course everyone thinks I'm jumping up and down because the men on the loudspeaker have finally gotten themselves together and compared notes and are announcing "In first place—Miss Hazel Elizabeth Deborah Parker." (Dig that.) "In second place—Miss Gretchen P. Lewis." And I look over at Gretchen wondering what the *P* stands for. And I smile. Cause she's good, no doubt about it. Maybe she'd like to help me coach Raymond; she obviously is serious about running, as any fool can see. And she nods to congratulate me and she smiles. And I smile. We stand there with this big smile of respect between us. It's about as real a smile as girls can do for each other, considering we don't practice real smiling every day, you know, cause maybe we too busy being flowers or fairies or strawberries instead of something honest and worthy of respect . . . you know . . . like being people.

And it occurs to me, watching how smoothly he climbs hand over hand and remembering how he looked running with his arms down to his side and with the wind pulling his mouth back and his teeth showing and all, it occurred to me that Raymond would make a very fine runner. Doesn't he always keep up with me on my trots? And he surely knows how to breathe in counts of seven cause he's always doing it at the

Raymond's Run   **27**

Reading Check

1. What is Squeaky's only chore at home?
2. Why does Squeaky have to take care of Raymond, who is older and bigger?
3. Where does Squeaky live?
4. What does she do while she walks with Raymond?
5. Who wins the fifty-yard dash?

For Study and Discussion

Analyzing and Interpreting the Story

1. In "Raymond's Run," a girl who believes in herself discovers the joy of believing in other people as well. What does Squeaky believe about her own abilities?

2. Squeaky believes in being honest. What actions of Cynthia Procter's irritate her?

3. Some people in the story think Squeaky should be a different kind of person. **a.** What would Squeaky's mother like her to do? **b.** What would Mr. Pearson like her to do?

4. Squeaky knows that she can win medals and "become a star." But she asks herself, "What has Raymond got to call his own?" After Raymond's run, what does Squeaky plan to do for her brother?

5. Squeaky also discovers something about her rival, Gretchen. Why do she and Gretchen smile at each other after the race?

6. Why do you think the author called this story "Raymond's Run"?

Literary Elements

Drawing Conclusions About a Character

In some stories, the writer may tell you directly that a character is loyal, or courageous, or mean, or dishonest. But in most stories, the writer lets you draw your own conclusions about a character's personal qualities.

In "Raymond's Run," for example, you learn a great deal about Squeaky from what she says and does, and even from what she thinks. But you are not told directly what her personal qualities are.

One way to learn about Squeaky's personal qualities is to notice how she acts toward Raymond. It would be easy to be cruel to Raymond, as some of the characters are. Name at least two of Squeaky's actions that reveal that she is loyal and kind to Raymond.

What personal qualities does Squeaky reveal by each of the following actions?

Squeaky admits that she needs to practice her running and her spelling.

Squeaky does not hide from the girls she meets on the street.

Squeaky smiles at Gretchen and admits that her rival is a good runner.

Language and Vocabulary

Recognizing Informal Language

Since Squeaky is the narrator in "Raymond's Run," the story is told from her point of view. To make Squeaky seem real, the author has her speak the same kind of informal language and slang that a tough, streetwise girl might use.

On page 27 Squeaky says:

And I have a big rep as the baddest thing around.

This sentence sounds like Squeaky speaking.

In slang, the word *bad* means "very good." Someone writing more formally might put the idea this way:

> I have a well-deserved reputation in the neighborhood for accomplishing anything I set out to do and, when I choose, for winning any contest I enter.

Some other slang and informal expressions from the story are italicized below. What does each italicized word mean?

> . . . run *smack* into the fence . . .
> . . . and *stomp* away I'm so *burnt*.
> But that's *chicken* . . .
> . . . I don't *feature* a whole lot of chitchat.

Rewrite these quotations substituting more formal words for the italicized ones. Do they still sound like Squeaky talking?

Narrative Writing

Writing from Another Point of View

With Squeaky as narrator, you cannot know what the other characters in "Raymond's Run" are thinking. You know only what they say and what Squeaky sees them doing.

Reread the paragraph beginning "Every time, just before I take off in a race . . . ." (page 25). Imagine that this same scene is being narrated by Gretchen. What is Gretchen thinking about as she prepares for the race? What is she thinking about during the race? What does she think about Squeaky?

Write a paragraph telling about the race, using Gretchen as the narrator. Begin with the words: "Every time, just before I take off in a race . . . ."

About the Author

Toni Cade Bambara   (1939–   )

Toni Cade Bambara has written many short stories, one novel (*The Salt Eaters*, 1980), and television scripts. In 1970 she edited and published the anthology *The Black Woman* and the next year edited the anthology *Tales and Stories for Black Folks*. In her own fiction, Bambara uses black-speech styles, and focuses on lives and relationships of blacks. She also is interested in the history, myths, and music of her race.

Like her character Squeaky, Bambara grew up in New York City. She now lives in Atlanta, Georgia. She became active in civil rights issues in the 1960s and 1970s. She has lectured extensively, and has been involved in many neighborhood programs and community art groups. She also has worked as a social worker and a therapist at a psychiatric unit. She took the name Bambara from a signature on a sketchbook she found in her great-grandmother's trunk. (Bambara is the name of a people of northwest Africa, who are famous for their delicate woodcarvings.)

The Sea Devil

ARTHUR GORDON

Nature can provide sudden, unexpected challenges that demand intelligence rather than strength for survival. As you read this story, think about how you would react in a similar situation.

The man came out of the house and stood quite still, listening. Behind him, the lights glowed in the cheerful room, the books were neat and orderly in their cases, the radio talked importantly to itself. In front of him, the bay stretched dark and silent, one of the countless lagoons that border the coast where Florida thrusts its green thumb deep into the tropics.

It was late in September. The night was breathless; summer's dead hand still lay heavy on the land. The man moved forward six paces and stood on the sea wall. He dropped his cigarette and noted where the tiny spark hissed and went out. The tide was beginning to ebb.

Somewhere out in the blackness a mullet jumped and fell back with a sullen splash. Heavy with roe,[1] they were jumping less often, now. They would not take a hook, but a practiced eye could see the swirls they made in the glassy water. In the dark of the moon, a skilled man with a cast net might take half a dozen in an hour's work. And a big mullet makes a meal for a family.

The man turned abruptly and went into the garage, where his cast net hung. He was in his late twenties, wide-shouldered and strong. He did not have to fish for a living, or even for food. He was a man who worked with his head, not with his hands. But he liked to go casting alone at night.

He liked the loneliness and the labor of it. He liked the clean taste of salt when he gripped the edge of the net with his teeth as a cast netter must. He liked the arching flight of sixteen pounds of lead and linen against the starlight, and the weltering crash[2] of the net into the unsuspecting water. He liked the harsh tug of the retrieving rope around his wrist, and the way the net came alive when the cast was true, and the thud of captured fish on the floorboards of the skiff.

He liked all that because he found in it a reality that seemed to be missing from his twentieth-century job and from his daily life. He liked being the hunter, skilled and solitary and elemental. There was no conscious cruelty in the way he felt. It was the way things had been in the beginning.

The man lifted the net down carefully and lowered it into a bucket. He put a paddle beside the bucket. Then he went into the house. When

---

1. **roe:** fish eggs.

2. **weltering crash:** a crash that causes a great disturbance in the water.

he came out, he was wearing swimming trunks and a pair of old tennis shoes. Nothing else.

The skiff, flat-bottomed, was moored off the sea wall. He would not go far, he told himself. Just to the tumbledown dock half a mile away. Mullet had a way of feeding around old pilings after dark. If he moved quietly, he might pick up two or three in one cast close to the dock. And maybe a couple of others on the way down or back.

He shoved off and stood motionless for a moment, letting his eyes grow accustomed to the dark. Somewhere out in the channel a porpoise blew with a sound like steam escaping. The man smiled a little; porpoises were his friends. Once, fishing in the Gulf, he had seen the charter-boat captain reach overside and gaff[3] a baby porpoise through the sinewy part of the tail. He had hoisted it aboard, had dropped it into the bait well, where it thrashed around, puzzled and unhappy. And the mother had swum alongside the boat and under the boat and around the boat, nudging the stout planking with her back, slapping it with her tail, until the man felt sorry for her and made the captain let the baby porpoise go.

He took the net from the bucket, slipped the noose in the retrieving rope over his wrist, pulled the slipknot tight. It was an old net, but still serviceable; he had rewoven the rents[4] made by underwater snags. He coiled the

3. **gaff:** spear.
4. **rents:** holes.

The Sea Devil **31**

thirty-foot rope carefully, making sure there were no kinks. A tangled rope, he knew, would spoil any cast.

The basic design of the net had not changed in three thousand years. It was a mesh circle with a diameter of fourteen feet. It measured close to fifteen yards around the circumference and could, if thrown perfectly, blanket a hundred fifty square feet of sea water. In the center of this radial trap[5] was a small iron collar where the retrieving rope met the twenty-three separate drawstrings leading to the outer rim of the net. Along this rim, spaced an inch and a half apart, were the heavy lead sinkers.

The man raised the iron collar until it was a foot above his head. The net hung soft and pliant and deadly. He shook it gently, making sure that the drawstrings were not tangled, that the sinkers were hanging true. Then he eased it down and picked up the paddle.

The night was black as a witch's cat; the stars looked fuzzy and dim. Down to the southward, the lights of a causeway made a yellow necklace across the sky. To the man's left were the tangled roots of a mangrove swamp; to his right, the open waters of the bay. Most of it was fairly shallow, but there were channels eight feet deep. The man could not see the old dock, but he knew where it was. He pulled the paddle quietly through the water, and the phosphorescence[6] glowed and died.

For five minutes he paddled. Then, twenty feet ahead of the skiff, a mullet jumped. A big fish, close to three pounds. For a moment it hung in the still air, gleaming dully. Then it vanished. But the ripples marked the spot, and where there was one there were often others.

The man stood up quickly. He picked up the coiled rope, and with the same hand grasped

the net at a point four feet below the iron collar. He raised the skirt to his mouth, gripped it strongly with his teeth. He slid his free hand as far as it would go down the circumference of the net, so that he had three points of contact with the mass of cordage and metal. He made sure his feet were planted solidly. Then he waited, feeling the tension that is older than the human race, the fierce exhilaration of the hunter at the moment of ambush, the atavistic desire[7] to capture and kill and ultimately consume.

A mullet swirled, ahead and to the left. The man swung the heavy net back, twisting his body and bending his knees so as to get more upward thrust. He shot it forward, letting go simultaneously with rope hand and with teeth, holding a fraction of a second longer with the other hand so as to give the net the necessary spin, impart the centrifugal force[8] that would make it flare into a circle. The skiff ducked sideways, but he kept his balance. The net fell with a splash.

The man waited for five seconds. Then he began to retrieve it, pulling in a series of sharp jerks so that the drawstrings would gather the net inward, like a giant fist closing on this segment of the teeming sea. He felt the net quiver, and he knew it was not empty. He swung it, dripping, over the gunwale,[9] saw the broad silver side of the mullet quivering, saw too the gleam of a smaller fish. He looked closely to make sure no stingray[10] was hidden in the mesh, then raised the iron collar and shook the net out. The mullet fell with a thud and flapped wildly. The other victim was an

5. **radial** (rā′dē-əl) **trap:** The drawstrings of the net lead out from a small iron collar, like spokes from the center of a wheel.

6. **phosphorescence** (fŏs′fə-rĕs′əns): glowing light.

7. **atavistic** (ăt′ə-vĭs′tĭk) **desire:** a desire that his earliest ancestors would have had.

8. **centrifugal** (sĕn-trĭf′yə-gəl) **force:** the force that makes an object moving in a circle (here, the net) move away from the center of the circle (here, the man).

9. **gunwale** (gŭn′əl): the upper edge of the side of the boat.

10. **stingray:** a fish with a long, whiplike tail, which has one or more dangerous spines.

angelfish, beautifully marked, but too small to keep. The man picked it up gently and dropped it overboard. He coiled the rope, took up the paddle. He would cast no more until he came to the dock.

The skiff moved on. At last, ten feet apart, a pair of stakes rose up gauntly out of the night. Barnacle-encrusted, they once had marked the approach from the main channel. The man guided the skiff between them, then put the paddle down softly. He stood up, reached for the net, tightened the noose around his wrist. From here he could drift down upon the dock. He could see it now, a ruined skeleton in the starshine. Beyond it a mullet jumped and fell back with a flat, liquid sound. The man raised the edge of the net, put it between his teeth. He would not cast at a single swirl, he decided; he would wait until he saw two or three close together. The skiff was barely moving. He felt his muscles tense themselves, awaiting the signal from the brain.

Behind him in the channel he heard the porpoise blow again, nearer now. He frowned in the darkness. If the porpoise chose to fish this area, the mullet would scatter and vanish. There was no time to lose.

A school of sardines surfaced suddenly, skittering along like drops of mercury. Something, perhaps the shadow of the skiff, had frightened them. The old dock loomed very close. A mullet broke water just too far away; then another, nearer. The man marked[11] the spreading ripples and decided to wait no longer.

He swung back the net, heavier now that it was wet. He had to turn his head, but out of the corner of his eye he saw two swirls in the black water just off the starboard bow.[12] They were about eight feet apart, and they had the sluggish oily look that marks the presence of

11. **marked:** here, noticed.
12. **starboard bow:** the right-hand side of the front of the boat.

something big just below the surface. His conscious mind had no time to function, but instinct told him that the net was wide enough to cover both swirls if he could alter the direction of his cast. He could not halt the swing, but he shifted his feet slightly and made the cast off balance. He saw the net shoot forward, flare into an oval, and drop just where he wanted it.

Then the sea exploded in his face. In a frenzy of spray, a great horned thing shot like a huge bat out of the water. The man saw the mesh of his net etched against the mottled blackness of its body and he knew, in the split second in which thought was still possible, that those twin swirls had been made not by two mullet, but by the wing tips of the giant ray of the Gulf Coast, *Manta birostris,* also known as clam cracker, devil ray, sea devil.

The man gave a hoarse cry. He tried to claw the slipknot off his wrist, but there was no time. The quarter-inch line snapped taut. He shot over the side of the skiff as if he had roped a runaway locomotive. He hit the water head first and seemed to bounce once. He plowed a blinding furrow for perhaps ten yards. Then the line went slack as the sea devil jumped again. It was not the full-grown manta of the deep Gulf, but it was close to nine feet from tip to tip and it weighed over a thousand pounds. Up into the air it went, pearl-colored underbelly gleaming as it twisted in a frantic effort to dislodge the clinging thing that had fallen upon it. Up into the starlight, a monstrous survival from the dawn of time.

The water was less than four feet deep. Sobbing and choking, the man struggled for a foothold on the slimy bottom. Sucking in great gulps of air, he fought to free himself from the rope. But the slipknot was jammed deep into his wrist; he might as well have tried to loosen a circle of steel.

The ray came down with a thunderous splash and drove forward again. The flexible net followed every movement, impeding it hardly at all. The man weighed a hundred seventy-five pounds, and he was braced for the shock, and he had the desperate strength that comes from looking into the blank eyes of death. It was useless. His arm straightened out with a jerk that seemed to dislocate his shoulder; his feet shot out from under him; his head went under again. Now at last he knew how the fish must feel when the line tightens and drags him toward the alien element that is his doom. Now he knew.

Desperately he dug the fingers of his free hand into the ooze, felt them dredge a futile channel through broken shells and the ribbon-like sea grasses. He tried to raise his head, but could not get it clear. Torrents of spray choked him as the ray plunged toward deep water.

His eyes were of no use to him in the foam-streaked blackness. He closed them tight, and at once an insane sequence of pictures flashed through his mind. He saw his wife sitting in their living room, reading, waiting calmly for his return. He saw the mullet he had just caught, gasping its life away on the floorboards of the skiff. He saw the cigarette he had flung from the sea wall touch the water and expire with a tiny hiss. He saw all these things and many others simultaneously in his mind as his body fought silently and tenaciously for its existence. His hand touched something hard and closed on it in a death grip, but it was only

the sharp-edged helmet of a horseshoe crab, and after an instant he let it go.

He had been underwater perhaps fifteen seconds now, and something in his brain told him quite calmly that he could last another forty or fifty and then the red flashes behind his eyes would merge into darkness, and the water would pour into his lungs in one sharp painful shock, and he would be finished.

This thought spurred him to a desperate effort. He reached up and caught his pinioned wrist with his free hand. He doubled up his knees to create more drag. He thrashed his body madly, like a fighting fish, from side to side. This did not disturb the ray, but now one of the great wings tore through the mesh, and the net slipped lower over the fins projecting like horns from below the nightmare head, and the sea devil jumped again.

And once more the man was able to get his feet on the bottom and his head above water, and he saw ahead of him the pair of ancient stakes that marked the approach to the channel. He knew that if he was dragged much beyond those stakes he would be in eight feet of water, and the ray would go down to hug the bottom as rays always do, and then no power on earth could save him. So in the moment of respite[13] that was granted him, he flung himself toward them.

For a moment he thought his captor yielded a bit. Then the ray moved off again, but more slowly now, and for a few yards the man was able to keep his feet on the bottom. Twice he hurled himself back against the rope with all his strength, hoping that something would break. But nothing broke. The mesh of the net was ripped and torn, but the draw lines were strong, and the stout perimeter cord threaded through the sinkers was even stronger.

The man could feel nothing now in his trapped hand, it was numb; but the ray could feel the powerful lunges of the unknown thing that was trying to restrain it. It drove its great wings against the unyielding water and forged ahead, dragging the man and pushing a sullen wave in front of it.

The man had swung as far as he could toward the stakes. He plunged toward one and missed it by inches. His feet slipped and he went down on his knees. Then the ray swerved sharply and the second stake came right at him. He reached out with his free hand and caught it.

He caught it just above the surface, six or eight inches below high-water mark. He felt the razor-sharp barnacles bite into his hand, collapse under the pressure, drive their tiny slime-covered shell splinters deep into his flesh. He felt the pain, and he welcomed it, and he made his fingers into an iron claw that would hold until the tendons were severed or the skin was shredded from the bone. The ray felt the pressure increase with a jerk that stopped it dead in the water. For a moment all was still as the tremendous forces came into equilibrium.[14]

Then the net slipped again, and the perimeter cord came down over the sea devil's eyes, blinding it momentarily. The great ray settled to the bottom and braced its wings against the mud and hurled itself forward and upward.

The stake was only a four-by-four of creosoted[15] pine, and it was old. Ten thousand tides had swirled around it. Worms had bored; parasites had clung. Under the crust of barnacles it still had some heart left, but not enough. The man's grip was five feet above the floor of the bay; the leverage was too great. The stake snapped off at its base.

The ray lunged upward, dragging the man

13. **respite** (rĕs′pĭt): relief.

14. **equilibrium** (ē′kwə-lĭb′rē-əm): balance.
15. **creosoted** (krē′ə-sōt′ĭd): treated with creosote, a preservative.

and the useless timber. The man had his lungs full of air, but when the stake snapped he thought of expelling the air and inhaling the water so as to have it finished quickly. He thought of this, but he did not do it. And then, just at the channel's edge, the ray met the porpoise, coming in.

The porpoise had fed well this night and was in no hurry, but it was a methodical creature and it intended to make a sweep around the old dock before the tide dropped too low. It had no quarrel with any ray, but it feared no fish in the sea, and when the great black shadow came rushing blindly and unavoidably, it rolled fast and struck once with its massive horizontal tail.

The blow descended on the ray's flat body with a sound like a pistol shot. It would have broken a buffalo's back, and even the sea devil was half stunned. It veered wildly and turned back toward shallow water. It passed within ten feet of the man, face down in the water. It slowed and almost stopped, wing tips moving faintly, gathering strength for another rush.

The man had heard the tremendous slap of the great mammal's tail and the snorting gasp as it plunged away. He felt the line go slack again, and he raised his dripping face, and he reached for the bottom with his feet. He found it, but now the water was up to his neck. He plucked at the noose once more with his lacerated hand, but there was no strength in his fingers. He felt the tension come back into the line as the ray began to move again, and for half a second he was tempted to throw himself backward and fight as he had been doing, pitting his strength against the vastly superior strength of the brute.

But the acceptance of imminent death had done something to his brain. It had driven out the fear, and with the fear had gone the panic. He could think now, and he knew with absolute certainty that if he was to make any use of this last chance that had been given him, it would have to be based on the one faculty that had carried man to his preeminence above all beasts, the faculty of reason. Only by using his brain could he possibly survive, and he called on his brain for a solution, and his brain responded. It offered him one.

He did not know whether his body still had the strength to carry out the brain's commands, but he began to swim forward, toward the ray that was still moving hesitantly away from the channel. He swam forward, feeling the rope go slack as he gained on the creature.

Ahead of him he saw the one remaining stake, and he made himself swim faster until he was parallel with the ray and the rope trailed behind both of them in a deep U. He swam with a surge of desperate energy that came from nowhere, so that he was slightly in the lead as they came to the stake. He passed on one side of it; the ray was on the other.

Then the man took one last deep breath, and he went down under the black water until he was sitting on the bottom of the bay. He put one foot over the line so that it passed under his bent knee. He drove both his heels into the mud, and he clutched the slimy grass with his bleeding hand, and he waited for the tension to come again.

The ray passed on the other side of the stake, moving faster now. The rope grew taut again, and it began to drag the man back toward the stake. He held his prisoned wrist close to the bottom, under his knee, and he prayed that the stake would not break. He felt the rope vibrate as the barnacles bit into it. He did not know whether the rope would crush the barnacles, or whether the barnacles would cut the rope. All he knew was that in five seconds or less he would be dragged into the stake and cut to ribbons if he tried to hold on, or drowned if he didn't.

He felt himself sliding slowly, and then

faster, and suddenly the ray made a great leap forward, and the rope burned around the base of the stake, and the man's foot hit it hard. He kicked himself backward with his remaining strength, and the rope parted, and he was free.

He came slowly to the surface. Thirty feet away the sea devil made one tremendous leap and disappeared into the darkness. The man raised his wrist and looked at the frayed length of rope dangling from it. Twenty inches, perhaps. He lifted his other hand and felt the hot blood start instantly, but he didn't care. He put his hand on the stake above the barnacles and held on to the good, rough, honest wood. He heard a strange noise, and realized that it was himself, sobbing.

High above, there was a droning sound, and looking up he saw the nightly plane from New Orleans inbound for Tampa. Calm and serene, it sailed, symbol of man's proud mastery over nature. Its lights winked red and green for a moment; then it was gone.

Slowly, painfully, the man began to move through the placid water. He came to the skiff at last and climbed into it. The mullet, still alive, slapped convulsively with its tail. The man reached down with his torn hand, picked up the mullet, let it go.

He began to work on the slipknot doggedly with his teeth. His mind was almost a blank, but not quite. He knew one thing. He knew he would do no more casting alone at night. Not in the dark of the moon. No, not he.

Reading Check

1. What is the setting of the story?
2. What does the man catch first in his net?
3. When he throws out the net a second time, what does he catch in it?
4. What animal helps him escape being pulled out to deep water?
5. What does the man decide he will never again do alone at night?

For Study and Discussion

Analyzing and Interpreting the Story

1. The man in this story doesn't need to fish for a living, or even for food. Why does he go casting alone at night?

2. This story is about a fisherman who becomes the "fish." How does the man become trapped by the sea devil?

3. Like a fighting fish, the man at first uses his strength to try to save himself. Why is his strength useless against the monster?

4. The porpoise plays a part in saving the man. **a.** How does the man feel about porpoises? **b.** How does the porpoise give the man one last chance?

5. The man finally realizes that only his intelligence can save him. What solution does his reason offer him?

6. After his struggle is over, the man looks up at the sky and sees a plane, which is described in this way: "Calm and serene, it sailed, symbol of man's proud mastery over nature." **a.** What is the man's condition as he looks up at the plane from the water? **b.** Is he calm and serene? **c.** Do you think this man believes that human beings have complete "mastery over nature"? Explain your answer.

7. Why do you think the man releases the mullet after his ordeal?

Literary Elements

Finding the Main Idea of the Story

"The Sea Devil" is an exciting story written for entertainment. But there are clues that the author also wants to share a serious idea with us.

Here is a key passage from "The Sea Devil." Which sentence or phrase in this paragraph would you say states the main idea of this story? Restate this idea in your own words.

> But the acceptance of imminent death had done something to his brain. It had driven out the fear, and with the fear had gone the panic. He could think now, and he knew with absolute certainty that if he was to make any use of this last chance that had been given him, it would have to be based on the one faculty that had carried man to his preeminence above all beasts, the faculty of reason. Only by using his brain could he possibly survive, and he called on his brain for a solution, and his brain responded. It offered him one.

Language and Vocabulary

Finding the Meanings of Prefixes and Suffixes

You can figure out the meanings of many unfamiliar words if you know the meanings of some common prefixes and suffixes. A **prefix** is a word element added at the beginning of a word to change its meaning. The prefix *un-*, for example, means "not." When the author of this story says that the water is *unyielding*, what does he mean?

A **suffix** is a word element added at the end of a word to change its meaning. The suffix *-less* means "without." When the author says that the man stood *motionless,* what does he mean?

In the following lists of words from the story, the prefixes and suffixes are italicized. What meaning does each prefix or suffix add to the rest of the word? Use your dictionary to find out.

breath*less*   *in*sane   ribbon*like*
cheer*ful*   master*y*   slugg*ish*
*dis*locate   *re*woven   thunder*ous*

Descriptive Writing

Using Specific Details in Description

Here is how the sea devil in this story is described:

> In a frenzy of spray, a great horned thing shot like a huge bat out of the water. The man saw the mesh of his net etched against the mottled blackness of its body and he knew, in the split second in which thought was still possible, that those twin swirls had been made not by two mullet, but by the wing tips of the giant ray of the Gulf Coast, *Manta birostris,* also known as clam cracker, devil ray, sea devil. . . . It was not the full-grown manta of the deep Gulf, but it was close to nine feet from tip to tip and it weighed over a thousand pounds. Up into the air it went, pearl-colored underbelly gleaming as it twisted in a frantic effort to dislodge the clinging thing that had fallen upon it. Up into the starlight, a monstrous survival from the dawn of time.

What is the ray compared to? What are its colors? What is its scientific name? What are its "popular" names? How big is it?

Using this passage as a model, write several sentences describing an animal, either a "monstrous" animal or a domestic animal. Give the reader specific details about its appearance and about its movements. Does it have distinctive colors or sounds? Tell what names it is known by, both its scientific names and its "popular" names.

About the Author

Arthur Gordon (1912–)

Arthur Gordon is noted as a magazine editor and free-lance magazine writer. Gordon was born in Savannah, Georgia. He graduated from Yale University and then attended Oxford University. He has served as managing editor of *Good Housekeeping* magazine, editor of *Cosmopolitan* magazine, and roving editor of *Guideposts*. Gordon has written more than two hundred stories and articles for magazines, a novel, and several nonfiction books. He coauthored *The American Heritage Book of Flight.* "The Sea Devil" reflects his interests in fishing, hunting, and boating.

Up the Slide

JACK LONDON

Clay had a sharp eye, but he would need more than a sharp eye to save himself from the harsh elements of the Yukon Territory.

When Clay Dilham left the tent to get a sled load of firewood, he expected to be back in half an hour. So he told Swanson, who was cooking the dinner. Swanson and he belonged to different outfits, located about twenty miles apart on the Stuart River;[1] but they had become traveling partners on a trip down the Yukon to Dawson[2] to get the mail.

Swanson had laughed when Clay said he would be back in half an hour. It stood to reason, Swanson said, that good, dry firewood could not be found so close to Dawson; that whatever firewood there was originally had long since been gathered in; that firewood would not be selling at forty dollars a cord[3] if any man could go out and get a sled load and be back in the time Clay expected to make it.

Then it was Clay's turn to laugh, as he sprang on the sled and *mushed*[4] the dogs on the river trail. For, coming up from the Siwash village the previous day, he had noticed a small dead pine in an out-of-the-way place, which had defied discovery by eyes less sharp than his. And his eyes were both young and sharp, for his seventeenth birthday was just cleared.

1. **Stuart River:** in British Columbia, Canada.
2. **Dawson:** a city in the Yukon Territory in northern Canada, center of the Klondike mining region.
3. **cord:** wood cut for fuel in a stack measuring 8 feet long, 4 feet wide, and 4 feet high.
4. *mushed:* traveled with a dog team.

A swift ten minutes over the ice brought him to the place, and figuring ten minutes to get the tree and ten minutes to return made him certain that Swanson's dinner would not wait.

Just below Dawson, and rising out of the Yukon itself, towered the great Moosehide Mountain, so named by Lieutenant Schwatka long ere the Klondike became famous. On the river side the mountain was scarred and gullied and gored; and it was up one of these gores or gullies that Clay had seen the tree.

Halting his dogs beneath, on the river ice, he looked up, and after some searching, rediscovered it. Being dead, its weather-beaten gray so blended with the gray wall of rock that a thousand men could pass by and never notice it. Taking root in a cranny, it had grown up, exhausted its bit of soil, and perished. Beneath it the wall fell sheer for a hundred feet to the river. All one had to do was to sink an ax into the dry trunk a dozen times and it would fall to the ice, and most probably smash conveniently to pieces. This Clay had figured on when confidently limiting the trip to half an hour.

He studied the cliff thoroughly before attempting it. So far as he was concerned, the longest way round was the shortest way to the tree. By making a long zigzag across the face of this slide and back again, he would arrive at the pine.

Fastening his ax across his shoulders so that it would not interfere with his movements, he clawed up the broken rock, hand and foot, like a cat, till the twenty feet were cleared and he could draw breath on the edge of the slide.

The slide was steep and its snow-covered surface slippery. Further, the heelless, walrus-hide soles of his *muclucs* were polished by much ice travel, and by his second step he realized how little he could depend upon them for clinging purposes. A slip at that point meant a plunge over the edge and a twenty-foot fall to the ice. A hundred feet farther along, and a slip would mean a fifty-foot fall.

He thrust his mittened hand through the snow to the earth to steady himself, and went on. But he was forced to exercise such care that the first zigzag consumed five minutes. Then, returning across the face of the slide toward the pine, he met with a new difficulty. The slope steepened considerably, so that little snow collected, while bent flat beneath this thin covering were long, dry last-year's grasses.

The surface they presented was as glassy as that of his muclucs, and when both surfaces came together his feet shot out, and he fell on his face, sliding downward, and convulsively clutching for something to stay himself.

This he succeeded in doing, although he lay quiet for a couple of minutes to get back his nerve. He would have taken off his muclucs and gone at it in his socks, only the cold was thirty below zero, and at such temperature his feet would quickly freeze. So he went on, and after ten minutes of risky work made the safe and solid rock where stood the pine.

A few strokes of the ax felled it into the chasm, and peeping over the edge, he indulged a laugh at the startled dogs. They were on the verge of bolting when he called aloud to them, soothingly, and they were reassured.

Then he turned about for the back trip.

Going down, he knew, was even more dangerous than coming up, but how dangerous he did not realize till he had slipped half a dozen times, and each time saved himself by what appeared to him a miracle.

He sat down and looked at the treacherous snow-covered slope. It was manifestly impossible for him to make it with a whole body, and he did not wish to arrive at the bottom shattered like the pine tree.

But while he sat inactive the frost was stealing in on him, and the quick chilling of his body warned him that he could not delay. He must be doing something to keep his blood circulating. If he could not get down by going down, there only remained to him to get down by going up. It was a herculean task, but it was the only way out of the predicament.

From where he was he could not see the top of the cliff, but he reasoned that the gully in which lay the slide must give inward more and more as it approached the top. From what little he could see, the gully displayed this tendency; and he noticed, also, that the slide extended for many hundreds of feet upward, and that where it ended the rock was well broken up and favorable for climbing.

So instead of taking the zigzag which led downward, he made a new one leading upward and crossing the slide at an angle of thirty degrees. The grasses gave him much trouble, and made him long for soft-tanned moosehide moccasins, which could make his feet cling like a second pair of hands.

He soon found that thrusting his mittened hands through the snow and clutching the grass roots was uncertain and unsafe. His mittens were too thick for him to be sure of his grip, so he took them off. But this brought with it new trouble. When he held on to a bunch of roots the snow, coming in contact with his bare warm hand, was melted, so that his hands and the wristbands of his woolen shirt were dripping with water. This the frost was quick to attack, and his fingers were numbed and made worthless.

Then he was forced to seek good footing, where he could stand erect unsupported, to put on his mittens, and to thrash his hands against his sides until the heat came back into them.

While beating his hands against his sides he turned and looked down the long slippery slope, and figured, in case he slipped, that he would be flying with the speed of an express train ere he took the final plunge into the icy bed of the Yukon.

He passed the first outcropping rock, and the second, and at the end of an hour found himself above the third, and fully five hundred feet above the river. And here, with the end nearly two hundred feet above him, the pitch of the slide was increasing.

Each step became more difficult and perilous, and he was faint from exertion and from lack of Swanson's dinner. Three or four times he slipped slightly and recovered himself; but, growing careless from exhaustion and the long tension on his nerves, he tried to continue with too great haste, and was rewarded by a double slip of each foot, which tore him loose and started him down the slope.

On account of the steepness there was little snow; but what little there was was displaced by his body, so that he became the nucleus of a young avalanche. He clawed desperately with his hands, but there was little to cling to, and he sped downward faster and faster.

The first and second outcroppings were below him, but he knew that the first was almost out of line, and pinned his hope on the second. Yet the first was just enough in line to catch one of his feet and to whirl him over and head downward on his back.

The shock of this was severe in itself, and the fine snow enveloped him in a blinding, mad-dening cloud; but he was thinking quickly and clearly of what would happen if he brought up head first against the second outcropping. He twisted himself over on his stomach, thrust both hands out to one side, and pressed them heavily against the flying surface.

This had the effect of a brake, drawing his head and shoulders to the side. In this position he rolled over and over a couple of times, and then, with a quick jerk at the right moment, he got his body the rest of the way round.

And none too soon, for the next moment his feet drove into the outcropping, his legs doubled up, and the wind was driven from his stomach with the abruptness of the stop.

There was much snow down his neck and up his sleeves. At once and with unconcern he shook this out, only to discover, when he looked up to where he must climb again, that he had lost his nerve. He was shaking as if with a palsy, and sick and faint from a frightful nausea.

Fully ten minutes passed ere he could master these sensations and summon sufficient strength for the weary climb. His legs hurt him and he was limping, and he was conscious of a sore place in his back, where he had fallen on the ax.

In an hour he had regained the point of his tumble, and was contemplating the slide, which so suddenly steepened. It was plain to him that he could not go up with hands and feet alone, and he was beginning to lose his nerve again when he remembered the ax.

Reaching upward the distance of a step, he brushed away the snow, and in the frozen gravel and crumbled rock of the slide chopped a shallow resting place for his foot. Then he came up a step, reached forward, and repeated the maneuver. And so, step by step, foothole by foothole, a tiny speck of toiling life poised like a fly on the face of Moosehide Mountain, he fought his upward way.

Twilight was beginning to fall when he gained the head of the slide and drew himself into the rocky bottom of the gully. At this point the shoulder of the mountain began to bend back toward the crest, and in addition to its being less steep, the rocks afforded better handhold and foothold. The worst was over, and the best yet to come!

The gully opened out into a miniature basin, in which a floor of soil had been deposited, out of which, in turn, a tiny grove of pines had sprung. The trees were all dead, dry and seasoned, having long since exhausted the thin skin of earth.

Clay ran his experienced eye over the timber, and estimated that it would chop up into fifty cords at least. Beyond, the gully closed in and became barren rock again. On every hand was barren rock, so the wonder was small that the trees had escaped the eyes of men. They were only to be discovered as he had discovered them—by climbing after them.

He continued the ascent, and the white moon greeted him when he came out upon the crest of Moosehide Mountain. At his feet, a thousand feet below, sparkled the lights of Dawson.

But the descent on that side was precipitate[5]

5. **precipitate** (prĭ-sĭp′ə-tĭt,-tāt′): very steep.

and dangerous in the uncertain moonshine, and he elected to go down the mountain by its gentler northern flank. In a couple of hours he reached the Yukon at the Siwash village, and took the river trail back to where he had left the dogs. There he found Swanson, with a fire going, waiting for him to come down.

And although Swanson had a hearty laugh at his expense, nevertheless, a week or so later, in Dawson, there were fifty cords of wood sold at forty dollars a cord, and it was he and Swanson who sold them.

Reading Check

1. What is Clay's purpose in going out before dinner?
2. Why are Clay's shoes undependable for climbing the cliff?
3. Why is he unable to return the way he came?
4. What tool does he use to ascend the slide?
5. What does he find when he reaches the gully?

For Study and Discussion

Analyzing and Interpreting the Story

1. At the beginning of the story, Clay is confident that he can return in half an hour. **a.** What does he fail to take into consideration when he begins his climb? **b.** At what point does he realize that he has underestimated the difficulties of the task? **c.** When does he become aware of the dangers involved?

2a. What does Clay decide to do to get out of his predicament? **b.** What new difficulties does he encounter when he puts this plan into operation? **c.** How does he finally succeed in solving the problem of the climb?

3. Suspense in a story makes us wonder what will happen next. What parts of this story did you find most suspenseful?

Literary Elements

Identifying Similes and Metaphors

When London describes Clay as clawing up the rock "like a cat," he is using a **simile.** A simile is a figure of speech that compares two basically unlike things by using a word such as *like* or *as.* London's simile suggests that Clay's actions in climbing the rock are similar to the actions of a cat as it climbs.

We are told in one passage that fine snow enveloped Clay "in a blinding, maddening cloud." This comparison, which identifies the snow with a cloud, is a **metaphor.** A metaphor says that one thing *is* another, different thing.

Tell whether each of the following comparisons is a simile or a metaphor. Explain each comparison in your own words.

as glassy as that of his muclucs
nucleus of a young avalanche
like a fly
thin skin of earth

Writing About Literature

Discussing Problems Faced by the Character

While Clay climbs the slide he is in conflict with the bitterly cold weather, the harsh terrain, and his own fears. Write a paragraph in which you discuss one of the problems Clay encounters. In your paper refer to specific details in the story.

About the Author

Jack London   (1876–1916)

Jack London joined the Klondike gold rush and hunted for gold in the Yukon in 1897. He found little gold, but did find a lot of material for stories. He became famous when *The Call of the Wild* was published in 1903. The next year *The Sea-Wolf* came out. He wrote some fifty volumes in the last sixteen years of his life. Many of his novels and short stories are classic works showing human beings struggling against nature. Many of his tales, such as *The Iron Heel,* fall in the science-fiction genre.

London's own early life was a struggle. He was born in San Francisco to a spiritualist mother and an astrologer father. By the time he was eighteen, London had been an illegal "oyster pirate," had worked on a sealing schooner in the North Pacific, had marched across the country with an "army" of unemployed men, had shoveled coal in a power station, had been a hobo, and had spent a month in prison. Throughout it all, London loved to read, and eventually settled upon a writing career.

The Street

RICHARD WRIGHT

The boy was so full of fear he could hardly breathe. But he had an adult's responsibility now. He had to make the journey down those streets.

Hunger stole upon me so slowly that at first I was not aware of what hunger really meant. Hunger had always been more or less at my elbow when I played, but now I began to wake up at night to find hunger standing at my bedside, staring at me gauntly. The hunger I had known before this had been no grim, hostile stranger; it had been a normal hunger that had made me beg constantly for bread, and when I ate a crust or two I was satisfied. But this new hunger baffled me, scared me, made me angry and insistent. Whenever I begged for food now my mother would pour me a cup of tea which would still the clamor[1] in my stomach for a moment or two; but a little later I would feel hunger nudging my ribs, twisting my empty guts until they ached. I would grow dizzy and my vision would dim. I became less active in my play, and for the first time in my life I had to pause and think of what was happening to me.

"Mama, I'm hungry," I complained one afternoon.

"Jump up and catch a kungry," she said, trying to make me laugh and forget.

"What's a *kungry?*"

"It's what little boys eat when they get hungry," she said.

"What does it taste like?"

"I don't know."

"Then why do you tell me to catch one?"

"Because you said that you were hungry," she said, smiling.

I sensed that she was teasing me and it made me angry.

"But I'm hungry. I want to eat."

"You'll have to wait."

"But I want to eat now."

"But there's nothing to eat," she told me.

"Why?"

"Just because there's none," she explained.

"But I want to eat," I said, beginning to cry.

"You'll just have to wait," she said again.

"But why?"

"For God to send some food."

"When is He going to send it?"

"I don't know."

"But I'm hungry!"

She was ironing and she paused and looked at me with tears in her eyes.

"Where's your father?" she asked me.

I stared in bewilderment. Yes, it was true that my father had not come home to sleep for many days now and I could make as much noise as I wanted. Though I had not known why he was absent, I had been glad that he was not there to shout his restrictions at me. But it had never occurred to me that his absence would mean that there would be no food.

"I don't know," I said.

"Who brings food into the house?" my mother asked me.

---

1. **clamor:** noise.

"Papa," I said. "He always brought food."

"Well, your father isn't here now," she said.

"Where is he?"

"I don't know," she said.

"But I'm hungry," I whimpered, stomping my feet.

"You'll have to wait until I get a job and buy food," she said.

As the days slid past, the image of my father became associated with my pangs of hunger, and whenever I felt hunger I thought of him with a deep biological bitterness.

My mother finally went to work as a cook and left me and my brother alone in the flat[2] each day with a loaf of bread and a pot of tea. When she returned at evening she would be tired and dispirited and would cry a lot. Sometimes, when she was in despair, she would call us to her and talk to us for hours, telling us that we now had no father, that our lives would be different from those of other children, that we must learn as soon as possible to take care of ourselves, to dress ourselves, to prepare our own food; that we must take upon ourselves the responsibility of the flat while she worked. Half frightened, we would promise solemnly. We did not understand what had happened between our father and our mother and the most that these long talks did to us was to make us feel a vague dread. Whenever we asked why Father had left, she would tell us that we were too young to know.

One evening my mother told me that thereafter I would have to do the shopping for food. She took me to the corner store to show me the way. I was proud; I felt like a grown-up. The next afternoon I looped the basket over my arm and went down the pavement toward the store. When I reached the corner, a gang of boys grabbed me, knocked me down, snatched the basket, took the money, and sent me run-

ning home in panic. That evening I told my mother what had happened, but she made no comment; she sat down at once, wrote another note, gave me more money, and sent me out to the grocery again. I crept down the steps and saw the same gang of boys playing down the street. I ran back into the house.

"What's the matter?" my mother asked.

"It's those same boys," I said. "They'll beat me."

"You've got to get over that," she said. "Now, go on."

"I'm scared," I said.

"Go on and don't pay any attention to them," she said.

I went out of the door and walked briskly down the sidewalk, praying that the gang would not molest me. But when I came abreast of them someone shouted.

"There he is!"

They came toward me and I broke into a wild run toward home. They overtook me and flung me to the pavement. I yelled, pleaded, kicked, but they wrenched the money out of my hand. They yanked me to my feet, gave me a few slaps, and sent me home sobbing. My mother met me at the door.

"They b-beat m-me," I gasped. "They t-t-took the m-money."

I started up the steps, seeking the shelter of the house.

"Don't you come in here," my mother warned me.

I froze in my tracks and stared at her.

"But they're coming after me," I said.

"You just stay right where you are," she said in a deadly tone. "I'm going to teach you this night to stand up and fight for yourself."

She went into the house and I waited, terrified, wondering what she was about. Presently, she returned with more money and another note; she also had a long heavy stick.

"Take this money, this note, and this stick,"

2. **flat:** an apartment.

she said. "Go to the store and buy those groceries. If those boys bother you, then fight."

I was baffled. My mother was telling me to fight, a thing that she had never done before.

"But I'm scared," I said.

"Don't you come into this house until you've gotten those groceries," she said.

"They'll beat me; they'll beat me," I said.

"Then stay in the streets; don't come back here!"

I ran up the steps and tried to force my way past her into the house. A stinging slap came on my jaw. I stood on the sidewalk, crying.

"Please, let me wait until tomorrow," I begged.

"No," she said. "Go now! If you come back into this house without those groceries, I'll whip you!"

She slammed the door and I heard the key turn in the lock. I shook with fright. I was alone upon the dark, hostile streets and gangs were after me, I had the choice of being beaten at home or away from home. I clutched the stick, crying, trying to reason. If I were beaten at home, there was absolutely nothing that I could do about it; but if I were beaten in the streets, I had a chance to fight and defend myself. I walked slowly down the sidewalk, coming closer to the gang of boys, holding the stick tightly. I was so full of fear that I could scarcely breathe. I was almost upon them now.

"There he is again!" the cry went up.

They surrounded me quickly and began to grab for my hand.

"I'll kill you!" I threatened.

They closed in. In blind fear I let the stick fly, feeling it crack against a boy's skull. I swung again, lamming another skull, then another. Realizing that they would retaliate if I let up for but a second, I fought to lay them low, to knock them cold, to kill them so that they could not strike back at me. I flayed with tears in my eyes, teeth clenched, stark fear making

me throw every ounce of my strength behind each blow. I hit again and again, dropping the money and the grocery list. The boys scattered, yelling, nursing their heads, staring at me in utter disbelief. They had never seen such frenzy. I stood panting, egging them on, taunting them to come on and fight. When they refused, I ran after them and they tore out for their homes, screaming. The parents of the boys rushed into the streets and threatened me, and for the first time in my life I shouted at grown-ups, telling them that I would give them the same if they bothered me. I finally found my grocery list and the money and went to the store. On my way back I kept my stick poised for instant use, but there was not a single boy in sight. That night I won the right to the streets of Memphis.

For Study and Discussion

Analyzing and Interpreting the Selection

1. In this true story, a boy battled a street gang. But the boy's family faced another "enemy" at home. Look back at the opening paragraph. **a.** What enemy did the family face? **b.** How did this enemy hurt the boy?

2. When a hero in a story has to fight, it is usually for some purpose that we understand and sympathize with. Sometimes a hero is unwilling to fight. Why do you think the mother forced the boy to face the gang in the street?

3. What do you think the boy proved, to his mother and to himself, by winning the street battle?

Literary Elements

Responding to Figurative Language

Wright wants to impress upon the reader how hunger haunted his family. To do this, he describes hunger as if it were a person: "Hunger had always been more or less at my elbow when I played." Where does he find hunger at night? What does hunger look like to him?

Wright is using **figurative language** here. He is comparing hunger to a person. Figurative language is not literally, or factually, true. Hunger does not really have eyes, and it can't actually stand or move. But figurative language helps you see things in sharp, new ways. How did Wright's unusual description of hunger affect you?

About the Author

Richard Wright   (1908–1960)

This selection is taken from *Black Boy,* the autobiography of Richard Wright. Wright's childhood was full of heartbreak. It was disrupted by family problems and by his mother's long illness. When he was very young, Wright learned to escape through listening to stories. With his mother's help, he learned to read before he entered school. His formal schooling didn't last long. Wright was only fifteen years old when he left home and set off on his own. Later in his life he said that it had been only through books that he had managed to keep himself alive. Whenever his environment failed to support or nourish him, he clutched at books. Wright is now recognized as one of the important American writers of the twentieth century.

Top Man

JAMES RAMSEY ULLMAN

"The mountain, to all of us, was no longer a mere giant of rock and ice; it had become a living thing, an enemy, watching us, waiting for us, hostile, relentless, and aware."

The gorge bent. The walk fell suddenly away, and we came out on the edge of a bleak, boulder-strewn valley. . . . *And there it was.*

Osborn saw it first. He had been leading the column, threading his way slowly among the huge rock masses of the gorge's mouth. Then he came to the first flat bare place and stopped. He neither pointed nor cried out, but every man behind him knew instantly what it was. The long file sprang taut, like a jerked rope. As

swiftly as we could, but in complete silence, we came out one by one into the open space where Osborn stood, and we raised our eyes with his.

In the records of the Indian Topographical Survey it says: "Kalpurtha: altitude 27,930 feet. The highest peak in the Garhwal Himalayas and probably fourth highest in the world. Also known as K3. A Tertiary formation of sedimentary limestone. . . ."

There were men among us who had spent

months of their lives—in some cases years—reading, thinking, planning about what now lay before us; but at that moment statistics and geology, knowledge, thought, and plans, were as remote and forgotten as the faraway western cities from which we had come. We were men bereft of everything but eyes, everything but the single electric perception: *there it was!*

Before us the valley stretched into miles of rocky desolation. To right and left it was bounded by low ridges, which, as the eye followed them, slowly mounted and drew closer together, until the valley was no longer a valley at all, but a narrowing, rising corridor between the cliffs. What happened then I can describe only as a stupendous crash of music. At the end of the corridor and above it—so far above it that it shut out half the sky—hung the blinding white mass of K3.

It was like the many pictures I had seen, and at the same time utterly unlike them. The shape was there, and the familiar distinguishing features: the sweeping skirt of glaciers; the monstrous vertical precipices of the face and the jagged ice-line of the east ridge; finally, the symmetrical summit pyramid that transfixed the sky. But whereas in the pictures the mountain had always seemed unreal—a dream-image of cloud, snow, and crystal—it was now no longer an image at all. It was a mass: solid, immanent, appalling. We were still too far away to see the windy whipping of its snow plumes or to hear the cannonading of its avalanches, but in that sudden silent moment every man of us was for the first time aware of it not as a picture in his mind, but as a thing, an antagonist. For all its twenty-eight thousand feet of lofty grandeur it seemed, somehow, less to tower than to crouch—a white-hooded giant, secret and remote, but living. Living and on guard.

I turned my eyes from the dazzling glare and looked at my companions. Osborn still stood a little in front of the others. He was absolutely motionless, his young face tense and shining, his eyes devouring the mountain as a lover's might devour the form of his beloved. One could feel in the very set of his body the overwhelming desire that swelled in him to act, to come to grips, to conquer. A little behind him were ranged the other white men of the expedition: Randolph, our leader, Wittmer and Johns, Dr. Schlapp and Bixler. All were still, their eyes cast upward. Off to one side a little stood Nace, the Englishman, the only one among us who was not staring at K3 for the first time. He had been the last to come up out of the gorge and stood now with arms folded on his chest, squinting at the great peak he had known so long and fought so tirelessly and fiercely. His lean British face, under its mask of stubble and windburn, was expressionless. His lips were a thin line, and his eyes seemed almost shut. Behind the sahibs[1] ranged the porters, bent forward over their staffs, their brown seamed faces straining upward from beneath their loads.

For a long while no one spoke or moved. The only sounds between earth and sky were the soft hiss of our breathing and the pounding of our hearts.

Through the long afternoon we wound slowly between the great boulders of the valley and at sundown pitched camp in the bed of a dried-up stream. The porters ate their rations in silence, wrapped themselves in their blankets, and fell asleep under the stars. The rest of us, as was our custom, sat close about the fire that blazed in the circle of tents, discussing the events of the day and the plans for the next. It was a flawlessly clear Himalayan night, and K3 tiered[2] up into the blackness like a monstrous beacon lighted from within. There was no

---

1. **sahibs** (sä'ĭbz): *Sahib* is a title of respect used in India.
2. **tiered** (tērd) **up:** rose upward in rows or *tiers*.

wind, but a great tide of cold air crept down the valley from the ice fields above, penetrating our clothing, pressing gently against the canvas of the tents.

"Another night or two and we'll be needing the sleeping bags," commented Randolph.

Osborn nodded. "We could use them tonight would be my guess."

Randolph turned to Nace. "What do you say, Martin?"

The Englishman puffed at his pipe a moment. "Rather think it might be better to wait," he said at last.

"Wait? Why?" Osborn jerked his head up.

"Well, it gets pretty nippy high up, you know. I've seen it thirty below at twenty-five thousand on the east ridge. Longer we wait for the bags, better acclimated we'll get."

Osborn snorted. "A lot of good being acclimated will do, if we have frozen feet."

"Easy, Paul, easy," cautioned Randolph. "It seems to me Martin's right."

Osborn bit his lip, but said nothing. The other men entered the conversation, and soon it had veered to other matters: the weather, the porters and pack animals, routes, camps, and strategy, the inevitable, inexhaustible topics of the climber's world.

There were all kinds of men among the eight of us, men with a great diversity of background and interest. Sayre Randolph, whom the Alpine Club had named leader of our expedition, had for years been a well-known explorer and lecturer. Now in his middle fifties, he was no longer equal to the grueling physical demands of high climbing, but served as planner and organizer of the enterprise. Wittmer was a Seattle lawyer, who had recently made a name for himself by a series of difficult ascents in the Coast Range of British Columbia. Johns was an Alaskan, fantastically strong, able sourdough,[3] who had been a ranger in the U.S. Forestry Service and had accompanied many famous Alaskan expeditions. Schlapp was a practicing physician from Milwaukee, Bixler a government meteorologist with a talent for photography. I, at the time, was an assistant professor of geology at an eastern university.

Finally, and preeminently, there were Osborn and Nace. I say "preeminently" because, even at this time, when we had been together as a party for little more than a month, I believe all of us realized that these were the two key men of our venture. None, to my knowledge, ever expressed it in words, but the conviction was none the less there that if any of us were eventually to stand on the summit of K3, it would be one of them, or both. They were utterly dissimilar men. Osborn was twenty-three and a year out of college, a compact, buoyant mass of energy and high spirits, He seemed to be wholly unaffected by either the physical or mental hazards of mountaineering and had already, by virtue of many spectacular ascents in the Alps and Rockies, won a reputation as the most skilled and audacious of younger American climbers. Nace was in his forties—lean, taciturn,[4] introspective. An official in the Indian Civil Service, he had explored and climbed in the Himalayas for twenty years. He had been a member of all five of the unsuccessful British expeditions to K3, and in his last attempt had attained to within five hundred feet of the summit, the highest point which any man had reached on the unconquered giant. This had been the famous, tragic attempt in which his fellow climber and lifelong friend, Captain Furness, had slipped and fallen ten thousand feet to his death. Nace

rarely mentioned his name, but on the steel head of his ice ax were engraved the words: TO MARTIN FROM JOHN. If fate were to grant that the ax of any one of us should be planted upon the summit of K3, I hoped it would be this one.

Such were the men who huddled about the fire in the deep, still cold of a Himalayan night. There were many differences among us, in temperament as well as in background. In one or two cases, notably that of Osborn and Nace, there had already been a certain amount of friction, and as the venture continued and the struggles and hardships of the actual ascent began, it would, I knew, increase. But differences were unimportant. What mattered—all that mattered—was that our purpose was one: to conquer the monster of rock and ice that now loomed above us in the night; to stand for a moment where no man, no living thing, had ever stood before. To that end we had come from half a world away, across oceans and continents to the fastnesses[5] of inner Asia. To that end we were prepared to endure cold, exhaustion, and danger, even to the very last extremity of human endurance. . . . Why? There is no answer, and at the same time every man among us knew the answer; every man who has ever looked upon a great mountain and felt the fever in his blood to climb and conquer knows the answer. George Leigh Mallory, greatest of mountaineers, expressed it once and for all when he was asked why he wanted to climb unconquered Everest.

"I want to climb it," said Mallory, "because it is there."

Day after day we crept on and upward. Sometimes the mountain was brilliant above us, as it had been when we first saw it; sometimes it was

3. **sourdough:** a slang word meaning "pioneer" or "prospector."
4. **taciturn** (tăs′ə-tûrn): reserved, quiet.

5. **fastnesses:** fortresses or strongholds. Here, the author is comparing the mountains to fortresses.

partially or wholly obscured by tiers of clouds. The naked desolation of the valley was unrelieved by any motion, color, or sound; and as we progressed, the great rock walls that enclosed it grew so high and steep that its floor received the sun for less than two hours each day. The rest of the time it lay in ashen half-light, its gloom intensified by the dazzling brilliance of the ice slopes above. As long as we remained there we had the sensation of imprisonment; it was like being trapped at the bottom of a deep well or in a sealed court between great skyscrapers. Soon we were thinking of the ascent of the shining mountain not only as an end in itself, but as an escape.

In our nightly discussions around the fire our conversation narrowed more and more to the immediate problems confronting us, and during them I began to realize that the tension between Osborn and Nace went deeper than I had at first surmised. There was rarely any outright argument between them—they were both far too able mountain men to disagree on fundamentals—but I saw that at almost every turn they were rubbing each other the wrong way. It was a matter of personalities, chiefly. Osborn was talkative, enthusiastic, optimistic, always chafing to be up and at it, always wanting to take the short straight line to the given point. Nace, on the other hand, was matter-of-fact, cautious, slow. He was the apostle of trial-and-error and watchful waiting. Because of his far greater experience and intimate knowledge of K3, Randolph almost invariably followed his advice, rather than Osborn's, when a difference of opinion arose. The younger man usually capitulated with good grace, but I could tell that he was irked.

During the days in the valley I had few occasions to talk privately with either of them, and only once did either mention the other in any but the most casual manner. Even then, the remarks they made seemed unimportant and I remember them only in view of what happened later.

My conversation with Osborn occurred first. It was while we were on the march, and Osborn, who was directly behind me, came up suddenly to my side. "You're a geologist, Frank," he began without preamble. "What do you think of Nace's theory about the ridge?"

"What theory?" I asked.

"He believes we should traverse[6] under it from the glacier up. Says the ridge itself is too exposed."

"It looks pretty mean through the telescope."

"But it's been done before. He's done it himself. All right, it's tough—I'll admit that. But a decent climber could make it in half the time the traverse will take."

"Nace knows the traverse is longer," I said. "But he seems certain it will be much easier for us."

"Easier for *him* is what he means." Osborn paused, looking moodily at the ground. "He was a great climber in his day. It's a shame a man can't be honest enough with himself to know when he's through." He fell silent and a moment later dropped back into his place in line.

It was that same night, I think, that I awoke to find Nace sitting up in his blanket and staring at the mountain.

"How clear it is!" I whispered.

The Englishman pointed. "See the ridge?"

I nodded, my eyes fixed on the great, twisting spine of ice that limbed into the sky. I could see now, more clearly than in the blinding sunlight, its huge indentations and jagged, wind-swept pitches. "It looks impossible," I said.

"No, it can be done. Trouble is, when you've made it you're too done in for the summit."

"Osborn seems to think its shortness would make up for its difficulty."

6. **traverse** (trăv′ərs, trə-vûrs′): To traverse a mountain is to crisscross it instead of climbing straight up.

mountain as we could, less than half a mile from the tongue of its lowest glacier, and plunged into the arduous tasks of preparation for the ascent. Our food and equipment were unpacked, inspected and sorted, and finally repacked in lighter loads for transportation to more advanced camps. Hours were spent poring over maps and charts and studying the monstrous heights above us through telescope and binoculars. Under Nace's supervision, a thorough reconnaissance of the glacier was made and the route across it laid out; then began the backbreaking labor of moving up supplies and establishing the chain of camps.

Camps I and II were set up on the glacier itself, in the most sheltered sites we could find. Camp III we built at its upper end, as near as possible to the point where the great rock spine of K3 thrust itself free of ice and began its precipitous ascent. According to our plans, this would be the advance base of operations during the climb. The camps to be established higher up, on the mountain proper, would be too small and too exposed to serve as anything more than one or two nights' shelter. The total distance between the base camp and Camp III was only fifteen miles, but the utmost daily progress of our porters was five miles, and it was essential that we should never be more than twelve hours' march from food and shelter. Hour after hour, day after day, the long file of men wound up and down among the hummocks[7] and crevasses of the glacier, and finally the time arrived when we were ready to advance.

Leaving Dr. Schlapp in charge of eight porters at the base camp, we proceeded easily and on schedule, reaching Camp I the first night, Camp II the second, and the advance base the third. No men were left at Camps I and II, inasmuch as they were designed simply

Nace was silent a long moment before answering. Then for the first and only time I heard him speak the name of his dead companion. "That's what Furness thought," he said quietly. Then he lay down and wrapped himself in his blanket.

For the next two weeks the uppermost point of the valley was our home and workshop. We established our base camp as close to the

7 **hummocks:** here, mounds of ice.

as caches for food and equipment; and furthermore we knew we would need all the manpower available for the establishment of the higher camps on the mountain proper.

For more than three weeks now the weather had held perfectly, but on our first night at the advance base, as if by malignant prearrangement of nature, we had our first taste of the fury of a high Himalayan storm. It began with great streamers of lightning that flashed about the mountain like a halo; then heavily through the weird glare, snow began to fall. The wind rose. At first it was only sound—a remote, desolate moaning in the night high above us—but soon it descended, sucked down the deep valley as if into a gigantic funnel. Hour after hour it howled about the tents with hurricane frenzy, and the wild flapping of the canvas dinned in our ears like machine-gun fire.

There was no sleep for us that night or the next. For thirty-six hours the storm raged without lull, while we huddled in the icy gloom of the tents, exerting our last ounce of strength to keep from being buried alive or blown into eternity. At last, on the third morning, it was over, and we came out into a world transformed by a twelve-foot cloak of snow. No single landmark remained as it had been before, and our supplies and equipment were in the wildest confusion. Fortunately there had not been a single serious injury, but it was another three days before we had regained our strength and put the camp in order.

Then we waited. The storm did not return, and the sky beyond the ridges gleamed flawlessly clear; but night and day we could hear the roaring thunder of avalanches on the mountain above us. To have ventured so much as one step into that savage vertical wilderness before the new-fallen snow froze tight would have been suicidal. We chafed or waited patiently, according to our individual temperaments, while the days dragged by.

It was late one afternoon that Osborn returned from a short reconnaissance up the ridge. His eyes were shining and his voice jubilant.

"It's tight!" he cried. "Tight as a drum. We can go!" All of us stopped whatever we were doing. His excitement leaped like an electric spark from one to another. "I went about a thousand feet, and it's sound all the way. What do you say, Sayre? Tomorrow?"

Randolph hesitated, then looked at Nace.

"Better give it another day or two," said the Englishman.

Osborn glared at him. "Why?" he challenged.

"It's usually safer to wait till——"

"Wait! Wait!" Osborn exploded. "Don't you ever think of anything but waiting? My God, man, the snow's firm, I tell you!"

"It's firm down here," Nace replied quietly, "because the sun hits it only two hours a day. Up above it gets the sun twelve hours. It may not have frozen yet."

"The avalanches have stopped."

"That doesn't necessarily mean it will hold a man's weight."

"It seems to me Martin's point——" Randolph began.

Osborn wheeled on him. "Sure," he snapped. "I know. Martin's right. The cautious bloody English are always right. Let him have his way, and we'll be sitting here chewing our nails until the mountain falls down on us." His eyes flashed to Nace. "Maybe with a little less of that bloody cautiousness you English wouldn't have made such a mess of Everest. Maybe your pals Mallory and Furness wouldn't be dead."

"Osborn!" commanded Randolph sharply.

The youngster stared at Nace for another moment, breathing heavily. Then abruptly he turned away.

The next two days were clear and windless, but we still waited, following Nace's advice. There were no further brushes between him and Osborn, but an unpleasant air of restlessness and tension hung over the camp. I found myself chafing almost as impatiently as Osborn himself for the moment when we would break out of that maddening inactivity and begin the assault.

At last the day came. With the first paling of the sky a roped file of men, bent almost double beneath heavy loads, began slowly to climb the ice slope, just beneath the jagged line of the great east ridge. In accordance with prearranged plan, we proceeded in relays, this first group consisting of Nace, Johns, myself, and eight porters. It was our job to ascend approximately two thousand feet in a day's climbing and establish Camp IV at the most level and sheltered site we could find. We would spend the night there and return to the advance base next day, while the second relay, consisting of Osborn, Wittmer, and eight more porters, went up with their loads. This process was to continue until all necessary supplies were at Camp IV, and then the whole thing would be repeated between Camps IV and V and V and VI. From VI, at an altitude of about twenty-six thousand feet, the ablest and fittest men—presumably Nace and Osborn—would make the direct assault on the summit. Randolph and Bixler were to remain at the advance base thoughout the operations, acting as directors and co-ordinators. We were under the strictest orders that any man—sahib or porter—who suffered illness or injury should be brought down immediately.

How shall I describe those next two weeks beneath the great ice ridge of K3? In a sense there was no occurrence of importance, and at the same time everything happened that could possibly happen, short of actual disaster. We established Camp IV, came down again, went up again, came down again. Then we crept laboriously higher. With our axes we hacked uncountable thousands of steps in the gleam-

ing walls of ice. Among the rocky outcroppings of the cliffs we clung to holds and strained at ropes until we thought our arms would spring from their sockets. Storms swooped down on us, battered us, and passed. The wind increased, and the air grew steadily colder and more difficult to breathe. One morning two of the porters awoke with their feet frozen black; they had to be sent down. A short while later Johns developed an uncontrollable nosebleed and was forced to descend to a lower camp. Wittmer was suffering from racking headaches and I from a continually dry throat. But providentially, the one enemy we feared the most in that icy gale-lashed hell did not again attack us. No snow fell. And day by day, foot by foot, we ascended.

It is during ordeals like this that the surface trappings of a man are shed and his secret mettle[8] laid bare. There were no shirkers or quitters among us—I had known that from the beginning—but now, with each passing day, it became more manifest which were the strongest and ablest among us. Beyond all argument, these were Osborn and Nace.

Osborn was magnificent. All the boyish impatience and moodiness which he had exhibited earlier were gone, and, now that he was at last at work in his natural element, he emerged as the peerless mountaineer he was. His energy was inexhaustible, his speed, both on rock and ice, almost twice that of any other man in the party. He was always discovering new routes and shortcuts. Often he ascended by the ridge itself, instead of using the traverse beneath it, as had been officially prescribed; but his craftsmanship was so sure and his performance so brilliant that no one ever thought of taking him to task. Indeed, there was such vigor, buoyancy, and youth in everything he did that it gave heart to all the rest of us.

8. **mettle** (mět′l): courage, spirit.

In contrast, Nace was slow, methodical, unspectacular. Since he and I worked in the same relay, I was with him almost constantly, and to this day I carry in my mind the clear image of the man: his tall body bent almost double against endless shimmering slopes of ice; his lean brown face bent in utter concentration on the problem in hand, then raised searchingly to the next; the bright prong of his ax rising, falling, rising, falling, with tireless rhythm, until the steps in the glassy incline were so wide and deep that the most clumsy of the porters could not have slipped from them had he tried. Osborn attacked the mountain head-on. Nace studied it, sparred with it, wore it down. His spirit did not flap from his sleeve like a pennon;[9] it was deep inside him— patient, indomitable.

The day soon came when I learned from him what it is to be a great mountaineer. We

9. **pennon** (pĕn'ən): flag.

were making the ascent from Camp IV to V, and an almost perpendicular ice wall had made it necessary for us to come out for a few yards on the exposed crest of the ridge. There were six of us in the party, roped together, with Nace leading, myself second, and four porters bringing up the rear. The ridge at this particular point was free of snow, but razor-thin, and the rocks were covered with a smooth glaze of ice. On either side the mountain dropped away in sheer precipices of five thousand feet.

Suddenly the last porter slipped. I heard the ominous scraping of boot nails behind me and, turning, saw a gesticulating figure plunge sideways into the abyss. There was a scream as the next porter was jerked off too. I remember trying frantically to dig into the ridge with my ax, realizing at the same time it would no more hold against the weight of the falling men than a pin stuck in a wall. Then I heard Nace shout, "Jump!" As he said it, the rope went tight about my waist, and I went hurtling after him into

space on the opposite side of the ridge. After me came the nearest porter. . . .

What happened then must have happened in five yards and a fifth of a second. I heard myself cry out, and the glacier, a mile below, rushed up at me, spinning. Then both were blotted out in a violent spasm, as the rope jerked taut. I hung for a moment, an inert mass, feeling that my body had been cut in two; then I swung in slowly to the side of the mountain. Above me the rope lay tight and motionless across the crest of the ridge, our weight exactly counterbalancing that of the men who had fallen on the far slope.

Nace's voice came up from below. "You chaps on the other side!" he shouted. "Start climbing slowly. We're climbing too."

In five minutes we had all regained the ridge. The porters and I crouched panting on the jagged rocks, our eyes closed, the sweat beading our faces in frozen drops. Nace carefully examined the rope that again hung loosely between us.

"All right, men," he said presently. "Let's get on to camp for a cup of tea."

Above Camp V the whole aspect of the ascent changed. The angle of the ridge eased off, and the ice, which lower down had covered the mountain like a sheath, lay only in scattered patches between the rocks. Fresh enemies, however, instantly appeared to take the place of the old. We were now laboring at an altitude of more than twenty-five thousand feet—well above the summits of the highest surrounding peaks—and day and night, without protection or respite, we were buffeted by the fury of the wind. Worse than this was that the atmosphere had become so rarefied it could scarcely support life. Breathing itself was a major physical effort, and our progress upward consisted of two or three painful steps followed by a long period of rest in which our hearts pounded

wildly and our burning lungs gasped for air. Each of us carried a small cylinder of oxygen in his pack, but we used it only in emergencies and found that, while its immediate effect was salutary, it left us later even worse off than before. My throat dried and contracted until it felt as if it were lined with brass. The faces of all of us, under our beards and windburn, grew haggard and strained.

But the great struggle was now mental as much as physical. The lack of air induced a lethargy of mind and spirit; confidence and the powers of thought and decision waned, and dark foreboding crept out from the secret recesses of the subconscious. The wind seemed to carry strange sounds, and we kept imagining we saw things which we knew were not there. The mountain, to all of us, was no longer a mere giant of rock and ice; it had become a living thing, an enemy, watching us, waiting for us, hostile, relentless, and aware. Inch by inch we crept upward through that empty forgotten world above the world, and only one last thing remained to us of human consciousness and human will: to go on. To go on.

On the fifteenth day after we had first left the advance base we pitched Camp VI at an altitude of almost twenty-six thousand feet. It was located near the uppermost extremity of the great east ridge, directly beneath the so-called shoulder of the mountain. On the far side of the shoulder the monstrous north face of K3 fell sheer to the glaciers, two miles below. And above it and to the left rose the symmetrical bulk of the summit pyramid. The topmost rocks of its highest pinnacle were clearly visible from the shoulder, and the intervening two thousand feet seemed to offer no insuperable obstacles.

Camp VI, which was in reality no camp at all, but a single tent, was large enough to accommodate only three men. Osborn established it with the aid of Wittmer and one porter; then, the following morning, Wittmer and the porter descended to Camp V, and Nace and I went up. It was our plan that Osborn and Nace should launch the final assault—the next day, if the weather held—with myself in support, following their progress through binoculars and going to their aid or summoning help from below if anything went wrong. As the three of us lay in the tent that night, the summit seemed already within arm's reach, victory securely in our grasp.

And then the blow fell. With malignant timing, which no power on earth could have made us believe was a simple accident of nature, the mountain hurled at us its last line of defense. It snowed.

For a day and a night the great flakes drove down on us, swirling and swooping in the wind, blotting out the summit, the shoulder, everything beyond the tiny white-walled radius of our tents. Hour after hour we lay in our sleeping bags, stirring only to eat or to secure the straining rope and canvas. Our feet froze under their thick layers of wool and rawhide. Our heads and bodies throbbed with a dull nameless aching, and time crept over our numbed minds like a glacier. At last, during the morning of the following day, it cleared. The sun came out in a thin blue sky, and the summit pyramid again appeared above us, now whitely robed in fresh snow. But still we waited. Until the snow either froze or was blown away by the wind it would have been the rashest courting of destruction for us to have ascended a foot beyond the camp. Another day passed. And another.

By the third nightfall our nerves were at the breaking point. For hours on end we had scarcely moved or spoken, and the only sounds in all the world were the endless moaning of the wind outside and the harsh sucking noise of our breathing. I knew that, one way or another, the end had come. Our meager food supply was running out; even with careful rationing there was enough left for only two more days.

Presently Nace stirred in his sleeping bag and sat up. "We'll have to go down tomorrow," he said quietly.

For a moment there was silence in the tent. Then Osborn struggled to a sitting position and faced him.

"No," he said.

"There's still too much loose snow above. We can't make it,"

"But it's clear. As long as we can see——"

Nace shook his head. "Too dangerous. We'll go down tomorrow and lay in a fresh supply. Then we'll try again."

"Once we go down we're licked. You know it."

Nace shrugged. "Better to be licked than . . ." The strain of speech was suddenly too much for him and he fell into a violent paroxysm of coughing. When it had passed there was a long silence.

Then suddenly Osborn spoke again. "Look, Nace," he said, "I'm going up tomorrow."

The Englishman shook his head.

"I'm going—understand?"

For the first time since I had known him I saw Nace's eyes flash in anger. "I'm the senior member of this group," he said, "I forbid you to go!"

Osborn jerked himself to his knees, almost upsetting the tiny tent. "You forbid me? This may be your sixth time on this mountain, and all that, but you don't *own* it! I know what you're up to. You haven't got it in you to make the top yourself, so you don't want anyone else to make it. That's it, isn't it? Isn't it?" He sat down again suddenly, gasping for breath.

Nace looked at him with level eyes. "This mountain has beaten me five times," he said softly. "It killed my best friend. It means more to me to climb it than anything else in the

world. Maybe I'll make it and maybe I won't. But if I do, it will be as a rational intelligent human being—not as a fool throwing my life away. . . ."

He collapsed into another fit of coughing and fell back in his sleeping bag. Osborn, too, was still. They lay there inert, panting, too exhausted for speech.

It was hours later that I awoke from dull, uneasy sleep. In the faint light I saw Nace fumbling with the flap of the tent.

"What is it?" I asked.

"Osborn. He's gone."

The words cut like a blade through my lethargy. I struggled to my feet and followed Nace from the tent.

Outside, the dawn was seeping up the eastern sky. It was very cold, but the wind had fallen and the mountain seemed to hang suspended in a vast stillness. Above us the summit pyramid climbed bleakly into space, like the last outpost of a spent and lifeless planet. Raising my binoculars, I swept them over the gray waste. At first I saw nothing but rock and ice; then, suddenly, something moved.

"I've got him," I whispered.

As I spoke, the figure of Osborn sprang into clear focus against a patch of ice. He took three or four slow upward steps, stopped, went on again. I handed the glasses to Nace.

The Englishman squinted through them, returned them to me, and reentered the tent. When I followed, he had already laced his boots and was pulling on his outer gloves.

"He's not far," he said. "Can't have been gone more than half an hour." He seized his ice ax and started out again.

"Wait," I said. "I'm going with you."

Nace shook his head. "Better stay here."

"I'm going with you," I said.

He said nothing further, but waited while I made ready. In a few moments we left the tent, roped up, and started off.

Almost immediately we were on the shoulder and confronted with the paralyzing two-mile drop of the north face; but we negotiated the short exposed stretch without mishap, and in ten minutes were working up the base of the summit pyramid. The going here was easier, in a purely climbing sense: the angle of ascent was not steep, and there was firm rock for hand- and foot-holds between the patches of snow and ice. Our progress, however, was creepingly slow. There seemed to be literally no air at all to breathe, and after almost every step we were forced to rest, panting and gasping as we leaned forward against our axes. My heart swelled and throbbed with every movement until I thought it would explode.

The minutes crawled into hours and still we climbed. Presently the sun came up. Its level rays streamed across the clouds, far below, and glinted from the summits of distant peaks. But, although the pinnacle of K3 soared a full three thousand feet above anything in the surrounding world, we had scarcely any sense of height. The wilderness of mountain valley and glacier that spread beneath us to the horizon was flattened and remote, an unreal, insubstantial landscape seen in a dream. We had no connection with it, or it with us. All living, all awareness, purpose, and will, was concentrated in the last step and the next: to put one foot before the other; to breathe; to ascend. We struggled on in silence.

I do not know how long it was since we had left the camp—it might have been two hours, it might have been six—when we suddenly sighted Osborn. We had not been able to find him again since our first glimpse through the binoculars; but now, unexpectedly and abruptly, as we came up over a jagged outcropping of rock, there he was. He was at a point, only a few yards above us, where the mountain steepened into an almost vertical wall. The smooth surface directly in front of him was

obviously unclimbable, but two alternate routes were presented. To the left, a chimney[10] cut obliquely across the wall, forbiddingly steep, but seeming to offer adequate holds. To the right was a gentle slope of snow that curved upward and out of sight behind the rocks. As we watched, Osborn ascended to the edge of the snow, stopped, and probed it with his ax. Then, apparently satisfied that it would bear his weight he stepped out on the slope.

I felt Nace's body tense. "Paul!" he cried out.

His voice was too weak and hoarse to carry. Osborn continued his ascent.

Nace cupped his hands and called his name again, and this time Osborn turned. "Wait!" cried the Englishman.

Osborn stood still, watching us, as we struggled up the few yards to the edge of the snow slope. Nace's breath came in shuddering gasps, but he climbed faster than I had ever seen him climb before.

"Come back!" he called. "Come off the snow!"

"It's all right. The crust is firm," Osborn called back.

"But it's melting. There's . . ." Nace paused, fighting for air. "There's nothing underneath!"

In a sudden sickening flash I saw what he meant. Looked at from directly below, at the point where Osborn had come to it, the slope on which he stood appeared as a harmless covering of snow over the rocks. From where we were now, however, a little to one side, it could be seen that it was in reality no covering at all, but merely a cornice or unsupported platform clinging to the side of the mountain. Below it was not rock, but ten thousand feet of blue air.

"Come back!" I cried. "Come back!"

Osborn hesitated, then took a downward step. But he never took the next. For in that same instant the snow directly in front of him

10. **chimney:** formation of rock resembling a chimney.

disappeared. It did not seem to fall or to break away. It was just soundlessly and magically no longer there. In the spot where Osborn had been about to set his foot there was now revealed the abysmal drop of the north face of K3.

I shut my eyes, but only for a second, and when I reopened them Osborn was still, miraculously, there. Nace was shouting, "Don't move! Don't move an inch!"

"The rope—" I heard myself saying.

The Englishman shook his head. "We'd have to throw it, and the impact would be too much. Brace yourself and play it out." As he spoke, his eyes were traveling over the rocks that bordered the snow bridge. Then he moved forward.

I wedged myself into a cleft in the wall and let out the rope which extended between us. A few yards away Osborn stood in the snow, transfixed, one foot a little in front of the other. But my eyes now were on Nace. Cautiously, but with astonishing rapidity, he edged along the rocks beside the cornice. There was a moment when his only support was an inch-wide ledge beneath his feet, another where there was nothing under his feet at all, and he supported himself wholly by his elbows and hands. But he advanced steadily and at last reached a shelf wide enough for him to turn around on. At this point he was perhaps six feet away from Osborn.

"It's wide enough here to hold both of us," he said in a quiet voice. "I'm going to reach out my ax. Don't move until you're sure you have a grip on it. When I pull, jump."

He searched the wall behind him and found a hold for his left hand. Then he slowly extended his ice ax, head foremost, until it was within two feet of Osborn's shoulder. "Grip it!" he cried suddenly. Osborn's hands shot out and seized the ax. "Jump!"

There was a flash of steel in the sunlight and a hunched figure hurtled inward from the snow to the ledge. Simultaneously another figure hurtled out. The haft[11] of the ax jerked suddenly from Nace's hand, and he lurched forward and downward. A violent spasm convulsed his body as the rope went taut. Then it was gone. Nace did not seem to hit the snow; he simply disappeared through it, soundlessly. In the same instant the snow itself was gone. The frayed, yellow end of broken rope spun lazily in space. . . .

Somehow my eyes went to Osborn. He was crouched on the ledge where Nace had been a moment before, staring dully at the ax he held in his hands. Beyond his head, not two hundred feet above, the white untrodden pinnacle of K3 stabbed the sky.

Perhaps ten minutes passed, perhaps a half hour. I closed my eyes and leaned forward motionless against the rock, my face against my arm. I neither thought nor felt; my body and mind alike were enveloped in a suffocating numbness. Through it at last came the sound of Osborn moving. Looking up, I saw he was standing beside me.

"I'm going to try for the top," he said tonelessly.

I merely stared at him.

"Will you come?"

"No," I said.

Osborn hesitated; then turned and began slowly climbing the steep chimney above us. Halfway up he paused, struggling for breath. Then he resumed his laborious upward progress and presently disappeared beyond the crest.

I stayed where I was, and the hours passed. The sun reached its zenith above the peak and sloped away behind it. And at last I heard above me the sound of Osborn returning. As I looked up, his figure appeared at the top of the

11. **haft:** handle.

chimney and began the descent. His clothing was in tatters, and I could tell from his movements that only the thin flame of his will stood between him and collapse. In another few minutes he was standing beside me.

"Did you get there?" I asked dully.

He shook his head. "I couldn't make it," he answered. "I didn't have what it takes."

We roped together silently and began the descent to the camp.

There is nothing more to be told of the sixth assault on K3—at least not from the experiences of the men who made it. Osborn and I reached Camp V in safety, and three days later the entire expedition gathered at the advance base. It was decided, in view of the tragedy that had occurred, to make no further attempt on the summit, and by the end of the week we had begun the evacuation of the mountain.

It remained for another year and other men to reveal the epilogue.

The summer following our attempt a combined English-Swiss expedition stormed the peak successfully. After weeks of hardship and struggle they attained the topmost pinnacle of the giant, only to find that what should have been their great moment of triumph was, instead, a moment of the bitterest disappointment. For when they came out at last upon the summit they saw that they were *not* the first. An ax stood there. Its haft was embedded in rock and ice and on its steel head were the engraved words: TO MARTIN FROM JOHN.

They were sporting men. On their return to civilization they told their story, and the name of the conqueror of K3 was made known to the world.

Reading Check

1. What mountain are the men trying to climb?
2. Why do they want to conquer the mountain?
3. After the storm, why must the men wait until the snow freezes before they can advance?
4. Why, above twenty-five thousand feet, does their struggle become mental as well as physical?
5. Which climber reaches the peak and what does he leave there?

For Study and Discussion

Analyzing and Interpreting the Story

1a. Describe the two conflicts in this story: the conflict between Nace and Osborn and the conflict between the exploring party and the natural obstacles they faced. **b.** In which conflict were you more interested? Why?

2a. In what ways are Nace and Osborn different? **b.** Refer to paragraphs in the story that bring out these differences.

3. The two conflicts are resolved at the end of the story. How do they turn out?

4a. What do you think the ax symbolizes or means in the story? **b.** Why does Osborn place it on top of the mountain?

5. In what ways does K3 function as a character in this story?

Language and Vocabulary

Using Context Clues

You can often find the meaning of an unfamiliar word by using clues provided by the word's **context,** the rest of the words in the sentence or passage. In the following sentence from the story, you can use context clues to find the meaning of *accommodate*:

> Camp VI, which was in reality no camp at all, but a single tent, was large enough to *accommodate* only three men.

What clues tell you that the word *accommodate* means "to supply room for"?

Use context clues to determine the meanings of the italicized words in the following passages from the story. Check your answers in the glossary or in a dictionary.

> The naked *desolation* of the valley was unrelieved by any motion, color, or sound . . .

> . . . with each passing day, it became more *manifest* which were the strongest and ablest among us.

> . . . while its immediate effect was *salutary*, it left us later even worse off than before.

Descriptive Writing

Using Sensory Appeal in Description

Notice that the italicized words in the following sentence from "Top Man" help you to see the fury of the Himalayan storm:

> It began with *great streamers of lightning* that *flashed* about the mountain like a *halo;* then *heavily* through the *weird glare, snow* began to fall.

This passage describing the storm continues with the following sentences. Point out the words in these sentences which appeal to your sense of hearing:

> The wind rose. At first it was only sound — a remote, desolate moaning in the night high above us — but soon it descended, sucked down the deep valley as if into a gigantic funnel. Hour after hour it howled about the tents with hurricane frenzy, and the wild flapping of the canvas dinned in our ears like machine-gun fire.

Write several sentences of your own about a game, a fight, a race, or other contest, in which you try to describe an action vividly by choosing words with sensory appeal.

About the Author

James Ramsey Ullman (1907–1971)

James Ramsey Ullman was born in New York City and attended Andover and Princeton. After his senior thesis won a prize, he decided on a writing career. He worked as a reporter and as a producer of plays before settling down to full-time writing.

Ullman is best known for his books on mountains and mountain climbing. *High Conquest* is a history of mountaineering. His novel *The White Tower* is a dramatic story about mountain climbing in the Alps.

Antigone°

Retold by
REX WARNER

Many Greek myths center on the ancient city of Thebes and its royal family. In this myth, Thebes has been torn by a civil war. The war was caused by two brothers who claimed the right to the throne. As the myth opens, the two brothers lie dead: they have killed each other in battle. Their uncle, Creon, has become king. Antigone is the sister of the two dead men.

In reading this story, you must know about the religious law of the ancient Greeks, which obliged them to perform burial rites for their dead. The Greeks believed that if burial rites were not performed, the soul of a dead person would wander forever in search of rest.

Creon became king of Thebes at a time when the city had lost half its army and at least half of its best warriors in civil war. The war was over. Eteocles,[1] the king, was dead; dead also was his brother Polynices,[2] who had come with the army of the Argives[3] to fight for his own right to the kingdom.

Creon, as the new king, decided first of all to show his people how unforgivable it was to make war upon one's own country. To Eteocles, who had reigned in Thebes, he gave a splendid burial; but he ordered that, upon pain of death, no one was to prepare for funeral or even sprinkle earth upon the body of Polynices. It was to lie as it had fallen in the plain for birds and beasts to devour. To make certain that his orders should be carried out Creon set a patrol of men to watch the body night and day.

Antigone and Ismene,[4] sisters of Polynices, heard the king's orders with alarm and shame. They had loved both their brothers, and hated the thought that one of them should lie unburied, unable to join the world of the ghosts, mutilated and torn by the teeth of dogs and jackals and by the beaks and talons of birds. Ismene, in spite of her feelings, did not dare oppose the king; but Antigone stole out of the city by night, and, after searching among the piled-up bodies of those who had died in the great battle, found the body of her brother. She lightly covered it with dust, and said for it the prayers that ought to be said for the dead.

Next day it was reported to Creon that someone (the guards did not know who) had disobeyed the king's orders and scattered earth over the body of Polynices. Creon swore an oath that if the guilty person should be found, even though that person was a member of his own family, he or she should die for it. He

°**Antigone** (ăn-tĭg′ə-nē′).
1. **Eteocles** (ĭ-tē′ə-klēz′).
2. **Polynices** (pŏl′ĭ-nī′sēz).
3. **Argives** (är′gīvz′): people of the city of Argos.

4. **Ismene** (ĭs-mē′nē).

Antigone Between Two Guards Before Creon. Dolon Painter (c. 380–370 B.C.).
Greek Vase.

threatened the guards also with death if they failed to find the criminal, and told them immediately to uncover the body and leave it to the birds and beasts of prey.

That day a hot wind blew from the south. Clouds of dust covered the plain, and Antigone again stole out of the city to complete her work of burying her brother. This time, however, the guards kept better watch. They seized her and brought her before King Creon.

Creon was moved by no other feelings than the feelings of one whose orders have been disobeyed. "Did you know," he asked Antigone, "the law that I made and the penalty that I laid down for those who broke the law?"

"I knew it," Antigone replied, "but there are other laws, made not by men but by the gods.

There is a law of pity and of mercy. That law is to be obeyed first. After I have obeyed that, I will, if I may, obey the laws that are made by men."

"If you love your brother," said Creon, "more than the established laws of your country and your king, then you must bear the penalty of the laws, loving your brother in the world of the dead."

"You may kill me with your laws," Antigone replied, " but to me death is, in all these sufferings, less of an evil than would be treachery to my brother or cowardice when the time came to help him."

Her confident and calm words stirred Creon to even greater anger. Now her sister Ismene, who had at first been too frightened to help Antigone in her defiance of the law, came for-

Antigone **69**

ward and asked to be allowed to share in Antigone's punishment; but Antigone would not permit her to claim a share with her in the deed or in its results. Nor would Creon listen to any appeal for mercy. Not wishing to have the blood of his niece upon his own hands, he gave orders that she should be put into an underground chamber, walled up from the light and then left to die.

So Antigone was carried away to a slow and lingering death, willing to suffer it, since she had obeyed the promptings of her heart. She had been about to marry Haemon,[5] the king's son, but, instead of the palace that she would have entered as a bride, she was now going to the house of death.

Haemon himself came to beg his father to be merciful. He spoke mildly, but let it clearly be understood that neither he nor the rest of the people of Thebes approved of so savage a sentence. It was true that Antigone had broken the law; but it was also true that she had acted as a sister ought to act when her brother was unburied. And, Haemon said, though most people did not dare oppose the king in his anger, nevertheless most people in their hearts felt as *he* did.

Haemon's love for Antigone and even his good will toward his father only increased the fury of the king. With harsh words he drove his son from him.

Next came the blind prophet Tiresias[6] to warn King Creon that the gods were angry with him both for his merciless punishment of Antigone and for leaving the body of Polynices to be desecrated[7] by the wild beasts and birds. Creon might have remembered how often in the past the words of Tiresias had been fulfilled, but now, in his obstinate rage, he

merely insulted the prophet. "You have been bribed," he said, "either by Haemon or by some traitor to try and save the life of a criminal by dishonest threats that have nothing to do with the gods at all."

Tiresias turned his sightless eyes on the king. "This very day," he said, "before the sun sets, you will pay twice, yes, with two dead bodies, for the sin which you could easily have avoided. As for me, I shall keep far away from one who, in his own pride, rejects the gods and is sure to suffer."

Tiresias went away, and now Creon for the first time began to feel that it was possible that his punishments had been too hard. For the first time, but too late, he was willing to listen to the advice of his council, who begged him to be merciful, to release Antigone and to give burial to the body of Polynices.

With no very good grace Creon consented to do as he had been advised. He gave orders for the burial of Polynices and went himself to release Antigone from the prison in which she had been walled away from the light. Joyfully his son Haemon went ahead of the rest with pickaxes and bars for breaking down the wall. But when they broke the stones of the wall they found that Antigone had made a noose out of the veil which she was wearing and hanged herself. Haemon could not bear to outlive her. He drew his sword and plunged it into his heart before the eyes of his father. Then he fell forward dead on the body of the girl whom he had wished to be his wife.

As for Creon he had scarcely time to lament for his son when news reached him of another disaster. His wife had heard of Haemon's death and she too had taken her own life. So the words of Tiresias were fulfilled.

5. **Haemon** (hē′mŏn).
6. **Tiresias** (tī-rē′sē-əs).
7. **desecrated** (dĕs′ə-krāt′ĭd) treated in a way that did not show reverence.

Reading Check

1. Why did Polynices fight his brother Eteocles?
2. Who became king when Eteocles died?
3. What sentence did the king order for anyone who tried to bury Polynices?
4. What did Antigone do after she was put in the chamber to die?
5. Why did Haemon take his own life?

For Study and Discussion

Analyzing and Interpreting the Myth

1. In heroic stories, a conflict takes place between the hero or heroine and an enemy. In many stories, the conflict involves physical strength. However, in this myth, the conflict involves two strong wills. **a.** Why does Creon forbid burial to Polynices? **b.** Why does Antigone defy the king's law?

2. The tragedy that occurs could have been prevented if Creon had not been so proud and stubborn. **a.** Which two people come to Creon and ask him to show mercy to Antigone? **b.** How does each one try to persuade the king to change his mind?

3. What are the tragic results of Creon's stubbornness and pride?

4. In one sense, Antigone loses to Creon in their conflict of wills. But, in another sense, how does she also win?

5. Is Creon a loser or a winner or both at the end of this story? Explain your answer.

6. In most myths and legends, some characters have supernatural powers that set them apart from ordinary people. In this story, how does the prophet Tiresias show that he possesses such powers?

Literary Elements

Interpreting Values from a Myth

Myths are stories that reveal the important beliefs of a people. A myth like "Antigone" can tell us a great deal about what qualities the ancient Greek people valued and what kind of behavior they admired.

In this myth, two people obey two conflicting laws. The major problem in this myth is, which law must be obeyed?

Find the words spoken by Antigone that tell what laws she believes must be valued more than the king's laws. What does Antigone say on page 69 about reverence and family loyalty?

The blind prophet Tiresias is important in this myth. The prophet is a holy man who can interpret the will of the gods. According to the prophet, Creon is sure to suffer. Why? What does Creon value more than the will of the gods?

About the Author

Rex Warner   (1905–1986)

Rex Warner was born in Birmingham, England, and attended Wadham College, Oxford. He worked as a teacher in England and Egypt, and also had positions in Germany and Greece, before coming to the United States in 1961. He taught English at the University of Connecticut. Warner was known as a novelist, a poet, an essayist, and a translator of Greek classics. Among his novels are *The Wild Goose Chase* and *The Converts*.

DEVELOPING SKILLS
IN CRITICAL THINKING

Analyzing a Literary Work

A question may ask you to *analyze* some aspect of a literary work. When you analyze something, you take it apart to see how each part works. In literary analysis you generally focus on some limited aspect of a work in order to better understand and appreciate the work as a whole. For example you might analyze the motives of the mother who, in "The Street," makes her son fight; you might analyze the meaning of the title "Raymond's Run" and its relation to the story as a whole; you might analyze the way in which setting affects or influences characters in "Up the Slide" and "Top Man."

Suppose you have decided to analyze the sources of humor in "The No-Talent Kid." To begin your analysis, ask the following questions about the story:

1. *Does the author's style and choice of words evoke humor?* Vonnegut uses exaggerated, humorous figures of speech: ". . . members of the C Band dropped out of the waltz, one by one, as though mustard gas were coming out of the ventilators . . ."; he refers to the Johnstown High School drum as "this eighth wonder of the world."

2. *Do the characters' actions and dialogue reveal humor?* Some of Plummer's actions are so extreme that they are laughable: Plummer, the worst member of C Band, challenges Flammer, the best clarinetist in the A Band. Plummer misunderstands and then reverses the point of Helmholtz's lecture about people being unable

to do everything well: "With a job as big as you've got, it'd be a miracle if you did the whole thing right."

3. *Do unexpected situations or events provide humor?* Members of A Band get their letters for musical accomplishments; Plummer succeeds in getting an A Band letter because he owns a large drum (which he cannot play) and pulls it well.

Why do you suppose Vonnegut decided to write about Plummer and Helmholtz in an entertaining, comic manner? Do you think the two characters' problems deserve a serious treatment?

Choose a topic for analysis from a selection in this unit or, if you wish, use one of the topics listed in the first paragraph above. Then write a short analysis showing how the topic relates to the selection as a whole.

PRACTICE IN READING AND WRITING

The Writing Process

The word *process* refers to a series of actions or some method of doing something in a number of steps. The writing process consists of several important stages or phases: *prewriting, writing a first draft, evaluating, revising, proofreading,* and *writing the final version.* Much of the work that goes into a paper actually precedes the writing. In the prewriting stage, writers make decisions about what to say and how to say it. Prewriting activities include choosing and limiting a topic, identifying purpose and audience, gathering ideas, organizing ideas, and arriving at a controlling idea for the paper. Some people do most of the planning in their heads; other people like to jot down their ideas on note cards or on a sheet of paper. During the prewriting stage some people find it helpful to make an outline. In the next stage, the writer uses notes or an outline to prepare a first draft of the paper. The writer then evaluates, or judges, the work and considers how it might be improved. In the revising stage, the writer rewrites the draft, often several times, adding or deleting ideas, rearranging sentences, rephrasing for clarity. The writer then proofreads the paper for errors in spelling, punctuation, and grammar. After the final corrections are made, the writer produces a clean copy and proofreads it.

The steps in this process are interdependent. Writers often find that even after they have rewritten a paper more than once, they want to make changes in its organization or to add new ideas.

Descriptive Writing

Description is the kind of writing that creates a picture of something—of a person, a scene, an object, or an action. This passage of description is from Arthur Gordon's story "The Sea Devil" (page 30). It helps you picture a setting.

> The man came out of the house and stood quite still, listening. Behind him, the lights glowed in the cheerful room, the books were neat and orderly in their cases, the radio talked importantly to itself. In front of him, the bay stretched dark and silent, one of the countless lagoons that border the coast where Florida thrusts its green thumb deep into the tropics.
>
> It was late in September. The night was breathless; summer's dead hand still lay heavy on the land. The man moved forward six paces and stood on the sea wall. He dropped his cigarette and noted where the tiny spark hissed and went out. The tide was beginning to ebb.

1. What specific sights and sounds does Gordon help you experience?
2. How does Gordon give you the impression that the house represents the comfort and security of civilization?
3. What words give the impression that the natural world is mysterious?
4. Where does Gordon use figurative language in the first paragraph? What does he mean by calling the night "breathless"?

Suggestions for Writing

Write a paragraph describing one of the following people, places, or things, or choose a subject of your own. Tell what your subject looks like. If you want to, tell also how it smells, sounds, tastes, or feels, or what it reminds you of.

> An unusual person you see often
> A traffic accident
> A crowd
> Something from nature; a beach, a forest, a swamp
> An amusement park

Here are some guidelines to help you plan, write, and revise your paper.

Prewriting

- Decide on the impression or mood you want to create. In "Top Man" the author gives the mountain human characteristics to make it seem alive and more deadly or menacing: "The wind seemed to carry strange sounds, and we kept imagining we saw things which we knew were not there. The mountain, to all of us, was no longer a mere giant of rock and ice; it had become a living thing, an enemy, watching us, waiting for us, hostile, relentless, and aware."
- Choose specific details that help your reader imagine how something looks, sounds, smells, tastes, or feels. Make sure these details strengthen the mood of your paragraph. Comic-book writers communicate sounds with words like *pow, wham,* and *ugh.* Kurt Vonnegut, in his story "The No-Talent Kid," helps us hear a sound when he says that the music director "*clattered* his stick against the music stand." Arthur Gordon helps us share the fisherman's sensations when he says, "he felt the *hot* blood start instantly. . . ."

- Use precise nouns, verbs, and modifiers to sustain your mood. In "The Sea Devil" the author says: "A school of sardines surfaced suddenly, *skittering* along like drops of mercury." *Skitter,* which means "to skim rapidly along a surface," helps us picture exactly how the fish move, and tells us that they are frightened.
- Arrange details in a logical order. In "Top Man" the author arranges details to direct us in a clear, orderly way from left to right and up: "To the left, a chimney cut obliquely across the wall, forbiddingly steep, but seeming to offer adequate holds. To the right was a gentle slope of snow that curved upward and out of sight behind the rocks."

Writing

- Open with a statement giving your impression of the subject.
- Use your prewriting notes as a guide for choosing specific details to support the mood of your paragraph.
- Arrange your details in spatial order.

Evaluating and Revising

- Does the paragraph focus on a person, place, object, or event and create a particular mood or impression?
- Are enough specific details included to give the reader a mental picture of your subject?
- Is every sentence directly related to the main impression?
- Are the details arranged in spatial order?
- Add, cut, replace, or reorder details until you are satisfied with your paragraph.

Proofreading and Making a Final Copy

- Check your revised paper for errors in grammar, usage, and mechanics.
- Prepare a final copy and check it for accuracy.

For Further Reading

Bolton, Carole, *Never Jam Today* (Atheneum, 1971; paperback, Atheneum)

In this novel, which is set in the early 1900s, seventeen-year-old Maddy Franklin joins the movement to give women the right to vote.

Drimmer, Frederick, *The Elephant Man* (Putnam, 1985)

Here is the dramatic story of John Merrick, called the elephant man.

Gannon, Robert, editor, *Great Survival Adventures* (Random House, 1973)

This collection includes nine first-person accounts of struggles to survive fearful disasters.

Gibson, Althea, *I Always Wanted to Be Somebody* (Harper & Row, 1958; paperback, Noble & Noble)

This famous athlete's autobiography tells of her childhood in Harlem, and of how she became one of America's great tennis players.

Gunther, John, *Death Be Not Proud: A Memoir* (Harper & Row, 1949; paperback, Harper, 1965)

A father tells of his seventeen-year-old son's battle against cancer. This true story is painful to read, but it reveals the grace and strength that people are capable of.

Holman, Felice, *Slake's Limbo* (Scribner, 1974)

Thirteen-year-old Slake spends 121 days underground in the New York City subway system as a refuge from his unhappiness.

London, Jack, *The Call of the Wild* and *White Fang* (Many editions)

These are two of the most famous animal stories in literature.

Morris, Jeannie, *Brian Piccolo: A Short Season* (Rand McNally, 1971; paperback, Dell)

This biography covers Brian Piccolo's life from his high school years, through his career as a running back with the Chicago Bears, to his battle with cancer at the age of twenty-six.

Portis, Charles, *True Grit* (Simon & Schuster, 1968; paperback, New American Library)

Fourteen-year-old Mattie, who has "true grit," hires Rooster G. Cogburn, an old U.S. marshal, to help her track down her father's murderer.

Taylor, Theodore, *The Cay* (Doubleday, 1969; paperback, Avon, 1976)

The young man and the old man in this novel must survive together on a small coral island after their ship is torpedoed.

Ullman, James Ramsey, *Banner in the Sky* (paperback, Archway, 1984)

Here is an exciting mountaineering story.

Viereck, Phillip, *The Summer I Was Lost* (John Day, 1965; paperback titled *Terror on the Mountain*, Starline)

A boy discovers that it takes more than muscle to survive when he gets lost in the woods.

White, Robb *Deathwatch* (Doubleday, 1972; paperback, Dell)

In this suspenseful novel, a young man finds himself pursued in the desert by a vicious killer.

Woltizer, Meg, *The Dream Book* (Greenwillow Books, 1986)

Here is a story about two friends, timid and shy Claudia, and tough and fearless Mindy.

GENERATIONS

Two people can see the same situation, or the same event, in different ways. In this unit, you will find clashes that result from people thinking, "But that's not the way *I* see it." In some of these selections, young people disagree with adults.

One of the values of literature is that it can expand our experience. Perhaps in some of these selections you will recognize your own point of view. But you might also discover the pleasure of seeing some aspect of life through another person's eyes.

The Hatch Family (1871) by Eastman Johnson (1824–1906). Oil on Canvas.
The Metropolitan Museum of Art, gift of Frederic H. Hatch, 1926.

A Cap for Steve

MORLEY CALLAGHAN

How can something as trivial as a baseball cap divide and then unite a father and son?

Dave Diamond, a poor man, a carpenter's assistant, was a small, wiry, quick-tempered individual who had learned how to make every dollar count in his home. His wife, Anna, had been sick a lot, and his twelve-year-old son, Steve, had to be kept in school. Steve, a big-eyed, shy kid, ought to have known the value of money as well as Dave did. It had been ground into him.

But the boy was crazy about baseball, and after school, when he could have been working as a delivery boy or selling papers, he played ball with the kids. His failure to appreciate that the family needed a few extra dollars disgusted Dave. Around the house he wouldn't let Steve talk about baseball, and he scowled when he saw him hurrying off with his glove after dinner.

When the Phillies came to town to play an exhibition game with the home team and Steve pleaded to be taken to the ballpark, Dave, of course, was outraged. Steve knew they couldn't afford it. But he had got his mother on his side. Finally Dave made a bargain with them. He said that if Steve came home after school and worked hard helping to make some kitchen shelves, he would take him that night to the ballpark.

Steve worked hard, but Dave was still resentful. They had to coax him to put on his good suit. When they started out, Steve held aloof, feeling guilty, and they walked down the street like strangers; then Dave glanced at Steve's face and, half ashamed, took his arm more cheerfully.

As the game went on, Dave had to listen to Steve's recitation of the batting average of every Philly that stepped up to the plate; the time the boy must have wasted learning these averages began to appall him. He showed it so plainly that Steve felt guilty again and was silent.

After the game Dave let Steve drag him onto the field to keep him company while he tried to get some autographs from the Philly players, who were being hemmed in by gangs of kids blocking the way to the clubhouse. But Steve, who was shy, let the other kids block him off from the players. Steve would push his way in, get blocked out, and come back to stand mournfully beside Dave. And Dave grew impatient. He was wasting valuable time. He wanted to get home; Steve knew it and was worried.

Then the big, blond Philly outfielder, Eddie Condon, who had been held up by a gang of kids tugging at his arm and thrusting their score cards at him, broke loose and made a run for the clubhouse. He was jostled, and his blue cap with the red peak, tilted far back on his head, fell off. It fell at Steve's feet, and Steve stooped quickly and grabbed it. "Okay, son,"

the outfielder called, turning back. But Steve, holding the hat in both hands, only stared at him.

"Give him his cap, Steve," Dave said, smiling apologetically at the big outfielder, who towered over them. But Steve drew the hat closer to his chest. In an awed trance he looked up at big Eddie Condon. It was an embarrassing moment. All the other kids were watching. Some shouted, "Give him his cap."

"My cap, son," Eddie Condon said, his hand out.

"Hey, Steve," Dave said, and he gave him a shake. But he had to jerk the cap out of Steve's hands.

"Here you are," he said.

The outfielder, noticing Steve's white, worshiping face and pleading eyes, grinned and then shrugged. "Aw, let him keep it," he said.

"No, Mister Condon, you don't need to do that," Steve protested.

"It's happened before. Forget it," Eddie Condon said, and he trotted away to the clubhouse.

Dave handed the cap to Steve; envious kids circled around them and Steve said, "He said I could keep it, Dad. You heard him, didn't you?"

"Yeah, I heard him," Dave admitted. The wonder in Steve's face made him smile. He took the boy by the arm and they hurried off the field.

On the way home Dave couldn't get him to talk about the game; he couldn't get him to take his eyes off the cap. Steve could hardly believe in his own happiness. "See," he said suddenly, and he showed Dave that Eddie Condon's name was printed on the sweatband. Then he went on dreaming. Finally he put the cap on his head and turned to Dave with a slow, proud smile. The cap was away too big for him; it fell down over his ears. "Never mind," Dave said. "You can get your mother to take a tuck in the back."

When they got home, Dave was tired and his wife didn't understand the cap's importance, and they couldn't get Steve to go to bed. He swaggered around wearing the cap and looking in the mirror every ten minutes. He took the cap to bed with him.

Dave and his wife had a cup of coffee in the kitchen, and Dave told her again how they had got the cap. They agreed that their boy must have an attractive quality that showed in his face, and that Eddie Condon must have been drawn to him—why else would he have singled Steve out from all the kids?

But Dave got tired of the fuss Steve made over that cap and of the way he wore it from the time he got up in the morning until the

time he went to bed. Some kid was always coming in, wanting to try on the cap. It was childish, Dave said, for Steve to go around assuming that the cap made him important in the neighborhood, and to keep telling them how he had become a leader in the park a few blocks away where he played ball in the evenings. And Dave wouldn't stand for Steve's keeping the cap on while he was eating. He was always scolding his wife for accepting Steve's explanation that he'd forgotten he had it on. Just the same, it was remarkable what a little thing like a ball cap could do for a kid, Dave admitted to his wife as he smiled to himself.

One night Steve was late coming home from the park. Dave didn't realize how late it was until he put down his newspaper and watched his wife at the window. Her restlessness got on his nerves. "See what comes from encouraging the boy to hang around with those park loafers," he said. "I don't encourage him," she protested. "You do," he insisted irritably, for he was really worried now. A gang hung around the park until midnight. It was a bad park. It was true that on one side there was a good district with fine, expensive apartment houses, but the kids from that neighborhood left the park to the kids from the poorer homes. When his wife went out and walked down to the corner, it was his turn to wait and worry and watch at the open window. Each waiting moment tortured him. At last he heard his wife's voice and Steve's voice, and he relaxed and sighed; then he remembered his duty and rushed angrily to meet them.

"I'll fix you, Steve, once and for all," he said. "I'll show you you can't start coming into the house at midnight."

"Hold your horses, Dave," his wife said. "Can't you see the state he's in?" Steve looked utterly exhausted and beaten.

"What's the matter?" Dave asked quickly.

"I lost my cap," Steve whispered; he walked

past his father and threw himself on the couch in the living room and lay with his face hidden.

"Now, don't scold him, Dave," his wife said.

"Scold him. Who's scolding him?" Dave asked, indignantly. "It's his cap, not mine. If it's not worth his while to hang on to it, why should I scold him?" But he was implying resentfully that he alone recognized the cap's value.

"So you are scolding him," his wife said. "It's his cap. Not yours. What happened, Steve?"

Steve told them he had been playing ball and he found that when he ran the bases the cap fell off; it was still too big despite the tuck his mother had taken in the band. So the next time he came to bat he tucked the cap in his hip pocket. Someone had lifted it, he was sure.

"And he didn't even know whether it was still in his pocket," Dave said sarcastically.

"I wasn't careless, Dad," Steve said. For the last three hours he had been wandering around to the homes of the kids who had been in the park at the time; he wanted to go on, but he was too tired. Dave knew the boy was apologizing to him, but he didn't know why it made him angry.

"If he didn't hang on to it, it's not worth worrying about now," he said, and he sounded offended.

After that night they knew that Steve didn't go to the park to play ball; he went to look for the cap. It irritated Dave to see him sit around listlessly, or walk in circles, trying to force his memory to find a particular incident which would suddenly recall to him the moment when the cap had been taken. It was no attitude for a growing, healthy boy to take, Dave complained. He told Steve firmly once and for all that he didn't want to hear any more about the cap.

One night, two weeks later, Dave was walking home with Steve from the shoemaker's. It was a hot night. When they passed an ice-cream parlor, Steve slowed down. "I guess I

couldn't have a soda, could I?" Steve said. "Nothing doing," Dave said firmly. "Come on now," he added as Steve hung back, looking in the window.

"Dad, look!" Steve cried suddenly, pointing at the window. "My cap! There's my cap! He's coming out!"

A well-dressed boy was leaving the ice-cream parlor; he had on a blue ball cap with a red peak, just like Steve's cap. "Hey, you!" Steve cried, and he rushed at the boy, his small face fierce and his eyes wild. Before the boy could back away, Steve had snatched the cap from his head. "That's my cap!" he shouted.

"What's this?" the bigger boy said. "Hey, give me my cap or I'll give you a poke on the nose."

Dave was surprised that his own shy boy did not back away. He watched him clutch the cap in his left hand, half crying with excitement as he put his head down and drew back his right fist: he was willing to fight. And Dave was proud of him.

"Wait, now," Dave said. "Take it easy, son," he said to the other boy, who refused to back away.

"My boy says it's his cap," Dave said.

"Well, he's crazy. It's my cap."

"I was with him when he got this cap. When the Phillies played here. It's a Philly cap."

"Eddie Condon gave it to me," Steve said. "And you stole it from me, you jerk."

"Don't call me a jerk, you little squirt. I never saw you before in my life."

"Look," Steve said, pointing to the printing on the cap's sweatband. "It's Eddie Condon's cap. See? See, Dad?"

"Yeah. You're right, Son. Ever see this boy before, Steve?"

"No," Steve said reluctantly.

The other boy realized he might lose the cap. "I bought it from a guy," he said. "I paid him. My father knows I paid him." He said he got the cap at the ballpark. He groped for some magically impressive words and suddenly found them. "You'll have to speak to my father," he said.

"Sure, I'll speak to your father," Dave said. "What's your name? Where do you live?"

"My name's Hudson. I live about ten minutes away on the other side of the park." The boy appraised Dave, who wasn't much bigger than he was and who wore a faded blue windbreaker and no tie. "My father is a lawyer," he said boldly. "He wouldn't let me keep the cap if he didn't think I should."

"Is that a fact?" Dave asked belligerently.

"Well, we'll see. Come on. Let's go." And he got between the two boys and they walked along the street. They didn't talk to each other. Dave knew the Hudson boy was waiting to get to the protection of his home, and Steve knew it, too, and he looked up apprehensively at Dave. And Dave, reaching for his hand, squeezed it encouragingly and strode along, cocky and belligerent, knowing that Steve relied on him.

The Hudson boy lived in that row of fine apartment houses on the other side of the park. At the entrance to one of these houses, Dave tried not to hang back and show he was impressed, because he could feel Steve hanging back. When they got into the small elevator, Dave didn't know why he took off his hat. In the carpeted hall on the fourth floor, the Hudson boy said, "Just a minute," and entered his own apartment. Dave and Steve were left alone in the corridor, knowing that the other boy was preparing his father for the encounter. Steve looked anxiously at his father, and Dave said, "Don't worry, Son," and he added resolutely, "No one's putting anything over on us."

A tall, balding man in a brown velvet smoking jacket suddenly opened the door. Dave had never seen a man wearing one of those jackets, although he had seen them in department store windows. "Good evening," he said, making a deprecatory[1] gesture at the cap Steve clutched tightly in his hand. "My boy didn't get your name. My name is Hudson."

"Mine's Diamond."

"Come on in," Mr. Hudson said, putting out his hand and laughing good-naturedly. He led Dave and Steve into his living room. "What's this about that cap?" he asked. "The way kids can get excited about a cap. Well, it's understandable, isn't it?"

"So it is," Dave said, moving closer to Steve, who was awed by the broadloom rug and the

---

1. **deprecatory** (dĕp′rə-kə-tôr′ē): apologetic.

fine furniture. He wanted to show Steve he was at ease himself, and he wished Mr. Hudson wouldn't be so polite. That meant Dave had to be polite and affable, too, and it was hard to manage when he was standing in the middle of the floor in his old windbreaker.

"Sit down, Mr. Diamond," Mr. Hudson said. Dave took Steve's arm and sat him down beside him on the chesterfield.[2] The Hudson boy watched his father. And Dave looked at Steve and saw that he wouldn't face Mr. Hudson or the other boy; he kept looking up at Dave, putting all his faith in him.

"Well, Mr. Diamond, from what I gathered from my boy, you're able to prove this cap belonged to your boy."

"That's a fact," Dave said.

"Mr. Diamond, you'll have to believe my boy bought that cap from some kid in good faith."

"I don't doubt it," Dave said. "But no kid can sell something that doesn't belong to him. You know that's a fact, Mr. Hudson."

"Yes, that's a fact," Mr. Hudson agreed. "But that cap means a lot to my boy, Mr. Diamond."

"It means a lot to my boy, too, Mr. Hudson."

"Sure it does. But supposing we called in a policeman. You know what he'd say? He'd ask you if you were willing to pay my boy what he paid for the cap. That's usually the way it works out," Mr. Hudson said, friendly and smiling, as he eyed Dave shrewdly.

"But that's not right. It's not justice," Dave protested. "Not when it's my boy's cap."

"I know it isn't right. But that's what they do."

"All right. What did you say your boy paid for the cap?" Dave said reluctantly.

"Two dollars."

"Two dollars!" Dave repeated. Mr. Hudson's smile was still kindly, but his eyes were shrewd, and Dave knew the lawyer was counting on his not having the two dollars; Mr. Hudson thought he had Dave sized up; he had looked at him and decided he was broke. Dave's pride was hurt, and he turned to Steve. What he saw in Steve's face was more powerful than the hurt to his pride: it was the memory of how difficult it had been to get an extra nickel, the talk he heard about the cost of food, the worry in his mother's face as she tried to make ends meet, and the bewildered embarrassment that he was here in a rich man's home, forcing his father to confess that he couldn't afford to spend two dollars. Then Dave grew angry and reckless. "I'll give you the two dollars," he said.

Steve looked at the Hudson boy and grinned brightly. The Hudson boy watched his father.

"I suppose that's fair enough," Mr. Hudson said. "A cap like this can be worth a lot to a kid. You know how it is. Your boy might want to sell—I mean be satisfied. Would he take five dollars for it?"

"Five dollars?" Dave repeated. "Is it worth five dollars, Steve?" he asked uncertainly.

Steve shook his head and looked frightened.

"No, thanks, Mr. Hudson," Dave said firmly. "I'll tell you what I'll do," Mr. Hudson said. "I'll give you ten dollars. The cap has a sentimental value for my boy, a Philly cap, a big-leaguer's cap. It's only worth about a buck and a half really," he added. But Dave shook his head again. Mr. Hudson frowned. He looked at his own boy with indulgent concern, but now he was embarrassed. "I'll tell you what I'll do," he said. "This cap—well, it's worth as much as a day at the circus to my boy. Your boy should be recompensed.[3] I want to be fair. Here's twenty dollars," and he held out two ten-dollar bills to Dave.

That much money for a cap, Dave thought, and his eyes brightened. But he knew what the cap had meant to Steve; to deprive him of it now that it was within his reach would be

---

2. **chesterfield** (chĕs′tər-fēld): a kind of sofa.

3. **recompensed** (rĕk′əm-pĕnst′): paid.

unbearable. All the things he needed in his life gathered around him; his wife was there, saying he couldn't afford to reject the offer, he had no right to do it; and he turned to Steve to see if Steve thought it wonderful that the cap could bring them twenty dollars.

"I don't know," Steve said. He was in a trance. When Dave smiled, Steve smiled too, and Dave believed that Steve was as impressed as he was, only more bewildered, and maybe even more aware that they could not possibly turn away that much money for a ball cap.

"Well, here you are," Mr. Hudson said, and he put the two bills in Steve's hand. "It's a lot of money. But I guess you had a right to expect as much."

With a dazed, fixed smile Steve handed the money slowly to his father, and his face was white.

Laughing jovially, Mr. Hudson led them to the door. His own boy followed a few paces behind.

In the elevator Dave took the bills out of his pocket. "See, Stevie," he whispered eagerly. "That windbreaker you wanted! And ten dollars for your bank! Won't Mother be surprised?"

"Yeah," Steve whispered, the little smile still on his face. But Dave had to turn away quickly so their eyes wouldn't meet, for he saw that it was a scared smile.

Outside, Dave said, "Here, you carry the money home, Steve. You show it to your mother."

"No, you keep it," Steve said, and then there was nothing to say. They walked in silence.

"It's a lot of money," Dave said finally. When Steve didn't answer him, he added angrily, "I turned to you, Steve. I asked you, didn't I?"

"That man knew how much his boy wanted that cap," Steve said.

"Sure. But he recognized how much it was worth to us."

"No, you let him take it away from us," Steve blurted.

"That's unfair," Dave said. "Don't dare say that to me."

"I don't want to be like you," Steve muttered, and he darted across the road and walked along on the other side of the street.

"It's unfair," Dave said angrily, only now he didn't mean that Steve was unfair. He meant that what had happened in the prosperous Hudson home was unfair, and he didn't know quite why. He had been trapped, not just by Mr. Hudson, but by his own life.

Across the road Steve was hurrying along with his head down, wanting to be alone. They walked most of the way home on opposite sides of the street, until Dave could stand it no longer. "Steve," he called, crossing the street. "It was very unfair. I mean, for you to say . . ." but Steve started to run. Dave walked as fast as he could and Steve was getting beyond him, and he felt enraged and suddenly he yelled, "Steve!" and he started to chase his son. He wanted to get hold of Steve and pound him, and he didn't know why. He gained on him, he gasped for breath and he almost got him by the shoulder. Turning, Steve saw his father's face in the streetlight and was terrified; he circled away, got to the house, and rushed in, yelling, "Mother!"

"Son, Son!" she cried, rushing from the kitchen. As soon as she threw her arms around Steve, shielding him, Dave's anger left him and he felt stupid. He walked past them into the kitchen.

"What happened?" she asked anxiously. "Have you both gone crazy? What did you do, Steve?"

"Nothing," he said sullenly.

"What did your father do?"

"We found the boy with my ball cap, and he let the boy's father take it from us."

"No, no," Dave protested. "Nobody pushed

us around. The man didn't put anything over on us." He felt tired and his face was burning. He told what had happened; then he slowly took the two ten-dollar bills out of his wallet and tossed them on the table and looked up guiltily at his wife.

It hurt him that she didn't pick up the money and that she didn't rebuke him. "It is a lot of money, Son," she said slowly. "Your father was only trying to do what he knew was right, and it'll work out, and you'll understand." She was soothing Steve, but Dave knew she felt that she needed to be gentle with him, too, and he was ashamed.

When she went with Steve to his bedroom, Dave sat by himself. His son, for the first time, had seen how easy it was for another man to handle him, and he had judged him and had wanted to walk alone on the other side of the street. He looked at the money and he hated the sight of it.

His wife returned to the kitchen, made a cup of tea, talked soothingly, and said it was incredible that he had forced the Hudson man to pay him twenty dollars for the cap, but all Dave could think of was Steve was scared of me.

Finally, he got up and went into Steve's room. The room was in darkness, but he could see the outline of Steve's body on the bed, and he sat down beside him and whispered, "Look, Son, it was a mistake. I know why. People like us—in circumstances where money can scare us. No, no," he said, feeling ashamed and shaking his head apologetically; he was taking the wrong way of showing the boy they were together; he was covering up his own failure. The failure had been his, and it had come out of being so separated from his son that he had been blind to what was beyond the price in a boy's life. He longed now to show Steve he could be with him

from day to day. His hand went out hesitantly to Steve's shoulder. "Steve, look," he said eagerly. "The trouble was I didn't realize how much I enjoyed it that night at the ballpark. If I had watched you playing for your own team—the kids around here say you could be a great pitcher. We could take that money and buy a new pitcher's glove for you, and a catcher's mitt. Steve, Steve, are you listening? I could catch for you, work with you in the lane. Maybe I could be your coach . . . watch you become a great pitcher." In the half-darkness he could see the boy's pale face turn to him.

Steve, who had never heard his father talk like this, was shy and wondering. All he knew was that his father, for the first time, wanted to be with him in his hopes and adventures. He said, "I guess you do know how important that cap was." His hand went out to his father's arm. "With that man the cap was—well, it was just something he could buy, eh, Dad?" Dave gripped his son's hand hard. The wonderful generosity of childhood—the price a boy was willing to pay to be able to count on his father's admiration and approval—made him feel humble, then strangely exalted.

Reading Check

1. What does Steve do after school instead of working?
2. What does Dave promise to do if Steve helps make kitchen shelves?
3. Why doesn't Steve get autographs after the game?
4. What does the outfielder give Steve?
5. How much does Mr. Hudson pay Steve for the cap?

A Cap for Steve   **85**

For Study and Discussion

Analyzing and Interpreting the Story

1. In this story, Dave Diamond and his son, Steve, are divided and then brought closer together because of a conflict over money. **a.** What does the first paragraph tell about the father's attitude toward money? **b.** According to the second paragraph, how has money caused hard feelings between father and son?

2. The baseball cap has a meaning for Steve that his father does not understand. **a.** Why does the cap mean so much to Steve? **b.** What does Dave think of Steve's attachment to the cap at first?

3. The bargaining for the cap that takes place at the Hudson apartment becomes a kind of test for the two fathers. Mr. Hudson "passes" the test because he has enough money to pay any price for the cap. **a.** Why does Dave "fail" the test? **b.** What should Dave have done in order to "pass" the test in his son's eyes?

4. Later, Dave looks at the money he has accepted for the cap and hates the sight of it. What has Dave realized is more important than money?

5. What does Dave finally say to make Steve see that he does know what is "beyond the price" in his son's life?

6. This story begins with a conflict. Do you think it ends with peace? Explain your answer.

Literary Elements

Recognizing the Causes of a Character's Actions

An important moment in this story occurs when the two fathers bargain for the baseball cap. At first, Dave offers to pay two dollars for the cap. But by the end of the scene, he has decided to give up the cap entirely.

What causes Dave to change his mind and take the money instead of the cap? The answer is in this paragraph.

> That much money for a cap, Dave thought, and his eyes brightened. But he knew what the cap had meant to Steve; to deprive him of it now that it was within his reach would be unbearable. All the things he needed in his life gathered around him; his wife was there, saying he couldn't afford to reject the offer, he had no right to do it; and he turned to Steve to see if Steve thought wonderful that the cap could bring them twenty dollars.

The turning point of the story occurs when Dave goes into Steve's bedroom and tries to explain why he gave up the cap. Steve is angry with his father. He has already said, "I don't want to be like you." According to the last paragraph of the story, what causes Steve to forgive his father and to forget about the cap?

Language and Vocabulary

Recognizing Multiple Meanings of Words

The meaning of a word is usually clear from its **context**—that is, from the other words in the sentence or paragraph. On page 80, Dave says, "See what comes from encouraging the boy to hang around with those park *loafers*." Clearly, *loafers* doesn't mean a pair of shoes; it means a group of lazy people. How do you know?

What does each italicized word or phrase mean in the following quotations from the story? Write a sentence using each word or phrase in another context, to indicate a different meaning. Do some words have more than two meanings? Your dictionary will help.

> Steve . . . ought to have known the value of money as well as Dave did. It had been *ground* into him.

> . . . Eddie Condon must have been *drawn* to him . . .

> . . . Mr. Hudson thought he had Dave *sized* up; he had looked at him and decided he was *broke*.

> ". . . the kids around here say you could be a great *pitcher*."

Narrative Writing

Writing a Dialogue

In a story or play, what the characters say to each other is called **dialogue.** Characters can address each other and respond to what other characters say, just as people do in a conversation. What each character says is enclosed in quotation marks.

Dialogue makes a character come alive. It can also add excitement to a story. For example, the scene in which Steve returns home after losing the cap could have been written in this way:

> Dave was angry at Steve and yelled at him. His wife told Dave to stop, because Steve was exhausted. When Dave asked Steve what was wrong, Steve said that he'd lost his cap.

Instead, the author wrote a dialogue.

> "I'll fix you, Steve, once and for all," he said. "I'll show you you can't start coming into the house at midnight."
>
> "Hold your horses, Dave," his wife said. "Can't you see the state he's in?" Steve looked utterly exhausted and beaten.
>
> "What's the matter?" Dave asked quickly.
>
> "I lost my cap," Steve whispered. . . .

Write a dialogue that could have taken place between Mr. Hudson and his son while Steve and Dave were waiting outside their apartment (page 82). What do you think the Hudson boy said to his father about how he got the cap? How did he explain who the Diamonds were and what they wanted? What do you think Mr. Hudson said to his son just before he let the Diamonds in?

About the Author

Morley Callaghan   (1903–   )

Morley Callaghan is a major Canadian novelist, playwright and short-story writer. He was a member of the "lost generation"—a group of writers and artists of the 1920s who gathered mostly in Paris, searching for new ways to express their ideas. His first published novel appeared in 1928. His work is concerned with the condition and conscience of the ordinary man. Some of his novels are *Strange Fugitive, Such Is My Beloved, They Shall Inherit the Earth,* and *A Passion in Rome.* His stories are written in a plain and straightforward style, like those of the writer he most admires, Ernest Hemingway.

The Apprentice

<u>DOROTHY CANFIELD</u>

As you read this story, think of an apprentice as a learner or beginner. What do you think this apprentice learns by the end of the story?

The day had been one of those unbearable ones, when every sound had set her teeth on edge like chalk creaking on a blackboard, when every word her father or mother said to her or did not say to her seemed an intentional injustice. And of course it would happen, as the end to such a day, that just as the sun went down back of the mountain and the long twilight began, she noticed that Rollie was not around.

Tense with exasperation—she would simply explode if Mother got going—she began to call him in a carefully casual tone: "Here, Rollie! He-ere, boy! Want to go for a walk, Rollie?" Whistling to him cheerfully, her heart full of wrath at the way the world treated her, she made the rounds of his haunts; the corner of the woodshed, where he liked to curl up on the wool of Father's discarded old windbreaker; the hay barn, the cow barn, the sunny spot on the side porch—no Rollie.

Perhaps he had sneaked upstairs to lie on her bed where he was not supposed to go—not that *she* would have minded! That rule was a part of Mother's fussiness, part too of Mother's bossiness. It was *her* bed, wasn't it? But was she allowed the say-so about it? Not on your life. They told her she could have things the way she wanted in her own room, now she was in her teens, but—her heart raged against unfairness as she took the stairs stormily, two steps at a time, her pigtails flopping up and down on her back. If Rollie was on her bed, she was just going to let him stay right there, and Mother could shake her head and frown all she wanted to.

But he was not there. The bedspread and pillow were crumpled, but not from his weight. She had flung herself down to cry there that afternoon. And then she couldn't. Every nerve in her had been twanging, but she couldn't cry. She could only lie there, her hands doubled up hard, furious that she had nothing to cry

about. Not really. She was too big to cry just over Father's having said to her, severely, "I told you if I let you take the chess set you were to put it away when you got through with it. One of the pawns was on the floor of our bedroom this morning. I stepped on it. If I'd had my shoes on, I'd have broken it."

Well, he *had* told her to be sure to put them away. And although she had forgotten and left them, he hadn't forbidden her ever to take the set again. No, the instant she thought about that, she knew she couldn't cry about it. She could be, and she was, in a rage about the way Father kept on talking, long after she'd got his point, "It's not that I care so much about the chess set," he said, just leaning with all his weight on being right, "it's because if you don't learn how to take care of things, you yourself will suffer for it, later. You'll forget or neglect something that will be really important, for *you*. We *have* to try to teach you to be responsible for what you've said you'll take care of. If we . . ." on and on, preaching and preaching.

She heard her mother coming down the hall, and hastily shut her door. She had a right to shut the door to her own room, hadn't she? She had *some* rights, she supposed, even if she was only thirteen and the youngest child. If her mother opened it to ask, smiling, "What are you doing in here that you don't want me to see?" she'd say—she'd just say—

She stood there, dry-eyed, by the bed that Rollie had not crumpled, and thought, "I hope Mother sees the spread and says something about Rollie—I just hope she does."

But her mother did not open the door. Her feet went steadily on along the hall, and then, carefully, slowly, down the stairs. She probably had an armful of winter things she was bringing down from the attic. She was probably thinking that a tall, thirteen-year-old daughter was big enough to help with a chore like that.

But she wouldn't *say* anything. She would just get out that insulting look of a grown-up silently putting up with a crazy, unreasonable kid. She had worn that expression all day; it was too much to be endured.

Up in her bedroom behind her closed door the thirteen-year-old stamped her foot in a rage, none the less savage and heart-shaking because it was mysterious to her.

But she had not located Rollie. Before she would let her father and mother know she had lost sight of him, forgotten about him, she would be cut into little pieces. They would not scold her, she knew. They would do worse. They would look at her. And in their silence she would hear droning on reproachfully what they had repeated and repeated when the sweet, woolly collie puppy had first been in her arms and she had been begging to keep him for her own.

How warm he had felt! Astonishing how warm and alive a puppy was compared to a doll! She had never liked her dolls much, after she had held Rollie, feeling him warm against her breast, warm and wriggling, bursting with life, reaching up to lick her face—he had loved her from that first instant. As he felt her arms around him, his beautiful eyes had melted in trusting sweetness. And they did now, whenever he looked at her. "My dog is the only one in the whole world who *really* loves me," she thought passionately.

Even then, at the very minute when as a darling baby dog he was beginning to love her, her father and mother were saying, so cold, so reasonable—gosh! how she *hated* reasonableness!—"Now, Peg, remember that, living where we do, with sheep on the farms around us, it is a serious responsibility to have a collie dog. If you keep him, you've got to be the one to take care of him. You'll have to be the one to train him to stay at home. We're too busy with you

children to start bringing up a puppy too." Rollie, nestling in her arms, let one hind leg drop awkwardly. It must be uncomfortable. She looked down at him tenderly, tucked his dangling leg up under him and gave him a hug. He laughed up in her face—he really did laugh, his mouth stretched wide in a cheerful grin.

All the time her parents kept hammering away: "If you want him, you can have him. But you must be responsible for him. If he gets to running sheep, he'll just have to be shot, you know that."

They had not said, aloud, "Like the Wilsons' collie." They never mentioned that awfulness—her racing unsuspectingly down across the fields just at the horrible moment when Mr. Wilson shot his collie caught in the very act of killing sheep. They probably thought that if they never spoke about it, she would forget it—*forget* the crack of that rifle, and the collapse of the great beautiful dog! Forget the red, red blood spurting from the hole in his head. She hadn't forgotten. She never would. She knew as well as they did how important it was to train a collie puppy about sheep. They didn't need to rub it in like that. They always rubbed everything in. She had told them, fervently, indignantly, that of *course* she would take care of him, be responsible for him, teach him to stay at home. Of course, of course. *She* understood!

And now, this afternoon, when he was six months old, tall, rangy,[1] powerful, standing up far above her knee, nearly to her waist, she didn't know where he was. But of course he must be somewhere around. He always was. She composed her face to look natural and went downstairs to search the house. He was probably asleep somewhere. She looked every room over carefully. Her mother was nowhere visible. It was safe to call him again, to give the special piercing whistle which always brought him racing to her, the white-feathered plume of his tail waving in elation that she wanted him.

But he did not answer. She stood still on the front porch to think.

Could he have gone up to their special place in the edge of the field where the three young pines, their branches growing close to the ground, made a triangular, walled-in space, completely hidden from the world? Sometimes he went up there with her. When she lay down on the dried grass to dream, he too lay down quietly, his head on his paws, his beautiful eyes fixed adoringly on her. He entered into her every mood. If she wanted to be quiet, all right, he did too.

It didn't seem as though he would have gone alone there. Still——She loped up the steep slope of the field rather fast, beginning to be anxious.

No, he was not there. She stood, irresolutely,[2] in the roofless, green-walled triangular hideout, wondering what to do next.

Then, before she knew what thought had come into her mind, its emotional impact knocked her down. At least her knees crumpled under her. Last Wednesday the Wilsons had brought their sheep down to the home farm from the upper pasture! She herself had seen them on the way to school, and like an idiot had not thought of Rollie. She had seen them grazing on the river meadow.

She was off like a racer at the crack of the starting pistol, her long, strong legs stretched in great leaps, her pigtails flying. She took the shortcut down to the upper edge of the meadow, regardless of the brambles. Their thorn-spiked, wiry stems tore at her flesh, but she did not care. She welcomed the pain. It was something she was doing for Rollie, for her Rollie.

She was tearing through the pine woods now, rushing down the steep, stony path, tripping over roots, half falling, catching herself just in time, not slackening her speed. She burst out on the open knoll above the river meadow, calling wildly, "Rollie, here, Rollie, here, boy! here! here!" She tried to whistle, but she was crying too hard to pucker her lips. She had not, till then, known she was crying.

There was nobody to see or hear her. Twilight was falling over the bare knoll. The sunless evening wind slid down the mountain like an

---

1. **rangy** (rān′jē): thin and long-limbed.

2. **irresolutely** (ĭ-rĕz′ə-loot′lē): in an undecided way.

invisible river, engulfing her in cold. Her teeth began to chatter. "Here, Rollie, here, boy, here!" She strained her eyes to look down into the meadow to see if the sheep were there. She could not be sure. She stopped calling him as if he were a dog, and called out his name despairingly, as if he were her child, "Rollie! oh, *Rollie*, where are you!"

The tears ran down her cheeks in streams. She sobbed loudly, terribly. Since there was no one to hear, she did not try to control herself.

"Hou! hou! hou!" she sobbed, her face contorted grotesquely. "Oh, Rollie! Rollie! Rollie!" She had wanted something to cry about. Oh, how terribly now she had something to cry about.

She saw him as clearly as if he were there beside her, his muzzle and gaping mouth all smeared with the betraying blood (like the Wilsons' collie). "But he didn't *know* it was wrong!" she screamed like a wild creature. "Nobody *told* him it was wrong. It was my fault. I should have taken better care of him. I will now. I will!"

But no matter how she screamed, she could not make herself heard. In the cold gathering darkness, she saw him stand, poor, guiltless victim of his ignorance, who should have been protected from his own nature, his soft eyes looking at her with love, his splendid plumed tail waving gently. "It was my fault. I promised I would bring him up. I should have *made* him stay at home. I was responsible for him. It was my fault."

But she could not make his executioners hear her. The shot rang out, Rollie sank down, his beautiful liquid eyes glazed, the blood spurting from the hole in his head—like the Wilsons' collie. She gave a wild shriek, long, soul-satisfying, frantic. It was the scream at sudden, unendurable tragedy of a mature, full-blooded woman. It drained dry the girl of thirteen. She came to herself. She was standing on the knoll, trembling and quaking with cold, the darkness closing in on her.

Her breath had given out. For once in her life she had wept all the tears there were in her body. Her hands were so stiff with cold she could scarcely close them. How her nose was running! Simply streaming down her upper lip. And she had no handkerchief. She lifted her skirt, fumbled for her slip, stooped, blew her nose on it, wiped her eyes, drew a long quavering breath—and heard something! Far off in the distance, a faint sound, like a dog's muffled bark.

She whirled on her heels and bent her head to listen. The sound did not come from the meadow below the knoll. It came from back of her higher up, from the Wilsons' maple grove. She held her breath. Yes, it came from there.

She began to run again, but now she was not sobbing. She was silent, absorbed in her effort to cover ground. If she could only live to get there, to see if it really were Rollie. She ran steadily till she came to the fence and went over this in a great plunge. Her skirt caught on a nail. She impatiently pulled at it, not hearing or not heeding the long sibilant[3] tear as it came loose. She was in the dusky maple woods, stumbling over the rocks as she ran. As she tore on up the slope, she heard the bark again, and knew it was Rollie's.

She stopped short and leaned weakly against a tree. She was sick with the breathlessness of her straining lungs, sick in the reaction of relief, sick with anger at Rollie, who had been here having a wonderful time while she had been dying, just dying in terror about him.

For she could now not only hear that it was Rollie's bark. She could hear, in the dog language she knew as well as he, what he was saying in those excited yips—that he had run a woodchuck into a hole in the tumbled stone wall, that he had almost had him, that the intoxicating wild-animal smell was as close to him—almost—as if he had his jaws on his quarry. Yip! Woof! Yip! Yip!

The wildly joyful quality of the dog-talk enraged the girl. She had been trembling in exhaustion. Now it was indignation. So that was where he had been—when *she* was *killing* herself trying to take care of him. Plenty near enough if he had paid attention to hear her calling and whistling to him. Just so set on hav-

ing his foolish good time, he never thought to listen for her call.

She stooped to pick up a stout stick. She would teach him. She was hot with anger. It was time he had something to make him remember to listen. She started forward on a run.

But after a few steps she stopped, stood thinking. One of the things to remember about collies, everybody knew that, was that a collie who had been beaten was never "right"

3. **sibilant** (sĭb′ə-lənt): making a hissing sound.

again. His spirit was broken. "Anything but a broken-spirited collie"—she had often heard a farmer say that. They were no good after that.

She threw down her stick. Anyhow, she thought, he was really too young to know that he had done wrong. He was still only a puppy. Like all puppies, he got perfectly crazy over wild-animal smells. Probably he truly hadn't heard her calling and whistling.

All the same, all the same—she stood stock-still, staring intently into the twilight—you couldn't let a puppy grow up just as he wanted to. It wouldn't be safe—for *him*. Somehow she would have to make him understand that he mustn't go off this way, by himself. He must be trained to know how to do what a good dog does—not because *she* wanted it, but for his own sake.

She walked on now, steady, purposeful, gathering her inner strength together, Olympian[4] in her understanding of the full meaning of the event.

When he heard his own special young god approaching, he turned delightedly and ran to meet her, panting, his tongue hanging out. His eyes shone. He jumped up on her in an ecstasy of welcome and licked her face.

She pushed him away. Her face and voice were grave. "No, Rollie, *no!*" she said severely. "You're *bad*. You know you're not to go off in the woods without me! You are—a—*bad—dog*."

He was horrified. Stricken into misery. He stood facing her, frozen. The gladness went out of his eyes, the waving plume of his tail slowly lowered to slinking, guilty dejection.

"I know you were all wrapped up in that woodchuck. But that's no excuse. You *could* have heard me, calling you, whistling for you,

if you'd paid attention," she went on. "You've got to learn, and I've got to teach you."

With a shudder of misery he lay down, his tail stretched out limp on the ground, his head flat on his paws, his ears drooping—ears ringing with the doomsday awfulness of the voice he loved and revered. To have it speak so to him, he must have been utterly wicked. He trembled, he turned his head away from her august[5] look of blame, he groveled in remorse for whatever mysterious sin he had committed.

As miserable as he, she sat down by him. "I don't *want* to scold you. But I have to! I have to bring you up right or you'll get shot, Rollie. You musn't go away from the house without me, do you hear, *never*."

His sharp ears, yearning for her approval, caught a faint overtone of relenting affection in her voice. He lifted his eyes to her, humbly, soft in imploring fondness.

"Oh, Rollie!" she said, stooping low over him, "I *do* love you. I do. But I *have* to bring you up. I'm responsible for you, don't you see."

He did not see. Hearing sternness, or something else he did not recognize, in the beloved voice, he shut his eyes tight in sorrow, and made a little whimpering lament in his throat.

She had never heard him cry before. It was too much. She sat down by him and drew his head to her, rocking him in her arms, soothing him with inarticulate small murmurs.

He leaped into her arms and wriggled happily as he had when he was a baby; he reached up to lick her face as he had then. But he was no baby now. He was half as big as she, a great, warm, pulsing, living armful of love. She clasped him closely. Her heart was brimming full, but calmed, quiet. The blood flowed strongly, steadily, all through her body. She was deliciously warm. Her nose was still running, a little. She sniffed and wiped it on her sleeve.

---

4. **Olympian** (ō-lĭm′pē-ən): godlike. The ancient Greek gods were believed to live on Mount Olympus in northeastern Greece.

5. **august** (ô-gŭst′): dignified; inspiring respect.

It was almost dark now. "We'll be late to supper, Rollie," she said, responsibly. Pushing him gently off she stood up. "Home, Rollie, home."

Here was a command he could understand. At once he trotted along the path towards home. His tail, held high, waved plumelike. His short dog-memory had forgotten the suffering just back of him.

Her human memory was longer. His prancing gait was as carefree as a young child's. She plodded behind him like a serious adult. Her very shoulders seemed bowed by what she had lived through. She felt, she thought, like an old woman of thirty. But it was all right now, she knew she had made an impression on him.

When they came out into the open pasture, Rollie ran back to get her to play with him. He leaped around her in circles, barking in cheerful yawps, jumping up on her, inviting her to run a race with him, to throw him a stick, to come alive.

His high spirits were ridiculous. But infectious. She gave one little leap to match his. Rollie took this as a threat, a pretend play-threat. He planted his forepaws low and barked loudly at her, laughing between yips. He was so funny, she thought, when he grinned that way. She laughed back, and gave another mock-threatening leap at him. Radiant that his sky was once more clear, he sprang high on his steel-spring muscles in an explosion of happiness, and bounded in circles around her.

Following him, not noting in the dusk where she was going, she felt the grassy slope drop steeply. Oh, yes, she knew where she was. They had come to the rolling-down hill just back of the house. All the kids rolled down there, even the littles ones, because it was soft grass without a stone. She had rolled down that slope a million times—years and years before, when she was a kid herself, six or seven years ago. It was fun. She remembered well the whirling dizziness of the descent, all the world turning crazily over and over. And the delicious giddy staggering when you first stood up, the earth still spinning under your feet.

"All right, Rollie, let's go," she cried, and flung herself down in the rolling position, her arms straight up over her head.

Rollie had never seen this skylarking before. It threw him into almost hysterical amusement. He capered around the rapidly rolling figure, half scared, mystified, enchanted.

His wild frolicsome barking might have come from her own throat, so accurately did it sound the way she felt—crazy, foolish—like a little kid, no more than five years old, the age she had been when she had last rolled down that hill.

At the bottom she sprang up, on muscles as steel-strong as Rollie's. She staggered a little, and laughed aloud.

The living-room windows were just before them. How yellow the lighted windows looked when you were in the darkness going home. How nice and yellow. Maybe Mother had waffles for supper. She was a swell cook, Mother was, and she certainly gave her family all the breaks, when it came to meals.

"Home, Rollie, home!" She burst open the door to the living room. "Hi, Mom, what'you got for supper?"

From the kitchen her mother announced coolly, "I hate to break the news to you, but it's waffles."

"Oh, *Mom!*" she shouted in ecstasy.

Her mother could not see her. She did not need to. "For goodness' sakes, go and wash," she called.

In the long mirror across the room she saw herself, her hair hanging wild, her long bare legs scratched, her broadly smiling face dirt-streaked, her torn skirt dangling, her dog laughing up at her. Gosh, was it a relief to feel your own age, just exactly thirteen years old!

Reading Check

1. At the opening of the story, where does Peg expect to find her dog?
2. Why has her father been severe with her?
3. What makes Peg think of the Wilsons' collie?
4. Where does she find Rollie?
5. Why does Peg decide not to beat her dog for running off?

For Study and Discussion

Analyzing and Interpreting the Story

1. At the beginning of the story, Peg is angry with her parents because they have been trying to teach her to take care of the things entrusted to her. What words spoken by her father on page 89 predict what actually does happen to Peg later that day?

2a. How does the author describe Peg's scream on page 92? **b.** What does this statement tell about the change that has taken place in Peg?

3. Peg is enraged at Rollie when she finds him. **a.** In what ways do Peg's actions become just like those she had resented in her parents? **b.** How is Rollie like Peg herself?

4. Look back at the passage describing Peg and Rollie's return home. **a.** What details indicate that Peg feels she is a different person? **b.** Do you think Peg has changed her attitude toward her mother? Why?

5. By the end of the story, why do you think Peg is relieved to feel thirteen again?

Literary Elements

Understanding the Title of a Story

One clue to the main idea of a story may be in its title. This story, for example, is called "The Apprentice." Yet no one in the story is an apprentice in the strict sense of the word. No one is really bound to some experienced person for a period of time in order to learn a trade or business.

But if we think of an apprentice as a learner, or beginner, we can understand why the story was given this title. Why can Peg be called an "apprentice"? Who are her teachers?

Often a story expresses some truth about life or people. Think about how the apprentice in this story learns her lesson. What idea do you think the story expresses about the way young people learn to be adults?

Narrative Writing

Writing from Another Point of View

"The Apprentice" is not told by Peg herself, but the author does tell you everything that Peg is thinking. You are *not* told what the other characters are thinking.

Here is how the author tells you what happens as Peg's mother goes past her bedroom door. Notice that you do not know what her mother is thinking. But you do know what is going on inside Peg's mind.

> But her mother did not open the door. Her feet went steadily on along the hall, and then, carefully, slowly, down the stairs. She probably had an armful of winter things she was bringing down from the attic. She was probably thinking that a tall, thirteen-year-old daughter was big enough to help with a chore like that. But she wouldn't *say* anything. She would just get out that insulting look of a grown-up silently putting up with a crazy, unreasonable kid. She had worn that expression all day; it was too much to be endured.

If this scene were told from the mother's point of view, it might begin in this way:

> She didn't knock on the door because she didn't want to irritate Peg. She went on along the hall, and then down the stairs. She walked slowly because she was trying to figure out what to do, trying not to let the closed door bother her. . . .

Using this beginning or one of your own, rewrite this scene from the mother's point of view. Write as if you know the mother's thoughts. What does she think is causing Peg's unhappiness? What does her expression really mean?

About the Author

Dorothy Canfield (1879–1958)

At the age of eighteen, Dorothy Canfield, also known as Dorothy Canfield Fisher, wrote, "I've lived long enough to know that life is a thing that can be saved or spent, but that it has value only as it's spent!" She spent her life in activity, and wrote constantly. She was born in Kansas, the daughter of an educator and an artist. She attended Ohio State University and in 1904 received a doctoral degree in philology (historical linguistics) from Columbia University. She married and began to raise a family in the country in Vermont. During World War I, she and her children joined her husband in France. She spent three years doing war work there. After the war she returned with her family to Vermont.

Whatever happened in her life, Canfield found time to write. She wrote many books for children. For adults she wrote novels, short stories, poems, and nonfiction on such topics as education and Vermont. She received many honors and awards for her writings. "The Apprentice" is one of her most famous stories, along with "The Heyday of the Blood" and "The Old Soldier." Canfield once said that no piece of fiction is "worth the reading unless it grapples with some problem of living."

old age sticks

E. E. CUMMINGS

Many of E. E. Cummings' poems look like puzzles. Often he does not begin his sentences with capital letters or end them with periods. Sometimes he stretches words out across a line, or squeezes them together, or divides them up in unusual ways.

This poem is made up of three sentences, each beginning with the words old age. *The first part of each sentence, in parentheses, tells what old age does to youth. The second part, the part not in parentheses, tells how youth responds.*

old age sticks
up Keep
Off
signs)&

youth yanks them   5
down(old
age
cries No

Tres)&(pas)
youth laughs   10
(sing
old age

scolds Forbid
den Stop
Must   15
n't Don't

&)youth goes
right on
gr
owing old   20

Analyzing and Interpreting the Poem

1. In this poem about the differences between generations, old age sticks up "Keep Off" signs. How does youth respond?

2. "No Trespassing" and "Keep Off" signs warn outsiders to keep off private property. However, in this poem, "No Trespassing" probably means more than this kind of warning. **a.** What else do you think old age is warning youth not to interfere with? **b.** How does youth respond to this cry of "No Trespassing"?

3a. Which lines in the poem suggest that the difference between generations will go on and on forever? **b.** Why will this happen?

Literary Elements

Understanding the Poet's Technique

Notice how Cummings divides the word *growing* in lines 19–20. By stretching out the word in such a way, he suggests that growing old is a long, slow process. How would you read these lines aloud?

The words *No Trespassing* are spread out over lines 8, 9, and 11. They are interrupted by *&* and *youth laughs*. Shifting back and forth from *No Trespassing* to *& youth laughs* creates the same effect as that of a motion-picture camera focusing first on one character and then on another. We see what both characters are doing at the same time. How would you read these lines aloud?

About the Author

E. E. Cummings (1894–1962)

By nature E. E. Cummings, whose full name was Edward Estlin Cummings, was shy and sensitive. A painter as well as a poet, he created many new ways of presenting a poem on a page. Some of his poems looked so unusual that they baffled typesetters and threw some readers into confusion.

Before the United States entered World War I, Cummings went to France as an ambulance driver. Because of a censor's error, he was placed in a French prison camp. There he gathered material for his book *The Enormous Room*, which has been called one of the best direct-observation books to come out of that war.

Cummings, however, is best known for his lyric poems, which are witty, emotional, and filled with striking images. He can make us look at the tiniest words and symbols in new ways. One of his books of poetry is called *&* [and].

Gentleman of Río en Medio

JUAN A. A. SEDILLO

Why would a man sell his land but not the trees on it?

It took months of negotiation to come to an understanding with the old man. He was in no hurry. What he had the most of was time. He lived up in Río en Medio, where his people had been for hundreds of years. He tilled the same land they had tilled. His house was small and wretched, but quaint. The little creek ran through his land. His orchard was gnarled and beautiful.

The day of the sale he came into the office. His coat was old, green and faded. I thought of Senator Catron,[1] who had been such a power with these people up there in the mountains. Perhaps it was one of his old Prince Alberts.[2] He also wore gloves. They were old and torn and his fingertips showed through them. He carried a cane, but it was only the skeleton of a worn-out umbrella. Behind him walked one of his innumerable kin—a dark young man with eyes like a gazelle.

The old man bowed to all of us in the room. Then he removed his hat and gloves, slowly and carefully. Chaplin[3] once did that in a picture, in a bank—he was the janitor. Then he handed his things to the boy, who stood obediently behind the old man's chair.

There was a great deal of conversation about rain and about his family. He was very proud of his large family. Finally we got down to business. Yes, he would sell, as he had agreed, for twelve hundred dollars, in cash. We would buy, and the money was ready. "Don[4] Anselmo," I said to him in Spanish, "we have made a discovery. You remember that we sent that surveyor, that engineer, up there to survey your land so as to make the deed. Well, he finds that you own more than eight acres. He tells us that your land extends across the river and that you own almost twice as much as you thought." He didn't know that. "And now, Don Anselmo," I added, "these Americans are *buena gente,* they are good people, and they are willing to pay you for the additional land as well, at the same rate per acre, so that instead of twelve hundred dollars you will get almost twice as much, and the money is here for you."

The old man hung his head for a moment in thought. Then he stood up and stared at me.

1. **Senator Catron:** Thomas Benton Catron, a Senator from New Mexico (1912–1917).
2. **Prince Alberts:** long, double-breasted coats named after Prince Albert, who later became King Edward VII of Great Britain.
3. **Chaplin:** Charlie Chaplin, a comic star of silent movies.

4. **Don:** a title of respect in Spanish, like *Sir* in English.

New Mexico Landscape (1929) by John Marin (1870–1953). Watercolor on paper.

"Friend," he said, "I do not like to have you speak to me in that manner." I kept still and let him have his say. "I know these Americans are good people, and that is why I have agreed to sell to them. But I do not care to be insulted. I have agreed to sell my house and land for twelve hundred dollars and that is the price."

I argued with him but it was useless. Finally he signed the deed and took the money but refused to take more than the amount agreed upon. Then he shook hands all around, put on his ragged gloves, took his stick and walked out with the boy behind him.

A month later my friends had moved into Río en Medio. They had replastered the old adobe house, pruned the trees, patched the fence, and moved in for the summer. One day they came back to the office to complain. The children of the village were overrunning their property. They came every day and played under the trees, built little play fences around them, and took blossoms. When they were spoken to, they only laughed and talked back good-naturedly in Spanish.

I sent a messenger up to the mountains for Don Anselmo. It took a week to arrange another meeting. When he arrived he repeated his previous preliminary performance. He wore the same faded cutaway,[5] carried the same stick and was accompanied by the boy again. He shook hands all around, sat down with the boy behind his chair, and talked about the weather. Finally I broached the subject. "Don Anselmo, about the ranch you sold to these people. They are good people and want to be your friends and neighbors always. When you sold to them you signed a document, a deed, and in that deed you agreed to several things. One thing was that they were to have the complete possession of the property.

Now, Don Anselmo, it seems that every day the children of the village overrun the orchard and spend most of their time there. We would like to know if you, as the most respected man in the village, could not stop them from doing so in order that these people may enjoy their new home more in peace."

Don Anselmo stood up. "We have all learned to love these Americans," he said, "because they are good people and good neighbors. I sold them my property because I knew they were good people, but I did not sell them the trees in the orchard."

This was bad. "Don Anselmo," I pleaded, "when one signs a deed and sells real property one sells also everything that grows on the land, and those trees, every one of them, are on the land and inside the boundaries of what you sold."

"Yes, I admit that," he said. "You know," he added, "I am the oldest man in the village. Almost everyone there is my relative and all the children of Río en Medio are my *sobrinos* and *nietos*,[6] my descendants. Every time a child has been born in Río en Medio since I took possession of that house from my mother I have planted a tree for that child. The trees in that orchard are not mine, *señor*, they belong to the children of the village. Every person in Río en Medio born since the railroad came to Santa Fe owns a tree in that orchard. I did not sell the trees because I could not. They are not mine."

There was nothing we could do. Legally we owned the trees but the old man had been so generous, refusing what amounted to a fortune for him. It took most of the following winter to buy the trees, individually, from the descendants of Don Anselmo in the valley of Río en Medio.

---

5. **cutaway:** a long coat with part of the lower front cut away, used for formal occasions.

6. **sobrinos** (sō-brē′nōs) **and** **nietos** (nyĕ′tōs): Spanish for "nephews and nieces" and "grandchildren."

Reading Check

1. For how much money does Don Anselmo agree to sell his land?
2. Why do the Americans return to the lawyer's office and complain?
3. What reason does Don Anselmo give the lawyer for not being able to sell the trees?
4. How do the Americans finally come to own the trees?

For Study and Discussion

Analyzing and Interpreting the Story

1. Don Anselmo and the Americans have different views about money and property. What surprising reply does Don Anselmo make when he is offered more money for his property?

2. The Americans believe they have a legal right to the entire property, but Don Anselmo has another surprise for them. Why does Don Anselmo feel he has no right to sell the trees?

3. Because of the unexpected turn of events, Don Anselmo's descendants receive some money at the end of this story. Do you think this solution is fair to everyone? Why or why not?

4. Don Anselmo is dressed in faded and tattered clothing. **a.** What details reveal that he wears these clothes like a dignified gentleman? **b.** In what other ways does Don Anselmo show that he is a true gentleman?

Language and Vocabulary

Recognizing Words That Create Tone

Formal speech is language that has a dignified tone. It is the language you use to write a seri-

ous paper or make an important speech. To use formal speech or writing, you must follow the rules of grammar, sentence construction, and spelling for standard English.

In "Gentleman of Río en Medio," the author uses language that reflects the dignity of his main character, Don Anselmo. The words of Don Anselmo are simple and direct, yet they command respect from those around him. His language clearly characterizes him as a gentleman.

Included in the dialogue are words and phrases from the Spanish language which contribute to the story's overall dignified tone. The social formalities which are observed by Don Anselmo also add to the feeling of formality. Find two examples of dialogue which show the author's use of formal tone. Tell why you think the overall tone of formality expressed in Don Anselmo's language makes the outcome of the story believable.

Writing About Literature

Comparing Values

In a brief essay compare Don Anselmo's ideas about money and property with those of the lawyer and his clients.

About the Author

Juan A. A. Sedillo   (1902–1982)

Juan A. A. Sedillo was born in New Mexico and was a descendant of early Spanish colonists. He was a lawyer and judge, and he held several public offices. For a number of years he wrote a weekly article on Mexico for New Mexico newspapers. The story "Gentleman of Río en Medio" is based on an incident that took place in his law office.

My Family and Other Animals

GERALD DURRELL

This true story is from a book of the same title. The narrator, who became a famous naturalist, was ten when this adventure took place. Even at that age, he was fascinated by all forms of life—including a community of scorpions he found one day in a plaster wall.

I grew very fond of these scorpions. I found them to be pleasant, unassuming creatures with, on the whole, the most charming habits. Provided you did nothing silly or clumsy (like putting your hand on one) the scorpions treated you with respect, their one desire being to get away and hide as quickly as possible. They must have found me rather a trial, for I was always ripping sections of the plaster away so that I could watch them, or capturing them and making them walk about in jam jars so that I could see the way their feet moved. By means of my sudden and unexpected assaults on the wall I discovered quite a bit about scorpions. I found that they would eat bluebottles[1] (though how they caught them was a mystery I never solved), grasshoppers, moths, and lacewing flies. Several times I found one of them eating another, a habit I found most distressing in a creature otherwise so impeccable.[2]

By crouching under the wall at night with a torch,[3] I managed to catch some brief glimpses of the scorpions' wonderful courtship dances. I saw them standing, claws clasped, their bodies raised to the skies, their tails lovingly entwined; I saw them waltzing slowly in circles among the moss cushions, claw in claw. But my view of these performances was all too short, for almost as soon as I switched on the torch the partners would stop, pause for a moment, and then, seeing that I was not going to extinguish the light, would turn round and walk firmly away, claw in claw, side by side. They were definitely beasts that believed in keeping themselves *to* themselves. If I could have kept a colony in captivity I would probably have been able to see the whole of the courtship, but the family had forbidden scorpions in the house, despite my arguments in favor of them.

Then one day I found a fat female scorpion in the wall, wearing what at first glance appeared to be a pale fawn fur coat. Closer inspection proved that this strange garment was made up of a mass of tiny babies clinging to the mother's back. I was enraptured by this family, and I made up my mind to smuggle them into the house and up to my bedroom so that I might keep them and watch them grow up. With infinite care I maneuvered the mother and family into a matchbox, and then

---

1. **bluebottles:** bluish flies.
2. **impeccable** (ĭm-pĕk′ə-bəl): faultless; perfect.
3. **torch:** here, a flashlight.

hurried to the villa. It was rather unfortunate that just as I entered the door lunch should be served; however, I placed the matchbox carefully on the mantelpiece in the drawing room, so that the scorpions should get plenty of air, and made my way to the dining room and joined the family for the meal. Dawdling over my food, feeding Roger[4] surreptitiously under the table, and listening to the family arguing, I completely forgot about my exciting new captures. At last, Larry,[5] having finished, fetched the cigarettes from the drawing room, and lying back in his chair he put one in his mouth and picked up the matchbox he had brought. Oblivious of my impending doom I watched him interestedly as, still talking glibly, he opened the matchbox.

Now I maintain to this day that the female scorpion meant no harm. She was agitated and a trifle annoyed at being shut up in a matchbox for so long, and so she seized the first opportunity to escape. She hoisted herself out of the box with great rapidity, her babies clinging on desperately, and scuttled onto the back of Larry's hand. There, not quite certain what to do next, she paused, her sting curved up at the ready. Larry, feeling the movement of her claws, glanced down to see what it was, and from that moment things got increasingly confused.

He uttered a roar of fright that made Lugaretzia[6] drop a plate and brought Roger out from beneath the table, barking wildly. With a flick of his hand he sent the unfortunate scorpion flying down the table, and she landed midway between Margo and Leslie,[7]

scattering babies like confetti as she thumped onto the cloth. Thoroughly enraged at this treatment, the creature sped towards Leslie, her sting quivering with emotion. Leslie leaped to his feet, overturning his chair, and flicked out desperately with his napkin, sending the scorpion rolling across the cloth towards Margo, who promptly let out a scream that any railway engine would have been proud to produce. Mother, completely bewildered by this sudden and rapid change from peace to chaos, put on her glasses and peered down the table to see what was causing the pandemonium, and at that moment Margo, in a vain attempt to stop the scorpion's advance, hurled a glass of water at it. The shower missed the animal completely, but successfully drenched Mother, who, not being able to stand cold water, promptly lost her breath and sat gasping at the end of the table, unable even to protest. The scorpion had now gone to ground under Leslie's plate, while her babies swarmed wildly all over the table. Roger, mystified by the panic, but determined to do his share, ran round and round the room, barking hysterically.

"It's that bloody boy again . . ." bellowed Larry.

"Look out! Look out! They're coming!" screamed Margo.

"All we need is a book," roared Leslie; "don't panic, hit 'em with a book."

"What on earth's the *matter* with you all?" Mother kept imploring, mopping her glasses.

"It's that bloody boy . . . he'll kill the lot of us. . . . Look at the table . . . knee-deep in scorpions. . . ."

"Quick . . . quick . . . do something. . . . Look out, look out!"

"Stop screeching and get a book. . . . You're worse than the dog. . . . Shut *up*, Roger. . . ."

"By the grace of God I wasn't bitten. . . ."

"Look out . . . there's another one. . . . Quick . . . quick . . ."

4. **Roger:** the narrator's big, black, woolly dog.
5. **Larry:** the narrator's twenty-three-year-old brother, who tends to be very dramatic.
6. **Lugaretzia** (lōō'gə-rĕt'sē-ə): the family's Greek maid, who is always worried about her health.
7. **Margo and Leslie:** Margo is the eighteen-year-old sister, and Leslie the nineteen-year-old brother.

"Oh, shut up and get me a book or something. . . ."

"But *how* did the scorpions get on the table, dear?"

"That bloody boy. . . . Every matchbox in the house is a deathtrap. . . ."

"Look out, it's coming towards me. . . . Quick, quick, do something. . . ."

"Hit it with your knife . . . *your knife.* . . . Go on, hit it. . . ."

Since no one had bothered to explain things to him, Roger was under the mistaken impression that the family were being attacked, and that it was his duty to defend them. As Lugaretzia was the only stranger in the room, he came to the logical conclusion that she must be the responsible party, so he bit her in the ankle. This did not help matters very much.

By the time a certain amount of order had been restored, all the baby scorpions had hidden themselves under various plates and bits of cutlery.[8] Eventually, after impassioned pleas on my part, backed up by Mother, Leslie's suggestion that the whole lot be slaughtered was quashed. While the family, still simmering with rage and fright, retired to the drawing room, I spent half an hour rounding up the babies, picking them up in a teaspoon, and returning them to their mother's back. Then I carried them outside on a saucer and, with the utmost reluctance, released them on the garden wall. Roger and I went and spent the afternoon on the hillside, for I felt it would be prudent to allow the family to have a siesta before seeing them again.

The results of this incident were numerous. Larry developed a phobia about matchboxes and opened them with the utmost caution, a handkerchief wrapped round his hand. Lugaretzia limped around the house, her ankle enveloped in yards of bandage, for

8. **cutlery:** knives, forks, and spoons.

weeks after the bite had healed, and came round every morning, with the tea, to show us how the scabs were getting on. But, from my point of view, the worst repercussion of the whole affair was that Mother decided I was running wild again, and that it was high time I received a little more education.

Reading Check

1. Where did Gerald find the scorpion colony?
2. Where did he put the mother scorpion and her babies?
3. What did Margo do in an attempt to stop the mother scorpion?
4. What did Roger do to the maid?
5. What did Gerald finally do with the scorpions?

For Study and Discussion

Analyzing and Interpreting the Selection

1. Living with the Durrells was like being in a comic movie. This part of the comedy began when Gerald found the scorpions. **a.** How did Gerald feel about the scorpions? **b.** Why were his feelings rather unusual?

2. The rest of the family didn't share Gerald's fascination with the scorpions. In a comic sequence, we are told about their reactions. The first one to react was Larry. What did he do?

3a. What did each of the other family members do? **b.** How did Lugaretzia get bitten in the ankle?

4. From the family's point of view, the scorpion invasion was bad enough. But from Gerald's point of view, what was the worst result of the whole affair?

5. What did Mother fail to realize about the kind of education Gerald was getting on his own?

Narrative Writing

Narrating a Series of Events

After Larry felt the movement of the scorpion's claws and saw what was crawling on the back of his hand, things reached a peak of comic confusion. Look at the paragraph on page 105, beginning "He uttered a roar of fright." As if he were shooting a film, Durrell moves from character to character, showing how each action produces a reaction.

The scene is full of frenzy because Durrell uses many lively verbs. Notice all the action he makes us see: *drop, barking, flying, scattering, thumped, sped, quivering, leaped, overturning, flicked, rolling, peered, hurled, drenched, gasping, swarmed, ran.*

Using this scene as a model, write a paragraph in which you narrate a series of related events. Use verbs that will help your reader see lively movement. Choose a series of humorous events, if you like. Perhaps you can think of a scene that involves an animal, or a family, or a sports event. Your subject can be entirely imaginary.

About the Author

Gerald Durrell (1925–   )

Gerald Durrell has a worldwide reputation as a naturalist and zoologist. He also is admired as a keenly observant writer of the animal world. Durrell was born in India. His lifelong interest in animals began on the Greek island of Corfu, where he lived with his parents for five years before World War II. His books *My Family and Other Animals, Birds, Beasts and Relatives,* and *Fauna and Family* are about those years. The first of these, from which this story of the scorpions is taken, was made into a motion picture. Durrell and his wife founded a zoo on the isle of Jersey in the English Channel, which they devote to the conservation of endangered species. He has led and underwritten zoological expeditions to remote parts of Africa, South America, Australia, and Southeast Asia. He wrote the script "Elephant Country" for NBC-TV in 1971. He has written many newspaper and magazine articles, as well as many novels, including *The Overloaded Ark* and *A Zoo in My Luggage.*

My Friend Flicka

MARY O'HARA

Kennie never seemed to do anything right. "If I could have a colt all for my own," he said, "I might do better."

Report cards for the second semester were sent out soon after school closed in mid-June.

Kennie's was a shock to the whole family.

"If I could have a colt all for my own," said Kennie, "I might do better."

Rob McLaughlin glared at his son. "Just as a matter of curiosity," he said, "how do you go about it to get a *zero* in an examination? Forty in arithmetic; seventeen in history! But a *zero?* Just as one man to another, what goes on in your head?"

"Yes, tell us how you do it, Ken," chirped Howard.

"Eat your breakfast, Howard," snapped his mother.

Kennie's blond head bent over his plate until his face was almost hidden. His cheeks burned.

McLaughlin finished his coffee and pushed his chair back. "You'll do an hour a day on your lessons all through the summer."

Nell McLaughlin saw Kennie wince as if something had actually hurt him.

Lessons and study in the summertime, when the long winter was just over and there weren't hours enough in the day for all the things he wanted to do!

Kennie took things hard. His eyes turned to the wide-open window with a look almost of despair.

The hill opposite the house, covered with arrow-straight jack pines, was sharply etched in the thin air of the eight-thousand-foot altitude. Where it fell away, vivid green grass ran up to meet it; and over range and upland poured the strong Wyoming sunlight that stung everything into burning color. A big jack rabbit sat under one of the pines, waving his long ears back and forth.

Ken had to look at his plate and blink back tears before he could turn to his father and say carelessly, "Can I help you in the corral with the horses this morning, Dad?"

"You'll do your study every morning before you do anything else." And McLaughlin's scarred boots and heavy spurs clattered across the kitchen floor. "I'm disgusted with you. Come, Howard."

Howard strode after his father, nobly refraining from looking at Kennie.

"Help me with the dishes, Kennie," said Nell McLaughlin as she rose, tied on a big apron, and began to clear the table.

Kennie looked at her in despair. She poured steaming water into the dishpan and sent him for the soap powder.

"If I could have a colt," he muttered again.

"Now get busy with that dish towel, Ken. It's eight o'clock. You can study till nine and then go up to the corral. They'll still be there."

At supper that night, Kennie said, "But Dad, Howard had a colt all of his own when he was only eight. And he trained it and schooled it all himself; and now he's eleven and Highboy is three, and he's riding him. I'm nine now, and even if you did give me a colt now, I couldn't catch up to Howard because I couldn't ride it till it was a three-year-old and then I'd be twelve."

Nell laughed, "Nothing wrong with that arithmetic."

But Rob said, "Howard never gets less than seventy-five average at school, and hasn't disgraced himself and his family by getting more demerits than any other boy in his class."

Kennie didn't answer. He couldn't figure it out. He tried hard; he spent hours poring over his books. That was supposed to get you good marks, but it never did. Everyone said he was bright; why was it that when he studied he didn't learn? He had a vague feeling that perhaps he looked out the window too much, or looked through the walls to see clouds and sky and hills and wonder what was happening out there. Sometimes it wasn't even a wonder but just a pleasant drifting feeling of nothing at all, as if nothing mattered, as if there was always plenty of time, as if the lessons would get done of themselves. And then the bell would ring and study period was over.

If he had a colt . . .

When the boys had gone to bed that night, Nell McLaughlin sat down with her overflowing mending basket and glanced at her husband.

He was at his desk as usual, working on account books and inventories.

Nell threaded a darning needle and thought, "It's either that whacking big bill from the vet for the mare that died or the last half of the tax bill."

It didn't seem just the auspicious moment to plead Kennie's cause. But then, these days, there was always a line between Rob's eyes and a harsh note in his voice.

"Rob," she began.

He flung down his pencil and turned around.

"That law!" he exclaimed.

"What law?"

"The state law that puts high taxes on pedigreed stock. I'll have to do as the rest of 'em do—drop the papers."

"Drop the papers! But you'll never get decent prices if you don't have registered horses."

"I don't get decent prices now."

"But you will someday, if you don't drop the papers."

"Maybe." He bent again over the desk.

Rob, thought Nell, was a lot like Kennie himself. He set his heart. Oh, how stubbornly he set his heart on just some one thing he wanted above everything else. He had set his heart on horses and ranching way back when he had been a crack rider at West Point; and he had resigned and thrown away his army career just for the horses. Well, he'd got what he wanted.

She drew a deep breath, snipped her thread, laid down the sock, and again looked across at her husband as she unrolled another length of darning cotton.

To get what you want is one thing, she was thinking. The three-thousand-acre ranch and the hundred head of horses. But to make it pay—for a dozen or more years they had been trying to make it pay. People said ranching hadn't paid since the beef barons ran their herds on public land; people said the only prosperous ranchers in Wyoming were the dude ranchers; people said . . .

But suddenly she gave her head a little rebellious, gallant shake. Rob would always be fighting and struggling against something, like Kennie, perhaps like herself too. Even those first years when there was no water piped into the house, when every day brought a new difficulty or danger, how she had loved it! How she still loved it!

She ran the darning ball into the toe of a sock, Kennie's sock. The length of it gave her a shock. Yes, the boys were growing up fast, and now Kennie—Kennie and the colt . . .

After a while she said, "Give Kennie a colt, Rob."

"He doesn't deserve it." The answer was short. Rob pushed away his papers and took out his pipe.

"Howard's too far ahead of him; older and bigger and quicker and his wits about him, and . . ."

"Ken doesn't half try, doesn't stick at anything."

She put down her sewing. "He's crazy for a colt of his own. He hasn't had another idea in his head since you gave Highboy to Howard."

"I don't believe in bribing children to do their duty."

"Not a bribe." She hesitated.

"No? What would you call it?"

She tried to think it out. "I just have a feeling Ken isn't going to pull anything off, and"—her eyes sought Rob's—"it's time he did. It isn't the school marks alone, but I just don't want things to go on any longer with Ken never coming out at the right end of anything."

"I'm beginning to think he's just dumb."

"He's not dumb. Maybe a little thing like this—if he had a colt of his own, trained him, rode him . . ."

Rob interrupted. "But it isn't a little thing, nor an easy thing, to break and school a colt the way Howard has schooled Highboy. I'm not going to have a good horse spoiled by Ken's careless ways. He goes woolgathering. He never knows what he's doing."

"But he'd *love* a colt of his own, Rob. If he could do it, it might make a big difference in him."

"*If* he could do it! But that's a big if."

At breakfast next morning, Kennie's father said to him, "When you've done your study, come out to the barn. I'm going in the car up to section twenty-one this morning to look over the brood mares.[1] You can go with me."

"Can I go too, Dad?" cried Howard.

McLaughlin frowned at Howard. "You turned Highboy out last evening with dirty legs."

Howard wriggled. "I groomed him. . . ."

"Yes, down to his knees."

"He kicks."

"And whose fault is that? You don't get on his back again until I see his legs clean."

The two boys eyed each other, Kennie secretly triumphant and Howard chagrined.[2] McLaughlin turned at the door, "And, Ken, a week from today I'll give you a colt. Between now and then you can decide what one you want."

Kennie shot out of his chair and stared at his father. "A—a—spring colt, Dad, or a yearling?"

McLaughlin was somewhat taken aback, but his wife concealed a smile. If Kennie got a yearling colt, he would be even up with Howard.

"A yearling colt, your father means, Ken," she said smoothly. "Now hurry with your lessons. Howard will wipe."

Kennie found himself the most important personage on the ranch. Prestige lifted his head, gave him an inch more of height and a bold stare, and made him feel different all the way through. Even Gus and Tim Murphy, the ranch hands, were more interested in Kennie's choice of a colt than anything else.

Howard was fidgety with suspense. "Who'll you pick, Ken? Say—pick Doughboy, why don't you? Then when he grows up, he'll be sort of twins with mine, in his name anyway. Doughboy, Highboy, see?"

---

1. **brood mares:** female horses kept for breeding.
2. **chagrined** (shə-grīnd′): embarrassed.

Scenes on pages 111, 113, 115, and 118
from the film *My Friend Flicka*.

The boys were sitting on the worn wooden step of the door which led from the tack room into the corral, busy with rags and polish, shining their bridles.

Ken looked at his brother with scorn. Doughboy would never have half of Highboy's speed.

"Lassie, then," suggested Howard. "She's black as ink, like mine. And she'll be fast. . . ."

"Dad says Lassie'll never go over fifteen hands."[3]

Nell McLaughlin saw the change in Kennie and her hopes rose. He went to his books in the morning with determination and really studied. A new alertness took the place of the daydreaming. Examples in arithmetic were neatly written out, and, as she passed his door before breakfast, she often heard the monotonous drone of his voice as he read his American history aloud.

Each night, when he kissed her, he flung his arms around her and held her fiercely for a moment, then, with a winsome and blissful smile into her eyes, turned away to bed.

He spent days inspecting the different bands of horses and colts. He sat for hours on the corral fence, very important, chewing straws. He rode off on one of the ponies for half the day, wandering through the mile-square pastures that ran down toward the Colorado border.

And when the week was up, he announced his decision. "I'll take that yearling filly of Rocket's. The sorrel[4] with the cream tail and mane.

His father looked at him in surprise. "The one that got tangled in the barbed wire?—that's never been named?"

In a second all Kennie's new pride was gone. He hung his head defensively. "Yes."

"You've made a bad choice, Son. You couldn't have picked a worse."

"She's fast, Dad. And Rocket's fast. . . ."

"It's the worst line of horses I've got. There's never one among them with real sense. The mares are hellions[5] and the stallions outlaws; they're untamable."

"I'll tame her."

Rob guffawed. "Not I, nor anyone, has ever really been able to tame any one of them."

Kennie's chest heaved.

"Better change your mind, Ken. You want a horse that'll be a real friend to you, don't you?"

"Yes"—Kennie's voice was unsteady.

3. **fifteen hands:** 60 inches (about 150 centimeters) in height.

4. **sorrel:** a horse of reddish-brown color.
5. **hellions:** troublemakers.

"Well, you'll never make a friend of that filly. She's all cut and scarred up already with tearing through barbed wire after that no-good mother of hers. No fence'll hold 'em. . . ."

"I know," said Kennie, still more faintly.

"Change your mind?" asked Howard briskly.

"No."

Rob was grim and put out. He couldn't go back on his word. The boy had to have a reasonable amount of help in breaking and taming the filly, and he could envision precious hours, whole days, wasted in the struggle.

Nell McLaughlin despaired. Once again Ken seemed to have taken the wrong turn and was back where he had begun, stoical, silent, defensive.

But there was a difference that only Ken could know. The way he felt about his colt. The way his heart sang. The pride and joy that filled him so full that sometimes he hung his head so they wouldn't see it shining out of his eyes.

He had known from the very first that he would choose that particular yearling because he was in love with her.

The year before, he had been out working with Gus, the big Swedish ranch hand, on the irrigation ditch, when they had noticed Rocket standing in a gully on the hillside, quiet for once and eyeing them cautiously.

"Ay bet she got a colt," said Gus, and they walked carefully up the draw.[6] Rocket gave a wild snort, thrust her feet out, shook her head wickedly, then fled away. And as they reached the spot, they saw standing there the wavering, pinkish colt, barely able to keep its feet. It gave a little squeak and started after its mother on crooked, wobbling legs.

"Yee whiz! Luk at de little *flicka!*" said Gus.

"What does *flicka* mean, Gus?"

"Swedish for 'little gurl,' Ken. . . ."

Ken announced at supper, "You said she'd never been named. I've named her. Her name is Flicka."

The first thing to do was to get her in. She was running with a band of yearlings on the saddleback,[7] cut with ravines and gullies, on section twenty.

They all went out after her, Ken, as owner, on old Rob Roy, the wisest horse on the ranch.

Ken was entranced to watch Flicka when the wild band of youngsters discovered that they were being pursued and took off across the mountain. Footing made no difference to her. She floated across the ravines, always two lengths ahead of the others. Her pink mane and tail whipped in the wind. Her long, delicate legs had only to aim, it seemed, at a particular spot for her to reach it and sail on. She seemed to Ken a fairy horse.

He sat motionless, just watching and holding Rob Roy in, when his father thundered past on Sultan and shouted, "Well, what's the matter? Why didn't you turn 'em?"

Kennie woke up and galloped after.

Rob Roy brought in the whole band. The corral gates were closed, and an hour was spent shunting the ponies in and out through the chutes, until Flicka was left alone in the small round corral in which the baby colts were branded. Gus drove the others away, out of the gate, and up the saddleback.

But Flicka did not intend to be left. She hurled herself against the poles which walled the corral. She tried to jump them. They were seven feet high. She caught her front feet over the top rung, clung, scrambled, while Kennie held his breath for fear the slender legs would be caught between the bars and snapped. Her hold broke; she fell over backward, rolled, screamed, tore around the corral. Kennie had

6. **draw:** gully.

7. **saddleback:** a hill or ridge with a depression at the top, like the back of a horse that has worn a saddle too long.

a sick feeling in the pit of his stomach, and his father looked disgusted.

One of the bars broke. She hurled herself again. Another went. She saw the opening and, as neatly as a dog crawls through a fence, inserted her head and forefeet, scrambled through, and fled away, bleeding in a dozen places.

As Gus was coming back, just about to close the gate to the upper range, the sorrel whipped through it, sailed across the road and ditch with her inimitable floating leap, and went up the side of the saddleback like a jack rabbit.

From way up the mountain, Gus heard excited whinnies, as she joined the band he had just driven up, and the last he saw of them they were strung out along the crest running like deer.

"Yee whiz!" said Gus, and stood motionless and staring until the ponies had disappeared over the ridge. Then he closed the gate, re-mounted Rob Roy, and rode back to the corral.

Rob McLaughlin gave Kennie one more chance to change his mind. "Last chance, Son. Better pick a horse that you have some hope of riding one day. I'd have got rid of this whole line of stock if they weren't so fast that I've had the fool idea that some day there might turn out one gentle one in the lot—and I'd have a racehorse. But there's never been one so far, and it's not going to be Flicka."

"It's not going to be Flicka," chanted Howard.

"Perhaps she *might* be gentled," said Kennie; and Nell, watching, saw that although his lips quivered, there was fanatical determination in his eye.

"Ken," said Rob, "it's up to you. If you say you want her, we'll get her. But she wouldn't be the first of that line to die rather than give in. They're beautiful and they're fast, but let me tell you this, young man, they're *loco!*"[8]

Kennie flinched under his father's direct glance.

"If I go after her again, I'll not give up whatever comes, understand what I mean by that?"

"Yes."

"What do you say?"

"I want her."

They brought her in again. They had better luck this time. She jumped over the Dutch half door of the stable and crashed inside. The men slammed the upper half of the door shut and she was caught.

The rest of the band were driven away, and Kennie stood outside the stable, listening to the wild hoofs beating, the screams, the crashes. His Flicka inside there! He was drenched with perspiration.

"We'll leave her to think it over," said Rob when dinnertime came. "Afterward, we'll go up and feed and water her."

But when they went up afterward there was no Flicka in the barn. One of the windows, higher than the mangers, was broken.

The window opened into a pasture an eighth of a mile square, fenced in barbed wire six feet high. Near the stable stood a wagonload of hay. When they went around the back of the stable to see where Flicka had hidden herself, they found her between the stable and the hay wagon, eating.

At their approach she leaped away, then headed east across the pasture.

"If she's like her mother," said Rob, "she'll go right through the wire."

"Ay bet she'll go over," said Gus. "She yumps like a deer."

"No horse can jump that," said McLaughlin.

Kennie said nothing because he could not

speak. It was, perhaps, the most terrible moment of his life. He watched Flicka racing toward the eastern wire.

A few yards from it, she swerved, turned, and raced diagonally south.

"It turned her! It turned her!" cried Kennie, almost sobbing. It was the first sign of hope for Flicka. "Oh, Dad! She has got sense. She has! She has!"

Flicka turned again as she met the southern boundary of the pasture; again at the northern; she avoided the barn. Without abating anything of her whirlwind speed, following a precise, accurate calculation and turning each time on a dime, she investigated every possibility. Then, seeing that there was no hope, she raced south toward the range where she had spent her life, gathered herself, and shot into the air.

Each of the three men watching had the impulse to cover his eyes, and Kennie gave a sort of howl of despair.

Twenty yards of fence came down with her as she hurled herself through. Caught on the upper strands, she turned a complete somersault, landing on her back, her four legs dragging the wire down on top of her, and tangling herself in them beyond hope of escape.

"Blasted wire!" said McLaughlin. "If I could afford decent fences . . ."

Kennie followed the men miserably as they walked to the filly. They stood in a circle, watching while she kicked and fought and thrashed until the wire was tightly wound and knotted about her, cutting, piercing, and tearing great three-cornered pieces of flesh and hide. At last she was unconscious, streams of blood running on her golden coat, and pools of crimson widening and spreading on the grass beneath her.

With the wire cutter which Gus always carried in the hip pocket of his overalls, he cut all the wire away, and they drew her into the pas-

8. *loco:* the Spanish word for "crazy."

ture, repaired the fence, placed hay, a box of oats, and a tub of water near her, and called it a day.

"I don't think she'll pull out of it," said McLaughlin.

Next morning Kennie was up at five, doing his lessons. At six he went out to Flicka.

She had not moved. Food and water were untouched. She was no longer bleeding, but the wounds were swollen and caked over.

Kennie got a bucket of fresh water and poured it over her mouth. Then he leaped away, for Flicka came to life, scrambled up, got her balance, and stood swaying.

Kennie went a few feet away and sat down to watch her. When he went into breakfast, she had drunk deeply of the water and was mouthing the oats.

There began, then, a sort of recovery. She ate, drank, limped about the pasture; stood for hours with hanging head and weakly splayed-out[9] legs, under the clump of cottonwood trees.

9. **splayed-out:** spread outward.

The swollen wounds scabbed and began to heal.

Kennie lived in the pasture, too. He followed her around; he talked to her. He too lay snoozing or sat under the cottonwoods; and often, coaxing her with hand outstretched, he walked very quietly toward her. But she would not let him come near her.

Often she stood with her head at the south fence, looking off to the mountain. It made the tears come to Kennie's eyes to see the way she longed to get away.

Still Rob said she wouldn't pull out of it. There was no use putting a halter on her. She had no strength.

One morning, as Ken came out of the house, Gus met him and said, "De filly's down."

Kennie ran to the pasture, Howard close behind him. The right hind leg, which had been badly swollen at the knee joint, had opened in a festering wound, and Flicka lay flat and motionless, with staring eyes.

"Don't you wish now you'd chosen Dough-boy?" asked Howard.

"Go away!" shouted Ken.

Howard stood watching while Kennie sat down on the ground and took Flicka's head on his lap. Though she was conscious and moved a little, she did not struggle or seem frightened. Tears rolled down Kennie's cheeks as he talked to her and petted her. After a few moments, Howard walked away.

"Mother, what do you do for an infection when it's a horse?" asked Kennie.

"Just what you'd do if it was a person. Wet dressings. I'll help you, Ken. We mustn't let those wounds close or scab over until they're clean. I'll make a poultice[10] for that hind leg and help you put it on. Now that she'll let us get close to her, we can help her a lot."

"The thing to do is see that she eats," said Rob. "Keep up her strength."

But he himself would not go near her. "She won't pull out if it," he said. "I don't want to see her or think about her."

Kennie and his mother nursed the filly. The big poultice was bandaged on the hind leg. It drew out much poisoned matter, and Flicka felt better and was able to stand again.

She watched for Kennie now and followed him like a dog, hopping on three legs, holding up the right hind leg with its huge knob of a bandage in comical fashion.

"Dad, Flicka's my friend now; she likes me," said Ken.

His father looked at him. "I'm glad of that, Son. It's a fine thing to have a horse for a friend."

Kennie found a nicer place for her. In the lower pasture the brook ran over cool stones. There was a grassy bank, the size of a corral, almost on a level with the water. Here she could lie softly, eat grass, drink fresh running water. From the grass, a twenty-foot hill sloped up, crested with overhanging trees. She was enclosed, as it were, in a green, open-air nursery.

Kennie carried her oats, morning and evening. She would watch for him to come, eyes and ears pointed to the hill. And one evening, Ken, still some distance off, came to a stop and a wide grin spread over his face. He had heard her nicker.[11] She had caught sight of him coming and was calling to him!

He placed the box of oats under her nose, and she ate while he stood beside her, his hand smoothing the satin-soft skin under her mane. It had a nap as deep as plush. He played with her long, cream-colored tresses, arranged her forelock neatly between her eyes. She was a bit dish-faced, like an Arab, with eyes set far apart. He lightly groomed and brushed her while she stood turning her head to him whichever way he went.

He spoiled her. Soon she would not step to the stream to drink but he must hold a bucket for her. And she would drink, then lift her dripping muzzle, rest it on the shoulder of his blue chambray shirt, her golden eyes dreaming off into the distance, then daintily dip her mouth to drink again.

When she turned her head to the south and pricked her ears and stood tense and listening, Ken knew she heard the other colts galloping on the upland.

"You'll go back there someday, Flicka," he whispered. "You'll be three and I'll be eleven. You'll be so strong you won't know I'm on your back, and we'll fly like the wind. We'll stand on the very top where we can look over the whole world and smell the snow from the Never-Summer Range. Maybe we'll see antelope. . . ."

This was the happiest month of Kennie's life.

With the morning, Flicka always had new strength and would hop three-legged up the

---

10. **poultice** (pōl′tĭs): a warm, moist dressing for a wound.

11. **nicker:** whinny.

hill to stand broadside to the early sun, as horses love to do.

The moment Ken woke, he'd go to the window and see her there; and when he was dressed and at his table studying, he sat so that he could raise his head and see Flicka.

After breakfast, she would be waiting for him and the box of oats at the gate, and for Nell McLaughlin with fresh bandages and buckets of disinfectant; and all three would go together to the brook, Flicka hopping along ahead of them, as if she were leading the way.

But Rob McLaughlin would not look at her.

One day all the wounds were swollen again. Presently they opened, one by one; and Kennie and his mother made more poultices.

Still the little filly climbed the hill in the early morning and ran about on three legs. Then she began to go down in flesh and almost overnight wasted away to nothing. Every rib showed; the glossy hide was dull and brittle, and was pulled over the skeleton as if she were a dead horse.

Gus said, "It's de fever. It burns up her flesh. If you could stop de fever she might get vell."

McLaughlin was standing in his window one morning and saw the little skeleton hopping about three-legged in the sunshine, and he said, "That's the end. I won't have a thing like that on my place."

Kennie had to understand that Flicka had not been getting well all this time; she had been slowly dying.

"She still eats her oats," he said mechanically.

They were all sorry for Ken. Nell McLaughlin stopped disinfecting and dressing the wounds. "It's no use Ken," she said gently. "You know Flicka's going to die, don't you?"

"Yes, Mother."

Ken stopped eating. Howard said, "Ken doesn't eat anything any more. Don't he have to eat his dinner, Mother?"

But Nell answered, "Leave him alone."

Because the shooting of wounded animals is all in the day's work on the Western plains, and sickening to everyone, Rob's voice, when he gave the order to have Flicka shot, was as flat as if he had been telling Gus to kill a chicken for dinner.

"Here's the Marlin, Gus. Pick out a time when Ken's not around and put the filly out of her misery."

Gus took the rifle. "*Ja*, Boss. . . ."

Ever since Ken had known that Flicka was to be shot, he had kept his eye on the rack which held the firearms. His father allowed no firearms in the bunkhouse. The gun rack was in the dining room of the ranch house; and, going through it to the kitchen three times a day for meals, Ken's eye scanned the weapons to make sure that they were all there.

That night they were not all there. The Marlin rifle was missing.

When Kennie saw that, he stopped walking. He felt dizzy. He kept staring at the gun rack, telling himself that it surely was there—he counted again and again—he couldn't see clearly. . . .

Then he felt an arm across his shoulder and heard his father's voice.

"I know, Son. Some things are awful hard to take. We just have to take 'em. I have to, too."

Kennie got hold of his father's hand and held on. It helped steady him.

Finally he looked up. Rob looked down and smiled at him and gave him a little shake and squeeze. Ken managed a smile too.

"All right now?"

"All right, Dad."

They walked in to supper together.

Ken even ate a little. But Nell looked thoughtfully at the ashen color of his face, and at the little pulse that was beating in the side of his neck.

After supper he carried Flicka her oats, but he had to coax her and she would only eat a little. She stood with her head hanging, but when he stroked it and talked to her, she pressed her face into his chest and was content. He could feel the burning heat of her body. It didn't seem possible that anything so thin could be alive.

Presently Kennie saw Gus come into the pasture, carrying the Marlin. When he saw Ken, he changed his direction and sauntered along as if he were out to shoot some cottontails.

Ken ran to him. "When are you going to do it, Gus?"

"Ay was goin' down soon now, before it got dark...."

"Gus, don't do it tonight. Wait till morning. Just one more night, Gus."

"Vell, in de morning, den, but it got to be done, Ken. Yer fader gives de order."

"I know. I won't say anything more."

An hour after the family had gone to bed, Ken got up and put on his clothes. It was a warm moonlit night. He ran down to the brook, calling softly, "Flicka! Flicka!"

But Flicka did not answer with a little nicker, and she was not in the nursery nor hopping about the pasture. Ken hunted for an hour.

At last he found her down the creek, lying in the water. Her head had been on the bank, but as she lay there, the current of the stream had sucked and pulled at her, and she had had no strength to resist; and little by little her head had slipped down until when Ken got there only the muzzle was resting on the bank, and the body and legs were swinging in the stream.

Kennie slid into the water, sitting on the bank, and he hauled at her head. But she was heavy, and the current dragged like a weight; and he began to sob because he had no strength to draw her out.

Then he found a leverage for his heels against some rocks in the bed of the stream, and he braced himself against these and pulled with all his might; and her head came

up onto his knees, and he held it cradled in his arms.

He was glad that she had died of her own accord, in the cool water, under the moon, instead of being shot by Gus. Then, putting his face close to hers and looking searchingly into her eyes, he saw that she was alive and looking back at him.

And then he burst out crying and hugged her and said, "Oh, my little Flicka, my little Flicka."

The long night passed.

The moon slid slowly across the heavens.

The water rippled over Kennie's legs and

over Flicka's body. And gradually the heat and fever went out of her. And the cool running water washed and washed her wounds.

When Gus went down in the morning with the rifle, they hadn't moved. There they were, Kennie sitting in water over his thighs and hips, with Flicka's head in his arms.

Gus seized Flicka by the head and hauled her out on the grassy bank, and then, seeing that Kennie couldn't move, cold and stiff and half paralyzed as he was, lifted him in his arms and carried him to the house.

"Gus," said Ken through chattering teeth, "don't shoot her, Gus."

"It ain't fur me to say, Ken. You know dat."

"But the fever's left her, Gus."

"Ay wait a little, Ken. . . ."

Rob McLaughlin drove to Laramie to get the doctor, for Ken was in violent chills that would not stop. His mother had him in bed, wrapped in hot blankets, when they got back.

He looked at his father imploringly as the doctor shook down the thermometer.

"She might get well now, Dad. The fever's left her. It went out of her when the moon went down."

"All right, Son. Don't worry. Gus'll feed her, morning and night, as long as she's . . ."

"As long as I can't do it," finished Ken happily.

The doctor put the thermometer in his mouth and told him to keep it shut.

All day Gus went about his work, thinking of Flicka. He had not been back to look at her. He had been given no more orders. If she was alive, the order to shoot her was still in effect. But Kennie was ill; McLaughlin, making his second trip to town, taking the doctor home, would not be back till long after dark.

After their supper in the bunkhouse, Gus and Tim walked down to the brook. They did not speak as they approached the filly, lying stretched out flat on the grassy bank, but their eyes were straining at her to see if she was dead or alive.

She raised her head as they reached her.

"By the powers!" exclaimed Tim; "there she is!"

She dropped her head, raised it again, and moved her legs and became tense as if struggling to rise. But to do so she must use her right hind leg to brace herself against the earth. That was the damaged leg, and at the first bit of pressure with it, she gave up and fell back.

"We'll swing her onto the other side," said Tim. "Then she can help herself."

"Ja. . . ."

Standing behind her, they leaned over, grabbed hold of her left legs, front and back, and gently hauled her over. Flicka was as lax and willing as a puppy. But the moment she found herself lying on her right side, she began to scramble, braced herself with her good left leg, and tried to rise.

"Yee whiz!" said Gus. "She got plenty strength yet."

"Hi!" cheered Tim. "She's up!"

But Flicka wavered, slid down again, and lay flat. This time she gave notice that she would not try again by heaving a deep sigh and closing her eyes.

Gus took his pipe out of his mouth and thought it over. Orders or no orders, he would try to save the filly. Ken had gone too far to be let down.

"Ay'm goin' to rig a blanket sling fur her, Tim, and get her on her feet and keep her up."

There was bright moonlight to work by. They brought down the posthole digger and set two aspen poles deep into the ground on either side of the filly, then, with ropes attached to the blanket, hoisted her by a pulley.

Not at all disconcerted, she rested comfortably in the blanket under her belly, touched her feet on the ground, and reached for the bucket of water Gus held for her.

Kennie was sick a long time. He nearly died. But Flicka picked up. Every day Gus passed the word to Nell, who carried it to Ken. "She's cleaning up her oats. . . . She's out of the sling. . . . She bears a little weight on the bad leg."

Tim declared it was a real miracle. They argued about it, eating their supper.

"Na," said Gus. "It was de cold water, washin' de fever outa her. And more dan dot—it was Ken—you tink it don't count? All night dot boy sits dere and says, 'Hold on, Flicka, Ay'm here wid you. Ay'm standin' by, two of us togedder.' . . ."

Tim stared at Gus without answering, while he thought it over. In the silence, a coyote yapped far off on the plains, and the wind made a rushing sound high up in the jack pines on the hill.

Gus filled his pipe.

"Sure," said Tim finally. "Sure, that's it."

Then came the day when Rob McLaughlin stood smiling at the foot of Kennie's bed and said, "Listen! Hear your friend?"

Ken listened and heard Flicka's high, eager whinny.

"She don't spend much time by the brook any more. She's up at the gate of the corral half the time, nickering for you."

"For me!"

Rob wrapped a blanket around the boy and carried him out to the corral gate.

Kennie gazed at Flicka. There was a look of marveling in his eyes. He felt as if he had been living in a world where everything was dreadful and hurting but awfully real; and *this*

couldn't be real; this was all soft and happy, nothing to struggle over or worry about or fight for any more. Even his father was proud of him! He could feel it in the way Rob's big arms held him. It was all like a dream and far away. He couldn't, yet, get close to anything.

But Flicka—Flicka—alive, well, pressing up to him, recognizing him, nickering . . .

Kennie put out a hand—weak and white— and laid it on her face. His thin little fingers straightened her forelock the way he used to do, while Rob looked at the two with a strange expression about his mouth and a glow in his eyes that was not often there.

"She's still poor, Dad, but she's on four legs now."

"She's picking up."

Ken turned his face up, suddenly remembering. "Dad! She did get gentled, didn't she?"

"Gentle—as—a kitten. . . ."

They put a cot down by the brook for Ken, and boy and filly got well together.

Reading Check

1. What does Kennie believe will help him do better in school?
2. Who persuades Kennie's father to give him a colt?
3. Why does Kennie pick Rocket's yearling filly?
4. How does Flicka injure herself?
5. How does Kennie treat Flicka's infection?

For Study and Discussion

Analyzing and Interpreting the Story

1. In this story, both Kennie and Flicka have to go through long and painful ordeals before they prove themselves to the people around them. Give examples to show how both the boy and filly are considered "misfits" or "losers" when we first meet them.

2. Kennie's father tries to get his son to change his mind about Flicka. Why does Kennie insist on his choice?

3. In what ways is Kennie like his father?

4a. What was perhaps "the most terrible moment" in Kennie's life (page 114)? **b.** What happens to Flicka in her leap for freedom?

5. On page 116 you are told: "This was the happiest month of Kennie's life." What makes this time so special for Kennie?

6a. What does Kennie do on the night before the filly is to be shot that proves his love for his "friend" Flicka? **b.** According to Gus, what saved Flicka?

7a. How do we know by the end of the story that Rob McLaughlin has changed his mind about Kennie and Flicka? **b.** How have Kennie and Flicka changed by the end of the story?

Language and Vocabulary

Using Context Clues

What context clues in the following sentences help you define the italicized words? Check your answers in a dictionary.

> Nell McLaughlin saw Kennie *wince* as if something had actually hurt him.

> "I'm not going to have a good horse spoiled by Ken's careless ways. He goes *woolgathering*. He never knows what he's doing."

> . . . she often heard the monotonous *drone* of his voice as he read his American history aloud.

Descriptive Writing

Creating a Strong Impression

In this paragraph from "My Friend Flicka," the author creates a vivid impression of the filly's enchanted lightness and speed. Notice how the words in italics help to suggest this impression:

> Ken was entranced to watch Flicka when the wild band of youngsters discovered that they were being pursued and took off across the mountain. Footing made no difference to her. She *floated* across the ravines, always two lengths ahead of the others. Her pink mane and tail *whipped in the wind*. Her long, *delicate* legs had only to aim, it seemed, at a particular spot for her to reach it and *sail* on. She seemed to Ken a *fairy* horse.

Write a short paragraph describing a person, an animal, or a place. Select specific words that will create a single strong impression. Before you write, decide the impression you want to create—for example, power, playfulness, or beauty.

About the Author

Mary O'Hara   (1885–1980)

Mary O'Hara is a name special to readers of all ages who love horses. She created the classic story of a boy and his horse, *My Friend Flicka*, in 1941. The story grew out of her experiences and impressions while living in Wyoming. A critic wrote that the story "makes you smell the grass and feel the coolness of the wind." She followed its success with two more novels about the Wyoming range country, *Thunderhead, Son of Flicka* and *The Green Grass of Wyoming*, and a diary, *Wyoming Summer*. The three novels were made into successful motion pictures, and *My Friend Flicka* also became a television series. O'Hara was a native of New Jersey. She worked for a time as a screenwriter in California and also composed piano music.

DEVELOPING SKILLS
IN CRITICAL THINKING

Making Generalizations About Theme

The *theme* of a story is its main idea about life or human nature. Usually, an author does not state the theme of a work directly. Readers must infer or make a reasonable guess about the theme from evidence in the story.

To find the theme of a story, first determine the story's central purpose or what the writer is trying to show about human nature in general. To do this you might ask the following questions:

1. *How have characters changed through the story?* For example, does an irresponsible character become responsible? Does a coward save someone's life?

2. *What major conflicts occur during the story?* Do the conflicts end with characters understanding more about themselves or with your understanding the characters better?

3. *Does the title give a clue to the theme?*

After you determine the theme, state it in a complete sentence as a *generalization* about life. (That means the statement will apply to many people, not just to those in the story.) The theme of "A Cap for Steve" (page 78) may be stated as the following generalization: *Winning and keeping the love and respect of a son can prove to be more important to a parent than having money.*

Using the questions above as guidelines, state, as a generalization, the theme of "The Apprentice" (page 88).

PRACTICE IN READING AND WRITING

Narrative Writing

A narrative relates a story or a series of events. To make a narrative clear, a writer must arrange the events in some kind of logical order—usually the order in which they occur. A good narrative also has unity—all the events deal with one main action.

The following passage from "My Family and Other Animals" illustrates several characteristics basic to good narrative writing. You will recall that when this passage begins, Larry opens the matchbox and the scorpion escapes with her babies.

He uttered a roar of fright that made Lugaretzia drop a plate and brought Roger out from beneath the table, barking wildly. With a flick of his hand he sent the unfortunate scorpion flying down the table, and she landed midway between Margo and Leslie, scattering babies like confetti as she thumped onto the cloth. Thoroughly enraged at this treatment, the creature sped towards Leslie, her sting quivering with emotion. Leslie leaped to his feet, overturning his chair, and flicked out desperately with his napkin, sending the scorpion rolling across the cloth towards Margo, who promptly let out a scream that any railway engine would have been proud to produce. Mother, completely bewildered by this sudden and rapid change from peace to chaos, put on her glasses and peered down the table to see what was causing the pandemonium, and at that moment Margo, in a vain attempt to stop the scorpion's advance, hurled a glass of water at it. The shower missed the animal completely, but successfully drenched Mother, who, not being able to stand cold water, promptly lost her breath and sat gasping at the end of the table, unable even to protest. The scorpion had now gone to ground under Leslie's plate, while her babies swarmed wildly all over the table.

1. What are the events that make up this narrative passage?
2. What order is used for the events in the model passage?
3. What is the main action of this passage?

Suggestions for Writing

Write a narrative, using one of these topics or a topic of your own:

A pet runs away
Winning the big game
Lost on a camping trip
A tornado hits town

Here are some guidelines to help you plan and write your paper.

Prewriting

• Choose a conflict or problem for your characters to face. Will they struggle against forces of nature, other characters, rules that are unjust or unfair?

- Use the *5 W-How?* questions (*Who? What? Where? When? Why?* and *How?*) to help you gather details and plan the sequence of events in your story.
- Develop an outline that shows events in the beginning (introducing characters and conflict), the middle, and the end (where the conflicts are resolved).
- Choose a point of view for telling your story. Will you have the story told by an all-knowing narrator, who can tell everyone's thoughts? Will you have a character tell the story in first-person, using the pronoun *I*?

Writing

- Open your story with a sentence that captures your reader's attention. For example: *Larry knew that gold coins lay buried under the oak stump in front of the police station.*
- Include only events that create interest or move the story along.
- Arrange your events in chronological order— the order in which events occur.
- Make your characters' words reveal their personalities and reasons for their actions.

Evaluating and Revising

- Are events in the story arranged logically?
- Are characters believable? Do their words reveal their personalities and feelings?

Proofreading

- Check your revised paper for errors in grammar, usage, and mechanics.
- Prepare a final copy and check it for accuracy.

Writing Dialogue

Dialogue is often an important part of narrative writing. Remember these points:
- Begin a new paragraph for each speaker.
- Use quotation marks to enclose each speaker's words.
- Begin each quotation with a capital letter. If the sentence is divided into two parts, begin the second part with a small letter.
- Use commas to separate a quotation from the rest of the sentence.
- Do not use quotation marks unless you are quoting a person's exact words.

Choose a passage of narrative from one of the selections in this unit, and rewrite it as dialogue.

For Further Reading

Behn, Harry, *The Faraway Lurs* (G.K. Hall, 1981)
Two young people from warring tribes meet and fall in love in this novel set in ancient Denmark.

Bell, Margaret, *The Totem Casts a Shadow* (Morrow, 1949)
White and Indian cultures clash in this novel set in Alaska in the 1890s.

Borland, Hal, *When the Legends Die* (Lippincott, 1963; paperback, Bantam, 1972)
The Ute boy in this novel flees into the wilderness. Thomas Black Bull is a character you are not likely to forget.

Bradbury, Ray, *The Martian Chronicles* (Doubleday, 1958; paperback, Bantam, 1974)
The first colonists came to Mars for many reasons, but none of them realized they were destroying a magnificent civilization.

Landon, Margaret, *Anna and the King of Siam* (Harper & Row, 1944; paperback, Pocket Books)
This true story of an English governess' experiences at the court of Siam was the basis for the musical *The King and I*.

Mather, Melissa, *One Summer in Between* (Harper & Row, 1967)
A black college student from the South keeps a diary during the summer she spends in Vermont.

Miller, Helen, *Kirsti* (Doubleday, 1964)
In this novel, set in Idaho in 1901, a Finnish girl falls in love with an American and tries to reconcile two cultures and two generations.

Papashvily, George, and Helen Papashvily, *Anything Can Happen* (St. Martin, 1984)
A young Russian who arrives in America with no money and high hopes tells his own humorous story.

Richter, Conrad, *The Light in the Forest* (Knopf, 1966; paperback, Bantam)
The boy in this novel is raised by Delawares, but when he is fifteen he finds himself suddenly returned to his white family.

Saroyan, William, *The Human Comedy* (Harcourt Brace Jovanovich, 1944; paperback, Dell)
This is a short novel about a family in southern California who try to make sense out of things that baffle all of us: love, work, war, loneliness, death. Many people read right through this little novel in one sitting, but the characters remain in one's memory for a long time.

Sone, Monica, *Nisei Daughter* (University of Washington Press, 1979)
This true story tells of a Japanese-American girl's experiences in a "relocation center" during World War II.

Speare, Elizabeth, *The Witch of Blackbird Pond* (Houghton Mifflin, 1958; paperback, Dell)
A girl rebels against the narrow-mindedness of the witch-hunters in Puritan New England and finds herself suspected of witchcraft.

Wojciechowska, Maia, *Shadow of a Bull* (Macmillan, 1964; paperback)
Everyone else in this novel expects Manolo to follow in his dead father's footsteps and become a bullfighter, but Manolo wants something else.

AMERICAN HERITAGE

The literature in this unit reveals something about how Americans—past and present—have seen themselves and their society. Here are images of heroes, of national ordeals, of the frontier, and of our institutions. Certain beliefs expressed in these selections have been part of America's heritage for centuries. These are beliefs in independence, tolerance, and personal freedom.

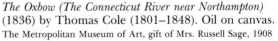

The Oxbow (The Connecticut River near Northampton) (1836) by Thomas Cole (1801–1848). Oil on canvas.
The Metropolitan Museum of Art, gift of Mrs. Russell Sage, 1908

127

Mission San Carlos de Rio Carmelo by Oriana Day.
Oil on canvas.

By Permission of The Fine Arts Museums of San Francisco,
gift of Mrs. Eleanor Martin

The Old House of Representatives (1822)
by Samuel Finley Breese Morse (1791–1872).
Oil on canvas.

The Corcoran Gallery of Art, Museum purchase,
Gallery Fund, 1911

The Jolly Flatboatmen (1846)
by George Caleb Bingham
(1811–1879). Oil on canvas.
Private Collection, on loan to the
National Gallery of Art, Washington

The County Election (1851–1852)
by George Caleb Bingham
(1811–1879). Oil on canvas.
The Saint Louis Art Museum,
Museum purchase

The Clipper Ship "Flying Cloud" by Frank Vining
Smith (1879–1967). Oil on canvas on masonite.
Courtesy of the Seamen's Bank for Savings, FSB

Sioux War Council by
George Catlin (1796–1872).
Oil on canvas.
John F. Eulich Collection,
Dallas, Texas

Westward Ho (1867–1868)
by Otto Sommer.
Oil on canvas.
Private Collection

Cincinnati, Queen of the West in 1876 (1972) by John Stobart (1929–   ).
Oil on canvas.
Private Collection

The Bowery at Night (c. 1895) by W. Louis Sonntag, Jr. (1822–1900).
Watercolor.
The Museum of the City of New York

American Astronaut Edgar D. Mitchell standing on the moon's surface in the hilly upland region north of the Fra Mauro crater (February 5, 1971).

Sandlot Game (1954) by Ralph Fasanella (1914–   ).
Oil on canvas.
Collection of Mr. and Mrs. John DePolo

Centennial of Statue of Liberty
(July 4, 1986).

Independence Hall, Philadelphia
(September 18, 1987). Bicentennial
celebration of signing of the United
States Constitution.

Reverend Martin Luther King, Jr., in
Jackson, Mississippi, 1966. Reverend
King was awarded
a Nobel Peace Prize
in 1964.

In Cold Storm Light

LESLIE MARMON SILKO

*American writers often describe nature both literally and fig-
uratively. What kind of animal would you use to describe a
winter storm figuratively?*

In cold storm light
I watch the sandrock
    canyon rim.

    The wind is wet
        with the smell of piñon.
    The wind is cold
        with the sound of juniper.
            And then
                out of the thick ice sky
                    running swiftly
                    pounding
                    swirling above the treetops
                The snow elk come,
              Moving, moving
                    white song
                    storm wind in the branches.
And when the elk have passed
    behind them
            a crystal train of snowflakes
            strands of mist
                tangled in rocks
                and leaves.

For Study and Discussion

Analyzing and Interpreting the Poem

1. Elk are large deer. Why do you think the poet chose elk to represent a winter storm?

2a. How might the pattern of the poem—its arrangement of lines—suggest the movement of elk? **b.** What words in the poem describe the movements of the elk?

3. The word *train* has several meanings. What is its meaning in the phrase "train of snowflakes"?

4. How would you describe the poet's attitude toward the storm? For example, is she sad, happy, solemn, awed?

About the Author

Leslie Marmon Silko   (1948–   )

Leslie Marmon Silko was born in Albuquerque and attended the University of New Mexico. She has referred to herself as "a mixed-breed Laguna Pueblo woman." She brings a direct knowledge of Indian lore and tradition to her writing. She has published short stories, poetry, and a novel. Her works include *Laguna Woman, Ceremony,* and *The Storyteller.* She now lives in Tucson, Arizona.

Paul Revere's Ride

HENRY WADSWORTH LONGFELLOW

Some say "the United States" began on the night of April 18, 1775. On that night, British soldiers went to raid the Massachusetts towns of Lexington and Concord. But the colonists had been warned that the soldiers were coming. Fully armed, they met the British in battle the next morning. About eighty years after this first battle of the American Revolution, Longfellow wrote the following poem.

Listen, my children, and you shall hear
Of the midnight ride of Paul Revere,
On the eighteenth of April, in Seventy-five;
Hardly a man is now alive
Who remembers that famous day and year.   5

He said to his friend, "If the British march
By land or sea from the town tonight,
Hang a lantern aloft in the belfry arch
Of the North Church tower as a signal light—
One, if by land, and two, if by sea;   10
And I on the opposite shore will be,
Ready to ride and spread the alarm
Through every Middlesex° village and farm,
For the country folk to be up and to arm."

13. **Middlesex:** a county in Massachusetts.

Then he said "Good night!" and with muffled oar   15
Silently rowed to the Charlestown° shore,
Just as the moon rose over the bay,
Where swinging wide at her moorings lay
The *Somerset,* British man-of-war;
A phantom ship, with each mast and spar   20
Across the moon, like a prison bar,
And a huge black hulk, that was magnified
By its own reflection in the tide.

16. **Charlestown:** a former city on Boston Harbor, now a part of Boston.

Meanwhile, his friend, through alley and street,
Wanders and watches with eager ears,   25
Till in the silence around him he hears

The muster of men at the barrack door,
The sound of arms, and the tramp of feet,
And the measured tread of the grenadiers
Marching down to their boats on the shore.   30

Then he climbed the tower of the Old North Church,
By the wooden stairs, with stealthy tread,
To the belfry chamber overhead,
And startled the pigeons from their perch
On the somber rafters, that round him made   35
Masses and moving shapes of shade—
By the trembling ladder, steep and tall,
To the highest window in the wall,
Where he paused to listen and look down
A moment on the roofs of the town,   40
And the moonlight flowing over all.

Beneath, in the churchyard, lay the dead,
In their night encampment on the hill,
Wrapped in silence so deep and still
That he could hear, like a sentinel's tread,   45
The watchful night wind, as it went
Creeping along from tent to tent,
And seeming to whisper, "All is well!"
A moment only he feels the spell
Of the place and the hour, and the secret dread   50
Of the lonely belfry and the dead;
For suddenly all his thoughts are bent
On a shadowy something far away,
Where the river widens to meet the bay—
A line of black that bends and floats   55
On the rising tide, like a bridge of boats.

Meanwhile, impatient to mount and ride,
Booted and spurred, with a heavy stride
On the opposite shore walked Paul Revere.
Now he patted his horse's side.   60
Now gazed at the landscape far and near,
Then, impetuous, stamped the earth,
And turned and tightened his saddle girth;
But mostly he watched with eager search
The belfry tower of the Old North Church,   65
As it rose above the graves on the hill,

Lonely and spectral and somber and still.
And lo! as he looks, on the belfry's height
A glimmer, and then a gleam of light!
He springs to the saddle, the bridle he turns,   70
But lingers and gazes, till full on his sight
A second lamp in the belfry burns!

A hurry of hoofs in a village street,
A shape in the moonlight, a bulk in the dark,
And beneath, from the pebbles, in passing, a spark   75
Struck out by a steed flying fearless and fleet:
That was all! And yet, through the gloom and the light,
The fate of a nation was riding that night;
And the spark struck out by that steed, in his flight,
Kindled the land into flame with its heat.   80

He has left the village and mounted the steep,
And beneath him, tranquil and broad and deep,
Is the Mystic, meeting the ocean tides;
And under the alders that skirt its edge,
Now soft on the sand, now loud on the ledge,   85
Is heard the tramp of his steed as he rides.

It was twelve by the village clock,
When he crossed the bridge into Medford town.
He heard the crowing of the cock,
And the barking of the farmer's dog,   90
And felt the damp of the river fog,
That rises after the sun goes down.

It was one by the village clock,
When he galloped into Lexington.
He saw the gilded weathercock   95
Swim in the moonlight as he passed,
And the meetinghouse windows, blank and bare,
Gaze at him with a spectral glare,
As if they already stood aghast
At the bloody work they would look upon.   100

It was two by the village clock,
When he came to the bridge in Concord town.
He heard the bleating of the flock,
And the twitter of birds among the trees,

And felt the breath of the morning breeze
Blowing over the meadows brown.
And one was safe and asleep in his bed
Who at the bridge would be first to fall,
Who that day would be lying dead,
Pierced by a British musket ball.

You know the rest. In the books you have read
How the British Regulars fired and fled—
How the farmers gave them ball for ball,
From behind each fence and farmyard wall,
Chasing the redcoats down the lane,
Then crossing the fields to emerge again
Under the trees at the turn of the road,
And only pausing to fire and load.

105

110

115

Midnight Ride of Paul Revere
(1931) by Grant Wood
(1892–1942).
Oil on composition board.
The Metropolitan Museum of Art,
Arthur Hoppock Hearn Fund, 1950

So through the night rode Paul Revere;
And so through the night went his cry of alarm   120
To every Middlesex village and farm—
A cry of defiance and not of fear,
A voice in the darkness, a knock at the door,
And a word that shall echo forevermore!
For, borne on the night wind of the Past,   125
Through all our history, to the last,
In the hour of darkness and peril and need,
The people will waken and listen to hear
The hurrying hoofbeats of that steed,
And the midnight message of Paul Revere.   130

For Study and Discussion

Analyzing and Interpreting the Poem

1. The poet says in line 78: "The fate of a nation was riding that night." **a.** What do you think this line means? **b.** What does it suggest *might* have happened if Paul Revere had not been successful?

2. In lines 79–80, the poet says that "the spark struck out" by Paul Revere's horse "kindled the land into flame with its heat." You know that the horse's iron horseshoes did not actually set the land on fire. **a.** What event in American history is the poet comparing to a fire? **b.** How is this a good comparison?

3. In the last six lines of the poem, the poet says that Paul Revere's message will be heard by people throughout our history. What do you think this "message" is? Try to express it in your own words.

Literary Elements

Responding to a Narrative Poem

A **narrative poem** is a poem that tells a story. Like all good storytellers, Longfellow wants to hold your attention and keep you in suspense. In fact, the first word of his poem is a direction: "Listen."

Beginning with line 15, the poet gives details that help you experience the tension felt by Revere and his friend as they wait for the British to reveal their plans. Which details in lines 24–56 help you see and hear what Revere's friend sees and hears as he walks the streets, climbs the tower, and waits?

Once the British plans are known, the famous ride begins. Which details in lines 87–110 help you hear the country sounds that Revere hears as he gallops through the sleeping villages?

This poem has a strong, galloping rhythm. Does the rhythm help hold your attention? Why or why not?

For Oral Reading

Preparing a Presentation

Plan an oral reading of "Paul Revere's Ride" that will convey the changes in mood. What tone of voice will you use for the opening stanza? How will you shift that tone in line 6? How will you convey the sense of mystery and danger as Paul Revere and his friend wait for the British to reveal their plans? How will you signal the change in line 57 as the scene switches? How will you show the rider's impatience and the excitement of the ride?

If you like, practice reading with a partner or with a group of students who will join in a choral reading of the poem.

Extending Your Study

Finding the Historical Facts

If Longfellow had not written this poem, Paul Revere might be a footnote in history books. In fact, his companions that night are little known because Longfellow decided not to name them.

In a history book or an encyclopedia, look up the historical facts about all the riders who warned the farmers to arm and meet the British. In a paragraph, tell how the details in the poem differ from the details in history. What were the names of the other riders? Did Paul Revere ever reach Concord?

Why do you think people have remembered the poem long after they have forgotten the historical facts?

About the Author

Henry Wadsworth Longfellow   (1807–1882)

Henry Wadsworth Longfellow was the most popular poet America has ever had. During his lifetime, people eagerly awaited each new poem, and his works were translated into twenty-four languages. In addition to writing, Longfellow taught at Harvard University for eighteen years. He then retired to lead a quiet life, devoting himself fully to writing poetry for his admiring public. But a catastrophe almost destroyed his desire to create. His wife died as a result of a fire in their home, and the poet needed great courage and patience to overcome his grief and begin writing again.

Longfellow was inspired by the American past. His long poems, *The Courtship of Miles Standish, Evangeline,* and *The Song of Hiawatha,* show Longfellow's talent for using history as a background for poems of action and romance.

The Man Without a Country

EDWARD EVERETT HALE

"Prisoner, hear the sentence of the court! The court decides, subject to the approval of the President, that you never hear the name of the United States again."

I suppose that very few readers of the New York Herald of August 13, 1863, observed in an obscure corner, among the "Deaths," the announcement:

NOLAN. Died on board the U.S. Corvette *Levant*, Lat. 2° 11′ S., Long. 131° W., on May 11, PHILIP NOLAN.

Hundreds of readers would have paused at that announcement, if it had read thus: "DIED, MAY 11, THE MAN WITHOUT A COUNTRY." For it was as "The Man Without a Country" that poor Philip Nolan had generally been known by the officers who had him in charge during some fifty years, as, indeed, by all the men who sailed under them.

There can now be no possible harm in telling this poor creature's story. Reason enough there has been till now for very strict secrecy, the secrecy of honor itself, among the gentlemen of the navy who have had Nolan in charge. And certainly it speaks well for the profession and the personal honor of its members that to the press this man's story has been wholly unknown—and, I think, to the country at large also. This I do know, that no naval officer has mentioned Nolan in his report of a cruise.

But there is no need for secrecy any longer. Now the poor creature is dead, it seems to me worthwhile to tell a little of his story, by way of showing young Americans of today what it is to be "A Man Without a Country."

Nolan's Fatal Wish

Philip Nolan was as fine a young officer as there was in the "Legion of the West," as the Western division of our army was then called. When Aaron Burr[1] made his first dashing expedition down to New Orleans in 1805, he met this gay, bright, young fellow. Burr marked[2] him, talked to him, walked with him, took him a day or two's voyage in his flatboat, and, in short, fascinated him. For the next year, barrack life was very tame to poor Nolan. He occasionally availed himself of the permission the great man had given him to write to

1. **Aaron Burr:** a controversial American political figure (1756–1836). Burr was Vice-President of the United States from 1801 to 1805. He killed Alexander Hamilton in a duel in 1804. At one time he was suspected of plotting to set up an empire in the Southwest.
2. **marked:** here, noticed.

Seascape (1906) by Thomas Moran (1837–1926). Oil on canvas.
The Brooklyn Museum, gift of the Executors, Estate of Michael Friedsam

him. Long, stilted letters the poor boy wrote and rewrote and copied. But never a line did he have in reply. The other boys in the garrison sneered at him, because he lost the fun which they found in shooting or rowing while he was working away on these grand letters to his grand friend. But before long, the young fellow had his revenge. For this time His Excellency, Honorable Aaron Burr, appeared again under a very different aspect. There were rumors that he had an army behind him and an empire before him. At that time the youngsters all envied him. Burr had not been talking twenty minutes with the commander before he asked him to send for Lieutenant Nolan. Then, after a little talk, he asked Nolan if he could show him something of the great river and the plans for the new post. He asked Nolan to take him out in his skiff to show him a canebrake[3] or a cottonwood tree, as he said—really to win

3. **canebrake:** a dense growth of cane plant.

Illustrations on pages 144–145, 148 149, 150, 152, and 154 by Everett Shinn (1876–1953) from *The Man Without a Country* (1940).

him over; and by the time the sail was over, Nolan was enlisted body and soul. From that time, though he did not yet know it, he lived as a man without a country.

What Burr meant to do I know no more than you. It is none of our business just now. Only, when the grand catastrophe came, Burr's treason trial at Richmond, Fort Adams[4] got up a string of courts-martial on the officers there. One and another of the colonels and majors were tried, and, to fill out the list, little Nolan, against whom there was evidence enough that he was sick of the service, had been willing to be false to it, and would have obeyed any order to march anywhere had the order been signed, "By command of his Exc. A. Burr." The courts dragged on. The big flies[5] escaped—rightly for all I know. Nolan was proved guilty enough, yet you and I would never have heard of him but that, when the president of the court asked him at the close whether he wished to say anything to show that he had always been faithful to the United States, he cried out in a fit of frenzy: "Damn the United States! I wish I may never hear of the United States again!"

Nolan's Punishment

I suppose he did not know how the words shocked old Colonel Morgan, who was holding the court. Half the officers who sat in it had served through the Revolution, and their lives had been risked for the very idea which he cursed in his madness. He, on his part, had grown up in the West of those days. He had been educated on a plantation where the finest company was a Spanish officer or a French merchant from Orleans. His education had been perfected in commercial expeditions to Veracruz,[6] and I think he told me his father once hired an Englishman to be a private tutor for a winter on the plantation. He had spent half his youth with an older brother, hunting horses in Texas; and to him *United States* was

4. **Fort Adams:** the fort where Nolan was stationed.
5. **the big flies:** Burr and the other important men who may have plotted with him.

6. **Veracruz** (věr′ə-krōōz′): a seaport in Mexico.

George," Morgan would not have felt worse. He called the court into his private room and returned in fifteen minutes, with a face like a sheet, to say: "Prisoner, hear the sentence of the court! The court decides, subject to the approval of the President, that you never hear the name of the United States again."

Nolan laughed. But nobody else laughed. Old Morgan was too solemn, and the whole room was hushed dead as night for a minute. Even Nolan lost his swagger in a moment. Then Morgan added: "Mr. Marshal, take the prisoner to Orleans, in an armed boat, and deliver him to the naval commander there."

The marshal gave his orders and the prisoner was taken out of court.

"Mr. Marshal," continued old Morgan," see that no one mentions the United States to the prisoner. Mr. Marshal, make my respects to Lieutenant Mitchell at Orleans, and request him to order that no one shall mention the United States to the prisoner while he is on board ship. You will receive your written orders from the officer on duty here this evening. The court is adjourned."

Before the *Nautilus*[7] got round from New Orleans to the northern Atlantic coast with the prisoner on board, the sentence had been approved by the President, and he was a man without a country.

The plan then adopted was substantially the same which was necessarily followed ever after. The Secretary of the Navy was requested to put Nolan on board a government vessel bound on a long cruise, and to direct that he should be only so far confined there as to make it certain that he never saw or heard of the country. We had few long cruises then, and I do not know certainly what his first cruise was. But the commander to whom he was entrusted regulated the etiquette and the precautions of

scarcely a reality. I do not excuse Nolan; I only explain to the reader why he damned his country and wished he might never hear her name again.

From that moment, September 23, 1807, till the day he died, May 11, 1863, he never heard her name again. For that half-century and more, he was a man without a country.

Old Morgan, as I said, was terribly shocked. If Nolan had compared George Washington to Benedict Arnold, or had cried, "God save King

---

7. *Nautilus:* the naval ship to which Nolan was delivered.

the affair, and according to his scheme they were carried out till Nolan died.

When I was second officer of the *Intrepid*, some thirty years after, I saw the original paper of instructions. I have been sorry ever since that I did not copy the whole of it. It ran, however, much in this way:

Washington [with a date, which must have been late in 1807]

Sir:

You will receive from Lieutenant Neale the person of Philip Nolan, late a lieutenant in the United States Army.

This person on trial by court-martial expressed, with an oath, the wish that he might "never hear of the United States again."

The court sentenced him to have his wish fulfilled.

For the present, the execution of the order is entrusted by the President to this department.

You will take the prisoner on board your ship, and keep him there with such precautions as shall prevent his escape.

You will provide him with such quarters, rations, and clothing as would be proper for an officer of his late rank, if he were a passenger on your vessel on the business of his government.

The gentlemen on board will make any arrangements agreeable to themselves regarding his society. He is to be exposed to no indignity of any kind, nor is he ever unnecessarily to be reminded that he is a prisoner.

But under no circumstances is he ever to hear of his country or to see any information regarding it; and you will especially caution all the officers under your command to take care that this rule, in which his punishment is involved, shall not be broken.

It is the intention of the government that he shall never again see the country which he has disowned. Before the end of your cruise, you will receive orders which will give effect to this intention.

Respectfully yours,
W. Southard,
for the Secretary of the Navy

The rule adopted on board the ships on which I have met "The Man Without a Country" was, I think, transmitted from the beginning. No mess[8] liked to have him permanently, because his presence cut off all talk of home or of the prospect of return, of politics or letters, of peace or of war—cut off more than half the talk men liked to have at sea. But it was always thought too hard that he should never meet the rest of us, except to touch hats, and we finally sank into one system. He was not permitted to talk with the men unless an officer was by. With officers he had unrestrained intercourse, as far as they and he chose. But he grew shy, though he had favorites: I was one. Then the captain always asked him to dinner on Monday. Every mess in succession took up the invitation in its turn. According to the size of the ship, you had him at your mess more or less often at dinner. His breakfast he ate in his own stateroom. Whatever else he ate or drank, he ate or drank alone. Sometimes, when the marines or sailors had any special jollification,[9] they were permitted to invite Plain Buttons, as they called him. Then Nolan was sent with some officer, and the men were forbidden to speak of home while he was there. I believe the theory was that the sight of his punishment did them good. They called him Plain Buttons, because, while he always chose to wear a regulation army uniform, he was not permitted to wear the army button, for the reason that it bore either the initials or the insignia of the country he had disowned.

8. **mess:** a group of people who eat meals together.
9. **jollification:** merrymaking.

The Reading

I remember, soon after I joined the navy, I was on shore with some of the older officers from our ship, and some of the gentlemen fell to talking about Nolan, and someone told the system which was adopted from the first about his books and other reading. As he was almost never permitted to go on shore, even though the vessel lay in port for months, his time at the best hung heavy. Everybody was permitted to lend him books, if they were not published in America and made no allusion to it. These were common enough in the old days. He had almost all the foreign papers that came into the ship, sooner or later; only somebody must go over them first, and cut out any advertisement or stray paragraph that referred to America. This was a little cruel sometimes, when the back of what was cut out might be innocent. Right in the midst of one of Napoleon's battles poor Nolan would find a great hole, because on the back of the page of that paper there had been an advertisement of a packet[10] for New York, or a scrap from the President's message. This was the first time I ever heard of this plan. I remember it, because poor Phillips, who was of the party, told a story of something which happened at the Cape of Good Hope[11] on Nolan's first voyage. They had touched at the Cape, paid their respects to the English admiral and the fleet, and then Phillips had borrowed a lot of English books from an officer. Among them was *The Lay of the Last Minstrel*,[12] which they had all of them heard of, but which most of them had never seen. I think it could not have been published long. Well, nobody thought there could be any risk of anything national in that. So Nolan was permitted to join the circle one afternoon when a lot of them sat on deck smoking and reading aloud. In his turn, Nolan took the book and read to the others; and he read very well, as I know. Nobody in the circle knew a line of the poem, only it was all magic and chivalry, and was ten thousand years ago. Poor Nolan read steadily through the fifth canto,[13] stopped a minute and drank something, and then began, without a thought of what was coming:

Breathes there the man with soul so dead,
Who never to himself hath said . . .

It seems impossible to us that anybody ever heard this for the first time; but all these fellows did then, and poor Nolan himself went on, still unconsciously or mechanically:

This is my own, my native land!

Then they all saw that something was to pay; but he expected to get through, I suppose, turned a little pale, but plunged on:

Whose heart hath ne'er within him burned,
As home his footsteps he hath turned
From wandering on a foreign strand!
If such there breathe, go, mark him well . . .

By this time, the men were all beside themselves, wishing there was any way to make him turn over two pages; but he had not quite presence of mind for that; he gagged a little, colored crimson, and staggered on:

For him no minstrel raptures swell;
High though his titles, proud his name,
Boundless his wealth as wish can claim;
Despite these titles, power, and pelf.[14]
The wretch, concentered all in self . . .

10. **packet:** a boat that travels a regular route, carrying passengers, freight, and mail.
11. **Cape of Good Hope:** a projection of land on the southwestern coast of Africa.
12. ***The Lay of the Last Minstrel:*** a long narrative poem by Sir Walter Scott (1771–1832).

13. **canto:** a main division of certain long poems.
14. **pelf:** wealth.

Here the poor fellow choked, could not go on, but started up, swung the book into the sea, vanished into his stateroom, "And by Jove," said Phillips, "we did not see him for two months again. And I had to make up some story to that English surgeon why I did not return his Walter Scott to him."

That story shows about the time when Nolan's braggadocio[15] must have broken down. At first, they said, he took a very high tone, considered his imprisonment a mere farce, affected to enjoy the voyage, and all that; but Phillips said that after he came out of his state-room he never was the same man again. He never read aloud again, unless it was the Bible or Shakespeare, or something else he was sure of. But it was not that merely. He never entered in with the other young men exactly as a companion again. He was always shy afterward, when I knew him—very seldom spoke unless he was spoken to, except to a very few friends. He lighted up occasionally, but generally he had the nervous, tired look of a heart-wounded man.

The Ball

When Captain Shaw was coming home, rather to the surprise of everybody they made one of the Windward Islands,[16] and lay off and on for nearly a week. The boys said the officers were sick of salt junk,[17] and meant to have turtle soup before they came home. But after several days, the *Warren* came to the same rendezvous; they exchanged signals; she told them she was outward bound, perhaps to the Mediterranean, and took poor Nolan and his traps[18] on the boat to try his second cruise. He looked very blank when he was told to get ready to join her. He had known enough of the signs of the sky to know that till that moment he was going "home." But this was a distinct evidence of something he had not thought of, perhaps—that there was no going home for him, even to a prison. And this was the first of some twenty such transfers, which brought him sooner or later into half our best vessels, but which kept him all his life at least some hundred miles from the country he had hoped he might never hear of again.

It may have been on that second cruise—it was once when he was up the Mediterranean —that Mrs. Graff, the celebrated Southern

---

15. **braggadocio** (brăg'ə-dō'shē-ō): pretended courage; in this case, Nolan's pretense that he does not mind his punishment.

16. **Windward Islands:** a group of islands in the West Indies.
17. **salt junk:** dried beef salted for preservation.
18. **traps:** here, luggage.

beauty of those days, danced with him. The ship had been lying a long time in the Bay of Naples, and the officers were very intimate in the English fleet, and there had been great festivities, and our men thought they must give a great ball on board the ship. They wanted to use Nolan's stateroom for something, and they hated to do it without asking him to the ball; so the captain said they might ask him, if they would be responsible that he did not talk with the wrong people, "who would give him intelligence."[19] So the dance went on. For ladies they had the family of the American consul, one or two travelers who had adventured so far, and a nice bevy of English girls and matrons.

Well, different officers relieved each other in standing and talking with Nolan in a friendly way, so as to be sure that nobody else spoke to him. The dancing went on with spirit, and after a while even the fellows who took this honorary guard of Nolan ceased to fear any trouble.

As the dancing went on, Nolan and our fellows all got at ease, as I said—so much that it seemed quite natural for him to bow to that splendid Mrs. Graff, and say, "I hope you have not forgotten me, Miss Rutledge. Shall I have the honor of dancing?"

He did it so quickly that Fellows, who was with him, could not hinder him. She laughed and said, "I am not Miss Rutledge any longer, Mr. Nolan; but I will dance all the same." She nodded to Fellows, as if to say he must leave Mr. Nolan to her, and led Nolan off to the place where the dance was forming.

Nolan thought he had got his chance. He had known her at Philadelphia. He said boldly—a little pale, she said, as she told me the story years after— "And what do you hear from home, Mrs. Graff?"

And that splendid creature looked *through*

EVERETT SHINN 1940

him. Jove! How she *must* have looked through him!

"Home! Mr. Nolan! I thought you were the man who never wanted to hear of home again!"—and she walked directly up the deck to her husband and left poor Nolan alone. He did not dance again.

The Battle

A happier story than either of these I have told is of the war.[20] That came along soon after. I have heard this affair told in three or four ways—and, indeed, it may have happened

19. **intelligence:** here, information about his country.

20. **the war:** the War of 1812, between the United States and Great Britain.

more than once. In one of the great frigate[21] duels with the English, in which the navy was really baptized, it happened that a round shot[22] from the enemy entered one of our ports[23] square, and took right down the officer of the gun himself and almost every man of the gun's crew. Now you may say what you choose about courage, but that is not a nice thing to see. But, as the men who were not killed picked themselves up, and as they and the surgeon's people were carrying off the bodies, there appeared Nolan, in his shirtsleeves, with the rammer in

21. **frigate** (frĭg'ĭt): a sailing ship equipped with war guns.
22. **round shot:** a cannonball.
23. **ports:** here, portholes for cannons.

his hand, and, just as if he had been the officer, told them off with authority—who should go to the cockpit with the wounded men, who should stay with him—perfectly cheery, and with that way which makes men feel sure all is right and is going to be right. And he finished loading the gun with his own hands, aimed it, and bade the men fire. And there he stayed, captain of that gun, keeping those fellows in spirits, till the enemy struck[24]—sitting on the carriage while the gun was cooling, though he was exposed all the time, showing them easier ways to handle heavy shot, making the raw hands laugh at their own blunders, and when the gun cooled again, getting it loaded and fired twice as often as any other gun on the ship. The captain walked forward by way of encouraging the men, and Nolan touched his hat and said, "I am showing them how we do this in the artillery, sir."

And this is the part of the story where all the legends agree; the commodore said, "I see you are, and I thank you, sir; and I shall never forget this day, sir, and you never shall, sir."

After the whole thing was over, and the commodore had the Englishman's sword,[25] in the midst of the state and ceremony of the quarterdeck, he said, "Where is Mr. Nolan? Ask Mr. Nolan to come here."

And when Nolan came, he said, "Mr. Nolan, we are all very grateful to you today; you are one of us today; you will be named in the dispatches."

And then the old man took off his own sword of ceremony, gave it to Nolan, and made him put it on. The man who told me this saw it. Nolan cried like a baby, and well he might. He had not worn a sword since that infernal day at Fort Adams. But always afterward on occasions

24. **struck:** struck their colors, or lowered their flag to admit defeat.
25. **the Englishman's sword:** A defeated commander used to give up his sword to the victor.

of ceremony he wore that quaint old sword of the commodore.

The captain did mention him in the dispatches. It was always said he asked that Nolan might be pardoned. He wrote a special letter to the Secretary of War, but nothing ever came of it.

All that was nearly fifty years ago. If Nolan was thirty then, he must have been near eighty when he died. He looked sixty when he was forty. But he never seemed to me to change a hair afterward. As I imagine his life, from what I have seen and heard of it, he must have been in every sea, and yet almost never on land. Till he grew very old, he went aloft a great deal. He always kept up his exercise, and I never heard that he was ill. If any other man was ill, he was the kindest nurse in the world; and he knew more than half the surgeons do. Then if anybody was sick or died, or if the captain wanted him to, or on any other occasion, he was always ready to read prayers. I have said that he read beautifully.

The Slaves

My own acquaintance with Philip Nolan began six or eight years after the English war, on my first voyage after I was appointed a midshipman. From the time I joined, I believe I thought Nolan was a sort of lay chaplain—a chaplain with a blue coat. I never asked about him. Everything in the ship was strange to me. I knew it was green to ask questions, and I suppose I thought there was a Plain Buttons on every ship. We had him to dine in our mess once a week, and the caution was given that on that day nothing was to be said about home. But if they had told us not to say anything about the planet Mars or the Book of Deuteronomy,[26] I should not have asked why;

there were a great many things which seemed to me to have as little reason. I first came to understand anything about "The Man Without a Country" one day when we overhauled a dirty little schooner which had slaves[27] on board. An officer named Vaughan was sent to take charge of her, and, after a few minutes, he sent back his boat to ask that someone might be sent who could speak Portuguese. None of the officers did; and just as the captain was sending forward to ask if any of the people could, Nolan stepped out and said he should be glad to interpret, if the captain wished, as he understood the language. The captain thanked him, fitted out another boat with him, and in this boat it was my luck to go.

When we got there, it was such a scene as you seldom see—and never want to. Nastiness beyond account, and chaos ran loose in the midst of the nastiness. There were not a great many of the Negroes. By way of making what there were understand that they were free, Vaughan had had their handcuffs and ankle-cuffs knocked off. The Negroes were, most of them, out of the hold and swarming all around the dirty deck, with a central throng surrounding Vaughan and addressing him in every dialect.

As we came on deck, Vaughan looked down from a hogshead,[28] which he had mounted in desperation, and said, "Is there anybody who can make these wretches understand something?"

Nolan said he could speak Portuguese, and one or two fine-looking Krumen[29] who had worked for the Portuguese on the coast were dragged out.

---

26. **Book of Deuteronomy** (do͞o′tə-rŏn′ə-mē): the fifth book of the Bible.

27. **slaves:** In 1808 the United States made it illegal to bring slaves into the country. In 1842 America and Great Britain agreed to patrol the African coast with ships to prevent any more people from being shipped off as slaves.
28. **hogshead** (hôgz′hĕd′): a large cask.
29. **Krumen** (kro͞o′mĕn): members of a tribe in northern Africa.

"Tell them they are free," said Vaughan.

Nolan explained it in such Portuguese as the Krumen could understand, and they in turn to such of the Negroes as could understand them. Then there was a yell of delight, clenching of fists, leaping and dancing, and kissing of Nolan's feet by way of spontaneous celebration of the occasion.

"Tell them," said Vaughan, well pleased, "that I will take them all to Cape Palmas."[30]

This did not answer so well. Cape Palmas was practically as far from the homes of most of them as New Orleans or Rio de Janeiro was; that is, they would be eternally separated from home there. And their interpreters, as we could understand, instantly said, "*Ah, non Palmas*" and began to protest loudly. Vaughan was rather disappointed at this result of his liberality, and he asked Nolan eagerly what they said. The drops stood on poor Nolan's white forehead, as he hushed the men down, and said, "He says, 'Not Palmas.' He says, 'Take us home; take us to our own country; take us to our own house; take us to our own children and our own women.' He says he has an old father and mother who will die if they do not see him. And this one says that he left his people all sick, and paddled down to Fernando to beg the white doctor to come and help them, and that these devils caught him in the bay just in sight of home, and that he has never seen anybody from home since then. And this one says," choked out Nolan, "that he has not heard a word from his home in six months."

Vaughan always said Nolan grew gray himself while he struggled through this interpretation. I, who did not understand anything of the passion involved in it, saw that the very elements were melting with fervent heat and that something was to pay somewhere. Even the Negroes themselves stopped howling as they saw Nolan's agony and Vaughan's almost equal agony of sympathy. As quick as he could get words, Vaughan said, "Tell them yes, yes, yes; tell them they shall go to the Mountains of the Moon,[31] if they will. If I sail the schooner through the Great White Desert,[32] they shall go home!"

And after some fashion, Nolan said so. And then they all fell to kissing him again and wanted to rub his nose with theirs.

---

30. **Cape Palmas** (päl'məs): a point on the southern border of Liberia, on the western coast of Africa—about 2,000 miles (about 3,200 kilometers) from the home of these Africans.

31. **Mountains of the Moon:** a mountain range in East Central Africa.
32. **Great White Desert:** probably the Great Salt Desert in Iran.

But he could not stand it long; and getting Vaughan to say he might go back, he beckoned me down into our boat. As we started back he said to me: "Youngster, let that show you what it is to be without a family, without a home, and without a country. If you are ever tempted to say a word or to do a thing that shall put a bar between you and your family, your home, and your country, pray God in His mercy to take you that instant home to His own heaven. Think of your home, boy; write and send and talk about it. Let it be nearer and nearer to your thought the farther you have to travel from it, and rush back to it when you are free, as that poor slave is doing now. And for your country, boy," and the words rattled in his throat, "and for that flag," and he pointed to the ship, "never dream a dream but of serving her as she bids you, though the service carry you through a thousand hells. No matter what happens to you, no matter who flatters you or who abuses you, never look at another flag, never let a night pass but you pray God to bless the flag. Remember, boy, that behind all these men you have to do with, behind officers, and government, and people even, there is the Country herself, your Country, and that you belong to her as you belong to your own mother. Stand by her, boy, as you would stand by your mother!"

I was frightened to death by his calm, hard passion; but I blundered out that I would, by all that was holy, and that I had never thought of doing anything else. He hardly seemed to hear me; but he did, almost in a whisper, say, "Oh, if anybody had said so to me when I was of your age!"

I think it was this half-confidence of his, which I never abused, that afterward made us great friends. He was very kind to me. Often he sat up, or even got up, at night, to walk the deck with me when it was my watch. He explained to me a great deal of my mathemat-

ics, and I owe him my taste for mathematics. He lent me books and helped me about my reading. He never referred so directly to his story again; but from one and another officer, I have learned, in thirty years, what I am telling.

Nolan's Repentance

After that cruise I never saw Nolan again. The other men tell me that in those fifteen years he aged very fast, but he was still the same gentle, uncomplaining, silent sufferer that he ever was, bearing as best he could his self-appointed punishment. And now it seems that the dear old fellow is dead. He has found a home at last, and a country.

Since writing this, and while considering whether or not I would print it, as a warning to the young Nolans of today of what it is to throw away a country, I have received from Danforth, who is on board the *Levant*, a letter which gives an account of Nolan's last hours. It removes all my doubts about telling this story.

Here is the letter:

Dear Fred,

I try to find heart and life to tell you that it is all over with dear old Nolan. I have been with him on this voyage more that I ever was, and I can understand wholly now the way in which you used to speak of the dear old fellow. I could see that he was not strong, but I had no idea the end was so near. The doctor has been watching him very carefully, and yesterday morning he came to me and told me that Nolan was not so well and had not left his stateroom—a thing I never remember before. He had let the doctor come and see him as he lay there—the first time the doctor had been in the stateroom—and he said he should like to see me. Do you remember the mysteries we boys used to invent about his room in the old *Intrepid* days? Well, I went in, and there, to be sure, the poor fellow lay in his berth, smiling pleasantly as he gave me his hand but looking very frail. I could not help a glance round, which showed me what a little shrine he had made of the box he was lying in. The Stars and Stripes were draped up above and around a picture of Washington, and he had painted a majestic eagle, with lightnings blazing from his beak and his foot just clasping the whole globe, which his wings overshadowed. The dear old boy saw my glance, and said, with a sad smile, "Here, you see, I have a country!" Then he pointed to the foot of his bed, where I had not seen before a great map of the United States, as he had drawn it from memory, and which he had there to look upon as he lay. Quaint, queer old names were on it, in large letters: "Indiana Territory," "Mississippi Territory," and "Louisiana Territory," as I suppose our fathers learned such things: but the old fellow had patched in Texas, too; he had carried his western boundary all the way to the Pacific, but on that shore he had defined nothing.

"O Captain," he said, "I know I am dying. I cannot get home. Surely you will tell me something now? . . . Stop! Stop! . . . Do not speak till I say what I am sure you know, that there is not in this ship, that there is not in America—God bless her!—a more loyal man than I. There cannot be a man who loves the old flag as I do, or prays for it as I do, or hopes for it as I do. There are thirty-four stars in it now, Danforth. I thank God for that, though I do not know what their names are. There has never been one taken away; I thank God for that. I know by that that there has never been any successful Burr. O Danforth, Danforth," he sighed out, "how like a wretched night's dream a boy's idea of personal fame or of separate sovereignty seems, when one looks back on it after such a life as mine! But tell me—tell me something—tell me everything, Danforth, before I die!"

I swear to you that I felt like a monster because I had not told him everything before. "Mr. Nolan," said I, "I will tell you everything you ask about. Only, where shall I begin?"

Oh, the blessed smile that crept over his white face! He pressed my hand and said, "God bless you! Tell me their names," and he pointed to the stars on the flag. "The last I know is Ohio. My father lived in Kentucky. But I have guessed Michigan, and Indiana, and Mississippi—that is where Fort Adams was— they make twenty. But where are your other fourteen? You have not cut up any of the old ones, I hope?"

Well, that was not a bad text, and I told him the names in as good order as I could, and he bade me take down his beautiful map and draw them in as I best could with my pencil. He was wild with delight about Texas, told me how his cousin died there; he had marked a gold cross near where he supposed his grave was; and he had guessed at Texas. Then he was delighted as he saw California and Oregon—that, he said, he had suspected partly, because he had never been permitted to land on that shore, though the ships were there so much. Then he asked about the old war—told me the story of his serving the gun the day we took the *Java*. Then he settled down more quietly, and very happily, to hear me tell in an hour the history of fifty years.

How I wish it had been somebody who knew something! But I did as well as I could. I told him of the English war. I told him of Fulton[33] and the steamboat beginning. I told him about old Scott,[34] and Jackson,[35] told him all I could think of about the Mississippi, and New Orleans, and Texas, and his own old Kentucky.

I tell you, It was a hard thing to condense the history of half a century into that talk with a sick man. And I do not now know what I told him—of emigration and the means of it—of steamboats, and railroads, and telegraphs—of inventions and books, and literature—of the colleges, and West Point, and the Naval School, but with the queerest interruptions that ever you heard. You see it was Robinson Crusoe asking all the accumulated questions of fifty-six years!

I remember he asked, all of a sudden, who was President now; and when I told him, he asked if Old Abe was General Benjamin Lincoln's son. He said he met old General

Lincoln, when he was quite a boy himself, at some Indian treaty. I said no, that Old Abe was a Kentuckian like himself, but I could not tell him of what family; he had worked up from the ranks. "Good for him!" cried Nolan; "I am glad of that." Then I got talking about my visit to Washington. I told him everything I could think of that would show the grandeur of his country and its prosperity.

And he drank it in and enjoyed it as I cannot tell you. He grew more and more silent, yet I never thought he was tired or faint. I gave him a glass of water, but he just wet his lips, and told me not to go away. Then he asked me to bring the Presbyterian Book of Public Prayer which lay there, and said, with a smile, that it would open at the right place—and so it did. There was his double red mark down the page; and I knelt down and read, and he repeated with me:

For ourselves and our country, O gracious God, we thank Thee, that, notwithstanding our manifold transgressions of Thy Holy laws, Thou hast continued to us Thy marvelous kindness . . .

and so to the end of that thanksgiving. Then he turned to the end of the same book, and I read the words more familiar to me:

Most heartily we beseech Thee with Thy favor to behold and bless Thy servant, the President of the United States, and all others in authority.

"Danforth," said he, "I have repeated those prayers night and morning—it is now fifty-five years." And then he said he would go to sleep. He bent me down over him and kissed me; and he said, "Look in my Bible, Captain, when I am gone." And I went away.

But I had no thought it was the end. I

---

33. **Fulton:** Robert Fulton (1765–1815), the inventor of the steamboat.
34. **Scott:** General Winfield Scott (1786–1866), a commander in the War of 1812 and in the Mexican War.
35. **Jackson:** Andrew Jackson (1767–1845), a general in the War of 1812 and the seventh President of the United States (1829–1837).

thought he was tired and would sleep. I knew he was happy, and I wanted him to be alone.

But in an hour, when the doctor went in gently, he found Nolan had breathed his life away with a smile.

We looked in his Bible, and there was a slip of paper at the place where he had marked the text:

They desire a country, even a heavenly: where God is not ashamed to be called their God: for he hath prepared for them a city.[36]

On this slip of paper he had written this:

Bury me in the sea; it has been my home, and I love it. But will not someone set up a stone for my memory, that my disgrace may not be more than I ought to bear? Say on it:

In Memory of
PHILIP NOLAN
Lieutenant in the Army
of the United States

HE LOVED HIS COUNTRY
AS NO OTHER MAN HAS LOVED HER;
BUT NO MAN DESERVED LESS
AT HER HANDS.

36. **They desire . . . a city:** The passage is from Hebrews 11:16.

Reading Check

1. What was the name of the man without a country?
2. Where was he educated?
3. What did the men on the ships call him?
4. What did he receive from the commodore after the battle with the English?
5. What was his last request?

The Star Spangled Banner published by Currier and Ives. Colored lithograph.

Print Collection, Miriam and Ira D. Wallach Division, Division of Art, Prints and Photographs, The New York Public Library, Astor, Lenox and Tilden Foundations

For Study and Discussion

Analyzing and Interpreting the Story

1. Who is telling this story? Why does he believe the story of Philip Nolan should be told?

2. What facts does the narrator give about Nolan's early life that might explain why he joined Aaron Burr and why he later renounced the United States?

3a. What was Nolan's punishment? **b.** How was the punishment carried out?

4. How did Nolan change during his years at sea?

5. After Nolan dies, the narrator tells you on page 153: "He has found a home at last, and a country." What do you think the narrator means by "home" and "country" here?

6. This story was written in 1863, when the United States was in danger of being destroyed by the Civil War. Which passages in the story show that the author wants to impress upon the reader the importance of national unity?

7. Look back at the passage from *The Lay of the Last Minstrel* on page 147. Which lines from this poem could be used to express the main idea of this story?

Literary Elements

Noting Details That Suggest Authenticity

"The Man Without a Country" is not a true story. However, the author uses certain techniques to make the reader think it is true, or to give it the appearance of *authenticity*. For example, the story opens with a quotation from the "Deaths" column of a real newspaper, a source most people trust. The author cites the date of the newspaper and even the name and the exact position of the ship. What real people and historical events does the author use to suggest authenticity?

Language and Vocabulary

Learning Special Vocabulary

In "The Man Without a Country" we are told that Philip Nolan was invited to dine in the officers' mess. The word *mess*, in this context, refers to the group of people who eat their meals together and also to the place where these meals are eaten.

Here are some other military and naval terms that appear in the story. Tell what each word means. Use a dictionary to check your answers.

barrack (page 142)
garrison (page 143)
court-martial (page 144)
insignia (page 146)
commodore (page 150)
quarter-deck (page 150)
dispatch (page 151)
midshipman (page 151)

Expository Writing

Supporting an Opinion

A statement of your opinion is always more forceful when you present clear, logical reasons for holding it.

Do you think Philip Nolan deserved his punishment? Answer this question in a paragraph. Give at least two reasons explaining why you hold the opinion you do. Be sure to state your opinion in your opening sentence.

About the Author

Edward Everett Hale   (1822–1909)

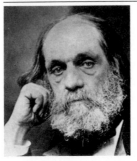

Edward Everett Hale, a grandnephew of the famous Nathan Hale of the American Revolution, was a highly respected clergyman, journalist, and teacher. Hale worked for many social reforms in his lifetime, including education, housing, and world peace. In 1863 he published "The Man Without a Country" to try to inspire greater patriotism during the Civil War. The story became very popular as a blend of fiction and history. In 1903 Hale was named chaplain of the United States Senate.

The Gettysburg Address

ABRAHAM LINCOLN

On November 19, 1863, President Abraham Lincoln delivered this speech at a ceremony to dedicate the Soldiers' National Cemetery at Gettysburg, Pennsylvania. Gettysburg had been the scene of one of the most terrible battles of the Civil War. Edward Everett, who spoke before Lincoln, said that the President came closer to expressing the importance of the occasion in two minutes than Everett himself had done in two hours.

Four score and seven years ago our fathers brought forth on this continent a new nation, conceived in liberty, and dedicated to the proposition that all men are created equal.

Now we are engaged in a great civil war, testing whether that nation, or any nation so conceived and dedicated, can long endure. We are met on a great battlefield of that war. We have come to dedicate a portion of that field as a final resting place for those who here gave their lives that that nation might live. It is altogether fitting and proper that we should do this.

But, in a larger sense, we cannot dedicate — we cannot consecrate — we cannot hallow — this ground. The brave men, living and dead, who struggled here, have consecrated it far above our poor power to add or detract. The world will little note nor long remember what we say here, but it can never forget what they did here. It is for us, the living, rather, to be dedicated here to the unfinished work which they who fought here have thus far so nobly advanced. It is rather for us to be here dedicated to the great task remaining before us — that from these honored dead we take increased devotion to that cause for which they gave the last full measure of devotion — that we here highly resolve that these dead shall not have died in vain — that this nation, under God, shall have a new birth of freedom — and that government of the people, by the people, for the people, shall not perish from the earth.

Abraham Lincoln, November 15, 1863.
This photograph was taken by Alexander
Gardner (1821–1882) four days before the
Gettysburg Address was delivered.

For Study and Discussion

Analyzing and Interpreting the Speech

1. In the Gettysburg Address, Abraham Lincoln presents three images of America— one from the past, one of the present, one for the future. In the first paragraph how does he describe the nation that was created "four score and seven years ago"?

2. In the second and third paragraphs, Lincoln speaks of the present time. Why can't the people at the ceremony make the battleground any more sacred than it already is?

3. The last part of the third paragraph focuses on the future. What national purpose does the President set for the people?

4. Where does President Lincoln present an image of the nation as something alive?

O Captain! My Captain!

WALT WHITMAN

Walt Whitman wrote this poem during a tragic time in America's history. In 1865 the American people were relieved that the Civil War was ending. But the relief turned to sadness again when the news came that President Abraham Lincoln had been assassinated.

O Captain! my Captain! our fearful trip is done,
The ship has weathered every rack,° the prize we sought is won,
The port is near, the bells I hear, the people all exulting,
While follow eyes the steady keel, the vessel grim and daring;
But O heart! heart! heart!   5
O the bleeding drops of red,
Where on the deck my Captain lies,
Fallen cold and dead.

O Captain! my Captain! rise up and hear the bells;
Rise up — for you the flag is flung — for you the bugle trills,   10
For you bouquets and ribboned wreaths — for you the shores
a-crowding,
For you they call, the swaying mass, their eager faces turning;
Here Captain! dear father!
This arm beneath your head!
It is some dream that on the deck   15
You've fallen cold and dead.

My Captain does not answer, his lips are pale and still,
My father does not feel my arm, he has no pulse nor will,
The ship is anchored safe and sound, its voyage closed and done,
From fearful trip the victor ship comes in with object won;   20
Exult O shores! and ring O bells!
But I with mournful tread
Walk the deck my Captain lies,
Fallen cold and dead.

2. **rack:** here an upheaval caused by a storm.

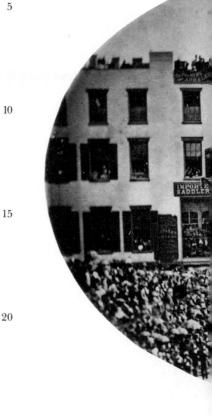

Analyzing and Interpreting the Poem

1. Whitman does not tell you directly who the "Captain" is. However, the readers of his day knew that the "Captain" was President Lincoln, and that the "ship" was the country. **a.** In what ways are a President and a ship's captain alike? **b.** In what ways is a nation like a ship? **c.** What else does Whitman call Lincoln?

2. This ship has been through a "fearful trip." What does this "fearful trip" stand for?

3. The ship is coming into "port." The "port" is the peace that the country has finally found. Is "port" a good way to describe peace? Why or why not?

Walt Whitman   (1819–1892)

Walt Whitman was born on Long Island, New York. For several years he worked as a newspaperman, but he was fired from his job for his strong antislavery views. Trips to Chicago and New Orleans intensified his appreciation of his country, and he soon began to write poetry. In 1855 Whitman published a collection of his own poems called *Leaves of Grass*. It was an extraordinary work, unlike any poetry that had appeared before. The public was astonished by the driving rhythms, the enthusiastic statements, and the frank language. Throughout his life Whitman continued to revise and add poems to *Leaves of Grass*. The book has had a tremendous influence on later poets.

During the Civil War, Whitman served as a volunteer nurse, caring for the wounded who filled the military hospitals. A great lover of America, Whitman was deeply affected by the assassination of Abraham Lincoln. His greatest poem about Lincoln's death is "When Lilacs Last in the Dooryard Bloomed."

Photograph of Lincoln's funeral showing the catafalque passing through the streets of Springfield, Illinois.

Too Soon a Woman

DOROTHY M. JOHNSON

We left the home place behind, mile by slow mile, heading for mountains, across the prairie where the wind blew forever.

At first there were four of us with the one-horse wagon and its skimpy load. Pa and I walked, because I was a big boy of eleven. My two little sisters romped and trotted until they got tired and had to be boosted up into the wagon bed.

That was no covered Conestoga,[1] like Pa's folks came West in, but just an old farm wagon, drawn by one weary horse, creaking and rumbling westward to the mountains, toward the little woods town where Pa thought he had an old uncle who owned a little two-bit sawmill.

Two weeks we had been moving when we picked up Mary, who had run away from somewhere that she wouldn't tell. Pa didn't want her along, but she stood up to him with no fear in her voice.

"I'd rather go with a family and look after kids," she said, "but I ain't going back. If you won't take me, I'll travel with any wagon that will."

Pa scowled at her, and her wide blue eyes stared back.

"How old are you?" he demanded.

"Eighteen," she said. "There's teamsters come this way sometimes. I'd rather go with you folks. But I won't go back."

"We're prid'near out of grub," my father told her. "We're clean out of money. I got all I can handle without taking anybody else." He turned away as if he hated the sight of her. "You'll have to walk," he said.

So she went along with us and looked after the little girls, but Pa wouldn't talk to her.

On the prairie, the wind blew. But in the mountains, there was rain. When we stopped at little timber claims along the way, the homesteaders said it had rained all summer. Crops among the blackened stumps were rotted and spoiled. There was no cheer anywhere, and little hospitality. The people we talked to were past worrying. They were scared and desperate.

So was Pa. He traveled twice as far each day as the wagon, ranging through the woods with his rifle, but he never saw game. He had been depending on venison,[2] but we never got any except as a grudging gift from the homesteaders.

He brought in a porcupine once, and that was fat meat and good. Mary roasted it in chunks over the fire, half crying with the smoke. Pa and I rigged up the tarp sheet for a shelter to keep the rain from putting the fire clean out.

The porcupine was long gone, except for some of the tried-out fat[3] that Mary had saved, when we came to an old, empty cabin. Pa said

---

1. **Conestoga** (kŏn′ĭs-tō′gə): a covered wagon with broad wheels, used by American pioneers in crossing the prairies.

2. **venison** (vĕn′ə-sən, -zən): deer meat.
3. **tried-out fat:** fat that is rendered, or melted down.

we'd have to stop. The horse was wore out, couldn't pull anymore up those grades on the deep-rutted roads in the mountains.

At the cabin, at least there was shelter. We had a few potatoes left and some corn meal. There was a creek that probably had fish in it, if a person could catch them. Pa tried it for half a day before he gave up. To this day I don't care for fishing. I remember my father's sunken eyes in his gaunt, grim face.

He took Mary and me outside the cabin to talk. Rain dripped on us from branches overhead.

"I think I know where we are," he said. "I calculate to get to old John's and back in about four days. There'll be grub in the town, and they'll let me have some whether old John's still there or not."

He looked at me. "You do like she tells you," he warned. It was the first time he had admitted Mary was on earth since we picked her up two weeks before.

"You're my pardner," he said to me, "but it might be she's got more brains. You mind what she says."

He burst out with bitterness. "There ain't anything good left in the world, or people to care if you live or die. But I'll get grub in the town and come back with it."

He took a deep breath and added, "If you get too all-fired hungry, butcher the horse. It'll be better than starvin'."

He kissed the little girls goodbye and plodded off through the woods with one blanket and the rifle.

The cabin was moldy and had no floor. We kept a fire going under a hole in the roof, so it was full of blinding smoke, but we had to keep the fire so as to dry out the wood.

The third night we lost the horse. A bear scared him. We heard the racket, and Mary and I ran out, but we couldn't see anything in the pitch-dark.

In gray daylight I went looking for him, and I must have walked fifteen miles. It seemed like I had to have that horse at the cabin when Pa came or he'd whip me. I got plumb lost two or three times and thought maybe I was going to die there alone and nobody would ever know it, but I found the way back to the clearing.

That was the fourth day, and Pa didn't come. That was the day we ate up the last of the grub.

The fifth day, Mary went looking for the horse. My sisters whimpered, huddled in a quilt by the fire, because they were scared and hungry.

I never did get dried out, always having to bring in more damp wood, and going out to yell to see if Mary would hear me and not get lost. But I couldn't cry like the little girls did, because I was a big boy, eleven years old.

It was near dark when there was an answer to my yelling, and Mary came into the clearing.

Mary didn't have the horse—we never saw hide nor hair of that old horse again—but she was carrying something big and white that looked like a pumpkin with no color to it.

She didn't say anything, just looked around and saw Pa wasn't there yet, at the end of the fifth day.

"What's that thing?" my sister Elizabeth demanded.

"Mushroom," Mary answered. "I bet it hefts[4] ten pounds."

"What are you going to do with it now?" I sneered. "Play football here?"

"Eat it—maybe," she said, putting it in a corner. Her wet hair hung over her shoulders. She huddled by the fire.

My sister Sarah began to whimper again. "I'm hungry!" she kept saying.

"Mushrooms ain't good eating," I said. "They can kill you."

4. **hefts:** weighs.

Too Soon a Woman **163**

"Maybe," Mary answered. "Maybe they can. I don't set up to know all about everything, like some people."

"What's that mark on your shoulder?" I asked here. "You tore your dress on the brush."

"What do you think it is?" she said, her head bowed in the smoke.

"Looks like scars," I guessed.

"'Tis scars. They whipped me. Now mind your own business. I want to think."

Elizabeth whimpered, "Why don't Pa come back?"

"He's coming," Mary promised. "Can't come in the dark. Your pa'll take care of you soon's he can."

She got up and rummaged around in the grub box.

"Nothing here but empty dishes," I growled. "If there was anything, we'd know it."

Mary stood up. She was holding the can with the porcupine grease.

"I'm going to have something to eat," she said coolly. "You kids can't have any yet. And I don't want any squalling, mind."

It was a cruel thing, what she did then. She sliced that big, solid mushroom and heated grease in a pan.

The smell of it brought the little girls out of their quilt, but she told them to go back in so fierce a voice that they obeyed. They cried to break your heart.

I didn't cry. I watched, hating her.

I endured the smell of the mushroom frying as long as I could. Then I said, "Give me some."

"Tomorrow," Mary answered. "Tomorrow, maybe. But not tonight." She turned to me with a sharp command: "Don't bother me! Just leave me be."

She knelt there by the fire and finished frying the slice of mushroom.

If I'd had Pa's rifle, I'd have been willing to kill her right then and there.

She didn't eat right away. She looked at the brown, fried slice for a while and said, "By tomorrow morning, I guess you can tell whether you want any."

The little girls stared at her as she ate. Sarah was chewing an old leather glove.

When Mary crawled into the quilts with them, they moved away as far as they could get.

I was so scared that my stomach heaved, empty as it was.

Mary didn't stay in the quilts long. She took a drink out of the water bucket and sat down by the fire and looked through the smoke at me.

She said in a low voice, "I don't know how it will be if it's poison. Just do the best you can with the girls. Because your pa will come back, you know. . . . You better go to bed. I'm going to sit up."

And so would you sit up. If it might be your last night on earth and the pain of death might seize you at any moment, you would sit up by the smoky fire, wide-awake, remembering whatever you had to remember, savoring life.

We sat in silence after the girls had gone to sleep. Once I asked, "How long does it take?"

"I never heard," she answered. "Don't think about it."

I slept after a while, with my chin on my chest. Maybe Peter[5] dozed that way at Gethsemane[6] as the Lord knelt praying.

Mary's moving around brought me wide-awake. The black of night was fading.

"I guess it's all right," Mary said. "I'd be able to tell by now, wouldn't I?"

I answered gruffly, "I don't know."

Mary stood in the doorway for a while, looking out at the dripping world as if she found it beautiful. Then she fried slices of the mushroom while the little girls danced with anxiety.

We feasted, we three, my sisters and I, until

---

5. **Peter:** one of the twelve apostles, also called Simon Peter or Saint Peter.
6. **Gethsemane** (gĕth-sĕm′ə-nē): the garden outside Jerusalem where Jesus was arrested (Matthew 26:36-57).

Mary ruled, "That'll hold you," and would not cook any more. She didn't touch any of the mushroom herself.

That was a strange day in the moldy cabin. Mary laughed and was gay; she told stories, and we played "Who's Got the Thimble?" with a pine cone.

In the afternoon we heard a shout, and my sisters screamed and I ran ahead of them across the clearing.

The rain had stopped. My father came plunging out of the woods leading a pack horse—and well I remember the treasures of food in that pack.

He glanced at us anxiously as he tore at the ropes that bound the pack.

"Where's the other one?" he demanded.

Mary came out of the cabin then, walking sedately. As she came toward us, the sun began to shine.

My stepmother was a wonderful woman.

Reading Check

1. How old is the boy in the story?
2. What is the family's destination?
3. What happens to the horse?
4. How many days do the children and Mary spend in the cabin?
5. What does the father bring on the pack horse?

For Study and Discussion

Analyzing and Interpreting the Story

1. Pa allows Mary to travel with his wagon. Why, then, won't he speak to her?

2. Why is it difficult for the family to find food?

3. Why is the father forced to leave his family in Mary's care?

4. Consider Mary's behavior after she finds the mushroom. Why is her harsh treatment of the children necessary?

5. How are you prepared early in the story for the strength in Mary's character?

6. Were you surprised by the conclusion of the story? Tell why or why not.

Writing About Literature

Relating Fiction to History

In a short essay, show how this story reveals the hardships faced by many early settlers in moving west across the prairie.

About the Author

Dorothy Johnson   (1905–   )

Dorothy Johnson is a well-known author of novels, biographies and short stories that portray the American West in a realistic and sympathetic manner. Johnson's writings include *Buffalo Woman* and *All the Buffalo Returning*. The movies *The Man Who Shot Liberty Valance* and *A Man Called Horse* were based on Johnson stories. Her work has been widely translated, and she has received numerous awards. Johnson is an honorary member of the Blackfeet tribe in Montana. She was born in Iowa and graduated from Montana State University. She has worked as a magazine editor, a news editor, and a journalism instructor.

The Oklahoma Land Run

EDNA FERBER

Exactly at noon on April 22, 1889, two million acres of Oklahoma territory were opened for settlement. On the border, some 50,000 land-seekers massed for the biggest stampede in the history of the West. This was the Oklahoma Land Run, a historical event that Edna Ferber used in her famous novel Cimarron.

The following selection is a scene from that novel. The Venables, a wealthy Kansas family, are listening to Yancey Cravat, a son-in-law, as he relates his adventures in the Land Run.

"I had planned to try and get a place on the Santa Fe train that was standing, steam up, ready to run into the Nation.[1] But you couldn't get on. There wasn't room for a flea. They were hanging on the cowcatcher[2] and swarming all over the engine, and sitting on top of the cars. It was keyed down to make no more speed than a horse. It turned out they didn't even do that. They went twenty miles in ninety minutes. I decided I'd use my Indian pony. I knew I'd get endurance, anyway, if not speed. And that's what counted in the end.

"There we stood, by the thousands, all night. Morning, and we began to line up at the Border, as near as they'd let us go. Militia all along to keep us back. They had burned the prairie ahead for miles into the Nation, so as to keep the grass down and make the way clearer. To smoke out the Sooners,[3] too, who had sneaked in and were hiding in the scrub oaks, in the draws,[4] wherever they could. Most of the killing was due to them. They had crawled in and staked the land and stood ready to shoot those of us who came in, fair and square, in the Run. I knew the piece I wanted. An old freighters' trail, out of use, but still marked with deep ruts, led almost straight to it, once you found the trail, all overgrown as it was. A little creek ran through the land, and the prairie rolled a little there, too. Nothing but blackjacks[5] for miles around it, but on that section, because of the water, I suppose, there were elms and persimmons and cottonwoods and even a grove of pecans. I had noticed it many a time, riding the range. . . .

"Ten o'clock, and the crowd was nervous and restless. Hundreds of us had been followers of Payne and had gone as Boomers[6] in the old Payne colonies, and had been driven out, and had come back again. Thousands from all parts of the country had waited ten years for

1. **the Nation:** the territory formerly occupied by five American Indian nations—the Cherokees, Creeks, Choctaws, Chickasaws, and Seminoles.
2. **cowcatcher:** a metal frame set on the front of a locomotive to remove obstructions, such as cows, from the tracks.
3. **Sooners:** people who occupied homestead land "sooner" than the authorized time for doing so.

From *Cimarron* by Edna Ferber. Copyright © 1930 by Edna Ferber; copyright © renewed 1957 by Edna Ferber. Reprinted by permission of Harriet F. Pilpel, as trustee and attorney for the Ferber Proprietors.

4. **draws:** gullies or ravines.
5. **blackjacks:** short oaks with black bark.
6. **Payne. . .Boomers:** David L. Payne was one of the leaders of the Boomers, people who settled illegally on the Unassigned Lands of central Oklahoma, but who were evicted by United States soldiers.

this day when the land-hungry would be fed. They were like people starving. I've seen the same look exactly on the faces of men who were ravenous for food.

"Well, eleven o'clock, and they were crowding and cursing and fighting for places near the Line. They shouted and sang and yelled and argued, and the sound they made wasn't human at all, but like thousands of wild animals penned up. The sun blazed down. It was cruel. The dust hung over everything in a thick cloud, blinding you and choking you. The black dust of the burned prairie was over everything. We were like a horde of fiends with our red eyes and our cracked lips and our blackened faces. Eleven thirty. It was a picture straight out of hell. The roar grew louder. People fought for an inch of gain on the Border. Just next to me was a girl who looked about eighteen—she turned out to be twenty-five—and a beauty she was, too—on a coal-black thoroughbred....

"On the other side was an old fellow with a long gray beard—a plainsman, he was—a six-shooter in his belt, one wooden leg, and a flask of whiskey. He took a pull out of that every

The Oklahoma Land Rush (1938). Sketch for mural for Department of Interior Building, Washington, D.C., by John Steuart Curry (1847–1946). Oil on canvas.

of anyone that saw her, even in that crazy mob. The better to cut the wind, she had shortened sail and wore a short skirt, black tights, and a skullcap. . . .

"It turned out that the three of us, there in the front line, were headed down the old freighters' trail toward the creek land. I said, 'I'll be the first in the Run to reach Little Bear.' That was the name of the creek on the section. The girl pulled her cap down tight over her ears. 'Follow me,' she laughed. 'I'll show you the way.' Then the old fellow with the wooden leg and the whiskers yelled out, 'Whoop-ee! I'll tell 'em along the Little Bear you're both a-comin'.'"

"There we were, the girl on my left, the old plainsman on my right. Eleven forty-five. Along the Border were the soldiers, their guns in one hand, their watches in the other. Those last five minutes seemed years long; and funny, they'd quieted till there wasn't a sound. Listening. The last minute was an eternity. Twelve o'clock. There went up a roar that drowned the crack of the soldiers' musketry as they fired in the air as the signal of noon and the start of the Run. You could see the puffs of smoke from their guns, but you couldn't hear a sound. The thousands surged over the Line. It was like water going over a broken dam. The rush had started, and it was devil take the hindmost. We swept across the prairie in a cloud of black and red dust that covered our faces and hands in a minute, so that we looked like black demons from hell. Off we went, down the old freight trail that was two wheel ruts, a foot wide each, worn into the prairie soil. The old man on his pony kept in one rut, the girl on her thoroughbred in the other, and I on my White-

minute or two. He was mounted on an Indian pony like mine. Every now and then he'd throw back his head and let out a yell that would curdle your blood, even in that chorus of fiends. As we waited we fell to talking, the three of us, though you couldn't hear much in that uproar. The girl said she had trained her thoroughbred for the race. He was from Kentucky, and so was she. She was bound to get her hundred and sixty acres, she said. She had to have it. She didn't say why, and I didn't ask her. We were all too keyed up, anyway, to make sense. Oh, I forgot. She had on a get-up that took the attention

foot on the raised place in the middle. That first half mile was almost a neck-and-neck race. The old fellow was yelling and waving one arm and hanging on somehow. He was beating his pony with the flask on his flanks. Then he began to drop behind. Next thing I heard a terrible scream and a great shouting behind me. I threw a quick glance over my shoulder. The old plainsman's pony had stumbled and fallen. His bottle smashed into bits, his six-shooter flew in another direction, and he lay sprawling full length in the rut of the trail. The next instant he was hidden in a welter[7] of pounding hoofs and flying dirt and cinders and wagon wheels."

A dramatic pause. . . . The faces around the table were balloons pulled by a single string. They swung this way and that with Yancey Cravat's pace as he strode the room, his Prince Albert[8] coattails billowing. This way—the faces turned toward the sideboard. That way— they turned toward the windows. Yancey held the little moment of silence like a jewel in the circlet of faces. Sabra Cravat's voice, high and sharp with suspense, cut the stillness.

"What happened? What happened to the old man?"

Yancey's pliant hands flew up in a gesture of inevitability. "Oh, he was trampled to death in the mad mob that charged over him. Crazy. They couldn't stop for a one-legged old whiskers with a quart flask. . . .

"The girl and I—funny, I never did learn her name—were in the lead because we had stuck to the old trail, rutted though it was, rather than strike out across the prairie that by this time was beyond the burned area and was covered with a heavy growth of blue stem grass almost six feet high in places. A horse could only be forced through that at a slow pace.

That jungle of grass kept many a racer from winning his section that day.

"The girl followed close behind me. That thoroughbred she rode was built for speed, not distance. A racehorse, blooded. I could hear him blowing. He was trained to short bursts. My Indian pony was just getting his second wind as her horse slackened into a trot. We had come nearly sixteen miles. I was well in the lead by that time, with the girl following. She was crouched low over his neck, like a jockey, and I could hear her talking to him, low and sweet and eager, as if he were a human being. We were far in the lead now. We had left the others behind, hundreds going this way, hundreds that, scattering for miles over the prairie. Then I saw that the prairie ahead was afire. The tall grass was blazing. Only the narrow trail down which we were galloping was open. On either side of it was a wall of flame. Some skunk of a Sooner, sneaking in ahead of the Run, had set the blaze to keep the Boomers off, saving the land for himself. The dry grass burned like oiled paper. I turned around. The girl was there, her racer stumbling, breaking and going on, his head lolling now. I saw her motion with her hand. She was coming. I whipped off my hat and clapped it over White-foot's eyes, gave him the spurs, crouched down low and tight, shut my own eyes, and down the trail we went into the furnace. Hot! It was hell! The crackling and snapping on either side was like a fusillade.[9] I could smell the singed hair on the flanks of the mustang. My own hair was singeing. I could feel the flames licking my legs and back. Another hundred yards and neither the horse nor I could have come through it. But we broke out into the open choking and blinded and half suffocated. I looked down the lane of flame. The girl hung on her horse's neck. Her skullcap was pulled down over her

7. **welter:** great confusion or turmoil.
8. **Prince Albert:** a long, double-breasted coat.

9. **fusillade** (fyo͞oʹsə-lād'): a burst of firearms.

eyes. She was coming through, game. I knew that my land—the piece that I had come through hell for—was not more than a mile ahead. I knew that hanging around here would probably get me a shot through the head, for the Sooner that started that fire must be lurking somewhere in the high grass ready to kill anybody that tried to lay claim to his land. I began to wonder, too, if that girl wasn't headed for the same section that I was bound for. I made up my mind that, woman or no woman, this was a race, and devil take the hindmost. My poor little pony was coughing and sneezing and trembling. Her racer must have been ready to drop. I wheeled and went on. I kept thinking how, when I came to Little Bear Creek, I'd bathe my little mustang's nose and face and his poor heaving flanks, and how I mustn't let him drink too much, once he got his muzzle in the water.

"Just before I reached the land I was riding for I had to leave the trail and cut across the prairie. I could see a clump of elms ahead. I knew the creek was nearby. But just before I got to it I came to one of those deep gullies you find in the plains country. Drought does it—a crack in the dry earth to begin with, widening with every rain until it becomes a small canyon. Almost ten feet across this one was, and deep. No way around it that I could see, and no time to look for one. I put Whitefoot to the leap and . . . he took it, landing on the other side with hardly an inch to spare. I heard a wild scream behind me. I turned. The girl on her spent racer had tried to make the gulch. He had actually taken it—a thoroughbred and a gentleman, that animal—but he came down on his knees just on the farther edge, rolled, and slid down the gully side into the ditch. The girl had flung herself free. My claim was fifty yards away. So was the girl, with her dying horse. She lay there on the prairie. As I raced toward her—my own poor little mount was nearly

gone by this time—she scrambled to her knees. I can see her face now, black with cinders and soot and dirt, her hair all over her shoulders, her cheek bleeding where she had struck a stone in her fall, her black tights torn, her little short skirt sagging. She sort of sat up and looked around her, and stood there swaying, and pushing her hair out of her eyes like someone who'd been asleep. She pointed down the gully. The black of her face was streaked with tears.

"'Shoot him!' she said, 'I can't. His two forelegs are broken. I heard them crack. Shoot him!' . . .

"So I off my horse and down to the gully's edge. There the animal lay, his eyes all whites, his poor legs doubled under him, his flanks black and sticky with sweat and dirt. He was done for, all right. I took out my six-shooter and aimed right between his eyes. He kicked once, sort of leaped—or tried to, and then lay still. I stood there a minute, to see if he had to have another. He was so game that, some way, I didn't want to give him more than he needed.

"Then something made me turn around. The girl had mounted my mustang. She was off toward the creek section. Before I had moved ten paces she had reached the very piece I had marked in my mind for my own. She leaped from the horse, ripped off her skirt, tied it to her riding whip that she still held tight in her hand, dug the whip butt into the soul of the prairie—planted her flag—and the land was hers by right of claim."

Reading Check

1. Why had the prairie been burned?
2. What dangers did the Sooners represent?
3. What was the signal to begin the Run?
4. What happened to the plainsman?
5. Which piece of land did the girl get?

Analyzing and Interpreting the Selection

1. This realistic description of the Oklahoma Land Run shows how desperate people were for new, free land. What does Yancey say the land-hungry people were like, in the third and fourth paragraphs?

2a. Which details in the fourth paragraph make you picture the scene as something from hell? **b.** How do you think the author wants you to feel about the Land Run?

3. The girl next to Yancey turns out to be his chief competitor in the race. What does Yancey tell you about the girl?

4a. How does the girl manage to stake her claim ahead of Yancey? **b.** What personal qualities cause Yancey's failure? **c.** What qualities make the girl the winner?

5. What do you think of the girl's actions?

Language and Vocabulary

Recognizing Americanisms

Each region of the United States has contributed words to the national vocabulary. For example, this story of the Oklahoma Land Run contains the words *range* and *gulch*. These are examples of *Americanisms*—that is, words that originated in America or that came to have distinctive meanings in American English. Use a dictionary to find the origins and meanings of these Americanisms:

aggie	moccasin
Annie Oakley	OK
billboard	shoofly pie
French fry	tin lizzie

Writing About Literature

Comparing Characters

Compare the character of Mary in "Too Soon a Woman" (page 162) with the character of the girl in "The Oklahoma Land Run." Show how both women display courage and strength of will.

About the Author

Edna Ferber (1885–1968)

Edna Ferber, one of the most popular novelists in America, at first wanted to be an actress. She abandoned this ambition after her father became blind and she had to take a job as a newspaper reporter for three dollars a week. She threw her first novel away, but her mother rescued the manuscript and sent it to a publisher. Edna Ferber later admitted that she had never written a book she was fully satisfied with. Her first best seller, *Show Boat,* was made into a stage musical and three movies. She won the Pulitzer Prize for *So Big,* a novel about a woman whose rugged individualism helps her triumph over disaster. *Cimarron* was a big hit as a movie, as was *Giant,* a novel about modern life in Texas. Though she had never intended to be a writer, Edna Ferber loved her profession. She once remarked that "life can't ever defeat a writer who is in love with writing."

American Folk Tales

Paul Bunyan's Been There

Retold by
MAURICE DOLBIER

Tales about Paul Bunyan, the giant logger, were first told in the northern lumber camps. Paul became popular with the general public when a logging company began using the stories in advertising brochures, to attract new workers. Since then, generations of storytellers have helped old Paul's tales grow taller and taller.

Wherever you go in this big country, you're likely to find somebody who'll tell you that Paul Bunyan's been there. Been there and done things. Like digging the Great Lakes so that Babe would have watering troughs that wouldn't run dry, or digging a canal that turned out to be the Mississippi River.

You'll hear that the dirt he threw off to the right became the Rocky Mountains, and the dirt he threw off to the left became the Appalachians.

You'll hear that Kansas used to be full of mountains before Paul Bunyan came. He turned it upside-down. Now it's flat as a pancake because all its mountain peaks are inside the ground, pointing to the center of the earth.

You'll hear that Paul got so sad at what he saw going on in New York City that he fell to crying, and his tears started the Hudson River.

Western deserts or Southern swamps, Eastern shores or Northern forests, Paul is said to have been there and done things. And if by chance you can't find any stories about his having been in your neck of the woods, fix some up. Everybody else has.

Right now, let's stick to the Northern forests, because we know for sure that Paul was there. Paul and his men and the Blue Ox. They logged all through Michigan and Minnesota and the Dakotas, North and South, and they were always pushing westward to where the redwoods waited.

Maybe you'd like to know what life was like in those lumber camps of Paul Bunyan?

Well, the day started when the owls in the woods thought it was still night. The Little Chore Boy would blow his horn, and the men would tumble out of their bunks for chow.

There were always flapjacks for breakfast.

These were made on a big round griddle about two city blocks wide. Before the batter was poured on, five men used to skate up and down and around on it with slabs of bacon tied on their feet. It'd take an ordinary man a week to eat one of the flapjacks that came off that griddle. Paul used to eat five or six every morning.

After breakfast came the work. The loggers tramped off to the woods. One crowd cleared the paths, another cut down the trees, another cut them up into logs, another piled them on carts or sledges. Then Babe the Blue Ox hauled the carts down to the water.

Soon after sunset, the men would all be back at the camp for supper. That was either baked beans or pea soup. Sometimes the cooks would surprise them, and serve pea soup or baked beans.

Sourdough Sam never liked to work very hard. One time he just dumped some split peas in the lake and then boiled the lake water and served it.

Matter of fact, Sam didn't stay with Paul Bunyan long. The men didn't mind that he was lazy, but they got almighty tired of sourdough. That's a kind of fermented dough that rises like yeast, and Sam used it in all his recipes. He put it in the coffee one morning. The Little Chore Boy drank a cup, and then started to rise into the air and float across the lake. They had to lasso him and pull him down.

After supper, they'd sit around and talk and sing and tell yarns so whopping that you'd never believe them.

Then, about nine o'clock, they turned in.

Of course, it wasn't all work at Paul's camp. The men would hunt and fish, and sometimes they'd have logrolling contests. That's when you stand on a log in the middle of the water and start the log rolling under you, trying to keep your balance as long as you can. Joe Murfraw used to win, mostly. Paul Bunyan himself never took part, except to demonstrate, because nobody could beat him anyway. He used to get the logs rolling so fast under foot that they set up a foam solid enough for him to walk to the shore on.

These are the things that went on fairly regularly, but I couldn't tell you what a typical day at Paul's camp was like. No day was typical. They were all special, and so was the weather.

There were fogs so thick that you could cut houses out of them, the way they do with snow and ice in the far north.

There were winds that blew up and down and in every direction at once.

There were thaws so quick that when the snow melted it just stayed there in big drifts of water for a week.

There was one time when all four seasons hit at once, and the whole camp came down with frostbite, sunstroke and spring fever.

There was another time when the rain didn't come from the skies at all. It came up from China, away underneath the world. Up from the ground it came, first in a drizzle and then in a pour, and it went straight up into the air. It got the sky so wet that the clouds were slipping and slopping around in the mud for a month.

But most of the stories you hear are about the winters that Paul Bunyan's loggers had to put up with. No one ever had winters like them before or since.

The cold was mighty intense. It went down to 70 degrees below zero, and each degree was 16 inches long. The men couldn't blow out the candles at night, because the flames were frozen, so they had to crack the flames off and toss them outdoors. (When the warm weather came, the flames melted and started quite a forest fire.)

It was so cold that the words froze in mid-air right after they'd come out of people's mouths, and all the next summer nobody had to talk. They had a winter's supply of conversation on hand.

The cold wasn't the only thing that was peculiar. Sometimes the snow was too. One winter it came down in big blue flakes, and Johnny Inkslinger used the icicles to write down the figures in his books. That's how he got the idea for inventing fountain pens. And the men used to have snowball fights until they were blue in the face.

Yes, the weather did all it could to upset Paul Bunyan's operations. And when the weather gave up, the mosquitoes tried.

One spring day, the men were working in a swamp, near a lake in northern Michigan, when they heard a droning noise. They looked up to see the whole stretch of western horizon black with flying creatures heading right toward them. The men didn't stop to inquire. They dropped their tools and went hotfoot back to the camp and locked themselves up in the bunkhouse.

Pretty soon they heard a terrible racket overhead, and then long things like sword blades began piercing through the tin roof. Paul Bunyan grabbed a sledgehammer and began pounding those stingers flat, so the mosquitoes couldn't get out. The rest of the mosquito army saw that it was no use and flew away.

Paul figured they'd be back with some new ideas, and he'd better have a new idea, too, just in case. So he sent Swede Charlie on a trip down into Indiana. He'd heard they had a special kind of monster bumblebee there. Charlie brought some of these back, and Paul trained them to fly in a protective circle around the camp. He thought that the next time the mosquitoes came they'd have a surprise. They did, and he did too. The bumblebees and the mosquitoes liked each other so much that they married and had children, and the children grew up with stingers in back and in front.

You won't hear anyone say that Paul Bunyan was ever stumped by any problem that came up. I won't say, either. But that section of timberland up in Michigan was the only place that Bunyan's men moved away from while there were still trees to be cut. I suppose they got a better offer.

Reading Check

1. According to this tale, how did Paul Bunyan create the Rocky Mountains?
2. What was the name of Bunyan's ox?
3. Identify Sourdough Sam.
4. What happened when Bunyan brought in monster bumblebees?

Analyzing and Interpreting the Selection

1. A **tall tale** is an exaggerated humorous story. Like the heroes of myths and legends, tall-tale figures often have superhuman characteristics. What exaggerated characteristics does the super-logger Paul Bunyan have?

2. Americans have become known as a people who are good problem-solvers. It isn't surprising that Paul Bunyan also has a reputation for being skilled at solving problems. How does he solve the mosquito problem?

3. Some tall-tale figures are so gigantic and powerful that their casual movements form lakes, rivers, deserts, and mountains. According to this tale, how did Paul Bunyan affect the geography of North America?

4. Tall-tale heroes of the frontier always live in the wilderness. Many of their stories show a distrust of city life and of the "city slicker." What passage in this story reveals that Paul dislikes city life?

Literary Elements

Recognizing Figures of Speech

Every language has expressions called **figures of speech.** Figures of speech are not literally, or factually, true. For example, the expression *on hand* in this sentence is used as a figure of speech:

> They had a winter's supply of conversation *on hand.*

The supply of conversation is not literally on top of anybody's hand. *On hand* here means "available; ready for use."

This story is told in a relaxed, informal style, the way that a storyteller might tell it aloud. It uses several figures of speech that are common in informal American usage. Explain the meaning of each of the italicized figures of speech in the following sentences from the story. Use your imagination to explain how each one might have originated.

> And if by chance you can't find any stories about his having been in *your neck of the woods,* fix some up.

> And the men used to have snowball fights until they were *blue in the face.*

> They dropped their tools and *went hotfoot* back to the camp and locked themselves up in the bunkhouse.

Creative Writing

Writing a Tall Tale

The teller of these tall tales about Paul Bunyan says: "And if by chance you can't find any stories about his having been in your neck of the woods, fix some up. Everybody else has."

Make up a brief story about Paul Bunyan that is set in your state or community. What natural features (mountain, river, cave, lake, swamp, cliff) can you explain with a tall tale about Paul Bunyan? What problems are perplexing people in your area? What does ol' Paul do to solve them?

You might want to read more about Paul Bunyan. Two good collections are *Ol' Paul* by Glen Rounds and *Paul Bunyan* by Esther Shephard.

Comin' Through the Rye (1902). Bronze sculpture by Frederic Remington (1861–1909).

Pecos Bill, Coyote Cowboy

Retold by
<u>ADRIEN STOUTENBURG</u>

Before Pecos Bill came along, cowhands didn't know much about their jobs. The only way they knew to catch a steer was to hide behind a bush, lay a looped rope on the ground, and wait for the steer to step into the loop. Pecos Bill changed that the minute he reached the Dusty Dipper Ranch. But before that, he had lived as a coyote.

There aren't as many coyotes in Texas now as there were when Pecos Bill was born. But the ones that there are still do plenty of howling at night, sitting out under the sagebrush like thin, gray shadows, and pointing their noses at the moon.

Some of the cowboys around the Pecos River country claim that the oldest coyotes remember the time when Bill lived with them and are howling because they are lonesome for him. It's not often that coyotes have a boy grow up with them like one of their own family.

Bill had over a dozen older brothers and sisters for playmates, but they were ordinary boys and girls and no match for him. When Bill was two weeks old, his father found a half-grown bear and brought the bear home.

"You treat this bear nice, now," Bill's father said.

The bear didn't feel friendly and threatened to take a bite out of Bill. Bill wrestled the bear and tossed it around until the bear put its paws over its head and begged for mercy. Bill couldn't talk yet, but he patted the bear to show that he didn't have any hard feelings. After that, the bear followed Bill around like a big, flat-footed puppy.

Pecos Bill's father was one of the first settlers in the West. There was lots of room in Texas, with so much sky that it seemed as if there couldn't be any sky left over for the rest of the United States. There weren't many people, and it was lonesome country, especially on nights when the wind came galloping over the land, rattling the bear grass and the yucca plants and carrying the tangy smell of greasewood. However, Bill didn't feel lonely often, with all the raccoons, badgers, and jack rabbits he had for friends. Once he made the mistake of trying to pet a skunk. The skunk sprayed Bill with its strongest scent. Bill's mother had to hang Bill on the clothesline for a week to let the smell blow off him.

Bill was a little over one year old when another family of pioneers moved into the country. The new family settled about fifty miles from where Bill's folks had built their homestead.

"The country's getting too crowded," said Bill's father. "We've got to move farther west."

So the family scrambled back into their big wagon and set out, the oxen puffing and snorting as they pulled the wagon toward the Pecos River. Bill was sitting in the rear of the wagon when it hit some rocks in a dry stream bed. There was a jolt, and Bill went flying out of the wagon. He landed so hard that the wind was knocked out of him and he couldn't even cry out to let his folks know. It might not have made any difference if he had, because all his brothers and sisters were making such a racket and the wagon wheels were creaking so loudly that no one could have heard him. In fact, with so many other children in the family besides Bill, it was four weeks before Bill's folks even missed him. Then, of course, it was too late to find him.

Young Bill sat there in the dry stream bed awhile, wondering what to do. Wherever he looked there was only the prairie and the sky, completely empty except for a sharp-shinned hawk floating overhead. Bill felt more lonely than he ever had in his life. Then, suddenly, he saw a pack of coyotes off in the distance, eating the remains of a dead deer. The coyotes looked at Bill, and Bill looked at them. These coyotes had never seen a human baby before, and they didn't know quite what to think. Apparently, they decided Bill was some new kind of hairless animal, for one of the female coyotes took a hunk of deer meat in her teeth and trotted over to Bill with it. She put it in front of him and stood back, waiting for him to eat it.

Bill had not eaten much raw meat before, but he knew that the female coyote meant well, and he didn't want to hurt her feelings. So he picked the meat up and began chewing. It tasted so good that he walked over and joined the other coyotes.

From that time on, Bill lived with the coyotes, going wherever they went, joining in their hunts, and even learning their language. Those years he lived with the coyotes were happy ones. He ran with them through the moonlit nights, curled up with them in their shady dens, and howled with them when they sang to the stars.

By the time Bill was ten years old, he could outrun and outhowl any coyote in the Southwest. And since he had not seen any other human beings in all that time, he thought he was a coyote himself.

He might have gone on believing this forever if one day a cowboy hadn't come riding through the sagebrush. The cowboy stopped, stared, and rubbed his eyes, because he could scarcely believe what he saw. There in front of him stood a ten-year-old boy, as naked as a cow's hoof, wrestling with a giant grizzly bear. Nearby sat a dozen coyotes, their tongues hanging out. Before the cowboy could say, "Yipee yi-yo!" or plain "Yipee!" the boy had hugged the bear to death.

When Pecos Bill saw the cowboy, he snarled like a coyote and put his head down between his shoulders, ready to fight.

"What's your name?" the cowboy asked. "What are you doing out here?"

Since Bill didn't know anything but coyote talk, he naturally didn't understand a word.

The cowboy tossed Bill a plug of tobacco. Bill ate it and decided it tasted pretty good, so when the cowboy came up close, Bill didn't bite him.

The cowboy stayed there for three days, teaching Bill to talk like a human. Then he tried to prove to Bill that Bill wasn't a coyote.

"I must be a coyote," Bill said. "I've got fleas, haven't I? And I can howl the moon out of the sky. And I can run a deer to death."

"All Texans have got fleas and can howl," the cowboy said. "In order to be a true coyote, you have to have a bushy tail."

Bill looked around and realized for the first time that he didn't have a nice bushy, waving tail like his coyote friends. "Maybe I lost it somewhere."

"No siree," the cowboy said. "You're a human being, sure as shooting. You'd better come along with me."

Being human was a hard thing for Bill to face up to, but he realized that the cowboy must be right. He told his coyote friends goodbye and thanked them for all that they had taught him. Then he straddled a mountain lion he had tamed and rode with the cowboy toward the cowboy's ranch. On the way to the ranch, a big rattlesnake reared up in front of them. The cowboy galloped off, but Bill jumped from his mount and faced the snake.

"I'll let you have the first three bites, Mister Rattler, just to be fair. Then I'm going to beat the poison out of you until you behave yourself!"

That is just what Bill did. He whipped the snake around until it stretched out like a thirty-foot rope. Bill looped the rattler-rope in one hand, got back on his lion, and caught up with the cowboy. To entertain himself, he made a loop out of the snake and tossed it over the head of an armadillo plodding along through the cactus. Next, he lassoed several Gila monsters.[1]

"I never saw anybody do anything like that before," said the cowboy.

"That's because nobody invented the lasso before," said Pecos Bill.

Before Pecos Bill came along, cowboys didn't know much about their job. They didn't know anything about rounding up cattle, or branding them, or even about ten-gallon hats. The only way they knew to catch a steer was to hide behind a bush, lay a looped rope on the

---

1. **Gila** (hē′lə) **monsters:** large, poisonous lizards.

ground, and wait for the steer to step into the loop.

Pecos Bill changed all that the minute he reached the Dusty Dipper Ranch. He slid off his mountain lion and marched up to the biggest cowboy there.

"Who's the boss here?" he asked.

The man took one look at Bill's lion and at the rattlesnake-rope, and said, "I *was*."

Young though he was, Bill took over. At the Dusty Dipper and at other ranches, Bill taught the cowboys almost everything they know today. He invented spurs for them to wear on their boots. He taught them how to round up the cattle and drive the herds to railroad stations where they could be shipped to market. One of the finest things Bill did was to teach the cowboys to sing cowboy songs.

Bill made himself a guitar. On a night when the moon was as reddish-yellow as a ripe peach, though fifty times as large, he led some of the fellows at the ranch out to the corral and set himself down on the top rail.

"I don't want to brag," he told the cowhands, "but I learned my singing from the coyotes, and that's about the best singing there is."

He sang a tune the coyotes had taught him, and made up his own words:

"My seat is in the saddle, and my saddle's in
    the sky,
And I'll quit punchin' cows in the sweet by
    and by."

He made up many more verses and sang many other songs. When Bill was through, the roughest cowboy of all, Hardnose Hal, sat wiping tears from his eyes because of the beauty of Bill's singing. Lefty Lightning, the smallest cowboy, put his head down on his arms and wept. All the cowboys there vowed they would learn to sing and make up songs. And they did make up hundreds of songs about the lone prairie, and the Texas sky, and the wind blowing over the plains. That's why we have so many cowboy songs today.

Pecos Bill invented something else almost as useful as singing. This happened after a band of cattle rustlers came to the ranch and stole half a hundred cows.

"You boys", said Bill, "have to get something to protect yourselves with besides your fists. I can see I'll have to think up a six-shooter."

"What's a six-shooter?" asked Broncobuster Bertie. (Bill had taught horses how to buck and rear so that cowboys could learn broncobusting.)

"Why," said Bill, "that's a gun that holds six bullets."

Bill sat down in the shade of a yucca tree and figured out how to make a six-shooter. It was a useful invention, but it had its bad side. Some of the cowboys started shooting at each other. Some even went out and held up trains and stagecoaches.

One of the most exciting things Bill did was to find himself the wildest, strongest, most beautiful horse that ever kicked up the Texas dust. He was a mighty, golden mustang, and even Bill couldn't outrun that horse. To catch the mustang, Bill had the cowboys rig up a huge slingshot and shoot him high over the cactus and greasewood. When Bill landed in front of the mustang, the horse was so surprised he stopped short, thrusting out his front legs stiff as rifle barrels. The mustang had been going so fast that his hoofs drove into the ground, and he was stuck. Bill leaped on the animal's back, yanked on his golden mane, and pulled him free. The mustang was so thankful for being pulled from the trap that he swung his head around and gave Pecos Bill a smacking kiss. From then on, the horse was as gentle as a soft wind in a thatch of Jimson weed.

No one else could ride him, however. Most of the cowboys who tried ended up with broken necks. That's why Bill called his mustang Widow-Maker.

Bill and Widow-Maker traveled all over the western range, starting new ranches and helping out in the long cattle drives. In stormy weather they often holed up with a band of coyotes. Bill would strum his guitar and the coyotes would sing with him.

Then came the year of the Terrible Drought. The land shriveled for lack of water, and the droves of cattle stood panting with thirst.

The cowboys and the ranch bosses from all around came to Bill, saying, "The whole country's going to dry up and blow away, Bill, unless you can figure out some way to bring us rain."

"I'm figuring," Bill told them. "But I've never tried making rain before, so I'll have to think a little."

While Bill thought, the country grew so dry it seemed that there would be nothing but bones and rocks left. Even cactus plants, which could stand a lot of dryness, began to turn brown. The pools where the cattle drank dried up and turned to cracked mud. All the snakes hid under the ground in order to keep from frying. Even the coyotes stopped howling, because their throats were too dry for them to make any sound.

Bill rode around on Widow-Maker, watching the clear, burning sky and hoping for the sight of a rain cloud. All he saw were whirls of dust, called dust devils, spinning up from the yellowing earth. Then, toward noon one day, he spied something over in Oklahoma which looked like a tall whirling tower of black bees. Widow-Maker reared up on his hind legs, his eyes rolling.

"It's just a cyclone," Pecos Bill told his horse, patting the golden neck.

But Widow-Maker was scared and began bucking around so hard that even Bill had a time staying in the saddle.

"Whoa there!" Bill commanded. "I could ride that cyclone as easy as I can ride you, the way you're carrying on."

That's when Bill had an idea. There might be rain mixed up in that cyclone tower. He nudged Widow-Maker with his spurs and yelled, "Giddap!"

What Bill planned to do was leap from his horse and grab the cyclone by the neck. But as he came near and saw how high the top of the whirling tower was, he knew he would have to do something better than that. Just as he and Widow-Maker came close enough to the cyclone to feel its hot breath, a knife of lightning streaked down into the ground. It stuck there, quivering, just long enough for Bill to reach out and grab it. As the lightning bolt whipped back up into the sky, Bill held on. When he was as high as the top of the cyclone, he jumped and landed astraddle its black, spinning shoulders.

By then, everyone in Texas, New Mexico, Arizona, and Oklahoma was watching. They saw Bill grab hold of that cyclone's shoulders and haul them back. They saw him wrap his legs around the cyclone's belly and squeeze so hard the cyclone started to pant. Then Bill got out his lasso and slung it around the cyclone's neck. He pulled it tighter and tighter until the cyclone started to choke, spitting out rocks and dust. All the rain that was mixed up in it started to fall.

Down below, the cattle and the coyotes, the jack rabbits and the horned toads, stuck out their tongues and caught the sweet, blue, falling rain. Cowboys on the ranches and people in town ran around whooping and cheering, holding out pans and kettles to catch the raindrops.

Bill rode the cyclone across three states. By the time the cyclone reached California, it was all out of steam, and out of rain, too. It gave a big sigh, trembled weakly, and sank to earth. Bill didn't have time to jump off. He fell hard, scooping out a few thousand acres of sand and rock and leaving a big basin below sea level. That was what made Death Valley.

Bill was a greater hero than ever after that. Yet at times, he felt almost as lonely as on the day when he had bounced out of his folks' wagon and found himself sitting alone under the empty sky. Widow-Maker was good company most of the time, but Bill felt there was something missing in his life.

One day, he wandered down to the Rio Grande and stood watching the brown river flow slowly past. Suddenly, he saw a catfish as big as a whale jumping around on top of the water, its whiskers shining like broomsticks. On top of the catfish was a brown-eyed, brown-haired girl.

Somebody beside Bill exclaimed, "Look at Slue-Foot Sue ride that fish!"

Pecos Bill felt his heart thump and tingle in a way it had never done before. "That's the girl I want to marry!" he said. He waded out into the Rio Grande, poked the catfish in the nose, and carried Slue-Foot Sue to a church. "You're going to be my bride," he said.

"That's fine with me," said Sue, looking Pecos Bill over and seeing that he was the biggest, boldest, smartest cowboy who had ever happened to come along beside the Rio Grande.

That was the beginning of a very happy life for Bill. He and Sue raised a large family. All of the boys grew up to be fine cowboys, and the girls grew up to be cowgirls. The only time Bill and Sue had any trouble was when Bill wanted to adopt a batch of baby coyotes who were orphans.

"We're human beings," Sue said, "and we can't be raising a bunch of varmints."

"I was a varmint once myself," said Bill. He argued so much that Sue agreed to take the coyotes in and raise them as members of the family. The coyotes grew to be so human that two of them were elected to the House of Representatives.

Pecos Bill grew old, as everyone and everything does in time. Even so, there wasn't a bronco he couldn't bust, or a steer he couldn't rope, or a bear he couldn't hug to death faster and better than anyone else.

No one knows, for sure, how he died, or even if he did die. Some say that he mixed barbed wire in his coffee to make it strong enough for his taste, and that the wire rusted in his stomach and poisoned him. Others say that one day he met a dude cowboy, all dressed up in fancy clothes, who didn't know the front end of a cow from the side of a boxcar. The dude asked so many silly questions about cowpunching that Pecos Bill lay down in the dust and laughed himself to death.

But the cowboys back in the Pecos River country say that every once in a while, when the moon is full and puffing its white cheeks out and the wind is crooning softly through the bear grass, Pecos Bill himself comes along and sits on his haunches and sings right along with the coyotes.

Reading Check

1. How did Bill get separated from his family?
2. How did Bill learn that he wasn't a coyote?
3. What did Bill do with the rattler?
4. How did Bill learn to sing?
5. How did Widow-Maker get his name?

Analyzing and Interpreting the Selection

1. It is not surprising that a tall-tale figure, whose life is one long exaggeration, should have an extraordinary childhood. What was remarkable about Bill's younger years?

2. Pecos Bill is credited with inventing many of the cowhand's tools and skills. List all the things Pecos Bill is supposed to have done for his people.

3. According to the story, what natural wonders were caused by Bill's activities?

4a. What disaster does Pecos Bill save his people from? **b.** What words on page 181 describe this enemy as if it were a living monster? **c.** How does Bill conquer this monster?

Language and Vocabulary

Recognizing Words from Spanish

It is easy to see why many terms used by cowhands are direct borrowings of Spanish words. Many Spanish-speaking Mexican-Americans live in the Southwest, where the cowhands live and work. Here are three cowhand terms borrowed from Spanish:

mustang (from Mexican Spanish *mestengo,* "stray horse"): a wild horse.

lariat (from Spanish *la reata,* "the rope"): a long rope used to catch or tie up animals.

bronco (from Mexican Spanish *bronco,* "rough"): an untamed horse.

The following words are not all cowhand terms, but they all came into English from Spanish. Two go back originally to Nahuatl, an ancient Mexican Indian language, which was spoken before the Spanish came to Mexico. Use a dictionary to find the original meaning of each word. Have any of the words taken on new meanings?

alfalfa	chocolate	hurricane
bonanza	coyote	mesa

Extending Your Study

Reporting on American Tall-Tale Heroes

Stories about Pecos Bill and Paul Bunyan are examples of occupational lore: stories about heroes associated with a particular kind of work. Here are some other tall-tale figures from American folk tales, and the work they are associated with:

Mike Fink, riverboatman
Casey Jones, railroad engineer
Joe Margarac, steelworker
Stormalong, sea captain

Choose one of these characters (or some other tall-tale figure you are interested in) and find one story about him. Write a brief report summing up the character's life and telling what impossible feats he achieved.

Information on these figures can be found in a book on American folklore or in an encyclopedia. A good source for stories of American folk heroes is *Yankee Doodle's Cousins* by Anne Malcolmson.

A Sensible Varmint

DAVY CROCKETT

Some people become legends after they die, but the American frontiersman Davy Crockett (1786–1836) became a legend in his own time. Davy helped create his own legend with stories like this one, which is surely one of the tallest tales about hunting ever told. The story is written just as a back-country yarn spinner might write it.

Almost every boddy that knows the forrest, understands parfectly well that Davy Crockett never loses powder and ball, havin' ben brort up to blieve it a sin to throw away amminition, and that is the bennefit of a vartuous eddikation. I war out in the forrest won arternoon, and had jist got to a plaice called the grate gap, when I seed a rakkoon setting all alone upon a tree. I klapped the breech of Brown Betty to my sholder, and war jist a-going to put a piece of led between his sholders, when he lifted one paw, and sez he, "Is your name Crockett?"

Sez I, "You are rite for wonst, my name is Davy Crockett."

"Then," sez he, "you needn't take no further trubble, for I may as well cum down without another word"; and the cretur wauked rite down from the tree, for he considered himself shot.

I stoops down and pats him on the head, and sez I, "I hope I may be shot myself before I hurt a hare of your head, for I never had sich a kompliment in my life."

"Seeing as how you say that," sez he, "I'll jist walk off for the present, not doubting your word a bit, d'ye see, but lest you should kinder happen to change your mind."

John Henry

John Henry was a real person, a steel driver, who is remembered for what he did
and how he died. In 1870 John Henry raced an automatic steam drill in the
Big Bend Tunnel of the Chesapeake and Ohio Railroad in the West Virginia
mountains. What happened? The story is immortalized in this famous folk
ballad.

John Henry was a little baby boy,
You could hold him in the palm of your hand,
He gave a long and lonesome cry,
"Gonna be a steel-drivin' man, Lawd, Lawd,
Gonna be a steel-drivin' man."   5

They took John Henry to the tunnel,
Put him in the lead to drive,
The rock was so tall, John Henry so small,
That he lied down his hammer and he cried, Lawd, Lawd,
Lied down his hammer and he cried.   10

John Henry started on the right hand,
The steam drill started on the left,
"Fo' I'd let that steam drill beat me down,
I'd hammer my fool self to death, Lawd, Lawd,
I'd hammer my fool self to death."   15

John Henry told his Captain,
"A man ain't nothin' but a man,
Fo' I let your steam drill beat me down
I'll die with this hammer in my hand, Lawd, Lawd,
I'll die with this hammer in my hand."   20

John Henry had a little woman
Her name were Polly Anne,
John Henry took sick and he had to go to bed,
Polly Anne drove steel like a man, Lawd, Lawd,
Polly Anne drove steel like a man.   25

Now the Captain told John Henry,
"I b'lieve my tunnel's sinkin' in."
"Stand back, Captain, and doncha be afraid,
That's nothin' but my hammer catchin' wind, Lawd, Lawd,
That's nothin' but my hammer catchin' wind."   30

John Henry he told his shaker,°
"Now shaker, why don't you sing?
I'm throwin' nine pounds from my hips on down,
Just listen to the cold steel ring, Lawd, Lawd,
Just listen to the cold steel ring."   35

John Henry he told his shaker,
"Now shaker, why don't you pray?
For if I miss this six-foot steel
Tomorrow'll be your buryin' day, Lawd, Lawd,
Tomorrow'll be your buryin' day."   40

John Henry he told his Captain,
"Looky yonder, boy, what do I see?
Your drill's done broke and your hole's done choke,
And you can't drive steel like me, Lawd, Lawd,
And you can't drive steel like me."   45

John Henry hammerin' in the mountain
Till the handle of his hammer caught on fire,
He drove so hard till he broke his poor heart,
Then he lied down his hammer and he died, Lawd, Lawd,
Then he lied down his hammer and he died.   50

Women in the West heard of John Henry's death
They couldn't hardly stay in bed,
Stood in the rain, flagged that eastbound train
"Goin' where that man fell dead, Lawd, Lawd,
Goin' where that man fell dead."   55

They took John Henry to the tunnel,
And they buried him in the sand,
An' every locomotive come rollin' by
Say, "There lays a steel-drivin' man, Lawd, Lawd,
There lays a steel-drivin' man."   60

31. **shaker:** steel driver's assistant.

Now some say he come from England,
And some say he come from Spain,
But I say he's nothin' but a Lou'siana man,
Leader of a steel-drivin' gang, Lawd, Lawd,
Leader of a steel-drivin' gang.

65

For Study and Discussion

Analyzing and Interpreting the Song

1. Many folk heroes show unusual talents or promise when they are only babies. Pecos Bill, for example, was only two weeks old when he made a bear beg for mercy (page 178). What ambition did John Henry reveal when he was so little he could be held in the palm of a hand?

2. The famous contest with the machine starts in the third stanza. How was John Henry both a winner and a loser in that battle?

3. According to the next-to-last stanza, how is John Henry's memory kept alive?

4a. How is Polly Anne also a heroic figure? **b.** How did the actions of other women show how people felt about John Henry's tragic death?

Creative Writing

Writing a Ballad

Make up a brief song that tells a story about a colorful hero, perhaps Paul Bunyan, Pecos Bill, or someone else, real or imaginary. You might choose one of these episodes:

> Paul Bunyan's conquest of the giant mosquitoes
> Pecos Bill's life with the coyotes

The words to many ballads are composed to old melodies. Here are three good ones:

> "On Top of Old Smoky"
> "My Darling Clementine"
> "Sweet Betsy from Pike"

Barrio Boy

ERNESTO GALARZA

"The melting pot" is an expression often used to describe the United States. In "the melting pot," all nationalities are mixed together, so that they assimilate, or absorb, one another's ways. Ernesto Galarza says that his public school was not a melting pot. He thinks of it as a griddle, where knowledge was warmed into students and racial hatreds roasted out of them.

In this excerpt from Barrio° Boy, *his autobiography, Ernesto and his mother have just arrived in Sacramento, California, from their native Mexico. They are on their way to enroll Ernesto in public school.*

The two of us walked south on Fifth Street one morning to the corner of Q street and turned right. Half of the block was occupied by the Lincoln School. It was a three-story wooden building, with two wings that gave it the shape of a double-T connected by a central hall. It was a new building, painted yellow, with a shingled roof that was not like the red tile of the school in Mazatlán.[1] I noticed other differences, none of them very reassuring.

We walked up the wide staircase hand in hand and through the door, which closed by itself. A mechanical contraption screwed to the top shut it behind us quietly.

Up to this point the adventure of enrolling me in the school had been carefully rehearsed. Mrs. Dodson[2] had told us how to find it and we had circled it several times on our walks. Friends in the barrio explained that the *director*

°**Barrio:** the neighborhood or district of a city where Spanish-speaking people live.
1. **Mazatlán** (mä′sät-län′): a city in Mexico, where Ernesto lived before coming to the United States.
2. **Mrs. Dodson:** the landlady of the boardinghouse in which the Galarzas lived.

was called a principal, and that it was a lady and not a man. They assured us that there was always a person at the school who could speak Spanish.

Exactly as we had been told, there was a sign on the door in both Spanish and English: "Principal." We crossed the hall and entered the office of Miss Nettie Hopley.

Miss Hopley was at a roll-top desk to one side, sitting in a swivel chair that moved on wheels. There was a sofa against the opposite wall, flanked by two windows and a door that opened on a small balcony. Chairs were set around a table and framed pictures hung on the walls of a man with long white hair and another with a sad face and a black beard.

The principal half turned in the swivel chair to look at us over the pinch glasses crossed on the ridge of her nose. To do this she had to duck her head slightly as if she were about to step through a low doorway.

What Miss Hopley said to us we did not know but we saw in her eyes a warm welcome and when she took off her glasses and straightened up she smiled wholeheartedly, like Mrs. Dodson. We were, of course, saying nothing, only catching the friendliness of her voice and the sparkle in her eyes while she said words we did not understand. She signaled us to the table. Almost tiptoeing across the office, I maneuvered myself to keep my mother between me and the gringo[3] lady. In a matter of seconds I had to decide whether she was a possible friend or a menace. We sat down.

Then Miss Hopley did a formidable thing. She stood up. Had she been standing when we entered she would have seemed tall. But rising from her chair she soared. And what she carried up and up with her were firm shoulders, a straight sharp nose, full cheeks slightly molded by a curved line along the nostrils, thin lips that moved like steel springs, and a high forehead topped by hair gathered in a bun. Miss Hopley was not a giant in body but when she mobilized it to a standing position she seemed a match for giants. I decided I liked her.

She strode to a door in the far corner of the office, opened it and called a name. A boy of about ten years appeared in the doorway. He sat down at one end of the table. He was brown like us, a plump kid with shiny black hair combed straight back, neat, cool, and faintly obnoxious.

Miss Hopley joined us with a large book and some papers in her hand. She, too, sat down and the questions and answers began by way of our interpreter. My name was Ernesto. My mother's name was Henriqueta. My birth certificate was in San Blas. Here was my last report card from the Escuela Municipal Número 3 para Varones of Mazatlán, and so forth. Miss Hopley put things down in the book and my mother signed a card.

As long as the questions continued, Doña Henriqueta could stay and I was secure. Now

that they were over, Miss Hopley saw her to the door, dismissed our interpreter and without further ado took me by the hand and strode down the hall to Miss Ryan's first grade.

Miss Ryan took me to a seat at the front of the room, into which I shrank—the better to survey her. She was, to skinny, somewhat runty me, of a withering height when she patrolled the class. And when I least expected it, there she was, crouching by my desk, her blond, radiant face level with mine, her voice patiently maneuvering me over the awful idiocies of the English language.

During the next few weeks Miss Ryan overcame my fears of tall, energetic teachers as she bent over my desk to help me with a word in the preprimer. Step by step, she loosened me and my classmates from the safe anchorage of the desks for recitations at the blackboard and consultations at her desk. Frequently she burst into happy announcements to the whole class. "Ito can read a sentence," and small Japanese Ito slowly read aloud while the class listened in wonder: "Come, Skipper, come. Come and run." The Korean, Portuguese, Italian, and Polish first-graders had similar moments of glory, no less shining than mine the day I conquered *butterfly*, which I had been persistently pronouncing in standard Spanish as "boo-ter-flee." "Children," Miss Ryan called for attention. "Ernesto has learned how to pronounce *butterfly!*" And I proved it with a perfect imitation of Miss Ryan. From that celebrated success, I was soon able to match Ito's progress as a sentence reader with "Come, butterfly, come fly with me."

Like Ito and several first-graders who did not know English, I received private lessons from Miss Ryan in the closet, a narrow hall off the classroom with a door at each end. Next to one of these doors Miss Ryan placed a large chair for herself and a small one for me. Keeping an eye on the class through the open door

3. **gringo:** a Spanish-American term for a foreigner.

EACH PUPIL REPRESENTS A DIFFERENT RACE—21 DIFFERENT NATIONALITIES

Photographs of the Lincoln School on pages 190 and 191 from the Sacramento City School District's Superintendent's Annual Reports for 1913–14 and 1917–18.

she read with me about sheep in the meadow and a frightened chicken going to see the king, coaching me out of my phonetic ruts in words like *pasture, bow-wow-wow, hay* and *pretty,* which to my Mexican ear and eye had so many unnecessary sounds and letters. She made me watch her lips and then close my eyes as she repeated words I found hard to read. When we came to know each other better, I tried interrupting to tell Miss Ryan how we said it in Spanish. It didn't work. She only said "oh" and went on with *pasture, bow-wow-wow,* and *pretty.* It was as if in that closet we were both discovering together the secrets of the English language and grieving together over the tragedies of Bo-Peep. The main reason I was graduated with honors from the first grade was that I had fallen in love with Miss Ryan. Her radiant, no-nonsense character made us either afraid not to love her or love her so we would not be afraid, I am not sure which. It was not only that we sensed she was with it, but also that she was with us.

Like the first grade, the rest of the Lincoln School was a sampling of the lower part of town where many races made their home. My pals in the second grade were Kazushi, whose parents spoke only Japanese; Matti, a skinny Italian boy; and Manuel, a fat Portuguese who would never get into a fight but wrestled you to the ground and just sat on you. Our assortment of nationalities included Koreans, Yugoslavs, Poles, Irish, and home-grown Americans.

Miss Hopley and her teachers never let us forget why we were at Lincoln: for those who were alien, to become good Americans; for those who were so born, to accept the rest of us. Off the school grounds we traded the same insults we heard from our elders. On the playground we were sure to be marched up to the principal's office for calling someone an insulting name. The school was not so much a melting pot as a griddle where Miss Hopley and her helpers warmed knowledge into us and roasted racial hatreds out of us.

At Lincoln, making us into Americans did not mean scrubbing away what made us originally foreign. The teachers called us as our parents did, or as close as they could pronounce our names in Spanish or Japanese. No one was ever scolded or punished for speaking in his native tongue on the playground. Matti told the class about his mother's down quilt, which she had made in Italy with the fine feathers of a thousand geese. Encarnación acted out how boys learned to fish in the Philippines. I astounded the third grade with the story of my travels on a stagecoach, which nobody else in the class had seen except in the museum at Sutter's Fort. After a visit to the Crocker Art Gallery and its collection of heroic paintings of the golden age of California, someone showed a silk scroll with a Chinese painting. Miss Hopley herself had a way of expressing wonder over these matters before a class, her eyes wide open until they popped slightly. It was easy for me to feel that becom-

ing a proud American, as she said we should, did not mean feeling ashamed of being a Mexican.

The Americanization of Mexican me was no smooth matter. I had to fight one lout[4] who made fun of my travels on the *diligencia*,[5] and my barbaric translation of the word into "diligence." He doubled up with laughter over the word until I straightened him out with a kick. In class I made points explaining that in Mexico roosters said *"qui-qui-ri-qui"* and not "cock-a-doodle-doo," but after school I had to put up with the taunts of a big Yugoslav who said Mexican roosters were crazy.

4. **lout:** a clumsy, stupid person.
5. *diligencia* (dē′lē-hĕn′syä): a Spanish word meaning "a fast coach." At one time, the English word *diligence* meant "speed" or "haste." Now *diligence* means "careful effort" or "hard work."

LINCOLN PRIMARY.

But it was Homer who gave the most lasting lesson for a future American.

Homer was a chunky Irishman who dressed as if every day was Sunday. He slicked his hair between a crew cut and a pompadour.[6] And Homer was smart, as he clearly showed when he and I ran for president of the third grade.

Everyone understood that this was to be a demonstration of how the American people vote for president. In an election, the teacher explained, the candidates could be generous and vote for each other. We cast our ballots in a shoebox and Homer won by two votes. I polled my supporters and came to the conclusion that I had voted for Homer and so had he. After class he didn't deny it, reminding me of what the teacher had said—we could vote for each other but didn't have to.

The lower part of town was a collage[7] of nationalities in the middle of which Miss Nettie Hopley kept school with discipline and compassion. She called assemblies in the upper hall to introduce celebrities like the police sergeant or the fire chief, to lay down the law of the school, to present awards to our athletic champions, and to make important announcements. One of these was that I had been proposed by my school and accepted as a member of the newly formed Sacramento Boys Band. "Now, isn't that a wonderful thing?" Miss Hopley asked the assembled school, all eyes on me. And everyone answered in a chorus, including myself, "Yes, Miss Hopley."

It was not only the parents who were summoned to her office and boys and girls who served sentences there who knew that Nettie Hopley meant business. The entire school witnessed her sizzling Americanism in its awful majesty one morning at flag salute.

All the grades, as usual, were lined up in the courtyard between the wings of the building, ready to march to class after the opening bell. Miss Shand was on the balcony of the second floor off Miss Hopley's office, conducting us in our lusty singing of "My Country tiz-a-thee." Our principal, as always, stood there like us, joining in the song.

Halfway through the second stanza she stepped forward, held up her arm in a sign of command, and called loud and clear: "Stop the singing." Miss Shand looked flabbergasted. We were frozen with shock.

Miss Hopley was now standing at the rail of the balcony, her eyes sparking, her voice low and resonant, the words coming down to us distinctly and loaded with indignation.

"There are two gentlemen walking on the school grounds with their hats on while we are singing," she said, sweeping our ranks with her eyes. "We will remain silent until the gentlemen come to attention and remove their hats." A minute of awful silence ended when Miss Hopley, her gaze fixed on something behind us, signaled Miss Shand and we began once more the familiar hymn. That afternoon, when school was out, the word spread. The two gentlemen were the Superintendent of Schools and an important guest on an inspection.

6. **pompadour:** a hair style in which the hair is combed or brushed up high away from the forehead.
7. **collage** (kō-läzh'): a collection of bits and pieces.

Reading Check

1. Who was the principal at Lincoln School?
2. How did the principal communicate with Ernesto?
3. What word did Ernesto struggle to pronounce correctly?
4. Where did Ernesto receive private tutoring from his teacher?
5. What was the goal set for the students at Lincoln?

For Study and Discussion

Analyzing and Interpreting the Selection

1. When Ernesto came to school in the United States, he did not understand English. How did Miss Hopley, the principal, make him feel at ease?

2. Miss Ryan was a patient and encouraging teacher with a "blond, radiant face." What did she do to make Ernesto and the other first-graders enjoy learning English?

3. The teachers at the Lincoln School never let the students forget why they were there. **a.** According to the teachers, what was the purpose of school? **b.** In your own words, explain what you think the teachers meant by "good Americans" (page 190).

4. Ernesto and his classmates also kept their pride in their own backgrounds. How did the teachers encourage the students to remember their own cultures?

5a. What lesson in "sizzling Americanism" did Miss Hopley give to the Superintendent of Schools and his important guest? **b.** How would you describe what Ernesto and his classmates learned from this "lesson"?

Language and Vocabulary

Comparing Words That Imitate Sounds

Ernesto discovered something about language when he realized that a Mexican rooster and an American rooster make different sounds. An American rooster is supposed to say "cock-a-doodle-doo." What does a Mexican rooster say? If there were Norwegians in Ernesto's class, they could have told him that Norwegian roosters go *"kykkeliky."*

Here are some other words that are supposed to echo natural sounds. Notice that people in different lands seem to "hear" the sounds in different ways.

bow-wow: *oua-oua* (French); *wan-wan* (Japanese); *bu-bu* (Italian)
bang: *pum* (Spanish)
knock-knock: *pom-pom* (French)
purr: *ron-ron* (French); *schnurr* (German)

The English words *hiss, rustle,* and *tap* are supposed to echo or imitate natural sounds. Do any of your classmates know the words for these sounds in another language?

About the Author

Ernesto Galarza (1905–1984)

Ernesto Galarza's popular autobiography *Barrio Boy* began as stories he told his own children about Jalcocotán, the remote mountain village in Mexico where he was born. The Galarza family suffered great hardship during the Mexican revolution, and some of them finally made their way to Sacramento, California. There young Ernesto had his first experience with American education. Galarza went on to receive a Ph.D. from Columbia University and become a teacher and writer. His other books include several textbooks on the Mexican-American heritage.

I Have a Dream

MARTIN LUTHER KING, JR.

On August 28, 1963, a quarter of a million Americans marched peacefully to Washington, D.C., to urge Congress to pass civil rights legislation. This is part of the speech delivered by Dr. King on that summer day.

Martin Luther King, Jr., speaking to crowd at Freedom Rally, 1963.

I say to you today, my friends, that in spite of the difficulties and frustrations of the moment, I still have a dream. It is a dream deeply rooted in the American dream.

I have a dream that one day this nation will rise up and live out the true meaning of its creed: "We hold these truths to be self-evident: that all men are created equal."

I have a dream that one day on the red hills of Georgia the sons of former slaves and the sons of former slave owners will be able to sit down together at the table of brotherhood.

I have a dream that my four little children will one day live in a nation where they will not be judged by the color of their skin but the content of their character.

I have a dream today.

I have a dream that one day every valley

shall be exalted, every hill and mountain shall be made low, the rough places will be made plains, and the crooked places will be made straight, and the glory of the Lord shall be revealed, and all flesh shall see it together.

This is our hope. This is the faith with which I return to the South. With this faith we will be able to hew out of the mountains of despair a stone of hope. With this faith we will be able to transform the jangling discords of our nation into a beautiful symphony of brotherhood. With this faith we will be able to work together, to pray together, to struggle together, to go to jail together, to stand up for freedom together, knowing that we will be free one day.

This will be the day when all of God's children will be able to sing with new meaning, "My country, 'tis of thee, sweet land of liberty, of thee I sing. Land where my fathers died, land of the Pilgrim's pride, from every mountainside, let freedom ring."

And if America is to be a great nation, this must become true. So let freedom ring from the prodigious hilltops of New Hampshire. Let freedom ring from the mighty mountains of New York. Let freedom ring from the heightening Alleghenies of Pennsylvania. Let freedom ring from the curvaceous peaks of California!

Let freedom ring from Stone Mountain of Georgia!

Let freedom ring from every hill and mole-hill of Mississippi. From every mountainside, let freedom ring.

When we let freedom ring, when we let it ring from every village and every hamlet, from every state and every city, we will be able to speed up that day when all of God's children, black men and white men, Jews and Gentiles, Protestants and Catholics, will be able to join hands and sing in the words of that old Negro spiritual, "Free at last! Free at last! Thank God almighty, we are free at last!"

For Study and Discussion

Analyzing and Interpreting the Selection

1. Martin Luther King, Jr., uses several images, or pictures, to express his dream. What are some of the pictures that he sees when he dreams of the perfect America?

2. King repeats "Let freedom ring!" **a.** What song is this line from? **b.** How do you think King's use of this line would affect an audience?

3. In paragraph 6, King quotes from the Biblical prophet Isaiah. Isaiah looked forward to the time when the Israelites would be led out of exile and bondage, back to their own home. Isaiah imagined that for his people's triumphant march home, mountains would be lowered, rocky places would be made into plains, and so on. What connection do you think King saw between his dream and Isaiah's?

About the Author

Martin Luther King, Jr. (1929–1968)

Martin Luther King, Jr., was a Baptist minister with a doctorate in theology from Boston University. During his graduate studies, he read from the works of the American writer Henry David Thoreau and the Indian leader Mahatma Gandhi. Both of these men advocated using nonviolent resistance to bring about social and political change. Their writings convinced King that these principles could be used to win civil rights for black people in America. Dr. King worked tirelessly for his goals. In 1957 alone, he traveled 700,000 miles and delivered 200 speeches. He spent time in jail. He preached, he marched, he wrote. In 1964 Dr. King was awarded the Nobel Prize for Peace. In 1968 he was killed by an assassin's bullet.

DEVELOPING SKILLS
IN CRITICAL THINKING

Predicting Probable Future Actions and Outcomes

When we read, we constantly make predictions about what will happen next. A good story inspires us to anticipate actions. In fact, some stories leave the ending entirely to the reader's imagination.

In "Too Soon a Woman" (page 162), the narrator gives clues to what will happen between Mary and the father. As Pa leaves the family to find food, he directs the eleven-year-old to do as Mary tells him. He shows that he trusts Mary with his children and has confidence in her judgment. When Pa returns with the pack horse and the children run out to meet him, he asks, "Where's the other one?" Here he shows a guarded interest in Mary, although he does not even call her by name. The narrator's observation that "The sun began to shine" gives a clue to what will happen. It does not come as a surprise that Mary marries Pa and becomes the children's stepmother.

Choose one of the stories you have read. Pick out clues that allow you to anticipate the outcome of events or the ending of the story. For example, how does the author of "Raymond's Run" (page 21) prepare you for the narrator's decision to coach Raymond? How does the characterization of Nace in "Top Man" (page 51) prepare you for his valiant rescue of Osborn?

PRACTICE IN READING AND WRITING

Expository Writing

The form of writing we use most frequently is exposition. Exposition is the kind of writing that explains something or gives information. Science and history books, reports, and even directions on how to assemble a piece of furniture all make use of exposition.

This paragraph from the true story "Barrio Boy" (page 188) is a good example of effective exposition. In it, the author gives specific examples to illustrate how, at his school, making students into "Americans" did not scrub away what made them originally "foreign."

At Lincoln, making us into Americans did not mean scrubbing away what made us originally foreign. The teachers called us as our parents did, or as close as they could pronounce our names in Spanish or Japanese. No one was ever scolded or punished for speaking in his native tongue on the playground. Matti told the class about his mother's down quilt, which she had made in Italy with the fine feathers of a thousand geese. Encarnación acted out how boys learned to fish in the Philippines. I astounded the third grade with the story of my travels on a stagecoach, which nobody else in the class had seen except in the museum at Sutter's Fort. After a visit to the Crocker Art Gallery and its collection of heroic paintings of the golden age of California, someone showed a silk scroll with a Chinese painting. Miss Hopley herself had a way of expressing wonder over these matters before a class, her eyes wide open until they popped slightly. It was easy for me to feel that becoming a proud American, as she said we should, did not mean feeling ashamed of being a Mexican.

1. What is the sentence that states the topic, or main idea?
2. What details or examples support the topic sentence?

Suggestions for Writing

Write an expository composition in which you explain something to your readers or audience. You might explain how to get somewhere, how to make or do something, or how something works. If you wish, write an essay informing your audience of something: for example, the importance of ironclad ships during the Civil War.

Here are some guidelines to help you plan, write, and revise your composition.

Prewriting
- Choose a subject and limit it to a topic that you can treat adequately in a short composition.
- Identify your audience. What do they already know about the topic? Will you need to give background information on your topic? Use the *5 W-How?* questions (*Who? What? Where? When? Why?* and *How?*) to gather specific details, examples, or reasons to support your topic.

- Use an outline to organize your topic logically. If you are giving information on how to make fried chicken, you will have to organize your details in chronological order—the order in which the preparations take place. If you are giving examples to support an opinion, you might want to begin or end your paper with your most forceful statement.
- Decide on the main idea for each paragraph and provide specific details to support each main idea.

Writing
- Begin your composition with a *thesis statement*. It states the purpose of your paper and tells what you will write about.
- Use your outline as a guide to help you develop each paragraph in your paper.
- Support each main idea with specific details, examples, reasons.

Evaluating and Revising
- Is the topic limited enough for your paper?
- Did you begin with a thesis statement?
- Have you given enough information for your audience to understand the topic?
- Does each paragraph discuss only one main idea?
- Are the ideas arranged in a logical order?
- Add, cut, replace, or reorder details until you are satisfied with your paper.

Proofreading and Making a Final Copy
- Check your paper for errors in grammar, usage, and mechanics.
- Prepare a final copy and check it for accuracy.

For Further Reading

Cather, Willa, *My Ántonia* (Houghton Mifflin, 1918; paperback, Houghton; repr. Thorndike, 1986)

This novel of pioneer days in Nebraska centers around the struggles of a poor immigrant family from Bohemia. Ántonia is the family's lively, beautiful daughter.

Clapp, Patricia, *Constance: A Story of Early Plymouth* (Lothrop, Lee & Shepard, 1968; paperback, Dell)

A fifteen-year-old girl begins her journal when the *Mayflower* arrives in the New World.

Collier, James Lincoln, and Christopher Collier, *Jump Ship to Freedom* (Delacorte Press, 1981)

Jack, a slave in the 1700s, earns his family's freedom by fighting in the Revolutionary War. When the papers granting freedom to Jack's family are lost, his fourteen-year-old son makes a daring attempt to get them but winds up as a slave on a ship bound for the West Indies.

Edmonds, Walter, *Bert Breen's Barn* (Little Brown, 1975)

This suspenseful novel centers around a poor boy who acquires a barn that may have a treasure hidden in it.

Freedman, Benedict, and Nancy Freedman, *Mrs. Mike* (Coward-McCann, 1947; paperback, Berkley, 1984)

A young Boston woman, Kathie O'Fallon, goes with her husband, a Canadian mountie, to live in a cabin near the Arctic Circle.

Hunt, Irene, *Across Five Aprils* (Follett Publishing, 1964; paperback, Ace Books, 1984)

The five Aprils are the years of the Civil War, which profoundly affect young Jethro Creighton and his family, who live on a farm in Illinois.

Keith, Harold, *Rifles for Watie* (Thomas Y. Crowell, 1957)

Young Jeff Bussey longs to be a Union soldier, but he soon learns that war is not glamorous and that enemies are human.

Lane, Rose Wilder, *Let the Hurricane Roar* (Longmans, Green, 1933; paperback, Harper, 1985)

This novel tells about a young homesteading couple in the Dakotas who must face the grim realities of pioneer life. The story is told by the daughter of Laura, one of the sisters in the *Little House on the Prairie* books.

Sandburg, Carl, *Abe Lincoln Grows Up* (Harcourt Brace Jovanovich, 1940, repr. 1985; paperback)

The greatest biographer of Lincoln tells the story, with illustrations, of Lincoln's boyhood years on the prairie.

Taylor, Mildred O., *Let the Circle Be Unbroken* (Dial Press, 1981)

The year is 1935 and the Logan family experiences many hardships living in Mississippi. The entire family regains pride and self-respect from their unsettling experiences.

Uchida, Yoshiko, *A Jar of Dreams* (McElderry Books, 1981)

Rinko, an eleven-year-old girl, and her family have a hard time living in California because they are Japanese. Aunt Wuka helps the family deal with their problems and encourages Rinko to pursue her dream of becoming a teacher.

Wartski, Maureen Crane, *A Long Way from Home* (Signet Vista Books, 1982)

A Vietnamese boy is unable to adjust to his new family in America and runs away. He comes to realize the only way to solve his problems is to face up to them.

Wibberley, Leonard, *John Treegate's Musket* (Farrar, Straus & Giroux, 1959)

In this first of a series of four novels about the Treegate family, young Peter becomes involved in murder and shipwreck in the years preceding the Revolutionary War.

PART II

FORMS OF LITERATURE

SHORT STORIES

The Blue Pool (1911) by Augustus John (1878–1961).
Oil on panel.
Aberdeen Art Gallery and Museums

CLOSE READING
OF A SHORT STORY

Developing Skills in Critical Thinking

A short story is like a little piece of life. A short-story writer creates characters and places them in a situation. In a good story, you keep on reading because you are eager to find out what happens to the characters. You have become interested in them as if they were living people.

Some stories are told purely for fun. "The Rule of Names" in this unit is an example of a story that is told just to entertain you. But most stories also have something serious to say about life and people.

A short story is made up of certain basic elements: *plot* (the sequence of related events); *characters* (persons, animals, or things presented as persons); *point of view* (the standpoint from which the writer tells the story); *setting* (the time and place of the action); and *theme* (the underlying idea about human life). The better you, the individual reader, understand how these elements work together, the better you will understand and appreciate the author's intent and meaning.

Here is a brief story that has been read carefully by an experienced reader. The notes in the margin show how this reader thinks in working through a story. Read the story at least twice before proceeding to the analysis on page 207. You may wish to make notes of your own on a separate piece of paper as you read.

The Gift
RAY BRADBURY

Tomorrow would be Christmas, and even while the three of them rode to the rocket port the mother and father were worried. It was the boy's first flight into space, his very first time in a rocket, and they wanted everything to be perfect. So when, at the

Thinking Model

First clue that this is science fiction. Space travel has become commonplace, even for children.

customs table,[1] they were forced to leave behind his gift, which exceeded the weight limit by no more than a few ounces, and the little tree with the lovely white candles, they felt themselves deprived of the season and their love.

The boy was waiting for them in the Terminal room. Walking toward him, after their unsuccessful clash with the Interplanetary officials, the mother and father whispered to each other.

"What shall we do?"

"Nothing, nothing, What *can* we do?"

"Silly rules!"

"And he so wanted the tree!"

The siren gave a great howl and people pressed forward into the Mars Rocket. The mother and father walked at the very last, their small pale son between them, silent.

"I'll think of something," said the father.

"What . . .?" asked the boy.

And the rocket took off and they were flung headlong into dark space.

The rocket moved and left fire behind and left Earth behind on which the date was December 24, 2052, heading out into a place where there was no time at all, no month, no year, no hour. They slept away the rest of the first "day." Near midnight, by their Earth-time New York watches, the boy awoke and said, "I want to go look out the porthole."

There was only one port, a "window" of immensely thick glass of some size, up on the next deck.

"Not quite yet," said the father. "I'll take you up later."

"I want to see where we are and where we're going."

"I want you to wait for a reason," said the father.

---

1. **customs table:** an area in an airport or pier where goods and baggage coming into or leaving a country are inspected and duties are paid.

Opening paragraph brings together the old and the new—Christmas, with its tradition of gift-giving, and transportation by spaceship.

A problem develops when the boy's Christmas gift must be left behind.

How is the author going to make use of this problem in the story?

Why is the tree so important to the boy?

Special equipment for space travel is no longer required.

The concept of Earth time is not relevant in outer space, yet passengers still use their watches to tell time.

Space travelers are no longer troubled by weightlessness; they can move about freely.

He had been lying awake, turning this way and that, thinking of the abandoned gift, the problem of the season, the lost tree and the white candles. And at last, sitting up, no more than five minutes ago, he believed he had found a plan. He need only carry it out and this journey would be fine and joyous indeed.

What is the father's plan?

"Son," he said, "in exactly one half hour it will be Christmas."

"Oh," said the mother, dismayed that he had mentioned it. Somehow she had rather hoped that the boy would forget.

The boy's face grew feverish and his lips trembled. "I know, I know. Will I get a present, will I? Will I have a tree? Will I have a tree? You promised—"

"Yes, yes, all that, and more," said the father.

The mother started. "But—"

"I mean it," said the father. "I really mean it. All and more, much more. Excuse me, now. I'll be back."

How will the father keep his promise?

He left them for about twenty minutes. When he came back, he was smiling. "Almost time."

Where has he gone, and what has he done?

"Can I hold your watch?" asked the boy, and the watch was handed over and he held it ticking in his fingers as the rest of the hour drifted by in fire and silence and unfelt motion.

"It's Christmas *now!* Christmas! Where's my present?"

How will the family celebrate Christmas in deep space?

"Here we go," said the father and took his boy by the shoulder and led him from the room, down the hall, up a rampway, his wife following.

"I don't understand," she kept saying.

"You will. Here we are," said the father.

They had stopped at the closed door of a large cabin. The father tapped three times and then twice in a code. The door opened and the light in the cabin went out and there was a whisper of voices.

"Go on in, son," said the father.

"It's dark."

"I'll hold your hand. Come on, Mama."

They stepped into the room and the door shut, and the room was very dark indeed. And before them loomed a great glass eye, the porthole, a window four feet high and six feet wide, from which they could look out into space.

The boy gasped.

Behind him, the father and the mother gasped with him, and then in the dark room some people began to sing.

"Merry Christmas, son," said the father.

And the voices in the room sang the old, the familiar carols, and the boy moved slowly until his face was pressed against the cool glass of the port. And he stood there for a long, long time, just looking and looking out into space and the deep night at the burning and the burning of ten billion billion white and lovely candles. . . .

The code signals, darkness, and whispering suggest secrecy. What kind of surprise is coming?

Author builds suspense by recording the characters' reactions.

The climax, the most exciting part of the story, resolves the problem in a logical and satisfying way. The boy gets his wish.

A new concept of gift-giving emerges. The "gift" is the beauty of the stars.

Analysis

In science-fiction stories, it is customary for human beings to encounter unusual life forms and strange experiences in outer space. In Ray Bradbury's story "The Gift," there are no fantastic creatures or time warps. Bradbury's concern is with what happens to old, familiar traditions as they pass into the world of the future. How will we be affected by the changes?

"The Gift" takes place in the middle of the twenty-first century. Interplanetary travel has become so commonplace that it is conducted very much as air travel is today. The problems caused by weightlessness in space have been solved; the passengers need no special equipment to make the trip to Mars. There are baggage limitations for the rocket ship, just as there are for commercial air carriers today. Space travel is safe enough for children.

The opening paragraph establishes the situation concisely. We learn that a family is going to spend the Christmas season away from Earth. This is obviously a special trip for the family, perhaps a holiday trip planned for the boy's first flight into space. A problem develops when their baggage is weighed and found to exceed the limit. The boy's Christmas present and a little tree with white candles must be left behind.

The Christmas tree is obviously important to the boy. Perhaps the Christmas tree has a special meaning to him because he is leaving Earth for Mars, and the tree reminds him of past holidays spent at home. Traditions are important to this boy. Later in the story he wishes to hold his father's watch so that he can mark the moment when Christmas arrives. Like most children, he can hardly wait for Christmas to come so that he can "open" his present. The parents, too, feel "deprived of the season and their love." They wish to give the boy what he wants.

The solution of this dilemma forms the main action of the story. The father puzzles over the problem for an entire day. Finally, he has a plan for a new gift to take the place of the tree. As the story builds toward the climax in the port cabin, there are hints of what the surprise will be. When the boy asks to look out the porthole, the father asks him to wait "for a reason." The father's plan takes into account the "abandoned gift" and the season. He promises his son that he will have a tree "and more."

At midnight the father leads the boy and his mother to a large cabin. He signals by a prearranged code, and the family is admitted to the port cabin. The father has arranged for a group of passengers to meet at twelve o'clock to celebrate Christmas. The "gift" to his son is a spectacular view of the galaxy, with the night sky lighted by innumerable brilliant stars.

The joyous ending of Bradbury's story resolves the problem in a logical and satisfying way. The boy gets his wish, but instead of an artificial tree with white candles, he is treated to a dazzling display of lighting effects that no celebration on Earth could equal. The ending also affirms the spirit of Christmas as a tradition that will continue to form a bond among future generations, whether they are earthbound or space travelers.

This analysis of "The Gift" tells more than the events of the story as they happen. It analyzes the *structure* of the story, making apparent the interconnection of setting, characters, and events. It explains how the major action of the story develops out of a problem—the abandoned Christmas gift—and how the ending of the story provides the solution for the problem. It also suggests that the underlying meaning of the story is concerned with the continuity and evolution of traditions.

The purpose of this exercise has been to demonstrate what is meant by the *close reading* of a story. When you read a story carefully, you read actively, responding to clues, anticipating outcomes, seeking to understand how different elements are related to the overall structure of the story.

With practice you can develop skill in reading and analyzing a literary work. Here are some guidelines for reading a short story.

Guidelines for Reading a Short Story

1. *Look up unfamiliar words and references.* In Ray Bradbury's story, the phrase "customs table" is defined in a footnote. If you feel uncertain about the meaning of a word and cannot get the meaning from context clues, be sure to check in a standard dictionary or other reference work.

2. *Learn to draw inferences.* The author does not tell you directly that the boy is disappointed and upset. However, you are told that the boy enters the rocket ship "pale" and "silent." When his father announces that it is almost Christmas day, the boy's face grows "feverish," and his lips tremble.

3. *Actively question the author's purpose and method.* Ask yourself what significance there might be to details that the author gives you. Why, for example, does the father want the boy to wait before going up to the port? Where does the father go when he leaves the family for twenty minutes? As you read, try to anticipate what is coming.

4. *Probe for the central idea or point.* "The Gift," like many of the stories included in this textbook, has an underlying meaning, or *theme*, which makes a comment on human nature. The story suggests that human beings will hold on to their time-honored customs, and that traditions will continue to form a bond between future generations. Theme is seldom stated directly. Generally, it must be inferred from the characters and their actions.

A Retrieved Reformation

O. HENRY

People don't always behave in predictable ways—in fact, they often do things that can't be easily explained. In this story, a sequence of events leads more than one character to a change of heart.

A guard came to the prison shoeshop, where Jimmy Valentine was assiduously[1] stitching uppers, and escorted him to the front office. There the warden handed Jimmy his pardon, which had been signed that morning by the Governor. Jimmy took it in a tired kind of way. He had served nearly ten months of a four-year sentence. He had expected to stay only about three months, at the longest. When a man with as many friends on the outside as Jimmy Valentine had is received in the "stir," it is hardly worthwhile to cut his hair.

"Now, Valentine," said the warden, "you'll go out in the morning. Brace up, and make a man of yourself. You're not a bad fellow at heart. Stop cracking safes, and live straight."

"Me?" said Jimmy, in surprise. "Why, I never cracked a safe in my life."

"Oh, no," laughed the warden. "Of course not. Let's see, now. How was it you happened to get sent up on that Springfield job? Was it because you wouldn't prove an alibi for fear of compromising somebody in extremely high-toned society? Or was it simply a case of a mean old jury that had it in for you? It's always one or the other with you innocent victims."

"Me?" said Jimmy, still blankly virtuous. "Why, Warden, I never was in Springfield in my life!"

"Take him back, Cronin," smiled the warden, "and fix him with outgoing clothes. Unlock him at seven in the morning, and let him come to the bullpen.[2] Better think over my advice, Valentine."

At a quarter past seven on the next morning Jimmy stood in the warden's outer office. He had on a suit of the villainously fitting, ready-made clothes and a pair of the stiff, squeaky shoes that the state furnishes to its discharged compulsory guests.

The clerk handed him a railroad ticket and the five-dollar bill with which the law expected him to rehabilitate himself into good citizenship and prosperity. The warden gave him a cigar, and shook hands. Valentine, 9762, was chronicled on the books "Pardoned by Governor," and Mr. James Valentine walked out into the sunshine.

Disregarding the song of the birds, the waving green trees, and the smell of the flowers, Jimmy headed straight for a restaurant. There

---

1. **assiduously** (ə-sĭj′ōō-əs-lē): steadily and busily.

2. **bullpen:** a barred room where prisoners are held temporarily.

he tasted the first sweet joys of liberty in the shape of a broiled chicken and a bottle of white wine—followed by a cigar a grade better than the one the warden had given him. From there he proceeded leisurely to the depot. He tossed a quarter into the hat of a blind man sitting by the door and boarded his train. Three hours set him down in a little town near the state line. He went to the café of one Mike Dolan and shook hands with Mike, who was alone behind the bar.

"Sorry we couldn't make it sooner, Jimmy, me boy," said Mike. "But we had that protest from Springfield to buck against, and the Governor nearly balked. Feeling all right?"

"Fine," said Jimmy. "Got my key?"

He got his key and went upstairs, unlocking the door of a room at the rear. Everything was just as he had left it. There on the floor was still Ben Price's collar button that had been torn from that eminent detective's shirt band when they had overpowered Jimmy to arrest him.

Pulling out from a wall a folding bed, Jimmy slid back a panel in the wall and dragged out a dust-covered suitcase. He opened this and gazed fondly at the finest set of burglar's tools in the East. It was a complete set, made of specially tempered steel, the latest designs in drills, punches, braces and bits, jimmies, clamps, and augers,[3] with two or three novelties invented by Jimmy himself, in which he took pride. Over nine hundred dollars they had cost him to have made at——, a place where they make such things for the profession.

In half an hour Jimmy went downstairs and through the café. He was now dressed in tasteful and well-fitting clothes and carried his dusted and cleaned suitcase in his hand.

"Got anything on?" asked Mike Dolan genially.

"Me?" said Jimmy, in a puzzled tone. "I don't understand. I'm representing the New York Amalgamated Short Snap Biscuit Cracker and Frazzled Wheat Company."

This statement delighted Mike to such an extent that Jimmy had to take a seltzer and milk on the spot. He never touched "hard" drinks.

A week after the release of Valentine, 9762, there was a neat job of safe burglary done in Richmond, Indiana, with no clue to the author. A scant eight hundred dollars was all that was secured. Two weeks after that a patented, improved, burglarproof safe in Logansport was opened like a cheese to the tune of fifteen hundred dollars, currency; securities and silver untouched. That began to interest the rogue-catchers.[4] Then an old-fashioned bank safe in Jefferson City became active and threw out of its crater an eruption of bank notes amounting to five thousand dollars. The losses were now high enough to bring the matter up into Ben Price's class of work. By comparing notes, a remarkable similarity in the methods of the burglaries was noticed. Ben Price investigated the scenes of the robberies and was heard to remark:

"That's Dandy Jim Valentine's autograph. He's resumed business. Look at that combination knob—jerked out as easy as pulling up a radish in wet weather. He's got the only clamps that can do it. And look how clean those tumblers were punched out! Jimmy never has to drill but one hole. Yes, I guess I want Mr. Valentine. He'll do his bit next time without any short-time or clemency foolishness."

Ben Price knew Jimmy's habits. He had learned them while working up the Springfield case. Long jumps, quick getaways, no confederates,[5] and a taste for good society—these ways

---

3. **drills . . . augers** (ô′gərz): tools for working with metal.

4. **rogue-catchers:** an elaborate way of describing the police.
5. **confederates:** accomplices.

had helped Mr. Valentine to become noted as a successful dodger of retribution.[6] It was given out that Ben Price had taken up the trail of the elusive cracksman, and other people with burglarproof safes felt more at ease.

One afternoon Jimmy Valentine and his suitcase climbed out of the mail hack[7] in Elmore, a little town five miles off the railroad down in the blackjack country of Arkansas. Jimmy, looking like an athletic young senior just home from college, went down the board sidewalk toward the hotel.

A young lady crossed the street, passed him at the corner, and entered a door over which was the sign "The Elmore Bank." Jimmy Valentine looked into her eyes, forgot what he was, and became another man. She lowered her eyes and colored slightly. Young men of Jimmy's style and looks were scarce in Elmore.

Jimmy collared a boy that was loafing on the steps of the bank as if he were one of the stockholders, and began to ask him questions about the town, feeding him dimes at intervals. By and by the young lady came out, looking royally unconscious of the young man with the suitcase, and went her way.

"Isn't that young lady Miss Polly Simpson?" asked Jimmy with specious guile.[8]

"Naw," said the boy. "She's Annabel Adams. Her pa owns this bank. What'd you come to Elmore for? Is that a gold watch chain? I'm going to get a bulldog. Got any more dimes?"

6. **retribution:** (rĕt′rə-byōō′shən): punishment.
7. **mail hack:** a horse-drawn carriage used to carry mail from one town to another.
8. **with specious** (spē′shəs) **guile** (gīl): in a tricky way that appears to be innocent.

Safe Money (c. 1889) by Victor Dubreuil.
Oil on canvas.
Collection of The Corcoran Gallery of Art, Museum Purchase through a gift from the heirs of George E. Lemon

Jimmy went to Planters' Hotel, registered as Ralph D. Spencer, and engaged a room. He leaned on the desk and declared his platform[9] to the clerk. He said he had come to Elmore to look for a location to go into business. How was the shoe business, now, in the town? He had thought of the shoe business. Was there an opening?

The clerk was impressed by the clothes and manner of Jimmy. He, himself, was something of a pattern of fashion to the thinly gilded[10] youth of Elmore, but now he perceived his shortcomings. While trying to figure out Jimmy's manner of tying his four-in-hand,[11] he cordially gave information.

Yes, there ought to be a good opening in the shoe line. There wasn't an exclusive shoe store in the place. The dry goods and general stores handled them. Business in all lines was fairly good. Hoped Mr. Spencer would decide to locate in Elmore. He would find it a pleasant town to live in, and the people very sociable.

Mr. Spencer thought he would stop over in the town a few days and look over the situation. No, the clerk needn't call the boy. He would carry up his suitcase, himself; it was rather heavy.

Mr. Ralph Spencer, the phoenix[12] that arose from Jimmy Valentine's ashes—ashes left by the flame of a sudden and alterative[13] attack of love—remained in Elmore and prospered. He opened a shoe store and secured a good run of trade.

Socially he was also a success and made many friends. And he accomplished the wish of his heart. He met Miss Annabel Adams and

9. **platform:** here, intentions; plans.
10. **thinly gilded:** only seeming to be well-dressed. To be *gilded* is to be covered with a layer of gold.
11. **four-in-hand:** a necktie.
12. **phoenix:** (fē′nĭks): a bird in ancient Egyptian mythology. It was believed that the phoenix burned itself up and that from its ashes a new bird arose.
13. **alterative** (ôl′tə-rā′tĭv): causing an alteration, or change. Jimmy's love changed him.

Scenes on pages 214 and 217 are from the Broadway theater production of *Alias Jimmy Valentine* (1910).

became more and more captivated by her charms.

At the end of a year the situation of Mr. Ralph Spencer was this: he had won the respect of the community, his shoe store was flourishing, and he and Annabel were engaged to be married in two weeks. Mr. Adams, the typical, plodding country banker, approved of Spencer. Annabel's pride in him almost equaled her affection. He was as much at home in the family of Mr. Adams and that of Annabel's married sister as if he were already a member.

One day Jimmy sat down in his room and wrote this letter, which he mailed to the safe address of one of his old friends in St. Louis:

Dear Old Pal:

I want you to be at Sullivan's place in Little Rock, next Wednesday night, at nine o'clock. I want you to wind up some little matters for me. And, also, I want to make you a present of my little kit of tools. I know you'll be glad to get them—you couldn't duplicate the lot for a thousand dollars. Say, Billy, I've quit the old business—a year ago. I've got a nice store. I'm making an honest living, and I'm going to marry the finest girl on earth two weeks from now. It's the only life, Billy—the straight one. I wouldn't touch a dollar of another man's money now for a million. After I get married I'm going to sell out and go West, where there won't be so much danger of having old scores brought up against me. I tell you, Billy, she's an angel. She believes in me; and I wouldn't do another crooked thing for the whole world. Be sure to be at Sully's, for I must see you. I'll bring along the tools with me.

Your old friend,
Jimmy

On the Monday night after Jimmy wrote this letter, Ben Price jogged unobtrusively[14] into Elmore in a livery buggy.[15] He lounged about town in his quiet way until he found out what he wanted to know. From the drugstore across the street from Spencer's shoe store, he got a good look at Ralph D. Spencer.

"Going to marry the banker's daughter, are you, Jimmy?" said Ben to himself softly. "Well, I don't know!"

The next morning Jimmy took breakfast at the Adamses'. He was going to Little Rock that day to order his wedding suit and buy something nice for Annabel. That would be the first time he had left town since he came to Elmore. It had been more than a year now since those last professional "jobs," and he thought he could safely venture out.

After breakfast quite a family party went downtown together—Mr. Adams, Annabel, Jimmy, and Annabel's married sister with her two little girls, aged five and nine. They came

by the hotel where Jimmy still boarded, and he ran up to his room and brought along his suitcase. Then they went on to the bank. There stood Jimmy's horse and buggy and Dolph Gibson, who was going to drive him over to the railroad station.

All went inside the high, carved oak railings into the banking room—Jimmy included, for Mr. Adams' future son-in-law was welcome anywhere. The clerks were pleased to be greeted by the good-looking, agreeable young man who was going to marry Miss Annabel. Jimmy set his suitcase down. Annabel, whose heart was bubbling with happiness and lively youth, put on Jimmy's hat and picked up the suitcase. "Wouldn't I make a nice drummer?"[16] asked Annabel. "My! Ralph, how heavy it is! Feels like it was full of gold bricks."

"Lot of nickel-plated shoehorns in there," said Jimmy coolly, "that I'm going to return. Thought I'd save express charges by taking them up. I'm getting awfully economical."

The Elmore Bank had just put in a new safe and vault. Mr. Adams was very proud of it and insisted on an inspection by everyone. The vault was a small one, but it had a new patented door. It fastened with three solid steel bolts thrown simultaneously with a single handle, and had a time lock. Mr. Adams beamingly explained its workings to Mr. Spencer, who showed a courteous but not too intelligent interest. The two children, May and Agatha, were delighted by the shining metal and funny clock and knobs.

While they were thus engaged, Ben Price sauntered in and leaned on his elbow, looking casually inside between the railings. He told the teller that he didn't want anything; he was just waiting for a man he knew.

Suddenly there was a scream or two from the women and a commotion. Unperceived by

14. **unobtrusively** (ŭn′əb-trōō′sĭv-lē): without attracting attention.
15. **livery buggy:** a hired horse and carriage.

16. **drummer:** here, a traveling salesman.

the elders, May, the nine-year-old girl, in a spirit of play had shut Agatha in the vault. She had then shot the bolts and turned the knob of the combination as she had seen Mr. Adams do.

The old banker sprang to the handle and tugged at it for a moment. "The door can't be opened," he groaned. "The clock hasn't been wound nor the combination set."

Agatha's mother screamed again, hysterically.

"Hush!" said Mr. Adams, raising his trembling hand. "All be quiet for a moment. Agatha!" he called as loudly as he could. "Listen to me." During the following silence they could just hear the faint sound of the child wildly shrieking in the dark vault in a panic of terror.

"My precious darling!" wailed the mother. "She will die of fright! Open the door! Oh, break it open! Can't you men do something?"

"There isn't a man nearer than Little Rock who can open that door," said Mr. Adams, in a shaky voice. "Spencer, what shall we do? That child—she can't stand it long in there. There isn't enough air, and, besides, she'll go into convulsions from fright."

Agatha's mother, frantic now, beat the door of the vault with her hands. Somebody wildly suggested dynamite. Annabel turned to Jimmy, her large eyes full of anguish, but not yet despairing. To a woman nothing seems quite impossible to the powers of the man she worships.

"Can't you do something, Ralph—try, won't you?"

He looked at her with a queer, soft smile on his lips and in his keen eyes.

"Annabel," he said, "give me that rose you are wearing, will you?"

Hardly believing that she heard him aright, she unpinned the bud from the bosom of her dress, and placed it in his hand. Jimmy stuffed it into his vest pocket, threw off his coat, and pulled up his shirt sleeves. With that act Ralph D. Spencer passed away, and Jimmy Valentine took his place.

"Get away from the door, all of you," he commanded, shortly.

He set his suitcase on the table, and opened it out flat. From that time on he seemed to be unconscious of the presence of anyone else. He laid out the shining, queer implements swiftly and orderly, whistling softly to himself as he always did when at work. In a deep silence and immovable, the others watched him as if under a spell.

In a minute Jimmy's pet drill was biting smoothly into the steel door. In ten minutes—breaking his own burglarious record—he threw back the bolts and opened the door.

Agatha, almost collapsed, but safe, was gathered into her mother's arms.

Jimmy Valentine put on his coat, and walked outside the railings toward the front door. As he went he thought he heard a faraway voice that he once knew call "Ralph!" But he never hesitated.

At the door a big man stood somewhat in his way.

"Hello, Ben!" said Jimmy, still with his strange smile. "Got around at last, have you? Well, let's go. I don't know that it makes much difference, now."

And then Ben Price acted rather strangely.

"Guess you're mistaken, Mr. Spencer," he said. "Don't believe I recognize you. Your buggy's waiting for you, ain't it?"

And Ben Price turned and strolled down the street.

Reading Check

1. Why had Jimmy Valentine been in prison?
2. What is unusual about the contents of Jimmy's suitcase?
3. Identify Ben Price.
4. What business does Jimmy go into in Elmore?
5. How does Agatha get locked in the vault?

For Study and Discussion

Analyzing and Interpreting the Story

1. At the beginning of the story, the prison warden tells Jimmy Valentine to stop cracking safes and reform. What does Jimmy do after his release that shows he plans to ignore the warden's advice?

2a. How does the power of love make Jimmy decide to "go straight"? **b.** Describe the new life that Jimmy has created for himself at the end of a year in Elmore.

3. The reader knows that Ben Price, the great detective, is on Jimmy's trail. But Jimmy himself is unaware of this danger. How do you think Ben Price finds out that Jimmy is in Elmore?

4. When he opens the safe to free Agatha, Jimmy believes he is destroying his chances for a new life. However, opening the safe actually *saves* Jimmy's happiness. Why doesn't Ben Price arrest Jimmy?

5. *Retrieved* means "brought back" or "recaptured." A *reformation* is a "change" or "improvement." **a.** How was Jimmy's reformation endangered? **b.** How was it "retrieved"?

6. What other stories, films, or television shows do you know that feature a good-hearted detective like Ben Price, or a tough character like Jimmy Valentine transformed by the power of love?

Literary Elements

Following the Plot

At the beginning of this story, you meet Jimmy Valentine in jail, where he has already spent ten months for breaking the law. At the end of the story, Jimmy is a reformed character. The series of events in the story, or the **plot,** tells you how this change occurs in the hero. In other words, plot is "what happens" in a story.

At the heart of every plot there is a **conflict,** or struggle. Often the character wants something that pits him or her in a struggle against someone or something else.

Conflicts with another person, an animal, or a force of nature, such as a hurricane, are called **external conflicts.** What is Jimmy's external conflict? Many stories also include **internal conflicts.** These are struggles that take place within a character's mind or feel-ings. Internal conflicts often involve decisions. How does Agatha's imprisonment in the vault force Jimmy into a difficult internal conflict?

In most stories there is a **climax,** or turning point. At this point you know whether the story will end happily or unhappily. The climax is a time of great suspense or emotion. It is usually the most exciting and tense part of the story. Which scene in this story would you say is the climax? What were your feelings at that point?

One of Jimmy's conflicts is finally resolved when he meets Ben Price after the safecracking scene. Were you surprised at Ben's actions at the end of the story? Did this ending satisfy you? Why or why not?

Recognizing Irony

If you were to say "That's just great!" when you really mean that something is terrible, you would be using **irony.** When people speak ironically, they are saying just the opposite of what they mean, or the opposite of what is true. Can you explain the irony in O. Henry's description of prisoners as "compulsory guests"?

Often an entire situation is ironic. In other words, it turns out to be exactly the opposite of what should happen, or the opposite of what we would expect to happen. O. Henry is famous for the humorously ironic situations in his stories.

Why is it ironic that Jimmy Valentine, the notorious safecracker, should win the hand of the banker's daughter, with the banker's approval?

Why is it ironic that Jimmy thought that opening the safe to free Agatha would ruin his chances for happiness? (Would Ben Price have let Jimmy go if he hadn't observed what Jimmy did to save Agatha?)

Language and Vocabulary

Understanding Denotation and Connotation

In addition to their dictionary meanings, or **denotations,** words have suggested meanings, or **connotations.** We are told that when Jimmy leaves the prison, he is wearing *ready-made* clothes. The literal meaning, or denotation, of *ready-made* is "ready for use" or "not made for any particular customer." The suggested meaning, or connotation, of *ready-made* is "ordinary" or "commonplace." We can infer from context that Jimmy has been accustomed to having his clothes made to order.

In these sentences from the story, what do the italicized words denote, and what additional feelings and qualities do they connote?

A guard came to the prison shoeshop, where Jimmy Valentine was assiduously stitching uppers, and *escorted* him to the front office.

Then an old-fashioned bank safe in Jefferson City became active and threw out of its crater an *eruption* of bank notes amounting to five thousand dollars.

There wasn't an *exclusive* shoe store in the place.

Creative Writing

Writing a Letter to an Imaginary Character

"A Retrieved Reformation" ends with the idea that Jimmy has truly reformed and will not go back to jail. Imagine that Jimmy and Annabel marry and have children and that Jimmy decides to explain his former life and his change of heart to their children. Assume that you are Jimmy. Write a letter to your children in which you explain your life of crime and why you decided to "go straight." You might enjoy reading your letter to a small group of your classmates.

About the Author

O. Henry (1862–1910)

O. Henry wrote "A Retrieved Reformation" while he was a prisoner in the Ohio federal penitentiary, serving time for embezzling funds from a Texas bank. The character of Jimmy Valentine—the criminal with a heart—was based on a safecracker that O. Henry knew in prison. As *Alias Jimmy Valentine*, O. Henry's story became a successful Broadway play.

O. Henry was the pen name of William Sydney Porter, who grew up in Greensboro, North Carolina, and became an apprentice to a pharmacist. He moved to Texas to work on an uncle's ranch. Later he was a bookkeeper, a bank teller, a newspaper writer, and owner of a weekly newspaper called *The Rolling Stone.* When he was summoned for trial on the embezzlement charge, he jumped bail and fled to Honduras. A year and a half later, when he returned to Texas to visit his dying wife, he was arrested and spent the next three years in jail. By 1903 he was in New York City, where he roamed the parks, streets, and restaurants, talking to people and collecting story material. His stories—more than two hundred fifty in all—became immensely popular.

You can almost count on an O. Henry story to have a surprise ending. Two of his other stories that you might enjoy are "The Gift of the Magi" and "The Ransom of Red Chief."

The Rule of Names

URSULA K. LE GUIN

In this story of magic and mystery, one of the characters is a mighty dragon in disguise. As you read the story, pay attention to the author's clever clues about the dragon's disguise.

Mr. Underhill came out from under his hill, smiling and breathing hard. Each breath shot out of his nostrils as a double puff of steam, snow-white in the morning sunshine. Mr. Underhill looked up at the bright December sky and smiled wider than ever, showing snow-white teeth. Then he went down to the village.

"Morning, Mr. Underhill," said the villagers as he passed them in the narrow street between houses with conical, overhanging roofs like the fat red caps of toadstools. "Morning, morning!" he replied to each. (It was of course bad luck to wish anyone a *good* morning; a simple statement of the time of day was quite enough, in a place so permeated with Influences as Sattins Island, where a careless adjective might change the weather for a week.) All of them spoke to him, some with affection, some with affectionate disdain. He was all the little island had in the way of a wizard, and so deserved respect—but how could you respect a little fat man of fifty who waddled along with his toes turned in, breathing steam and smiling? He was no great shakes as a workman either. His fireworks were fairly elaborate but his elixirs[1] were weak. Warts he charmed off frequently reappeared after three days; tomatoes he enchanted grew no bigger

than cantaloupes; and those rare times when a strange ship stopped at Sattins Harbor, Mr. Underhill always stayed under his hill—for fear, he explained, of the evil eye. He was, in other words, a wizard the way walleyed[2] Gan was a carpenter: by default. The villagers made do with badly-hung doors and inefficient spells, for this generation, and relieved their annoyance by treating Mr. Underhill quite familiarly, as a mere fellow villager. They even asked him to dinner. Once he asked some of them to dinner, and served a splendid repast, with silver, crystal, damask,[3] roast goose, sparkling Andrades '639,[4] and plum pudding with hard sauce; but he was so nervous all through the meal that it took the joy out of it, and besides, everybody was hungry again half an hour afterward. He did not like anyone to visit his cave, not even the anteroom, beyond which in fact nobody had ever got. When he saw people approaching the hill he always came trotting out to meet them. "Let's sit out here under the pine trees!" he would say, smiling and waving towards the fir grove, or if it was raining, "Let's go have a drink at the inn,

1. **elixirs** (ĭ-lĭk′sərz): magic remedies.

2. **walleyed** (wôl′īd′): having eyes that turn outward.
3. **damask** (dăm′əsk): a fine fabric, which has a design woven into it. Here, the word refers to a tablecloth and napkins made from this fabric.
4. **Andrades '639:** a vintage of wine. The number '639 indicates the year.

Illustration by Wayne Anderson for *The Flight of Dragons* by
Peter Dickinson (1979).

eh?" though everybody knew he drank nothing stronger than well-water.

Some of the village children, teased by that
locked cave, poked and pried and made raids
while Mr. Underhill was away; but the small
door that led into the inner chamber was spell-
shut, and it seemed for once to be an effective
spell. Once a couple of boys, thinking the wizard was over on the West Shore curing Mrs.
Ruuna's sick donkey, brought a crowbar and a
hatchet up there, but at the first whack of the
hatchet on the door there came a roar of wrath

from inside, and a cloud of purple steam. Mr.
Underhill had got home early. The boys fled.
He did not come out, and the boys came to no
harm, though they said you couldn't believe
what a huge hooting howling hissing horrible
bellow that little fat man could make unless
you'd heard it.

His business in town this day was three
dozen fresh eggs and a pound of liver; also a
stop at Seacaptain Fogeno's cottage to renew
the seeing-charm on the old man's eyes (quite
useless when applied to a case of detached

retina,[5] but Mr. Underhill kept trying), and finally a chat with old Goody[6] Guld, the concertina[7]-maker's widow. Mr. Underhill's friends were mostly old people. He was timid with the strong young men of the village, and the girls were shy of him. "He makes me nervous he smiles so much" they all said, pouting, twisting silky ringlets round a finger. *Nervous* was a newfangled word, and their mothers all replied grimly, "Nervous my foot, *silliness* is the word for it. Mr. Underhill is a very respectable wizard!"

After leaving Goody Guld, Mr. Underhill passed by the school, which was being held this day out on the common. Since no one on Sattins Island was literate, there were no books to learn to read from and no desks to carve initials on and no blackboards to erase, and in fact no schoolhouse. On rainy days the children met in the loft of the Communal Barn, and got hay in their pants; on sunny days the schoolteacher, Palani, took them anywhere she felt like. Today, surrounded by thirty interested children under twelve and forty uninterested sheep under five, she was teaching an important item on the curriculum: the Rules of Names. Mr. Underhill, smiling shyly, paused to listen and watch. Palani, a plump, pretty girl of twenty, made a charming picture there in the wintry sunlight, sheep and children around her, a leafless oak above her, and behind her the dunes and sea and clear, pale sky. She spoke earnestly, her face flushed pink by wind and words. "Now you know the Rules of Names already, children. There are two, and they're the same on every island in the world. What's one of them?"

"It ain't polite to ask anybody what his name is," shouted a fat, quick boy, interrupted by a little girl shrieking, "You can't never tell your own name to nobody, my ma says!"

"Yes, Suba. Yes, Popi dear, don't screech. That's right. You never ask anybody his name. You never tell your own. Now think about that a minute and then tell me why we call our wizard Mr. Underhill." She smiled across the curly heads and the woolly backs at Mr. Underhill, who beamed, and nervously clutched his sack of eggs.

" 'Cause he lives under a hill!" said half the children.

"But is it his truename?"

"No!" said the fat boy, echoed by little Popi shrieking, "No!"

"How do you know it's not?"

" 'Cause he came here all alone and so there wasn't anybody knew his truename so they couldn't tell, and *he* couldn't——"

"Very good, Suba. Popi, don't shout. That's right. Even a wizard can't tell his truename. When you children are through school and go through the Passage, you'll leave your childnames behind and keep only your truenames, which you must never ask for and never give away. Why is that the rule?"

The children were silent. The sheep bleated gently. Mr. Underhill answered the question: "Because the name is the thing," he said in his shy, soft, husky voice, "and the truename is the true thing. To speak the name is to control the thing. Am I right, Schoolmistress?"

She smiled and curtsied, evidently a little embarrassed by his participation. And he trotted off towards his hill, clutching his eggs to his bosom. Somehow the minute spent watching Palani and the children had made him very hungry. He locked his inner door behind him with a hasty incantation,[8] but there must

---

5. **detached retina** (rĕt'n-ə): a serious visual disorder caused by damaged nerve tissue at the back of the eyeball.
6. **Goody:** a shortened form of *goodwife*, a title once used for married women of low social status.
7. **concertina:** a musical instrument similar to a small accordion.

8. **incantation:** a series of magic words used to cast a spell.

have been a leak or two in the spell, for soon the bare anteroom of the cave was rich with the smell of frying eggs and sizzling liver.

The wind that day was light and fresh out of the west, and on it at noon a little boat came skimming the bright waves into Sattins Harbor. Even as it rounded the point a sharp-eyed boy spotted it, and knowing, like every child on the island, every sail and spar of the forty boats of the fishing fleet, he ran down the street calling out, "A foreign boat, a foreign boat!" Very seldom was the lonely isle visited by a boat from some equally lonely isle of the East Reach, or an adventurous trader from the Archipelago.[9] By the time the boat was at the pier half the village was there to greet it, and fishermen were following it homewards, and cowherds and clam-diggers and herb-hunters were puffing up and down all the rocky hills, heading towards the harbor.

But Mr. Underhill's door stayed shut.

There was only one man aboard the boat. Old Seacaptain Fogeno, when they told him that, drew down a bristle of white brows over his unseeing eyes. "There's only one kind of man," he said, "that sails the Out Reach alone. A wizard, or a warlock, or a Mage. . . ."

So the villagers were breathless hoping to see for once in their lives a Mage, one of the mighty White Magicians of the rich, towered, crowded inner islands of the Archipelago. They were disappointed, for the voyager was quite young, a handsome black-bearded fellow who hailed them cheerfully from his boat, and leaped ashore like any sailor glad to have made port. He introduced himself at once as a sea-peddler. But when they told Seacaptain Fogeno that he carried an oaken walking-stick around with him, the old man nodded. "Two wizards in one town," he said. "Bad!" And his mouth snapped shut like an old carp's.

9. **Archipelago** (är′kə-pĕl′ə-gō′): a large group of islands.

As the stranger could not give them his name, they gave him one right away: Black-beard. And they gave him plenty of attention. He had a small mixed cargo of cloth and sandals and piswi feathers for trimming cloaks and cheap incense and levity stones and fine herbs and great glass beads from Venway—the usual peddler's lot. Everyone on Sattins Island came to look, to chat with the voyager, and perhaps to buy something—"Just to remember him by!" cackled Goody Guld, who like all the women and girls of the village was smitten with Blackbeard's bold good looks. All the boys hung round him too, to hear him tell of his voyages to far, strange islands of the Reach or describe the great rich islands of the Archipelago, the Inner Lanes, the roadsteads white with ships, and the golden roofs of Havnor. The men willingly listened to his tales; but some of them wondered why a trader should sail alone, and kept their eyes thoughtfully upon his oaken staff.

But all this time Mr. Underhill stayed under his hill.

"This is the first island I've ever seen that had no wizard," said Blackbeard one evening to Goody Guld, who had invited him and her nephew and Palani in for a cup of rushwash tea. "What do you do when you get a toothache, or the cow goes dry?"

"Why, we've got Mr. Underhill!" said the old woman.

"For what that's worth," muttered her nephew Birt, and then blushed purple and spilled his tea. Birt was a fisherman, a large, brave, wordless young man. He loved the schoolmistress, but the nearest he had come to telling her of his love was to give baskets of fresh mackerel to her father's cook.

"Oh, you do have a wizard?" Blackbeard asked. "Is he invisible?"

"No, he's just very shy," said Palani. "You've only been here a week, you know, and we see so few strangers here. . . ." She also blushed a little, but did not spill her tea.

Blackbeard smiled at her. "He's a good Sattinsman, then, eh?"

"No," said Goody Guld, "no more than you are. Another cup, nevvy?[10] — keep it in the cup this time. No, my dear, he came in a little bit of a boat, four years ago was it? — just a day after the end of the shad-run, I recall, for they was taking up the nets over in East Creek, and Pondi Cowherd broke his leg that very morning — five years ago it must be. No, four. No, five it is, 'twas the year the garlic didn't sprout. So he sails in on a bit of a sloop loaded full up with great chests and boxes and says to Seacaptain Fogeno, who wasn't blind then, though old enough goodness knows to be blind twice over, 'I hear tell,' he says, 'you've got no wizard nor warlock at all, might you be wanting one?' 'Indeed, if the magic's white!' says the Captain, and before you could say 'cuttlefish' Mr. Underhill had settled down in the cave under the hill and was charming the mange off Goody Beltow's cat. Though the fur grew in gray, and 'twas an orange cat. Queer-looking thing it was after that. It died last winter in the cold spell. Goody Beltow took on so at the cat's death, poor thing, worse than when her man was drowned on the Long Banks, the year of the long herring-runs, when nevvy Birt here was but a babe in petticoats." Here Birt spilled his tea again, and Blackbeard grinned, but Goody Guld proceeded undismayed, and talked on till nightfall.

Next day Blackbeard was down at the pier, seeing after the sprung board in his boat which he seemed to take a long time fixing, and as usual drawing the taciturn[11] Sattinsmen into talk. "Now which of these is your wizard's craft?" he asked. "Or has he got one of those

the Mages fold up into a walnut shell when they're not using it?"

"Nay," said a stolid fisherman. "She's oop in his cave, under hill."

"He carried the boat he came in up to his cave?"

"Aye. Clear opp. I helped. Heavier as lead she was. Full oop with great boxes, and they full oop with books o' spells, he says. Heavier as lead she was." And the stolid fisherman turned his back, sighing stolidly. Goody Guld's nephew, mending a net nearby, looked up from his work and asked with equal stolidity, "Would ye like to meet Mr. Underhill, maybe?"

Blackbeard returned Birt's look. Clever black eyes met candid blue ones for a long moment; then Blackbeard smiled and said, "Yes. Will you take me up to the hill, Birt?"

"Aye, when I'm done with this," said the fisherman. And when the net was mended, he and the Archipelagan set off up the village street towards the high green hill above it. But as they crossed the common Blackbeard said, "Hold on awhile, friend Birt, I have a tale to tell you, before we meet your wizard."

"Tell away," says Birt, sitting down in the shade of a live oak.

"It's the story that started a hundred years ago, and isn't finished yet — though it soon will be, very soon. . . . In the very heart of the Archipelago, where the islands crowd thick as flies on honey, there's a little isle called Pendor. The sealords of Pendor were mighty men, in the old days of war before the League. Loot and ransom and tribute came pouring into Pendor, and they gathered a great treasure there, long ago. Then from somewhere away out in the West Reach, where dragons breed on the lava isles, came one day a very mighty dragon. Not one of those overgrown lizards most of you Outer Reach folk call dragons, but a big, black, winged, wise, cunning monster, full of strength and subtlety, and like all drag-

10. **nevvy:** a dialectal form of *nephew*.
11. **taciturn** (tăs′ə-tərn): quiet; having little to say.

ons loving gold and precious stones above all things. He killed the Sealord and his soldiers, and the people of Pendor fled in their ships by night. They all fled away and left the dragon coiled up in Pendor Towers. And there he stayed for a hundred years, dragging his scaly belly over the emeralds and sapphires and coins of gold, coming forth only once in a year or two when he must eat. He'd raid nearby islands for his food. You know what dragons eat?"

Birt nodded and said in a whisper, "Maidens."

"Right," said Blackbeard. "Well, that couldn't be endured forever, nor the thought of his sitting on all that treasure. So after the League grew strong, and the Archipelago wasn't so busy with wars and piracy, it was decided to attack Pendor, drive out the dragon, and get the gold and jewels for the treasury of the League. They're forever wanting money, the League is. So a huge fleet gathered from fifty islands, and seven Mages stood in the prows of the seven strongest ships, and they sailed towards Pendor. . . . They got there. They landed. Nothing stirred. The houses all stood empty, the dishes on the tables full of a hundred years' dust. The bones of the old Sealord and his men lay about in the castle courts and on the stairs. And the Tower rooms reeked of dragon. But there was no dragon. And no treasure, not a diamond the size of a poppyseed, not a single silver bead. . . . Knowing that he couldn't stand up to seven Mages, the dragon had skipped out. They tracked him, and found he'd flown to a deserted island up north called Udrath; they followed his trail there, and what did they find? Bones again. His bones—the dragon's. But no treasure. A wizard, some unknown wizard from somewhere, must have met him singlehanded, and defeated him—and then made off with the treasure, right under the League's nose!"

The fisherman listened, attentive and expressionless.

"Now that must have been a powerful wizard and a clever one, first to kill a dragon, and second to get off without leaving a trace. The lords and Mages of the Archipelago couldn't track him at all, neither where he'd come from nor where he'd made off to. They were about to give up. That was last spring; I'd been off on a three-year voyage up in the North Reach, and got back about that time. And they asked me to help them find the unknown wizard. That was clever of them. Because I'm not only a wizard myself, as I think some of the oafs here have guessed, but I am also a descendant of the Lords of Pendor. That treasure is mine. It's mine, and knows that it's mine. Those fools of the League couldn't find it, because it's not theirs. It belongs to the House of Pendor, and the great emerald, the star of the hoard, Inalkil the Greenstone, knows its master. Behold!" Blackbeard raised his oaken staff and cried aloud, "Inalkil!" The tip of the staff began to glow green, a fiery green radiance, a dazzling haze the color of April grass, and at the same moment the staff tipped in the wizard's hand, leaning, slanting till it pointed straight at the side of the hill above them.

"It wasn't so bright a glow, far away in Havnor," Blackbeard murmured, "but the staff pointed true. Inalkil answered when I called. The jewel knows its master. And I know the thief, and I shall conquer him. He's a mighty wizard, who could overcome a dragon. But I am mightier. Do you want to know why, oaf? Because I know his name!"

As Blackbeard's tone got more arrogant, Birt had looked duller and duller, blanker and blanker, but at this he gave a twitch, shut his mouth, and stared at the Archipelagan. "How did you . . . learn it?" he asked very slowly.

Blackbeard grinned, and did not answer.

"Black magic?"

"How else?"

Birt looked pale, and said nothing.

"I am the Sealord of Pendor, oaf, and I will have the gold my fathers won, and the jewels my mothers wore, and the Greenstone! For they are mine. Now, you can tell your village boobies the whole story after I have defeated this wizard and gone. Wait here. Or you can come and watch, if you're not afraid. You'll never get the chance again to see a great wizard in all his power." Blackbeard turned, and without a backward glance strode off up the hill towards the entrance to the cave.

Very slowly, Birt followed. A good distance from the cave he stopped, sat down under a hawthorn tree, and watched. The Archipelagan had stopped; a stiff, dark figure alone on the green swell of the hill before the gaping cave-mouth, he stood perfectly still. All at once he swung his staff up over his head, and the emerald radiance shone about him as he shouted, "Thief, thief of the Hoard of Pendor, come forth!"

There was a crash, as of dropped crockery, from inside the cave, and a lot of dust came spewing out. Scared, Birt ducked. When he looked again he saw Blackbeard still standing motionless, and at the mouth of the cave, dusty and disheveled, stood Mr. Underhill. He looked small and pitiful, with his toes turned in as usual, and his little bowlegs in black tights, and no staff—he never had had one, Birt suddenly thought. Mr. Underhill spoke. "Who are you?" he said in his husky little voice.

"I am the Sealord of Pendor, thief, come to claim my treasure!"

At that, Mr. Underhill slowly turned pink, as he always did when people were rude to him. But he then turned something else. He turned yellow. His hair bristled out, he gave a coughing roar—and was a yellow lion leaping down the hill at Blackbeard, white fangs gleaming.

But Blackbeard no longer stood there. A gigantic tiger, color of night and lightning, bounded to meet the lion. . . .

The lion was gone. Below the cave all of a sudden stood a high grove of trees, black in the winter sunshine. The tiger, checking himself in mid-leap just before he entered the shadow of the trees, caught fire in the air, became a tongue of flame lashing out at the dry black branches. . . .

But where the trees had stood a sudden cataract[12] leaped from the hillside, an arch of silvery crashing water, thundering down upon the fire. But the fire was gone. . . .

For just a moment before the fisherman's staring eyes two hills rose—the green one he knew, and a new one, a bare, brown hillock ready to drink up the rushing waterfall. That passed so quickly it made Birt blink, and after blinking he blinked again, and moaned, for what he saw now was a great deal worse. Where the cataract had been there hovered a dragon. Black wings darkened all the hill, steel claws reached groping, and from the dark, scaly, gaping lips fire and steam shot out.

Beneath the monstrous creature stood Blackbeard, laughing.

"Take any shape you please, little Mr. Underhill!" he taunted. "I can match you. But the game grows tiresome. I want to look upon my treasure, upon Inalkil. Now, big dragon, little wizard, take your true shape. I command you by the power of your truename—Yevaud!"

Birt could not move at all, not even to blink. He cowered, staring whether he would or not. He saw the black dragon hang there in the air above Blackbeard. He saw the fire lick like many tongues from the scaly mouth, the steam jet from the red nostrils. He saw Blackbeard's face grow white, white as chalk, and the beard-fringed lips trembling.

"Your name is Yevaud!"

12. **cataract** (kăt′ə-răkt′): a waterfall.

"Yes," said a great, husky, hissing voice. "My truename is Yevaud, and my true shape is this shape."

"But the dragon was killed—they found dragon bones on Udrath Island —"

"That was another dragon," said the dragon, and then stooped like a hawk, talons outstretched. And Birt shut his eyes.

When he opened them the sky was clear, the hillside empty, except for a reddish-blackish trampled spot, and a few talon-marks in the grass.

Birt the fisherman got to his feet and ran.

He ran across the common, scattering sheep to right and left, and straight down to the village street to Palani's father's house. Palani was out in the garden weeding the nasturtiums. "Come with me!" Birt gasped. She stared. He grabbed her wrist and dragged her with him. She screeched a little, but did not resist. He ran with her straight to the pier, pushed her into his fishing sloop the *Queenie,* untied the painter,[13] took up the oars and set off rowing like a demon. The last that Sattins Island saw

13. **painter:** here, a rope attached to a boat.

Lacquer chest with incised design (Cheng Te Reign 1306–1321).

of him and Palani was the *Queenie*'s sail vanishing in the direction of the nearest island westward.

The villagers thought they would never stop talking about it, how Goody Guld's nephew Birt had lost his mind and sailed off with the schoolmistress on the very same day that the peddler Blackbeard disappeared without a trace, leaving all his feathers and beads behind. But they did stop talking about it, three days later. They had other things to talk about, when Mr. Underhill finally came out of his cave.

Mr. Underhill had decided that since his truename was no longer a secret, he might as well drop his disguise. Walking was a lot harder than flying, and besides, it was a long, long time since he had had a real meal.

Reading Check

1. What kind of work does Mr. Underhill do on Sattins Island?
2. Why are there no books on Sattins Island?
3. When are the children allowed to keep their truenames?
4. Why has the Sealord of Pendor come to Sattins Island?
5. What is Mr. Underhill's true identity?

For Study and Discussion

Analyzing and Interpreting the Story

1. By the end of this story we know that Yevaud, the powerful dragon, came to Sattins Island disguised as Mr. Underhill. **a.** What does Mr. Underhill keep hidden in his cave? **b.** Why does Blackbeard, the Sealord of Pendor, come to Sattins Island?

2. Mr. Underhill does not seem to be much of an opponent for Blackbeard. How do they differ in appearance?

3. According to the magical Rule of Names, if you say someone's "truename," you can gain control over that person. **a.** How does Blackbeard plan to conquer Mr. Underhill? **b.** Why doesn't his plan work?

4. The author doesn't tell you directly what happened to Blackbeard. Find the passage toward the end of the story that reveals what became of the handsome stranger.

5a. According to Blackbeard, what do dragons eat? **b.** At the end of the story, Birt runs away with Palani, the schoolteacher. Why do you think he does this?

6a. After destroying Blackbeard, why does Mr. Underhill decide to drop his disguise? **b.** What do you think this decision will mean for the people living on Sattins Island?

7. Perhaps you've heard the saying: "There's an exception to every rule." How does this saying apply to the story?

Literary Elements

Noting Techniques That Create Suspense

Ursula Le Guin gains interest and creates suspense by dropping clues about what is going to happen. This technique is called **foreshadowing.**

For example, the opening paragraph of this story describes Mr. Underhill breathing a "double puff of steam" and showing "snow-white teeth." These clues hint that he is a dragon. You get another hint of his true nature when you are told that "the minute spent watching Palani and the children had made him very hungry." Later you learn that a dragon eats maidens. Can you find other clues that foreshadow Mr. Underhill's identity?

Sometimes this author drops false clues to put you off balance and to keep you in suspense. For example, from Blackbeard's story, you are led to think that a great wizard killed the dragon, stole its treasure, and fled to Sattins Island. What actually happened?

Language and Vocabulary

Looking Up Word Histories

In this story of fantasy, Seacaptain Fogeno knows that the mysterious Blackbeard is a wizard when he hears that the stranger carries an "*oaken* walking stick." Thousands of years ago in Europe, many people considered the oak to be a sacred tree with magical properties. In ancient Greece, the oak was the special tree of Zeus, the chief god.

Using a dictionary or an encyclopedia, find the meaning and history of these words:

dragon	mage	warlock
incantation	magic	wizard

Writing About Literature

Analyzing Foreshadowing in a Story

Foreshadowing is a technique used by writers and filmmakers alike. Choose a suspenseful story, movie, or television program you have enjoyed recently. In a paragraph, discuss how clues in the work—the foreshadowing—contribute to the story's suspense. You may need to include a sentence that gives a brief summary of the story if your readers are not familiar with it.

About the Author

Ursula Le Guin   (1929–   )

Ursula K. Le Guin is considered one of today's most important writers of science fiction and fantasy. She was born in California, and started writing at about age five. Some of her best-known stories deal with events on the planet Hain and on the dream landscape of Earthsea. She is the author of such award-winning novels as *The Left Hand of Darkness* and *The Dispossessed*. She helped with the screenplay for a 1980 television film of her novel *The Lathe of Heaven*. "The Rule of Names" is from her short-story collection *The Wind's Twelve Quarters* and is, Le Guin says, one of her first "explorations" of Earthsea.

Thank You, M'am

LANGSTON HUGHES

Sometimes characters do not act as you might expect they would. As you read this story, notice how the characters gradually reveal themselves through what they do, say, and think.

She was a large woman with a large purse that had everything in it but hammer and nails. It had a long strap and she carried it slung across her shoulder. It was about eleven o'clock at night, and she was walking alone, when a boy ran up behind her and tried to snatch her purse. The strap broke with the single tug the boy gave it from behind. But the boy's weight, and the weight of the purse combined, caused him to lose his balance so, instead of taking off full blast as he had hoped, the boy fell on his back on the sidewalk, and his legs flew up. The large woman simply turned around and kicked him right square in his blue-jeaned sitter. Then she reached down, picked the boy up by his shirt front, and shook him until his teeth rattled.

After that the woman said, "Pick up my pocketbook, boy, and give it here."

She still held him. But she bent down enough to permit him to stoop and pick up her purse. Then she said, "Now ain't you ashamed of yourself?"

Firmly gripped by his shirt front, the boy said, "Yes'm."

The woman said, "What did you want to do it for?"

The boy said, "I didn't aim to."

She said, "You a lie!"

By that time two or three people passed, stopped, turned to look, and some stood watching.

"If I turn you loose, will you run?" asked the woman.

"Yes'm," said the boy.

"Then I won't turn you loose," said the woman. She did not release him.

"I'm very sorry, lady, I'm sorry," whispered the boy.

"Um-hum! And your face is dirty. I got a great mind to wash your face for you. Ain't you got nobody home to tell you to wash your face?"

"No'm," said the boy.

"Then it will get washed this evening," said the large woman starting up the street, dragging the frightened boy behind her.

He looked as if he were fourteen or fifteen, frail and willow-wild, in tennis shoes and blue jeans.

The woman said, "You ought to be my son. I

Mother Courage II (1974) by Charles White (1918–1979). Oil on canvas.
The National Academy of Design, New York
Courtesy Heritage Gallery, Los Angeles

would teach you right from wrong. Least I can do right now is to wash your face. Are you hungry?"

"No'm," said the being-dragged boy. "I just want you to turn me loose."

"Was I bothering *you* when I turned that corner?" asked the woman.

"No'm."

"But you put yourself in contact with *me*." said the woman. "If you think that that contact is not going to last awhile, you got another thought coming. When I get through with you, sir, you are going to remember Mrs. Luella Bates Washington Jones."

Sweat popped out on the boy's face and he began to struggle. Mrs. Jones stopped, jerked him around in front of her, put a half nelson[1] about his neck, and continued to drag him up the street. When she got to her door, she dragged the boy inside, down a hall, and into a large kitchenette-furnished room at the rear of the house. She switched on the light and left the door open. The boy could hear other roomers laughing and talking in the large house. Some of their doors were opened, too, so he knew he and the woman were not alone. The woman still had him by the neck in the middle of her room.

She said, "What is your name?"

"Roger," answered the boy.

"Then, Roger, you go to that sink and wash your face," said the woman, whereupon she turned him loose—at last. Roger looked at the door—looked at the woman—looked at the door—*and went to the sink.*

"Let the water run until it gets warm," she said. "Here's a clean towel."

"You gonna take me to jail?" asked the boy, bending over the sink.

"Not with that face, I would not take you nowhere," said the woman. "Here I am trying

1. **half nelson:** a wrestling hold made with one arm.

to get home to cook me a bite to eat and you snatch my pocketbook! Maybe you ain't been to your supper either, late as it be. Have you?"

"There's nobody home at my house," said the boy.

"Then we'll eat," said the woman. "I believe you're hungry—or been hungry—to try to snatch my pocketbook."

"I wanted a pair of blue suede shoes," said the boy.

"Well, you didn't have to snatch *my* pocketbook to get some suede shoes," said Mrs. Luella Bates Washington Jones. "You could of asked me."

"M'am?"

The water dripping from his face, the boy looked at her. There was a long pause. A very long pause. After he had dried his face and not knowing what else to do dried it again, the boy turned around, wondering what next. The door was open. He could make a dash for it down the hall. He could run, run, run, run, *run!*

The woman was sitting on the daybed. After a while she said, "I were young once and I wanted things I could not get."

There was another long pause. The boy's mouth opened. Then he frowned, but not knowing he frowned.

The woman said, "Um-hum! You thought I was going to say *but,* didn't you? You thought I was going to say, *but I didn't snatch people's pocketbooks.* Well, I wasn't going to say that." Pause. Silence. "I have done things, too, which I would not tell you, son—neither tell God, if he didn't already know. So you set down while I fix us something to eat. You might run that comb through your hair so you will look presentable."

In another corner of the room behind a screen was a gas plate and an icebox. Mrs. Jones got up and went behind the screen. The woman did not watch the boy to see if he was going to run now, nor did she watch her purse which she left behind her on the daybed. But the boy took care to sit on the far side of the room where he thought she could easily see him out of the corner of her eye, if she wanted to. He did not trust the woman *not* to trust him. And he did not want to be mistrusted now.

"Do you need somebody to go to the store," asked the boy, "maybe to get some milk or something?"

"Don't believe I do," said the woman, "unless you just want sweet milk yourself. I was going to make cocoa out of this canned milk I got here."

"That will be fine," said the boy.

She heated some lima beans and ham she had in the icebox, made the cocoa, and set the table. The woman did not ask the boy anything about where he lived, or his folks, or anything else that would embarrass him. Instead, as they ate, she told him about her job in a hotel beauty shop that stayed open late, what the work was like, and how all kinds of women came in and out, blondes, redheads, and Spanish. Then she cut him a half of her ten-cent cake.

"Eat some more, son," she said.

When they were finished eating she got up and said, "Now, here, take this ten dollars and buy yourself some blue suede shoes. And next time do not make the mistake of latching on to *my* pocketbook *nor nobody else's*—because shoes come by devilish like that will burn your feet. I got to get my rest now. But I wish you would behave yourself, son, from here on in."

She led him down the hall to the front door and opened it. "Good night! Behave yourself, boy!" she said, looking out into the street.

The boy wanted to say something else other than, "Thank you, m'am," to Mrs. Luella Bates Washington Jones, but he couldn't do so as he turned at the barren stoop and looked back at the large woman in the door. He barely managed to say, "Thank you," before she shut the door. And he never saw her again.

Reading Check

1. What does Roger try to do to Mrs. Jones?
2. How old is Roger?
3. Why does Mrs. Jones take Roger home?
4. What does Roger want to buy?
5. What does Mrs. Jones give to Roger?

For Study and Discussion

Analyzing and Interpreting the Story

1. Many people who are robbed would call for help or call the police. What does Mrs. Jones do instead?

2. Most people in Roger's situation would run when they had a chance. Why do you think Roger decides not to run away when he can?

3a. What does Mrs. Jones reveal about her past when she and Roger are in her home? **b.** How do you think this information makes Roger feel?

4a. During the time that Roger is in her apartment, how does Mrs. Jones show that she does not want to embarrass him or hurt his feelings? **b.** What does this concern reveal about her character?

5. What do Mrs. Jones's home and the meal she serves reveal about her own financial situation?

6a. In your opinion, why does Mrs. Jones give Roger the ten dollars? **b.** What do you think he learns from her warmth and generosity?

7. Why do you suppose Roger cannot say more than "Thank you, m'am"?

Literary Elements

Recognizing Techniques of Characterization

Characterization is the means an author uses to reveal the characters in a story. When writers *tell* what characters are like through description, they are using **direct characterization.** For example, in the first sentence of this story, Langston Hughes describes Mrs. Jones as "a large woman with a large purse that had everything in it but hammer and nails." Later he also describes Roger, saying, "He looked as if he were fourteen or fifteen, frail and willow-wild, in tennis shoes and blue jeans." These are examples of direct characterization. They are the only direct statements made about the two characters in the story.

Yet you know much more about these two characters because you have watched their actions and listened to their conversations and thoughts. When writers let you know characters in this way — they are using **indirect characterization.** What incident in the story lets you know, for example, that Mrs. Jones is physically strong?

Writing About Literature

Analyzing Indirect Characterization

Write a paragraph in which you explain how details in "Thank You, M'am" *indirectly* reveal Mrs. Jones as a kind and generous person. You might use this as your topic sentence: *In "Thank You, M'am," Mrs. Jones's actions toward Roger show that she is a kind and generous person.* As you write, be sure to enclose any direct quotations from the story in quotation marks.

About the Author

Langston Hughes (1902–1967)

"Mightily did he use the street," poet Gwendolyn Brooks has written about her friend Langston Hughes. "He found its multiple heart, its tastes, smells, alarms, formulas, flowers, garbage, and confusions. He brought them all to his tabletop. . . ." During his long and diverse career, Hughes wrote poems, short stories, novels, plays, songs, and essays, though he is best known for his poems. He attended Columbia University in New York City for a year, but left to write and travel. He worked as a seaman on transatlantic ships and as a cook in Paris. In 1925 he took a job as a busboy in a Washington, D.C., hotel where the poet Vachel Lindsay was staying. Hughes left three of his poems next to Lindsay's plate one day. Lindsay, recognizing their merit, read them to his audience that night and introduced a new young poet to the world of literature. One critic has said that Hughes has written "some of the saddest, most humorous, and beautiful insights ever given into the heart of a race." One of his famous poems is "Mother to Son."

The Parachutist

D'ARCY NILAND

In this story, the fierce conflict between a hawk and a kitten reflects the fierceness of the setting—a land ravaged by a hurricane. As you read, notice how the natural environment brings out each animal's instinct for survival.

The hurricane came down from Capricorn,[1] and for two days and a night it rained.

In the darkness of the second night, softening away to dawn, there was silence. There was only the gurgle and drip of the wet world, and the creatures that lived on the earth began to appear, freed from the tyranny of the elements.

1. **Capricorn:** the Tropic of Capricorn. The story is set in the Southern Hemisphere.

The hawk, ruffled in misery, brooding in ferocity, came forth in hunger and hate. It struck off into the abyss of space, scouring the earth for some booty of the storm—the sheep lying like a heap of wet kapok[2] in the sodden paddocks,[3] the bullock like a dark bladder carried down on the swollen stream and washing

2. **kapok** (kā'pŏk'): silky fiber from the seeds of a tropical tree, used for padding in pillows and mattresses.
3. **paddocks** (păd'əks): fenced-in land.

The Parachutist **235**

against a tree on the river flats, the rabbit, driven from its flooded warren[4] and squeezed dead against a log.

With practiced eye it scrutinized the floating islands of rubble and the wracks[5] of twigs lying askew on the banks for sign of lizard or snake, dead or alive. But there was nothing. Once, in the time before, there had been a rooster, daggled,[6] forlorn derelict riding a raft of flotsam: too weak to fight and too sick to care about dying or the way it died.

The hawk rested on a crag of the gorge and conned the terrain with a fierce and frowning eye. The lice worried its body with the sting of nettles. Savagely it plucked with its beak under the fold of its wings, first on one side, then on the other. It rasped its bill on the jagged stone, and dropped over the lip. It climbed in a gliding circle, widening its field of vision.

The earth was yellow and green. On the flats were chains of lagoons as if the sky had broken and fallen in sheets of blue glass. The sun was hot and the air heavy and humid.

Swinging south, the hawk dropped over a vast graveyard of dead timber. The hurricane had ravaged the gaunt trees, splitting them, falling them, tearing off their naked arms and strewing the ground with pieces, like a battlefield of bones, gray with exposure and decay.

A rabbit sprang twenty yards like a bobbing wheel, and the sight drew the hawk like a plummet, but the rabbit vanished in a hollow log, and stayed there, and there was no other life.

Desperate, weak, the hawk alighted on a bleak limb and glared in hate. The sun was a fire on its famished body. Logs smoked with steam and the brightness of water on the earth reflected like mirrors. The telescopic eye

inched over the ground—crawled infallibly over the ground, and stopped. And then suddenly the hawk swooped to the ground and tore at the body of a dead field mouse—its belly bloated and a thin vapor drifting from the gray, plastered pelt.

The hawk did not sup as it supped on the hot running blood of the rabbit in the trap—squealing in eyeless terror; it did not feast in stealthy leisure as it did on the sheep paralyzed in the drought, tearing out bit by bit its steaming entrails. Voraciously it ripped at the mouse, swallowing fast and finishing the meal in a few seconds.

But the food was only a tantalization, serving to make the hawk's appetite more fierce,

4. **warren** (wôr′ən, wŏr′-): a place where rabbits live in their burrows.
5. **wracks** (răks): fragments.
6. **daggled** (dă′gəld): wet and dirty.

more lusty. It flew into a tree, rapaciously scanning the countryside. It swerved into space and climbed higher and higher in a vigilant circle, searching the vast expanse below, even to its uttermost limits.

Hard to the west something moved on the earth, a speck: and the hawk watched it: and the speck came up to a walnut, and up to a plum, and up to a ball striped with white and gray.

The hawk did not strike at once. Obedient to instinct, it continued to circle, peering down at the farmhouse and outbuildings, suspicious; seeing the draft horses in the yard and the fowls in the hen coop, the pigs in the sty, and the windmill twirling, and watching for human life in their precincts.

Away from them all, a hundred yards or more, down on the margin of the fallowed[7] field, the kitten played, leaping and running and tumbling, pawing at a feather and rolling on its back biting at the feather between its forepaws.

Frenzied with hunger, yet ever cautious, the hawk came down in a spiral, set itself, and swooped. The kitten propped[8] and froze with its head cocked on one side, unaware of danger but startled by this new and untried sport. It was no more than if a piece of paper had blown past it in a giant brustle[9] of sound. But in the next moment the hawk fastened its talons in the fur and the fat belly of the kitten, and the kitten spat and twisted, struggling against the power that was lifting it.

Its great wings beating, paddling with the rhythm of oars, the hawk went up a slope of space with its cargo, and the kitten, airborne for the first time in its life, the earth running under it in a blur, wailed in shrill terror. It squirmed frantically as the world fell away in the distance, but the hawk's talons were like the grabs of an iceman.

The air poured like water into the kitten's eyes and broke against its triangular face, streaming back against its rippling furry sides. It howled in infinite fear, and gave a sudden desperate twist, so that the hawk was jolted in its course and dropped to another level, a few feet below the first.

Riding higher and higher on the wind, the hawk went west by the dam like a button of silver far below. The kitten cried now with a new note. Its stomach was wambling.[10] The air gushing into its mouth and nostrils set up a humming in its ears and an aching dizziness in its head. As the hawk turned on its soundless orbit, the sun blazed like flame in the kitten's eyes, leaving its sight to emerge from a blinding grayness.

The kitten knew that it had no place here in the heart of space, and its terrified instincts told it that its only contact with solidity and safety was the thing that held it.

Then the hawk was ready to drop its prey. It was well practiced. Down had gone the rabbit, a whistle in space, to crash in a quiver of death on the ruthless earth. And the hawk had followed to its gluttonous repast.

Now there at two thousand feet the bird hovered. The kitten was alarmingly aware of the change, blinking at the pulsations of beaten air as the wings flapped, hearing only that sound. Unexpectedly, it stopped, and the wings were still—outstretched, but rigid, tilting slightly with the poised body, only the fanned tail lifting and lowering with the flow of the currents.

The kitten felt the talons relax slightly, and that was its warning. The talons opened, but in the first flashing shock of the movement the kitten completed its twist and slashed at the hawk's legs and buried its claws in the flesh like

7. **fallowed** (făl′ōd): plowed.
8. **propped** (prŏpt): stopped suddenly.
9. **brustle:** a dialect variation of *bristle*.

10. **wambling** (wŏm′blĭng, wăm′-): turning.

fishhooks. In the next fraction of a second the kitten had consolidated its position, securing its hold, jabbing in every claw except those on one foot which thrust out in space, pushing against insupportable air. And then the claws on this foot were dug in the breast of the hawk.

With a cry of pain and alarm the bird swooped crazily, losing a hundred feet like a dropping stone. And then it righted itself, flying in a drunken sway that diminished as it circled.

Blood from its breast beaded and trickled down the paw of the kitten and spilled into one eye. The kitten blinked, but the blood came and congealed, warm and sticky. The kitten could not turn its head. It was frightened to risk a change of position. The blood slowly built over its eye a blinding pellicle.[11]

The hawk felt a spasm of weakness, and out of it came an accentuation of its hunger and a lust to kill at all costs the victim it had claimed and carried to this place of execution. Lent an access of power by its ferocity, it started to climb again, desperately trying to dislodge the kitten. But the weight was too much and it could not ascend. A great tiredness came in its dragging body; an ache all along the frames of its wings. The kitten clung tenaciously, staring down at the winding earth and mewling in terror.

For ten minutes the hawk gyrated on a level, defeated and bewildered. All it wanted to do now was to get rid of the burden fastened to its legs and body. It craved respite, a spell on the tallest trees, but it only flew high over these trees, knowing it was unable to perch. Its beak gaped under the harsh ruptures of its breath. It descended three hundred feet. The kitten, with the wisdom of instinct, never altered its position, but rode down like some fantastic parachutist.

11. **pellicle** (pĕl′ ĭ-kəl): a thin film.

In one mighty burst the hawk with striking beak and a terrible flapping of its wings tried finally to cast off its passenger—and nearly succeeded. The kitten miauled[12] in a frenzy of fear at the violence of the sound and the agitation. Its back legs dangled in space, treading air, and like that it went around on the curves of the flight for two minutes. Then it secured a foothold again, even firmer than the first.

In a hysterical rage, the hawk tried once more to lift itself, and almost instantly began to sweep down in great, slow, gliding eddies that became narrower and narrower.

The kitten was the pilot now and the hawk no longer the assassin of the void, the lord of the sky and the master of the wind. The ache coiled and throbbed in its breast. It fought against the erratic disposition of its wings and the terror of its waning strength. Its heart bursting with the strain, its eyes dilated wild and yellow, it came down until the earth skimmed under it; and the kitten cried at the silver glare of the roofs not far off, and the expanding earth, and the brush of the grass.

The hawk lobbed and flung over, and the kitten rolled with it. And the hawk lay spraddled in exhaustion, its eyes fiercely, cravenly aware of the danger of its forced and alien position. The kitten staggered giddily, unhurt, towards the silver roofs, wailing loudly as if in answer to the voice of a child.

12. **miauled** (mē-ôld′): meowed.

Reading Check

1. Where does the story take place?
2. What is the hawk searching for?
3. Why is the hawk's search so difficult?
4. What does the kitten do to save itself?

Analyzing and Interpreting the Story

1. Sometimes a writer suggests certain details of setting in a story. **a.** At what time of day does this story occur? **b.** How do you know?

2. Every story centers on **conflict**, the struggle between two opposing forces. **a.** What is the conflict in this story? **b.** Is there more than one conflict?

3. Although the hawk is lord of the sky at the beginning of the story, its rule is challenged by the end of the story. How does the situation of control change?

4. Why do you think the author ends the story with the kitten crying as if in answer to a child's voice?

5. The characters an author chooses convey a certain message to the reader. **a.** Why do you think the author chose a hawk and a kitten as the characters in this story? **b.** How would you feel about the story if the author had used a bobcat instead of a kitten?

6. A reader learns a great deal about characters through the words the author uses to describe them. **a.** Considering how Niland describes the hawk, how would you characterize it? **b.** What kind of character is the kitten?

7. Why do you think the author titled this story "The Parachutist"?

Literary Elements

Recognizing the Importance of Setting

Setting is the time and place in which a story occurs. The setting also includes background information that relates to the action of a story. In "The Parachutist," the general setting is the countryside, but, as the hawk travels, the specifics of the setting change.

How many different settings are actually described in the story? What are the conditions of the hawk's environment before it comes across the kitten? How is the environment different after the hawk spots the kitten? How do you think the story would change if the setting were in the city and the kitten were a household animal instead of a farm animal?

Creative Writing

Writing a Short Story

Write a short story that occurs in a vivid setting. Remember that the characters should face some kind of conflict and that they should reveal themselves through what they do, say, and think. Also be sure to create a setting that relates to the conflict in the story. You and your classmates might enjoy reading one another's stories.

About the Author

D'Arcy Niland   (1920–   )

D'Arcy Niland's birthplace of Glen Innes, New South Wales, Australia, serves as a backdrop for many of his works. It has been said that his writing presents an authentic picture of life in the Australian outback—vigorous and harsh, lonely, and sometimes heartbreaking. Throughout his career as a writer and journalist, Niland has written for radio and television. He has contributed many of his short stories to anthologies and periodicals while writing articles for newspapers and magazines. His other works include *The Shiralee* and his autobiography, *The Drums Go Bang*.

Flowers for Algernon

DANIEL KEYES

The doctors told Charlie that if he volunteered for this experiment he might "get smart." If the operation worked, Charlie would be the first of a new breed of intellectual supermen. As you read, notice how the first-person point of view helps us to understand the remarkable but tragic changes that Charlie undergoes.

progris riport—martch 5 1965

Dr. Strauss says I shud rite down what I think and evrey thing that happins to me from now on. I dont know why but he says its importint so they will see if they will use me. I hope they use me. Miss Kinnian says maybe they can make me smart. I want to be smart. My name is Charlie Gordon. I am 37 years old and 2 weeks ago was my brithday. I have nuthing more to rite now so I will close for today.

progris riport 2—martch 6

I had a test today. I think I faled it. and I think that maybe now they wont use me. What happind is a nice young man was in the room and he had some white cards with ink spillled all over them. He sed Charlie what do you see on this card. I was very skared even tho I had my rabits foot in my pockit because when I was a kid I always faled tests in school and I spillled ink to.

I told him I saw an inkblot. He said yes and it made me feel good. I thot that was all but when I got up to go he stopped me. He said now sit down Charlie we are not thru yet. Then I dont remember so good but he wantid me to say what was in the ink. I dint see nuthing in the ink but he said there was picturs there other pepul saw some picturs. I coudnt see any picturs. I reely tried to see. I held the card close up and then far away. Then I said if I had my glases I coud see better I usally only ware my glases in the movies or TV but I said they are in the closit in the hall. I got them. Then I said let me see that card agen I bet Ill find it now.

I tryed hard but I still coudnt find the picturs I only saw the ink. I told him maybe I need new glases. He rote somthing down on a paper and I got skared of faling the test. I told him it was a very nice inkblot with littel points all around the eges. He looked very sad so that wasnt it. I said please let me try agen. Ill get it in a few minits becaus Im not so fast somtimes. Im a slow reeder too in Miss Kinnians class for slow adults but I'm trying very hard.

He gave me a chance with another card that had 2 kinds of ink spillled on it red and blue.

He was very nice and talked slow like Miss Kinnian does and he explaned to me that it was a *raw shok*.[1] He said pepul see things in the ink. I said show me where. He said think. I told him I think a inkblot but that wasnt rite eather. He said what does it remind you—pretend something. I closd my eyes for a long time to pretend. I told him I pretned a fowntan pen with ink leeking all over a table cloth. Then he got up and went out.

I dont think I passd the *raw shok* test.

progris report 3—martch 7

Dr Strauss and Dr Nemur say it dont matter about the inkblots. I told them I dint spill the ink on the cards and I coudnt see anything in the ink. They said that maybe they will still use me. I said Miss Kinnian never gave me tests like that one only spelling and reading. They said Miss Kinnian told that I was her bestist pupil in the adult nite scool becaus I tryed the hardist and I reely wantid to lern. They said how come you went to the adult nite scool all by yourself Charlie. How did you find it. I said I askd pepul and sumbody told me where I shud go to lern to read and spell good. They said why did you want to. I told them becaus all my life I wantid to be smart and not dumb. But its very hard to be smart. They said you know it will probly be tempirery. I said yes. Miss Kinnian told me. I dont care if it herts.

Later I had more crazy tests today. The nice lady who gave it me told me the name and I asked her how do you spellit so I can rite it in my progris riport. THEMATIC APPERCEPTION TEST. I dont know the frist 2 words but I know what *test* means. You got to pass it or you get bad marks. This test lookd easy becaus I coud see the picters. Only this time she dint want me to tell her the picters. That mixd me up. I said the man yesterday said I shoud tell him what I saw in the ink she said that dont make no difrence. She said make up storys about the pepul in the picters.

I told her how can you tell storys about pepul you never met. I said why shud I make up lies. I never tell lies any more becaus I always get caut.

She told me this test and the other one the raw-shok was for getting personalty. I laffed so hard. I said how can you get that thing from inkblots and fotos. She got sore and put her picters away. I dont care. It was sily. I gess I faled that test too.

Later some men in white coats took me to a difernt part of the hospitil and gave me a game to play. It was like a race with a white mouse. They called the mouse Algernon. Algernon was in a box with a lot of twists and turns like all kinds of walls and they gave me a pencil and a paper with lines and lots of boxes. On one side it said START and on the other end it said FINISH. They said it was *amazed*[2] and that Algernon and me had the same *amazed* to do. I dint see how we could have the same *amazed* if Algernon had a box and I had a paper but I dint say nothing. Anyway there wasnt time because the race started.

One of the men had a watch he was trying to hide so I wouldnt see it so I tryed not to look and that made me nervus.

Anyway that test made me feel worser than all the others because they did it over 10 times with difernt *amazeds* and Algernon won every time. I dint know that mice were so smart.

1. **raw shok:** Charlie means the *Rorschach* (rôr′shäk) test, a personality test in which people tell what is suggested to them by a series of inkblot designs.

2. **amazed:** Charlie means *a maze,* a series of winding paths with one exit and many dead ends. The intelligence of laboratory animals is measured by the amount of time it takes them to find the exit.

Maybe thats because Algernon is a white mouse. Maybe white mice are smarter then other mice.

Their going to use me! Im so exited I can hardly write. Dr Nemur and Dr Strauss had a argament about it first. Dr Nemur was in the office when Dr Strauss brot me in. Dr Nemur was worryed about using me but Dr Strauss told him Miss Kinnian rekemmended me the best from all the people who she was teaching. I like Miss Kinnian becaus shes a very smart teacher. And she said Charlie your going to have a second chance. If you volenteer for this experament you mite get smart. They dont know if it will be perminint but theirs a chance. Thats why I said ok even when I was scared because she said it was an operashun. She said dont be scared Charlie you done so much with so little I think you deserv it most of all.

So I got scaird when Dr Nemur and Dr Strauss argud about it. Dr Strauss said I had something what was very good. He said I had a good *motor-vation*.[3] I never even knew I had that. I felt proud when he said that not every body with an eye-q of 68 had that thing. I dont know what it is or where I got it but he said Algernon had it too. Algernons *motor-vation* is the cheese they put in his box. But it cant be that because I didnt eat any cheese this week.

Then he told Dr Nemur something I dint understand so while they were talking I wrote down some of the words.

He said Dr Nemur I know Charlie is not what you had in mind as the first of your new brede of intelek** (couldnt get the word)

superman. But most people of his low ment** are host** and uncoop** they are usualy dull apath** and hard to reach. He has a good natcher hes intristed and eager to please.

Dr Nemur said remember he will be the first human beeng ever to have his intelijence trippled by surgicle meens.

Dr Strauss said exakly. Look at how well hes lerned to read and write for his low mentel age its as grate an acheve** as you and I lerning einstines therey of **vity without help. That shows the intenss motor-vation. Its comparat** a tremen** achev** I say we use Charlie.

I dint get all the words and they were talking to fast but it sounded like Dr Strauss was on my side and like the other one wasnt.

Then Dr Nemur nodded he said all right maybe your right. We will use Charlie. When he said that I got so exited I jumped up and shook his hand for being so good to me. I told him thank you doc you wont be sorry for giving me a second chance. And I mean it like I told him. After the operashun Im gonna try to be smart. Im gonna try awful hard.

Im skared. Lots of people who work here and the nurses and the people who gave me the tests came to bring me candy and wish me luck. I hope I have luck. I got my rabits foot and my lucky penny and my horse shoe. Only a black cat crossed me when I was comming to the hospitil. Dr Strauss says dont be supersitis Charlie this is sience. Anyway Im keeping my rabits foot with me.

I asked Dr Strauss if Ill beat Algernon in the race after the operashun and he said maybe. If the operashun works Ill show that mouse I can be as smart as he is. Maybe smarter. Then Ill be abel to read better and spell the words good and know lots of things and be like other peo-

---

3. **motor-vation:** Charlie means *motivation* (mō′tə-vā′shən), the inner drive to work hard at something.

ple. I want to be smart like other people. If it works perminint they will make everybody smart all over the wurld.

They dint give me anything to eat this morning. I dont know what that eating has to do with getting smart. Im very hungry and Dr Nemur took away my box of candy. That Dr Nemur is a grouch. Dr Strauss says I can have it back after the operashun. You cant eat befor a operashun . . .

that happin to me but he says I shoud tell more about what I feel and what I think. When I told him I dont know how to think he said try. All the time when the bandijis were on my eyes I tryed to think. Nothing happened. I dont know what to think about. Maybe if I ask him he will tell me how I can think now that Im suppose to get smart. What do smart people think about. Fancy things I suppose. I wish I knew some fancy things alredy.

Progress Report 6—Mar 15

The operashun dint hurt. He did it while I was sleeping. They took off the bandijis from my eyes and my head today so I can make a PROGRESS REPORT. Dr Nemur who looked at some of my other ones says I spell PROGRESS wrong and he told me how to spell it and REPORT too. I got to try and remember that.

I have a very bad memary for spelling. Dr Strauss says its ok to tell about all the things

Progress Report 7—mar 19

Nothing is happining. I had lots of tests and different kinds of races with Algernon. I hate that mouse. He always beats me. Dr Strauss said I got to play those games. And he said some time I got to take those tests over again. Those inkblots are stupid. And those pictures are stupid too. I like to draw a picture of a man and a woman but I wont make up lies about people.

Scenes on pages 243, 246, 250, 253 and 260 are from the film *Charly.*

I got a headache from trying to think so much. I thot Dr Strauss was my frend but he dont help me. He dont tell me what to think or when Ill get smart. Miss Kinnian dint come to see me. I think writing these progress reports are stupid too.

Progress Report 8—Mar 23

Im going back to work at the factery. They said it was better I shud go back to work but I cant tell anyone what the operashun was for and I have come to the hospitil for an hour evry night after work. They are gonna pay me mony every month for lerning to be smart.

Im glad Im going back to work because I miss my job and all my frends and all the fun we have there.

Dr Strauss says I shud keep writing things down but I dont have to do it every day just when I think of something or something speshul happins. He says dont get discoridged because it takes time and it happins slow. He says it took a long time with Algernon before he got 3 times smarter than he was before. Thats why Algernon beats me all the time because he had that operashun too. That makes me feel better. I coud probly do that *amazed* faster than a reglar mouse. Maybe some day Ill beat Algernon. Boy that would be something. So far Algernon looks like he mite be smart perminent.

Mar 25 (I dont have to write PROGRESS REPORT on top any more just when I hand it in once a week for Dr Nemur to read. I just have to put the date on. That saves time)

We had a lot of fun at the factery today. Joe Carp said hey look where Charlie had his operashun what did they do Charlie put some brains in. I was going to tell him but I remembered Dr Strauss said no. Then Frank Reilly said what did you do Charlie forget your key and open your door the hard way. That made me laff. Their really my friends and they like me.

Sometimes somebody will say hey look at Joe or Frank or George he really pulled a Charlie Gordon. I dont know why they say that but they always laff. This morning Amos Borg who is the 4 man at Donnegans used my name when he shouted at Ernie the office boy. Ernie lost a packige. He said Ernie what are you trying to be a Charlie Gordon. I dont understand why he said that. I never lost any packiges.

Mar 28 Dr Strauss came to my room tonight to see why I dint come in like I was suppose to. I told him I dont like to race with Algernon any more. He said I dont have to for a while but I shud come in. He had a present for me only it wasnt a present but just for lend. I thot it was a little television but it wasnt. He said I got to turn it on when I go to sleep. I said your kidding why shud I turn it on when Im going to sleep. Who ever herd of a thing like that. But he said if I want to get smart I got to do what he says. I told him I dint think I was going to get smart and he put his hand on my sholder and said Charlie you dont know it yet but your getting smarter all the time. You wont notice for a while. I think he was just being nice to make me feel good because I dont look any smarter.

Oh yes I almost forgot. I asked him when I can go back to the class at Miss Kinnians school. He said I wont go their. He said that soon Miss Kinnian will come to the hospitil to start and teach me speshul. I was mad at her for not comming to see me when I got the operashun but I like her so maybe we will be frends again.

Mar 29 That crazy TV kept me up all night. How can I sleep with something yelling crazy things all night in my ears. And the nutty pictures. Wow. I dont know what it says when Im up so how am I going to know when Im sleeping.

Dr Strauss says its ok. He says my brains are lerning when I sleep and that will help me when Miss Kinnian starts my lessons in the hospitl (only I found out it isnt a hospitil its a labatory). I think its all crazy. If you can get smart when your sleeping why do people go to school. That thing I dont think will work. I use to watch the late show and the late late show on TV all the time and it never made me smart. Maybe you have to sleep while you watch it.

PROGRESS REPORT 9—April 3

Dr Strauss showed me how to keep the TV turned low so now I can sleep. I dont hear a thing. And I still dont understand what it says. A few times I play it over in the morning to find out what I lerned when I was sleeping and I dont think so. Miss Kinnian says Maybe its another langwidge or something. But most times it sounds american. It talks so fast faster than even Miss Gold who was my teacher in 6 grade and I remember she talked so fast I couldnt understand her.

I told Dr Strauss what good is it to get smart in my sleep. I want to be smart when Im awake. He says its the same thing and I have two minds. Theres the *subconscious* and the *conscious* (thats how you spell it). And one dont tell the other one what its doing. They dont even talk to each other. Thats why I dream. And boy have I been having crazy dreams. Wow. Ever since that night TV. The late late late late late show.

I forgot to ask him if it was only me or if everybody had those two minds.

(I just looked up the word in the dictionary Dr Strauss gave me. The word is *subconscious.*

adj. Of the nature of mental operations yet not present in consciousness; as, subconscious conflict of desires.) Theres more but I still don't know what it means. This isnt a very good dictionary for dumb people like me.

Anyway the headache is from the party. My frends from the factery Joe Carp and Frank Reilly invited me to go with them to Muggsys Saloon for some drinks. I dont like to drink but they said we will have lots of fun. I had a good time.

Joe Carp said I shoud show the girls how I mop out the toilet in the factory and he got me a mop. I showed them and everyone laffed when I told that Mr Donnegan said I was the best janiter he ever had because I like my job and do it good and never come late or miss a day except for my operashun.

I said Miss Kinnian always said Charlie be proud of your job because you do it good.

Everybody laffed and we had a good time and they gave me lots of drinks and Joe said Charlie is a card. I dont know what that means but everybody likes me and we have fun. I cant wait to be smart like my best friends Joe Carp and Frank Reilly.

I dont remember how the party was over but I think I went out to buy a newspaper and coffe for Joe and Frank and when I came back there was no one their. I looked for them all over till late. Then I dont remember so good but I think I got sleepy or sick. A nice cop brot me back home. Thats what my landlady Mrs Flynn says.

But I got a headache and a big lump on my head and black and blue all over. I think maybe I fell. Anyway I got a bad headache and Im sick and hurt all over. I dont think Ill drink anymore.

April 6 I beat Algernon! I dint even know I beat him until Burt the tester told me. Then the second time I lost because I got so exited I fell off the chair before I finished. But after that I beat him 8 more times. I must be getting smart to beat a smart mouse like Algernon. But I dont *feel* smarter.

I wanted to race Algernon some more but Burt said thats enough for one day. They let me hold him for a minit. Hes not so bad. Hes soft like a ball of cotton. He blinks and when he opens his eyes their black and pink on the eges.

I said can I feed him because I felt bad to beat him and I wanted to be nice and make frends. Burt said no Algernon is a very specshul mouse with an operashun like mine, and he was the first of all the animals to stay smart so long. He told me Algernon is so smart that every day he has to solve a test to get his food. Its a thing like a lock on a door that changes every time Algernon goes in to eat so he has to lern something new to get his food. That made me sad because if he couldnt lern he woud be hungry.

I dont think its right to make you pass a test to eat. How woud Dr Nemur like it to have to pass a test every time he wants to eat. I think Ill be frends with Algernon.

April 9 Tonight after work Miss Kinnian was at the laboratory. She looked like she was glad to see me but scared. I told her dont worry Miss Kinnian Im not smart yet and she laffed. She said I have confidence in you Charlie the way you struggled so hard to read and right better than all the others. At werst you will have it for a little wile and your doing somthing for sience.

We are reading a very hard book. I never read such a hard book before. Its called *Robinson Crusoe* about a man who gets merooned on a dessert Iland. Hes smart and figers out all kinds of things so he can have a house and food and hes a good swimmer. Only I feel sorry because hes all alone and has no frends. But I think their must be somebody else on the iland because theres a picture with

his funny umbrella looking at footprints. I hope he gets a frend and not be lonly.

April 10   Miss Kinnian teaches me to spell better. She says look at a word and close your eyes and say it over and over until you remember. I have lots of truble with *through* that you say *threw* and *enough* and *tough* that you dont say *enew* and *tew*. You got to say *enuff* and *tuff*. Thats how I use to write it before I started to get smart. Im confused but Miss Kinnian says theres no reason in spelling.

Apr 14   Finished *Robinson Crusoe*. I want to find out more about what happens to him but Miss Kinnian says thats all there is. *Why*

Apr 15   Miss Kinnian says Im lerning fast. She read some of the Progress Reports and she looked at me kind of funny. She says Im a fine person and Ill show them all. I asked her why. She said never mind but I shouldnt feel bad if I find out that everybody isnt nice like I think. She said for a person who god gave so little to you done more then a lot of people with brains they never even used. I said all my frends are smart people but there good. They like me and they never did anything that wasnt nice. Then she got something in her eye and she had to run out to the ladys room.

Apr 16   Today, I lerned, the *comma,* this is a comma (,) a period, with a tail, Miss Kinnian, says its important, because it makes writing, better, she said, somebody, coud lose, a lot of money, if a comma, isnt, in the, right place, I dont have, any money, and I dont see, how a comma, keeps you, from losing it,

But she says, everybody, uses commas, so Ill use, them too,

Apr 17   I used the comma wrong. Its punctuation. Miss Kinnian told me to look up long words in the dictionary to lern to spell them. I said whats the difference if you can read it anyway. She said its part of your education so now on Ill look up all the words Im not sure how to spell. It takes a long time to write that way but I think Im remembering. I only have to look up once and after that I get it right. Anyway thats how come I got the word *punctuation* right. (Its that way in the dictionary). Miss Kinnian says a period is punctuation too, and there are lots of other marks to lern. I told her I thot all the periods had to have tails but she said no.

You got to mix them up, she showed? me" how. to mix! them(up,. and now; I can! mix up all kinds" of punctuation, in! my writing? There, are lots! of rules? to lern; but Im gettin'g them in my head.

One thing I? like about, Dear Miss Kinnian: (thats the way it goes in a business letter if I ever go into business) is she, always gives me' a reason" when—I ask. She's a gen'ius! I wish! I cou'd be smart" like, her;

(Punctuation, is ; fun!)

Apr 18   What a dope I am! I didn't even understand what she was talking about. I read the grammar book last night and it explanes the whole thing. Then I saw it was the same way as Miss Kinnian was trying to tell me, but I didn't get it. I got up in the middle of the night, and the whole thing straightened out in my mind.

Miss Kinnian said that the TV working in my sleep helped out. She said I reached a plateau. Thats like the flat top of a hill.

After I figgered out how punctuation worked, I read over all my old Progress Reports from the beginning. Boy, did I have crazy spelling and punctuation! I told Miss Kinnian I ought to go over the pages and fix all the mistakes but she said, "No, Charlie, Dr. Nemur wants them just as they are. That's why he let you keep them after they were photostated, to see your own progress. You're coming along fast, Charlie."

That made me feel good. After the lesson I went down and played with Algernon. We don't race any more.

April 20   I feel sick inside. Not sick like for a doctor, but inside my chest it feels empty like getting punched and a heartburn at the same time.

I wasn't going to write about it, but I guess I got to, because it's important, Today was the first time I ever stayed home from work.

Last night Joe Carp and Frank Reilly invited me to a party. There were lots of girls and some men from the factory. I remembered how sick I got last time I drank too much, so I told Joe I didn't want anything to drink. He gave me a plain Coke instead. It tasted funny, but I thought it was just a bad taste in my mouth.

We had a lot of fun for a while. Joe said I should dance with Ellen and she would teach me the steps. I fell a few times and I couldn't understand why because no one else was dancing besides Ellen and me. And all the time I was tripping because somebody's foot was always sticking out.

Then when I got up I saw the look on Joe's face and it gave me a funny feeling in my stomack. "He's a scream," one of the girls said. Everybody was laughing.

Frank said, "I ain't laughed so much since we sent him off for the newspaper that night at Muggsy's and ditched him."

"Look at him. His face is red."

"He's blushing. Charlie is blushing."

"Hey, Ellen, what'd you do to Charlie? I never saw him act like that before."

I didn't know what to do or where to turn. Everyone was looking at me and laughing and I felt naked. I wanted to hide myself. I ran out into the street and I threw up. Then I walked home. It's a funny thing I never knew that Joe and Frank and the others liked to have me around all the time to make fun of me.

Now I know what it means when they say "to pull a Charlie Gordon."

I'm ashamed.

PROGRESS REPORT 10

April 21   Still didn't go into the factory. I told Mrs. Flynn my landlady to call and tell Mr. Donnegan I was sick. Mrs. Flynn looks at me very funny lately like she's scared of me.

I think it's a good thing about finding out how everybody laughs at me. I thought about it a lot. It's because I'm so dumb and I don't even know when I'm doing something dumb. People think it's funny when a dumb person can't do things the same way they can.

Anyway, now I know I'm getting smarter every day. I know punctuation and I can spell good. I like to look up all the hard words in the dictionary and I remember them. I'm reading a lot now, and Miss Kinnian says I read very fast. Sometimes I even understand what I'm reading about, and it stays in my mind. There are times when I can close my eyes and think of a page and it all comes back like a picture.

Besides history, geography, and arithmetic, Miss Kinnian said I should start to learn a few foreign languages. Dr. Strauss gave me some more tapes to play while I sleep. I still don't understand how that conscious and unconscious mind works, but Dr. Strauss says not to worry yet. He asked me to promise that when I start learning college subjects next week I wouldn't read any books on psychology—that is, until he gives me permission.

I feel a lot better today, but I guess I'm still a little angry that all the time people were laughing and making fun of me because I wasn't so smart. When I become intelligent like Dr. Strauss says, with three times my I.Q. of 68, then maybe I'll be like everyone else and people will like me and be friendly.

I'm not sure what an I.Q. is. Dr. Nemur said it was something that measured how intelligent you were—like a scale in the drugstore weighs pounds. But Dr. Strauss had a big argument with him and said an I.Q. didn't weigh intelligence at all. He said an I.Q. showed how much intelligence you could get, like the numbers on the outside of a measuring cup. You still had to fill the cup up with stuff.

Then when I asked Burt, who gives me my intelligence tests and works with Algernon, he said that both of them were wrong (only I had to promise not to tell them he said so). Burt says that the I.Q. measures a lot of different things including some of the things you learned already, and it really isn't any good at all.

So I still don't know what I.Q. is except that mine is going to be over 200 soon. I didn't want to say anything, but I don't see how if they don't know *what* it is, or *where* it is—I don't see how they know *how much* of it you've got.

Dr. Nemur says I have to take a *Rorschach Test* tomorrow. I wonder what *that* is.

April 22 I found out what a *Rorschach* is. It's the test I took before the operation—the one with the inkblots on the pieces of cardboard. The man who gave me the test was the same one.

I was scared to death of those inkblots. I knew he was going to ask me to find the pictures and I knew I wouldn't be able to. I was thinking to myself, if only there was some way of knowing what kind of pictures were hidden there. Maybe there weren't any pictures at all. Maybe it was just a trick to see if I was dumb enough to look for something that wasn't there. Just thinking about that made me sore at him.

"All right, Charlie," he said, "you've seen these cards before, remember?"

"Of course I remember."

The way I said it, he knew I was angry, and he looked surprised. "Yes, of course. Now I want you to look at this one. What might this be? What do you see on this card? People see all sorts of things in these inkblots. Tell me what it might be for you—what it makes you think of."

I was shocked. That wasn't what I had expected him to say at all. "You mean there are no pictures hidden in those inkblots?"

He frowned and took off his glasses. "What?"

"Pictures. Hidden in the inkblots. Last time you told me that everyone could see them and you wanted me to find them too."

He explained to me that the last time he had used almost the exact same words he was using now. I didn't believe it, and I still have the suspicion that he misled me at the time just for the fun of it. Unless—I don't know any more—could I have been *that* feeble-minded?

We went through the cards slowly. One of them looked like a pair of bats tugging at something. Another one looked like two men fencing with swords. I imagined all sorts of things. I guess I got carried away. But I didn't trust him any more, and I kept turning them around and even looking on the back to see if there was anything there I was supposed to catch. While he was making his notes, I peeked out of the corner of my eye to read it. But it was all in code that looked like this:

WF + A   DdF − Ad orig.   WF−A   SF + obj

The test still doesn't make sense to me. It seems to me that anyone could make up lies about things that they didn't really see. How could he know I wasn't making a fool of him by mentioning things that I didn't really imagine? Maybe I'll understand it when Dr. Strauss lets me read up on psychology.

April 25 I figured out a new way to line up the machines in the factory, and Mr. Donnegan says it will save him ten thousand dollars a year in labor and increased production. He gave me a twenty-five-dollar bonus.

I wanted to take Joe Carp and Frank Reilly out to lunch to celebrate, but Joe said he had to buy some things for his wife, and Frank said he was meeting his cousin for lunch. I guess it'll take a little time for them to get used to the changes in me. Everybody seems to be frightened of me. When I went over to Amos Borg and tapped him on the shoulder, he jumped up in the air.

People don't talk to me much any more or kid around the way they used to. It makes the job kind of lonely.

April 27 I got up the nerve today to ask Miss Kinnian to have dinner with me tomorrow night to celebrate my bonus.

At first she wasn't sure it was right, but I asked Dr. Strauss and he said it was okay. Dr. Strauss and Dr. Nemur don't seem to be getting along so well. They're arguing all the time. This evening when I came in to ask Dr. Strauss about having dinner with Miss Kinnian, I heard them shouting. Dr. Nemur was saying that it was *his* experiment and *his* research, and Dr. Strauss was shouting back that he contributed just as much, because he found me through Miss Kinnian and he performed the operation. Dr. Strauss said that someday thousands of neurosurgeons might be using his technique all over the world.

Dr. Nemur wanted to publish the results of the experiment at the end of this month. Dr. Strauss wanted to wait a while longer to be sure. Dr. Strauss said that Dr. Nemur was more interested in the Chair[4] of Psychology at

4. **Chair:** here, a professorship.

Princeton than he was in the experiment. Dr. Nemur said that Dr. Strauss was nothing but an opportunist who was trying to ride to glory on *his* coattails.

When I left afterwards, I found myself trembling. I don't know why for sure, but it was as if I'd seen both men clearly for the first time. I remember hearing Burt say that Dr. Nemur had a shrew of a wife who was pushing him all the time to get things published so that he could become famous. Burt said that the dream of her life was to have a big-shot husband.

Was Dr. Strauss really trying to ride on his coattails?

April 28 I don't understand why I never noticed how beautiful Miss Kinnian really is. She has brown eyes and feathery brown hair that comes to the top of her neck. She's only thirty-four! I think from the beginning I had the feeling that she was an unreachable genius—and very, very old. Now, every time I see her she grows younger and more lovely.

We had dinner and a long talk. When she said that I was coming along so fast that soon I'd be leaving her behind, I laughed.

"It's true, Charlie. You're already a better reader than I am. You can read a whole page at a glance while I can take in only a few lines at a time. And you remember every single thing you read. I'm lucky if I can recall the main thoughts and the general meaning."

"I don't feel intelligent. There are so many things I don't understand."

She took out a cigarette and I lit it for her. "You've got to be a *little* patient. You're accomplishing in days and weeks what it takes normal people to do in half a lifetime. That's what makes it so amazing. You're like a giant sponge now, soaking things in. Facts, figures, general knowledge. And soon you'll begin to connect them, too. You'll see how the different branches of learning are related. There are many levels, Charlie, like steps on a giant ladder that take you up higher and higher to see more and more of the world around you.

"I can see only a little bit of that, Charlie, and I won't go much higher than I am now, but you'll keep climbing up and up, and see more and more, and each step will open new worlds that you never even knew existed." She frowned. "I hope . . . I just hope to God—"

"What?"

"Never mind, Charles. I just hope I wasn't wrong to advise you to go into this in the first place."

I laughed. "How could that be? It worked, didn't it? Even Algernon is still smart."

We sat there silently for a while and I knew what she was thinking about as she watched me toying with the chain of my rabbit's foot and my keys. I didn't want to think of that possibility any more than elderly people want to think of death. I *knew* that this was only the beginning. I knew what she meant about levels because I'd seen some of them already. The thought of leaving her behind made me sad.

I'm in love with Miss Kinnian.

PROGRESS REPORT 11

April 30 I've quit my job with Donnegan's Plastic Box Company. Mr. Donnegan insisted that it would be better for all concerned if I left. What did I do to make them hate me so?

The first I knew of it was when Mr. Donnegan showed me the petition. Eight hundred and forty names, everyone connected with the factory, except Fanny Girden. Scanning the list quickly, I saw at once that hers was the only missing name. All the rest demanded that I be fired.

Joe Carp and Frank Reilly wouldn't talk to me about it. No one else would either, except

Fanny. She was one of the few people I'd known who set her mind to something and believed it no matter what the rest of the world proved, said, or did—and Fanny did not believe that I should have been fired. She had been against the petition on principle and despite the pressure and threats she'd held out.

"Which don't mean to say," she remarked, "that I don't think there's something mighty strange about you, Charlie. Them changes. I don't know. You used to be a good, dependable, ordinary man—not too bright maybe, but honest. Who knows what you done to yourself to get so smart all of a sudden. Like everybody around here's been saying, Charlie, it's not right."

"But how can you say that, Fanny? What's wrong with a man becoming intelligent and wanting to acquire knowledge and understanding of the world around him?"

She stared down at her work and I turned to leave. Without looking at me, she said: "It was evil when Eve[5] listened to the snake and ate from the tree of knowledge. It was evil when she saw that she was naked. If not for that none of us would ever have to grow old and sick, and die."

Once again now I have the feeling of shame burning inside me. This intelligence has driven a wedge between me and all the people I once knew and loved. Before, they laughed at me and despised me for my ignorance and dullness; now, they hate me for my knowledge and understanding. What do they want of me?

They've driven me out of the factory. Now I'm more alone than ever before. . . .

May 15   Dr. Strauss is very angry at me for not having written any progress reports in two weeks. He's justified because the lab is now pay-ing me a regular salary. I told him I was too busy thinking and reading. When I pointed out that writing was such a slow process that it made me impatient with my poor handwriting, he suggested that I learn to type. It's much easier to write now because I can type nearly seventy-five words a minute. Dr. Strauss continually reminds me of the need to speak and write simply so that people will be able to understand me.

I'll try to review all the things that happened to me during the last two weeks. Algernon and I were presented to the American Psychological Association sitting in convention with the World Psychological Association last Tuesday. We created quite a sensation. Dr. Nemur and Dr. Strauss were proud of us.

I suspect that Dr. Nemur, who is sixty—ten years older than Dr. Strauss—finds it necessary to see tangible results of his work. Undoubtedly the result of pressure by Mrs. Nemur.

Contrary to my earlier impressions of him, I realize that Dr. Nemur is not at all a genius. He has a very good mind, but it struggles under the specter of self-doubt. He wants people to take him for a genius. Therefore, it is important for him to feel that his work is accepted by the world. I believe that Dr. Nemur was afraid of further delay because he worried that someone else might make a discovery along these lines and take the credit from him.

Dr. Strauss on the other hand might be called a genius, although I feel that his areas of knowledge are too limited. He was educated in the tradition of narrow specialization; the broader aspects of background were neglected far more than necessary—even for a neurosurgeon.

I was shocked to learn that the only ancient languages he could read were Latin, Greek, and Hebrew, and that he knows almost nothing of mathematics beyond the elementary levels of the calculus of variations. When he admit-

5. **Eve:** The story of Adam and Eve is told in Genesis 2–3.

ted this to me, I found myself almost annoyed. It was as if he'd hidden this part of himself in order to deceive me, pretending—as do many people I've discovered—to be what he is not. No one I've ever known is what he appears to be on the surface.

Dr. Nemur appears to be uncomfortable around me. Sometimes when I try to talk to him, he just looks at me strangely and turns away. I was angry at first when Dr. Strauss told me I was giving Dr. Nemur an inferiority complex. I thought he was mocking me and I'm oversensitive at being made fun of.

How was I to know that a highly respected psychoexperimentalist like Nemur was unacquainted with Hindustani and Chinese? It's absurd when you consider the work that is being done in India and China today in the very field of his study.

I asked Dr. Strauss how Nemur could refute Rahajamati's attack on his method and results if Nemur couldn't even read it in the first place. The strange look on Dr. Strauss's face can only mean one of two things. Either he doesn't want to tell Nemur what they're saying in India, or else—and this worries me—Dr. Strauss doesn't know either. I must be careful to speak and write clearly and simply so that people won't laugh.

May 18   I am very disturbed. I saw Miss Kinnian last night for the first time in over a week. I tried to avoid all discussions of intellectual concepts and to keep the conversation on a simple, everyday level, but she just stared at me blankly and asked me what I meant about the mathematical variance equivalent in Dobermann's Fifth Concerto.

When I tried to explain she stopped me and laughed. I guess I got angry, but I suspect I'm approaching her on the wrong level. No matter what I try to discuss with her, I am unable to communicate. I must review Vrostadt's equations on *Levels of Semantic Progression.* I find that I don't communicate with people much any more. Thank God for books and music and things I can think about. I am alone in my apartment at Mrs. Flynn's boardinghouse most of the time and seldom speak to anyone.

May 20   I would not have noticed the new dishwasher, a boy of about sixteen, at the corner diner where I take my evening meals if not for the incident of the broken dishes.

They crashed to the floor, shattering and sending bits of white china under the tables. The boy stood there, dazed and frightened, holding the empty tray in his hand. The whistles and catcalls from the customers (the cries of "Hey, there go the profits!" . . . "*Mazel tov!*"[6] . . . and "Well, *he* didn't work here very long. . . ." which invariably seem to follow the breaking of glass or dishware in a public restaurant) all seemed to confuse him.

When the owner came to see what the excitement was about, the boy cowered as if he expected to be struck and threw up his arms as if to ward off the blow.

"All right! All right, you dope," shouted the owner, "don't just stand there! Get the broom and sweep that mess up. A broom . . . a broom, you idiot! It's in the kitchen. Sweep up all the pieces."

The boy saw that he was not going to be punished. His frightened expression disappeared and he smiled and hummed as he came back with the broom to sweep the floor. A few of the rowdier customers kept up the remarks, amusing themselves at his expense.

"Here, sonny, over here there's a nice piece behind you. . . ."

"C'mon, do it again. . . ."

"He's not so dumb. It's easier to break 'em than to wash 'em. . . ."

6. *Mazel tov!* (mä´zəl tôf): Hebrew for "Congratulations!"

As his vacant eyes moved across the crowd of amused onlookers, he slowly mirrored their smiles and finally broke into an uncertain grin at the joke which he obviously did not understand.

I felt sick inside as I looked at his dull, vacuous smile, the wide, bright eyes of a child, uncertain but eager to please. They were laughing at him because he was mentally retarded.

And I had been laughing at him too.

Suddenly, I was furious at myself and all those who were smirking at him. I jumped up and shouted, "Shut up! Leave him alone! It's not his fault he can't understand! He can't help what he is! But . . . he's still a human being!"

The room grew silent. I cursed myself for losing control and creating a scene. I tried not to look at the boy as I paid my check and walked out without touching my food. I felt ashamed for both of us.

How strange it is that people of honest feelings and sensibility, who would not take advantage of a man born without arms or legs or eyes—how such people think nothing of abusing a man born with low intelligence. It infuriated me to think that not long ago, I, like this boy, had foolishly played the clown.

And I had almost forgotten.

I'd hidden the picture of the old Charlie Gordon from myself because now that I was intelligent it was something that had to be pushed out of my mind. But today in looking at that boy, for the first time I saw what I had been. *I was just like him!*

Only a short time ago, I learned that people laughed at me. Now I can see that unknowingly I had joined with them in laughing at myself. That hurts most of all.

I have often reread my progress reports and seen the illiteracy, the childish naiveté, the mind of low intelligence peering from a dark room, through the keyhole, at the dazzling light outside. I see that even in my dullness I knew that I was inferior, and that other people had something that I lacked—something denied me. In my mental blindness, I thought that it was somehow connected with the ability to read and write, and I was sure that if I could get those skills I would automatically have intelligence too.

Even a feebleminded man wants to be like other men.

A child may not know how to feed itself, or what to eat, yet it knows of hunger.

This then is what I was like; I never knew. Even with my gift of intellectual awareness, I never really knew.

This day was good for me. Seeing the past more clearly, I have decided to use my knowledge and skills to work in the field of increasing human intelligence levels. Who is better equipped for this work? Who else has lived in both worlds? These are my people. Let me use my gift to do something for them.

Tomorrow, I will discuss with Dr. Strauss the manner in which I can work in this area. I may be able to help him work out the problems of widespread use of the technique which was used on me. I have several good ideas of my own.

There is so much that might be done with this technique. If I could be made into a genius, what about thousands of others like myself? What fantastic levels might be achieved by using this technique on normal people? On *geniuses?*

There are so many doors to open. I am impatient to begin.

PROGRESS REPORT 12

May 23 It happened today. Algernon bit me. I visited the lab to see him as I do occasionally, and when I took him out of his cage, he snapped at my hand. I put him back and watched him for a while. He was unusually disturbed and vicious.

May 24   Burt, who is in charge of the experimental animals, tells me that Algernon is changing. He is less cooperative; he refuses to run the maze any more; general motivation has decreased. And he hasn't been eating. Everyone is upset about what this may mean.

May 25   They've been feeding Algernon, who now refuses to work the shifting-lock problem. Everyone identifies me with Algernon. In a way we're both the first of our kind. They're all pretending that Algernon's behavior is not necessarily significant for me. But it's hard to hide the fact that some of the other animals who were used in the experiment are showing strange behavior.

Dr. Strauss and Dr. Nemur have asked me not to come to the lab any more. I know what they're thinking but I can't accept it. I am going ahead with my plans to carry their research forward. With all due respect to both of these fine scientists, I am well aware of their limitations. If there is an answer, I'll have to find it out for myself. Suddenly, time has become very important to me.

May 29   I have been given a lab of my own and permission to go ahead with the research. I'm on to something. Working day and night. I've had a cot moved into the lab. Most of my writing time is spent on the notes which I keep in a separate folder, but from time to time I feel it necessary to put down my moods and my thoughts out of sheer habit.

I find the *calculus of intelligence* to be a fascinating study. Here is the place for the application of all the knowledge I have acquired. In a sense it's the problem I've been concerned with all my life.

May 31   Dr. Strauss thinks I'm working too hard. Dr. Nemur says I'm trying to cram a lifetime of research and thought into a few weeks. I know I should rest, but I'm driven on by something inside that won't let me stop. I've got to find the reason for the sharp regression in Algernon. I've got to know *if* and *when* it will happen to me.

June 4
LETTER TO DR. STRAUSS *(copy)*

Dear Dr. Strauss

Under separate cover I am sending you a copy of my report entitled "The Algernon-Gordon Effect: A Study of Structure and Function of Increased Intelligence," which I would like to have you read and have published.

As you can see, my experiments are completed. I have included in my report all of my formulae, as well as mathematical analysis in the appendix. Of course, these should be verified.

Because of its importance to both you and Dr. Nemur (and need I say to myself, too?) I have checked and rechecked my results a dozen times in the hope of finding an error.

I am sorry to say the results must stand. Yet for the sake of science, I am grateful for the little bit that I here add to the knowledge of the function of the human mind and of the laws governing the artificial increase of human intelligence.

I recall your saying to me once that an experimental *failure* or the *disproving* of a theory was as important to the advancement of learning as a success would be. I know now that this is true. I am sorry, however, that my own contribution to the field must rest upon the ashes of the work of two men I regard so highly.

Yours truly,
Charles Gordon

June 5 I must not become emotional. The facts and the results of my experiments are clear, and the more sensational aspects of my own rapid climb cannot obscure the fact that the tripling of intelligence by the surgical technique developed by Drs. Strauss and Nemur must be viewed as having little or no practical applicability (at the present time) to the increase of human intelligence.

As I review the records and data on Algernon, I see that although he is still in his physical infancy, he has regressed mentally. Motor activity[7] is impaired; there is a general reduction of glandular activity; there is an accelerated loss of coordination.

There are also strong indications of progressive amnesia.

As will be seen by my report, these and other physical and mental deterioration syndromes can be predicted with statistically significant results by the application of my formula.

The surgical stimulus to which we were both subjected has resulted in an intensification and acceleration of all mental processes. The unforeseen development, which I have taken the liberty of calling the "Algernon-Gordon Effect," is the logical extension of the entire intelligence speedup. The hypothesis here proven may be described simply in the following terms: Artificially increased intelligence deteriorates at a rate of time directly proportional to the quantity of the increase.

I feel that this, in itself, is an important discovery.

7. **Motor activity:** movement.

As long as I am able to write, I will continue to record my thoughts in these progress reports. It is one of my few pleasures. However, by all indications, my own mental deterioration will be very rapid.

I have already begun to notice signs of emotional instability and forgetfulness, the first symptoms of the burnout.

June 10 Deterioration progressing. I have become absent-minded. Algernon died two days ago. Dissection shows my predictions were right. His brain had decreased in weight and there was a general smoothing out of cerebral convolutions[8] as well as a deepening and broadening of brain fissures.[9]

I guess the same thing is or soon will be happening to me. Now that's it's definite, I don't want it to happen.

I put Algernon's body in a cheese box and buried him in the backyard. I cried.

June 15 Dr. Strauss came to see me again. I wouldn't open the door and told him to go away. I want to be left to myself. I have become touchy and irritable. I feel the darkness closing in. It's hard to throw off thoughts of suicide. I keep telling myself how important this introspective journal will be.

It's a strange sensation to pick up a book that you've read and enjoyed just a few months ago and discover that you don't remember it. I remembered how great I thought John Milton was, but when I picked up *Paradise Lost* I couldn't understand it at all. I got so angry I threw the book across the room.

I've got to try to hold on to some of it. Some of the things I've learned. Oh, God, please don't take it all away.

8. **cerebral** (sə-rē′brəl) **convolutions** (kŏn′və-loo′shənz): irregular folds in the cerebrum, the part of the brain where thinking takes place.
9. **fissures** (fĭsh′ərz): deep cracks or grooves.

June 19 Sometimes, at night, I go out for a walk. Last night I couldn't remember where I lived. A policeman took me home. I have the strange feeling that this has all happened to me before—a long time ago. I keep telling myself I'm the only person in the world who can describe what's happening to me.

June 21 Why can't I remember? I've got to fight. I lie in bed for days and I don't know who or where I am. Then it all comes back to me in a flash. Fugues of amnesia.[10] Symptoms of senility—second childhood. I can watch them coming on. It's so cruelly logical. I learned so much and so fast. Now my mind is deteriorating rapidly. I won't let it happen. I'll fight it. I can't help thinking of the boy in the restaurant, the blank expression, the silly smile, the people laughing at him. No—please—not that again . . .

June 22 I'm forgetting things that I learned recently. It seems to be following the classic pattern—the last things learned are the first things forgotten. Or is that the pattern? I'd better look it up again. . . .

I reread my paper on the "Algernon-Gordon Effect" and I get the strange feeling that it was written by someone else. There are parts I don't even understand.

Motor activity impaired. I keep tripping over things, and it becomes increasingly difficult to type.

June 23 I've given up using the typewriter completely. My coordination is bad. I feel that I'm moving slower and slower. Had a terrible shock today. I picked up a copy of an article I used in my research, Krueger's "Über psychi-

sche Ganzheit," to see if it would help me understand what I had done. First I thought there was something wrong with my eyes. Then I realized I could no longer read German. I tested myself in other languages. All gone.

June 30 A week since I dared to write again. It's slipping away like sand through my fingers. Most of the books I have are too hard for me now. I get angry with them because I know that I read and understood them just a few weeks ago.

I keep telling myself I must keep writing these reports so that somebody will know what is happening to me. But it gets harder to form the words and remember spellings. I have to look up even simple words in the dictionary now and it makes me impatient with myself.

Dr. Strauss comes around almost every day, but I told him I wouldn't see or speak to anybody. He feels guilty. They all do. But I don't blame anyone. I knew what might happen. But how it hurts.

July 7 I don't know where the week went. Todays Sunday I know becuase I can see through my window people going to church. I think I stayed in bed all week but I remember Mrs. Flynn bringing food to me a few times. I keep saying over and over I've got to do something but then I forget or maybe its just easier not to do what I say Im going to do.

I think of my mother and father a lot these days. I found a picture of them with me taken at a beach. My father has a big ball under his arm and my mother is holding me by the hand. I dont remember them the way they are in the picture. All I remember is my father arguing with mom about money. He never shaved much and he used to scratch my face when he hugged me. He said he was going to take me to see cows on a farm once but he never did. He never kept his promises . . .

10. **Fugues** (fyo͞ogz) **of amnesia** (ăm-nē′zhə): periods of time in which a person behaves normally but later has no memory of what has happened.

July 10   My landlady Mrs Flynn is very worried about me. She said she doesnt like loafers. If Im sick its one thing, but if Im a loafer thats another thing and she wont have it. I told her I think Im sick.

I try to read a little bit every day, mostly stories, but sometimes I have to read the same thing over and over again because I dont know what it means. And its hard to write. I know I should look up all the words in the dictionary but its so hard and Im so tired all the time.

Then I got the idea that I would only use the easy words instead of the long hard ones. That saves time. I put flowers on Algernons grave about once a week. Mrs Flynn thinks Im crazy to put flowers on a mouses grave but I told her that Algernon was special.

July 14   Its sunday again. I dont have anything to do to keep me busy now because my television set is broke and I dont have any money to get it fixed. (I think I lost this months check from the lab. I don't remember)

I get awful headaches and asperin doesnt help me much. Mrs Flynn knows Im really sick and she feels sorry for me. Shes a wonderful woman whenever someone is sick.

July 22   Mrs Flynn called a strange doctor to see me. She was afraid I was going to die. I told the doctor I wasnt too sick and that I only forget sometimes. He asked me did I have any friends or relatives and I said no I dont have any. I told him I had a friend called Algernon once but he was a mouse and we used to run races together. He looked at me kind of funny like he thought I was crazy.

He smiled when I told him I used to be a genius. He talked to me like I was a baby and he winked at Mrs Flynn. I got mad and chased him out because he was making fun of me the way they all used to.

July 24   I have no money and Mrs Flynn says I got to go to work somewhere and pay the rent because I havent paid for over two months. I dont know any work but the job I used to have at Donnegans Plastic Box Company. I dont want to go back there because they all knew me when I was smart and maybe theyll laugh at me. But I dont know what else to do to get money.

July 25   I was looking at some of my old progress reports and its very funny but I cant read what I wrote. I can make out some of the words but they don't make sense.

Miss Kinnian came to the door but I said go away I dont want to see you. She cried and I cried too but I wouldnt let her in because I didnt want her to laugh at me. I told her I didn't like her any more. I told her I didnt want to be smart any more. Thats not true. I still love her and I still want to be smart but I had to say that so shed go away. She gave Mrs Flynn money to pay the rent. I dont want that. I got to get a job.

Please . . . please let me not forget how to read and write . . .

July 27   Mr Donnegan was very nice when I came back and asked him for my old job of janitor. First he was very suspicious but I told him what happened to me and then he looked very sad and put his hand on my shoulder and said Charlie Gordon you got guts.

Everybody looked at me when I came downstairs and started working in the toilet sweeping it out like I used to. I told myself Charlie if they make fun of you dont get sore because you remember their not so smart as you once thot they were. And besides they were once your friends and if they laughed at you that doesn't mean anything because they liked you too.

One of the new men who came to work there

after I went away made a nasty crack he said hey Charlie I hear your a very smart fella a real quiz kid. Say something intelligent. I felt bad but Joe Carp came over and grabbed him by the shirt and said leave him alone or Ill break your neck. I didnt expect Joe to take my part so I guess hes really my friend.

Later Frank Reilly came over and said Charlie if anybody bothers you or trys to take advantage you call me or Joe and we will set em straight. I said thanks Frank and I got choked up so I had to go into the supply room so he wouldn't see me cry. Its good to have friends.

July 28 I did a dumb thing today I forgot I wasnt in Miss Kinnians class at the adult center any more like I use to be. I went in and sat down in my old seat in the back of the room and she looked at me funny and she said Charles. I dint remember she ever called me that before only Charlie so I said hello Miss Kinnian Im redy for my lesin today only I lost my reader that we was using. She startid to cry and run out of the room and everybody looked at me and I saw they wasnt the same pepul who used to be in my class.

Then all of a suddin I rememberd some things about the operashun and me getting smart and I said holy smoke I reely pulled a Charlie Gordon that time. I went away before she came back to the room.

Thats why Im going away from New York for

good. I dont want to do nothing like that agen. I dont want Miss Kinnian to feel sorry for me. Evry body feels sorry at the factery and I dont want that eather so Im going someplace where nobody knows that Charlie Gordon was once a genus and now he cant even reed a book or rite good.

Im taking a cuple of books along and even if I cant reed them Ill practise hard and maybe I wont forget every thing I lerned. If I try reel hard maybe Ill be a littel bit smarter then I was before the operashun. I got my rabits foot and my luky penny and maybe they will help me.

If you ever reed this Miss Kinnian dont be sorry for me Im glad I got a second chanse to be smart becaus I lerned a lot of things that I never even new were in this world and Im grateful that I saw it all for a littel bit. I dont know why Im dumb agen or what I did wrong maybe its becaus I dint try hard enuff. But if I try and practis very hard maybe Ill get a littl smarter and know what all the words are. I remember a littel bit how nice I had a feeling with the blue book that has the torn cover when I red it. Thats why Im gonna keep trying to get smart so I can have that feeling agen. Its a good feeling to know things and be smart. I wish I had it rite now if I did I would sit down and reed all the time. Anyway I bet Im the first dumb person in the world who ever found out something important for sience. I remember I did somthing but I dont remember what. So I guess its like I did it for all the dumb pepul like me.

Good-by Miss Kinnian and Dr Strauss and evreybody. And P.S. please tell Dr Nemur not to be such a grouch when pepul laff at him and he woud have more frends. Its easy to make frends if you let pepul laff at you. Im going to have lots of frends where I go. P.P.S. Please if you get a chanse put some flowrs on Algernons grave in the bak yard . . .

Reading Check

1. Who suggests that Charlie volunteer for the experiment?
2. What is Charlie's job at the factory?
3. How does Charlie learn while he is asleep?
4. What is the first sign of change in Algernon?
5. What are the first symptoms of the deterioration of Charlie's intelligence?

For Study and Discussion

Analyzing and Interpreting the Story

1. "Flowers for Algernon" is a story about a young man who undergoes a remarkable transformation, or change, through surgery. According to the Progress Report dated March 8, what are the doctors planning to do with their daring techniques?

2. What evidence in the entries of March 10 through April 18 shows Charlie's increase in intelligence?

3. In the entry of April 20, Charlie's feelings change. What happens to make him feel ashamed?

4a. As Charlie becomes *more* intelligent, how do his relations with other people change? b. How do the doctors, Miss Kinnian, and the people at the factory treat him when he *loses* his intelligence?

5. Charlie feels shame again in the entry of May 20. a. What does Charlie learn about himself in the scene with the dishwasher? b. What resolution does he make at the end of this entry?

6. The entry of May 23 opens with the dramatic words: "It happened today." What hap-

pened, and why does Charlie see such significance in it?

7. In his P.S., Charlie says, "Its easy to make frends if you let pepul laff at you. Im going to have lots of frends where I go." Why is this statement sad?

8. In the entry of April 30, one of Charlie's co-workers, Fanny, says that it was evil when Eve listened to the snake and ate from the tree of knowledge. **a.** Why do you think she reminds Charlie of the temptation of Adam and Eve? **b.** How does Charlie, like Adam and Eve, have to pay a terrible price for his decision?

9a. What is going to happen to Charlie? **b.** How do you know?

10. Why is Algernon so important to Charlie?

11a. If Charlie had understood what would happen to him, do you think he would still have chosen to be intelligent, or to be limited mentally, as he is in the beginning and the end of this story? **b.** What evidence from his own reports can you find to support your answer?

Literary Elements

Understanding Point of View

"Flowers for Algernon" is written from the point of view of Charlie Gordon, the narrator. You learn about the characters and events in the story only through what Charlie writes in his reports. A story told by one of its characters is written in the **first-person point of view.** (The first-person pronoun is *I,* and it is an *I* who tells the story.)

The first-person point of view enables you to learn the narrator's thoughts and feelings, but it limits your understanding of other characters. First-person narrators can report only conversations and events they are aware of. Charlie's limited understanding of the people around him is clear at the beginning of his story. For example, what is really happening to Miss Kinnian in this entry of April 15?

> I said all my frends are smart people but there good. They like me and they never did anything that wasnt nice. Then she got something in her eye and she had to run out to the ladys room.

A writer may choose any of the characters in the story to be the narrator. Why do you think Daniel Keyes made Charlie Gordon the narrator, instead of Miss Kinnian or one of the doctors? Why do you think he chose to write the story in the form of personal reports, which are like diary entries?

Language and Vocabulary

Identifying Levels of Usage

As Charlie Gordon's intelligence changes, his use of language also changes. Notice the dramatic contrast in the following sentences.

> I dint see nuthing in the ink but he said there was picturs there other pepul saw some picturs.

> I am sorry, however, that my own contribution to the field must rest upon the ashes of the work of two men I regard so highly.

What mistakes can you find in the first sentence? This type of language, or level of usage, is called **nonstandard English** because it does not follow the generally accepted rules of English usage and English spelling.

The second sentence is an example of **standard English,** the level of usage most widely accepted by English-speaking people. When Charlie Gordon begins to write in standard English, what do you realize is happening to him mentally?

Charlie's command of vocabulary also changes in this story. His intelligence is probably at its peak on June 4 and 5. How do the reports written on these two days show that he has acquired an extensive scientific vocabulary? Contrast these reports with the one written on March 8.

Despite the different levels of usage in his Progress Reports, Charlie Gordon retains the same human feelings. Did your own feelings for Charlie change after his writing improved? Why or why not?

Creative Writing

Writing from a Different Point of View

Choose an incident from this story, and retell it from the point of view of a character other than Charlie Gordon. Have your new narrator write a diary entry telling what happened, what was said, and how he or she felt about the incident. You may choose any episode in the story. Here are some suggestions:

April 20. Joe Carp gets Charlie to dance with Ellen. (Use Ellen as the narrator.)

April 28. Miss Kinnian and Charlie have dinner together and talk about how Charlie has changed. (Use Miss Kinnian as the narrator.)

May 15. Dr. Nemur is uncomfortable around Charlie. (Use Dr. Nemur as the narrator.)

July 27. Joe Carp comes to Charlie's rescue when a new man makes a nasty crack about Charlie's former intelligence. (Use Joe Carp as the narrator.)

About the Author

Daniel Keyes (1927–   )

Daniel Keyes says he is "fascinated by the complexities of the human mind," as "Flowers for Algernon" shows. The story won the Hugo Award given by the Science Fiction Writers of America in 1959, and it has been translated into many languages. Keyes expanded the story into a novel, which won the Nebula Award for science fiction in 1966. The story was also successful as a television play called *The Two Worlds of Charlie Gordon* and as a movie called *Charly*. The novel was adapted into a stage musical in 1980. Keyes won a special award from the Mystery Writers of America for *The Minds of Billy Milligan*, his 1981 novel, which continues his interest in psychological themes.

Keyes was born in New York City and graduated from Brooklyn College. He has worked as a merchant seaman, a fiction editor, and a photographer. He has taught English at Ohio University in Athens, Ohio, since 1962, and is director of the university's creative writing center.

The Land and The Water

SHIRLEY ANN GRAU

At some point in our lives, we all realize that death can touch us at any time.
Read the story to see how the author explores this theme.

From the open Atlantic beyond Timbalier Head[1] a few scattered foghorns grunted, muffled and faint. That bank[2] had been hanging offshore for days. We'd been watching the big draggers[3] chug up to it, get dimmer and dimmer, and finally disappear in its grayness, leaving only the stifled sounds of their horns behind. It had been there so long we got used to it, and came to think of it as always being there, like another piece of land, maybe.

The particular day I'm thinking about started out clear and hot with a tiny breeze—a perfect day for a snipe or a sailfish.[4] There were a few of them moving on the big bay, not many. And they stayed close to shore, for the barometer was drifting slowly down in its tube and the wind was shifting slowly backward around the compass.[5]

Larger sailboats never came into the bay—it was too shallow for them—and these small ones, motorless, moving with the smallest stir of air, could sail for home, if the fog came in, by following the shore—or if there was really no wind at all, they could be paddled in and beached. Then their crews could walk to the nearest phone and call to be picked up. You had to do it that way, because the fog always came in so quick. As it did that morning.

My sister and I were working by our dock, scraping and painting the little dinghy.[6] Because the spring tides washed over this stretch, there were no trees, no bushes even, just snail grass and beach lettuce and pink flowering sea lavender, things that liked salt. All morning it had been bright and blue and shining. Then all at once it turned gray and wet, like an unfalling rain, moveless and still. We went right on sanding and from being sweaty hot we turned sweaty cold, the fog chilling and dripping off our faces.

"It isn't worth the money," my sister said. She is ten and that is her favorite sentence. This time it wasn't even true. She was the one who'd talked my father into giving us the job.

I wouldn't give her the satisfaction of an answer, though I didn't like the wet any more

---

1. **Timbalier** (tăm′bəl-yā′) **Head:** the part of Louisiana that juts into Tambalier Bay.
2. **bank:** a mass of fog.
3. **draggers:** trawlers, or fishing boats that use huge nets to catch fish.
4. **snipe . . . sailfish:** sailboats.
5. **the barometer . . . compass:** A drop in atmospheric pressure and a change in wind direction are signs that a storm is approaching.

6. **dinghy** (dĭng′ē): a small rowboat.

than she did. It was sure to make my hair roll up in tight little curls all over my head and I would have to wash it again and sleep on the hard metal curlers to get it back in shape.

Finally my sister said, "Let's go get a Coke."

When we turned around to go back up to the house, we found that it had disappeared. It was only a couple of hundred yards away, right behind us and up a little grade, a long slope of beach plum and poison ivy, saltburned and scrubby. You couldn't see a thing now, except gray. The land and the water all looked the same; the fog was that thick.

There weren't any Cokes. Just some bottles of Dr. Pepper and a lot of empties waiting in cases on the back porch. "Well," my sister said, "let's go tell her."

She meant my mother, of course, and we didn't have to look for her very hard. The house wasn't big, and being a summer house, it had very thin walls: we could hear her playing cards with my father in the living room.

They were sitting by the front window. On a clear day there was really something to see out there: the sweep of the bay and the pattern of the inlets and, beyond it all, the dark blue of the Atlantic. Today there was nothing, not even a bird, if you didn't count the occasional yelp of a sea gull off high overhead somewhere.

"There's no Cokes," my sister said. "Not a single one."

"Tomorrow's grocery day," my mother said. "Go make a lemonade."

"Look," my father said, "why not go back to work on the dinghy? You'll get your money faster."

So we went, only stopping first to get our oil-skin hats. And pretty soon, fog was dripping from the brims like a kind of gentle rain.

But we didn't go back to work on the dinghy. For a while we sat on the edge of the dock and looked at the minnow-flecked water, and then we got out the crab nets and went over to the tum-

bled heap of rocks to see if we could catch anything. We spent a couple of hours out there, skinning our knees against the rough barnacled[7] surfaces. Once a sea gull swooped down so low he practically touched the tops of our hats. Almost but not quite. I don't think we even saw a crab, though we dragged our nets around in the water just for the fun of it. Finally we dug a dozen or so clams, ate them, and tried to skip the shells along the water. That was how the afternoon passed, with one thing or the other, and us not hurrying, not having anything we'd rather be doing.

We didn't have a watch with us, but it must have been late afternoon when they all came down from the house. We heard them before we saw them, heard the brush of their feet on the grass path.

It was my mother and my father and Robert, my biggest brother, the one who is eighteen. My father had the round black compass and a coil of new line. Robert had a couple of gas lanterns and a big battery one. My mother had the life jackets and a little wicker basket and a thermos bottle. They all went out along the narrow rickety dock and began to load the gear into my father's *Sea Skiff.* It wasn't a big boat and my father had to take a couple of minutes to pack it, stowing the basket way up forward under the cowling[8] and wedging the thermos bottle on top of that. Robert, who'd left his lanterns on the ground to help him, came back to fetch them.

"I thought you were at the McKays," I said. "How'd you get over here?"

"Dad called me." He lifted one eyebrow. "Remember about something called the telephone?" And he picked up his gear and walked away.

"Well," my sister said.

They cast off; the big outboard sputtered gen-

7. **barnacled** (bär'nə-kəld): covered with barnacles, tiny shellfish that cling to rocks and wood.
8. **cowling:** a metal lid that covers an engine.

tly, throttled way down. They would have to move very slowly in the fog. As they swung away, Robert at the tiller, we saw my father set out his compass and take a bearing off it.

My mother watched them out of sight, which didn't take more than a half-minute. Then she stood watching the fog for a while and, I guess, following the sound of the steady put-put. It seemed to me, listening to it move off and blend with the sounds of the bay—the sounds of a lot of water, of tiny waves and fish feeding—that I could pick out two or three other motors.

Finally my mother got tired of standing on the end of the dock and she turned around and walked up to us. I expected her to pass right by and go on up to the house. But she didn't. We

could hear her stop and stand looking at us. My sister and I just scraped a little harder, pretending we hadn't noticed.

"I guess you're wondering what that was all about?" she said finally.

"I don't care," my sister said. She was lying. She was just as curious as I was.

My mother didn't seem to have heard her. "It's Linda Holloway and Stan Mitchell and Butch Rodgers."

We knew them. They were sailing people, a little older than I. A little younger than my brother Robert. They lived in three houses lined up one by the other on the north shore of Marshall's Inlet. They were all-right kids, nothing special either way, sort of a gang, living as close as they did. This year they had turned up with a new sailboat, a twelve-foot fiberglass job that somebody had designed and built for Stan Mitchell as a birthday present.

"What about them?" my sister asked, forgetthing that she wasn't interested.

"They haven't come home."

"Oh," I said.

"They were sailing," my mother said. "The Brewers think they saw them off their place just before the fog. They were sort of far out."

"You mean Dad's gone to look for them?"

She nodded.

"Is that all?" my sister said. "Just somebody going to have to sit in their boat and wait until the fog lifts."

My mother looked at us. Her curly red hair was dripping with the damp of the fog and her face was smeared with dust. "The Lord save me from children," she said quietly. "The glass is twenty-nine eighty and it's still going down fast."

We went back up to the house with her, to help fix supper—a quiet nervous kind of supper. The thick luminous fish-colored fog turned into deep solid night fog. Just after supper, while we were drying the dishes, the wind sprang up. It shook the whole line of windows in the kitchen and knocked over every single pot of geraniums on the back porch.

"Well," my mother said, "it's square into the east now."

A low barometer and a wind that had gone backwards into the east—there wasn't one of us didn't know what that meant. And it wasn't more than half an hour before there was a grumble of approaching thunder and the fog began to swirl around the windows, streaming like torn cotton as the wind increased.

"Dad'll come back now, huh?" my sister asked.

"Yes," my mother said. "All the boats'll have to come back now."

We settled down to television, half watching it and half listening to the storm outside. In a little

while, an hour or so, my mother said, "Turn off that thing."

"What?"

"Turn if off, quick." She hurried on the porch, saying over her shoulder: "I hear something."

The boards of the wide platform were wet and slippery under our feet, and the eaves of the house poured water in steady small streams that the wind grabbed and tore away. Between the crashes of thunder, we heard it too. There was a boat coming into our cove. By the sound of it, it would be my father and Robert.

"Is that the motor?" my mother asked.

"Sure," I said. It had a little tick and it was higher pitched than any of the others. You couldn't miss it.

Without another word to us she went scuttling across the porch and down the stairs toward the cove. We followed and stood close by, off the path and a little to one side. It was tide marsh there, and salt mud oozed over the tops of our sneakers. The cove itself was sheltered—it was in the lee[9] of Cedar Tree Neck—but even so it was pretty choppy. Whitecaps were beginning to run high and broken, wind against tide, and the spume from them stung as it hit your face and your eyes. You could hear the real stuff blowing overhead, with the peculiar sound wind has when it gets past half a gale.

My father's boat was sidling up to the dock now, pitching and rolling in the broken water. Its motor sputtered into reverse and then the hull rubbed gently against the pilings. They had had a bad time. In the quick lightning flashes you could see every scupper[10] pouring water. You could see the slow weary way they made the lines fast.

"There wasn't anything else to do," my father was saying as they came up the path, beating their arms for warmth; "with it blowing straight

9. **lee:** the side away from the wind; the protected side.
10. **scupper:** an opening in a ship's side at deck level that allows water to run off the deck.

out of the east, we had to come in."

Robert stopped a moment to pull off his oil-skins. Under them his shirt was as drenched as if he hadn't had any protection at all.

"We came the long way around," my father said, "hugging the lee as much as we could."

"We almost swamped," Robert said.

Then we were at the house and they went off to dry their clothes, and that was that. They told us later that everybody had come in, except only for the big Coast Guard launch. And with only one boat it was no wonder they didn't find them.

The next morning was bright and clear and a lot cooler. The big stretch of bay was still shaken and tousled-looking, spotted with whitecaps. Soon as it was light, my father went to the front porch and looked and looked with his glasses. He checked the anemometer[11] dial and shook his head. "It's still too rough for us." In a bit the coast Guard boats—two of them—appeared, and a helicopter began its chopping noisy circling.

It was marketing day too, so my mother, my sister, and I went off, as we always did. We stopped at the laundromat and the hardware, and then my mother had to get some pine trees for the slope behind the house. It was maybe four o'clock before we got home.

The wind had dropped; the bay was almost quiet again. Robert and my father were gone, and so was the boat. "I thought they'd go out again," my mother said. She got a cup of coffee and the three of us sat watching the fleet of boats work their way back and forth across the bay, searching.

Just before dark—just when the sky was beginning to take its twilight color—my father and Robert appeared. They were burned lobster-red with great white circles around their eyes where their glasses had been.

"Did you find anything?" my sister asked.

My father looked at my mother, who was opening a can of beer for him.

"You might as well tell them," she said. "They'll know anyway."

"Well," my father said, "they found the boat."

"That's what they were expecting to find, wasn't it?" my mother asked quietly.

He nodded. "It's kind of hard to say what happened. But it looks like they got blown on East Shoal with the tide going down and the chop tearing the keel out."[12]

"Oh," my mother said.

"Oh," my sister said.

"They found the boat around noon."

My mother said: "Have they found them?"

"Not that I heard."

"You think," my mother said, "they could have got to shore way out on Gull Point or some place like that?"

"No place is more than a four-hour walk," my father said. "They'd have turned up by now."

And it was later still, after dark, ten o'clock or so, that Mr. Robinson, who lived next door, stopped on the porch on his way home. "Found one," he said wearily. "The Mitchell boy."

"Oh," my mother said, "oh, oh."

"Where?" my father asked.

"Just off the shoal, they said, curled up in the eelgrass."

"My God," my mother said softly.

Mr. Robinson moved off without so much as a goodbye. And after a while my sister and I went to bed.

But not to sleep. We played cards for an hour or so, until we couldn't stand that any more. Then we did a couple of crossword puzzles together. Finally we just sat in our beds, in the chilly night, and listened. There were the usual sounds from outside the open windows, sounds of the land and the water. Deer moving about in

11. **anemometer** (ăn′ə-mŏm′ə-tər): an instrument that measures wind speed.

12. **the chop tearing the keel out:** the choppy waves tearing out the keel, or supporting beam at the bottom of the boat.

the brush on their way to eat the wild watercress and wild lettuce that grew around the spring. The deep pumping sounds of an owl's wings in the air. Little splashes from the bay—the fishes and the muskrats and the otters.

"I didn't know there'd be so many things moving at night," my sister said.

"You just weren't ever awake."

"What do you reckon it's like," she said, "being on the bottom in the eelgrass?"

"Shut up," I told her.

"Well," she said, "I just asked. Because I was wondering."

"Don't."

Her talking had started a funny shaking quivering feeling from my navel right straight back to my backbone. The tips of my fingers hurt too, the way they always did.

"I thought the dogs would howl," she said.

"They can't smell anything from the water," I told her. "Now quit."

She fell asleep then and maybe I did too, because the night seemed awful short. Or maybe the summer dawns really come that quick. Not dawn, no. The quiet deep dark that means dawn is just about to come. The birds started whistling and the gulls started shrieking. I got up and looked out at the dripping beach plum bushes and the twisted, salt-burned jack pines, then I slipped out the window. I'd done it before. You lifted the screen and lowered yourself down. It wasn't anything of a drop—all you had to watch was the patch of poison ivy. I circled around the house and took the old deer trail down to the bay. It was chilly, and I began to wish I had brought my robe or a coat. With just cotton pajamas my teeth would begin chattering very soon.

I don't know what I expected to see. And I didn't see anything at all. Just some morning fog in the hollows and around the spring. And the dock, with my father's boat bobbing in the run of the tide.

The day was getting close now. The sky over-head turned a sort of luminous dark blue. As it did, the water darkened to a lead-colored gray. It looked heavy and oily and impenetrable.[13] I tried to imagine what would be under it. I always thought I knew. There would be horseshoe crabs and hermit crabs and blue crabs, and scallops squirting their way along, and there'd be all the different kinds of fish, and the eels. I kept telling myself that that was all.

But this time I couldn't seem to keep my thoughts straight. I kept wondering what it must be like to be dead and cold and down in the sand and mud with the eelgrass brushing you and the crabs bumping you and the fish—I had felt their little sucking mouths sometimes when I swam.

The water was thick and heavy and the color of a mirror in a dark room. Minnows broke the surface right under the wharf. I jumped. I couldn't help it.

And I got to thinking that something might come out of the water. It didn't have a name or a shape. But it was there.

I stood where I was for a while, trying to fight down the idea. When I found I couldn't do that, I decided to walk slowly back to the house. At least I thought I was going to walk, but the way the boards of the wharf shook under my feet I know that I must have been running. On the path up to the house my bare feet hit some of the sharp cut-off stubs of the rosa rugosa bushes, but I didn't stop. I went crashing into the kitchen because that was the closest door.

The room was thick with the odor of frying bacon, the softness of steam: my mother had gotten up early. She turned around when I came in, not seeming surprised—as if it was the most usual thing in the world for me to be wandering around before daylight in my pajamas.

"Go take those things off, honey," she said. "You're drenched."

---

13. **impenetrable** (ĭm-pĕn'ə-trə-bəl): Unable to be penetrated or pierced; also, unable to be understood.

"Yes ma'am," I told her.

I stripped off the clothes and saw that they really were soaking. I knew it was just the dew and the fog. But I couldn't help thinking it was something else. Something that had reached for me, and missed. Something that was wet, that had come from the water, something that had splashed me as it went past.

Reading Check

1. Which ocean serves as the setting in the story?
2. What are the narrator and her sister doing at the beginning of the story?
3. Why do the narrator's father and brother go out in the boat?
4. What news does Mr. Robinson bring?

For Study and Discussion

Analyzing and Interpreting the Story

1. At the beginning of this story, a girl and her sister are peacefully scraping their dinghy near a dock on a bright, sunny day. At the end of the story, the girl runs in terror from the same dock in the darkness just before dawn. **a.** What tragedy has occurred to bring about this change in her feelings? **b.** What details show that she now views the water as a frightening place, a place where death lives?

2. The land and the water produce very different feelings in this story. Find passages in the story that suggest that the land is a safe and comfortable place.

3. Why do you suppose the girl goes down to the dock in the darkness before dawn?

4. A young person's first reaction to death is a common subject in stories. Do you think the

girl's reactions in this story are believable? Why or why not?

5. Why do you think the author titled the story "The Land and the Water"?

Literary Elements

Stating the Theme

Many stories are written purely for entertainment. Detective stories, Westerns, love stories—many of these are written just to be enjoyed. But many stories are also written to illustrate some central idea or truth about human life or experience. This central idea is called the **theme** of the story. Writers do not generally state the theme in their stories. They expect the reader to derive the theme from all the events that take place in the story.

The theme of a story is different from the **plot,** which is the sequence of events that occur in the story. Plot is what happens in the story. Theme is what the story means.

Here are two statements about this story. One is a statement of the plot. The other is a statement about the theme. Which one states the theme?

1. The narrator hears that three of her young neighbors are missing on a sailboat. The fog is coming in, and a storm is expected. She waits while her father and older brother aid in the search. Late the next day she hears that the three young people have been lost. One of them is found dead in the eelgrass. Shortly before dawn the next day, she goes to the dock. There she feels some terror in the water and rushes home.

2. A girl learns for the first time that death can touch young people like her. She discovers how fragile and vulnerable human life is. Though nature can seem mild and pleasant, beneath its surface are destructive forces which can destroy without warning and without reason. She has escaped death this time, but she realizes that it can reach out for her just as it has reached out and caught her young neighbors.

This story might have suggested other meanings to you. Why do you think the author associates death with *water*? Do you know of any other stories where something evil and fearful is associated with the sea?

Language and Vocabulary

Analyzing Words with Greek and Latin Roots

At one point in this story, the father checks the *anemometer* dial. As the footnote on page 269 indicates, an *anemometer* is a device for measuring the speed of wind. It comes from *anemos*, a Greek root word meaning "wind," and *metron*, a Greek root word meaning "a measure."

What Latin and Greek roots are used to form these words? A dictionary will help.

anemone	meter	thermometer
barometer	pedometer	thermos

Descriptive Writing

Writing a Paragraph

Although the sea is often associated with death and fearful images, it is also associated with life. The narrator in the story, for example, talks about what she had always thought of as being below the surface of the ocean—different kinds of crabs and fish, scallops, and eels. Write a paragraph in which you describe the images that you associate with the sea. As you write, use vivid and specific words to create striking pictures for your readers. You might also enjoy illustrating your paragraph with a drawing or photograph.

About the Author

Shirley Ann Grau (1929–   )

Shirley Ann Grau won the Pulitzer Prize for fiction in 1965 for her third novel, *The Keepers of the House*. The story is set in a small Alabama town and revolves around three generations of a family. She said the book considers "the whole human plight of how do you cope with evil." Her early novels and short-story collections established Grau as an important new Southern writer. She says that the goal of all her fiction is to make more understandable, more bearable, the muddle of human life.

Grau lives in a suburb of New Orleans, where she was born. She graduated from Sophie Newcomb College, Tulane University. She and her husband, a philosophy professor and writer, have five children.

The Tell-Tale Heart

EDGAR ALLAN POE

*Edgar Allan Poe's stories linger in our memories. As you read, try to figure out
how Poe creates an unforgettable atmosphere for a chilling tale.*

True!—nervous—very, very dreadfully nervous I had been and am; but why *will* you say that I am mad? The disease had sharpened my senses—not destroyed—not dulled them. Above all was the sense of hearing acute. I heard all things in the heaven and in the earth. I heard many things in hell. How, then, am I mad? Hearken! and observe how healthily—how calmly I can tell you the whole story.

It is impossible to say how first the idea entered my brain; but once conceived, it haunted me day and night. Object there was none. Passion there was none. I loved the old man. He had never wronged me. He had never given me insult. For his gold I had no desire. I think it was his eye! yes, it was this! He had the eye of a vulture—a pale blue eye, with a film over it. Whenever it fell upon me, my blood ran cold; and so by degrees—very gradually—I made up my mind to take the life of the old man, and thus rid myself of the eye forever.

Now this is the point. You fancy[1] me mad. Madmen know nothing. But you should have seen *me*. You should have seen how wisely I proceeded—with what caution—with what foresight—with what dissimulation[2] I went to work! I was never kinder to the old man than during the whole week before I killed him. And every

night, about midnight, I turned the latch of his door and opened it—oh, so gently! And then, when I had made an opening sufficient for my head, I put in a dark lantern,[3] all closed, closed, so that no light shone out, and then I thrust in my head. Oh, you would have laughed to see how cunningly I thrust it in! I moved it slowly—very, very slowly, so that I might not disturb the old man's sleep. It took me an hour to place my whole head within the opening so far that I could see him as he lay upon his bed. Ha!—would a madman have been so wise as this? And then, when my head was well in the room, I undid the lantern cautiously—oh, so cautiously—cautiously (for the hinges creaked)—I undid it just so much that a single thin ray fell upon the vulture eye. And this I did for seven long nights—every night just at midnight—but I found the eye always closed; and so it was impossible to do the work; for it was not the old man who vexed me, but his Evil Eye. And every morning, when the day broke, I went boldly into the chamber, and spoke courageously to him, calling him by name in a hearty tone, and inquiring how he had passed the night. So you see he would have been a very profound old man, indeed, to suspect that every night, just at twelve, I looked in upon him while he slept.

1. **fancy:** imagine.
2. **dissimulation** (dĭ-sĭm′yə-lā′shən): concealment of plans or intentions.

3. **dark lantern:** a lantern with a shutter that can conceal its light.

Upon the eighth night I was more than usually cautious in opening the door. A watch's minute hand moves more quickly than did mine. Never before that night had I *felt* the extent of my own powers—of my sagacity.[4] I could scarcely contain my feelings of triumph. To think that there I was, opening the door, little by little, and he not even to dream of my secret deeds or thoughts. I fairly chuckled at the idea; and perhaps he heard me; for he moved on the bed suddenly, as if startled. Now you may think that I drew back—but no. His room was black as pitch with the thick darkness (for the shutters were close fastened, through fear of robbers), and so I knew that he could not see the opening of the door, and I kept pushing it on steadily, steadily.

I had my head in, and was about to open the lantern, when my thumb slipped upon the tin fastening, and the old man sprang up in bed, crying out—"Who's there?"

I kept quite still and said nothing. For a whole hour I did not move a muscle, and in the meantime I did not hear him lie down. He was still sitting up in the bed listening—just as I have done, night after night, hearkening to the deathwatches[5] in the wall.

Presently I heard a slight groan, and I knew it was the groan of mortal terror. It was not a groan of pain or of grief—oh, no!—it was the low stifled sound that arises from the bottom of the soul when overcharged with awe. I knew the sound well. Many a night, just at midnight, when all the world slept, it has welled up from my own bosom, deepening, with its dreadful echo, the terrors that distracted me. I say I knew it well. I knew what the old man felt, and pitied him, although I chuckled at heart. I

knew that he had been lying awake ever since the first slight noise, when he had turned in the bed. His fears had been ever since growing upon him. He had been trying to fancy them causeless, but could not. He had been saying to himself, "It is nothing but the wind in the chimney—it is only a mouse crossing the floor," or "It is merely a cricket which has made a single chirp." Yes, he had been trying to comfort himself with these suppositions: but he had found all in vain. *All in vain;* because Death, in approaching him, had stalked with his black shadow before him, and enveloped the victim. And it was the mournful influence of the unperceived shadow that caused him to feel—although he neither saw nor heard—to *feel* the presence of my head within the room.

When I had waited a long time, very patiently, without hearing him lie down, I resolved to open a little—a very, very little crevice[6] in the lantern. So I opened it—you cannot imagine how stealthily, stealthily—until, at length, a simple dim ray, like the thread of the spider, shot from out the crevice and fell full upon the vulture eye.

It was open—wide, wide open—and I grew furious as I gazed upon it. I saw it with perfect distinctness—all a dull blue, with a hideous veil over it that chilled the very marrow in my bones; but I could see nothing else of the old man's face or person: for I had directed the ray as if by instinct, precisely upon the damned spot.

And have I not told you that what you mistake for madness is but overacuteness of the senses?—now, I say, there came to my ears a low, dull, quick sound, such as a watch makes when enveloped in cotton. I knew *that* sound well, too. It was the beating of the old man's heart. It increased my fury, as the beating of a drum stimulates the soldier into courage.

---

4. **sagacity** (sə-găs′ə-tē): keen intelligence and good judgment.
5. **deathwatches:** small insects which make a ticking sound, believed by superstitious people to be a forewarning of death.

6. **crevice:** an opening. The shutter opens to let the light shine out.

But even yet I refrained and kept still. I scarcely breathed. I held the lantern motionless. I tried how steadily I could maintain the ray upon the eye. Meantime the hellish tattoo[7] of the heart increased. It grew quicker and quicker, and louder and louder every instant. The old man's terror *must* have been extreme! It grew louder, I say, louder every moment!—do you mark[8] me well? I have told you that I am nervous: so I am. And now at the dead hour of the night, amid the dreadful silence of that old house, so strange a noise as this excited me to uncontrollable terror. Yet, for some minutes longer I refrained and stood still. But the beating grew louder, louder! I thought the heart must burst. And now a new anxiety seized me—the sound would be heard by a neighbor! The old man's hour had come! With a loud yell, I threw open the lantern and leaped into the room. He shrieked once—once only. In an instant I dragged him to the floor, and pulled the heavy bed over him. I then smiled gaily, to find the deed so far done. But, for many minutes, the heart beat on with a muffled sound. This, however, did not vex me; it would not be heard through the wall. At length it ceased. The old man was dead. I removed the bed and examined the corpse. Yes, he was stone, stone dead. I placed my hand upon the heart and held it there many minutes. There was no pulsation. He was stone dead. His eye would trouble me no more.

If still you think me mad, you will think so no longer when I describe the wise precautions I took for the concealment of the body. The night waned,[9] and I worked hastily, but in silence. First of all I dismembered the corpse. I cut off the head and the arms and the legs.

I then took up three planks from the flooring of the chamber, and deposited all between the scantlings.[10] I then replaced the boards so cleverly, so cunningly, that no human eye—not even *his*—could have detected anything wrong. There was nothing to wash out—no stain of any kind—no blood spot whatever. I had been too wary for that. A tub had caught all—ha! ha!

When I had made an end of these labors, it was four o'clock—still dark as midnight. As the bell sounded the hour, there came a knocking at the street door. I went down to open it with a light heart, for what had I *now* to fear? There entered three men, who introduced themselves, with perfect suavity,[11] as officers of the police. A shriek had been heard by a neighbor during the night; suspicion of foul play had been aroused; information had been lodged at the police office, and they (the officers) had been deputed to search the premises.

I smiled, for *what* had I to fear? I bade the gentlemen welcome. The shriek, I said, was my own in a dream. The old man, I mentioned, was absent in the country. I took my visitors all over the house. I bade them search—search *well*. I led them, at length, to *his* chamber. I showed them his treasures, secure, undisturbed. In the enthusiasm of my confidence, I brought chairs into the room, and desired them *here* to rest from their fatigues, while I myself, in the wild audacity[12] of my perfect triumph, placed my own seat upon the very spot beneath which reposed the corpse of the victim.

The officers were satisfied. My *manner* had convinced them. I was singularly at ease. They sat, and while I answered cheerily, they chatted of familiar things. But, ere long, I felt myself getting pale and wished them gone. My head ached, and I fancied a ringing in my ears; but still they sat and still they chatted. The

---

7. **tattoo:** here, a rhythmic beating.
8. **mark:** here, pay attention to.
9. **waned** (wānd): drew to a close.

10. **scantlings:** crosspieces of wood.
11. **suavity** (swäv′ə-tē): politeness.
12. **audacity** (ô-dăs′ə-tē): daring.

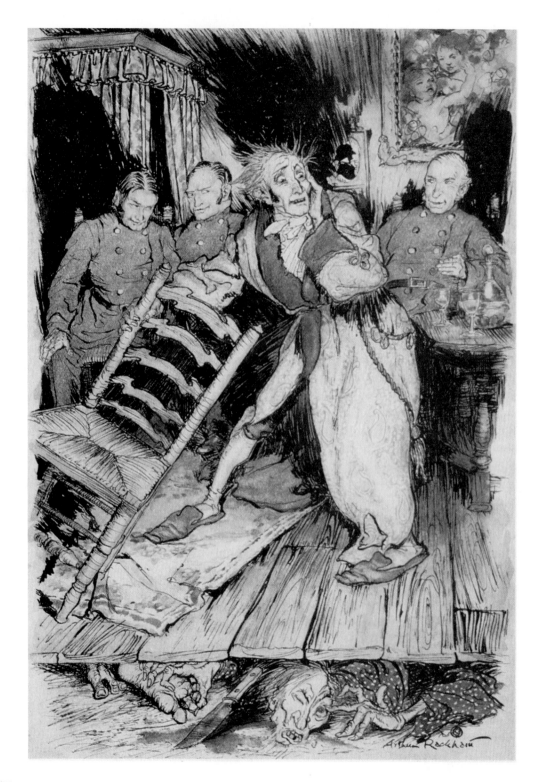

ringing became more distinct—it continued and became more distinct; I talked more freely to get rid of the feeling; but it continued and gained definiteness—until, at length, I found that the noise was *not* within my ears.

No doubt, I now grew *very* pale—but I talked more fluently, and with a heightened voice. Yet the sound increased—and what could I do? It was *a low, dull, quick sound—much such a sound as a watch makes when enveloped in cotton.* I gasped for breath—and yet the officers heard it not. I talked more quickly—more vehemently; but the noise steadily increased. I arose and argued about trifles, in a high key and with violent gesticulations;[13] but the noise steadily increased. Why *would* they not be gone? I paced the floor to and fro with heavy strides, as if excited to fury by the observations of the men—but the noise steadily increased. Oh what *could* I do? I foamed—I raved—I swore! I swung the chair upon which I had been sitting, and grated it upon the boards, but the noise arose over all and continually increased. It grew louder—louder—*louder!* And still the men chatted pleasantly, and smiled. Was it possible they heard not? No, no! They heard!—they suspected—they *knew!*—they were making a *mockery* of my horror—this I thought, and this I think. But anything was better than this agony! Anything was more tolerable than this derision![14] I could bear those hypocritical smiles no longer! I felt that I must scream or die!—and now—again!—hark! louder! louder! louder! *louder!*—

13. **gesticulations** (jĕ-stĭk'yə-lā'shənz): gestures; movements of the arms and legs.
14. **derision** (dĭ-rĭzh'ən): mockery.

Frontispiece by Arthur Rackham (1867–1939) from *Tales of Mystery and Imagination* (1935) by Edgar Allan Poe.

Print Collection, Miriam and Ira D. Wallach Division, Division of Art, Prints and Photographs, The New York Public Library, Astor, Lenox and Tilden Foundations

"Villains!" I shrieked, "dissemble[15] no more! I admit the deed!—tear up the planks!—here, here!—it is the beating of his hideous heart!"

15. **dissemble** (dĭ-sĕm'bəl): pretend.

Reading Check

1. What is the narrator's sharpest sense?
2. What is it about the old man that disturbs the narrator?
3. How does the narrator treat the old man during the week before he kills him?
4. How does the narrator try to hide his crime?
5. What causes the narrator to admit his crime?

For Study and Discussion

Analyzing and Interpreting the Story

1. In the first sentence of this horror story, the narrator asks a question: ". . . but why *will* you say that I am mad?" How does the narrator try to convince you that he is sane?

2. What does the narrator claim is his motive for killing the old man?

3. The narrator tells how he opens the old man's door every night for seven nights. Why doesn't he kill the man until the eighth night?

4. Find the passage in which the narrator first describes hearing the sound of the old man's heart (page 274). How does this sound affect him?

5. At first, the narrator is able to convince the three police officers that nothing is wrong. What do you think makes him reveal where the old man's body is hidden?

Literary Elements

Responding to Atmosphere

Poe once said that he wanted to give the readers of his stories a "single overwhelming impression." In other words, he wanted to create a certain **atmosphere**, or emotional effect. Poe uses several techniques to create the atmosphere in this unusual story.

The very first word of the first sentence is set off with an exclamation point: "True!" In what other ways does the first sentence emphasize the narrator's nervousness?

Sometimes Poe uses short, jerky sentences and dashes to create an effect of nervousness and tension. Look back at the passage on page 277 beginning "No doubt, I now grew *very* pale. . . ." Which details in this passage make you feel the narrator's excitement and increasing nervousness?

A single word can help create atmosphere. For example, Poe compares the old man's eye to the eye of a *vulture*. What kind of bird is a vulture? Suppose Poe had compared the eye to the eye of a robin, or the eye of a kitten. How would the effect be different?

If you had to identify the "single overwhelming impression" that this story created for you, what would you say it was: horror, pity, sadness, fear, or something entirely different?

Language and Vocabulary

Recognizing Analogies

Vocabulary questions that ask you to identify synonyms or antonyms usually involve a pair of words. Some other vocabulary questions, called **analogies**, involve two pairs of words. You must first decide what relationship exists between the words in the first pair. The same relationship applies to the second pair.

An analogy question has a special format and uses special symbols. This is one type of analogy question:

bright : cheerful :: fierce : _____
a. happy **b.** gentle **c.** savage **d.** fearful

The two dots (:) stand for "is to"; the four dots (::) stand for "as." The example, therefore, reads "Bright *is to* cheerful *as* fierce *is to* _____ ." Since the first two words, *bright* and *cheerful,* are synonyms, the correct answer is **c.** The word that means the same thing as *fierce* is *savage.*

Complete the following analogies:

Synonyms

1. coax : persuade :: vex : _____
   a. annoy   **c.** walk
   b. rave   **d.** dare

2. alien : foreign :: cunning : _____
   a. soothing   **c.** sad
   b. alarming   **d.** clever

3. savor : enjoy :: stifle : _____
   a. squirm   **c.** confess
   b. move   **d.** smother

Antonyms

4. courageous : cowardly :: profound : _____
   a. deep   **c.** simply
   b. shallow   **d.** brave

5. good : evil :: vehement : _____
   a. reckless   **c.** unemotional
   b. tricky   **d.** angry

6. brief: lengthy :: hypocritical : _____
   a. unusual   **c.** envious
   b. friendly   **d.** honest

Writing About Literature

Explaining an Impression

Write a paragraph in which you explain which details in Poe's story create a "single overwhelming impression" for you as a reader. Begin your paragraph with a topic sentence that states the effect Poe creates. Then include incidents, details, and quotations from the story that explain or support your point of view. Be sure to enclose direct quotations from the story in quotation marks. You and your classmates might enjoy reading one another's paragraphs.

For Oral Reading

Reading a Story Aloud

Read "The Tell-Tale Heart" aloud. Make your voice sound the way you imagine the narrator would sound. At different points in the story, he sounds nervous, calm, excited, frightened, pleased with himself, or almost hysterical.

Be sure to notice the punctuation marks as you read. The dashes signal places where the narrator interrupts his thoughts, and the exclamation marks signal strong feeling or excitement. Notice especially the last paragraphs of the story. How would you read these sentences to suggest the narrator's panic?

About the Author

Edgar Allan Poe (1809–1849)

Edgar Allan Poe—poet, short-story writer, and literary critic—is one of the most important American writers of the nineteenth century. He is called "the father of the American short story" and "the inventor of the detective story."

Poe was the son of professional actors. He was orphaned by the age of three and was raised and educated by a wealthy couple in Richmond, Virginia, named Allan. As Poe grew older, he came into conflict with his foster father, who disapproved of his literary ambitions. Poe attended the University of Virginia briefly and then enlisted in the army. Hoping to win back the favor of his foster father, he served for a short time as a West Point cadet. But he purposely got himself dismissed when he realized that reconciliation with the Allan family was impossible.

Marriage to his young cousin Virginia Clemm provided Poe with some affection and family life. He eked out a meager living by writing for newspapers and literary magazines. Though he was a good editor, Poe was unable to hold a job for long. His temper was erratic, and he always seemed to be exhausted and underfed. In 1847 his young wife died of tuberculosis. Poe, grief-stricken and ill, survived her by only two years.

One of Poe's most famous poems is "The Raven." Some of Poe's other famous horror stories are "The Fall of the House of Usher," "The Pit and the Pendulum," "The Cask of Amontillado," and "The Masque of the Red Death."

DEVELOPING SKILLS
IN CRITICAL THINKING

Establishing Criteria for Evaluation

In this unit you have studied the elements that make up short stories. You should also consider some standards for evaluating, or judging, the quality of any short story you read.

1. *Is the conflict in the story clear, well-developed, and believable?* Even stories with surprise endings, such as O. Henry's "A Retrieved Reformation," should end with a believable solution to the conflict.

2. *Is foreshadowing used to create interest and suspense?* For example, in "The Rule of Names," the author describes Mr. Underhill as breathing a "double puff of steam" and as showing "snow-white teeth," both hints to the reader that he is actually the dragon.

3. *Do the characters' actions match their words and thoughts and the author's descriptions of them? Are their actions clearly motivated by events in the story? Are the characters clearly individuals, or are they merely predictable and shallow?* You should expect that some characters in a story will be more fully developed than others. Think about Charlie Gordon in "Flowers for Algernon." How is Charlie revealed as a unique character, different from Miss Kinnian or Dr. Strauss?

4. *What role does the setting play? Does it have an important connection to the plot, or could the story have been set in any time and place?* Think, for instance, about "The Land and the Water." The coastal setting helps the narrator to learn that the sea can be a deadly enemy, and the dark skies create a somber atmosphere.

5. *How does the point of view contribute to the story?* For example, Edgar Allan Poe uses the first-person point of view to bring the reader closer to the terrible events in "The Tell-Tale Heart."

6. *Does the story offer some insight into human experience?* Some stories merely tell about an exciting episode. In others, such as "The Land and the Water," the main character learns a valuable lesson about life. More often than not, the reader draws a conclusion about the theme from what happens in the story.

Select a short story from this unit. Evaluate the story by answering each of the preceding questions. Be prepared to discuss your evaluation.

PRACTICE IN READING AND WRITING

Writing Stories

Stories do not need to be lengthy. This action story, told to writer Claude Brown by one of his teachers, takes only a single paragraph.

> There were two frogs sitting on a milk vat one time. The frogs fell into the milk vat. It was very deep. They kept swimming and swimming around, and they couldn't get out. They couldn't climb out because they were too far down. One frog said, "Oh, I can't make it, and I'm going to give up." And the other frog kept swimming and swimming. His arms became more and more tired, and it was harder and harder and harder for him to swim. Then he couldn't do another stroke. He couldn't throw one more arm into the milk. He kept trying and trying; it seemed as if the milk was getting hard and heavy. He kept trying; he knew that he was going to die, but as long as he had that little bit of life in him, he was going to keep on swimming. On his last stroke, it seemed as though he had to pull a whole ocean back, but he did it and found himself sitting on a vat of butter.

Answer the following four questions about this short story. Notice, too, that you can ask yourself the same questions about almost any story ever written or told.

1. Who are the characters and what do they want?
2. What is the conflict in the story?
3. What happens? In other words, what is the story's plot?

4. What does the story mean? Does it express a theme, or an idea about life and people? In a sentence or two, explain the meaning you find in this story.

Suggestions for Writing

Write a short story. Professional novelists and short-story writers usually tell young writers to write about what they know best. Many writers' first stories are about their own childhoods or about characters or events they know from their own towns. Perhaps you can get an idea for a story from one of the following situations. Your story can be based on a true event, or it can be something that takes place only in your imagination.

A child's first experience with a bully
A dream that became a nightmare
How a young person discovered adult responsibility
How a person did something that seemed impossible

Prewriting

- Think about the characters in your story. Who will the main characters be? What will they want?
- Decide what the conflict will be. What will your characters have to struggle against in order to get what they want?
- Gather details for your story by asking the 5 W-How? questions *(Who? What? When? Where? Why? How?)*
- Outline the main events that will make up your plot. What event will open your story?

What will happen in the middle? Will the characters get what they want at the end?

- Decide on a point of view. Through whose eyes will the reader see the action?

Writing

Remember that the opening of your story should "hook" the reader, by creating a mood or establishing the conflict for the story. As you write, use both direct and indirect methods of characterization, *telling* about the characters and *showing* the characters through their words and actions. If you use dialogue, make sure that the characters sound natural. Finally, maintain a consistent point of view.

Evaluating and Revising

Evaluate your short story by answering the following questions. Then revise your draft by adding, cutting, reordering, or replacing words.

- Does the beginning "hook" the reader?
- Have you clearly included a conflict?
- Have you developed the characters both directly and indirectly?
- Have you included a beginning, a middle, and an end for the story?
- Have you arranged the actions in the plot in chronological order?
- Is the dialogue lively and natural-sounding?
- Have you maintained one point of view throughout the story?

Proofreading

Reread your revised draft to correct any errors in grammar, usage, spelling, and mechanics. Pay special attention to the correct capitalization and punctuation of dialogue. Then prepare a final copy of your story, proofreading once more to catch any errors or omissions made in recopying. You might enjoy sharing your short story with your classmates by reading it in a small group or including it in a class anthology of stories.

For Further Reading

Aiken, Joan, *Up the Chimney Down and Other Stories* (Harper & Row, 1985)

> The theme of each story is pure imagination.

Daly, Maureen, editor, *My Favorite Suspense Stories* (Dodd, Mead, 1968)

> These eighteen exciting stories will keep you wondering what happens next.

Doyle, Sir Arthur Conan, *Adventures of Sherlock Holmes* (many editions)

> Here are a dozen stories of Sherlock Holmes's most famous cases of crime.

Du Maurier, Daphne, *Don't Look Now* (Doubleday, 1971; paperback, Dell, 1985)

> A famous writer's tales about strange and super-natural events.

Henry, O., *The Gift of the Magi and Five Other Stories* (Franklin Watts, 1967)

> These stories with surprise endings include "The Ransom of Red Chief," about two kidnappers who are tormented by a ten-year-old boy.

Lester, Julius, *This Strange New Feeling* (Dial Press, 1982)

> This collection includes three stories based on the lives of black couples who lived in the United States in the 1800s.

Manley, Seon, editor, *Ladies of Horror* (Lothrop, Lee & Shepard, 1971)

> Among the thirteen horror stories in this book are Daphne Du Maurier's "The Birds" and Shirley Jackson's "The Lovely House."

Poe, Edgar Allan, *Tales of Terror and Fantasy* (Dutton, 1972)

> Ten of Poe's most suspenseful stories are included in this anthology.

Schaefer, Jack, *The Plainsman* (Houghton Mifflin, 1963)

> This anthology of humorous Western stories includes one about how Cooter James cured his nervousness.

Schulman, L. M., editor, *Winners and Losers: An Anthology of Great Sports Fiction* (Macmillan, (1968)

> Here are twelve action narratives about sports by such writers as Ring Lardner, Jack London, Ernest Hemingway, and William Faulkner.

Sohn, David A., editor, *Ten Top Stories* (paperback, Bantam, 1964)

> Students selected these stories as their favorites. All of them are about young adults.

Stolz, Mary, *The Beautiful Friend and Other Stories* (Harper & Row, 1960)

> In these stories, young people face turning points in their lives and make important decisions.

Sutcliff, Rosemary, *Heather, Oak and Olive* (Dutton, 1972)

> Prehistoric times are relived in three tales by a skillful storyteller.

Wells, H. G., *The Complete Short Stories of H. G. Wells* (St. Martin's, 1971)

> Included in this collection are strange, fantastic, and humorous stories, such as "The Door in the Wall" and "The Country of the Blind."

Yolen, Jane, et al, editors, *Dragons and Dreams; A Collection of New Fantasy and Science Fiction Stories* (Harper & Row, 1986)

> Here are ten imaginative stories.

Zolotow, Charlotte, editor, *Early Sorrow: Ten Stories of Youth* (Harper & Row, 1986)

> Here are ten stories about the experiences of young people.

DRAMA

Scene from a modern production of Shakespeare's
Two Gentlemen of Verona at the Oregon
Shakespeare Festival in Ashland.

The word *drama* comes from a Greek word meaning "to do" or "to act." A drama is a story that is "acted" out, as if it were real life. If you have ever seen a live play, you know that the theater darkens, and that when the curtain rises, only the stage area is lit. This means that you are supposed to forget where you are sitting and think of the stage as a new world.

When you read a play, of course, you must let your imagination go to work. You must picture the stage in your mind. You must imagine how the actors and actresses speak their lines. If your imagination is allowed to do its job, this will be no problem. You will find that the story will easily come "alive" in your own mind.

CLOSE READING
OF A PLAY

*Developing
Skills in
Critical
Thinking*

While many of the elements studied in connection with short stories are relevant to the study of drama, there are several additional elements that need to be taken into account. Dramatists frequently make use of stage directions to create setting and to give players instructions for acting. Sound effects are often important in creating setting and mood. Sometimes a dramatist may use a narrator to comment on the action. Generally, however, dialogue is the dramatist's most important device for presenting character and for moving the action along.

The following play, *The Bishop's Candlesticks* by Van Dusen Rickert, Jr., is based on a famous episode in a nineteenth-century French novel, *Les Misérables* (*The Unfortunate Ones*), by Victor Hugo. The central figure in this story is a man named Jean Valjean, who is sentenced to prison for stealing food. During this time, ex-convicts were required to carry yellow passports, which made it difficult for them to find shelter or to earn a living.

Read the play carefully, using the notes in the margin as a guide. Then turn to the analysis on page 297.

The Bishop's Candlesticks

VAN DUSEN RICKERT, JR.

Characters

Monseigneur Bienvenu (môN-sĕ-nyœr′ byȧN′ və-nü′), Bishop of Digne (dēn′yə)[1]

Mademoiselle Baptistine (mȧd′mwȧ-zĕl′ bȧp′tē-stēn′), his sister

Madame Magloire (mȧ-dȧm′ mȧ-glwȧr′), their servant

Jean Valjean (zhäN vȧl-zhäN′), an ex-convict

A Sergeant and Two Police Officers

Scene: The home of the Bishop.

Scene 1

The living room of the Bishop of Digne, *a large, oblong room plainly furnished, scrupulously[2] neat. The walls are whitewashed. There is no carpet. A fire burns in the fireplace down right; an alcove, closed by portières,[3] occupies the upstage center. A door leading outdoors is in the wall left of the alcove. Against the wall up left stands a sturdy dresser. Down left a door leads to a passage.*

The Bishop *and his* Sister *are finishing their supper. It is late evening of a winter day. The room is lighted by firelight and two candles which stand on the table in handsome silver candlesticks.*

Mlle.[4] Baptistine. Will you have coffee, brother?

The Bishop. If you please.

Mlle. Baptistine. I'll ring for Madame Magloire. . . .

---

1. **Digne:** in southeast France, northeast of Marseilles.
2. **scrupulously** (skrōō′pyə-ləs-lē): with utmost care.
3. **portières** (pôr-tyârz′): heavy curtains.
4. **Mlle.:** an abbreviation for mademoiselle.

Thinking Model

Setting gives impression of simplicity, orderliness, and no luxury.

[Mme.[5] Magloire *enters from the passage.*]

The Bishop. But here she is—and bringing our coffee. Madame Magloire, you are wonderful; you read our minds.

Mme. Magloire. I should be able to, after all these years.

The Bishop. Of faithful service—and mind reading.

Mme. Magloire. Thank you, my lord.

Mlle. Baptistine. We'll drink our coffee in front of the fire, Madame Magloire.

Mme. Magloire. Yes, mademoiselle. Let me stir up that fire a little. Such a cold night!

Mlle. Baptistine. I'm glad all our poor have fuel and food. *(Sits at fireplace and pours coffee)*

The Bishop. Not all, I'm afraid.

Mlle. Baptistine. I meant all in the parish.

The Bishop. If we could only help them all! My heart aches on a night like this to think of poor homeless wanderers, lonely, hungry——

Mlle. Baptistine. Not all of them deserve help, I'm afraid. Some of them are good-for-nothing, ungrateful vagabonds.

Mme. Magloire. They say there's a tough-looking fellow in town now. He came along the boulevard and tried to get in to spend the night at the hotel. Of course they threw him out. A tramp with a sack over his shoulder and a terrible face. An ugly brute! *(She brings the candlesticks from the table and sets them on the mantelpiece above the fireplace.)*

The Bishop. There are no human brutes; there are only miserable men who have been unfortunate.

Mme. Magloire (*she is clearing the table*). You are as kindhearted as the good Lord himself, Bishop; but when there are fellows like that around, we say—mademoiselle and I...

This seems to be a peaceful and happy household.

Bishop sympathizes deeply with unfortunate human beings.

The women are not as kindhearted as the Bishop.

Bishop gently chides the servant.

5. **Mme.:** an abbreviation for madame.

Mlle. Baptistine. I have said nothing.

Mme. Magloire. Well . . . we say that this house isn't safe. If you don't mind, I'm going to send for the locksmith to put bolts on these doors. It's terrible to leave these doors unfastened, so that anybody can walk in. And the Bishop always calls "Come in!" the minute anyone knocks.

[*There is a loud knock.*]

The Bishop. Come in.

[Jean Valjean *appears in the doorway.* Mlle. Baptistine *gasps;* Mme. Magloire *suppresses a cry. There is a silence.*]

Valjean. My name's Jean Valjean. I'm a convict. I've been nineteen years in prison at hard labor. I got out four days ago, and I'm on my way to Pontarlier.[6] I've come twenty-five miles on foot today, and I'm tired and hungry. Nobody'll take me in, because I've got a convict's passport—yellow. See! They've kicked me out like a dog everywhere I stopped. I even went to the jail and asked for lodging, but the turnkey said. "Get yourself arrested, if you want to spend the night here." Then a good woman pointed out your door to me and said, "Knock there." So I did. I'm tired. Can I stay?

The Bishop. Madame Magloire, will you set another place and bring some food?

Valjean. Wait a minute. Did you understand? I'm a convict. There's my yellow passport. Take a look at it. It says nineteen years in prison—five years for burglary and fourteen for attempted escape. It says, "This man is dangerous." Dangerous! Well, are you going to take me in?

6. **Pontarlier** (pôn′tär-lyā′): in eastern France, near the Swiss border.

The Bishop is unconcerned about his safety.

Imagine the dramatic effect of this man's appearance.

This is the "ugly brute" Mme. Magloire mentioned.

The Bishop makes the stranger welcome.

The man cannot believe that anyone will allow him to stay.

The Bishop. Won't you sit down, monsieur?[7] Madame Magloire, you may make up the bed in the alcove.

Valjean (*lowers his sack to the floor*). "Monsieur!" You call me "monsieur!" And you're not going to put me out! (Mme. Magloire *places food on the table.*) That looks good. (*He sits.*) I've been starving for four days. (*He begins to eat avidly.*) I'll pay you for this. I've got some money to pay you with. . . . You're an innkeeper, aren't you?

The Bishop. I'm a priest.

Valjean. Oh, a priest . . . a good priest. . . . That's a good one! Then you don't want me to pay——

The Bishop. No, no. Keep your money. How much have you?

Valjean. One hundred and nine francs.

The Bishop. And how long did it take you to earn that?

Valjean. Nineteen years.

The Bishop. (*sighing*). Nineteen years.

Valjean. Yes, they pay us something for the work we do in prison. Not much, of course; but we get a little out of it. I really earned one hundred and seventy-one francs, but they didn't give me that much. I've still got all they paid me.

The Bishop. Madame Magloire, will you bring the candles to the table? It is a little dark over here.

Mlle. Baptistine (*timidly*). Did you . . . could you ever go to Mass while you were–in there?

Valjean. Yes, ma'am. They said Mass at an altar in the middle of the courtyard. You'll be interested in this, monsieur, since you're a priest. Once we had a bishop come to say Mass—"my lord," they called him. He's a priest who's over a lot of other priests. He

The Bishop treats the man respectfully.

The Bishop's sorrow indicates how small a sum it is.

He implies that he was cheated.

He doesn't realize that he is talking to a bishop.

---

7. **monsieur** (mə-syœ′): a title like "Mister" or "Sir" in English.

said Mass and wore a pointed gold thing on his head. He wasn't close to us. We were drawn up in lines on three sides of the courtyard. We couldn't understand what he said. That was the only time we ever saw a bishop.

The Bishop. That's very interesting.

Mlle. Baptistine. How happy your family will be to see you again after so many years.

Valjean. I haven't got any family.

Mlle. Baptistine. Haven't you any relatives at all? Is there no one waiting for you?

Valjean. No, nobody. I had a sister. I used to live with her and her children, but I don't know what's become of her. She may have gone to Paris.

Mlle. Baptistine. Didn't she write to you sometimes?

Valjean. I haven't heard from her in twelve years. I'll never bother her again.

The Bishop. And you're going to Pontarlier. Do you know anyone there?

Valjean. No, I don't. It's not my part of the country; but I visited there once when I was young, and I liked it—high mountains, good air, and not too many people. I thought about it often in prison and made up my mind to go there if ever—if I ever was free.

The Bishop. You're going to a fine country, and there is plenty of work there: paper mills, tanneries, copper and iron foundries; and there are dairy farms all through the region. You'll have to find work, of course. What do you want to do?

Valjean. It doesn't matter. I can do any kind of work. I'm as tough as steel. But, with a yellow passport, I don't know whether I can get a job.

The Bishop (*writing*). Here, take this card. If you will give it to Monsieur Doumic from me . . . he has a tannery at Pontarlier and, what is more important, he has a heart. He will not ask you too many questions.

the bishop's miter

Man is now all alone.

Bishop gives the ex-convict a recommendation.

Valjean. Thank you, monsieur. You've been so kind, giving me this good dinner and taking me in—and all. . . . I ought to tell you my name.

The Bishop. You have a name I know without your telling me.

Valjean. Is that right? You already knew my name?

The Bishop. Yes. Your name is . . . my brother. You need not tell me who you are. Those who come to this door are not asked "What is your name?" but "What is your need . . . or sorrow?"

Bishop reveals his humane nature.

Valjean. I've seen plenty of that. There's nothing else in prison. If you complain—solitary confinement. Double chains, just for nothing at all. A dog is better off than a convict! I had nineteen years of it— because I stole some food. And now I'm forty-six, and I have a yellow passport.

Punishment for crime was excessive.

The Bishop. You have left behind you a sad and terrible place. If you have come from it with a little kindness or peace in your heart, then you are better than any one of us.

Mme. Magloire. The bed is made now.

The Bishop. Thank you, Madame Magloire. You may clear the table. And, monsieur, we know you are very tired. My sister and I will leave you to your rest. Do you need anything else?

Valjean. No . . . thanks.

The Bishop. Then good night, monsieur.

Mlle. Baptistine. Good night, monsieur.

[*Exit left, followed by the* Bishop. Jean Valjean *carries his sack to the bed.* Mme. Magloire *comes from the kitchen carrying silver, which she puts away in the dresser.* Jean Valjean *watches her. When she leaves the room, he goes to the table and takes up one of the candlesticks. He looks toward the dresser. The* Bishop *enters.*]

Suspense mounts.

Is he going to steal the silver?

The Bishop. I've brought you an extra

cover, monsieur. It is a doeskin I bought in Germany, in the Black Forest. This is better than a blanket for warmth.

[Jean Valjean *puts down the candlestick as the* Bishop *speaks.*]

Valjean (*harshly*). Are you going to let me sleep in your house like this? You'd better think it over. I'm a thief, you know. How do you know I'm not a murderer?

Valjean seems to be warning the Bishop.

The Bishop. That is as God wills it, brother.

The Bishop's strength is his faith.

[*He blesses* Jean Valjean *and goes slowly out of the room.* Jean Valjean *looks after the* Bishop, *motionless and unyielding. Then he blows out the candles and goes to the alcove, where he lies down on the bed without undressing.*]

Valjean remains unmoved.

[*Curtain.*]

Scene 2

The room is dark. Jean Valjean *sits on the bed. After a moment he rises and takes up his pack and tiptoes toward the door. He hesitates, looking at the dresser; then he goes to it, opens it, and takes out silver; he crouches beside his pack, putting the silver into it. There is a sound as he thrusts the silver into the pack. Alarmed, he starts up, leaving the silver basket on the floor, catches up the pack, and goes hastily out of the door.*

After everyone else is asleep, Jean Valjean steals the silver.

[*Curtain.*]

Scene 3

It is morning. Mme. Magloire *enters with dishes. Going directly to the table, she notices that the bed is unoccupied. Without seeing the basket, she runs to the dresser and finds that the silver is gone.*

Mme. Magloire discovers the theft.

Mme. Magloire. Good heavens! Oh, good heavens! Mademoiselle! Monseigneur! What will the Bishop say! Oh, Mademoiselle!

[Mlle. Baptistine *enters.*]

Mlle. Baptistine. Good morning, Madame Magloire. What's the matter?

Mme. Magloire. Mademoiselle! The dresser is open–and that man is gone! The silver–all our knives and forks! Where are they?

Mlle. Baptistine. You put them away there last night?

Mme. Magloire. Yes, yes, just as I always do. And now there's nothing here! Oh, my lord.

[*The* Bishop *enters. He sees the silver basket and the empty alcove.*]

The Bishop. What is it, Madame Magloire?

Mme. Magloire. The silver! Does your lordship know where the silver basket is?

The Bishop. Yes.

Mme. Magloire. Oh, thank heaven! I didn't know what had become of it.

The Bishop (*picking up the empty basket and handing it to her*). Here it is.

Mme. Magloire. Well, but–there's nothing in it. Where's the silver?

The Bishop. Oh, then it's the silver you're worried about. I don't know where it is.

Mme. Magloire. Then it's stolen! Knives, forks, spoons–all gone. That vagabond stole them. He's gone, you see–cleared out before any of us were awake. The scoundrel!

The Bishop. Well, let's consider. In the first place, was the silver ours?

Mme. Magloire. Ours? And why not?

The Bishop. Madame Magloire, I had no right to keep that silver so long. It belonged

The Bishop seems unconcerned about the disappearance of the silver.

The Bishop again reveals his humane nature.

to the poor. And this man was one of the poor, wasn't he?

Mme. Magloire. Oh, it isn't that I mind for myself or mademoiselle. But, my lord, what will you eat with?

The Bishop. There are tin spoons.

Mme. Magloire (*with great disgust*). Tin smells.

The Bishop. And there are iron spoons.

Mme. Magloire. Iron tastes!

The Bishop (*chuckling*). Well, well—then there are wooden spoons. Tell me, sister, do you regret having given that poor fellow food and shelter?

Mme. Magloire. Not at all. I shall pray for him. Somehow I have a feeling that we may hear more from him.

[*They sit at the table.*]

Mme. Magloire. When I think of that cutthroat spending the night here! Suppose he had taken it into his head to kill us instead of stealing from us.

Mlle. Baptistine. He'll probably make haste to get as far away as he can. He wouldn't try to sell the silver in this neighborhood.

Mme. Magloire. I hope he'll take good care never to come this way again.

[*There is a knock at the door. Mme. Magloire and Mlle. Baptistine are startled.*]

The Bishop. Come in.

[A Sergeant *and two* Policemen, *guarding* Jean Valjean, *appear at the door.*]

Sergeant. Your excellency —

The Bishop. Come in, officer.

Valjean (*he looks up, surprised*). Excellency? Then he isn't a priest?

Policeman. Be quiet you. This is the Bishop.

Mme. Magloire's unforgiving response to the theft is contrasted with that of the Bishop.

The Bishop. Oh, it's you. I'm glad to see you. Why did you go off so early and without the candlesticks? They're solid silver and I gave them to you, as well as the other pieces. You can easily get two hundred francs for the pair.

Sergeant. Your excellency, we wanted to know if this fellow was telling the truth. We stopped him on suspicion and found that he had a yellow passport and this silver.

The Bishop. And he told you the silver was given him by a good old priest at whose house he spent last night.

Sergeant. He did, your excellency.

The Bishop. I see it all. Then you brought him back here. Well, it's just a misunderstanding.

Sergeant. Then we can let him go?

The Bishop. Of course, let him go.

[*The* Sergeant *hands the silver to* Valjean.]

Valjean. You mean I'm free?

Policeman. Yes, it's all right. You're free.

The Bishop. But, before you go, here are your candlesticks. Take them with you.

Valjean. Monsieur . . . monseigneur . . . I . . . (*he stands silent, with bowed head.*)

The Bishop. Ah—good morning, officer. You and your men were quite right in doing your duty. Good morning.

Sergeant. Good day, your excellency.

[*The* Sergeant *and* Policemen *close the door and leave.*]

Mlle. Baptistine (*very softly*). Come in Madame Magloire.

[*They slip discreetly out the door down left.*]

The Bishop. Now, Jean Valjean, you may go in peace. But never forget that you have

The Bishop shields Valjean.

Valjean cannot believe that someone would allow him to go unpunished for his theft.

promised to use that silver to make yourself an honest man.

Valjean (*slowly*). I didn't promise.... But I ...

The Bishop. Jean Valjean, my brother, you no longer belong to evil, but to good. It is your soul that I am buying for you. It belongs to God. Will you give it to Him?

Valjean (*almost inaudibly*). Yes, Father. (*He kneels.*)

There is a change in Valjean.

Valjean commits his life to good.

[*Curtain.*]

Analysis

The opening scene suggests that this is a play about the meaning of charity. The Bishop is shown to be a benevolent man. His humane nature is established in the opening lines of the play by his warm treatment of his servant and by his concern for wretched, poor, and homeless people. He does not agree with his sister and his servant that some human beings are undeserving of help. Rather, he believes that brutal behavior is the result of grave misfortunes. His home, like a church, is open to all.

The appearance of the ex-convict, Jean Valjean, is foreshadowed by Madame Magloire's mention of the stranger looking for lodging in town. To judge from her description, he is truly frightening: "tough-looking" with a "terrible face." She refers to him as a beast: "An ugly brute." We are prepared for the women's surprise and fear when Jean Valjean appears in the doorway.

The man speaks bluntly, getting to the point immediately. He has been traveling for four days. Because of his yellow passport, which he must present in order to prove his identity, no one will give him a lodging. He has a long prison record: nineteen years at hard labor.

When the Bishop offers him a place at the table, the ex-convict thinks that he has been misunderstood. He emphasizes that he has been labeled a dangerous man. He is stunned when the Bishop addresses him respectfully as "monsieur."

While the man eats greedily, the Bishop and his sister question him about his background. They learn that he no longer has any family, that he has no friends, and that he is virtually alone. He claims that he was imprisoned for nineteen years for stealing food. He tells of the excessive punishment in prison, and implies that he was exploited. Although he worked hard, he received very little money.

To help the man get a job in Pontarlier, the Bishop writes a recommendation for him. He brings him an extra cover for warmth. Before leaving for the night, he gives the man his blessing.

Despite the humane conduct of the Bishop, the scene ends ominously. When Madame Magloire puts away the silver, Jean Valjean watches her. After she leaves the room, he reaches for the candlestick and looks toward the dresser, where the silver is kept. He speaks harshly to the Bishop, warning him that he might be a murderer. Finally, his look at the end of the scene is "unyielding." We are not to expect that he has been softened or changed by the Bishop's kindness.

The second scene includes no dialogue. Valjean is alone on the stage in a dark room in the middle of the night. He is obviously preparing to leave the house while everyone else is asleep. Hesitating at the door, he goes back and takes the silver from the dresser.

In the third scene, Madame Magloire discovers that the silver is missing. She immediately assumes that "that man," who is also missing, has taken it. When she tells the Bishop that the silver is missing, he shows no alarm. Then, when Madame Magloire suggests that Valjean has stolen the silver, the Bishop comes to the convict's defense. He explains to Madame Magloire that the silver really belongs to the poor, not the church. Since Valjean is one of the poor, he has only taken what belongs to him.

This scene reveals the great contrast between the Bishop's humane concern for the poor and Madame Magloire's concern for the church's property. The Bishop's humility and sense of humor are also revealed, as he chuckles over their use of tin, iron, or wooden spoons to replace the silver.

When the policemen appear at the door with the captured Valjean, the Bishop shows no surprise. He tells the police that the affair is a misunderstanding: he has given Valjean the silver. Valjean, who has experienced nothing but injustice during his life, cannot believe what is happening. He cannot understand why the Bishop would forgive the theft and give the silver.

After the policemen and the two women leave the room, however, the Bishop reveals his motive. He demands that, in return for the silver and the freedom, Valjean become an honest man. Valjean hesitates, perhaps doubting his ability to do it, and then promises his soul to God.

Guidelines for Reading a Play

1. *Note any information that establishes the setting and the situation that will start the plot moving.* The opening scene of the play shows us a simple and utilitarian room. Its humble character implies that the Bishop who lives there is uninterested in possessions and lavish furnishings. It is apparent from the Bishop's concern with "poor homeless wanderers" and the servant's fear of vagabonds that the play will focus in some way on the outcast.

2. *Note clues that tell you what the players are doing or how the lines are spoken.* Stage directions, such as *timidly* and *harshly,* tell you how some lines are delivered. Other speeches have clues built into them. We can tell from the short sentences and plain language of Jean Valjean's speeches that he speaks bluntly and roughly.

3. *Anticipate the action that will develop out of each scene.* There are several warnings of danger before the curtain falls at the end of the first scene. Jean Valjean watches the servant put away the silver. When no one is watching, he grasps one of the silver candlesticks. He says openly that the Bishop may be showing hospitality to a murderer. Finally, he goes to bed without undressing, suggesting that he means to leave in a hurry.

4. *Be alert to the mood and theme of the play.* A somber mood is set by the many references to human suffering. We have the impression that Jean Valjean's character has been hardened by his life in prison and that he is untouched by the kindness and goodness of the Bishop. The play's theme, or central idea about life, may be stated this way: *Humane understanding and acts of genuine kindness may help transform a criminal into an honest person.*

The Ugly Duckling

A. A. MILNE

Nothing in this comical fairy-tale kingdom is quite the way we expect it to be. The King is not very kingly. The Queen is very bossy. The Princess is not beautiful, and the Prince can't swim. As you read, think about the details Milne has used to create a story that is not at all like the usual fairy tale. Can you predict what will happen after the play ends?

Characters

The King
The Queen
The Princess Camilla
The Chancellor
Dulcibella
Prince Simon
Carlo
A Voice

Scene: *The Throne Room of the palace, a room of many doors, or, if preferred, curtain openings, simply furnished with three thrones for Their Majesties and Her Royal Highness the* Princess Camilla—*in other words, with three handsome chairs. At each side is a long seat, reserved, as it might be, for His Majesty's Council (if any), but useful, as today, for other purposes.*

The King *is asleep on his throne, with a handkerchief over his face. He is a king of any country from any storybook, in whatever costume you please. But he should be wearing his crown.*

A Voice (*announcing*). His Excellency, the Chancellor!

[*The* Chancellor, *an elderly man in horn-rimmed spectacles, enters bowing. The* King *wakes up with a start and removes the handkerchief from his face.*]

King (*with simple dignity*). I was thinking.
Chancellor (*bowing*). Never, Your Majesty, was greater need for thought than now.
King. That's what I was thinking. (*He struggles into a more dignified position.*) Well, what is it? More trouble?
Chancellor. What we might call the old trouble, Your Majesty.
King. It's what I was saying last night to the Queen. "Uneasy lies the head that wears a crown,"[1] was how I put it.
Chancellor. A profound and original thought, which may well go down to posterity.
King. You mean it may go down well with posterity. I hope so. Remind me to tell you some time of another little thing I said to Her Majesty: something about a fierce light beating

---

1. **"Uneasy . . . crown":** This line is a quotation from *Henry IV, Part II* by William Shakespeare. Throughout the play, the King quotes from famous poets and claims to have made up the lines himself. He probably really thinks he has.

Scenes on pages 301, 304, 307, 311, 314–315 are from *The Ugly Duckling* performed by Music Mosaics, Canmore, Alberta, Canada. Puppets designed by Felix Mirbt. The King and the Chancellor are shown above.

on a throne.[2] Posterity would like that, too. Well, what is it?

Chancellor. It is in the matter of Her Royal Highness' wedding.

King. Oh . . . yes.

Chancellor. As Your Majesty is aware, the young Prince Simon arrives today to seek Her Royal Highness' hand in marriage. He has been traveling in distant lands and, as I understand, has not—er—has not——

King. You mean he hasn't heard anything.

2. **a fierce . . . throne:** These words are an approximate quotation from *Idylls of the King* by Alfred, Lord Tennyson.

Chancellor. It is a little difficult to put this tactfully, Your Majesty.

King. Do your best, and I will tell you afterwards how you got on.

Chancellor. Let me put it this way. The Prince Simon will naturally assume that Her Royal Highness has the customary—so customary as to be, in my own poor opinion, slightly monotonous—has what one might call the inevitable—so inevitable as to be, in my opinion again, almost mechanical—will assume, that she has the, as *I* think of it, faultily faultless, icily regular, splendidly—

King. What you are trying to say in the fewest words possible is that my daughter is not beautiful.

Chancellor. Her beauty is certainly elusive, Your Majesty.

King. It is. It has eluded you, it has eluded me, it has eluded everybody who has seen her. It even eluded the Court Painter. His last words were, "Well, I did my best." His successor is now painting the view across the water meadows from the West Turret. He says that his doctor has advised him to keep to landscape.

Chancellor. It is unfortunate, Your Majesty, but there it is. One just cannot understand how it could have occurred.

King. You don't think she takes after *me*, at all? You don't detect a likeness?

Chancellor. Most certainly not, Your Majesty.

King. Good. . . . Your predecessor did.

Chancellor. I have often wondered what happened to my predecessor.

King. Well, now you know.

[*There is a short silence.*]

Chancellor. Looking at the bright side, although Her Royal Highness is not, strictly speaking, beautiful——

King. Not, truthfully speaking, beautiful——

Chancellor. Yet she has great beauty of character.

King. My dear Chancellor, we are not considering her Royal Highness' character, but her chances of getting married. You observe that there is a distinction.

Chancellor. Yes, Your Majesty.

King. Look at it from the suitor's point of view. If a girl is beautiful, it is easy to assume that she has, tucked away inside her, an equally beautiful character. But it is impossible to assume that an unattractive girl, however elevated in character, has, tucked away inside her, an equally beautiful face. That is, so to speak, not where you want it—tucked away.

Chancellor. Quite so, Your Majesty.

King. This doesn't, of course, alter the fact that the Princess Camilla is quite the nicest person in the kingdom.

Chancellor (*enthusiastically*). She is indeed, Your Majesty. (*Hurriedly*) With the exception, I need hardly say, of Your Majesty—and Her Majesty.

King. Your exceptions are tolerated for their loyalty and condemned for their extreme fatuity.[3]

Chancellor. Thank you, Your Majesty.

King. As an adjective for your King, the word *nice* is ill-chosen. As an adjective for Her Majesty, it is—ill-chosen.

[*At which moment the* Queen *comes in. The* King *rises. The* Chancellor *puts himself at right angles.*]

Queen (*briskly*). Ah. Talking about Camilla? (*She sits down.*)

King (*returning to his throne*). As always, my dear, you are right.

Queen (*to the* Chancellor). This fellow, Simon—what's he like?

Chancellor. Nobody has seen him, Your Majesty.

Queen. How old is he?

---

3. **fatuity** (fə-to͞o′ə-tē): stupidity.

Chancellor. Five-and-twenty, I understand.

Queen. In twenty-five years he must have been seen by somebody.

King (*to the* Chancellor). Just a fleeting glimpse?

Chancellor. I meant, Your Majesty, that no detailed report of him has reached this country, save that he has the usual personal advantages and qualities expected of a prince and has been traveling in distant and dangerous lands.

Queen. Ah! Nothing gone wrong with his eyes? Sunstroke or anything?

Chancellor. Not that I am aware of, Your Majesty. At the same time, as I was venturing to say to His Majesty, Her Royal Highness' character and disposition are so outstandingly——

Queen. Stuff and nonsense. You remember what happened when we had the Tournament of Love last year.

Chancellor. I was not myself present, Your Majesty. I had not then the honor of—I was abroad, and never heard the full story.

Queen. No, it was the other fool. They all rode up to Camilla to pay their homage—it was the first time they had seen her. The heralds blew their trumpets and announced that she would marry whichever prince was left master of the field when all but one had been unhorsed. The trumpets were blown again, they charged enthusiastically into the fight, and——(*The* King *looks nonchalantly at the ceiling and whistles a few bars.*) Don't do that.

King. I'm sorry, my dear.

Queen (*to the* Chancellor). And what happened? They all simultaneously fell off their horses and assumed the posture of defeat.

King. One of them was not quite so quick as the others. I was very quick. I proclaimed him the victor.

Queen. At the Feast of Betrothal held that night——

King. We were all very quick.

Queen. ——the Chancellor announced that by the laws of the country the successful suitor had to pass a further test. He had to give the correct answer to a riddle.

Chancellor. Such undoubtedly is the fact, Your Majesty.

King. There are times for announcing facts, and times for looking at things in a broad-minded way. Please remember that, Chancellor.

Chancellor. Yes, Your Majesty.

Queen. I invented the riddle myself. Quite an easy one. What is it that has four legs and barks like a dog? The answer is, "A dog."

King (*to the* Chancellor). You see that?

Chancellor. Yes, Your Majesty.

King. It isn't difficult.

Queen. He, however, seemed to find it so. He said an eagle. Then he said a serpent; a very high mountain with slippery sides; two peacocks; a moonlight night; the day after tomorrow——

King. Nobody could accuse him of not trying.

Queen. *I* did.

King. I *should* have said that nobody could fail to recognize in his attitude an appearance of doggedness.

Queen. Finally he said death. I nudged the King——

King. Accepting the word *nudge* for the moment, I rubbed my ankle with one hand, clapped him on the shoulder with the other, and congratulated him on the correct answer. He disappeared under the table, and, personally, I never saw him again.

Queen. His body was found in the moat next morning.

Chancellor. But what was he doing in the moat, Your Majesty?

King. Bobbing about. Try not to ask needless questions.

Chancellor. It all seems so strange.

Queen. What does?

Chancellor. That Her Royal Highness, alone of all the princesses one has ever heard of, should lack that invariable attribute of royalty, supreme beauty.

Queen. (*to the* King). That was your Great-Aunt Malkin. She came to the christening. You know what she said.

King. It was cryptic.[4] Great-Aunt Malkin's

4. **cryptic** (krĭp′tĭk): puzzling.

besetting weakness. She came to *my* christening—she was one hundred and one then, and that was fifty-one years ago. (*To the* Chancellor) How old would that make her?

Chancellor. One hundred and fifty-two, your Majesty.

King (*after thought*). About that, yes. She promised me that when I grew up I should have all the happiness which my wife deserved. It struck me at the time—well, when I say "at the time," I was only a week old—but it did strike me as soon as anything could strike me—I mean of that nature—well, work it out for yourself, Chancellor. It opens up a most interesting field of speculation. Though naturally I have not liked to go into it at all deeply with Her Majesty.

Queen. I never heard anything less cryptic. She was wishing you extreme happiness.

King. I don't think she was *wishing* me anything. However.

Chancellor. (*to the* Queen). But what, Your Majesty, did she wish Her Royal Highness?

Queen. Her other godmother—on my side—had promised her the dazzling beauty for which all the women in my family are famous.

[*She pauses, and the* King *snaps his fingers surreptitiously[5] in the direction of the* Chancellor.]

Chancellor (*hurriedly*). Indeed, yes, Your Majesty.

[*The* King *relaxes.*]

Queen. And Great-Aunt Malkin said——(*To the* King) What were the words?

King.   I give you with this kiss
        A wedding-day surprise.
        Where ignorance is bliss
        'Tis folly to be wise.[6]
I thought the last two lines rather neat. But what it *meant*——

Queen. We can all see what it meant. She was given beauty—and where is it? Great-Aunt Malkin took it away from her. The wedding-day surprise is that there will never be a wedding day.

King. Young men being what they are, my dear, it would be much more surprising if there *were* a wedding day. So how——

5. **surreptitiously** (sûr′əp-tĭsh′əs-lē): secretly.
6. **Where . . . wise:** These lines come from a poem called "A Distant Prospect of Eton College" by Thomas Gray.

[*The* Princess *comes in. She is young, happy, healthy, but not beautiful. Or let us say that by some trick of makeup or arrangement of hair she seems plain to us, unlike the princesses of the storybooks.*]

Princess (*to the* King). Hallo, darling! (*Seeing the others*) Oh, I say! Affairs of state? Sorry.

King (*holding out his hand*). Don't go, Camilla.

[*She takes his hand.*]

Chancellor. Shall I withdraw, Your Majesty?

Queen. You are aware, Camilla, that Prince Simon arrives today?

Princess. He has arrived. They're just letting down the drawbridge.

King (*jumping up*). Arrived! I must—

Princess. Darling, you know what the drawbridge is like. It takes at *least* half an hour to let it down.

King (*sitting down*). It wants oil. (*To the* Chancellor) Have *you* been grudging it oil?

Princess. It wants a new drawbridge, darling.

Chancellor. Have I Your Majesty's permission—

King. Yes, yes.

[*The* Chancellor *bows and goes out.*]

Queen. You've told him, of course? It's the only chance.

King. Er—no. I was just going to, when——

Queen. Then I'd better. (*She goes to the door.*) You can explain to the girl; I'll have her sent to you. You've told Camilla?

King. Er—no. I was just going to, when——

Queen. Then you'd better tell her now.

King. My dear, are you sure——

Queen. It's the only chance left. (*Dramatically to heaven*) My daughter! (*She goes out. There is a little silence when she is gone.*)

King. Camilla, I want to talk seriously to you about marriage.

Princess. Yes, Father.

King. It is time that you learned some of the facts of life.

Princess. Yes, Father.

King. Now the great fact about marriage is that once you're married you live happy ever after. All our history books affirm this.

Princess. And your own experience too, darling.

King (*with dignity*). Let us confine ourselves to history for the moment.

Princess. Yes, Father.

King. Of course, there *may* be an exception here and there, which, as it were, proves the rule; just as—oh, well, never mind.

Princess (*smiling*). Go on, darling. You were going to say that an exception here and there proves the rule that all princesses are beautiful.

King. Well—leave that for the moment. The point is that it doesn't matter *how* you marry, or *who* you marry, as long as you *get* married. Because you'll be happy ever after in any case. Do you follow me so far?

Princess. Yes, Father.

King. Well, your mother and I have a little plan——

Princess. Was that it, going out of the door just now?

King. Er—yes. It concerns your waiting-maid.

Princess. Darling, I have several.

King. Only one that leaps to the eye, so to speak. The one with the—well, with everything.

Princess. Dulcibella?

King. That's the one. It is our little plan that at the first meeting she should pass herself off as the Princess—a harmless ruse,[7] of which you will find frequent record in the history books—and allure Prince Simon to his—that is to say, bring him up to the——In other words,

the wedding will take place immediately afterwards, and as quietly as possible—well, naturally in view of the fact that your Aunt Malkin is one hundred and fifty-two; and since you will be wearing the family bridal veil—which is no doubt how the custom arose—the surprise after the ceremony will be his. Are you following me at all? Your attention seems to be wandering.

Princess. I was wondering why you needed to tell me.

King. Just a precautionary measure, in case you happened to meet the Prince or his attendant before the ceremony; in which case, of course, you would pass yourself off as the maid——

Princess. A harmless ruse, of which, also, you will find frequent record in the history books.

King. Exactly. But the occasion need not arise.

A Voice (*announcing*). The woman Dulcibella!

King. Ah! (*To the* Princess) Now, Camilla, if you will just retire to your own apartments, I will come to you there when we are ready for the actual ceremony. (*He leads her out as he is talking, and as he returns calls out.*) Come in, my dear! (Dulcibella *comes in. She is beautiful, but dumb.*) Now don't be frightened, there is nothing to be frightened about. Has Her Majesty told you what you have to do?

Dulcibella. Y-yes, Your Majesty.

King. Well now, let's see how well you can do it. You are sitting here, we will say. (*He leads her to a seat.*) Now imagine that I am Prince Simon. (*He curls his mustache and puts his stomach in. She giggles.*) You are the beautiful Princess Camilla whom he has never seen. (*She giggles again.*) This is a serious moment in your life, and you will find that a giggle will not be helpful. (*He goes to the door.*) I am announced: "His Royal Highness Prince Simon!" That's me being announced. Remember what I said about giggling. You should have a faraway look upon the face. (*She does her best.*) Farther away than that.

---

7. **ruse** (rōōz): trick.

The King giving lessons to Dulcibella.

(*She tries again.*) No, that's too far. You are sitting there, thinking beautiful thoughts—in maiden meditation, fancy-free,[8] as I remember saying to Her Majesty once—speaking of somebody else—fancy-free, but with the

8. **in . . . fancy-free:** The King is quoting from Shakespeare again—this time from *A Midsummer Night's Dream*.

mouth definitely shut—that's better. I advance and fall upon one knee. (*He does so.*) You extend your hand graciously—*graciously*; you're not trying to push him in the face—that's better, and I raise it to my lips—so—and I kiss it (*He kisses it warmly*)—no, perhaps not so ardently as that, more like this (*He kisses it again*), and I say,

"Your Royal Highness this is the most—er—Your Royal Highness, I shall ever be—no—Your Royal Highness, it is the proudest—" Well, the point is that *he* will say it, and it will be something complimentary, and then he will take your hand in both of his and press it to his heart. (*He does so.*) And then—what do *you* say?

Dulcibella. Coo!

King. No, *not* "Coo."

Dulcibella. Never had anyone do *that* to me before.

King. That also strikes the wrong note. What you want to say is, "Oh, Prince Simon!" . . . Say it.

Dulcibella (*loudly*). Oh, Prince Simon!

King. No, no. You don't need to shout until he has said "What?" two or three times. Always consider the possibility that he *isn't* deaf. Softly, and giving the words a dying fall, letting them play around his head like a flight of doves.

Dulcibella (*still a little overloud*). O-o-o-o-h, Prinsimon!

King. Keep the idea in your mind of a flight of *doves* rather than a flight of panic-stricken elephants, and you will be all right. Now I'm going to get up, and you must, as it were, *waft*[9] me into a seat by your side. (*She starts wafting.*) *Not* rescuing a drowning man, that's another idea altogether, useful at times, but at the moment inappropriate. Wafting. Prince Simon will put the necessary muscles into play—all you require to do is indicate by a gracious movement of the hand the seat you require him to take. Now! (*He gets up, a little stiffly, and sits next to her.*) That was better. Well, here we are. Now, I think you give me a look: something, let us say, halfway between breathless adoration and regal dignity, touched, as it were, with good comradeship. Now try that. (*She gives him a vacant look of bewilderment.*) Frankly, that didn't quite get it. There was just

a little something missing. An absence, as it were, of all the qualities I asked for, and in their place an odd resemblance to an unsatisfied fish. Let us try to get at it another way. Dulcibella, have you a young man of your own?

Dulcibella (*eagerly, seizing his hand*). Oo, yes, he's ever so smart, he's an archer, well, not as you might say a real archer, he works in the armory, but old Bottlenose, *you* know who I mean, the Captain of the Guard, says the very next man they ever has to shoot, my Eg shall take his place, knowing Father and how it is with Eg and me, and me being maid to Her Royal Highness and can't marry me till he's a real soldier, but ever so loving, and funny like, the things he says, I said to him once, "Eg," I said——

King (*getting up*). I rather fancy, Dulcibella, that if you think of Eg all the time, *say* as little as possible, and, when thinking of Eg, see that the mouth is not more than partially open, you will do very well. I will show you where you are to sit and wait for His Royal Highness. (*He leads her out. On the way he is saying*) Now remember—waft—waft—not *hoick*.[10]

[*Prince Simon wanders in from the back unannounced. He is a very ordinary-looking young man in rather dusty clothes. He gives a deep sigh of relief as he sinks into the throne of the* King. . . . Camilla, *a new and strangely beautiful* Camilla, *comes in.*]

Princess (*surprised*). Well!

Prince. Oh, hallo!

Princess. Ought you?

Prince (*getting up*). Do sit down, won't you?

Princess. Who are you, and how did you get here?

Prince. Well, that's rather a long story. Couldn't

---

9. **waft** (wäft): carry gently, as if through the air.

10. **hoick**: yank or pull abruptly.

we sit down? You could sit here if you liked, but it isn't very comfortable.

Princess. That is the King's Throne.

Prince. Oh, is that what it is?

Princess. Thrones are not meant to be comfortable.

Prince. Well, I don't know if they're meant to be, but they certainly aren't.

Princess. Why were you sitting on the King's Throne, and who are you?

Prince. My name is Carlo.

Princess. Mine is Dulcibella.

Prince. Good. And now couldn't we sit down?

Princess (*sitting down on the long seat to the left of the throne, and, as it were, wafting him to a place next to her*). You may sit here, if you like. Why are you so tired?

[*He sits down.*]

Prince. I've been taking very strenuous exercise.

Princess. Is that part of the long story?

Prince. It is.

Princess (*settling herself*). I love stories.

Prince. This isn't a story really. You see, I'm attendant on Prince Simon, who is visiting here.

Princess. Oh? I'm attendant on Her Royal Highness.

Prince. Then you know what he's here for.

Princess. Yes.

Prince. She's very beautiful, I hear.

Princess. Did you hear that? Where have you been lately?

Prince. Traveling in distant lands—with Prince Simon.

Princess. Ah! All the same, I don't understand. Is Prince Simon in the palace now? The drawbridge *can't* be down yet!

Prince. I don't suppose it is. *And* what a noise it makes coming down!

Princess. Isn't it terrible?

Prince. I couldn't stand it any more. I just had to get away. That's why I'm here.

Princess. But how?

Prince. Well, there's only one way, isn't there? That beech tree, and then a swing and a grab for the battlements, and don't ask me to remember it all—— (*He shudders.*)

Princess. You mean you came across the moat by that beech tree?

Prince. Yes. I got so tired of hanging about.

Princess. But it's terribly dangerous!

Prince. That's why I'm so exhausted. Nervous shock. (*He lies back and breathes loudly.*)

Princess. Of course, it's different for *me*.

Prince (*sitting up*). Say that again. I must have got it wrong.

Princess. It's different for me, because I'm used to it. Besides, I'm so much lighter.

Prince. You don't mean that you—

Princess. Oh yes, often.

Prince. And I thought I was a brave man! At least, I didn't until five minutes ago, and now I don't again.

Princess. Oh, but you are! And I think it's wonderful to do it straight off the first time.

Prince. Well, *you* did.

Princess. Oh no, not the first time. When I was a child.

Prince. You mean that you crashed?

Princess. Well, you only fall into the moat.

Prince. Only! Can you *swim*?

Princess. Of course.

Prince. So you swam to the castle walls, and yelled for help and they fished you out and walloped you. And next day you tried again. Well, if *that* isn't pluck——

Princess. Of course I didn't. I swam back, and did it at once; I mean I tried again at once. It wasn't until the third time that I actually did it. You see, I was afraid I might lose my nerve.

Prince. Afraid she might lose her nerve!

Princess. There's a way of getting over from this side, too; a tree grows out from the wall and you jump into another tree—I don't think it's quite so easy.

The Ugly Duckling **309**

Prince. Not quite so easy. Good. You must show me.

Princess. Oh, I will.

Prince. Perhaps it might be as well if you taught me how to swim first. I've often heard about swimming, but never——

Princess. You can't swim?

Prince. No. Don't look so surprised. There are a lot of other things that I can't do. I'll tell you about them as soon as you have a couple of years to spare.

Princess. You can't swim and yet you crossed by the beech tree! And you're *ever* so much heavier than I am! Now who's brave?

Prince (*getting up*). You keep talking about how light you are. I must see if there's anything in it. Stand up! (*She stands obediently and he picks her up.*) You're right, Dulcibella. I could hold you here forever. (*Looking at her*) You're very lovely. Do you know how lovely you are?

Princess. Yes. (*She laughs suddenly and happily.*)

Prince. Why do you laugh?

Princess. Aren't you tired of holding me?

Prince. Frankly, yes. I exaggerated when I said I could hold you forever. When you've been hanging by the arms for ten minutes over a very deep moat, wondering if it's too late to learn how to swim—— (*He puts her down.*) What I meant was that I should *like* to hold you forever. Why did you laugh?

Princess. Oh, well, it was a little private joke of mine.

Prince. If it comes to that, I've got a private joke too. Let's exchange them.

Princess. Mine's very private. One other woman in the whole world knows, and that's all.

Prince. Mine's just as private. One other man knows, and that's all.

Princess. What fun. I love secrets. . . . Well, here's mine. When I was born, one of my godmothers promised that I should be very beautiful.

Prince. How right she was.

Princess. But the other one said this:

> I give you with this kiss
> A wedding-day surprise.
> Where ignorance is bliss
> 'Tis folly to be wise.

And nobody knew what it meant. And I grew up very plain. And then, when I was about ten, I met my godmother in the forest one day. It was my tenth birthday. Nobody knows this—except you.

Prince. Except us.

Princess. Except us. And she told me what her gift meant. It meant that I *was* beautiful—but everybody else was to go on being ignorant and thinking me plain, until my wedding day. Because, she said, she didn't want me to grow up spoiled and willful and vain, as I should have done if everybody had always been saying how beautiful I was; and the best thing in the world, she said, was to be quite sure of yourself, but not to expect admiration from other people. So ever since then my mirror has told me I'm beautiful, and everybody else thinks me ugly, and I get a lot of fun out of it.

Prince. Well, seeing that Dulcibella is the result, I can only say that your godmother was very, very wise.

Princess. And now tell me *your* secret.

Prince. It isn't such a pretty one. You see, Prince Simon was going to woo Princess Camilla, and he'd heard that she was beautiful and haughty and imperious—all *you* would have been if your godmother hadn't been so wise. And being a very ordinary-looking fellow himself, he was afraid she wouldn't think much of him, so he suggested to one of his attendants, a man called Carlo, of extremely attractive appearance, that *he* should pretend to be the Prince and win the Princess' hand; and then at the last moment they would change places——

Princess. How would they do that?

Prince. The Prince was going to have been married in full armor—with his visor down.

Princess (*laughing happily*). Oh, what fun!

Prince. Neat, isn't it?

Princess (*laughing*). Oh, very . . . very . . . very.

Prince. Neat, but not so terribly *funny*. Why do you keep laughing?

Princess. Well, that's another secret.

Prince. If it comes to that, *I've* got another one up my sleeve. Shall we exchange again?

Princess. All right. You go first this time.

Prince. Very well....I am not Carlo. (*Standing up and speaking dramatically*) I am Simon!—*ow!* (*He sits down and rubs his leg violently.*)

Princess (*alarmed*). What is it?

Prince. Cramp. (*In a mild voice, still rubbing*) I was saying that I was Prince Simon.

Princess. Shall I rub it for you? (*She rubs.*)

Prince (*still hopefully*). I am Simon.

Princess. Is that better?

Prince (*despairingly*). I am Simon.

Princess. I know.

Prince. How did you know?

Princess. Well, you told me.

Prince. But oughtn't you to swoon or something?

Princess. Why? History records many similar ruses.

Prince (*amazed*). Is that so? I've never read history. I thought I was being profoundly original.

Princess. Oh, no! Now I'll tell you *my* secret. For reasons very much like your own, the Princess Camilla, who is held to be extremely plain, feared to meet Prince Simon. Is the drawbridge down yet?

Prince. Do your people give a faint, surprised cheer every time it gets down?

Princess. Naturally.

Prince. Then it came down about three minutes ago.

Princess. Ah! Then at this very moment your man Carlo is declaring his passionate love for my maid, Dulcibella. That, I think, is funny. (*So does the* Prince. *He laughs heartily.*) Dulcibella, by the way, is in love with a man she calls Eg, so I hope Carlo isn't getting carried away.

Prince. Carlo is married to a girl he calls "the little woman," so Eg has nothing to fear.

Princess. By the way, I don't know if you heard, but I said, or as good as said, that I am the Princess Camilla.

Prince. I wasn't surprised. History, of which I read a great deal, records many similar ruses.

Princess (*laughing*). Simon!

Prince (*laughing*). Camilla! (*He stands up.*) May I try holding you again? (*She nods. He takes her in his arms and kisses her.*) Sweetheart!

Princess. You see, when you lifted me up before, you said, "You're very lovely," and my godmother said that the first person to whom I would seem lovely was the man I should marry; so I knew then that you were Simon and I should marry you.

Prince. I knew directly[11] I saw you that I should marry you, even if you were Dulcibella. By the way, which of you *am* I marrying?

Princess. When she lifts her veil, it will be Camilla. (*Voices are heard outside.*) Until then it will be Dulcibella.

Prince (*in a whisper*). Then goodbye, Camilla, until you lift your veil.

Princess. Goodbye, Simon, until you raise your visor.

[*The* King *and* Queen *come in arm-in-arm, followed by* Carlo *and* Dulcibella *also arm-in-arm. The* Chancellor *precedes them, walking backwards, at a loyal angle.*]

Prince (*supporting the* Chancellor *as an accident seems inevitable*). Careful!

[*The* Chancellor *turns indignantly round.*]

King. Who and what is this? More accurately who and what are all these?

Carlo. My attendant, Carlo, Your Majesty. He will, with Your Majesty's permission, prepare me for the ceremony.

[*The* Prince *bows.*]

King. Of course, of course!

Queen (*to* Dulcibella). Your maid, Dulcibella, is it not, my love? (Dulcibella *nods violently.*) I thought so. (*To* Carlo) She will prepare Her Royal Highness.

[*The* Princess *curtsies.*]

11. **directly:** here, as soon as.

King. Ah, yes. Yes. *Most* important.

Princess (*curtsying*). I beg your pardon, Your Majesty, if I've done wrong, but I found the gentleman wandering——

King (*crossing to her*). Quite right, my dear, quite right. (*He pinches her cheek and takes advantage of this kingly gesture to speak in a loud whisper.*) We've pulled it off!

[*They sit down: the* King *and* Queen *on their thrones,* Dulcibella *on the* Princess' *throne.* Carlo *stands behind* Dulcibella, *the* Chancellor *on the right of the* Queen, *and the* Prince *and* Princess *behind the long seat on the left.*]

Chancellor (*consulting documents*). H'r'm! Have I Your Majesty's authority to put the final test to His Royal Highness?

Queen (*whispering to the* King). Is this safe?

King (*whispering*). Perfectly, my dear. I told him the answer a minute ago. (*Over his shoulder, to* Carlo) Don't forget. "Dog." (*Aloud*) Proceed, Your Excellency. It is my desire that the affairs of my country should ever be conducted in a strictly constitutional manner.

Chancellor (*oratorically*). By the constitution of the country, a suitor to Her Royal Highness' hand cannot be deemed successful until he has given the correct answer to a riddle. (*Conversationally*) The last suitor answered incorrectly, and thus failed to win his bride.

King. By a coincidence he fell into the moat.

Chancellor (*to* Carlo). I have now to ask Your Royal Highness if you are prepared for the ordeal?

Carlo (*cheerfully*). Absolutely.

Chancellor. I may mention, as a matter possibly of some slight historical interest to our visitor, that by the constitution of the country, the same riddle is not allowed to be asked on two successive occasions.

King (*startled*). What's that?

Chancellor. This one, it is interesting to recall, was propounded exactly a century ago, and we must take it as a fortunate omen that it was well and truly solved.

King (*to the* Queen). I may want my sword directly.

Chancellor. The riddle is this: What is it that has four legs and mews like a cat?

Carlo (*promptly*). A dog.

King (*still more promptly*). Bravo, bravo! (*He claps loudly and nudges the* Queen, *who claps too.*)

Chancellor (*peering at his documents*). According to the records of the occasion to which I referred, the correct answer would seem to be——

Princess (*to the* Prince). Say something, quick!

Chancellor. ——not "dog," but——

Prince. Your Majesty, have I permission to speak? Naturally His Royal Highness could not think of justifying himself on such an occasion, but I think that with Your Majesty's gracious permission, I could——

King. Certainly, certainly.

Prince. In our country, we have an animal to which we have given the name "dog," or, in the local dialect of the more mountainous districts, "doggie." It sits by the fireside and purrs.

Carlo. That's right. It purrs like anything.

Prince. When it needs milk, which is its staple food, it mews.

Carlo (*enthusiastically*). Mews like nobody's business.

Prince. It also has four legs.

Carlo. One at each corner.

Prince. In some countries, I understand, this animal is called a "cat." In one distant country to which His Royal Highness and I penetrated, it was called by the very curious name of "hippopotamus."

Carlo. That's right. (*To the* Prince) Do you remember that ginger-colored hippopotamus which used to climb onto my shoulder and lick my ear?

The entire cast: (*left*) the Prince and the Princess; (*center*) the
Chancellor, the King, and the Queen; (*right*) Dulcibella and Carlo.

Prince. I shall never forget it, sir. (*To the* King) So you see, Your Majesty——

King. Thank you. I think that makes it perfectly clear. (*Firmly, to the* Chancellor) You are about to agree?

Chancellor. Undoubtedly, Your Majesty. May I be the first to congratulate His Royal Highness on solving the riddle so accurately?

King. You may be the first to see that all is in order for an immediate wedding.

Chancellor. Thank you, Your Majesty.

[*He bows and withdraws. The* King *rises, as do the* Queen *and* Dulcibella.]

King (*to* Carlo). Doubtless, Prince Simon, you will wish to retire and prepare yourself for the ceremony.

Carlo. Thank you, sir.

Prince. Have I Your Majesty's permission to attend His Royal Highness? It is the custom of his country for princes of the royal blood to be married in full armor, a matter which requires a certain adjustment——

King. Of course, of course. (Carlo *bows to the* King *and* Queen *and goes out. As the* Prince *is about to follow, the* King *stops him.*) Young man, you have a quality of quickness which I admire. It is my pleasure to reward it in any way which commends itself to you.

Prince. Your Majesty is ever gracious. May I ask for my reward *after* the ceremony?

[*The* Prince *catches the eye of the* Princess, *and they give each other a secret smile.*]

King. Certainly. (*The* Prince *bows and goes out. To* Dulcibella) Now, young woman, make yourself scarce. You have done your work excellently, and we will see that you and your——What was his name?

Dulcibella. Eg, Your Majesty.

King.——that you and your Eg are not forgotten.

Dulcibella. Coo! (*She curtsies and goes out.*)

Princess (*calling*). Wait for me, Dulcibella!

King (*to the* Queen). Well, my dear, we may congratulate ourselves. As I remember saying to somebody once, "You have not lost a daughter, you have gained a son." How does he strike you?

Queen. Stupid.

King. They made a very handsome pair, I thought, he and Dulcibella.

Queen. Both stupid.

King. I said nothing about stupidity. What I *said* was that they were both extremely handsome. That is the important thing. (*Struck by a sudden idea*) Or isn't it?

Queen. What do *you* think of Prince Simon, Camilla?

Princess. I adore him. We shall be so happy together.

King. Well, of course you will. I told you so. Happy ever after.

Queen. Run along now and get ready.

Princess. Yes, Mother, (*She throws a kiss to them and goes out.*)

King (*anxiously*). My dear, have we been wrong about Camilla all this time? It seemed to me that she wasn't looking *quite* so plain as usual just now. Did *you* notice anything?

Queen (*carelessly*). Just the excitement of the marriage.

King (*relieved*). Ah, yes, that would account for it.

[*Curtain.*]

Reading Check

1. Why are the King and the Queen worried about Prince Simon's arrival?

2. How do the King and Queen plan to trick Prince Simon?

3. How does Prince Simon plan to trick the Princess?

4. How do Prince Simon and Princess Camilla meet each other?

5. What riddle must the Prince solve in order to win the hand of Princess Camilla?

For Study and Discussion

Analyzing and Interpreting the Play

1. In the fairy tale "The Ugly Duckling" by Hans Christian Andersen, a young bird believes he is ugly until he grows into a beautiful swan. In this play, a young woman is believed to be very plain until love reveals her beauty. In the scene on page 310, what does the Princess say will happen on her wedding day?

2. Fairy tales are filled with characters such as a dignified king, a serene and ladylike queen, a beautiful princess, and a fearless and strong prince. But the characters in this humorous play are not at all what they would be in the usual fairy tale. **a.** What actions of the King show that he is undignified and a bit foolish? **b.** How does the Queen show she is bossy and quick-tempered? **c.** How do you learn that the Prince is not fearless and strong?

3. Fairy tales are also filled with trials and tests such as tournaments and riddles. But this comedy is filled with surprising twists. What humorous unexpected events occurred in the Tournament of Love that the King and Queen gave for Camilla?

4. The most important part of this story will take place after the play ends. **a.** What will happen then? **b.** What surprising discoveries will be made when all the disguises are removed?

5. Most comedies end with all problems solved and everyone living "happily ever after." **a.** Do you believe that Simon and Camilla will live "happily ever after"? **b.** What will happen to Dulcibella to help her and Eg live "happily ever after"?

Literary Elements

Recognizing the Elements of a Comedy

The Ugly Duckling is a **comedy**. In a comedy the characters often include some young lovers, the plot ends happily, and the theme often has something to do with love.

Comic Characters. One of the basic elements of humor is the unexpected. Characters like a king who is nagged by his queen and a prince who is timid are funny because they are different from what you expect them to be. Why is Dulcibella's attempt to act like a princess so funny? Why is it humorous to see a fairy-tale chancellor in horn-rimmed glasses?

Comic Plot. In every play, the characters face some struggle or conflict. The plot tells what they do to solve their problem. In a comedy, the characters solve the problem happily. In every play there is also a **climax**, or turning point, when we know whether the play will end happily or unhappily. The climax in this play comes when the Chancellor tests the fake "Prince" with the riddle (page 313). How does the real Prince win his bride and make the play end happily?

Comic Theme. Most comedies are about love or happiness. What does *The Ugly Duckling* say about the power of love? Look at the Princess' speech on page 310, in which she reveals her secret to the Prince. Which line sums up what this play says about happiness?

Understanding Stage Terms

The theater has its own technical terminology, just as baseball, medicine, and electronics do. If you ever stage a play, you'll have to know the vocabulary of the stage.

Almost every production of a play has people in charge of *sets, props, lighting,* and *costumes.* The *director* of the play supervises all aspects of the play's production.

Set: all the scenery and furniture used on the stage. Some plays use more than one set. Each time a play is produced, it usually has a different set. Describe (or draw) the set you would design for *The Ugly Duckling.* Would it be a reversal of what the audience expects a castle to be like, or would it be a typical fairy-tale castle?

Props: the properties, or objects that the characters need to use as they act out the play. Props may include a handkerchief, a glass of water, a sword, or a paper bag. Make a list of the props needed for this play. Start with the handkerchief.

Lighting: all the lights that are focused on the stage, including footlights and spotlights. Lighting must be planned to create the right mood for the play. What kind of lighting would you use for *The Ugly Duckling*?

Costumes: the clothes the characters wear. Each time a play is produced, the costumes may differ. If you were the costume designer for a production of *The Ugly Duckling,* you would need to tell exactly what each character would wear. Using words or drawings (or both), describe the costumes you would design for the characters in *The Ugly Duckling.* Would you have the King wear a business suit, a typical fairy-tale costume, or a humorous combination of both? (Notice that the stage direction at the opening of the play says, *"But he should be wearing his crown."*) How would you make Dulcibella's costume differ from Camilla's?

For Dramatization

Presenting a Scene

Perhaps the funniest scene in this play is the one in which the King tries to teach the giggling Dulcibella to act like a princess (page 306). Dulcibella tries hard—too hard—but she is a hilarious flop as a princess. You might try presenting this scene in class.

Read the scene carefully to find out what props you will need.

Pay close attention to the stage directions in parentheses. They tell how the characters should say their lines, and what they should be doing. For example, one stage direction to the King reads:

(*He curls his mustache and puts his stomach in.*)

What does Dulcibella do in response to this action?

You will also get clues to actions from the speeches of the characters. For example, the King tells Dulcibella to be "thinking beautiful thoughts." Then he adds, "but with the mouth definitely shut." What is Dulcibella doing to look as if she is having beautiful thoughts?

Creative Writing

Adapting a Fairy Tale

In this play, "The Ugly Duckling," A. A. Milne borrows the theme and title of a well-known fairy tale. He changes the ugly duckling to a plain princess, and he adds humorous details to change what was a serious story to a comedy. Choose a well-known fairy tale such as "The Three Bears" or "Little Red Riding Hood." Borrow the title and write a new story that presents a humorous variation of the same theme.

About the Author

A. A. Milne (1882–1956)

A. A. Milne was a British novelist and playwright whose stories of Winnie-the-Pooh and Christopher Robin (a character based on his own son) have overshadowed everything else he wrote. Milne worked for the British humor magazine *Punch*. He wrote his first play at the front lines during World War I. His plays were huge successes. Among them are *Mr. Pim Passes By* and a mystery called *The Perfect Alibi*.

Pyramus and Thisby

WILLIAM SHAKESPEARE

In Shakespeare's comedy A Midsummer Night's Dream, *a group of work-ingmen plan a play as entertainment for the wedding of their ruler, the Duke of Athens. The men can hardly read or write. They have difficulty figuring out the meaning of their lines and memorizing them. They decide to dramatize a tragic story that was well known in Shakespeare's day—a tale of two young lovers named Pyramus and Thisby. As you read, notice how seriously these actors take themselves and how the audience responds to their play.*

Characters

Peter Quince, a carpenter, the director of the play, who also delivers
   the Prologue
Nick Bottom, a weaver, who takes the part of the lover Pyramus
Francis Flute, a bellows-mender, who takes the part of Thisby
Robin Starveling, a tailor, who presents Moonshine
Tom Snout, a tinker, who plays the Wall
Snug, a joiner, or cabinetmaker, who plays the Lion
Theseus (thē′sē-əs, -syo͞os′), Duke of Athens
Hippolyta (hĭ-pŏl′ə-tə), queen of the Amazons and bride of Theseus
Philostrate (fĭ′lŏs-strä′tē), master of the revels
Courtiers, Ladies, and Attendants

Scene 1

[*Quince's house. Enter* Quince, Snug, Bottom, Flute, Snout, *and* Starveling.]

Quince. Is all our company here?
Bottom. You were best to call them generally,° man by man, according to the scrip.°
Quince. Here is the scroll of every man's name which is thought fit, through all Athens, to
   play in our interlude° before the Duke and the Duchess on his wedding day at night.
Bottom. First, good Peter Quince, say what the play treats on. Then read the names of the   5
   actors, and so grow to a point.°

---

2. **generally:** Bottom means "severally" or "separately."   **scrip:** list.   4. **interlude:** play.   6. **grow to a point:** conclude.

Quince. Marry,° our play is *The most lamentable comedy and most cruel death of Pyramus and Thisby.*

Bottom. A very good piece of work, I assure you, and a merry. Now, good Peter Quince, call forth your actors by the scroll. Masters, spread yourselves.   10

Quince. Answer as I call you. Nick Bottom, the weaver.

Bottom. Ready. Name what part I am for, and proceed.

Quince. You, Nick Bottom, are set down for Pyramus.

Bottom. What is Pyramus? A lover, or a tyrant?

Quince. A lover, that kills himself most gallant for love.   15

Bottom. That will ask some tears in the true performing of it. If I do it, let the audience look to their eyes, I will move storms, I will condole° in some measure. To the rest. Yet my chief humor° is for a tyrant. I could play Ercles° rarely, or a part to tear a cat in,° to make all split.

> "The raging rocks   20
> And shivering shocks
> Shall break the locks
>   Of prison gates.
> And Phibbus' car°
> Shall shine from far,   25
> And make and mar
>   The foolish Fates."

This was lofty! Now name the rest of the players. This is Ercles' vein, a tyrant's vein.° A lover is more condoling.

Quince. Francis Flute, the bellows-mender.   30

Flute. Here, Peter Quince.

Quince. Flute, you must take Thisby on you.

Flute. What is Thisby? A wandering knight?

Quince. It is the lady that Pyramus must love.

Flute. Nay, faith, let not me play a woman. I have a beard coming.   35

Quince. That's all one. You shall play it in a mask, and you may speak as small° as you will.

Bottom. An° I may hide my face, let me play Thisby too. I'll speak in a monstrous little voice, "Thisne, Thisne." "Ah Pyramus, my lover dear! Thy Thisby dear, and lady dear!"

Quince. No, no. You must play Pyramus, and Flute, you Thisby.

Bottom. Well, proceed.   40

Quince. Robin Starveling, the tailor.

Starveling. Here, Peter Quince.

Quince. Robin Starveling, you must play Thisby's mother. Tom Snout, the tinker.

Snout. Here, Peter Quince.

Quince. You, Pyramus' father. Myself, Thisby's father. Snug, the joiner, you, the lion's part.   45
And, I hope, here is a play fitted.

---

7. **Marry:** an exclamation.   17. **condole:** Bottom means "lament."   18. **humor:** whim.   **Ercles:** Hercules.   **tear a cat in:** to overact.   24. **Phibbus' car:** the chariot of Phoebus, the sun god.   28. **tyrant's vein:** In the old drama, Hercules was portrayed as a ranting character.   36. **small:** shrilly.   37. **An:** if.

Snug. Have you the lion's part written? Pray you, if it be, give it me, for I am slow of study.

Quince. You may do it extempore, for it is nothing but roaring.

Bottom. Let me play the lion too. I will roar that I will do any man's heart good to hear me; I will roar that I will make the Duke say, "Let him roar again, let him roar again." 50

Quince. An you should do it too terribly, you would fright the Duchess and the ladies, that they would shriek; and that were enough to hang us all.

All. That would hang us, every mother's son.

Bottom. I grant you, friends, if you should fright the ladies out of their wits, they would have no more discretion but to hang us. But I will aggravate° my voice so that I will roar you 55 as gently as any sucking dove, I will roar you an 'twere any nightingale.

Quince. You can play no part but Pyramus; for Pyramus is a sweet-faced man, a proper° man as one shall see in a summer's day, a most lovely, gentlemanlike man. Therefore you must needs play Pyramus.

Bottom. Well, I will undertake it. What beard were I best to play it in? 60

Quince. Why, what you will.

Bottom. I will discharge it in either your straw-color beard, your orange-tawny beard, your purple-in-grain° beard, or your French-crown-color beard, your perfect yellow.

Quince. Masters, here are your parts. And I am to entreat you, request you, and desire you, to con° them by tomorrow night; and meet me in the palace wood, a mile without the 65 town, by moonlight. There will we rehearse, for if we meet in the city, we shall be dogged with company, and our devices known. In the meantime I will draw a bill of properties such as our play wants. I pray you, fail me not.

Bottom. We will meet, and there we may rehearse most obscenely° and courageously. Take pains, be perfect. Adieu. 70

Quince. At the Duke's Oak we meet.

Scene 2

[*A wood near Athens. Enter* Quince, Snug, Bottom, Flute, Snout *and* Starveling.]

Bottom. Are we all met?

Quince. Pat,° pat, and here's a marvelous convenient place for our rehearsal. This green plot shall be our stage, this hawthorn brake° our tiring-house;° and we will do it in action as we will do it before the Duke.

Bottom. Peter Quince —— 5

Quince. What sayest thou, bully Bottom?

Bottom. There are things in this comedy of Pyramus and Thisby that will never please. First, Pyramus must draw a sword to kill himself, which the ladies cannot abide. How answer you that?

---

55. **aggravate:** Bottom means "restrain." 57. **proper:** handsome. 63. **purple-in-grain:** dyed purple. 65. **con;** learn. 69. **obscenely:** Bottom means "obscurely" or "off the scene."
    2. **Pat:** right on time. 3. **hawthorn brake:** thicket of hawthorn bushes. **tiring-house:** dressing room.

Snout. By'r lakin, a parlous° fear! 10

Starveling. I believe we must leave the killing out, when all is done.

Bottom. Not a whit. I have a device to make all well. Write me a prologue, and let the prologue seem to say we will do no harm with our swords, and that Pyramus is not killed
indeed. And, for the more better assurance, tell them that I Pyramus am not Pyramus,
but Bottom, the weaver. This will put them out of fear. 15

Quince. Well, we will have such a prologue, and it shall be written in eight and six.°

Bottom. No, make it two more. Let it be written in eight and eight.

Snout. Will not the ladies be afeard of the lion?

Starveling. I fear it, I promise you.

Bottom. Masters, you ought to consider with yourselves. To bring in—God shield us—a lion 20
among ladies is a most dreadful thing; for there is not a more fearful wildfowl than your
lion living, and we ought to look to 't.

Snout. Therefore another prologue must tell he is not a lion.

Bottom. Nay, you must name his name, and half his face must be seen through the lion's neck.
And he himself must speak through, saying thus, or to the same defect°—"Ladies"—or 25
"Fair ladies—I would wish you"—or "I would request you"—or "I would entreat you—
not to fear, not to tremble. My life for yours. If you think I come hither as a lion, it were
pity of my life. No, I am no such thing. I am a man as other men are." And there indeed
let him name his name, and tell them plainly he is Snug the joiner.

Quince. Well, it shall be so. But there is two hard things: that is, to bring the moonlight into a 30
chamber, for you know, Pyramus and Thisby meet by moonlight.

Snout. Doth the moon shine that night we play our play?

Bottom. A calendar, a calendar! Look in the almanac, find out moonshine, find out moonshine!

Quince. Yes, it doth shine that night. 35

Bottom. Why, then may you leave a casement of the great-chamber° window, where we play,
open, and then the moon may shine in at the casement.

Quince. Aye, or else one must come in with a bush of thorns and a lantern,° and say he comes
to disfigure,° or to present, the person of moonshine. Then, there is another thing. We
must have a wall in the great chamber, for Pyramus and Thisby, says the story, did talk 40
through the chink of a wall.

Snout. You can never bring in a wall. What say you, Bottom?

Bottom. Some man or other must present wall. And let him have some plaster, or some loam,
or some roughcast° about him, to signify wall. And let him hold his fingers thus, and
through that cranny shall Pyramus and Thisby whisper. 45

Quince. If that may be, then all is well. Come, sit down, every mother's son, and rehearse
your parts. Pyramus, you begin. When you have spoken your speech, enter into that
brake. And so everyone according to his cue. Speak, Pyramus, Thisby, stand forth.

Bottom (*as* **Pyramus**). "Thisby, the flowers of odious savors sweet —— "

---

10. **parlous:** perilous.   16. **eight and six:** Ballads were written in alternate lines of eight and six syllables.   25. **defect:** Bottom means "effect."   36. **great-chamber:** hall of a great house.   38. **bush . . . lantern:** supposedly carried by the man in
the moon.   39. **disfigure:** Quince means "figure" or "portray."   44. **roughcast:** rough plaster.

Scene from *A Midsummer Night's Dream* performed at the Stratford
Shakespeare Festival, Stratford, Ontario, Canada.

Quince. Odors, odors. 50

Bottom (*as* **Pyramus**). " —— odors savors sweet.
So hath thy breath, my dearest Thisby dear.
But hark, a voice! Stay thou but here awhile,
And by and by I will to thee appear." [*Exit.*]

Flute. Must I speak now? 55

Quince. Aye, marry must you, for you must understand he goes but to see a noise that he
heard, and is to come again.

Flute (*as* **Thisby**). "Most radiant Pyramus, most lily-white of hue,
Of color like the red rose on triumphant brier,
Most briskly juvenal,° and eke° most lovely too, 60

60. **juvenal:** youthful. **eke:** also.

Pyramus and Thisby **323**

As true as truest horse, that yet would never tire,
I'll meet thee, Pyramus, at Ninny's tomb."

Quince. "Ninus' tomb," man. Why, you must not speak that yet. That you answer to Pyramus.
You speak all your part at once, cues and all. Pyramus enter. Your cue is past. It is "never
tire."   65

Flute (*as* **Thisby**). Oh—
"As true as truest horse, that yet would never tire."

[*Reenter* Bottom.]

Bottom (*as* **Pyramus**). "If I were fair, Thisby, I were only thine."

[*At this point the rehearsal is broken up and the players scatter. They next meet to perform their play before
the Duke and his court.*]

Scene 3

[*Athens. The palace of* Theseus. *Enter* Theseus, Hippolyta, Philostrate, Lords, *and* Attendants.]

Theseus. Where is our usual manager of mirth?
What revels are in hand? Is there no play?
Call Philostrate.

Philostrate.   Here, mighty Theseus.

Theseus. Say, what abridgement° have you for this evening?
What masque?° What music? How shall we beguile   5
The lazy time, if not with some delight?

Philostrate. A play there is, my lord, some ten words long,
Which is as brief as I have known a play.
But by ten words, my lord, it is too long,
Which makes it tedious; for in all the play   10
There is not one word apt, one player fitted.
And tragical, my noble lord, it is,
For Pyramus therein doth kill himself.
Which, when I saw rehearsed, I must confess,
Made mine eyes water, but more merry tears   15
The passion of loud laughter never shed.

Theseus. What are they that do play it?

Philostrate. Hard-handed men that work in Athens here,
Which never labored in their minds till now.

4. **abridgement:** entertainment (to abridge, or shorten, the evening.)   5. **masque:** court entertainment.

324 DRAMA

And now have toiled their unbreathed° memories 20
With this same play, against° your nuptial.
Theseus. I will hear that play,
For never anything can be amiss,
When simpleness and duty tender it.
Go, bring them in, and take your places, ladies. 25

[*As* Philostrate *leaves to get the players,* Theseus *and the others arrange themselves on the side of the stage as an audience.* Philostrate *reenters.*]

Philostrate. So please your Grace, the Prologue is addressed.°

[*Flourish of trumpets. Enter* Quince *for the* Prologue.]

Quince (*as* **Prologue**). If° we offend, it is with our good will.
That you should think, we come not to offend,
But with good will. To show our simple skill,
That is the true beginning of our end. 30
Consider, then, we come but in despite.°
We do not come, as minding to content you,
Our true intent is. All for your delight,
We are not here. That you should here repent you,
The actors are at hand, and, by their show, 35
You shall know all, that you are like to know.
Theseus. This fellow does not stand upon points.°
First Courtier. He hath rid° his prologue like a rough colt, he knows not the stop. A good moral, my lord. It is not enough to speak, but to speak true.
Hippolyta. Indeed he hath played on his prologue like a child on a recorder—a sound, but 40 not in government.°
Theseus. His speech was like a tangled chain—nothing impaired, but all disordered. Who is next?

[*Enter* Pyramus *and* Thisby, Wall, Moonshine, *and* Lion.]

Quince (*as* **Prologue**). Gentles, perchance you wonder at this show,
But wonder on, till truth makes all things plain. 45
This man is Pyramus, if you would know.
This beauteous lady, Thisby is certáin.
This man, with lime and roughcast, doth present
Wall, that vile Wall which did these lovers sunder,°

20. **unbreathed:** unpracticed, inexperienced.   21. **against:** in anticipation of.   26. **addressed:** ready.   27. **If . . .:** Because the prologue is mispunctuated, the meaning of Quince's speech is comically distorted.   31. **despite:** ill will.   37. **stand upon points:** pay attention to punctuation marks.   38. **rid:** ridden.   41. **not in government:** undisciplined.   49. **sunder:** separate.

Scene from *A Midsummer Night's Dream* performed at the New York
Shakespeare Festival, New York City.

And through Wall's chink, poor souls, they are content   50
To whisper. At the which let no man wonder.
This man, with lantern, dog, and bush of thorn,
Presenteth Moonshine; for, if you will know,
By moonshine did these lovers think no scorn
To meet at Ninus' tomb, there, there to woo.   55
This grisly beast, which Lion hight° by name,
The trusty Thisby, coming first by night,
Did scare away, or rather did affright.
And, as she fled, her mantle she did fall,
Which Lion vile with bloody mouth did stain.   60

56. **hight:** is called.

Anon comes Pyramus, sweet youth and tall,
And finds his trusty Thisby's mantle slain.
Whereat, with blade, with bloody blameful blade,
He bravely broached° his boiling bloody breast.
And Thisby, tarrying in mulberry shade,   65
His dagger drew, and died. For all the rest,
Let Lion, Moonshine, Wall, and lovers twain
At large° discourse, while here they do remain.

[*Exeunt* Prologue, Pyramus, Thisby, Lion *and* Moonshine.]

Theseus. I wonder if the lion be to speak.
Second Courtier. No wonder, my Lord. One lion may, when many asses do.   70
Snout (*as* **Wall**). In this same interlude it doth befall
    That I, one Snout by name, present a wall,
    And such a wall, as I would have you think,
    That had in it a crannied hole or chink,
    Through which the lovers, Pyramus and Thisby,   75
    Did whisper often very secretly.
    This loam, this roughcast, and this stone doth show
    That I am that same wall. The truth is so.
    And this the cranny is, right and siníster,°
    Through which the fearful lovers are to whisper.   80
Theseus. Would you desire lime and hair to speak better?
Second Courtier. It is the wittiest partition that I have ever heard discourse, my lord.
Theseus. Pyramus draws near the wall! Silence!

[*Reenter* Pyramus.]

Bottom (*as* **Pyramus**). O grim-looked night! O night with hue so black!
    O night, which ever art when day is not!   85
    O night, O night! alack, alack, alack!
    I fear my Thisby's promise is forgot!
    And thou, O wall, O sweet, O lovely wall,
    That stand'st between her father's ground and mine!
    Thou wall, O wall, O sweet and lovely wall,   90
    Show me thy chink, to blink through with mine eyne!

[Wall *holds up his fingers.*]

Thanks, courteous wall. Jove shield thee well for this!

64. **broached:** stabbed.   68. **at large:** in full.   79. **siníster:** left.

But what see I? No Thisby do I see.
O wicked wall, through whom I see no bliss!
Cursed be thy stones for thus deceiving me! 95

Theseus. The wall, methinks, being sensible,° should curse again.

Bottom. No, in truth, sir, he should not. "Deceiving me" is Thisby's cue. She is to enter now, and I am to spy her through the wall. You should see it will fall pat as I told you. Yonder she comes.

[*Reenter* Thisby.]

Flute (*as* **Thisby**). O wall, full often has thou heard my moans, 100
For parting my fair Pyramus and me!
My cherry lips have often kissed thy stones,
Thy stones with lime and hair knit up in thee.

Bottom (*as* **Pyramus**). I see a voice. Now will I to the chink,
To spy an I can hear my Thisby's face. 105
Thisby!

Flute (*as* **Thisby**). My love thou art, my love I think.

Bottom (*as* **Pyramus**). Think what thou wilt, I am thy lover's grace;
And like Limander,° am I trusty still.

Flute (*as* **Thisby**). And I, like Helen,° till the Fates° me kill. 110

Bottom (*as* **Pyramus**). Oh, kiss me through the hole of this vile wall!

Flute (*as* **Thisby**). I kiss the wall's hole, not your lips at all.

Bottom (*as* **Pyramus**). Wilt thou at Ninny's tomb meet me straightway?

Flute (*as* **Thisby**). 'Tide° life, 'tide death, I come without delay.

[*Exeunt* Pyramus *and* Thisby.]

Snout (*as* **Wall**). Thus have I, Wall my part dischargèd so; 115
And, being done, thus Wall away doth go. [*Exit* Wall.]

Theseus. Now is the mural° down between the two neighbors.

Second Courtier. No remedy, my lord, when walls are so willful to hear without warning.

Hippolyta. This is the silliest stuff that I ever heard.

Theseus. The best in this kind are but shadows, and the worst are no worse if imagination 120
amend them.

Hippolyta. It must be your imagination then, and not theirs.

Theseus. If we imagine no worse of them than they of themselves, they may pass for excellent men. Here come two noble beasts in, a man and a lion.

[*Reenter* Lion *and* Moonshine.]

96. **being sensible:** having feeling. 109. **Limander:** instead of *Leander,* a legendary Greek lover. 110. **Helen:** instead of *Hero,* Leander's love. Helen was in another legend. **Fates:** in Greek mythology, the three goddesses who controlled the future. 114. **'Tide:** betide; happen. 117. **mural:** wall.

Snug (*as* **Lion**). You, ladies, you, whose gentle hearts do fear   125
    The smallest monstrous mouse that creeps on floor,
    May now perchance° both quake and tremble here,
    When lion rough in wildest rage doth roar.
    Then know that I, one Snug, the joiner, am
    A lion fell,° nor else no lion's dam;   130
    For, if I should as lion come in strife
    Into this place, 'twere pity on my life.°
Theseus. A very gentle beast, and of a good conscience.
Second Courtier. The very best at a beast, my lord, that e'er I saw.
First Courtier. This lion is a very fox for his valor.   135
Starveling (*as* **Moonshine**). This lantern doth the hornèd moon present,
    Myself the man i' the moon do seem to be.
Theseus. This is the greatest error of all the rest. The man should be put into the lantern.
    How is it else the man i' the moon?
First Courtier. Proceed, Moon.   140
Starveling. All that I have to say is, to tell you that the lantern is the moon; I, the man i' the
    moon; this thornbush, my thornbush; and this dog, my dog.
Second Courtier. Why, all these should be in the lantern, for all these are in the moon. But
    silence! Here comes Thisby.

[Reenter Thisby.]

Flute (*as* **Thisby**). This is old Ninny's tomb. Where is my love?   145
Snug (*as* **Lion**, *roaring*). Oh ——   [Thisby *runs off.*]
Second Courtier. Well roared, Lion!
Theseus. Well run, Thisby!
Hippolyta. Well shone, Moon! Truly, the moon shines with a good grace.
                               [Lion shakes Thisby's *mantle and exits.]*
Theseus. Well moused, Lion!   150
First Courtier. And so the lion vanished.
Second Courtier. And then came Pyramus.

[Reenter Pyramus.]

Bottom (*as* **Pyramus**). Sweet Moon, I thank thee for thy sunny beams,
    I thank thee, Moon, for shining now so bright.
    For by thy gracious, golden, glittering gleams,   155
    I trust to take of truest Thisby sight.
        But stay, oh spite!

---

127. **perchance:** perhaps.   130. **fell:** fierce. *Fell* also refers to an animal's hide or skin.   132. **'twere . . . life:** I should be
hanged for it.

But mark, poor knight,
What dreadful dole° is here!
Eyes, do you see? 160
How can it be?
Oh dainty duck! Oh dear!
Thy mantle good,
What, stained with blood!
Approach, ye Furies fell!° 165
O Fates, come, come,
Cut thread and thrum°
Quail, crush, conclude, and quell!°

Theseus. This passion,° and the death of a dear friend, would go near to make a man look
    sad. 170

Hippolyta. Beshrew my heart, but I pity the man.

Bottom (*as* **Pyramus**). O wherefore, Nature, didst thou lions frame?
    Since lion vile hath here deflowered my dear,
    Which is—no, no—which was the fairest dame
    That lived, that loved, that liked, that looked with cheer. 175
        Come, tears, confound!°
        Out, sword, and wound
        The pap° of Pyramus.
        Aye, that left pap,
        Where heart doth hop. [*Stabs himself.*] 180
    Thus die I, thus, thus, thus.
    Now am I dead,
    Now am I fled,
    My soul is in the sky.
    Tongue, lose thy light, 185
    Moon, take thy flight, [*Exit* Moonshine.]
    Now die, die, die, die, die. [*Dies.*]

Theseus. With the help of a surgeon he might yet recover, and prove an ass.

Hippolyta. How chance Moonshine is gone before Thisby comes back and finds her lover?

Theseus. She will find him by starlight. Here she comes, and her passion ends the play. 190

[*Reenter* Thisby.]

Flute (*as* **Thisby**). Asleep, my love?
    What, dead, my dove?
    O Pyramus, arise!

---

159. **dole:** sorrow. 165. **Furies fell:** In Greek mythology, the Furies avenged unpunished crimes. 167. **thrum:** the very end of the thread. One of the goddesses spun the thread of life, a second goddess determined its length, and a third cut it. 168. **quell:** slay. 169. **passion:** display of sorrow. 176. **confound:** destroy. 178. **pap:** breast.

Speak, speak. Quite dumb?
Dead, dead? A tomb   195
Must cover thy sweet eyes.
These lily lips,
This cherry nose,
These yellow cowslip cheeks,
Are gone, are gone.   200
Lovers, make moan.
His eyes were as green as leeks.
O Sisters Three,°
Come, come to me,
With hands as pale as milk;   205
Lay them in gore,
Since you have shore°
With shears his thread of silk.
Tongue, not a word.
Come trusty sword,   210
Come, blade, my breast imbrue!° [*Stabs herself.*]
And, farewell, friends.
Thus Thisby ends.
Adieu, adieu, adieu! [*Dies.*]

Theseus. Moonshine and Lion are left to bury the dead.   215

Second Courtier. Aye, and Wall too.

Bottom. (*starting up*). No, I assure you; the wall is down that parted their fathers. Will it please you to see the epilogue?

Theseus. No epilogue, I pray you, for your play needs no excuse. Never excuse, for when the players are all dead, there need none to be blamed. Marry, if he that writ it had played   220
Pyramus and hanged himself in Thisby's garter, it would have been a fine tragedy. And so it is, truly, and very notably discharged.

203. **Sisters Three:** the Fates.   207. **shore:** cut.   211. **imbrue:** drench with blood.

1. What is the occasion for the interlude the workingmen present?
2. Why does Bottom ask for a prologue to the play?
3. What do the players use to represent the wall and the moon?
4. How do Theseus and the other members of the audience react to the play?
5. In the play, how do Pyramus and Thisby die?

For Study and Discussion

Analyzing and Interpreting the Play

Scene 1

1. How can you tell that these workingmen are simple and uneducated?

2. How does the title of the interlude contribute to the humor of this scene?

3. Bottom often uses words without understanding what they mean. For example, in line 55 he says he will *aggravate* his voice when he means he will *restrain* it. Find several comic examples of his misuse of language.

4. How does Bottom show he is a "ham," a performer who tends to exaggerate his roles?

5. In lines 20–27, Bottom treats us to poetry in the "lofty" vein. Why is this speech so comical?

Scene 2

1a. What fears does Bottom express about the audience's reaction to certain parts of the play?   **b.** What solution does he offer to these problems?

2. Quince says in line 30 that there are "two hard things" to present in the interlude. How do the actors decide to handle these difficulties?

3. What problems does Quince have in directing the rehearsal?

Scene 3

1a. Why does Philostrate try to dissuade Theseus from having the play performed? **b.** Why does Theseus decide, nevertheless, to hear it?   **c.** What does his decision reveal about him as a ruler?

2. The story of Pyramus and Thisby was a well-known tragic legend in Shakespeare's day. Retell the story in your own words. Be sure to include the roles played by the wall and by the lion.

3. **Parody** is a humorous imitation of a serious work or style of writing for the purpose of amusement. In this play Shakespeare parodies certain techniques of his contemporaries. Find instances where he pokes fun at flowery language and ridiculous comparisons.

4. Read aloud Bottom's speech, lines 153–168. How does Bottom overuse such poetic devices as alliteration and rhyme?

5a. Find instances where the actors drop out of character to address members of the audience.   **b.** Why do these interruptions add to the comedy?

Language and Vocabulary

Understanding Meanings of Words

Notice that many words in *Pyramus and Thisby* are glossed at the bottom of the page. Some of the words are explained as comic misuse of the language by one of the characters. Others are defined because their meanings in the play are either out of use (**archaic**) or not commonly used. Shakespeare wrote *Pyramus and Thisby* more than three hundred and fifty years ago, and a number of the words he used have changed in meaning over the centuries.

Use an advanced dictionary to answer the following questions about words used in *Pyramus and Thisby*:

Does your dictionary list the same definition for the word *proper* as is listed on page 321? Is the definition marked *archaic*?

The meaning of *con* given on page 321 is "to learn." This meaning is not commonly used today. Explain the relationship between this meaning and the French word, *conduire*, meaning "to guide."

On page 325, the definition provided for *against* is "in anticipation of." Is that meaning archaic or is it just infrequently used?

The meaning given for *sinister* (page 327) is "left." That meaning for *sinister*, though rare today, is derived from the Latin word *sinister*, meaning "left." Can you think of any connection between the meaning of *left* and the meaning of *evil*, the common definition of *sinister* today?

Writing About Literature

Discussing Aspects of the Play

1. Shakespeare was an actor as well as a playwright. What aspects of his profession might he be poking fun at in this "interlude"? In your discussion refer to specific speeches.

2. Bottom is one of Shakespeare's great comic characters. Write an analysis of Bottom's character. Be sure to include his treatment of language.

3. All the workingmen are simple and uneducated. However, they are presented as individuals with distinguishing characteristics. Explain the differences you note in this group.

About the Author

William Shakespeare   (1564–1616)

William Shakespeare is generally regarded as the greatest English writer and the world's greatest dramatist. He was the son of a prominent merchant in the town of Stratford-on-Avon in England. When he was in his twenties, he went to London to seek his fortune. There he joined a famous acting company. For this company, he wrote thirty-seven brilliant plays, including tragedies, comedies, and history plays. Plays such as *Hamlet* and *Romeo and Juliet*, which were great successes in their own day, still are being read and performed all over the world. Shakespeare also wrote two narrative poems and many sonnets. Most of Shakespeare's plays were not published during his lifetime.

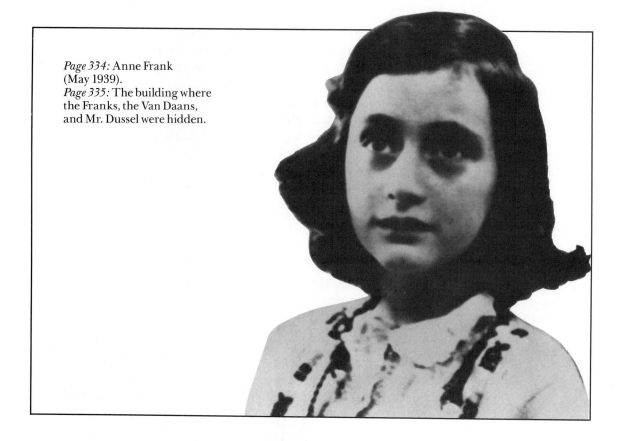

Page 334: Anne Frank (May 1939).
Page 335: The building where the Franks, the Van Daans, and Mr. Dussel were hidden.

The Diary of Anne Frank

FRANCES GOODRICH
AND
ALBERT HACKETT

The Diary of Anne Frank *is a play based upon a diary found at the end of World War II in a pile of rubbish in an old warehouse in Amsterdam. A young Jewish girl named Anne Frank had kept this diary for twenty-five months. In it, she had recorded the small details of domestic life and her own thoughts during the last years of one of the most terrible wars in history.*

To escape the Nazis, Anne Frank's family had moved from Germany to the Netherlands. But when the Nazis took over the Netherlands in 1940, they immediately began persecuting the Jews there.

In July 1942 Anne's family went into hiding in a secret apartment. Their hiding place was on the top floors of a building that Otto Frank, Anne's father, had used as his warehouse and business office. It was in these hidden rooms that Anne kept the diary that has since been translated into many languages. It was here that, in the midst of fear and suffering, she could write: "In spite of everything, I still believe that people are really good at heart."

As you read this play, consider how the characters deal with the terrible forces that are seeking to destroy them.

Characters

Mr. Frank	Mrs. Frank
Miep (mēp)	Margot Frank
Mrs. Van Daan	Anne Frank
Mr. Van Daan	Mr. Kraler
Peter Van Daan	Dussel

The Time: During the years of World War II and immediately thereafter.
The Place: Amsterdam.
There are two acts.

Act One

Scene 1

The scene remains the same throughout the play. It is the top floor of a warehouse and office building in Amsterdam, Holland. The sharply peaked roof of the building is outlined against a sea of other rooftops, stretching away into the distance. Nearby is the belfry of a church tower, the Westertoren, whose carillon rings out the hours. Occasionally faint sounds float up from below: the voices of children playing in the street, the tramp of marching feet, a boat whistle from the canal.

The Diary of Anne Frank Act One, Scene 1   **335**

The stage set for the original production of *The Diary of Anne Frank* (1955).
Designed by Boris Aronson.

The three rooms of the top floor and a small attic space above are exposed to our view. The largest of the rooms is in the center, with two small rooms, slightly raised, on either side. On the right is a bathroom, out of sight. A narrow, steep flight of stairs at the back leads up to the attic. The rooms are sparsely furnished with a few chairs, cots, a table or two. The windows are painted over, or covered with makeshift blackout curtains. In the main room there is a sink, a gas ring for cooking, and a wood-burning stove for warmth.

The room on the left is hardly more than a closet. There is a skylight in the sloping ceiling. Directly under this room is a small steep stairwell, with steps leading down to a door. This is the only entrance from the building below. When the door is opened we see that it has been concealed on the outer side by a bookcase attached to it.

The curtain rises on an empty stage. It is late afternoon, November, 1945.

The rooms are dusty, the curtains in rags. Chairs and tables are overturned.

The door at the foot of the small stairwell swings open. **Mr. Frank** *comes up the steps into view. He is a gentle, cultured European in his middle years. There is still a trace of a German accent in his speech.*

He stands looking slowly around, making a supreme effort at self-control. He is weak, ill. His clothes are threadbare.

After a second he drops his rucksack on the couch and moves slowly about. He opens the door to one of the smaller rooms and then abruptly closes it again, turning away. He goes to the window at the back, looking off at the Westertoren as its carillon strikes the hour of six; then he moves restlessly on.

From the street below we hear the sound of a barrel organ and children's voices at play. There is a many-colored scarf hanging from a nail. Mr. Frank *takes it, putting it around his neck. As he starts back for his rucksack, his eye is caught by something lying on the floor. It is a woman's white glove. He holds it in his hand and suddenly all of his self-control is gone. He breaks down, crying.*

We hear footsteps on the stairs. Miep Gies *comes up, looking for* Mr. Frank. Miep *is a Dutch girl of about twenty-two. She wears a coat and hat, ready to go home. She is pregnant. Her attitude toward* Mr. Frank *is protective, compassionate.*

Miep. Are you all right, Mr. Frank?

Mr. Frank (*quickly controlling himself*). Yes, Miep, yes.

Miep. Everyone in the office has gone home. . . . It's after six. (*Then pleading*) Don't stay up here, Mr. Frank. What's the use of torturing yourself like this?

Mr. Frank. I've come to say goodbye. . . . I'm leaving here, Miep.

Miep. What do you mean? Where are you going? Where?

Mr. Frank. I don't know yet, I haven't decided.

Miep. Mr. Frank, you can't leave here! This is your home! Amsterdam is your home. Your business is here, waiting for you. . . . You're needed here. . . . Now that the war is over, there are things that . . .

Mr. Frank. I can't stay in Amsterdam, Miep. It has too many memories for me. Everywhere there's something . . . the house we lived in . . . the school . . . that street organ playing out

there . . . I'm not the person you used to know, Miep. I'm a bitter old man. (*Breaking off*) Forgive me. I shouldn't speak to you like this . . . after all that you did for us . . . the suffering . . .

Miep. No. No. It wasn't suffering. You can't say we suffered. (*As she speaks, she straightens a chair which is overturned.*)

Mr. Frank. I know what you went through, you and Mr. Kraler. I'll remember it as long as I live. (*He gives one last look around.*) Come, Miep. (*He starts for the steps, then remembers his rucksack, going back to get it.*)

Miep (*hurrying up to a cupboard*). Mr. Frank, did you see? There are some of your papers here. (*She brings a bundle of papers to him.*) We found them in a heap of rubbish on the floor after . . . after you left.

Mr. Frank. Burn them. (*He opens his rucksack to put the glove in it.*)

Miep. But, Mr. Frank, there are letters, notes . . .

Mr. Frank. Burn them. All of them.

Miep. Burn *this*? (*She hands him a paperbound notebook.*)

Mr. Frank (*quietly*). Anne's diary. (*He opens the diary and begins to read.*) "Monday, the sixth of July, nineteen forty-two." (*To* Miep) Nineteen forty-two. Is it possible, Miep? . . . Only three years ago. (*As he continues his reading, he sits down on the couch.*) "Dear Diary, since you and I are going to be great friends, I will start by telling you about myself. My name is Anne Frank. I am thirteen years old. I was born in Germany the twelfth of June, nineteen twenty-nine. As my family is Jewish, we emigrated to Holland when Hitler came to power."

[*As* Mr. Frank *reads on, another voice joins his, as if coming from the air. It is* Anne's *voice.*]

Mr. Frank and **Anne.** "My father started a business, importing spice and herbs. Things went well for us until nineteen forty. Then the war came, and the Dutch capitulation,[1] followed by the arrival of the Germans. Then things got very bad for the Jews."

[Mr. Frank's *voice dies out.* Anne's *voice continues alone. The lights dim slowly to darkness. The curtain falls on the scene.*]

Anne's Voice. You could not do this and you could not do that. They forced Father out of his business. We had to wear yellow stars. I had to turn in my bike. I couldn't go to the movies, or ride in an automobile, or even on a streetcar, and a million other things. But somehow we children still managed to have fun. Yesterday Father told me we were going into hiding. Where, he wouldn't say. At five o'clock this morning Mother woke me and told me to hurry and get dressed. I was to put on as many clothes as I could. It would look too suspicious if we walked along carrying suitcases. It wasn't until we were on our way that I learned where we were going. Our hiding place was to be upstairs in the building where Father used to have his business. Three other people were coming in with us . . . the Van Daans and their son Peter. . . . Father knew the Van Daans but we had never met them. . . .

[*During the last lines the curtain rises on the scene. The lights dim on.* Anne's *voice fades out.*]

Scene 2

It is early morning, July, 1942. The rooms are bare, as before, but they are now clean and orderly.

Mr. Van Daan, *a tall, portly man in his late forties, is in the main room, pacing up and down, nervously smoking a cigarette. His clothes and overcoat are expensive and well cut.*

Mrs. Van Daan *sits on the couch, clutching her possessions—a hatbox, bags, etc. She is a pretty woman in her early forties. She wears a fur coat over her other clothes.*

Peter Van Daan *is standing at the window of the room on the right, looking down at the street below. He is a shy, awkward boy of sixteen. He wears a cap, a raincoat, and long Dutch trousers, like "plus fours."[2] At his feet is a black case, a carrier for his cat.*

The yellow Star of David[3] is conspicuous on all of their clothes.

Mrs. Van Daan (*rising, nervous, excited*). Something's happened to them! I know it!
Mr. Van Daan. Now, Kerli!
Mrs. Van Daan. Mr. Frank said they'd be here at seven o'clock. He said . . .
Mr. Van Daan. They have two miles to walk. You can't expect . . .
Mrs. Van Daan. They've been picked up. That's what's happened. They've been taken. . . .

[Mr. Van Daan *indicates that he hears someone coming.*]

Mr. Van Daan. You see?

[Peter *takes up his carrier and his schoolbag, etc., and goes into the main room as* Mr. Frank *comes up the stairwell from below.* Mr. Frank *looks much younger now. His movements are brisk, his manner confident. He wears an overcoat and carries his hat and a small cardboard box. He crosses to the* Van Daans, *shaking hands with each of them.*]

Mr. Frank. Mrs. Van Daan, Mr. Van Daan,

2. **"plus fours":** baggy trousers that are gathered in under the knee; also called *knickers.*
3. **Star of David:** a six-pointed star, an ancient symbol of Judaism. The Nazis required Jews to sew the Star of David onto all their clothing so that they would be immediately identifiable as Jews.

1. **capitulation** (kə-pĭ′choŏ-lā′shən): surrender. The Netherlands was taken over by the Nazis in May 1940. The Dutch underground, however, was active in helping escaped Allied prisoners and Jewish refugees.

Peter. (*Then, in explanation of their lateness*) There were too many of the Green Police[4] on the streets. . . . We had to take the long way around.

[*Up the steps come* Margot Frank, Mrs. Frank, Miep (*not pregnant now*), *and* Mr. Kraler. *All of them carry bags, packages, and so forth. The* Star *of* David *is conspicuous on all of the* Franks' *clothing.* Margot *is eighteen, beautiful, quiet, shy.* Mrs. Frank *is a young mother, gently bred, reserved. She, like* Mr. Frank, *has a slight German accent.* Mr. Kraler *is a Dutchman, dependable, kindly.*

As Mr. Kraler *and* Miep *go upstage to put down their parcels,* Mrs. Frank *turns back to call* Anne.]

Mrs. Frank. Anne?

[Anne *comes running up the stairs. She is thirteen, quick in her movements, interested in everything, mercurial[5] in her emotions. She wears a cape, long wool socks, and carries a schoolbag.*]

Mr. Frank (*introducing them*). My wife, Edith. Mr. and Mrs. Van Daan

[Mrs. Frank *hurries over, shaking hands with them.*]

. . . their son, Peter . . . my daughters, Margot and Anne.

[Anne *gives a polite little curtsy as she shakes* Mr. Van Daan's *hand. Then she immediately starts off on a tour of investigation of her new home, going upstairs to the attic room.*

Miep *and* Mr. Kraler *are putting the various things they have brought on the shelves.*]

Mr. Kraler. I'm sorry there is still so much confusion.

4. **Green Police:** the Nazi police, who wore green uniforms.
5. **mercurial** (mər-kyŏŏr′ē-əl): quickly changeable.

Mr. Frank. Please. Don't think of it. After all, we'll have plenty of leisure to arrange everything ourselves.

Miep (*to* Mrs. Frank). We put the stores of food you sent in here. Your drugs are here . . . soap, linen here.

Mrs. Frank. Thank you, Miep.

Miep. I made up the beds . . . the way Mr. Frank and Mr. Kraler said. (*She starts out.*) Forgive me. I have to hurry. I've got to go to the other side of town to get some ration books[6] for you.

Mrs. Van Daan. Ration books? If they see our names on ration books, they'll know we're here.

Mr. Kraler. There isn't anything . . .

Miep. Don't worry. Your names won't be on them. (*As she hurries out*) I'll be up later. } (*Together*)

Mr. Frank. Thank you, Miep.

Mrs. Frank (*to* Mr. Kraler). It's illegal, then, the ration books? We've never done anything illegal.

Mr. Frank. We won't be living here exactly according to regulations.

[*As* Mr. Kraler *reassures* Mrs. Frank, *he takes various small things, such as matches, soap, etc., from his pockets, handing them to her.*]

Mr. Kraler. This isn't the black market,[7] Mrs. Frank. This is what we call the white market . . . helping all of the hundreds and hundreds who are hiding out in Amsterdam.

[*The carillon is heard playing the quarter-hour before eight.* Mr. Kraler *looks at his watch.* Anne *stops at the window as she comes down the stairs.*]

6. **ration books:** books given to each citizen during wartime, containing a certain number of stamps for various items such as food, clothing, and gasoline. These items could not be purchased without the stamps. Ration books were used to make sure that scarce items would be rationed, or evenly distributed.
7. **black market:** an illegal system for buying and selling goods without ration stamps.

Anne. It's the Westertoren!

Mr. Kraler. I must go. I must be out of here and downstairs in the office before the workmen get here. (*He starts for the stairs leading out.*) Miep or I, or both of us, will be up each day to bring you food and news and find out what your needs are. Tomorrow I'll get you a better bolt for the door at the foot of the stairs. It needs a bolt that you can throw yourself and open only at our signal. (*To Mr. Frank*) Oh . . . You'll tell them about the noise?

Mr. Frank. I'll tell them.

Mr. Kraler. Goodbye then for the moment. I'll come up again, after the workmen leave.

Mr. Frank. Goodbye, Mr. Kraler.

Mrs. Frank (*shaking his hand*). How can we thank you?

[*The others murmur their goodbyes.*]

Mr. Kraler. I never thought I'd live to see the day when a man like Mr. Frank would have to go into hiding. When you think——

[*He breaks off, going out, Mr. Frank follows him down the steps, bolting the door after him. In the interval before he returns, Peter goes over to Margot, shaking hands with her. As Mr. Frank comes back up the steps, Mrs. Frank questions him anxiously.*]

Mrs. Frank. What did he mean, about the noise?

Mr. Frank. First let us take off some of these clothes.

[*They all start to take off garment after garment. On each of their coats, sweaters, blouses, suits, dresses, is another yellow Star of David. Mr. and Mrs. Frank are underdressed quite simply. The others wear several things—sweaters, extra dresses, bathrobes, aprons, nightgowns, etc.*]

Mr. Van Daan. It's a wonder we weren't arrested, walking along the streets . . . Petronella with a fur coat in July . . .

and that cat of Peter's crying all the way.

Anne. (*as she is removing a pair of panties*). A cat?

Mrs. Frank (*shocked*). Anne, please!

Anne. It's all right. I've got on three more.

[*She pulls off two more. Finally, as they have all removed their surplus clothes, they look to Mr. Frank, waiting for him to speak.*]

Mr. Frank. Now. About the noise. While the men are in the building below, we must have complete quiet. Every sound can be heard down there, not only in the workrooms, but in the offices too. The men come at about eight thirty, and leave at about five thirty. So, to be perfectly safe, from eight in the morning until six in the evening we must move only when it is necessary, and then in stockinged feet. We must not speak above a whisper. We must not run any water. We cannot use the sink, or even, forgive me, the w.c.[8] The pipes go down through the workrooms. It would be heard. No trash . . . (*Mr. Frank stops abruptly as he hears the sound of marching feet from the street below. Everyone is motionless, paralyzed with fear. Mr. Frank goes quietly into the room on the right to look down out of the window. Anne runs after him, peering out with him. The tramping feet pass without stopping. The tension is relieved. Mr. Frank, followed by Anne, returns to the main room and resumes his instructions to the group.*) . . . No trash must ever be thrown out which might reveal that someone is living up here . . . not even a potato paring. We must burn everything in the stove at night. This is the way we must live until it is over, if we are to survive.

[*There is silence for a second.*]

Mrs. Frank. Until it is over.

---

8. **w.c.:** water closet, or toilet.

Mr. Frank (*reassuringly*). After six we can move about . . . we can talk and laugh and have our supper and read and play games . . . just as we would at home. (*He looks at his watch.*) And now I think it would be wise if we all went to our rooms, and were settled before eight o'clock. Mrs. Van Daan, you and your husband will be upstairs. I regret that there's no place up there for Peter. But he will be here, near us. This will be our common room, where we'll meet to talk and eat and read, like one family.

Mr. Van Daan. And where do you and Mrs. Frank sleep?

Mr. Frank. This room is also our bedroom.

Mrs. Van Daan. That isn't right. We'll sleep here and you take the room upstairs. } (*Together*)

Mr. Van Daan. It's your place.

Mr. Frank. Please. I've thought this out for weeks. It's the best arrangement. The only arrangement.

Mrs. Van Daan (*to Mr. Frank*). Never, never can we thank you. (*Then, to Mrs. Frank*) I don't know what would have happened to us, if it hadn't been for Mr. Frank.

Mr. Frank. You don't know how your husband helped me when I came to this country . . . knowing no one . . . not able to speak the language. I can never repay him for that. (*Going to Mr. Van Daan*) May I help you with your things?

Mr. Van Daan. No. No. (*To Mrs. Van Daan*) Come along, *liefje.*[9]

Mrs. Van Daan. You'll be all right, Peter? You're not afraid?

Peter (*embarrassed*). Please, Mother.

[*They start up the stairs to the attic room above.* Mr. Frank *turns to* Mrs. Frank.]

Mr. Frank. You too must have some rest, Edith.

9. *liefje* (lēf'hyə): Dutch for "little loved one."

You didn't close your eyes last night. Nor you, Margot.

Anne. I slept, Father. Wasn't that funny? I knew it was the last night in my own bed, and yet I slept soundly.

Mr. Frank. I'm glad, Anne. Now you'll be able to help me straighten things in here. (*To* Mrs. Frank *and* Margot) Come with me. . . . You and Margot rest in this room for the time being. (*He picks up their clothes, starting for the room on the right.*)

Mrs. Frank. You're sure . . . ? I could help . . . And Anne hasn't had her milk . . .

Mr. Frank. I'll give it to her. (*To* Anne *and* Peter) Anne, Peter . . . it's best that you take off your shoes now, before you forget. (*He leads the way to the room, followed by* Margot.)

Mrs. Frank. You're sure you're not tired, Anne?

Anne. I feel fine. I'm going to help Father.

Mrs. Frank. Peter, I'm glad you are to be with us.

Peter. Yes, Mrs. Frank.

[Mrs. Frank *goes to join* Mr. Frank *and* Margot.

During the following scene Mr. Frank *helps* Margot *and* Mrs. Frank *to hang up their clothes. Then he persuades them both to lie down and rest. The* Van Daans *in their room above settle themselves. In the main room* Anne *and* Peter *remove their shoes.* Peter *takes his cat out of the carrier.*]

Anne. What's your cat's name?

Peter. Mouschi.

Anne. Mouschi! Mouschi! Mouschi! (*She picks up the cat, walking away with it. To* Peter) I love cats. I have one . . . a darling little cat. But they made me leave her behind. I left some food and a note for the neighbors to take care of her. . . . I'm going to miss her terribly. What is yours? A him or a her?

Photographs (pages 342, 344, 347, 351, 353, 360, 364, 371, 379, 381, 387, 388, 391, and 392) of the original stage production of *The Diary of Anne Frank*, which opened on Broadway on October 5, 1955.

Peter. He's a tom. He doesn't like strangers. (*He takes the cat from her, putting it back in its carrier.*)

Anne (*unabashed*). Then I'll have to stop being a stranger, won't I? Is he fixed?

Peter (*startled*). Huh?

Anne. Did you have him fixed?

Peter. No.

Anne. Oh, you ought to have him fixed—to keep him from—you know, fighting. Where did you go to school?

Peter. Jewish Secondary.

Anne. But that's where Margot and I go! I never saw you around.

Peter. I used to see you . . . sometimes . . .

Anne. You did?

Peter. . . . in the schoolyard. You were always in the middle of a bunch of kids. (*He takes a penknife from his pocket.*)

Anne. Why didn't you ever come over?

Peter. I'm sort of a lone wolf. (*He starts to rip off his Star of David.*)

Anne. What are you doing?

Peter. Taking it off.

Anne. But you can't do that. They'll arrest you if you go out without your Star. (*He tosses his knife on the table.*)

Peter. Who's going out?

Anne. Why, of course! You're right! Of course we don't need them any more. (*She picks up his knife and starts to take her Star off.*). I wonder what our friends will think when we don't show up today?

Peter. I didn't have any dates with anyone.

Anne. Oh, I did. I had a date with Jopie to go and play ping-pong at her house. Do you know Jopie deWall?

Peter. No.

Anne. Jopie's my best friend. I wonder what she'll think when she telephones and there's no answer? . . . Probably she'll go over to the house. . . . I wonder what she'll think . . . we left everything as if we'd suddenly been called away . . . breakfast dishes in the sink . . . beds not made. . . . (*As she pulls off her Star the cloth underneath shows clearly the color and form of the Star.*) Look! It's still there! (Peter *goes over to the stove with his Star.*) What're you going to do with yours?

Peter. Burn it.

Anne. (*She starts to throw hers in, and cannot.*) It's funny, I can't throw mine away. I don't know why.

Peter. You can't throw . . . ? Something they branded you with . . . ? That they made you wear so they could spit on you?

Anne. I know. I know. But after all, it *is* the Star of David, isn't it?

[*In the bedroom, right,* Margot *and* Mrs. Frank *are lying down.* Mr. Frank *starts quietly out.*]

Peter. Maybe it's different for a girl.

[Mr. Frank *comes into the main room.*]

Mr. Frank. Forgive me, Peter. Now let me see. We must find a bed for your cat. (*He goes to a cupboard.*) I'm glad you brought your cat. Anne was feeling so badly about hers. (*Getting a used small washtub*) Here we are. Will it be comfortable in that?

Peter (*gathering up his things*). Thanks.

Mr. Frank (*opening the door of the room on the left*). And here is your room. But I warn you, Peter, you can't grow any more. Not an inch, or you'll have to sleep with your feet out of the skylight. Are you hungry?

Peter. No.

Mr. Frank. We have some bread and butter.

Peter. No, thank you.

Mr. Frank. You can have it for luncheon then. And tonight we will have a real supper . . . our first supper together.

Peter. Thanks. Thanks. (*He goes into his room. During the following scene he arranges his possessions in his new room.*)

Mr. Frank. That's a nice boy, Peter.

Anne. He's awfully shy, isn't he?

Mr. Frank. You'll like him, I know.

Anne. I certainly hope so, since he's the only boy I'm likely to see for months and months.

[Mr. Frank *sits down, taking off his shoes.*]

Mr. Frank. Annele,[10] there's a box there. Will you open it?

[*He indicates a carton on the couch.* Anne *brings it to the center table. In the street below there is the sound of children playing*].

10. **Annele** (än′ə-lə): an affectionate form of the name Anne in Yiddish.

Anne (*as she opens the carton*). You know the way I'm going to think of it here? I'm going to think of it as a boardinghouse. A very peculiar summer boardinghouse, like the one that we ——(*She breaks off as she pulls out some photographs.*) Father! My movie stars! I was wondering where they were! I was looking for them this morning . . . and Queen Wilhelmina![11] How wonderful!

Mr. Frank. There's something more. Go on. Look further. (*He goes over to the sink, pouring a glass of milk from a thermos bottle.*)

Anne (*pulling out a pasteboard-bound book*). A diary! (*She throws her arms around her father.*) I've never had a diary. And I've always longed for one. (*She looks around the room.*) Pencil, pencil, pencil, pencil (*She starts down the stairs.*) I'm going down to the office to get a pencil.

Mr. Frank. Anne! No! (*He goes after her, catching her by the arm and pulling her back.*)

Anne (*startled*). But there's no one in the building now.

Mr. Frank. It doesn't matter. I don't want you ever to go beyond that door.

Anne (*sobered*). Never . . . ? Not even at nighttime, when everyone is gone? Or on Sundays? Can't I go down to listen to the radio?

Mr. Frank. Never, I am sorry, Anneke.[12] It isn't safe. No, you must never go beyond that door.

[*For the first time* Anne *realizes what "going into hiding" means.*]

Anne. I see.

Mr. Frank. It'll be hard, I know. But always remember this, Anneke. There are no walls, there are no bolts, no locks that anyone can put on your mind. Miep will bring us books. We will read history, poetry, mythology. (*He gives

11. **Queen Wilhelmina:** queen of the Netherlands from 1890 to 1948. She died in 1962.
12. **Anneke** (än′ə-kə): an affectionate form of the name Anne in German.

her the glass of milk.). Here's your milk. (*With his arm about her, they go over to the couch, sitting down side by side.*) As a matter of fact, between us, Anne, being here has certain advantages for you. For instance, you remember the battle you had with your mother the other day on the subject of overshoes? You said you'd rather die than wear overshoes? But in the end you had to wear them? Well now, you see, for as long as we are here you will never have to wear overshoes! Isn't that good? And the coat that you inherited from Margot, you won't have to wear that any more. And the piano! You won't have to practice on the piano. I tell you, this is going to be a fine life for you!

[*Anne's panic is gone.* Peter *appears in the doorway of his room, with a saucer in his hand. He is carrying his cat.*]

Peter. I . . . I . . . I thought I'd better get some water for Mouschi before . . .

Mr. Frank. Of course.

[*As he starts toward the sink the carillon begins to chime the hour of eight. He tiptoes to the window at the back and looks down at the street below. He turns to* Peter, *indicating in pantomime that it is too late.* Peter *starts back for his room. He steps on a creaking board. The three of them are frozen for a minute in fear. As* Peter *starts away again,* Anne *tiptoes over to him and pours some of the milk from her glass into the saucer for the cat.* Peter *squats on the floor, putting the milk before the cat.* Mr. Frank *gives* Anne *his fountain pen and then goes into the room at the right. For a second* Anne *watches the cat; then she goes over to the center table and opens her diary.*

In the room at the right, Mrs. Frank *has sat up*

quickly at the sound of the carillon. Mr. Frank comes in and sits down beside her on the settee, his arm comfortingly around her.

Upstairs, in the attic room, Mr. and Mrs. Van Daan have hung their clothes in the closet and are now seated on the iron bed. Mrs. Van Daan leans back exhausted. Mr. Van Daan fans her with a newspaper.

Anne starts to write in her diary. The lights dim out; the curtain falls.

In the darkness Anne's voice comes to us again, faintly at first, and then with growing strength.]

Anne's Voice. I expect I should be describing what it feels like to go into hiding. But I really don't know yet myself. I only know it's funny never to be able to go outdoors . . . never to breathe fresh air . . . never to run and shout and jump. It's the silence in the nights that frightens me most. Every time I hear a creak in the house, or a step on the street outside, I'm sure they're coming for us. The days aren't so bad. At least we know that Miep and Mr. Kraler are down there below us in the office. Our protectors, we call them. I asked Father what would happen to them if the Nazis found out they were hiding us. Pim said that they would suffer the same fate that we would. . . . Imagine! They know this, and yet when they come up here, they're always cheerful and gay as if there were nothing in the world to bother them. . . . Friday, the twenty-first of August, nineteen forty-two. Today I'm going to tell you our general news. Mother is unbearable. She insists on treating me like a baby, which I loathe. Otherwise things are going better. The weather is . . .

[*As Anne's voice is fading out, the curtain rises on the scene.*]

Scene 3

It is a little after six o'clock in the evening, two months later.

Margot is in the bedroom at the right, studying. Mr. Van Daan is lying down in the attic room above.

The rest of the "family" is in the main room. Anne and Peter sit opposite each other at the center table, where they have been doing their lessons. Mrs. Frank is on the couch. Mrs. Van Daan is seated with her fur coat, on which she has been sewing, in her lap. None of them are wearing their shoes.

Their eyes are on Mr. Frank, waiting for him to give them the signal which will release them from their day-long quiet. Mr. Frank, his shoes in his hand, stands looking down out of the window at the back, watching to be sure that all of the workmen have left the building below.

After a few seconds of motionless silence, Mr. Frank turns from the window.
Mr. Frank (*quietly, to the group*). It's safe now. The last workman has left.

[*There is an immediate stir of relief.*]

Anne (*Her pent-up energy explodes*). WHEE!
Mrs. Frank (*startled, amused*). Anne!
Mrs. Van Daan. I'm first for the w.c.

[*She hurries off to the bathroom. Mrs. Frank puts on her shoes and starts up to the sink to prepare supper. Anne sneaks Peter's shoes from under the table and hides them behind her back. Mr. Frank goes into Margot's room.*]

Mr. Frank (*to* Margot). Six o'clock. School's over.

[*Margot gets up, stretching. Mr. Frank sits down to put on his shoes. In the main room Peter tries to find his.*]

Peter (*to* Anne). Have you seen my shoes?

Anne (*innocently*). Your shoes?

Peter. You've taken them, haven't you?

Anne. I don't know what you're talking about.

Peter. You're going to be sorry!

Anne. Am I?

[Peter *goes after her.* Anne, *with his shoes in her hand, runs from him, dodging behind her mother.*]

Mrs. Frank (*protesting*). Anne, dear!

Peter. Wait till I get you!

Anne. I'm waiting! (Peter *makes a lunge for her. They both fall to the floor. Peter* pins *her down, wrestling with her to get the shoes.*) Don't! Don't! Peter, stop it. Ouch!

Mrs. Frank. Anne! . . . Peter!

[*Suddenly* Peter *becomes self-conscious. He grabs his shoes roughly and starts for his room.*]

Anne (*following him*). Peter, where are you going? Come dance with me.

Peter. I tell you I don't know how.

Anne. I'll teach you.

Peter. I'm going to give Mouschi his dinner.

Anne. Can I watch?

Peter. He doesn't like people around while he eats.

Anne. Peter, please.

Peter. No!

[He *goes into his room.* Anne *slams his door after him.*]

Mrs. Frank. Anne, dear, I think you shouldn't play like that with Peter. It's not dignified.

Anne. Who cares if it's dignified? I don't want to be dignified.

[Mr. Frank *and* Margot *come from the room on the right.* Margot *goes to help her mother.* Mr. Frank starts for the center table to correct* Margot's *school papers.*]

Mrs. Frank (*to* Anne). You complain that I don't treat you like a grown-up. But when I do, you resent it.

Anne. I only want some fun . . . someone to laugh and clown with. . . . After you've sat still all day and hardly moved, you've got to have some fun. I don't know what's the matter with that boy.

Mr. Frank. He isn't used to girls. Give him a little time.

Anne. Time? Isn't two months time? I could cry. (*Catching hold of* Margot) Come on, Margot . . . dance with me. Come on, please.

Margot. I have to help with supper.

Anne. You know we're going to forget how to dance. . . . When we get out we won't remember a thing.

[*She starts to sing and dance by herself.* Mr. Frank *takes her in his arms, waltzing with her.* Mrs. Van Daan *comes in from the bathroom.*]

Mrs. Van Daan. Next? (*She looks around as she starts putting on her shoes.*) Where's Peter?

Anne (*as they are dancing*). Where would he be!

Mrs. Van Daan. He hasn't finished his lessons, has he? His father'll kill him if he catches him in there with that cat and his work not done. (Mr. Frank *and* Anne *finish their dance. They bow to each other with extravagant formality.*) Anne, get him out of there, will you?

Anne (*at* Peter's *door*). Peter? Peter?

Peter (*opening the door a crack*). What is it?

Anne. Your mother says to come out.

Peter. I'm giving Mouschi his dinner.

Mrs. Van Daan. You know what your father says. (*She sits on the couch, sewing on the lining of her fur coat.*)

Peter. For heaven's sake, I haven't even looked at him since lunch.

Mrs. Van Daan. Look at him blush! Look at him!

Peter. Please! I'm not . . . anyway . . . let me alone, will you?

Mrs. Van Daan. He acts like it was something to be ashamed of. It's nothing to be ashamed of, to have a little girlfriend.

Peter. You're crazy. She's only thirteen.

Mrs. Van Daan. So what? And you're sixteen. Just perfect. Your father's ten years older than I am. (*To* Mr. Frank) I warn you, Mr. Frank, if this war lasts much longer, we're going to be related and then . . .

Mr. Frank. *Mazel tov!*[13]

Mrs. Frank (*deliberately changing the conversation*). I wonder where Miep is. She's usually so prompt.

[*Suddenly everything else is forgotten as they hear the sound of an automobile coming to a screeching stop in the street below. They are tense, motionless in their terror. The car starts away. A wave of relief sweeps over them. They pick up their occupations again.* Anne *flings open the door of* Peter's *room, making a dramatic entrance. She is dressed in* Peter's *clothes.* Peter *looks at her in fury. The others are amused.*]

Anne. Good evening, everyone. Forgive me if I don't stay. (*She jumps up on a chair.*) I have a friend waiting for me in there. My friend Tom. Tom Cat. Some people say that we look alike. But Tom has the most beautiful whiskers, and I have only a little fuzz. I am hoping . . . in time . . .

Peter. All right, Mrs. Quack Quack!

Anne (*outraged—jumping down*). Peter!

Peter. I heard about you. . . . How you talked so much in class they called you Mrs. Quack Quack. How Mr. Smitter made you write a composition . . . " 'Quack, quack,' said Mrs. Quack Quack."

Mrs. Van Daan. I'm just telling you, that's all.

Anne. I'll feed him.

Peter. I don't want you in there.

Mrs. Van Daan. Peter!

Peter (*to* Anne). Then give him his dinner and come right out, you hear?

[*He comes back to the table.* Anne *shuts the door of* Peter's *room after her and disappears behind the curtain covering his closet.*]

Mrs. Van Daan (*to* Peter). Now is that any way to talk to your little girlfriend?

Peter. Mother . . . for heaven's sake . . . will you please stop saying that?

13. *Mazel tov!* (mä′zəl tôf′): Hebrew for "Congratulations!"

Anne. Well, go on. Tell them the rest. How it was so good that he read it out loud to the class and then read it to all his other classes!

Peter. Quack! Quack! Quack . . . Quack . . . Quack . . .

[Anne *pulls off the coat and trousers.*]

Anne. You are the most intolerable, insufferable boy I've ever met!

[*She throws the clothes down the stairwell.* Peter *goes down after them.*]

Peter. Quack, quack, quack!

Mrs. Van Daan (*to* Anne). That's right, Anneke! Give it to him!

Anne. With all the boys in the world . . . Why I had to get locked up with one like you! . . .

Peter. Quack, quack, quack, and from now on stay out of my room!

[*As Peter* passes her, Anne *puts out her foot, tripping him. He picks himself up and goes on into his room.*]

Mrs. Frank (*quietly*). Anne, dear . . . your hair. (*She feels* Anne's *forehead.*) You're warm. Are you feeling all right?

Anne. Please, Mother. (*She goes over to the center table, slipping into her shoes.*)

Mrs. Frank (*following her*). You haven't a fever, have you?

Anne (*pulling away*). No. No.

Mrs. Frank. You know we can't call a doctor here, ever. There's only one thing to do . . . watch carefully. Prevent an illness before it comes. Let me see your tongue.

Anne. Mother, this is perfectly absurd.

Mrs. Frank. Anne, dear, don't be such a baby. Let me see your tongue. (*As Anne* refuses, Mrs. Frank *appeals to* Mr. Frank.) Otto . . . ?

Mr. Frank. You hear your mother, Anne.

[Anne *flicks out her tongue for a second, then turns away.*]

Mrs. Frank. Come on—open up! (*As* Anne *opens her mouth very wide*) You seem all right . . . but perhaps an aspirin . . .

Mrs. Van Daan. For heaven's sake, don't give that child any pills. I waited for fifteen minutes this morning for her to come out of the W.C.

Anne. I was washing my hair!

Mrs. Frank. I think there's nothing the matter with our Anne that a ride on her bike or a visit with her friend Jopie deWaal wouldn't cure. Isn't that so, Anne?

[Mr. Van Daan *comes down into the room. From outside we hear faint sounds of bombers going over and a burst of ack-ack.*[14]]

Mr. Van Daan. Miep not come yet?

Mrs. Van Daan. The workmen just left, a little while ago.

Mr. Van Daan. What's for dinner tonight?

Mrs. Van Daan. Beans.

Mr. Van Daan. Not again!

Mrs. Van Daan. Poor Putti! I know. But what can we do? That's all that Miep brought us.

[Mr. Van Daan *starts to pace, his hands behind his back.* Anne *follows behind him, imitating him.*]

Anne. We are now in what is known as the "bean cycle." Beans boiled, beans en casserole, beans with strings, beans without strings . . .

[Peter *has come out of his room. He slides into his place at the table, becoming immediately absorbed in his studies.*]

Mr. Van Daan (*to* Peter). I saw you . . . in there, playing with your cat.

14. **ack-ack:** antiaircraft fire.

Mrs. Van Daan. He just went in for a second, putting his coat away. He's been out here all the time, doing his lessons.

Mr. Frank (*looking up from the paper*). Anne, you got an excellent in your history paper today . . . and very good in Latin.

Anne (*sitting beside him*). How about algebra?

Mr. Frank. I'll have to make a confession. Up until now I've managed to stay ahead of you in algebra. Today you caught up with me. We'll leave it to Margot to correct.

Anne. Isn't algebra *vile*, Pim!

Mr. Frank. Vile!

Margot (*to Mr. Frank*). How did I do?

Anne (*getting up*). Excellent, excellent, excellent, excellent!

Mr. Frank (*to Margot*). You should have used the subjunctive here. . . .

Margot. Should I? . . . I thought . . . look here . . . I didn't use it here. . . .

[*The two become absorbed in the papers.*]

Anne. Mrs. Van Daan, may I try on your coat?

Mrs. Frank. No, Anne.

Mrs. Van Daan (*giving it to Anne*). It's all right . . . but careful with it. (Anne *puts it on and struts with it.*) My father gave me that the year before he died. He always bought the best that money could buy.

Anne. Mrs. Van Daan, did you have a lot of boyfriends before you were married?

Mrs. Frank. Anne, that's a personal question. It's not courteous to ask personal questions.

Mrs. Van Daan. Oh, I don't mind. (*To* Anne) Our house was always swarming with boys. When I was a girl we had . . .

Mr. Van Daan. Oh, God. Not again!

Mrs. Van Daan (*good-humored*). Shut up! (*Without a pause, to* Anne. Mr. Van Daan *mimics* Mrs. Van Daan, *speaking the first few words in unison with her.*) One summer we had a big house in Hilversum. The boys came buzzing round like bees around a jam pot. And when I was sixteen! . . . We were wearing our skirts very short those days and I had good-looking legs. (*She pulls up her skirt, going to* Mr. Frank) I still have 'em. I may not be as pretty as I used to be, but I still have my legs. How about it, Mr. Frank?

Mr. Van Daan. All right. All right. We see them.

Mrs. Van Daan. I'm not asking you. I'm asking Mr. Frank.

Peter. Mother, for heaven's sake.

Mrs. Van Daan. Oh, I embarrass you, do I? Well, I just hope the girl you marry has as good. (*Then, to* Anne) My father used to worry about me, with so many boys hanging round. He told me, if any of them gets fresh, you say to him . . . "Remember, Mr. So-and-So, remember I'm a lady."

Anne. "Remember, Mr. So-and-So, remember I'm a lady." (*She gives* Mrs. Van Daan *her coat.*)

Mr. Van Daan. Look at you, talking that way in front of her! Don't you know she puts it all down in that diary?

Mrs. Van Daan. So, if she does? I'm only telling the truth!

[Anne *stretches out, putting her ear to the floor, listening to what is going on below. The sound of the bombers fades away.*]

Mrs. Frank (*setting the table.*) Would you mind, Peter, if I moved you over to the couch?

Anne (*listening*). Miep must have the radio on.

[Peter *picks up his papers, going over to the couch beside* Mrs. Van Daan.]

Mr. Van Daan (*accusingly, to* Peter). Haven't you finished yet?

Peter. No.

Mr. Van Daan. You ought to be ashamed of yourself.

Peter. All right. I'm a dunce. I'm a hopeless case. Why do I go on?

Mrs. Van Daan. You're not hopeless. Don't talk that way. It's just that you haven't anyone to help you, like the girls have. *(To* Mr. Frank*)* Maybe you could help him, Mr. Frank?

Mr. Frank. I'm sure that his father . . . ?

Mr. Van Daan. Not me. I can't do anything with him. He won't listen to me. You go ahead . . . if you want.

Mr. Frank *(going to* Peter*).* What about it, Peter? Shall we make our school coeducational?

Mrs. Van Daan *(kissing* Mr. Frank*).* You're an angel, Mr. Frank. An angel. I don't know why I didn't meet you before I met that one there. Here, sit down, Mr. Frank. . . . *(She forces him down on the couch beside* Peter.*)* Now, Peter, you listen to Mr. Frank.

Mr. Frank. It might be better for us to go into Peter's room.

[Peter *jumps up eagerly, leading the way.*]

Mrs. Van Daan. That's right. You go in there, Peter. You listen to Mr. Frank. Mr. Frank is a highly educated man.

[As Mr. Frank *is about to follow* Peter *into his room,* Mrs. Frank *stops him and wipes the lipstick from his lips. Then she closes the door after them.*]

Anne *(on the floor, listening).* Shh! I can hear a man's voice talking.

Mr. Van Daan. *(to* Anne*).* Isn't it bad enough here without your sprawling all over the place?

[Anne *sits up.*]

Mrs. Van Daan *(to* Mr. Van Daan*).* If you didn't smoke so much, you wouldn't be so bad-tempered.

Mr. Van Daan. Am I smoking? Do you see me smoking?

Mrs. Van Daan. Don't tell me you've used up all those cigarettes.

Mr. Van Daan. One package. Miep only brought me one package.

Mrs. Van Daan. It's a filthy habit anyway. It's a good time to break yourself.

Mr. Van Daan. Oh, stop it, please.

Mrs. Van Daan. You're smoking up all our money. You know that, don't you?

Mr. Van Daan. Will you shut up? *(During this,* Mrs. Frank *and* Margot *have studiously kept their eyes down. But* Anne, *seated on the floor, has been following the discussion interestedly.* Mr. Van Daan *turns to see her staring up at him.)* And what are you staring at?

Anne. I never heard grown-ups quarrel before. I thought only children quarreled.

Mr. Van Daan. This isn't a quarrel! It's a discussion. And I never heard children so rude before.

Anne. *(rising indignantly).* I, rude!

Mr. Van Daan. Yes!

Mrs. Frank *(quickly).* Anne, will you get me my knitting? *(*Anne *goes to get it.)* I must remember, when Miep comes, to ask her to bring me some more wool.

Margot *(going into her room).* I need some hairpins and some soap. I made a list. *(She goes into her bedroom to get the list.)*

Mrs. Frank *(to* Anne*).* Have you some library books for Miep when she comes?

Anne. It's a wonder that Miep has a life of her own, the way we make her run errands for us. Please, Miep, get me some starch. Please take my hair out and get it cut. Tell me all the latest news, Miep. *(She goes over, kneeling on the couch beside* Mrs. Van Daan.*)* Did you know she was engaged? His name is Dirk, and Miep's afraid the Nazis will ship him off to Germany to work in one of their war plants. That's what they're doing with some of the young Dutchmen . . . they pick them up off the streets ——

Mr. Van Daan. *(interrupting).* Don't you ever get tired of talking? Suppose you try keeping still for five minutes. Just five minutes.

[*He starts to pace again. Again* Anne *follows him, mimicking him.* Mrs. Frank *jumps up and takes her by the arm up to the sink, and gives her a glass of milk.*]

Mrs. Frank. Come here, Anne. It's time for your glass of milk.

Mr. Van Daan. Talk, talk, talk. I never heard such a child. Where is my . . . ? Every evening it's the same, talk, talk, talk. (*He looks around.*) Where is my . . . ?

Mrs. Van Daan. What're you looking for?

Mr. Van Daan. My pipe. Have you seen my pipe?

Mrs. Van Daan. What good's a pipe? You haven't got any tobacco.

Mr. Van Daan. At least I'll have something to hold in my mouth! (*Opening* Margot's *bedroom door*) Margot, have you seen my pipe?

Margot. It was on the table last night.

[Anne *puts her glass of milk on the table and picks up his pipe, hiding it behind her back.*]

Mr. Van Daan. I know. I know. Anne, did you see my pipe? . . . Anne!

Mrs. Frank. Anne, Mr. Van Daan is speaking to you.

Anne. Am I allowed to talk now?

Mr. Van Daan. You're the most aggravating . . . The trouble with you is, you've been spoiled. What you need is a good old-fashioned spanking.

Anne (*mimicking* Mrs. Van Daan). "Remember, Mr. So-and-So, remember I'm a lady." (*She thrusts the pipe into his mouth, then picks up her glass of milk.*)

Mr. Van Daan. (*restraining himself with difficulty*). Why aren't you nice and quiet like your sister Margot? Why do you have to show off all the time? Let me give you a little advice, young lady. Men don't like that kind of thing in a girl. You know that? A man likes a girl who'll listen to him once in a while . . . a domestic girl, who'll keep her house shining for her husband . . . who loves to cook and sew and . . .

Anne. I'd cut my throat first! I'd open my veins! I'm going to be remarkable! I'm going to Paris . . .

Mr. Van Daan (*scoffingly*). Paris!

Anne. . . . to study music and art.

Mr. Van Daan. Yeah! Yeah!

Anne. I'm going to be a famous dancer or singer . . . or something wonderful.

[*She makes a wide gesture, spilling the glass of milk on the fur coat in* Mrs. Van Daan's *lap.* Margot *rushes quickly over with a towel.* Anne *tries to brush the milk off with her skirt.*]

Mrs. Van Daan. Now look what you've done . . . you clumsy little fool! My beautiful fur coat my father gave me . . .

Anne. I'm so sorry.

Mrs. Van Daan. What do you care? It isn't yours. . . . So go on, ruin it! Do you know what that coat cost? Do you? And now look at it! Look at it!

Anne. I'm very, very sorry.

Mrs. Van Daan. I could kill you for this. I could just kill you!

[Mrs. Van Daan *goes up the stairs, clutching the coat.* Mr. Van Daan *starts after her.*]

Mr. Van Daan. Petronella . . . *liefje! Liefje! . . .* Come back . . . the supper . . . come back!

Mrs. Frank. Anne, you must not behave in that way.

Anne. It was an accident. Anyone can have an accident.

Mrs. Frank. I don't mean that. I mean the answering back. You must not answer back. They are our guests. We must always show the greatest courtesy to them. We're all living under terrible tension. (*She stops as* Margot *indicates that* Mr. Van Daan *can hear. When he is gone, she continues.*) That's why we must control ourselves. . . . You don't hear Margot getting into arguments with them, do you? Watch Margot. She's always courteous with them. Never familiar. She keeps her distance. And they respect her for it. Try to be like Margot.

Anne. And have them walk all over me, the way they do her? No, thanks!

Mrs. Frank. I'm not afraid that anyone is going to walk all over you, Anne. I'm afraid for other people, that you'll walk on them. I don't know what happens to you, Anne. You are wild, self-willed. If I had ever talked to my mother as you talk to me . . .

Anne. Things have changed. People aren't like that any more. "Yes, Mother." "No, Mother."

"Anything you say, Mother." I've got to fight things out for myself! Make something of myself!

Mrs. Frank. It isn't necessary to fight to do it. Margot doesn't fight, and isn't she . . . ?

Anne (*violently, rebellious*). Margot! Margot! Margot! That's all I hear from everyone . . . how wonderful Margot is . . . "Why aren't you like Margot?"

Margot (*protesting*). Oh, come on, Anne, don't be so . . .

Anne (*paying no attention*). Everything she does is right, and everything I do is wrong! I'm the goat around here! . . . You're all against me! . . . And you worst of all!

[*She rushes off into her room and throws herself down on the settee, stifling her sobs.* Mrs. Frank *sighs and starts toward the stove.*]

Mrs. Frank (*to* Margot). Let's put the soup on the stove . . . if there's anyone who cares to eat. Margot, will you take the bread out? (Margot *gets the bread from the cupboard.*) I don't know how we can go on living this way . . . I can't say a word to Anne . . . she flies at me. . . .

Margot. You know Anne. In half an hour she'll be out here, laughing and joking.

Mrs. Frank. And . . . (She makes a motion *upwards, indicating the* Van Daans.) I told your father it wouldn't work . . . but no . . . no . . . he had to ask them, he said . . . he owed it to him, he said. Well, he knows now that I was right! These quarrels! . . . This bickering!

Margot (*with a warning look*). Shush. Shush.

[*The buzzer for the door sounds.* Mrs. Frank *gasps, startled.*]

Mrs. Frank. Every time I hear that sound, my heart stops!

Margot (*starting for* Peter's *door*). It's Miep. (*She knocks at the door.*) Father?

[Mr. Frank *comes quickly from* Peter's room.]

Mr. Frank. Thank you, Margot. (*As he goes down the steps to open the outer door*) Has everyone his list?

Margot. I'll get my books. (*Giving her mother a list*) Here's your list. (Margot *goes into her and* Anne's *bedroom on the right.* Anne *sits up, hiding her tears, as* Margot *comes in.*) Miep's here.

[Margot *picks up her books and goes back.* Anne *hurries over to the mirror, smoothing her hair.*]

Mr. Van Daan (*coming down the stairs*). Is it Miep?

Margot. Yes. Father's gone down to let her in.

Mr. Van Daan. At last I'll have some cigarettes!

Mrs. Frank (*to* Mr. Van Daan). I can't tell you how unhappy I am about Mrs. Van Daan's coat. Anne should never have touched it.

Mr. Van Daan. She'll be all right.

Mrs. Frank. Is there anything I can do?

Mr. Van Daan. Don't worry.

[*He turns to meet* Miep. *But it is not* Miep *who comes up the steps. It is* Mr. Kraler, *followed by* Mr. Frank. *Their faces are grave.* Anne *comes from the bedroom.* Peter *comes from his room.*]

Mrs. Frank. Mr. Kraler!

Mr. Van Daan. How are you, Mr. Kraler?

Margot. This is a surprise.

Mrs. Frank. When Mr. Kraler comes, the sun begins to shine.

Mr. Van Daan. Miep is coming?

Mr. Kraler. Not tonight. (Mr. Kraler *goes to* Margot *and* Mrs. Frank *and* Anne, *shaking hands with them.*)

Mrs. Frank. Wouldn't you like a cup of coffee? . . . Or, better still, will you have supper with us?

Mr. Frank. Mr. Kraler has something to talk

over with us. Something has happened, he says, which demands an immediate decision.

Mrs. Frank (*fearful*). What is it?

[Mr. Kraler *sits down on the couch. As he talks he takes bread, cabbages, milk, etc., from his briefcase, giving them to* Margot *and* Anne *to put away.*]

Mr. Kraler. Usually, when I come up here, I try to bring you some bit of good news. What's the use of telling you the bad news when there's nothing that you can do about it? But today something has happened. . . . Dirk . . . Miep's Dirk, you know, came to me just now. He tells me that he has a Jewish friend living near him. A dentist. He says he's in trouble. He begged me, could I do anything for this man? Could I find him a hiding place? . . . So I've come to you. . . . I know it's a terrible thing to ask of you, living as you are, but would you take him in with you?

Mr. Frank. Of course we will.

Mr. Kraler (*rising*). It'll be just for a night or two . . . until I find some other place. This happened so suddenly that I didn't know where to turn.

Mr. Frank. Where is he?

Mr. Kraler. Downstairs in the office.

Mr. Frank. Good. Bring him up.

Mr. Kraler. His name is Dussel . . . Jan Dussel.

Mr. Frank. Dussel . . . I think I know him.

Mr. Kraler. I'll get him.

[*He goes quickly down the steps and out.* Mr. Frank *suddenly becomes conscious of the others.*]

Mr. Frank. Forgive me. I spoke without consulting you. But I knew you'd feel as I do.

Mr. Van Daan. There's no reason for you to consult anyone. This is your place. You have a right to do exactly as you please. The only thing I feel . . . there's so little food as it is . . . and to take in another person . . .

[Peter *turns away, ashamed of his father.*]

Mr. Frank. We can stretch the food a little. It's only for a few days.

Mr. Van Daan. You want to make a bet?

Mrs. Frank. I think it's fine to have him. But, Otto, where are you going to put him? Where?

Peter. He can have my bed. I can sleep on the floor. I wouldn't mind.

Mr. Frank. That's good of you, Peter. But your room's too small . . . even for *you.*

Anne. I have a much better idea. I'll come in here with you and Mother, and Margot can take Peter's room, and Peter can go in our room with Mr. Dussel.

Margot. That's right. We could do that.

Mr. Frank. No, Margot. You mustn't sleep in that room . . . neither you nor Anne. Mouschi has caught some rats in there. Peter's brave. He doesn't mind.

Anne. Then how about *this?* I'll come in here with you and Mother, and Mr. Dussel can have my bed.

Mrs. Frank. No. No. *No!* Margot will come in here with us and he can have her bed. It's the only way. Margot, bring your things in here. Help her, Anne.

[Margot *hurries into her room to get her things.*]

Anne (*to her mother*). Why Margot? Why can't I come in here?

Mrs. Frank. Because it wouldn't be proper for Margot to sleep with a . . . Please, Anne. Don't argue. Please.

[Anne *starts slowly away.*]

Mr. Frank (*to* Anne). You don't mind sharing your room with Mr. Dussel, do you, Anne?

Anne. No. No, of course not.

Mr. Frank. Good. (Anne *goes off into her bedroom, helping* Margot. Mr. Frank *starts to search in the cupboards.*) Where's the cognac?

Mrs. Frank. It's there. But, Otto, I was saving it in case of illness.

Mr. Frank. I think we couldn't find a better time to use it. Peter, will you get five glasses for me?

[Peter *goes for the glasses.* Margot *comes out of her bedroom, carrying her possessions, which she hangs behind a curtain in the main room.* Mr. Frank *finds the cognac and pours it into the five glasses that* Peter *brings him.* Mr. Van Daan *stands looking on sourly.* Mrs. Van Daan *comes downstairs and looks around at all of the bustle.*]

Mrs. Van Daan. What's happening? What's going on?

Mr. Van Daan. Someone's moving in with us.

Mrs. Van Daan. In here? You're joking.

Margot. It's only for a night or two . . . until Mr. Kraler finds him another place.

Mr. Van Daan. Yeah! Yeah!

[Mr. Frank *hurries over as* Mr. Kraler *and* Dussel *come up.* Dussel *is a man in his late fifties, meticulous, finicky . . . bewildered now. He wears a raincoat. He carries a briefcase, stuffed full, and a small medicine case.*]

Mr. Frank. Come in, Mr. Dussel.

Mr. Kraler. This is Mr. Frank

Dussel. Mr. Otto Frank?

Mr. Frank. Yes. Let me take your things. (*He takes the hat and briefcase, but* Dussel *clings to his medicine case.*) This is my wife Edith . . . Mr. and Mrs. Van Daan . . . their son, Peter . . . and my daughters, Margot and Anne.

[Dussel *shakes hands with everyone.*]

Mr. Kraler. Thank you, Mr. Frank. Thank you all. Mr. Dussel, I leave you in good hands. Oh . . . Dirk's coat.

[Dussel *hurriedly takes off the raincoat, giving it to* Mr. Kraler. *Underneath is his white dentist's jacket, with a yellow Star of David on it.*]

Dussel (*to* Mr. Kraler). What can I say to thank you . . . ?

Mrs. Frank (*to* Dussel). Mr. Kraler and Miep . . . They're our lifeline. Without them we couldn't live.

Mr. Kraler. Please, please. You make us seem very heroic. It isn't that at all. We simply don't like the Nazis. (*To* Mr. Frank, *who offers him a drink*) No, thanks. (*Then going on*) We don't like their methods. We don't like . . .

Mr. Frank (*smiling*). I know. I know. "No one's going to tell us Dutchmen what to do with our damn Jews!"

Mr. Kraler (*to* Dussel). Pay no attention to Mr. Frank. I'll be up tomorrow to see that they're treating you right. (*To* Mr. Frank) Don't trouble to come down again. Peter will bolt the door after me, won't you, Peter?

Peter. Yes, sir.

Mr. Frank. Thank you, Peter. I'll do it.

Mr. Kraler. Good night, Good night.

Group. Good night, Mr. Kraler. We'll see you tomorrow, *etc. etc.*

[Mr. Kraler *goes out with* Mr. Frank. Mrs. Frank *gives each one of the "grown-ups" a glass of cognac.*]

Mrs. Frank. Please, Mr. Dussel, sit down.

[Mr. Dussel *sinks into a chair.* Mrs. Frank *gives him a glass of cognac.*]

Dussel. I'm dreaming. I know it. I can't believe my eyes. Mr. Otto Frank here! (*To* Mrs. Frank) You're not in Switzerland then? A woman told me . . . She said she'd gone to your house . . . the door was open, everything was in disorder, dishes in the sink. She said she found a piece of paper in the wastebasket with an address scribbled on it . . . an address in Zurich. She said you must have escaped to Zurich.

Anne. Father put that there purposely . . . just so people would think that very thing!

Dussel. And you've been *here* all the time?

Mrs. Frank. All the time . . . ever since July.

[Anne *speaks to her father as he comes back.*]

Anne. It worked, Pim . . . the address you left! Mr. Dussel says that people believe we escaped to Switzerland.

Mr. Frank. I'm glad . . . And now let's have a little drink to welcome Mr. Dussel. (*Before they can drink,* Dussel *bolts his drink.* Mr. Frank *smiles and raises his glass.*) To Mr. Dussel. Welcome. We're very honored to have you with us.

Mrs. Frank. To Mr. Dussel, welcome.

[*The* Van Daans *murmur a welcome. The "grownups" drink.*]

Mrs. Van Daan. Um. That was good.

Mr. Van Daan. Did Mr. Kraler warn you that you won't get much to eat here? You can imagine . . . three ration books among the seven of us . . . and now you make eight.

[Peter *walks away, humiliated. Outside a street organ is heard dimly.*]

Dussel (*rising*). Mr. Van Daan, you don't realize what is happening outside that you should warn me of a thing like that. You don't realize what's going on. . . . (*As* Mr. Van Daan *starts his characteristic pacing,* Dussel *turns to speak to the others.*) Right here in Amsterdam every day hundreds of Jews disappear. . . . They surround a block and search house by house. Children come home from school to find their parents gone. Hundreds are being deported . . . people that you and I know . . . the Hallensteins . . . the Wessels . . .

Mrs. Frank (*in tears*). Oh, no. No!

Dussel. They get their call-up notice . . . come to the Jewish theater on such and such a day and hour . . . bring only what you can carry in a rucksack. And if you refuse the call-up notice, then they come and drag you from your home and ship you off to Mauthausen. The death camp!

Mrs. Frank. We didn't know that things had got so much worse.

Dussel. Forgive me for speaking so.

Anne (*coming to* Dussel). Do you know the deWaals? . . . What's become of them? Their daughter Jopie and I are in the same class. Jopie's my best friend.

Dussel. They are gone.

Anne. Gone?

Dussel. With all the others.

Anne. Oh, no. Not Jopie!

[*She turns away, in tears.* Mrs. Frank *motions to* Margot *to comfort her.* Margot *goes to* Anne, *putting her arms comfortingly around her.*]

Mrs. Van Daan. There were some people called Wagner. They lived near us . . . ?

Mr. Frank (*interrupting with a glance at* Anne). I think we should put this off until later. We all have many questions we want to ask. . . . But I'm sure that Mr. Dussel would like to get settled before supper.

Dussel. Thank you. I would. I brought very little with me.

Mr. Frank (*giving him his hat and briefcase*). I'm sorry we can't give you a room alone. But I hope you won't be too uncomfortable. We've had to make strict rules here . . . a schedule of hours. . . . We'll tell you after supper. Anne, would you like to take Mr. Dussel to his room?

Anne (*controlling her tears*). If you'll come with me, Mr. Dussel? (*She starts for her room.*)

Dussel (*shaking hands with each in turn*). Forgive me if I haven't really expressed my gratitude to all of you. This has been such a shock to me. I'd always thought of myself as Dutch. I was born in Holland. My father was born in Holland, and my grandfather. And now . . . after all these years . . . (*He breaks off.*) If you'll excuse me.

[Dussel *gives a little bow and hurries off after* Anne. Mr. Frank *and the others are subdued.*]

Anne (*turning on the light*). Well, here we are.

[Dussel *looks around the room. In the main room* Margot *speaks to her mother.*]

Margot. The news sounds pretty bad, doesn't it? It's so different from what Mr. Kraler tells us. Mr. Kraler says things are improving.
Mr. Van Daan. I like it better the way Kraler tells it.

[*They resume their occupations, quietly.* Peter *goes off into his room. In* Anne's *room,* Anne *turns to* Dussel.]

Anne. You're going to share the room with me.
Dussel. I'm a man who's always lived alone. I haven't had to adjust myself to others. I hope you'll bear with me until I learn.
Anne. Let me help you. (*She takes his briefcase.*) Do you always live all alone? Have you no family at all?
Dussel. No one. (*He opens his medicine case and spreads his bottles on the dressing table.*)
Anne. How dreadful. You must be terribly lonely.
Dussel. I'm used to it.
Anne. I don't think I could ever get used to it. Didn't you even have a pet? A cat, or a dog?
Dussel. I have an allergy for fur-bearing animals. They give me asthma.
Anne. Oh, dear. Peter has a cat.
Dussel. Here? He has it here?

Anne. Yes. But we hardly ever see it. He keeps it in his room all the time. I'm sure it will be all right.
Dussel. Let us hope so. (*He takes some pills to fortify himself.*)
Anne. That's Margot's bed, where you're going to sleep. I sleep on the sofa there. (*Indicating the clothes hooks on the wall*) We cleared these off for your things. (*She goes over to the window.*) The best part about this room. . . you can look down and see a bit of the street and the canal. There's a houseboat . . . you can see the end of it . . . a bargeman lives there with his family. . . . They have a baby and he's just beginning to walk and I'm so afraid he's going to fall into the canal some day. I watch him. . . .
Dussel (*interrupting*). Your father spoke of a schedule.
Anne (*coming away from the window*). Oh, yes. It's mostly about the times we have to be quiet. And times for the w.c. You can use it now if you like.
Dussel (*stiffly*). No, thank you.
Anne. I suppose you think it's awful, my talking about a thing like that. But you don't know how important it can get to be, especially when you're frightened. . . . About this room, the way Margot and I did . . . she had it to herself in the afternoons for studying, reading . . . lessons, you know . . . and I took the mornings. Would that be all right with you?
Dussel. I'm not at my best in the morning.
Anne. You stay in here in the mornings then. I'll take the room in the afternoons.
Dussel. Tell me, when you're in here, what happens to me? Where am I spending my time? In there, with all the people?
Anne. Yes.
Dussel. I see. I see.
Anne. We have supper at half past six.
Dussel (*going over to the sofa*). Then, if you don't mind . . . I like to lie down quietly for ten minutes before eating. I find it helps the digestion.

Anne. Of course. I hope I'm not going to be too much of a bother to you. I seem to be able to get everyone's back up.

[Dussel *lies down on the sofa, curled up, his back to her.*]

Dussel. I always get along very well with children. My patients all bring their children to me, because they know I get on well with them. So don't you worry about that.

[Anne *leans over him, taking his hand and shaking it gratefully.*]

Anne. Thank you. Thank you, Mr. Dussel.

[*The lights dim to darkness. The curtain falls on the scene. Anne's voice comes to us faintly at first, and then with increasing power.*]

Anne's Voice. . . . And yesterday I finished Cissy Van Marxvelt's latest book. I think she is a first-class writer. I shall definitely let my children read her. Monday, the twenty-first of September, nineteen forty-two. Mr. Dussel and I had another battle yesterday. Yes, Mr. Dussel! According to him, nothing, I repeat . . . nothing, is right about me . . . my appearance, my character, my manners. While he was going on at me I thought . . . sometime I'll give you such a smack that you'll fly right up to the ceiling! Why is it that every grown-up thinks he knows the way to bring up children? Particularly the grown-ups that never had any. I keep wishing that Peter was a girl instead of a boy. Then I would have someone to talk to. Margot's a darling, but she takes everything too seriously. To pause for a moment on the subject of Mrs. Van Daan. I must tell you that her attempts to flirt with Father are getting her nowhere. Pim, thank goodness, won't play.

[*As she is saying the last lines, the curtain rises on the darkened scene. Anne's voice fades out.*]

Scene 4

It is the middle of the night, several months later. The stage is dark except for a little light which comes through the skylight in Peter's *room.*

Everyone is in bed. Mr. and Mrs. Frank *lie on the couch in the main room, which has been pulled out to serve as a makeshift double bed.*

Margot *is sleeping on a mattress on the floor in the main room, behind a curtain stretched across for privacy. The others are all in their accustomed rooms.*

From outside we hear two drunken soldiers singing "Lili Marlene." A girl's high giggle is heard. The sound of running feet is heard coming closer and then fading in the distance. Throughout the scene there is the distant sound of airplanes passing overhead.

A match suddenly flares up in the attic. We dimly see Mr. Van Daan. *He is getting his bearings. He comes quickly down the stairs and goes to the cupboard where the food is stored. Again the match flares up, and is as quickly blown out. The dim figure is seen to steal back up the stairs.*

There is quiet for a second or two, broken only by the sound of airplanes, and running feet on the street below.

Suddenly, out of the silence and the dark, we hear Anne *scream.*

Anne (*screaming*). No! No! Don't . . . don't take me!

[*She moans, tossing and crying in her sleep. The other people wake, terrified.* Dussel *sits up in bed, furious.*]

Dussel. Shush! Anne! Anne, for God's sake, shush!
Anne (*still in her nightmare*). Save me! Save me!

[*She screams and screams. Dussel gets out of bed, going over to her, trying to wake her.*]

Dussel. For God's sake! Quiet! Quiet! You want someone to hear?

[*In the main room Mrs. Frank grabs a shawl and pulls it around her. She rushes in to Anne, taking her in her arms. Mr. Frank hurriedly gets up, putting on his overcoat. Margot sits up, terrified. Peter's light goes on in his room.*]

Mrs. Frank (*to Anne, in her room*). Hush, darling, hush. It's all right. It's all right. (*Over her shoulder, to Dussel*) Will you be kind enough to turn on the light, Mr. Dussel? (*Back to Anne*) It's nothing, my darling. It was just a dream.

[*Dussel turns on the light in the bedroom. Mrs. Frank holds Anne in her arms. Gradually Anne comes out of her nightmare, still trembling with horror. Mr. Frank comes into the room and goes quickly to the window, looking out to be sure that no one outside has heard Anne's screams. Mrs. Frank holds Anne, talking softly to her. In the main room Margot stands on a chair, turning on the center hanging lamp. A light goes on in the Van Daans' room overhead. Peter puts his robe on, coming out of his room.*]

Dussel (*to Mrs. Frank, blowing his nose*). Something must be done about that child, Mrs. Frank. Yelling like that! Who knows but there's somebody on the streets? She's endangering all our lives.

Mrs. Frank. Anne, darling.

Dussel. Every night she twists and turns. I don't sleep. I spend half my night shushing her. And now it's nightmares!

[*Margot comes to the door of Anne's room, followed by Peter. Mr. Frank goes to them, indicating that everything is all right. Peter takes Margot back.*]

Mrs. Frank (*to Anne*). You're here, safe, you see? Nothing has happened. (*To Dussel*) Please, Mr. Dussel, go back to bed. She'll be herself in a minute or two. Won't you, Anne?

Dussel (*picking up a book and a pillow*). Thank you, but I'm going to the w.c. The one place where there's peace!

[*He stalks out. Mr. Van Daan, in underwear and trousers, comes down the stairs.*]

Mr. Van Daan (*to Dussel*). What is it? What happened?

Dussel. A nightmare. She was having a nightmare!

Mr. Van Daan. I thought someone was murdering her.

Dussel. Unfortunately, no.

[*He goes into the bathroom. Mr. Van Daan goes back up the stairs. Mr. Frank, in the main room, sends Peter back to his own bedroom.*]

Mr. Frank. Thank you, Peter. Go back to bed.

[*Peter goes back to his room. Mr. Frank follows him, turning out the light and looking out the window. Then he goes back to the main room and gets up on a chair, turning out the center hanging lamp.*]

Mrs. Frank (*to Anne*). Would you like some water? (*Anne shakes her head.*) Was it a very bad dream? Perhaps if you told me . . . ?

Anne. I'd rather not talk about it.

Mrs. Frank. Poor darling. Try to sleep then. I'll sit right here beside you until you fall asleep. (*She brings a stool over, sitting there.*)

Anne. You don't have to.

Mrs. Frank. But I'd like to stay with you . . . very much. Really.

Anne. I'd rather you didn't.

Mrs. Frank. Good night, then. (*She leans down to kiss Anne. Anne throws her arm up over her face,*

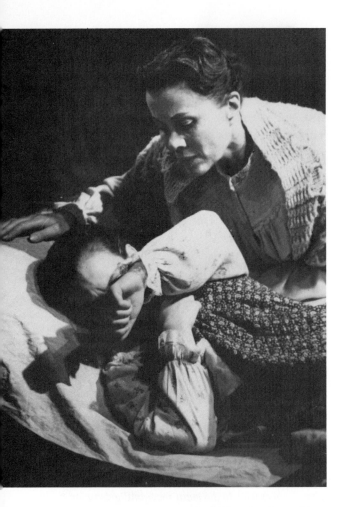

turning away. Mrs. Frank, *hiding her hurt, kisses* Anne's *arm.*) You'll be all right? There's nothing that you want?

Anne. Will you please ask Father to come.

Mrs. Frank (*after a second*). Of course, Anne dear. (*She hurries out into the other room.* Mr. Frank *comes to her as she comes in.*) *Sie verlangt nach Dir!*[15]

Mr. Frank (*sensing her hurt*). *Edith, Liebe, schau . . .*[16]

Mrs. Frank. *Es macht nichts! Ich danke dem lieben Herrgott, dass sie sich wenigstens an Dich wendet,*

15. *Sie verlangt nach Dir!*: She's asking to see you!
16. *Liebe, schau . . .*: dear, look . . .

wenn sie Trost braucht! Geh hinein, Otto, sie ist ganz hysterisch vor Angst.[17] (*As* Mr. Frank *hesitates*) *Geh zu ihr.*[18] (*He looks at her for a second and then goes to get a cup of water for* Anne. Mrs. Frank *sinks down on the bed, her face in her hands, trying to keep from sobbing aloud.* Margot *comes over to her, putting her arms around her.*) She wants nothing of me. She pulled away when I leaned down to kiss her.

Margot. It's a phase . . . You heard Father. . . . Most girls go through it . . . they turn to their fathers at this age . . . they give all their love to their fathers.

Mrs. Frank. You weren't like this. You didn't shut me out.

Margot. She'll get over it. . . .

[*She smooths the bed for* Mrs. Frank *and sits beside her a moment as* Mrs. Frank *lies down. In* Anne's *room* Mr. Frank *comes in, sitting down by* Anne. Anne *flings her arms around him, clinging to him. In the distance we hear the sound of ack-ack.*]

Anne. Oh, Pim. I dreamed that they came to get us! The Green Police! They broke down the door and grabbed me and started to drag me out the way they did Jopie.

Mr. Frank. I want you to take this pill.

Anne. What is it?

Mr. Frank. Something to quiet you.

[*She takes it and drinks the water. In the main room* Margot *turns out the light and goes back to her bed.*]

Mr. Frank (*to* Anne). Do you want me to read to you for a while?

Anne. No. Just sit with me for a minute. Was I

17. *Es macht . . . Angst:* It doesn't matter. I just thank the dear Lord that at least she turns to you when she needs comfort. Go, Otto, she's utterly hysterical with fear.
18. *Geh zu ihr:* Go to her.

awful? Did I yell terribly loud? Do you think anyone outside could have heard?

Mr. Frank. No. No. Lie quietly now. Try to sleep.

Anne. I'm a terrible coward. I'm so disappointed in myself. I think I've conquered my fear . . . I think I'm really grown-up . . . and then something happens . . . and I run to you like a baby. . . . I love you, Father. I don't love anyone but you.

Mr. Frank (*reproachfully*). Annele!

Anne. It's true. I've been thinking about it for a long time. You're the only one I love.

Mr. Frank. It's fine to hear you tell me that you love me. But I'd be happier if you said you loved your mother as well. . . . She needs your help so much . . . your love . . .

Anne. We have nothing in common. She doesn't understand me. Whenever I try to explain my views on life to her she asks me if I'm constipated.

Mr. Frank. You hurt her very much now. She's crying. She's in there crying.

Anne. I can't help it. I only told the truth. I didn't want her here. . . . (*Then, with sudden change*) Oh, Pim, I was horrible, wasn't I? And the worst of it is, I can stand off and look at myself doing it and know it's cruel and yet I can't stop doing it. What's the matter with me? Tell me. Don't say it's just a phase! Help me.

Mr. Frank. There is so little that we parents can do to help our children. We can only try to set a good example . . . point the way. The rest you must do yourself. You must build your own character.

Anne. I'm trying. Really I am. Every night I think back over all of the things I did that day that were wrong . . . like putting the wet mop in Mr. Dussel's bed . . . and this thing now with Mother. I say to myself, that was wrong. I make up my mind. I'm never going to do that again. Never! Of course I may do something worse . . . but at least I'll never do *that* again! . . . I

have a nicer side, Father . . . a sweeter, nicer side. But I'm scared to show it. I'm afraid that people are going to laugh at me if I'm serious. So the mean Anne comes to the outside and the good Anne stays on the inside, and I keep on trying to switch them around and have the good Anne outside and the bad Anne inside and be what I'd like to be . . . and might be . . . if only . . . only . . .

[*She is asleep.* Mr. Frank *watches her for a moment and then turns off the light and starts out. The lights dim out. The curtain falls on the scene.* Anne's *voice is heard dimly at first, and then with growing strength.*]

Anne's Voice. . . . The air raids are getting worse. They come over day and night. The noise is terrifying. Pim says it should be music to our ears. The more planes, the sooner will come the end of the war. Mrs. Van Daan pretends to be a fatalist. What will be, will be. But when the planes come over, who is the most frightened? No one else but Petronella! . . . Monday, the ninth of November, nineteen forty-two. Wonderful news! The Allies have landed in Africa. Pim says that we can look for an early finish to the war. Just for fun he asked each of us what was the first thing we wanted to do when we got out of here. Mrs. Van Daan longs to be home with her own things, her needlepoint chairs, the Beckstein piano her father gave her . . . the best that money could buy. Peter would like to go to a movie. Mr. Dussel wants to get back to his dentist's drill. He's afraid he is losing his touch. For myself, there are so many things . . . to ride a bike again . . . to laugh till my belly aches . . . to have new clothes from the skin out . . . to have a hot tub filled to overflowing and wallow in it for hours . . . to be back in school with my friends . . .

[*As the last lines are being said, the curtain rises on*

the scene. The lights dim on as Anne's *voice fades away.*]

Scene 5

It is the first night of the Hanukkah[19] celebration. Mr. Frank *is standing at the head of the table, on which is the menorah.[20] He lights the shamas,[21] or servant candle, and holds it as he says the blessing. Seated listening is all of the "family," dressed in their best. The men wear hats;* Peter *wears his cap.*

Mr. Frank (*reading from a prayer book*). "Praised be Thou, O Lord our God, Ruler of the universe, who hast sanctified us with Thy commandments and bidden us kindle the Hanukkah lights. Praised be Thou, O Lord our God, Ruler of the universe, who hast wrought wondrous deliverances for our fathers in days of old. Praised be Thou, O Lord our God, Ruler of the universe, that Thou hast given us life and sustenance and brought us to this happy season." (Mr. Frank *lights the one candle of the menorah as he continues.*) "We kindle this Hanukkah light to celebrate the great and wonderful deeds wrought through the zeal with which God filled the hearts of the heroic Maccabees, two thousand years ago. They fought against indifference, against tyranny and oppression, and they restored our Temple to us. May these lights remind us that we should ever look to God, whence cometh our help." Amen. (*Pronounced "O-mayn"*)

19. **Hanukkah** (кнä'noo-kə): a joyful holiday lasting eight days, usually in December, which celebrates a victorious fight for religious liberty in 165 B.C. At that time, a Greek king of Syria who ruled the Jews had been forcing them to worship Greek gods. Led by a family known as the Maccabees, the Jews won their independence from Syria and restored their holy Temple, which the Syrians had used to make offerings to Zeus.
20. **menorah** (mə-nôr'ə): a ritual candleholder. The Hanukkah menorah holds nine candles.
21. **shamas** (shä'məs): the central candle in the menorah, which is used to light the others.

All. Amen.

[Mr. Frank *hands* Mrs. Frank *the prayer book.*]

Mrs. Frank (*reading*). "I lift up mine eyes unto the mountains, from whence cometh my help. My help cometh from the Lord who made heaven and earth. He will not suffer thy foot to be moved. He that keepeth thee will not slumber. He that keepeth Israel doth neither slumber nor sleep. The Lord is thy keeper. The Lord is thy shade upon thy right hand. The sun shall not smite thee by day, nor the moon by night. The Lord shall keep thee from all evil. He shall keep thy soul. The Lord shall guard thy going out and thy coming in, from this time forth and forevermore." Amen.
All. Amen.

[Mrs. Frank *puts down the prayer book and goes to get the food and wine.* Margot *helps her.* Mr. Frank *takes the men's hats and puts them aside.*]

Dussel (*rising*). That was very moving.
Anne (*pulling him back*). It isn't over yet!
Mrs. Van Daan. Sit down! Sit down!
Anne. There's a lot more, songs and presents.
Dussel. Presents?
Mrs. Frank. Not this year, unfortunately.
Mrs. Van Daan. But always on Hanukkah everyone gives presents . . . everyone!
Dussel. Like our St. Nicholas' Day.[22]

[*There is a chorus of* no's *from the group.*]

Mrs. Van Daan. No! Not like St. Nicholas! What kind of a Jew are you that you don't know Hanukkah?
Mrs. Frank (*as she brings the food*). I remember

22. **our St. Nicholas' Day:** Christian children in the Netherlands receive gifts on St. Nicholas' Day, December 6. Mr. Dussel considers himself a Christian. However, he is one of the many people who were hunted by the Nazis because they had Jewish ancestry.

particularly the candles. . . . First one, as we have tonight. Then the second night you light two candles, the next night three . . . and so on until you have eight candles burning. When there are eight candles it is truly beautiful.

Mrs. Van Daan. And the potato pancakes.

Mr. Van Daan. Don't talk about them!

Mrs. Van Daan. I make the best *latkes* you ever tasted!

Mrs. Frank. Invite us all next year . . . in your own home.

Mr. Frank. God willing.

Mrs. Van Daan. God willing.

Margot. What I remember best is the presents we used to get when we were little . . . eight days of presents . . . and each day they got better and better.

Mrs. Frank. (*sitting down*). We are all here, alive. That is present enough.

Anne. No, it isn't. I've got something. . . . (*She rushes into her room, hurriedly puts on a little hat improvised from the lampshade, grabs a satchel bulging with parcels and comes running back.*)

Mrs. Frank. What is it?

Anne. Presents!

Mrs. Van Daan. Presents!

Dussel. Look!

Mr. Van Daan. What's she got on her head?

Peter. A lampshade!

Anne. (*She picks out one at random*). This is for Margot. (*She hands it to* Margot, *pulling her to her feet.*) Read it out loud.

Margot (*reading*).

"You have never lost your temper.

You never will, I fear,

You are so good.

But if you should,

Put all your cross words here."

(*She tears open the package.*) A new crossword puzzle book! Where did you get it?

Anne. It isn't new. It's one that you've done. But I rubbed it all out, and if you wait a little and forget, you can do it all over again.

Margot (*sitting*). It's wonderful, Anne. Thank you. You'd never know it wasn't new.

[*From outside we hear the sound of a streetcar passing.*]

Anne (*with another gift*). Mrs. Van Daan.

Mrs. Van Daan (*taking it*). This is awful. . . . I haven't anything for anyone. . . . I never thought . . .

Mr. Frank. This is all Anne's idea.

Mrs. Van Daan (*holding up a bottle*). What is it?

Anne. It's hair shampoo. I took all the odds and ends of soap and mixed them with the last of my toilet water.

Mrs. Van Daan. Oh, Anneke!

Anne. I wanted to write a poem for all of them, but I didn't have time. (*Offering a large box to Mr. Van Daan*) Yours, Mr. Van Daan, is *really* something . . . something you want more than anything. (*As she waits for him to open it*) Look! Cigarettes!

Mr. Van Daan. Cigarettes!

Anne. Two of them! Pim found some old pipe tobacco in the pocket lining of his coat . . . and we made them . . . or rather, Pim did.

Mrs. Van Daan. Let me see . . . Well, look at that! Light it, Putti! Light it.

[Mr. Van Daan *hesitates.*]

Anne. It's tobacco, really it is! There's a little fluff in it, but not much.

[*Everyone watches as* Mr. Van Daan *cautiously lights it. The cigarette flares up. Everyone laughs.*]

Peter. It works!

Mrs. Van Daan. Look at him.

Mr. Van Daan (*spluttering*). Thank you, Anne. Thank you.

[Anne *rushes back to her satchel for another present.*]

Anne (*handing her mother a piece of paper.*) For Mother, Hanukkah greeting. (*She pulls her mother to her feet.*)

Mrs. Frank. (*She reads*).

"Here's an IOU that I promise to pay.
Ten hours of doing whatever you say.
Signed Anne Frank." (Mrs. Frank, *touched, takes* Anne *in her arms, holding her close.*)

Dussel. (*to* Anne). Ten hours of doing what you're told? *Anything* you're told?

Anne. That's right.

Dussel. You wouldn't want to sell that, Mrs. Frank?

Mrs. Frank. Never! This is the most precious gift I've ever had.

[*She sits, showing her present to the others. Anne hurries back to the satchel and pulls out a scarf, the scarf that* Mr. Frank *found in the first scene.*]

Anne (*offering it to her father*). For Pim.

Mr. Frank. Anneke . . . I wasn't supposed to have a present! (*He takes it, unfolding it and showing it to the others.*)

Anne. It's a muffler . . . to put round your neck . . . like an ascot, you know. I made it myself out of odds and ends. . . . I knitted it in the dark each night, after I'd gone to bed. I'm afraid it looks better in the dark!

Mr. Frank (*putting it on*). It's fine. It fits me perfectly. Thank you, Annele.

[Anne *hands* Peter *a ball of paper, with a string attached to it.*]

Anne. That's for Mouschi.

Peter (*rising to bow*). On behalf of Mouschi, I thank you.

Anne (*hesitant, handing him a gift*). And . . . this is yours . . . from Mrs. Quack Quack. (*As he holds it gingerly in his hands*) Well . . . open it. . . . Aren't you going to open it?

Peter. I'm scared to. I know something's going to jump out and hit me.

Anne. No. It's nothing like that, really.

Mrs. Van Daan (*as he is opening it*). What is it, Peter? Go on. Show it.

Anne (*excitedly*). It's a safety razor!

Dussel. A what?

Anne. A razor!

Mrs. Van Daan (*looking at it*). You didn't make that out of odds and ends.

Anne (*to* Peter). Miep got it for me. It's not new. It's secondhand. But you really do need a razor now.

Dussel. For what?

Anne. Look on his upper lip . . . you can see the beginning of a mustache.

Dussel. He wants to get rid of that? Put a little milk on it and let the cat lick it off.

Peter (*starting for his room*). Think you're funny, don't you.

Dussel. Look! He can't wait! He's going to try it!

Peter. I'm going to give Mouschi his present! (*He goes into his room, slamming the door behind him.*)

Mr. Van Daan (*disgustedly*). Mouschi, Mouschi, Mouschi.

[*In the distance we hear a dog persistently barking. Anne brings a gift to Dussel.*]

Anne. And last but never least, my roommate, Mr. Dussel.

Dussel. For me? You have something for me? (*He opens the small box she gives him.*)

Anne. I made them myself.

Dussel. (*puzzled*). Capsules! Two capsules!

Anne. They're earplugs!

Dussel. Earplugs?

Anne. To put in your ears so you won't hear me when I thrash around at night. I saw them advertised in a magazine. They're not real ones. . . . I made them out of cotton and candle wax. Try them. . . . See if they don't work . . . see if you can hear me talk. . . .

Dussel (*putting them in his ears*). Wait now until I get them in . . . so.

Anne. Are you ready?

Dussel. Huh?

Anne. Are you ready?

Dussel. Good God! They've gone inside! I can't get them out! (*They laugh as Dussel jumps about, trying to shake the plugs out of his ears. Finally he gets them out. Putting them away*) Thank you, Anne! Thank you!

Mr. Van Daan. A real Hanukkah!

Mrs Van Daan. Wasn't it cute of her?

Mrs. Frank. I don't know when she did it.

Margot. I love my present.

(*Together*)

Anne (*sitting at the table*). And now let's have the song, Father . . . please. . . . (*To* Dussel) Have you heard the Hanukkah song, Mr. Dussel? The song is the whole thing! (*She sings.*) "Oh, Hanukkah! Oh, Hanukkah! The sweet celebration. . . ."

Mr. Frank (*quieting her*). I'm afraid, Anne, we shouldn't sing that song tonight. (*To* Dussel) It's a song of jubilation, of rejoicing. One is apt to become too enthusiastic.

Anne. Oh, please, please. Let's sing the song. I promise not to shout!

Mr. Frank. Very well. But quietly now . . . I'll keep an eye on you and when . . .

[*As* Anne *starts to sing, she is interrupted by* Dussel, *who is snorting and wheezing.*]

Dussel (*pointing to* Peter). You . . . you! (Peter *is coming from his bedroom, ostentatiously holding a bulge in his coat as if he were holding his cat, and dangling* Anne's *present before it.*) How many times . . . I told you . . . Out! Out!

Mr. Van Daan (*going to* Peter). What's the matter with you? Haven't you any sense? Get that cat out of here.

Peter (*innocently*). Cat?

Mr. Van Daan. You heard me. Get it out of here!

Peter. I have no cat.

[*Delighted with his joke, he opens his coat and pulls out a bath towel. The group at the table laugh, enjoying the joke.*]

Dussel (*still wheezing*). It doesn't need to be the cat . . . his clothes are enough . . . when he comes out of that room. . . .

Mr. Van Daan. Don't worry. You won't be bothered any more. We're getting rid of it.

Dussel. At last you listen to me. (*He goes off into his bedroom.*)

Mr. Van Daan (*calling after him*). I'm not doing it for you. That's all in your mind . . . all of it! (*He starts back to his place at the table.*) I'm doing it because I'm sick of seeing that cat eat all our food.

Peter. That's not true! I only give him bones . . . scraps . . .

Mr. Van Daan. Don't tell me! He gets fatter every day! Damn cat looks better than any of us. Out he goes tonight!

Peter. No! No!

Anne. Mr. Van Daan, you can't do that! That's Peter's cat. Peter loves that cat.

Mrs. Frank (*quietly*). Anne.

Peter (*to* Mr. Van Daan). If he goes, I go.

Mr. Van Daan. Go! Go!

Mrs. Van Daan. You're not going and the cat's not going! Now please . . . this is Hanukkah . . . Hanukkah . . . this is the time to celebrate. . . . What's the matter with all of you? Come on, Anne. Let's have the song.

Anne (*singing*).
"Oh, Hanukkah! Oh, Hanukkah!
The sweet celebration."

Mr. Frank (*rising*). I think we should first blow out the candle . . . then we'll have something for tomorrow night.

Margot. But, Father, you're supposed to let it burn itself out.

Mr. Frank. I'm sure that God understands shortages. (*Before blowing it out*) "Praised be Thou, O Lord our God, who hast sustained us and permitted us to celebrate this joyous festival."

[*He is about to blow out the candle when suddenly there is a crash of something falling below. They all freeze in horror, motionless. For a few seconds there is complete silence.* Mr. Frank *slips off his shoes. The others noiselessly follow his example.* Mr. Frank *turns out a light near him. He motions to* Peter *to turn off the center lamp.* Peter *tries to reach it, realizes he cannot and gets up on a chair. Just as he is touching the lamp he loses his balance. The chair goes out from under him. He falls. The iron lampshade crashes to the floor. There is a sound of feet below, running down the stairs.*]

Mr. Van Daan (*under his breath*). God almighty! (*The only light left comes from the Hanukkah candle.* Dussel *comes from his room.* Mr. Frank *creeps over to the stairwell and stands listening. The dog is heard barking excitedly.*) Do you hear anything?

Mr. Frank (*in a whisper*). No. I think they've gone.

Mrs. Van Daan. It's the Green Police. They've found us.

Mr. Frank. If they had, they wouldn't have left. They'd be up here by now.

Mrs. Van Daan. I know it's the Green Police. They've gone to get help. That's all, they'll be back.

Mr. Van Daan. Or it may have been the Gestapo,[23] looking for papers. . . .

Mr. Frank (*interrupting*). Or a thief, looking for money.

Mrs. Van Daan. We've got to do something. . . . Quick! Quick! Before they come back.

Mr. Van Daan. There isn't anything to do. Just wait.

[Mr. Frank *holds up his hand for them to be quiet. He is listening intently. There is complete silence as they all strain to hear any sound from below. Suddenly* Anne *begins to sway. With a low cry she falls to the floor in a faint.* Mrs. Frank *goes to her quickly, sitting beside her on the floor and taking her in her arms.*]

Mrs. Frank. Get some water, please! Get some water!

[Margot *starts for the sink.*]

Mr. Van Daan (*grabbing* Margot). No! No! No one's going to run water!

Mr. Frank. If they've found us, they've found us. Get the water. (Margot *starts again for the sink.* Mr. Frank, *getting a flashlight*) I'm going down.

[Margot *rushes to him, clinging to him.* Anne *struggles to consciousness.*]

Margot. No, Father, no! There may be someone there, waiting. . . . It may be a trap!

Mr. Frank. This is Saturday. There is no way for us to know what has happened until Miep or Mr. Kraler comes on Monday morning. We cannot live with this uncertainty.

Margot. Don't go, Father!

23. **Gestapo** (gə-stä′pō): the Nazi secret police.

Mrs. Frank. Hush, darling, hush. (Mr. Frank *slips quietly out, down the steps and out through the door below.*) Margot! Stay close to me.

[Margot *goes to her mother.*]

Mr. Van Daan. Shush! Shush!

[Mrs. Frank *whispers to* Margot *to get the water.* Margot *goes for it.*]

Mrs. Van Daan. Putti, where's our money? Get our money. I hear you can buy the Green Police off, so much a head. Go upstairs quick! Get the money!

Mr. Van Daan. Keep still!

Mrs. Van Daan (*kneeling before him, pleading*). Do you want to be dragged off to a concentration camp? Are you going to stand there and wait for them to come up and get you? Do something, I tell you!

Mr. Van Daan (*pushing her aside*). Will you keep still!

[He *goes over to the stairwell to listen.* Peter *goes to his mother, helping her up onto the sofa. There is a second of silence. Then* Anne *can stand it no longer.*]

Anne. Someone go after Father! Make Father come back!

Peter (*starting for the door*). I'll go.

Mr. Van Daan. Haven't you done enough?

[He *pushes* Peter *roughly away. In his anger against his father* Peter *grabs a chair as if to hit him with it, then puts it down, burying his face in his hands.* Mrs. Frank *begins to pray softly.*]

Anne. Please, please, Mr. Van Daan. Get Father.

Mr. Van Daan. Quiet! Quiet!

[Anne *is shocked into silence.* Mrs. Frank *pulls her closer, holding her protectively in her arms.*]

Mrs. Frank (*softly, praying*). "I lift up mine eyes unto the mountains, from whence cometh my help. My help cometh from the Lord who made heaven and earth. He will not suffer thy foot to be moved. . . . He that keepeth thee will not slumber. . . ."

[*She stops as she hears someone coming. They all watch the door tensely.* Mr. Frank *comes quietly in.* Anne *rushes to him, holding him tight.*]

Mr. Frank. It was a thief. That noise must have scared him away.
Mrs. Van Daan. Thank God.
Mr. Frank. He took the cashbox. And the radio. He ran away in such a hurry that he didn't stop to shut the street door. It was swinging wide open. (*A breath of relief sweeps over them.*) I think it would be good to have some light.
Margot. Are you sure it's all right?
Mr. Frank. The danger has passed. (Margot *goes to light the small lamp.*) Don't be so terrified, Anne. We're safe.
Dussel. Who says the danger has passed? Don't you realize we are in greater danger than ever?
Mr. Frank. Mr. Dussel, will you be still! (Mr. Frank *takes* Anne *back to the table, making her sit down with him, trying to calm her.*)
Dussel (*pointing to* Peter). Thanks to this clumsy fool, there's someone now who knows we're up here! Someone now knows we're up here, hiding!
Mrs. Van Daan (*going to* Dussel). Someone knows we're here, yes. But who is the someone? A thief! A thief! You think a thief is going to go to the Green Police and say . . . I was robbing a place the other night and I heard a noise up over my head? You think a thief is going to do that?

Dussel. Yes. I think he will.
Mrs. Van Daan (*hysterically*). You're crazy!

[*She stumbles back to her seat at the table.* Peter *follows protectively, pushing* Dussel *aside.*]

Dussel. I think someday he'll be caught and then he'll make a bargain with the Green Police . . . if they'll let him off, he'll tell them where some Jews are hiding!

[*He goes off into the bedroom. There is a second of appalled silence.*]

Mr. Van Daan. He's right.
Anne. Father, let's get out of here! We can't stay here now . . . Let's go. . . .
Mr. Van Daan. Go! Where?
Mrs. Frank (*sinking into her chair at the table*). Yes. Where?
Mr. Frank (*rising, to them all*). Have we lost all faith? All courage? A moment ago we thought that they'd come for us. We were sure it was the end. But it wasn't the end. We're alive, safe. (Mr. Frank *prays.*) "We thank Thee, O Lord our God, that in Thy infinite mercy Thou has again seen fit to spare us." (*He blows out the candle, then turns to* Anne.). Come on, Anne. The song! Let's have the song!

[*He starts to sing.* Anne *finally starts faltering to sing as* Mr. Frank *urges her on. Her voice is hardly audible at first.*]

Anne (*singing*).
"Oh, Hanukkah! Oh, Hanukkah!
The sweet . . . celebration. . . ."

[*As she goes on singing, the others gradually join in, their voices still shaking with fear.* Mrs. Van Daan *sobs as she sings.*]

Group.
"Around the feast . . . we . . . gather

In complete . . . jubilation. . . .

Happiest of sea . . . sons

Now is here.

Many are the reasons for good cheer.

(Dussel *comes from the bedroom. He comes over to the table, standing beside* Margot, *listening to them as they sing.*)

"Together

We'll weather

Whatever tomorrow may bring.

(*As they sing on with growing courage, the lights start to dim.*)

"So hear us rejoicing

And merrily voicing

The Hanukkah song that we sing.

Hoy!

(*The lights are out. The curtain starts slowly to fall.*)

"Hear us rejoicing

And merrily voicing

The Hanukkah song that we sing."

[*They are still singing as the curtain falls.*]

Reading Check

1. Why were Anne and her family forced into hiding?
2. Where did the Frank family hide?
3. Who else was forced into hiding with the Franks?
4. Who helped the Franks and the others to survive?
5. How old was Anne when she started her diary?

For Study and Discussion

Analyzing and Interpreting the Play

ACT ONE

Scene 1

1. *The Diary of Anne Frank* is about a group of people who are forced to leave the outside world and to retreat into a small, secret hiding place. What details of the set indicate that this will be a realistic, or lifelike, story?

2a. The play opens in November 1945. But in what year does most of this act take place? **b.** What prompts Mr. Frank's thoughts to flash back in time?

Scene 2

3. Anne's entrance is an important moment in the play. **a.** How does the stage direction on page 339, before her entrance, describe her personality? **b.** What does Anne do as soon as she comes onstage?

4. Why do you think Anne cannot destroy the Star of David, as Peter does?

5. When does Anne first realize what "going into hiding" means?

6a. What does Mr. Frank say cannot be locked up? **b.** What does he suggest he and Anne can do to hold on to one kind of freedom?

Scene 3

7. After several months together in their enclosed world, the "family" members find their tempers growing shorter. **a.** What do Anne and Peter argue about in this scene? **b.** What do the Van Daans quarrel about?

8. Anne has grown lonely and frustrated in the last several months. **a.** What are Anne's dreams for her future? **b.** What does she accuse her family of feeling about her?

9. Mr. Dussel brings the group the harsh news which they have been ignorant of. What

The Diary of Anne Frank Act One, Scene 5 **369**

does he tell them has been happening in the outside world?

Scene 4

10a. What is Anne's nightmare? **b.** How is it completely different from the dreams of her future that she expressed in Scene 3?

11. Anne says that there is a person inside her that is different from the one that people see. **a.** What kind of person remains hidden inside her? **b.** Why doesn't Anne allow this side of her nature to show?

Scene 5

12a. What gifts has Anne managed to gather together for the members of her "family"? **b.** How does the celebration help unite them in the midst of their suffering?

13. The Hanukkah song gives the characters hope and courage. Yet the words of the song do not at all describe their true situation. **a.** Tell how each of the following lines from the song differs from the real conditions of the singers:

> Around the feast . . . we . . . gather
> Many are the reasons for good cheer.
> So hear us rejoicing

b. Knowing what you do of the actual circumstances of the characters, tell how their singing of the Hanukkah song makes you feel.

14. Act One ends with the characters (and the audience) in a state of worry and suspense. What do the characters fear caused the noise downstairs?

Language and Vocabulary

Recognizing Exact Meanings

During the Hanukkah celebration in Scene 5, Mr. Frank tells about the Maccabees, who fought against "tyranny and oppression." The words *tyranny* and *oppression* are close in meaning but they are not synonyms. What is the exact meaning of each word? Check your answers in a dictionary. Show that you understand the precise meaning of each word by using it in a sentence.

Writing About Literature

Analyzing a Character

You have seen that in a short story a character is developed by direct and indirect methods. Consider what you have learned about Anne from direct statements included in stage directions, from her words and actions, and from the reactions of other characters to her. Write a paper in which you give your impression of her. If you wish, focus on two or three main characteristics and give evidence from the play that illustrates each characteristic. Be sure to enclose direct quotations in quotation marks.

Act Two

Scene 1

In the darkness we hear Anne's *voice, again reading from the diary.*

Anne's Voice. Saturday, the first of January, nineteen forty-four. Another new year has begun and we find ourselves still in our hiding place. We have been here now for one year, five months and twenty-five days. It seems that our life is at a standstill.

[*The curtain rises on the scene. It is late afternoon. Everyone is bundled up against the cold. In the main room* Mrs. Frank *is taking down the laundry, which is hung across the back.* Mr. Frank *sits in the chair down left, reading.* Margot *is lying on the couch with a blanket over her and the many-colored knitted scarf around her throat.* Anne *is seated at the center table, writing in her diary.* Peter, Mr. *and* Mrs. Van Daan, *and* Dussel *are all in their own rooms, reading or lying down.*

As the lights dim on, Anne's *voice continues, without a break.*]

Anne's Voice. We are all a little thinner. The Van Daans' "discussions" are as violent as ever. Mother still does not understand me. But then I don't understand her either. There is one great change, however. A change in myself. I read somewhere that girls of my age don't feel quite certain of themselves. That they become quiet within and begin to think of the miracle that is taking place in their bodies. I think that what is happening to me is so wonderful . . . not only what can be seen, but what is taking place inside. Each time it has happened I have a feeling that I have a sweet secret. (*We hear the chimes and then a hymn being played on the carillon outside.*) And in spite of any pain, I long for the time when I shall feel that secret within me again.

[*The buzzer of the door below suddenly sounds.*

Everyone is startled; Mr. Frank *tiptoes cautiously to the top of the steps and listens. Again the buzzer sounds, in* Miep's *V-for-Victory signal.*[1]]

Mr. Frank. It's Miep!

[*He goes quickly down the steps to unbolt the door.* Mrs. Frank *calls upstairs to the* Van Daans *and then to* Peter.]

Mrs. Frank. Wake up, everyone! Miep is here! (Anne *quickly puts her diary away.* Margot *sits up, pulling the blanket around her shoulders.* Dussel *sits on the edge of his bed, listening, disgruntled.* Miep *comes up the steps, followed by* Mr. Kraler. *They bring flowers, books, newspapers, etc.* Anne *rushes to* Miep, *throwing her arms affectionately around her.*) Miep . . . and Mr. Kraler . . . What a delightful surprise!

1. **V-for-Victory signal:** three short rings and one long ring, the Morse code for V, used as the Allied symbol for victory.

Mr. Kraler. We came to bring you New Year's greetings.

Mrs. Frank. You shouldn't . . . you should have at least one day to yourselves. (*She goes quickly to the stove and brings down teacups and tea for all of them.*)

Anne. Don't say that, it's so wonderful to see them! (*Sniffing at* Miep's *coat*) I can smell the wind and the cold on your clothes.

Miep (*giving her the flowers*). There you are. (*Then, to* Margot, *feeling her forehead*) How are you, Margot? . . . Feeling any better?

Margot. I'm all right.

Anne. We filled her full of every kind of pill so she won't cough and make a noise.

[*She runs into her room to put the flowers in water. Mr. and Mrs. Van Daan come from upstairs. Outside there is the sound of a band playing.*]

Mrs. Van Daan. Well, hello, Miep. Mr. Kraler.

Mr. Kraler (*giving a bouquet of flowers to* Mrs. Van Daan). With my hope for peace in the New Year.

Peter (*anxiously*). Miep, have you seen Mouschi? Have you seen him anywhere around?

Miep. I'm sorry, Peter. I asked everyone in the neighborhood had they seen a gray cat. But they said no.

[Mrs. Frank *gives* Miep *a cup of tea.* Mr. Frank *comes up the steps, carrying a small cake on a plate.*]

Mr. Frank. Look what Miep's brought for us!

Mrs. Frank (*taking it*). A cake!

Mr. Van Daan. A cake! (*He pinches* Miep's *cheeks gaily and hurries up to the cupboard.*) I'll get some plates.

[Dussel, *in his room, hastily puts a coat on and starts out to join the others.*]

Mrs. Frank. Thank you, Miepia. You shouldn't

have done it. You must have used all of your sugar ration for weeks. (*Giving it to* Mrs. Van Daan) It's beautiful, isn't it?

Mrs. Van Daan. It's been ages since I even saw a cake. Not since you brought us one last year. (*Without looking at the cake, to* Miep) Remember? Don't you remember, you gave us one on New Year's Day? Just this time last year? I'll never forget it because you had "Peace in nineteen forty-three" on it. (*She looks at the cake and reads.*) "Peace in nineteen forty-four!"

Miep. Well, it has to come sometime, you know. (*As* Dussel *comes from his room*) Hello, Mr. Dussel.

Mr. Kraler. How are you?

Mr. Van Daan (*bringing plates and a knife*). Here's the knife, *liefje*. Now, how many of us are there?

Miep. None for me, thank you.

Mr. Frank. Oh, please. You must.

Miep. I couldn't.

Mr. Van Daan. Good! That leaves one . . . two . . . three . . . seven of us.

Dussel. Eight! Eight! It's the same number as it always is!

Mr. Van Daan. I left Margot out. I take it for granted Margot wouldn't eat any.

Anne. Why wouldn't she?

Mrs. Frank. I think it won't harm her.

Mr. Van Daan. All right! All right! I just didn't want her to start coughing again, that's all.

Dussel. And please, Mrs. Frank should cut the cake.

Mr. Van Daan. What's the difference? ⎫
Mrs. Van Daan. It's not Mrs. Frank's cake, is it, Miep? It's for all of us. ⎬ (*Together*)

Dussel. Mrs. Frank divides things better.

Mrs. Van Daan (*going to* Dussel). What are you trying to say? ⎫
Mr. Van Daan. Oh, come on! Stop wasting time! ⎬ (*Together*)

Mrs. Van Daan (*to* Dussel). Don't I always give everybody exactly the same? Don't I?

Mr. Van Daan. Forget it, Kerli.

Mrs. Van Daan. No. I want an answer! Don't I?

Dussel. Yes. Yes. Everybody gets exactly the same . . . except Mr. Van Daan always gets a little bit more.

[Mr. Van Daan *advances on* Dussel, *the knife still in his hand.*]

Mr. Van Daan. That's a lie!

[Dussel *retreats before the onslaught of the* Van Daans.]

Mr. Frank. Please, please! (*Then, to* Miep) You see what a little sugar cake does to us? It goes right to our heads!

Mr. Van Daan (*handing* Mrs. Frank *the knife*). Here you are, Mrs. Frank.

Mrs. Frank. Thank you. (*Then, to* Miep *as she goes to the table to cut the cake*) Are you sure you won't have some?

Miep (*drinking her tea*). No, really, I have to go in a minute.

[*The sound of the band fades out in the distance.*]

Peter (*to* Miep). Maybe Mouschi went back to our house . . . they say that cats . . . Do you ever get over there . . . ? I mean . . . do you suppose you could . . . ?

Miep. I'll try, Peter. The first minute I get I'll try. But I'm afraid, with him gone a week . . .

Dussel. Make up your mind, already someone has had a nice big dinner from that cat!

[Peter *is furious, inarticulate. He starts toward* Dussel *as if to hit him.* Mr. Frank *stops him.* Mrs. Frank *speaks quickly to ease the situation.*]

Mrs. Frank (*to* Miep). This is delicious, Miep!

Mrs. Van Daan (*eating hers*). Delicious!

Mr. Van Daan (*finishing it in one gulp*). Dirk's in luck to get a girl who can bake like this!

Miep (*putting down her empty teacup*). I have to run. Dirk's taking me to a party tonight.

Anne. How heavenly! Remember now what everyone is wearing, and what you have to eat and everything, so you can tell us tomorrow.

Miep. I'll give you a full report! Goodbye, everyone!

Mr. Van Daan (*to* Miep). Just a minute. There's something I'd like you to do for me. (*He hurries off up the stairs to his room.*)

Mrs. Van Daan (*sharply*). Putti, where are you going? (*She rushes up the stairs after him, calling hysterically.*) What do you want? Putti, what are you going to do?

Miep (*to* Peter). What's wrong?

Peter (*His sympathy is with his mother*). Father says he's going to sell her fur coat. She's crazy about that old fur coat.

Dussel. Is it possible? Is is possible that anyone is so silly as to worry about a fur coat in times like this?

Peter. It's none of your darn business . . . and if you say one more thing . . . I'll, I'll take you and I'll . . . I mean it . . . I'll . . .

[*There is a piercing scream from* Mrs. Van Daan *above. She grabs at the fur coat as* Mr. Van Daan *is starting downstairs with it.*]

Mrs. Van Daan. No! No! No! Don't you dare take that! You hear? It's mine! (*Downstairs* Peter *turns away, embarrassed, miserable.*) My father gave me that! You didn't give it to me. You have no right. Let go of it . . . you hear?

[Mr. Van Daan *pulls the coat from her hands and hurries downstairs.* Mrs. Van Daan *sinks to the floor sobbing. As* Mr. Van Daan *comes into the main room the others look away, embarrassed for him.*]

Mr. Van Daan (*to* Mr. Kraler). Just a little—discussion over the advisability of selling this coat. As I have often reminded Mrs. Van Daan, it's very selfish of her to keep it when people outside are in such desperate need of clothing. . . . (*He gives the coat to* Miep.) So if you will please to sell it for us? It should fetch a good price. And by the way, will you get me cigarettes. I don't care what kind they are . . . get all you can.

Miep. It's terribly difficult to get them, Mr. Van Daan. But I'll try. Goodbye.

[*She goes.* Mr. Frank *follows her down the steps to bolt the door after her.* Mrs. Frank *gives* Mr. Kraler *a cup of tea.*]

Mrs. Frank. Are you sure you won't have some cake, Mr. Kraler?

Mr. Kraler. I'd better not.

Mr. Van Daan. You're still feeling badly? What does your doctor say?

Mr. Kraler. I haven't been to him.

Mrs. Frank. Now Mr. Kraler! . . .

Mr. Kraler (*sitting at the table*). Oh, I tried. But you can't get near a doctor these days . . . they're so busy. After weeks I finally managed to get one on the telephone. I told him I'd like an appointment . . . I wasn't feeling very well. You know what he answers . . . over the telephone . . . Stick out your tongue! (*They laugh. He turns to* Mr. Frank *as* Mr. Frank *comes back.*) I have some contracts here. . . . I wonder if you'd look over them with me. . . .

Mr. Frank (*putting out his hand*). Of course.

Mr. Kraler (*He rises*). If we could go downstairs . . . (Mr. Frank *starts ahead;* Mr. Kraler *speaks to the others.*) Will you forgive us? I won't keep him but a minute. (*He starts to follow* Mr. Frank *down the steps.*)

Margot (*with sudden foreboding*). What's happened? Something's happened! Hasn't it, Mr. Kraler?

[Mr. Kraler *stops and comes back, trying to reassure* Margot *with a pretense of casualness.*]

Mr. Kraler. No, really. I want your father's advice. . . .

Margot. Something's gone wrong! I know it!

Mr. Frank (*coming back, to* Mr. Kraler). If it's something that concerns us here, it's better that we all hear it.

Mr. Kraler (*turning to him, quietly*). But . . . the children . . . ?

Mr. Frank. What they'd imagine would be worse than any reality.

[*As* Mr. Kraler *speaks, they all listen with intense apprehension.* Mrs. Van Daan *comes down the stairs and sits on the bottom step.*]

Mr. Kraler. It's a man in the storeroom. . . . I don't know whether or not you remember him . . . Carl, about fifty, heavyset, near-sighted . . . He came with us just before you left.

Mr. Frank. He was from Utrecht?

Mr. Kraler. That's the man. A couple of weeks ago, when I was in the storeroom, he closed the door and asked me . . . how's Mr. Frank? What do you hear from Mr. Frank? I told him I only knew there was a rumor that you were in Switzerland. He said he'd heard that rumor too, but he thought I might know something more. I didn't pay any attention to it . . . but then a thing happened yesterday. . . . He'd brought some invoices to the office for me to sign. As I was going through them, I looked up. He was standing staring at the bookcase . . . your bookcase. He said he thought he remembered a door there. . . . Wasn't there a door there that used to go up to the loft? Then he told me he wanted more money. Twenty guilders[2] more a week.

Mr. Van Daan. Blackmail!

Mr. Frank. Twenty guilders? Very modest blackmail.

Mr. Van Daan. That's just the beginning.

2. **Twenty guilders:** about five dollars at the time.

Dussel (*coming to* Mr. Frank). You know what I think? He was the thief who was down there that night. That's how he knows we're here.

Mr. Frank (*to* Mr. Kraler). How was it left? What did you tell him?

Mr. Kraler. I said I had to think about it. What shall I do? Pay him the money? . . . Take a chance on firing him . . . or what? I don't know.

Dussel (*frantic*). For God's sake don't fire him! Pay him what he asks . . . keep him here where you can have your eye on him.

Mr. Frank. Is it so much that he's asking? What are they paying nowadays?

Mr. Kraler. He could get it in a war plant. But this isn't a war plant. Mind you, I don't know if he really knows . . . or if he doesn't know.

Mr. Frank. Offer him half. Then we'll soon find out if it's blackmail or not.

Dussel. And if it is? We've got to pay it, haven't we? Anything he asks we've got to pay!

Mr. Frank. Let's decide that when the time comes.

Mr. Kraler. This may be all imagination. You get to a point, these days, where you suspect everyone and everything. Again and again . . . on some simple look or word, I've found myself . . .

[*The telephone rings in the office below.*]

Mrs. Van Daan (*hurrying to* Mr. Kraler). There's the telephone! What does that mean, the telephone ringing on a holiday?

Mr. Kraler. That's my wife. I told her I had to go over some papers in my office . . . to call me there when she got out of church. (*He starts out.*) I'll offer him half then. Goodbye . . . we'll hope for the best!

[*The group call their goodbyes halfheartedly. Mr. Frank follows Mr. Kraler, to bolt the door below. During the following scene, Mr. Frank comes back up and stands listening, disturbed.*]

Dussel (*to* Mr. Van Daan). You can thank your son for this . . . smashing the light! I tell you, it's just a question of time now. (*He goes to the window at the back and stands looking out.*)

Margot. Sometimes I wish the end would come . . . whatever it is.

Mrs. Frank (*shocked*). Margot!

[Anne *goes to* Margot, *sitting beside her on the couch with her arms around her.*]

Margot. Then at least we'd know where we were.

Mrs. Frank. You should be ashamed of yourself! Talking that way! Think how lucky we are! Think of the thousands dying in the war, every day. Think of the people in concentration camps.

Anne (*interrupting*). What's the good of that? What's the good of thinking of misery when you're already miserable? That's stupid!

Mrs. Frank. Anne!

[As Anne *goes on raging at her mother,* Mrs. Frank *tries to break in, in an effort to quiet her.*]

Anne. We're young. Margot and Peter and I! You grown-ups have had your chance! But look at us. . . . If we begin thinking of all the horror in the world, we're lost! We're trying to hold on to some kind of ideals . . . when everything . . . ideals, hopes . . . everything, are being destroyed! It isn't our fault that the world is in such a mess! We weren't around when all this started! So don't try to take it out on us! (*She rushes off to her room, slamming the door after her. She picks up a brush from the chest and hurls it to the floor. Then she sits on the settee, trying to control her anger.*)

Mr. Van Daan. She talks as if we started the war! Did we start the war?

[*He spots* Anne's *cake. As he starts to take it,* Peter *anticipates him.*]

Peter. She left her cake. (*He starts for* Anne's *room with the cake. There is silence in the main room.* Mrs. Van Daan *goes up to her room, followed by* Mr. Van Daan. Dussel *stays looking out the window.* Mr. Frank *brings* Mrs. Frank *her cake. She eats it slowly, without relish.* Mr. Frank *takes his cake to* Margot *and sits quietly on the sofa beside her.* Peter *stands in the doorway of* Anne's *darkened room, looking at her, then makes a little movement to let her know he is there.* Anne *sits up, quickly, trying to hide the signs of her tears.* Peter *holds out the cake to her.*) You left this.
Anne (*dully*). Thanks.

[Peter *starts to go out, then comes back.*]

Peter. I thought you were fine just now. You know just how to talk to them. You know just how to say it. I'm no good . . . I never can think . . . especially when I'm mad. . . . That Dussel . . . when he said that about Mouschi . . . someone eating him . . . all I could think is . . . I wanted to hit him. I wanted to give him such a . . . a . . . that he'd . . . That's what I used to do when there was an argument at school. . . . That's the way I . . . but here . . . And an old man like that . . . it wouldn't be so good.
Anne. You're making a big mistake about me. I do it all wrong. I say too much. I go too far. I hurt people's feelings. . . .

[Dussel *leaves the window, going to his room.*]

Peter. I think you're just fine. . . . What I want to say . . . if it wasn't for you around here, I don't know. What I mean . . .

[Peter *is interrupted by* Dussel's *turning on the light.* Dussel *stands in the doorway, startled to see* Peter. Peter *advances toward him forbiddingly.* Dussel *backs out of the room.* Peter *closes the door on him.*]

Anne. Do you mean it, Peter? Do you really mean it?
Peter. I said it, didn't I?
Anne. Thank you, Peter!

[*In the main room* Mr. *and* Mrs. Frank *collect the dishes and take them to the sink, washing them.* Margot *lies down again on the couch.* Dussel, *lost, wanders into* Peter's *room and takes up a book, starting to read.*]

Peter (*looking at the photographs on the wall*). You've got quite a collection.
Anne. Wouldn't you like some in your room? I could give you some. Heaven knows you spend enough time in there . . . doing heaven knows what. . . .
Peter. It's easier. A fight starts, or an argument . . . I duck in there.
Anne. You're lucky, having a room to go to. His Lordship is always here. . . . I hardly ever get a minute alone. When they start in on me, I can't duck away. I have to stand there and take it.
Peter. You gave some of it back just now.
Anne. I get so mad. They've formed their opinions . . . about everything . . . but we . . . we're still trying to find out. . . . We have problems here that no other people our age have ever had. And just as you think you've solved them, something comes along and bang! You have to start all over again.
Peter. At least you've got someone you can talk to.
Anne. Not really. Mother . . . I never discuss anything serious with her. She doesn't understand. Father's all right. We can talk about everything . . . everything but one thing. Mother. He simply won't talk about her. I don't think you can be really intimate with anyone if he holds something back, do you?
Peter. I think your father's fine.
Anne. Oh, he is, Peter! He is! He's the only one

who's ever given me the feeling that I have any sense. But anyway, nothing can take the place of school and play and friends of your own age . . . or near your age . . . can it?

Peter. I suppose you miss your friends and all.

Anne. It isn't just . . . (*She breaks off, staring up at him for a second.*) Isn't it funny, you and I? Here we've been seeing each other every minute for almost a year and a half, and this is the first time we've ever really talked. It helps a lot to have someone to talk to, don't you think? It helps you to let off steam.

Peter (*going to the door*). Well, any time you want to let off steam, you can come into my room.

Anne (*following him*). I can get up an awful lot of steam. You'll have to be careful how you say that.

Peter. It's all right with me.

Anne. Do you really mean it?

Peter. I said it, didn't I?

[*He goes out.* Anne *stands in her doorway looking after him. As* Peter *gets to his door, he stands for a minute looking back at her. Then he goes into his room.* Dussel *rises as he comes in, and quickly passes him, going out. He starts across for his room.* Anne *sees him coming and pulls her door shut.* Dussel *turns back toward* Peter's *room.* Peter *pulls his door shut.* Dussel *stands there, bewildered, forlorn.*

The scene slowly dims out. The curtain falls on the scene. Anne's *voice comes over in the darkness . . . faintly at first, and then with growing strength.*]

Anne's Voice. We've had bad news. The people from whom Miep got our ration books have been arrested. So we have had to cut down on our food. Our stomachs are so empty that they rumble and make strange noises, all in different keys. Mr. Van Daan's is deep and low, like a bass fiddle. Mine is high, whistling like a flute. As we all sit around waiting for supper, it's like an orchestra tuning up. It only needs

Toscanini[3] to raise his baton and we'd be off in the "Ride of the Valkyries."[4] Monday, the sixth of March, nineteen forty-four. Mr. Kraler is in the hospital. It seems he has ulcers. Pim says we are his ulcers. Miep has to run the business and us too. The Americans have landed on the southern tip of Italy. Father looks for a quick finish to the war. Mr. Dussel is waiting every day for the warehouseman to demand more money. Have I been skipping too much from one subject to another? I can't help it. I feel that spring is coming. I feel it in my whole body and soul. I feel utterly confused. I am longing . . . so longing . . . for everything . . . for friends . . . for someone to talk to . . . someone who understands . . . someone young, who feels as I do. . . .

[*As these last lines are being said, the curtain rises on the scene. The lights dim on.* Anne's *voice fades out.*]

Scene 2

It is evening, after supper. From the outside we hear the sound of children playing. The "grown-ups," with the exception of Mr. Van Daan, *are all in the main room.* Mrs. Frank *is doing some mending.* Mrs. Van Daan *is reading a fashion magazine.* Mr. Frank *is going over business accounts.* Dussel, *in his dentist's jacket, is pacing up and down, impatient to get into his bedroom.* Mr. Van Daan *is upstairs working on a piece of embroidery in an embroidery frame.*

In his room Peter *is sitting before the mirror, smoothing his hair. As the scene goes on, he puts on his tie, brushes his coat and puts it on, preparing himself meticulously for a visit from* Anne. *On his*

3. **Toscanini** (tŏs′kə-nē′nē): Arturo Toscanini, a famous conductor.
4. **"Ride of the Valkyries"** (văl-kîr′ēz): a rousing piece of music from an opera by the German composer Richard Wagner.

wall are now hung some of Anne's *motion-picture stars.*

In her room Anne *too is getting dressed. She stands before the mirror in her slip, trying various ways of dressing her hair.* Margot *is seated on the sofa, hemming a skirt for* Anne *to wear.*

In the main room Dussel *can stand it no longer. He comes over, rapping sharply on the door of his and* Anne's *bedroom.*

Anne (*calling to him*). No, no, Mr. Dussel! I am not dressed yet. (Dussel *walks away, furious, sitting down and burying his head in his hands.* Anne *turn to* Margot.) How is that? How does that look?

Margot (*glancing at her briefly*). Fine.

Anne. You didn't even look.

Margot. Of course I did. It's fine.

Anne. Margot, tell me, am I terribly ugly?

Margot. Oh, stop fishing.

Anne. No. No. Tell me.

Margot. Of course you're not. You've got nice eyes . . . and a lot of animation, and . . .

Anne. A little vague, aren't you?

[*She reaches over and takes a brassière out of* Margot's *sewing basket. She holds it up to herself, studying the effect in the mirror. Outside,* Mrs. Frank, *feeling sorry for* Dussel, *comes over, knocking at the girls' door.*]

Mrs. Frank (*outside*). May I come in?

Margot. Come in, Mother.

Mrs. Frank (*shutting the door behind her*). Mr. Dussel's impatient to get in here.

Anne (*still with the brassière*). Heavens, he takes the room for himself the entire day.

Mrs. Frank (*gently*). Anne, dear, you're not going in again tonight to see Peter?

Anne (*dignified*). That is my intention.

Mrs. Frank. But you've already spent a great deal of time in there today.

Anne. I was in there exactly twice. Once to get the dictionary, and then three quarters of an hour before supper.

Mrs. Frank. Aren't you afraid you're disturbing him?

Anne. Mother, I have some intuition.

Mrs. Frank. Then may I ask you this much, Anne. Please don't shut the door when you go in.

Anne. You sound like Mrs. Van Daan!

[*She throws the brassière back in* Margot's *sewing basket and picks up her blouse, putting it on.*]

Mrs. Frank. No. No. I don't mean to suggest anything wrong. I only wish that you wouldn't expose yourself to criticism . . . that you wouldn't give Mrs. Van Daan the opportunity to be unpleasant!

Anne. Mrs. Van Daan doesn't need an opportunity to be unpleasant!

Mrs. Frank. Everyone's on edge, worried about Mr. Kraler. This is one more thing. . . .

Anne. I'm sorry, Mother. I'm going to Peter's room. I'm not going to let Petronella Van Daan spoil our friendship.

[Mrs. Frank *hesitates for a second, then goes out, closing the door after her. She gets a pack of playing cards and sits at the center table, playing solitaire. In* Anne's *room* Margot *hands the finished skirt to* Anne. *As* Anne *is putting it on,* Margot *takes off her high-heeled shoes and stuffs paper in the toes so that* Anne *can wear them.*]

Margot (*to* Anne). Why don't you two talk in the main room? It'd save a lot of trouble. It's hard on Mother, having to listen to those remarks from Mrs. Van Daan and not say a word.

Anne. Why doesn't she say a word? I think it's ridiculous to take it and take it.

Margot. You don't understand Mother at all, do you? She can't talk back. She's not like you. It's just not in her nature to fight back.

Anne. Anyway . . . the only one I worry about is

you. I feel awfully guilty about you. (*She sits on the stool near* Margot, *putting on* Margot's *high-heeled shoes.*)

Margot. What about?

Anne. I mean, every time I go into Peter's room, I have a feeling I may be hurting you. (Margot *shakes her head.*) I know if it were me, I'd be wild. I'd be desperately jealous, if it were me.

Margot. Well, I'm not.

Anne. You don't feel badly? Really? Truly? You're not jealous?

Margot. Of course I'm jealous . . . jealous that you've got something to get up in the morning for . . . But jealous of you and Peter? No.

[Anne *goes back to the mirror.*]

Anne. Maybe there's nothing to be jealous of. Maybe he doesn't really like me. Maybe I'm just taking the place of his cat. . . . (*She picks up a pair of short, white gloves, putting them on.*) Wouldn't you like to come in with us?

Margot. I have a book.

[*The sound of the children playing outside fades out. In the main room* Dussel *can stand it no longer. He jumps up, going to the bedroom door and knocking sharply.*]

Dussel. Will you please let me in my room!

Anne. Just a minute, dear, dear Mr. Dussel. (*She picks up her mother's pink stole and adjusts it elegantly over her shoulders, then gives a last look in the mirror.*) Well, here I go . . . to run the gantlet.[5] (*She starts out, followed by* Margot.)

Dussel (*as she appears—sarcastic*). Thank you so much.

[Dussel *goes into his room.* Anne *goes toward* Peter's *room, passing* Mrs. Van Daan *and her parents at the center table.*]

Mrs. Van Daan. My God, look at her! (Anne *pays no attention. She knocks at* Peter's *door.*) I don't know what good it is to have a son. I

5. **run the gantlet** (gônt′lĭt): go forward under attack from both sides.

never see him. He wouldn't care if I killed myself. (Peter *opens the door and stands aside for* Anne *to come in.*) Just a minute, Anne. (*She goes to them at the door.*) I'd like to say a few words to my son. Do you mind? (Peter *and* Anne *stand waiting.*) Peter, I don't want you staying up till all hours tonight. You've got to have your sleep. You're a growing boy. You hear?

Mrs. Frank. Anne won't stay late. She's going to bed promptly at nine. Aren't you, Anne?

Anne. Yes, Mother . . . (*to* Mrs. Van Daan) May we go now?

Mrs. Van Daan. Are you asking me? I didn't know I had anything to say about it.

Mrs. Frank. Listen for the chimes, Anne dear.

[*The two young people go off into* Peter's *room, shutting the door after them.*]

Mrs. Van Daan (*to* Mrs. Frank). In my day it was the boys who called on the girls. Not the girls on the boys.

Mrs. Frank. You know how young people like to feel that they have secrets. Peter's room is the only place where they can talk.

Mrs. Van Daan. Talk! That's not what they called it when I was young.

[Mrs. Van Daan *goes off to the bathroom.* Margot *settles down to read her book.* Mr. Frank *puts his papers away and brings a chess game to the center table. He and* Mrs. Frank *start to play. In* Peter's *room,* Anne *speaks to* Peter, *indignant, humiliated.*]

Anne. Aren't they awful? Aren't they impossible? Treating us as if we were still in the nursery.

[*She sits on the cot.* Peter *gets a bottle of pop and two glasses.*]

Peter. Don't let it bother you. It doesn't bother me.

Anne. I suppose you can't really blame them . . . they think back to what *they* were like at our age. They don't realize how much more advanced we are. . . . When you think what wonderful discussions we've had! . . . Oh, I forgot. I was going to bring you some more pictures.

Peter. Oh, these are fine, thanks.

Anne. Don't you want some more? Miep just brought me some new ones.

Peter. Maybe later. (*He gives her a glass of pop and, taking some for himself, sits down facing her.*)

Anne (*looking up at one of the photographs*). I remember when I got that. . . . I won it. I bet Jopie that I could eat five ice-cream cones. We'd all been playing ping-pong. . . . We used to have heavenly times . . . we'd finish up with ice cream at the Delphi, or the Oasis, where Jews were allowed . . . there'd always be a lot of boys . . . we'd laugh and joke . . . I'd like to go back to it for a few days or a week. But after that I know I'd be bored to death. I think more seriously about life now. I want to be a journalist . . . or something. I love to write. What do you want to do?

Peter. I thought I might go off someplace . . . work on a farm or something . . . some job that doesn't take much brains.

Anne. You shouldn't talk that way. You've got the most awful inferiority complex.

Peter. I know I'm not smart.

Anne. That isn't true. You're much better than I am in dozens of things . . . arithmetic and algebra and . . . well, you're a million times better than I am in algebra. (*With sudden directness*) You like Margot, don't you? Right from the start you liked her, liked her much better than me.

Peter (*uncomfortably*). Oh, I don't know.

[*In the main room* Mrs. Van Daan *comes from the bathroom and goes over to the sink, polishing a coffeepot.*]

Anne. It's all right. Everyone feels that way. Margot's so good. She's sweet and bright and beautiful and I'm not.

Peter. I wouldn't say that.

Anne. Oh, no, I'm not. I know that. I know quite well that I'm not a beauty. I never have been and never shall be.

Peter. I don't agree at all. I think you're pretty.

Anne. That's not true!

Peter. And another thing. You've changed . . . from at first, I mean.

Anne. I have?

Peter. I used to think you were awful noisy.

Anne. And what do you think now, Peter? How have I changed?

Peter. Well . . . er . . . you're . . . quieter.

[*In his room* Dussel *takes his pajamas and toilet articles and goes into the bathroom to change.*]

Anne. I'm glad you don't just hate me.

Peter. I never said that.

Anne. I bet when you get out of here you'll never think of me again.

Peter. That's crazy.

Anne. When you get back with all of your friends, you're going to say . . . now what did I ever see in that Mrs. Quack Quack.

Peter. I haven't got any friends.

Anne. Oh, Peter, of course you have. Everyone has friends.

Peter. Not me. I don't want any. I get along all right without them.

Anne. Does that mean you can get along without me? I think of myself as your friend.

Peter. No. If they were all like you, it'd be different.

[*He takes the glasses and the bottle and puts them away. There is a second's silence and then* Anne *speaks, hesitantly, shyly.*]

Anne. Peter, did you ever kiss a girl?

Peter. Yes. Once.

Anne (*to cover her feelings*). That picture's crooked. (Peter *goes over, straightening the photograph.*) Was she pretty?

Peter. Huh?

Anne. The girl that you kissed.

Peter. I don't know. I was blindfolded. (*He comes back and sits down again.*) It was at a party. One of those kissing games.

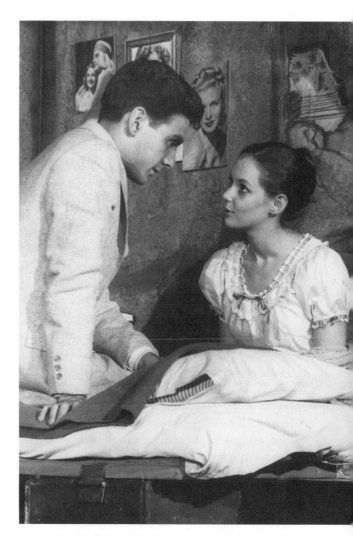

Anne (*relieved*). Oh, I don't suppose that really counts, does it?

Peter. It didn't with me.

Anne. I've been kissed twice. Once a man I'd never seen before kissed me on the cheek when he picked me up off the ice and I was crying. And the other was Mr. Koophuis, a friend of Father's who kissed my hand. You wouldn't say those counted, would you?

Peter. I wouldn't say so.

Anne. I know almost for certain that Margot would never kiss anyone unless she was engaged to them. And I'm sure too that Mother never touched a man before Pim. But I don't know . . . things are so different now. . . . What do you think? Do you think a girl shouldn't kiss anyone except if she's engaged or something? It's so hard to try to think what to do, when here we are with the whole world falling around our ears and you think . . . well . . . you don't know what's going to happen tomorrow and . . . What do you think?

Peter. I suppose it'd depend on the girl. Some girls, anything they do's wrong. But others . . . well . . . it wouldn't necessarily be wrong with them. (*The carillon starts to strike nine o'clock.*) I've always thought that when two people . . .

Anne. Nine o'clock. I have to go.

Peter. That's right.

Anne (*without moving*). Good night.

[*There is a second's pause; then* Peter *gets up and moves toward the door.*]

Peter. You won't let them stop you coming?

Anne. No. (*She rises and starts for the door.*) Sometime I might bring my diary. There are so many things in it that I want to talk over with you. There's a lot about you.

Peter. What kind of thing?

Anne. I wouldn't want you to see some of it. I thought you were a nothing, just the way you thought about me.

Peter. Did you change your mind, the way I changed my mind about you?

Anne. Well . . . You'll see. . . .

[*For a second* Anne *stands looking up at* Peter, *longing for him to kiss her. As he makes no move she turns away. Then suddenly* Peter *grabs her awkwardly in his arms, kissing her on the cheek.* Anne *walks out dazed. She stands for a minute, her back to the people in the main room. As she regains her poise she goes to her mother and father and* Margot, *silently kissing them. They murmur their good-nights*

to her. As she is about to open her bedroom door, she catches sight of* Mrs. Van Daan. *She goes quickly to her, taking her face in her hands and kissing her first on one cheek and then on the other. Then she hurries off into her room.* Mrs. Van Daan *looks after her and then looks over at* Peter's *room. Her suspicions are confirmed.*]

Mrs. Van Daan (*She knows*). Ah hah!

[*The lights dim out. The curtain falls on the scene. In the darkness* Anne's *voice comes faintly at first, and then with growing strength.*]

Anne's Voice. By this time we all know each other so well that if anyone starts to tell a story, the rest can finish it for him. We're having to cut down still further on our meals. What makes it worse, the rats have been at work again. They've carried off some of our precious food. Even Mr. Dussel wishes now that Mouschi was here. Thursday, the twentieth of April, nineteen forty-four. Invasion fever is mounting every day. Miep tells us that people outside talk of nothing else. For myself, life has become much more pleasant. I often go to Peter's room after supper. Oh, don't think I'm in love, because I'm not. But it does make life more bearable to have someone with whom you can exchange views. No more tonight. P.S. . . . I must be honest. I must confess that I actually live for the next meeting. Is there anything lovelier than to sit under the skylight and feel the sun on your cheeks and have a darling boy in your arms? I admit now that I'm glad the Van Daans had a son and not a daughter. I've outgrown another dress. That's the third. I'm having to wear Margot's clothes after all. I'm working hard on my French and am now reading *La Belle Nivernaise*.[6]

6. *La Belle Nivernaise:* a novel by the French writer Alphonse Daudet.

[As she is saying the last lines, the curtain rises on the scene. The lights dim on as Anne's voice fades out.]

Scene 3

It is night, a few weeks later. Everyone is in bed. There is complete quiet. In the Van Daans' *room a match flares up for a moment and then is quickly put out.* Mr. Van Daan, *in bare feet, dressed in underwear and trousers, is dimly seen coming stealthily down the stairs and into the main room, where* Mr. *and* Mrs. Frank *and* Margot *are sleeping. He goes to the food safe and again lights a match. Then he cautiously opens the safe, taking out a half-loaf of bread. As he closes the safe, it creaks. He stands rigid.* Mrs. Frank *sits up in bed. She sees him.*

Mrs. Frank (*screaming*). Otto! Otto! Komme schnell![7]

[The rest of the people wake, hurriedly getting up.]

Mr. Frank. Was ist los? Was ist passiert?[8]

[Dussel, followed by Anne, *comes from his room.]*

Mrs. Frank (*as she rushes over to* Mr. Van Daan). Er stiehlt das Essen![9]

Dussel (*grabbing* Mr. Van Daan). You! You! Give me that.

Mrs. Van Daan (*coming down the stairs*). Putti . . . Putti . . . what is it?

Dussel (*his hands on* Van Daan's *neck*). You dirty thief . . . stealing food . . . you good-for-nothing . . .

Mr. Frank. Mr. Dussel! For God's sake! Help me, Peter!

7. *Komme schnell!:* Come quickly!
8. *Was ist los? Was ist passiert?:* What's wrong? What happened?
9. *Er stiehlt das Essen!:* He's stealing the food!

[Peter comes over, trying, with Mr. Frank, *to separate the two struggling men.]*

Peter. Let him go! Let go!

[Dussel drops Mr. Van Daan, *pushing him away. He shows them the end of a loaf of bread that he has taken from* Mr. Van Daan.]*

Dussel. You greedy, selfish . . .

[Margot turns on the lights.]

Mrs. Van Daan. Putti . . . what is it?

[All of Mrs. Frank's *gentleness, her self-control, is gone. She is outraged, in a frenzy of indignation.]*

Mrs. Frank. The bread! He was stealing the bread!

Dussel. It was you, and all the time we thought it was the rats!

Mr. Frank. Mr. Van Daan, how could you!

Mr. Van Daan. I'm hungry.

Mrs. Frank. We're all of us hungry! I see the children getting thinner and thinner. Your own son Peter . . . I've heard him moan in his sleep, he's so hungry. And you come in the night and steal food that should go to them . . . to the children!

Mrs. Van Daan (*going to* Mr. Van Daan *protectively*). He needs more food than the rest of us. He's used to more. He's a big man.

[Mr. Van Daan breaks away, going over and sitting on the couch.]

Mrs. Frank (*turning on* Mrs. Van Daan). And you . . . you're worse than he is! You're a mother, and yet you sacrifice your child to this man . . . this . . . this . . .

Mr. Frank. Edith! Edith!

[Margot *picks up the pink woolen stole, putting it over her mother's shoulders.*]

Mrs. Frank (*paying no attention, going on to* Mrs. Van Daan). Don't think I haven't seen you! Always saving the choicest bits for him! I've watched you day after day and I've held my tongue. But not any longer! Not after this! Now I want him to go! I want him to get out of here!

Mr. Frank. Edith!

Mr. Van Daan. Get out of here? } (*Together*)

Mrs. Van Daan. What do you mean?

Mrs. Frank. Just that! Take your things and get out!

Mr. Frank (*to* Mrs. Frank). You're speaking in anger. You cannot mean what you are saying.

Mrs. Frank. I mean exactly that!

[Mrs. Van Daan *takes a cover from the* Franks' *bed, pulling it about her.*]

Mr. Frank. For two long years we have lived here, side by side. We have respected each other's rights . . . we have managed to live in peace. Are we now going to throw it all away? I know this will never happen again, will it, Mr. Van Daan?

Mr. Van Daan. No. No.

Mrs. Frank. He steals once! He'll steal again!

[Mr. Van Daan, *holding his stomach, starts for the bathroom.* Anne *puts her arms around him, helping him up the step.*]

Mr. Frank. Edith, please. Let us be calm. We'll all go to our rooms . . . and afterwards we'll sit down quietly and talk this out . . . we'll find some way . . .

Mrs. Frank. No! No! No more talk! I want them to leave!

Mrs. Van Daan. You'd put us out, on the streets?

Mrs. Frank. There are other hiding places.

Mrs. Van Daan. A cellar . . . a closet. I know. And we have no money left even to pay for that.

Mrs. Frank. I'll give you money. Out of my own pocket I'll give it gladly. (*She gets her purse from a shelf and comes back with it.*)

Mrs. Van Daan. Mr. Frank, you told Putti you'd never forget what he'd done for you when you came to Amsterdam. You said you could never repay him, that you . . .

Mrs. Frank (*counting out money*). If my husband had any obligation to you, he's paid it, over and over.

Mr. Frank. Edith, I've never seen you like this before. I don't know you.

Mrs. Frank. I should have spoken out long ago.

Dussel. You can't be nice to some people.

Mrs. Van Daan (*turning on* Dussel). There would have been plenty for all of us, if *you* hadn't come in here!

Mr. Frank. We don't need the Nazis to destroy us. We're destroying ourselves.

[He *sits down, with his head in his hands.* Mrs. Frank *goes to* Mrs. Van Daan.]

Mrs. Frank (*giving* Mrs. Van Daan *some money*). Give this to Miep. She'll find you a place.

Anne. Mother, you're not putting *Peter* out. Peter hasn't done anything.

Mrs. Frank. He'll stay, of course. When I say I must protect the children, I mean Peter too.

[Peter *rises from the steps where he has been sitting.*]

Peter. I'd have to go if Father goes.

[Mr. Van Daan *comes from the bathroom.* Mrs. Van Daan *hurries to him and takes him to the couch. Then she gets water from the sink to bathe his face.*]

Mrs. Frank (*while this is going on*). He's no

father to you . . . that man! He doesn't know what it is to be a father!

Peter (*starting for his room*). I wouldn't feel right. I couldn't stay.

Mrs. Frank. Very well, then. I'm sorry.

Anne (*rushing over to* Peter). No, Peter! No! (Peter *goes into his room, closing the door after him.* Anne *turns back to her mother, crying.*) I don't care about the food. They can have mine! I don't want it! Only don't send them away. It'll be daylight soon. They'll be caught. . . .

Margot (*putting her arms comfortingly around* Anne). Please, Mother!

Mrs. Frank. They're not going now. They'll stay here until Miep finds them a place. (*To* Mrs. Van Daan) But one thing I insist on! He must never come down here again! He must never come to this room where the food is stored! We'll divide what we have . . . an equal share for each! (Dussel *hurries over to get a sack of potatoes from the food safe.* Mrs. Frank *goes on, to* Mrs. Van Daan.) You can cook it here and take it up to him.

[Dussel *brings the sack of potatoes back to the center table.*]

Margot. Oh, no. No. We haven't sunk so far that we're going to fight over a handful of rotten potatoes.

Dussel (*dividing the potatoes into piles*). Mrs. Frank, Mr. Frank, Margot, Anne, Peter, Mrs. Van Daan, Mr. Van Daan, myself . . . Mrs. Frank . . .

[*The buzzer sounds in* Miep's *signal.*]

Mr. Frank. It's Miep! (*He hurries over, getting his overcoat and putting it on.*)

Margot. At this hour?

Mrs. Frank. It is trouble.

Mr. Frank (*as he starts down to unbolt the door*). I beg you, don't let her see a thing like this!

Mr. Dussel (*counting without stopping*). . . . Anne, Peter, Mrs. Van Daan, Mr. Van Daan, myself . . .

Margot (*to* Dussel). Stop it! Stop it!

Dussel. . . . Mr. Frank, Margot, Anne, Peter, Mrs. Van Daan, Mr. Van Daan, myself, Mrs. Frank . . .

Mrs. Van Daan. You're keeping the big ones for yourself! All the big ones . . . Look at the size of that! . . . And that! . . .

[Dussel *continues on with his dividing.* Peter, *with his shirt and trousers on, comes from his room.*]

Margot. Stop it! Stop it!

[*We hear* Miep's *excited voice speaking to* Mr. Frank *below.*]

Miep. Mr. Frank . . . the most wonderful news! . . . The invasion has begun!

Mr. Frank. Go on, tell them! Tell them!

[Miep *comes running up the steps, ahead of* Mr. Frank. *She has a man's raincoat on over her night-clothes and a bunch of orange-colored flowers in her hand.*]

Miep. Did you hear that, everybody? Did you hear what I said? The invasion has begun! The invasion!

[*They all stare at* Miep, *unable to grasp what she is telling them.* Peter *is the first to recover his wits.*]

Peter. Where?

Mrs. Van Daan. When? When, Miep?

Miep. It began early this morning. . . .

[*As she talks on, the realization of what she has said begins to dawn on them. Everyone goes crazy. A wild demonstration takes place.* Mrs. Frank *hugs* Mr. Van Daan.]

Mrs. Frank. Oh, Mr. Van Daan, did you hear that?

[Dussel *embraces* Mrs. Van Daan. Peter *grabs a frying pan and parades around the room, beating on it, singing the Dutch national anthem.* Anne *and* Margot *follow him, singing, weaving in and out among the excited grown-ups.* Margot *breaks away to take the flowers from* Miep *and distribute them to everyone. While this pandemonium is going on* Mrs. Frank *tries to make herself heard above the excitement.*]

Mrs. Frank (*to* Miep). How do you know?
Miep. The radio . . . The B.B.C.![10] They said they landed on the coast of Normandy!
Peter. The British?
Miep. British, Americans, French, Dutch, Poles, Norwegians . . . all of them! More than four thousand ships! Churchill[11] spoke, and General Eisenhower![12] D-Day they call it!
Mr. Frank. Thank God, it's come!
Mrs. Van Daan. At last!
Miep (*starting out*). I'm going to tell Mr. Kraler. This'll be better than any blood transfusion.
Mr. Frank (*stopping her*). What part of Normandy did they land, did they say?
Miep. Normandy . . . that's all I know now. . . . I'll be up the minute I hear some more! (*She goes hurriedly out.*)
Mr. Frank (*to* Mrs. Frank). What did I tell you? What did I tell you?

[Mrs. Frank *indicates that he has forgotten to bolt the door after* Miep. *He hurries down the steps.* Mr. Van Daan, *sitting on the couch, suddenly*

breaks into a convulsive sob. Everybody looks at him, bewildered.]

Mrs. Van Daan (*hurrying to him*). Putti! Putti! What is it? What happened?
Mr. Van Daan. Please. I'm so ashamed.

[Mr. Frank *comes back up the steps.*]

Dussel. Oh, for God's sake!
Mrs. Van Daan. Don't, Putti.
Margot. It doesn't matter now!
Mr. Frank (*going to* Mr. Van Daan). Didn't you hear what Miep said? The invasion has come! We're going to be liberated! This is a time to celebrate. (*He embraces* Mrs. Frank *and then hurries to the cupboard and gets the cognac and a glass.*)
Mr. Van Daan. To steal bread from children!
Mrs. Frank. We've all done things that we're ashamed of.
Anne. Look at me, the way I've treated Mother . . . so mean and horrid to her.
Mrs. Frank. No, Anneke, no.

[Anne *runs to her mother, putting her arms around her.*]

Anne. Oh, Mother, I was. I was awful.
Mr. Van Daan. Not like me. No one is as bad as me!
Dussel (*to* Mr. Van Daan). Stop it now! Let's be happy!
Mr. Frank (*giving* Mr. Van Daan *a glass of cognac*). Here! Here! *Schnapps! L'chaim!*[13]

[Mr. Van Daan *takes the cognac. They all watch him. He gives them a feeble smile.* Anne *puts up her fingers in a V-for-Victory sign. As* Mr. Van Daan *gives an answering V-sign, they are startled to hear a loud sob from behind them. It is* Mrs. Frank,

---

10. **B.B.C.:** British Broadcasting Corporation, a British radio network.
11. **Churchill:** Sir Winston Churchill (1874–1965), a British prime minister (1940–1945; 1951–1955).
12. **General Eisenhower:** Dwight D. Eisenhower (1890–1969), the commander of the Allied forces in Europe during World War II, and later the thirty-fourth President of the United States (1953–1961).

13. *Schnapps!* (shnäps) *L'chaim!* (lə-KHä´yĭm): *Schnapps* means "a drink" in German. *L'chaim* is a toast in Hebrew, meaning "To life!"

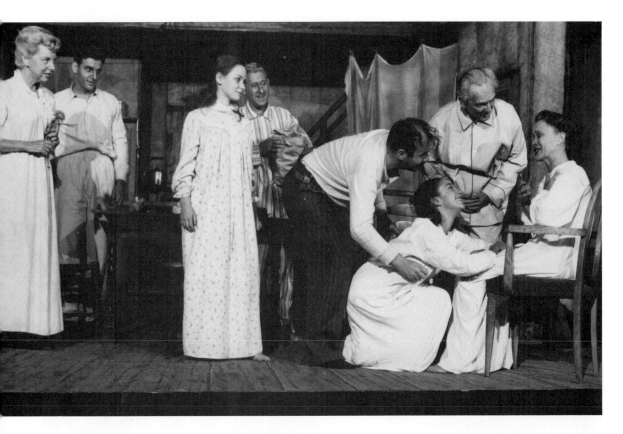

stricken with remorse. She is sitting on the other side of the room.]

Mrs. Frank (*through her sobs*). When I think of the terrible things I said . . .

[Mr. Frank, Anne *and* Margot *hurry to her, trying to comfort her.* Mr. Van Daan *brings her his glass of cognac.*]

Mr. Van Daan. No! No! You were right!

Mrs. Frank. That I should speak that way to you! . . . Our friends! . . . Our guests! (*She starts to cry again.*)

Dussel. Stop it, you're spoiling the whole invasion!

[*As they are comforting her, the lights dim out. The curtain falls.*]

Anne's Voice (*faintly at first, and then with growing strength*). We're all in much better spirits these days. There's still excellent news of the invasion. The best part about it is that I have a feeling that friends are coming. Who knows? Maybe I'll be back in school by fall. Ha, ha! The joke is on us! The warehouseman doesn't know a thing and we are paying him all that money! . . . Wednesday, the second of July, nineteen forty-four. The invasion seems temporarily to be bogged down. Mr. Kraler has to have an operation, which looks bad. The Gestapo have found the radio that was stolen. Mr. Dussel says they'll trace it back and back to the thief, and then, it's just a matter of time till they get to us. Everyone is low. Even poor Pim can't raise their spirits. I have often been downcast myself . . . but never in despair. I can shake off everything if I write. But . . . and that is the great question . . . will I ever be able to write well? I want to so much. I want to go on living even after my death. Another birthday has gone by, so now I am fifteen. Already I know what I want. I have a goal, an opinion.

[*As this is being said, the curtain rises on the scene, the lights dim on, and Anne's voice fades out.*]

Scene 4

It is an afternoon a few weeks later. . . . Everyone but Margot is in the main room. There is a sense of great tension.

Both Mrs. Frank *and* Mr. Van Daan *are nervously pacing back and forth;* Dussel *is standing at the window, looking down fixedly at the street below.* Peter *is at the center table, trying to do his lessons.* Anne *sits opposite him, writing in her diary.* Mrs. Van Daan *is seated on the couch, her eyes on* Mr. Frank *as he sits reading.*

The sound of a telephone ringing comes from the office below. They all are rigid, listening tensely. Dussel *rushes down to* Mr. Frank.

Dussel. There it goes again, the telephone! Mr. Frank, do you hear?

Mr. Frank (*quietly*). Yes. I hear.

Dussel (*pleading, insistent*). But this is the third time, Mr. Frank! The third time in quick succession! It's a signal! I tell you it's Miep, trying to get us! For some reason she can't come to us and she's trying to warn us of something!

Mr. Frank. Please. Please.

Mr. Van Daan (*to* Dussel). You're wasting your breath.

Dussel. Something has happened, Mr. Frank. For three days now Miep hasn't been to see us! And today not a man has come to work. There hasn't been a sound in the building!

Mrs. Frank. Perhaps it's Sunday. We may have lost track of the days.

Mr. Van Daan (*to* Anne). You with the diary there. What day is it?

Dussel (*going to* Mrs. Frank). I don't lose track of the days! I know exactly what day it is! It's Friday, the fourth of August. Friday, and not a man at work. (*He rushes back to* Mr. Frank, *pleading with him, almost in tears.*) I tell you Mr. Kraler's dead. That's the only explanation. He's dead and they've closed down the building, and Miep's trying to tell us!

Mr. Frank. She'd never telephone us.

Dussel (*frantic*). Mr. Frank, answer that! I beg you, answer it!

Mr. Frank. No.

Mr. Van Daan. Just pick it up and listen. You don't have to speak. Just listen and see if it's Miep.

Dussel (*speaking at the same time*). For God's sake . . . I ask you.

Mr. Frank. No. I've told you, no. I'll do nothing that might let anyone know we're in the building.

Peter. Mr. Frank's right.

Mr. Van Daan. There's no need to tell us what side you're on.

Mr. Frank. If we wait patiently, quietly, I believe that help will come.

[*There is silence for a minute as they all listen to the telephone ringing.*]

Dussel. I'm going down. (*He rushes down the steps.* Mr. Frank *tries ineffectually to hold him.* Dussel *runs to the lower door, unbolting it. The telephone*

stops ringing. Dussel *bolts the door and comes slowly back up the steps.*) Too late.

[Mr. Frank *goes to* Margot *in* Anne's *bedroom.*]

Mr. Van Daan. So we just wait here until we die.

Mrs. Van Daan (*hysterically*). I can't stand it. I'll kill myself! I'll kill myself!

Mr. Van Daan. For God's sake, stop it!

[*In the distance, a German military band is heard playing a Viennese waltz.*]

Mrs. Van Daan. I think you'd be glad if I did! I think you want me to die!

Mr. Van Daan. Whose fault is it we're here? (Mrs. Van Daan *starts for her room. He follows, talking at her.*) We could've been safe somewhere . . . in America or Switzerland. But no! No! You wouldn't leave when I wanted to. You couldn't leave your things. You couldn't leave your precious furniture.

Mrs. Van Daan. Don't touch me!

[*She hurries up the stairs, followed by* Mr. Van Daan. Peter, *unable to bear it, goes to his room.* Anne *looks after him, deeply concerned.* Dussel *returns to his post at the window.* Mr. Frank *comes back into the main room and takes a book, trying to read.* Mrs. Frank *sits near the sink, starting to peel some potatoes.* Anne *quietly goes to* Peter's *room, closing the door after her.* Peter *is lying face down on the cot.* Anne *leans over him, holding him in her arms, trying to bring him out of his despair.*]

Anne. Look, Peter, the sky. (*She looks up through the skylight.*) What a lovely, lovely day! Aren't the clouds beautiful? You know what I do when it seems as if I couldn't stand being cooped up for one more minute? I *think* myself out. I think myself on a walk in the park where I used to go with Pim. Where the jonquils and the crocuses and violets grow down the slopes. You know the most wonderful part about *thinking* yourself out? You can have it any way you like. You can have roses and violets and chrysanthemums all blooming at the same time. . . . It's funny . . . I used to take it all for granted . . . and now I've gone crazy about everything to do with nature. Haven't you?

Peter. I've just gone crazy. I think if something doesn't happen soon . . . if we don't get out of here . . . I can't stand much more of it!

Anne (*softly*). I wish you had a religion, Peter.

Peter. No, thanks! Not me!

Anne. Oh, I don't mean you have to be Orthodox[14]. . . or believe in heaven or hell and purgatory and things . . . I just mean some religion . . . it doesn't matter what. Just to believe in something! When I think of all that's out there . . . the trees . . . the flowers . . . and sea gulls . . . when I think of the dearness of you, Peter . . . and the goodness of the people we know . . . Mr. Kraler, Miep, Dirk, the vegetable man, all risking their lives for us every day . . . When I think of these good things, I'm not afraid any more . . . I find myself, and God, and I . . .

[Peter *interrupts, getting up and walking away.*]

Peter. That's fine! But when I begin to think, I get mad! Look at us, hiding out for two years. Not able to move! Caught here like . . . waiting for them to come and get us . . . and all for what?

Anne. We're not the only people that've had to suffer. There've always been people that've had to . . . sometimes one race . . . sometimes another . . . and yet . . .

Peter. That doesn't make me feel any better!

Anne (*going to him*). I know it's terrible, trying to have any faith . . . when people are doing such horrible . . . But you know what I sometimes think? I think the world may be going through a phase, the way I was with Mother. It'll pass, maybe not for hundreds of years, but someday . . . I still believe, in spite of everything, that people are really good at heart.

Peter. I want to see something now. . . . Not a thousand years from now!

[*He goes over, sitting down again on the cot.*]

Anne. But, Peter, if you'd only look at it as part of a great pattern . . . that we're just a little minute in the life . . . (*She breaks off.*) Listen to us, going at each other like a couple of stupid grown-ups! Look at the sky now. Isn't it lovely? (*She holds out her hand to him. Peter takes it and rises, standing with her at the window looking out, his arms around her.*) Someday, when we're outside again, I'm going to . . .

[*She breaks off as she hears the sound of a car, its brakes squealing as it comes to a sudden stop. The people in the other rooms also become aware of the sound. They listen tensely. Another car roars up to a screeching stop.* Anne *and* Peter *come from* Peter's *room.* Mr. *and* Mrs. Van Daan *creep down the stairs.* Dussel *comes out from his room. Everyone is listening, hardly breathing. A doorbell clangs again and again in the building below.* Mr. Frank *starts quietly down the steps to the door.* Dussel *and* Peter *follow him. The others stand rigid, waiting, terrified.*

In a few seconds, Dussel *comes stumbling back up the steps. He shakes off* Peter's *help and goes to his room.* Mr. Frank *bolts the door below and comes slowly back up the steps. Their eyes are all on him as he stands there for a minute. They realize what they feared has happened.* Mrs. Van Daan *starts to whimper.* Mr. Van Daan *puts her gently in a chair, and then hurries off up the stairs to their room to collect their things.* Peter *goes to comfort his mother. There is a sound of violent pounding on a door below.*]

14. **be Orthodox:** follow the most strictly traditional branch of Judaism.

Mr. Frank (*quietly*). For the past two years we have lived in fear. Now we can live in hope.

[*The pounding below becomes more insistent. There are muffled sounds of voices, shouting commands.*]

Men's Voices. *Aufmachen! Da drinnen! Aufmachen! Schnell! Schnell! Schnell!*[15] etc., etc.

[*The street door below is forced open. We hear the heavy tread of footsteps coming up.* Mr. Frank *gets two schoolbags from the shelves and gives one to* Anne *and the other to* Margot. *He goes to get a bag for* Mrs. Frank. *The sound of feet coming up grows louder.* Peter *comes to* Anne, *kissing her goodbye; then he goes to his room to collect his things. The buzzer of their door starts to ring.* Mr. Frank *brings* Mrs. Frank *a bag. They stand together, waiting. We hear the thud of gun butts on the door, trying to break it down.*

Anne *stands, holding her school satchel, looking over at her father and mother with a soft, reassuring smile. She is no longer a child, but a woman with courage to meet whatever lies ahead.*

The lights dim out. The curtain falls on the scene. We hear a mighty crash as the door is shattered. After a second Anne's *voice is heard.*]

Anne's Voice. And so it seems our stay is over. They are waiting for us now. They've allowed us five minutes to get our things. We can each take a bag and whatever it will hold of clothing. Nothing else. So, dear Diary, that means I must leave you behind. Goodbye for a while. P.S. Please, please, Miep, or Mr. Kraler, or anyone else. If you should find this diary, will you please keep it safe for me, because someday I hope . . .

[*Her voice stops abruptly. There is silence. After a second the curtain rises.*]

15. *Aufmachen! . . . Schnell!:* Open up! You in there! Open up! Quick! Quick! Quick!

Scene 5

It is again the afternoon in November 1945. The rooms are as we saw them in the first scene. Mr. Kraler *has joined* Miep *and* Mr. Frank. *There are coffee cups on the table. We see a great change in* Mr. Frank. *He is calm now. His bitterness is gone. He slowly turns a few pages of the diary. They are blank.*

Mr. Frank. No more. (*He closes the diary and puts it down on the couch beside him.*)
Miep. I'd gone to the country to find food.

When I got back the block was surrounded by police. . . .

Mr. Kraler. We made it our business to learn how they knew. It was the thief . . . the thief who told them.

[Miep *goes up to the gas burner, bringing back a pot of coffee.*]

Mr. Frank *(after a pause).* It seems strange to say this, that anyone could be happy in a concentration camp. But Anne was happy in the camp in Holland where they first took us. After two years of being shut up in these rooms, she could be out . . . out in the sunshine and the fresh air that she loved.

Miep *(offering the coffee to Mr. Frank).* A little more?

Mr. Frank *(holding out his cup to her).* The news of the war was good. The British and Americans were sweeping through France. We felt sure that they would get to us in time. In September we were told that we were to be shipped to Poland. . . . The men to one camp. The women to another. I was sent to Auschwitz. They went to Belsen. In January we were freed, the few of us who were left. The war wasn't yet over, so it took us a long time to get home. We'd be sent here and there behind the lines where we'd be safe. Each time our train would stop . . . at a siding, or a crossing . . . we'd all get out and go from group to group. . . . Where were you? Were you at Belsen? At Buchenwald? At Mauthausen? Is it possible that you knew my wife? Did you ever see my husband? My son? My daughter? That's how I found out about my wife's death . . . of Margot, the Van Daans . . . Dussel. But Anne . . . I still hoped . . . Yesterday I went to Rotterdam. I'd heard of a woman there . . . She'd been in Belsen with Anne. . . . I know now.

[*He picks up the diary again and turns the pages back to find a certain passage. As he finds it we hear Anne's voice.*]

Anne's Voice. In spite of everything, I still believe that people are really good at heart.

[Mr. Frank *slowly closes the diary.*]

Mr. Frank. She puts me to shame.

[*They are silent. The curtain falls.*]

> *Anne's actual diary ends on August 1, 1944. On August 4 the Nazis broke into the warehouse and sent all occupants to concentration camps. Anne's father was the only one to survive. Anne died of typhus fever at Bergen-Belsen in March 1945, two months before the liberation of the Netherlands.*

1. What does Miep bring on New Year's Day, 1944?

2. What does Mr. Van Daan want to do with his wife's fur coat?

3. What does Anne offer to give Peter for his room?

4. What good news does Miep bring as the families are arguing?

5. Why does Mr. Frank refuse to answer the telephone?

For Study and Discussion

Analyzing and Interpreting the Play

ACT TWO

Scene 1

1. Anne's voice reading from her diary provides basic information about the story. What facts does the diary relate at the opening of Act Two?

2. Most of the characters own a few small possessions that are very precious to them. **a.** What do you think Peter's cat means to him? **b.** Why is Mrs. Van Daan's coat so important to her?

3. The suspense in the play is increased by a new worry. What fear does Mr. Kraler's news bring?

Scene 2

4. Love, which unites some of the characters, also divides them. How would you describe Mrs. Van Daan's reaction to the interest that Anne and Peter show in each other?

5. Peter says that Anne has changed from the kind of girl she was when they first met. **a.** How has Anne changed? **b.** How does she explain her new relationship with Peter in her diary?

Scene 3

6. Mr. Frank says, "We don't need the Nazis to destroy us. We're destroying ourselves." The constant threat of the Nazis on the outside terrifies the characters. What human fears and weaknesses attack them from the inside?

7. In one moment the "family" realizes that their quarrels are unimportant compared to the greater evil in the outside world. **a.** What event changes their fear to hope, and their hatred to forgiveness? **b.** What is the first reaction of Mrs. Frank and Mr. Van Daan?

Scene 4

8. In spite of the great tension around her, Anne still has a way to escape to a happy and beautiful world. **a.** What does she do? **b.** Where does she go?

9a. How does Anne explain the war and the world's madness? **b.** What belief, in spite of everything, gives her hope?

10. At the opening of the play, Anne is a girl just beginning to understand the world around her. How has she changed by the end of the play?

Scene 5

11. This scene returns to the first scene of the play. Mr. Frank tells Miep about the concentration camps. What does he say happened to all the other members of the "family"?

12. Mr. Frank feels ashamed because he cannot share Anne's belief in the goodness of people. Do you think any events in the play support Anne's belief?

Literary Elements

Recognizing the Elements of a Tragedy

The Diary of Anne Frank is a **tragedy.** Most tragedies end with the hero or heroine suffering death or defeat.

Tragic Characters. In tragedies, attention is focused on one or two outstanding characters. These are people whose courage, dignity, or other heroic qualities strongly distinguish them from the rest of the people in the play. Which characters in this play are you most interested in? What makes you admire them?

Tragic Plot. In tragedies, the characters face some powerful force that finally overcomes them. What terrible outside forces are seeking to destroy the characters in this play? You knew from the beginning of the play that Anne would not survive. Did you want to read on, even though you knew that the story would end sadly for her?

Tragic Theme. Tragedies need not be depressing, even though they show people facing overwhelming odds and often death. In fact, many tragedies lift up our spirits. They make us see nobility and courage and dignity in people, despite the terrible things that happened to them. What would you say is the theme, or main idea about life, that this play expresses?

In what ways is Anne victorious, despite her tragedy?

Understanding Dramatic Terms

Here are some terms that are useful in understanding *The Diary of Anne Frank* and other plays.

Subplot: a second plot or "story" within the larger main plot. In *The Diary of Anne Frank,* the main plot tells what happens as the "family" hides from the Nazis. The subplot tells what happens between Anne and Peter. Plot and subplot are often related. Anne and Peter, for instance, must hide their world of love from the grown-ups, just as the whole "family" must hide from the hostile outside world. How does this subplot involving Anne and Peter add a hopeful mood to the play?

Flashback: a way of taking the audience back in time, in order to recall events already past. Almost all of *The Diary of Anne Frank* is a flashback. Who is remembering these events?

Monologue: a long speech delivered by one character. In English, the suffix *-logue* means "words." *Monologue* means "words spoken by one person." *Dialogue* means "conversation, or words exchanged between characters." Monologues often contain ideas that are important in the play. In this play, Anne delivers several monologues. Which sentence in Anne's monologue in Act Two, Scene 3, expresses an important wish?

Writing About Literature

Writing a Review of a Play

The review of *The Diary of Anne Frank* reproduced on page 395 was written by Walter F. Kerr for the *New York Herald Tribune.* Kerr begins his review with an evaluation of the play itself. He then describes what he thinks is the most touching scene in the play. Write your own review of the play. Include your personal reactions to the play and a description of the scene you think is the most touching. End your review with a comment about the appropriateness of the play for a teen-age audience.

NEW YORK
Herald ⚘ Tribune

October 6, 1955

THEATER

'The Diary of Anne Frank'

By WALTER F. KERR

NEARLY all of the characters in "The Diary of Anne Frank"—they are Dutch Jews hiding out from Hitler in a dingy and overcrowded garret—are doomed to death. Yet the precise quality of the new play at the Cort is the quality of glowing, ineradicable life—life in its warmth, its wonder, its spasms of anguish, and its wild and flaring humor.

Perhaps no scene in the play is more touching than that in which a fifteen-year-old girl and a nineteen-year-old boy enter into the formalities of courtship. They have, with their families, been cooped up on the top floor of an Amsterdam office building for nearly two years. They have seen each other morning, noon and night during all this time, eaten together, squabbled together, been terrified together, simply grown up together.

＊　＊　＊

When the time comes, though, for each to seek the other out in a shy, faltering, heartbreak-ing romance, they at once begin to behave like lovers who have just been introduced. In her own little corner of the densely populated living quarters, the girl piles her hair on top of her head and hopefully drapes a scarf about her shoulders; in his cubbyhole the boy puts on a jacket, straightens his tie, and trembles in expectation. The girl 'goes out' for the evening to see him—just across the room, past her chess-playing parents, past the boy's greedy father and frivolous mother—to a door that opens gently not more than twenty feet away.

＊　＊　＊

The circumstances around her are the circumstances of despair and decay. In the midst of this, a fresh and shining dignity, a springtime innocence and an instinctive honor rise to fill the shabby room. Since you know that Anne Frank's life is to end in the horrors of Belsen, the play cannot help but break your heart. But along the way it takes great care to let you know that the moments of living—short as they were—were all moments of growth and discovery and very great joy.

Frances Goodrich and Albert Hackett have fashioned a wonderfully sensitive and theatrically craftsmanlike narrative out of the real-life legacy left us by a spirited and straightforward Jewish girl. Garson Kanin has not so much staged it as orchestrated it—from the simple and homely rhythms of a silent couple doing the dinner dishes to the sudden, catlike tensions of an alarmed household listening in panic to a telephone bell that may be a warning.

Authors and director together have given us a series of vivid, utterly lifelike yet colorfully dramatic pictures: the happy new refugees stripping off layer after layer of concealed clothing, the night-time stir that responds to an adolescent's scream, the religious ritual by candlelight that turns into an antic round of gift-giving.

＊　＊　＊

And Mr. Kanin has found a superb company for the purpose. A few seasons ago young Susan Strasberg suggested, in an off-Broadway performance, that she had the magic of which stars are made. That star is beginning to shine now—not with absolute authority, perhaps, but with a puppyish effervescence that is like a promise of the world on a platter.

If Miss Strasberg has a little difficulty still with the reflective passages that come with the girl's new maturity, she has nothing but enchantment to bring the earlier scenes of tomboy fire and prankish ebullience. Clambering over the furniture, pounding her hands against her head excitedly, dancing demurely with her father, or donning oversize trousers for a flash of mimic impudence, she is breathtaking.

＊　＊　＊

Joseph Schildkraut's controlled and confident father is a tower of strength to the family—and to the play—he must hold together. David Levin's boy-next-door is quietly moving, Jack Gilford's fussy dentist, Lou Jacobi's eternally hungry business man, Dennie Moore's vain and pathetic wife, and Clinton Sundberg's restrained friend of the oppressed are all crystal-clear portraits. And you aren't likely to forget Gusti Huber's drawn face across a festive table as she realizes with absolute certainty that they are all bound to be discovered.

Boris Aronson's gabled setting, from which the homeless look out on a thousand homes, is brilliantly drawn, a stunning background for a play that is—for all its pathos—as bright and shining as a banner.

About the Authors

Frances Goodrich (1891–1984)
Albert Hackett (1900–)

Frances Goodrich and Albert Hackett, a husband-and-wife team, made an abrupt change in their careers with the writing of the play *The Diary of Anne Frank*. They had been writing scripts for light comedy movies since 1933. They began *The Thin Man* series in 1934. They also wrote the script for the popular movie musical *Seven Brides for Seven Brothers*. Writing Anne Frank's story took the couple two years. The script went through eight rewrites. The play won the Pulitzer Prize for drama in 1956.

DEVELOPING SKILLS
IN CRITICAL THINKING

Using Methods of Comparison and Contrast

To *compare* is to look for ways in which things are alike. To *contrast* is to look for ways in which they are different. The critical thinking skills of comparison and contrast can be used to develop a better understanding of something. You can gain greater insight into Anne's development, for example, by comparing and contrasting her speeches at the beginning of the play with those that come later on.

Read the following passages from the play. Identify points of similarity and difference. You may wish to keep a chart in two columns, labeled *Similarities* and *Differences,* to record your notes. Then write a short paper in which you present your findings.

I expect I should be describing what it feels like to go into hiding. But I really don't know yet myself. I only know it's funny never to be able to go outdoors . . . never to breathe fresh air . . . never to run and shout and jump. It's the silence in the nights that frightens me most. Every time I hear a creak in the house, or a step on the street outside, I'm sure they're coming for us. The days aren't so bad. At least we know that Miep and Mr. Kraler are down there below us in the office. Our protectors, we call them. I asked Father what would happen to them if the Nazis found out they were hiding us. Pim said that they would suffer the same fate that we would. . . . Imagine! They know this, and yet when they come up here, they're always cheerful and gay as if there were nothing in the world to bother them. . . .

Look, Peter, the sky. (*She looks up through the skylight.*) What a lovely, lovely day! Aren't the clouds beautiful? You know what I do when it seems as if I couldn't stand being cooped up for one more minute? I *think* myself out. I think myself on a walk in the park where I used to go with Pim. Where the jonquils and the crocuses and violets grow down the slopes. You know the most wonderful part about *thinking* yourself out? You can have it any way you like. You can have roses and violets and chrysanthemums all blooming at the same time. . . . It's funny . . . I used to take it all for granted . . . and now I've gone crazy about everything to do with nature. . . . When I think of all that's out there . . . the trees . . . the flowers . . . and sea gulls . . . when I think of the dearness of you, Peter . . . and the goodness of the people we know . . . Mr. Kraler, Miep, Dirk, the vegetable man, all risking their lives for us every day . . . When I think of these good things, I'm not afraid any more . . . I find myself, and God. . . . I know it's terrible, trying to have any faith . . . when people are doing such horrible . . . But you know what I sometimes think? I think the world may be going through a phase, the way I was with Mother. It'll pass, maybe not for hundreds of years, but someday. . . . I still believe, in spite of everything, that people are really good at heart.

PRACTICE IN READING AND WRITING

Writing a Play

Dialogue assumes great importance in drama, for the entire story must be told through the characters' conversations. Stage directions sometimes give the actors instructions, but for the most part, the clues are built right into the dialogue. In the following passage from *The Ugly Duckling,* note how Milne builds devices for interpretation into the characters' speeches:

> **King.** . . . and then he will take your hand in both of his and press it to his heart. (*He does so.*) And then—what do *you* say?
> **Dulcibella.** Coo!
> **King.** No, *not* "Coo."
> **Dulcibella.** Never had anyone do *that* to me before.
> **King.** That also strikes the wrong note. What you want to say is, "Oh, Prince Simon!" . . . Say it.
> **Dulcibella** (*loudly*). Oh, Prince Simon!
> **King.** No, no. You don't need to shout until he has said "What?" two or three times. Always consider the possibility that he *isn't* deaf. Softly, and giving the words a dying fall, letting them play around his head like a flight of doves.
> **Dulcibella** (*still a little overloud*). O-o-o-o-h, Prinsimon!
> **King.** Keep the idea in your mind of a flight of *doves* rather than a flight of panic-stricken elephants, and you will be all right. Now I'm going to get up, and you must, as it were, *waft* me into a seat by your side. (*She starts*

> *wafting.*) *Not* rescuing a drowning man, that's another idea altogether. . . .

1. *Note the stage directions that tell how speeches are to be spoken and what the players are to be doing.*

According to the stage directions, what does the King do in his first speech? How is Dulcibella instructed to deliver her "Oh, Prince Simon!" speeches?

2. *Note clues in the speeches themselves that tell what the players are doing, or how their speeches are to be delivered.*

For example, the King wants Dulcibella to "waft" him into a seat. How does Dulcibella actually move? (The clue is in the King's speech, when he says, "*Not* rescuing a drowning man. . . .") You will find an additional clue on how Dulcibella delivers her second. "Oh, Prince Simon!" speech by reading the King's response to it. (The clue is in his remark about a flight of panic-stricken elephants.)

3. *Imagine the actions taking place that are not indicated in stage directions or in the speeches.*

What do you imagine the King is doing as he gives his speech beginning "No, no. You don't need to shout . . ."? What expressions do you think Dulcibella has on her face during this scene?

Suggestions for Writing

Write a dialogue that might take place between the following characters or between two characters of your own choosing. Where you think necessary, use stage directions to tell how the characters are speaking or what they are doing.

A shy boy and a shy girl

An angry boss and a fast-talking young employee

A highly educated Martian and a five-year-old Earthling

An optimist and a pessimist

Here are some guidelines to follow.

Prewriting

To plan your dialogue, you must make several decisions:

- Identify the problem your characters must face. Every dramatic situation centers on some kind of problem.
- Decide on a setting for the scene. Where and when will these characters have their dialogue?
- Determine the personalities of the characters in your dialogue. Are they friendly, shy, bold, timid?
- Decide what, if any, stage directions you must include to suggest each character's actions or tone of voice. Do you need to identify any sounds or events?

Writing

As you write your dialogue, be sure that the language is appropriate for your characters and that it is natural-sounding. Be sure that the problem they face is clear.

Evaluating and Revising

Evaluate the draft of your dialogue by answering the following questions. Then revise your draft by adding, cutting, reordering, or replacing words.

- Have you provided any stage directions that are necessary to explain the character's actions or the setting?
- Does the dialogue sound appropriate for the characters? Does it sound natural?
- Do the characters' actions and words suggest something about their personalities?
- Have you included a problem that the characters encounter?

Proofreading

Reread your revised dialogue and correct any mistakes in spelling or capitalization. Then prepare a final copy. Be prepared to share your dialogue with your classmates, perhaps by having two or three students act out the parts.

For Further Reading

Davis, Ossie, *Langston: A Play* (Delacorte Press, 1982)
This play dramatizes important events in the life of the famous black poet.

Gibson, William, *The Miracle Worker* (Knopf, 1957; paperback, Bantam)
This play is based on the true story of how Annie Sullivan taught Helen Keller—a deaf and blind child—that there are words and ways to communicate.

Gies, Miep, *Anne Frank Remembered* (Simon & Schuster, 1987)
The woman who helped to hide the Frank family gives a new perspective on the tragedy.

Hamlett, Christina, *Humorous Plays for Teenagers* (Plays, 1986)
This is a collection of one-act plays based on real-life situations.

Hammerstein, Oscar, *Six Plays by Rodgers and Hammerstein* (Modern Library, 1955)
This collection contains the scripts and lyrics of some famous musical comedies: *Oklahoma, Carousel, South Pacific,* and *The King and I.*

Hansberry, Lorraine, *A Raisin in the Sun* (Random House, 1969; paperback, New American Library)
Three generations of a middle-class black family in Chicago face many troubles when Mama buys a house.

Kozelka, Paul, editor, *Fifteen American One-Act Plays* (paperback, Washington Square Press, 1980)
The outstanding plays here include comedies (*The Trysting Place* by Booth Tarkington), suspense stories (*Sorry, Wrong Number* by Lucille Fletcher), and fantasies (*The Devil and Daniel Webster* by Stephen Vincent Benét).

Laurents, Arthur, *West Side Story* (Random House, 1958; paperback, Dell)
This tragic Romeo and Juliet story, set in Spanish Harlem, tells of two opposing teen-age gangs who doom the love between Maria and Tony.

Schary, Dore, *Sunrise at Campobello* (Random House, 1958)
In this drama, Franklin D. Roosevelt is stricken by polio and struggles to regain an active life.

Sherwood, Robert, *Abe Lincoln in Illinois* (Scribner, 1937)
Lincoln comes alive as a very human figure in this play, which begins when he is a young man and ends when be becomes President.

Simon, Neil, *Brighton Beach Memoirs* (Random House, 1984)
To fifteen-year-old Eugene Jerome, baseball is the major focus of each day.

Stone, Peter, and Sherman Edwards, *1776: A Musical Play* (Viking, 1970; paperback, Penguin, 1976)
This musical gives you an unusual view of the people who shaped America's history in the struggle to adopt the Declaration of Independence.

Vidal, Gore, editor, *Visit to a Small Planet and Other Television Plays* (Little, Brown, 1957)
This collection includes Vidal's own satire about a visitor from outer space who is fascinated by life on our "primitive" planet.

Wilder, Thornton, *Our Town* (Harper & Row, 1960; paperback, 1985)
One of the most famous of American plays, this drama examines the priceless value of everyday life. The play is set in a small town called Grover's Corners, New Hampshire. Another famous Wilder play is *The Happy Journey to Trenton and Camden,* available in several collections.

NONFICTION

Little Greek Girl Mounting a Staircase (c. 1963)
by Henri Cartier-Bresson (1908–   ). Photograph.

The writings in this unit are *nonfiction*—that is, they are about actual people and actual events. Nonfiction can be about almost anything—sports, wars, inventions, adventures, disasters, people's lives. It can take the form of diaries, letters, biographies, magazine articles, speeches, or interviews.

Like all literature, nonfiction helps you share experiences. This unit includes an article about an eagle that became the mascot for a Wisconsin infantry company during the Civil War; a humorous essay about living with a bad-tempered dog; an excerpt from a biography of Harriet Tubman, a conductor on the Underground Railroad; a true narrative about a fight on a Mississippi steamboat; an autobiographical recollection of growing up in the South; and a true story of an artist's struggle to become successful at her craft.

You will be reading nonfiction all of your life. It is a form of writing that can give you information about the world and personal pleasure as well.

CLOSE READING
OF AN ESSAY

Developing Skills in Critical Thinking

The essay is a type of nonfiction that can be adapted to several purposes. An essay can be informative or instructive; it can be entertaining; it can be persuasive. Essays may be *formal* or *informal*. The formal essay is serious and impersonal. The informal essay is light, personal, and often humorous.

When you read an essay, determine the writer's *purpose*. Is the purpose chiefly to give information, to provide entertainment, to explain something, or to influence thinking and actions? Also pay close attention to *style*—the way the writer uses language.

Read the following essay carefully, using the marginal notes and questions as a guide to close reading. As you read, you may wish to make notes of your own on a separate sheet of paper. After reading the essay turn to the analysis on page 405.

The Pioneer Women

FABIOLA CABEZA DE BACA

The women on the *Llano*[1] and *Ceja*[2] played a great part in the history of the land. It was a difficult life for a woman, but she had made her choice when in the marriage ceremony she had promised to obey and follow her husband. It may not have been her choice, since parents may have decided for her. It was the Spanish custom to make matches for the children. Whether through choice or tradition, the women had to be a hardy lot in order to survive the long trips by wagon or carriage and the separation from their families, if their families were not among those who were settling on the Llano.

The women had to be versed in the curative powers of plants and in midwifery, for there were no doctors for two hundred miles or more.

The knowledge of plant medicine is an inheritance from the Moors[3] and brought to New Mexico by the first Spanish colonizers. From childhood, we are taught the names of herbs, weeds and plants that have curative potency; even today when we have doctors at immediate call, we still have great faith in plant medicine. Certainly this knowledge of home remedies was a source of comfort to the women who went out to the *Llano,* yet their faith in God helped more than anything in the survival.

Every village had its *curandera* or *medica*[4] and the ranchers rode many miles to bring

Thinking Model

The opening sentence states the topic of the essay—the contributions of pioneer women in the Southwest.

What hardships were faced by these women?

Author discusses women's roles on the Llano. *How did they serve as substitutes for doctors?*

What sustained them most in their hardships?

1. *Llano* (lăn′ō, lä′nō): a large grassy plain in southwestern United States.
2. *Ceja* (sā′hä): top of a mesa.
3. **Moors** (mŏŏrz): a Moslem people who invaded Spain in the eighth century.
4. *curandera* or *medica*: medicine woman, or doctor.

the medicine woman or midwife from a distant village or neighboring ranch.

Quite often, the wife of the *patron*[5] was well versed in plant medicine. I know that my grandmother, Dona Estefana Delgado de Baca, although not given the name of *medica*, because it was not considered proper in her social class, was called every day by some family in the village, or by their *empleados* (servants, or *hacienda* workers), to treat a child or some other person in the family. In the fall of the year, she went out to the hills and valleys to gather her supply of healing herbs. When she went to live in La Liendre, there were terrible outbreaks of smallpox, and she had difficulty convincing the villagers that vaccination was the solution. Not until she had a godchild in every family was she able to control the dreaded disease. In Spanish tradition, a godmother takes the responsibility of a real mother, and in that way grandmother conquered many superstitions which the people had. At least she had the power to decide what should be done for her godchildren.

Author gives a specific example of her grandmother, who served as the medicine woman for an entire community. What special responsibilities did she have?

From El Paso, Texas, she secured vaccines from her cousin, Doctor Samaniego. She vaccinated her children, grandchildren and godchildren against the disease. She vaccinated me when I was three years old and the vaccination has passed any doctor's inspections.

In what way did she help to bring progress to the settlement?

As did my grandmother, so all the wives of the *patrones* held a very important place in the villages and ranches on the *Llano*. The *patron* ruled the *rancho*, but his wife looked after the spiritual and physical welfare of of the *empleados* and their families. She was the first one called when there was death, illness, misfortune or good tidings in a family. She was a great social force in the commu-

What were the responsibilities of the wives of the ranch owners?

5. *patron* (pä-trōn'): the owner of a large ranch.

nity—more so than her husband. She held the purse strings, and thus she was able to do as she pleased in her charitable enterprises and help those who might seek her assistance. . . .

The women in these isolated areas had to be resourceful in every way. They were their own doctors, dressmakers, tailors and advisers.

The settlements were far apart and New Mexico was a poor territory trying to adapt itself to a new rule. The *Llano* people had no opportunity for public schools, before statehood, but there were men and women who held classes for the children of the *patrones* in private homes. They taught reading in Spanish and sometimes in English. Those who had means sent their children to school in Las Vegas, Santa Fe, or Eastern states. If no teachers were available, the mothers taught their own children to read and many of the wealthy ranchers had private teachers for their children until they were old enough to go away to boarding schools. . . .

How were children educated?

Without the guidance and comfort of the wives and mothers, life on the *Llano* would have been unbearable, and a great debt is owed to the brave pioneer women who ventured into the cruel life of the plains, far from contact with the outside world. Most of them have gone to their eternal rest, and God must have saved a very special place for them to recompense them for their contribution to colonization and religion in an almost savage country.

What is the author's conclusion? What has been her purpose in discussing the role of pioneer women in the Southwest?

Analysis

The purpose of Fabiola Cabeza de Baca's essay is stated explicitly in her conclusion: to make the reader appreciate the contributions of pioneer women to the colonization of the Southwest. Cabeza de Baca speaks from personal knowledge, for her grandmother was one of the women instrumental in looking after the physical and spiritual welfare of her community.

The essay focuses on the self-sufficient nature of the women who settled in New Mexico. After surviving a difficult trip by wagon or carriage and experiencing the loneliness and isolation of being far from their parents, these women had to make do without the services of doctors, dressmakers, or teachers. They became adept at using home remedies to doctor the sick. They learned to depend on plant medicine. Throughout their hardships they were sustained chiefly by their faith in God.

The wives of ranch owners, who occupied a special class, were responsible for the well-being of the ranch workers and their families. They helped in times of sickness, they gave advice, and they dispensed charity. The author's grandmother, who became godmother to a child in every family in her village, was able to exert great influence over the villagers and to overcome their superstitions against vaccination.

Since there were no public schools in the early settlements, and only the rich could afford to send their children away to school, mothers had to teach their own children to read.

Cabeza de Baca concludes that we are indebted to these pioneer women. Without their comfort and guidance, life on the *Llano* would have been intolerable.

Guidelines for Reading an Essay

1. *Determine the purpose of the essay.* The purpose may be to inform, to explain, to entertain, to persuade, or some combination of these objectives. Cabeza de Baca wishes to have the reader understand and appreciate the efforts of women who settled in the Southwest.

2. *Determine the tone of the essay.* A formal essay is serious in tone and generally objective. An informal essay, like that by Cabeza de Baca, is told from a personal point of view.

3. *Pay close attention to style.* Writers make use of different kinds of writing: *description,* to give a picture and to communicate sensory impressions; *narration,* to relate a series of events; *exposition,* to present information; and *persuasion,* to influence the reader's ideas. Note the effectiveness of including Spanish words, along with their translations, in Cabeza de Baca's essay.

4. *State the main idea of the essay.* Look for the single idea that gives focus to the essay. In Cabeza de Baca's essay, the main idea is stated explicitly. In other essays the main idea may be implied.

The Glorious Bird

GERALD CARSON

Although some of the stories about Old Abe may have been exaggerated, no one questions the fact that he performed his patriotic duties well. As you read this essay, note how Gerald Carson interweaves historical information with legend.

From time immemorial, birds have been held in particular esteem as omens and as totems, especially the eagle, whose soaring flights were interpreted in Homer's *Odyssey*[1] as signs of events yet to come in human affairs. And the eagle has been the symbol of Saint John the Evangelist, of imperial Rome, and of other proud empires that have since risen and passed away.

In our own American annals, no individual member of the zoological world can rival Old Abe, the Wisconsin Civil War eagle, in the nation's affections, although one might get an argument in favor of Jumbo, P. T. Barnum's[2] celebrated elephant, or of a magnificent, shaggy, American bull bison whose name may or may not have been Black Diamond and whose home was probably, but not certainly, New York's Central Park Zoo. The bison was real, all right, but the high regard in which he was held was due in part to an unfair advantage: he represented money since his profile appeared on the reverse of the "buffalo" nickel.

But on to our eagle, who was, after all, designated our national bird in 1782. Early in 1861, at sugar-making time, a Chippewa Indian called Chief Sky captured a young bald eagle at the headwaters of the Flambeau River near the line between Wisconsin's Ashland and Pierce counties. Finding a large, tublike nest of mud and sticks in a tall pine, the Indian felled the tree amid the screams and menaces of the parent birds. A few weeks later, when the Flambeau band moved south to dispose of baskets, furs, and moccasins, Chief Sky carried the young bird to Eagle Point. There a farmer named Dan McCann acquired the bird, now nearly grown and handsome, for a bushel of corn. McCann, in turn, took the eagle to Eau Claire, where members of the Eau Claire Badgers, later Company C of the Eighth Wisconsin Volunteer Infantry, chipped in to buy the appealing raptor for $5.00, although a variant account says the price was $2.50. The captain of the company gave the bird the felicitous name Old Abe in compliment to President Abraham Lincoln.

Old Abe was formally sworn into the service of the United States in a ceremony that included placing red, white, and blue ribbons around his graceful neck and a rosette of the same colors on his breast. A new rank, eagle

---

1. **Odyssey** (ŏd′ə-sē): a Greek epic poem about the wanderings of Odysseus. See the introduction to the epic on page 624.
2. **P. T. Barnum:** Phineas Taylor Barnum (1810–1891), a circus producer and showman.

Old Abe and Color Guard of the Eighth Wisconsin Volunteer Infantry, Vicksburg, Mississippi (July 1863).
State Historical Society of Wisconsin

bearer, was created, and a soldier was detailed to carry the eagle beside the regimental colors on a special perch. Little flags made by two patriotic ladies were placed on each side when the regiment was on the march. The bearer wore a belt with a socket to receive the butt end of the staff. The pole was about five feet long, which made it possible to carry the eagle three feet above the heads of the men. This, a member of Company C recalled, "made him quite conspicuous."

Early in September 1861, the Eau Claire Eagles (formerly Badgers) boarded the steamer *Stella Whipple* with banners flying. People shouted and wept, as they paid farewell to the young recruits departing for the war. The little steamer carried the soldiers downriver to the Mississippi where it was made fast to the levee at La Crosse. There the First Wisconsin Battery[3] boomed a salute. As the spectators shouted greetings, the war eagle was carried proudly above the line of march, the color bearer and the eagle bearer heading the column—the colors on the right, eagle on the left. At this time an offer for Old Abe, the first of many, was made and refused. The bird could not be bought, even for $200 on the barrelhead.[4]

The company traveled by rail from La Crosse to Madison, to join the regiment forming at Camp Randall, moving briskly at the quickstep past the capitol building to the gates of the camp. At that moment Old Abe became a celebrity. As the men of the Seventh Wisconsin lined up on each side of the entrance to greet the new men of the Eighth, and the band played "Yankee Doodle," the majestic bird cast an eye on the American flag floating above him, seized its starry folds in his beak, and spread his wings to their full extent—six and a half feet. It was an irresistible *tableau vivant*.[5] The crowds went wild when they grasped the symbolism—our national bird, the bird of freedom, aligning the natural world with the Union cause. Omen indeed!

At the time, Old Abe weighed about ten and a half pounds. His breast was broad and heavy;

3. **Battery:** heavy artillery.
4. **on the barrelhead:** in cash only.

5. ***tableau vivant*** (tă-blō′ vē-väɴ′): French for "a living picture," a scene in which figures pose without moving or making a sound.

his body symmetrical with a white tail, well rounded. He had a large, well-developed head, bright yellow legs, and talons sharp as grappling irons. The plumage was brown with hints of gold, the greater part of the neck a snowy white, the iris of the eyes a brilliant straw color, the pupils a piercing black. For this splendid creature a new, more elaborate, round wooden perch was designed. At each end were clusters of golden arrows, and underneath the crossbar, a shield with painted stars and stripes was attached. Below, there appeared the legend, "8th Reg. W.V." A leather ring was attached to one of the eagle's legs, with a stout cord about twenty feet long. On a march or during a bat-

tle, the eagle bearer took in the slack, giving the bird a free play of about three feet. . . .

The Eighth Wisconsin was assigned to the western theater of war, where it did railroad guard duty, manned rifle pits, and engaged in a number of skirmishes. On various occasions it took heavy casualties, being under heavy fire at the battles of Farmington and Corinth; the capture of Island No. 10; the assault on Jackson, Mississippi; the siege of Vicksburg. It took part in the Red River expedition, and later, toward the end of its period of enlistment, in the two-day battle at Nashville in 1864. The eagle was in the thick of it all, carried high on all marches, present at every battle in which the Eighth was engaged, spreading his wings when he heard the bugle calls, and screaming through the smoke and roar of battle. At Corinth, according to one version of the story, Old Abe's cord was cut by a bullet and the war eagle soared high above the battle, even dropping rocks upon the rebel forces. This may be carrying anthropomorphism[6] pretty far, but it is a fact that the phenomena[7] of war—the drums and rattle of musketry and the roar of cannon—did excite the bird, and the rest is, well, a matter of the will to believe. At any rate, the eagle undoubtedly lifted up the spirits of a whole regiment. And he survived. Once he wavered in the sky, but a solicitous examination showed that only a few tail feathers had been shot away.

Like all soldiers, Old Abe found that in war there is more waiting than fighting. When in quarters, Abe was allowed a good deal of freedom. He amused himself catching bugs, fishing in a creek, tipping over water pails, stealing baseballs, sneaking into the sutler's[8] tent for dainties. Old Abe never forgot a

6. **anthropomorphism** (ăn'thrə-pō-môr'fĭz'əm): assigning human behavior and characteristics to objects or animals.
7. **phenomena** (fĭ-nŏm'ə-nə): events.
8. **sutler** (sŭt'lər): camp cook.

grudge and punished any soldier foolish enough to "get fresh" with him. In general he was as independent as a hog on ice. Abe disliked dogs, except for Frank, the regimental dog, who brought in rabbits, squirrels, rats, and mice; as a gourmet, however, his preference was for Confederate chicken, which seemed to agree with his constitution remarkably well. Once Abe discovered a cup of peach brandy and swallowed it, thus rounding out his military experience by finding out what it was like to be drunk. . . .

A furlough home enabled the war eagle to celebrate the Fourth of July, 1864, in Chippewa Falls, and the *Wisconsin State Journal* noticed that he had put on weight and "acquired dignity and ease of bearing . . . the impersonation of haughty defiance." The eagle participated in his final battle at Hurricane Creek, Mississippi, in the late summer of 1864. At the time he was mustered out of service, P. T. Barnum, the great showman of the age, made an unsuccessful bid of $20,000 for the sacred bird. Governor Lewis received the bald eagle as an honored charge of the state. A large, airy cage in a special room was prepared for Old Abe in the capitol building, and he was given life tenancy in his quarters and the right to draw rations in perpetuity. On nice summer days, Abe, with his attendant, enjoyed the freedom of the capitol grounds under the shade of venerable oak trees.

But Old Abe's career was not over; he still had public duties to perform as a civilian. He was in demand as a star feature of sanitary fairs (to raise money for medical care for soldiers) and encampments of the Grand Army of the Republic, where the boys cheered, marched, ate hardtack and sowbelly, sang Civil War marching songs, and cheered for Old Abe—while he cheered back, after his fashion. On these occasions, devoted to nostalgia and charity, Abe lent a photograph or a tail feather

Old Abe, the Live Wisconsin War Eagle, Taking a Sun Bath (1879). Stereograph.
State Historical Society of Wisconsin

(worth $10) to raise funds for sick and wounded veterans. At a great fair in Chicago, for example, in 1865, the eagle raised about $16,000. In fact, in a souvenir book written about Old Abe, the author explained in a note that the volume was "prepared to furnish a means whereby a few veterans, maimed in the service of their country, might turn an honest penny." . . .

Eighteen-hundred and seventy-six—the centennial of American independence. It goes without saying that Old Abe attended the great

Centennial Exhibition in Philadelphia, the first of our great World's Fairs, in the United States. Abe was one of the chief attractions during that centennial summer, feted especially on Wisconsin Day. Standing on the national escutcheon,[9] supported on a lofty pole, he behaved with the dignity of a hero of some forty-two battles and skirmishes. Crowds were always at hand, and the bird surveyed the animated scene around him, a historian of the exposition wrote, "with an air of royal majesty."

Old Abe's death and apotheosis[10] were spectacular, not to say, Wagnerian,[11] and fully consistent with his extraordinary life. He didn't peg out until March 1881, when a paint-and-oil smudge fire in the capitol basement created a suffocating volume of oily smoke. The eagle was rescued but never recovered from smoke inhalation, refused all food, and died on March 26 in the arms of his keeper. A gracefully posed image of the bird was preserved by the art of taxidermy and displayed in the Capitol War Museum until February 1904. Then another fire swept through much of the museum, this time destroying all that remained of Old Abe. "The vision ends," wrote an amateur poet, "and we will leave him there,/And trust in God with faith and earnest prayer/That Victory's dream be fully realized,/And all the world be nobly eagleized!"

Old Abe's memory endures. Today on state highway 178, approximately eight miles northeast of Chippewa Falls and the Chippewa River, a historical marker commemorates the "glorious bird" at a wayside that is part of the old McCann farm, and an oil portrait by an unknown artist hangs in the state capitol in Madison, Wisconsin. It perpetuates a legend, yes, not of the Paul Bunyan[12] school of unnatural natural history, such as the Black Hodag,[13] *Bovinis spiritualis*, subject of many tall tales, but an affectionate legend, mostly true, based upon verifiable fact.

9. **escutcheon** (ĕ-skŭch′ən, ĭ-): shield or emblem.
10. **apotheosis** (ə-pŏth′ē-ō′sĭs, ăp′ə-thē′ə-sĭs): glorification.
11. **Wagnerian** (väg-nîr′ē-ən): referring to Richard Wagner (1813–1883), a German composer whose operas are known for their grand and often theatrical climaxes.

12. **Paul Bunyan:** in American folk tales, a giant logger. See page 173.
13. **Black Hodag** (hō′dăg): a mythical creature with horns and a hooked tail, known for its ugliness and ferocity.

Reading Check

1. How was the young eagle captured?
2. What group purchased the eagle?
3. How was Old Abe displayed in parades?
4. What did Old Abe do when he heard bugle calls?
5. What happened to Old Abe after he left military service?

Analyzing and Interpreting the Essay

1. When the company moved to Camp Randall, Old Abe put on quite a show for the crowd. What were Old Abe's actions interpreted to mean?

2. During the battle at Corinth, Old Abe was rumored to have bombed the rebel forces with rocks. How does the author indicate that this story may not actually be true?

3. What public duties did Old Abe perform as a "civilian"?

4. What do you think made Old Abe so appealing and memorable to people?

5. At the close of the essay, Gerald Carson says that the story of Old Abe is an "affectionate legend, mostly true, based upon verifiable fact." **a.** In your view, what in the essay is more legend than fact? **b.** Why do you think so?

Expository Writing

Supporting an Opinion

Ben Franklin believed that the turkey and not the bald eagle should have been chosen as the national emblem. He said:

> [The bald eagle] is a bird of bad moral character; he does not get his living honestly; you may have seen him perched on some dead tree near the river, where, too lazy to fish for himself, he watches the labor of the fishing-hawk; and, when that diligent bird has at length taken a fish and is bearing it to his nest for the support of his mate and young ones, the bald eagle pursues him and takes it from him. With all this injustice he is never in good case; but, like those among men who live by sharping and robbing, he is generally poor and often very lousy. . . . The turkey is in comparison a much more respectable bird, and withal a true original native of America. . . . He is (though a little vain and silly, it is true, but not the worse emblem for that) a bird of courage, and would not hesitate to attack a grenadier of the British Guards who should presume to invade his farmyard with a red coat on.

Why does Franklin think that the bald eagle is a bird of "bad moral character"? What are his reasons for preferring the turkey as a national emblem? Do you agree or disagree with Franklin? If you agree, what additional evidence can you offer to support his position? If you disagree, what can you tell about the eagle that presents a different image of the bird?

Write a paragraph in which you express your opinion about which bird should be our national emblem. Begin with a topic sentence that states your opinion and include evidence that supports your position.

About the Author

Gerald Carson (1899–   )

Gerald Carson has written for many years about American culture, manners, history, folkways, and economics. He received awards for his first book, *The Old Country Store* in 1954, and for *The Dentist and the Empress: The Adventures of Dr. Tom Evans in Gas-Lit Paris* in 1983. His books and articles for magazines and journals have covered a wide range of topics, such as animal cruelty, food, and personal income tax. He was born and educated in Illinois, and he has worked as a reporter and editor and in advertising.

The Dog That Bit People

JAMES THURBER

An informal essay often reveals as much about the personality of the author as it does about its subject. What impression do you form of Thurber from this informal essay?

Probably no one man should have as many dogs in his life as I have had, but there was more pleasure than distress in them for me except in the case of an Airedale named Muggs. He gave me more trouble than all the other fifty-four or -five put together, although my moment of keenest embarrassment was the time a Scotch terrier named Jeannie, who had just had four puppies in the shoe closet of a fourth-floor apartment in New York, had the fifth and last at the corner of—but we shall get around to that later on. Then, too, there was the prizewinning French poodle, a great big black poodle—none of your little, untroublesome white miniatures—who got sick riding in the rumble seat[1] of a car with me on her way to the Greenwich Dog Show. She had a red rubber bib tucked around her throat and, since a rainstorm came up when we were halfway through the Bronx, I had to hold over her a small green umbrella, really more of a parasol.

The rain beat down fearfully, and suddenly the driver of the car drove into a big garage filled with mechanics. It happened so quickly that I forgot to put the umbrella down, and I shall always remember the look of incredulity[2] that came over the face of the garageman who came over to see what we wanted. "Get a load of this, Mac," he called to someone behind him.

But the Airedale, as I have said, was the worst of all my dogs. He really wasn't my dog, as a matter of fact; I came home from a vacation one summer to find that my brother Robert had brought him while I was away. A big, burly, choleric[3] dog, he always acted as if he thought I wasn't one of the family. There was a slight advantage in being one of the family, for he didn't bite the family as often as he bit strangers. Still, in the years that we had him he bit everybody but Mother, and he made a pass at her once but missed. That was during the

---

1. **rumble seat:** an open seat in the back of some early automobiles. It could be folded shut when not in use.

2. **incredulity** (ĭn'krə-dōō'lə-tē): disbelief.
3. **choleric** (kŏl'ər-ĭk): bad-tempered.

month when we suddenly had mice, and Muggs refused to do anything about them. Nobody ever had mice exactly like the mice we had that month. They acted like pet mice, almost like mice somebody had trained. They were so friendly that one night when Mother entertained at dinner the Friraliras, a club she and my father had belonged to for twenty years, she put down a lot of little dishes with food in them on the pantry floor so that the mice would be satisfied with that and wouldn't come into the dining room. Muggs stayed out in the pantry with the mice, lying on the floor, growling to himself—not at the mice, but about all the people in the next room that he would have liked to get at. Mother slipped out into the pantry once to see how everything was going. Everything was going fine. It made her so mad to see Muggs lying there, oblivious of[4] the mice—they came running up to her—that she slapped him and he slashed at her, but didn't make it. He was sorry immediately, Mother said. He was always sorry, she said, after he bit someone, but we could not understand how she figured this out. He didn't act sorry.

Mother used to send a box of candy every Christmas to the people the Airedale bit. The list finally contained forty or more names. Nobody could understand why we didn't get rid of the dog. I didn't understand it very well myself, but we didn't get rid of him. I think that one or two people tried to poison Muggs—he acted poisoned once in a while—and old Major Moberly fired at him once with his service revolver near the Seneca Hotel on East Broad Street—but Muggs lived to be almost eleven years old, and even when he could hardly get around, he bit a congressman who had called to see my father on business. My mother had never liked the congressman—she said the signs of his horoscope showed he couldn't be

trusted (he was Saturn with the moon in Virgo)—but she sent him a box of candy that Christmas. He sent it right back, probably because he suspected it was trick candy. Mother persuaded herself it was all for the best that the dog had bitten him, even though Father lost an important business association because of it. "I wouldn't be associated with such a man," Mother said. "Muggs could read him like a book."

We used to take turns feeding Muggs to be on his good side, but that didn't always work. He was never in a very good humor, even after a meal. Nobody knew exactly what was the matter with him, but whatever it was it made him irascible,[5] especially in the mornings. Robert never felt very well in the morning either, especially before breakfast, and once when he came downstairs and found that Muggs had moodily chewed up the morning paper, he hit him in the face with a grapefruit and then jumped up on the dining-room table, scattering dishes and silverware and spilling the coffee. Muggs's first free leap carried him all the way across the table and into a brass fire screen in front of the gas grate, but he was back on his feet in a moment, and in the end he got Robert and gave him a pretty vicious bite in the leg. Then he was all over it; he never bit anyone more than once at a time. Mother always mentioned that as an argument in his favor; she said he had a quick temper but that he didn't hold a grudge. She was forever defending him. I think she liked him because he wasn't well. "He's not strong," she would say, pityingly, but that was inaccurate; he may not have been well, but he was terribly strong.

One time my mother went to the Chittenden Hotel to call on a woman mental healer who was lecturing in Columbus on the subject of "Harmonious Vibrations." She wanted to find out if it

---

4. **oblivious of:** forgetful of; not mindful of.

5. **irascible** (ĭ-răs′ə-bəl): irritable.

was possible to get harmonious vibrations into a dog. "He's a large, tan-colored Airedale," Mother explained. The woman said she had never treated a dog, but she advised my mother to hold the thought that he did not bite and would not bite. Mother was holding the thought the very next morning when Muggs got the iceman, but she blamed that slip-up on the iceman. "If you didn't think he would bite you, he wouldn't," Mother told him. He stomped out of the house in a terrible jangle of vibrations.

One morning when Muggs bit me slightly, more or less in passing, I reached down and grabbed his short stumpy tail and hoisted him into the air. It was a foolhardy thing to do, and the last time I saw my mother, about six months ago, she said she didn't know what possessed me. I don't know either, except that I was pretty mad. As long as I held the dog off the floor by his tail he couldn't get at me, but he twisted and jerked so, snarling all the time, that I realized I couldn't hold him that way very long. I carried him to the kitchen and flung him onto the floor and shut the door on him just as he crashed against it. But I forgot about the back stairs. Muggs went up the back stairs and down the front stairs and had me cornered in the living room. I managed to get up onto the mantelpiece above the fireplace, but it gave way and came down with a tremendous crash, throwing a large marble clock, several vases, and myself heavily to the floor. Muggs was so alarmed by the racket that when I picked myself up he had disappeared. We couldn't find him anywhere, although we whistled and shouted, until old Mrs. Detweiler called after dinner that night. Muggs had bitten her once, in the leg, and she came into the living room only after we assured her that Muggs had run away. She had just seated herself when, with a great growling and scratching of claws, Muggs emerged from under a davenport where he had been quietly hiding all the time and bit her again. Mother

examined the bite and put arnica[6] on it and told Mrs. Detweiler that it was only a bruise. "He just bumped you," she said. But Mrs. Detweiler left the house in a nasty state of mind.

Lots of people reported our Airedale to the police, but my father held a municipal office at the time and was on friendly terms with the police. Even so, the cops had been out a couple of times—once when Muggs bit Mrs. Rufus Sturtevant and again when he bit Lieutenant Governor Malloy—but Mother told them that it hadn't been Muggs's fault but the fault of the people who were bitten. "When he starts for them, they scream," she explained, "and that excites him." The cops suggested that it might be a good idea to tie the dog up, but Mother said that it mortified him to be tied up and he wouldn't eat when he was tied up.

Muggs at his meals was an unusual sight. Because of the fact that if you reached toward the floor he would bite you, we usually put his food plate on top of an old kitchen table with a bench alongside the table. Muggs would stand on the bench and eat. I remember that my mother's Uncle Horatio, who boasted that he was the third man up Missionary Ridge,[7] was splutteringly indignant when he found out that we fed the dog on a table because we were afraid to put his plate on the floor. He said he wasn't afraid of any dog that ever lived and that he would put the dog's plate on the floor if we would give it to him. Robert said that if Uncle Horatio had fed Muggs on the ground just before the battle, he would have been the first man up Missionary Ridge. Uncle Horatio was furious. "Bring him in! Bring him in now!" he shouted. "I'll feed the——on the floor!" Robert was all for giving him a chance, but my father wouldn't hear of it. He said that Muggs had

6. **arnica:** a preparation for sprains and bruises made from the arnica plant.
7. **Missionary Ridge:** a ridge in Tennessee and Georgia, the site of an important Civil War battle.

already been fed. "I'll feed him again!" bawled Uncle Horatio. We had quite a time quieting him.

In his last year Muggs used to spend practically all of his time outdoors. He didn't like to stay in the house for some reason or other—perhaps it held too many unpleasant memories for him. Anyway, it was hard to get him to come in, and as a result, the garbage man, the iceman, and the laundryman wouldn't come near the house. We had to haul the garbage down to the corner, take the laundry out and bring it back, and meet the iceman a block from home. After this had gone on for some time, we hit on an ingenious arrangement for getting the dog in the house so that we could lock him up while the gas meter was read, and so on. Muggs was afraid of only one thing, an electrical storm.

Thunder and lightning frightened him out of his senses (I think he thought a storm had broken the day the mantelpiece fell). He would rush into the house and hide under a bed or in a clothes closet. So we fixed up a thunder machine out of a long narrow piece of sheet iron with a wooden handle on one end. Mother would shake this vigorously when she wanted to get Muggs into the house. It made an excellent imitation of thunder, but I suppose it was the most roundabout system for running a household that was ever devised. It took a lot out of Mother.

A few months before Muggs died, he got to "seeing things." He would rise slowly from the floor, growling low, and stalk stiff-legged and menacing toward nothing at all. Sometimes the Thing would be just a little to the right or left of a visitor. Once a Fuller brush salesman got hysterics. Muggs came wandering into the room like Hamlet following his father's ghost. His eyes were fixed on a spot just to the left of the Fuller brush man, who stood it until Muggs was about three slow, creeping paces from him. Then he shouted. Muggs wavered on past him into the hallway, grumbling to himself, but the Fuller brush man went on shouting. I think Mother had to throw a pan of cold water on him before he stopped. That was the way she used to stop us boys when we got into fights.

Muggs died quite suddenly one night. Mother wanted to bury him in the family plot under a marble stone with some such inscription as "Flights of angels sing thee to thy rest,"[8] but we persuaded her it was against the law. In the end we just put up a smooth board above his grave along a lonely road. On the board I wrote with an indelible pencil *Cave Canem*.[9] Mother was quite pleased with the simple, classic dignity of the old Latin epitaph.

8. **"Flights . . . rest"**: words spoken to the dead Hamlet in Shakespeare's play.
9. *Cave Canem* (kä′vā kän′ĕm): Latin for "Beware of the dog." In ancient Rome, this warning was often put on the doorways of homes.

Reading Check

1. What family member was never bitten by the Airedale?
2. What did Thurber's mother do at Christmastime for the people that the Airedale had bitten?
3. Why did she refuse to keep the dog tied up?
4. Why was Muggs fed on a table?
5. What was the only thing that the Airedale feared?

For Study and Discussion

Analyzing and Interpreting the Essay

1. This essay is made up of a series of **anecdotes,** or amusing stories, about a particular subject—here, a dog. Thurber pokes fun at himself and his family as he tells how they tried to keep Muggs in a good mood. How does the opening incident with the prize poodle prepare you for a story about people who would do anything for their pets?

2. Part of the fun of this story lies in the ridiculous lengths a whole family went to, in order to stay on the good side of their dog. **a.** What did the family do about Muggs's food, and about their garbage, their laundry, and the iceman? **b.** Why did they rig up the thunder machine?

3. Thurber's mother saw Muggs as having human characteristics. **a.** What were some of the excuses she made for his behavior? **b.** Do you think many people see their pets in the same way that Mother saw Muggs? Explain your answer.

4a. What does Thurber reveal about himself in this essay? **b.** Would you say that he likes or dislikes dogs? **c.** Does he seem tolerant of people's (and dogs') quirks?

Narrative Writing

Writing an Anecdote

An **anecdote** is a brief story about a single incident, often humorous in tone. Write a paragraph telling of an amusing anecdote involving a pet. What individual characteristics does this pet possess? Convey the special personality of the animal in your narrative.

About the Author

James Thurber (1894–1961)

 James Thurber wrote about all kinds of animals—seals, dolphins, unicorns, polar bears, fiddler crabs, wombats, woggle-bugs, bowerbirds, bandicoots, and bristle worms. But he wrote enough dog stories to collect them into an entire book, called *Thurber's Dogs.* Thurber also wrote stories about the kind of person who is victimized by life and its problems. He gave this character a shape and a name in one of his most famous humorous stories, "The Secret Life of Walter Mitty."

Thurber was blinded in one eye in a childhood accident, and he became completely blind during the last years of his life. Nevertheless, he continued to write and he even appeared nightly as himself in *A Thurber Carnival,* a Broadway show based on his work. Thurber once said that humor was a serious thing, one of our greatest national resources, which must be preserved at all cost. One of his humorous twists on a familiar fairy-tale plot is called "The Princess and the Tin Box."

They Called Her Moses

ANN PETRY

This selection is from a biography called Harriet Tubman: Conductor on the Underground Railroad. *After Harriet Tubman made the perilous journey out of slavery herself, she returned to conduct others along the Underground Railroad to freedom. As you read, find out how she came to be called Moses.*

Along the Eastern Shore of Maryland, in Dorchester County, in Caroline County, the masters kept hearing whispers about the man named Moses, who was running off slaves. At first they did not believe in his existence. The stories about him were fantastic, unbelievable. Yet they watched for him. They offered rewards for his capture.

They never saw him. Now and then they heard whispered rumors to the effect that he was in the neighborhood. The woods were searched. The roads were watched. There was never anything to indicate his whereabouts. But a few days afterward, a goodly number of slaves would be gone from the plantation. Neither the master nor the overseer had heard or seen anything unusual in the quarter. Sometimes one or the other would vaguely remember having heard a whippoorwill call somewhere in the woods, close by, late at night. Though it was the wrong season for whippoorwills.

Sometimes the masters thought they had heard the cry of a hoot owl, repeated, and would remember having thought that the intervals between the low moaning cry were wrong, that it had been repeated four times in succession instead of three. There was never anything more than that to suggest that all was not well in the quarter. Yet when morning came, they invariably discovered that a group of the finest slaves had taken to their heels.

Unfortunately, the discovery was almost always made on a Sunday. Thus a whole day was lost before the machinery of pursuit could be set in motion. The posters offering rewards for the fugitives could not be printed until Monday. The men who made a living hunting for runaway slaves were out of reach, off in the woods with their dogs and their guns, in pursuit of four-footed game, or they were in camp meetings saying their prayers with their wives and families beside them.

Harriet Tubman could have told them that there was far more involved in this matter of running off slaves than signaling the would-be runaways by imitating the call of a whippoorwill, or a hoot owl, far more involved than a matter of waiting for a clear night when the North Star was visible.

In December, 1851, when she started out with the band of fugitives that she planned to take to Canada, she had been in the vicinity of the plantation for days, planning the trip, care-

fully selecting the slaves that she would take with her.

She had announced her arrival in the quarter by singing the forbidden spiritual[1]—"Go down, Moses, way down to Egypt Land"—singing it softly outside the door of a slave cabin, late at night. The husky voice was beautiful even when it was barely more than a murmur borne on the wind.

Once she had made her presence known, word of her coming spread from cabin to cabin. The slaves whispered to each other, ear to mouth, mouth to ear, "Moses is here." "Moses has come." "Get ready. Moses is back again." The ones who had agreed to go North with her put ashcake and salt herring in an old bandanna, hastily tied it into a bundle, and then waited patiently for the signal that meant it was time to start.

There were eleven in this party, including one of her brothers and his wife. It was the largest group that she had ever conducted, but she was determined that more and more slaves should know what freedom was like.

She had to take them all the way to Canada. The Fugitive Slave Law[2] was no longer a great many incomprehensible words written down

on the country's lawbooks. The new law had become a reality. It was Thomas Sims, a boy, picked up on the streets of Boston at night and shipped back to Georgia. It was Jerry and Shadrach, arrested and jailed with no warning.

She had never been in Canada. The route beyond Philadelphia was strange to her. But she could not let the runaways who accompanied her know this. As they walked along she told them stories of her own first flight, she kept painting vivid word pictures of what it would be like to be free.

But there were so many of them this time. She knew moments of doubt when she was half afraid, and kept looking back over her shoulder, imagining that she heard the sound of pursuit. They would certainly be pursued. Eleven of them. Eleven thousand dollars' worth of flesh and bone and muscle that belonged to Maryland planters. If they were caught, the eleven runaways would be whipped and sold South, but she—she would probably be hanged.

They tried to sleep during the day but they never could wholly relax into sleep. She could tell by the positions they assumed, by their restless movements. And they walked at night. Their progress was slow. It took them three nights of walking to reach the first stop. She had told them about the place where they would stay, promising warmth and good food, holding these things out to them as an incentive to keep going.

When she knocked on the door of a farmhouse, a place where she and her parties of runaways had always been welcome, always been given shelter and plenty to eat, there was no answer. She knocked again, softly. A voice from within said, "Who is it?" There was fear in the voice.

She knew instantly from the sound of the voice that there was something wrong. She

<hr>

1. **forbidden spiritual:** In 1831, a slave named Nat Turner led an unsuccessful uprising in Virginia. Turner used the Biblical account of the Israelites' escape from Egypt to encourage the rebellion. After this, slaves were forbidden to sing certain spirituals. It was feared that the songs about the Israelites' march to freedom would encourage more uprisings.
2. **Fugitive Slave Law:** part of the Compromise of 1850. According to this law, escaped slaves, even if found in free states, could be forced to return to their masters. Thus, the fugitives were not really safe until they reached Canada. Anyone caught aiding a fugitive slave could be punished with six months in prison and a thousand-dollar fine.

Harriet Tubman by H. B. Lindsley.
Photograph.
Library of Congress

They Called Her Moses   **421**

said, "A friend with friends," the password on the Underground Railroad.

The door opened, slowly. The man who stood in the doorway looked at her coldly, looked with unconcealed astonishment and fear at the eleven disheveled runaways who were standing near her. Then he shouted, "Too many, too many. It's not safe. My place was searched last week. It's not safe!" and slammed the door in her face.

She turned away from the house, frowning. She had promised her passengers food and rest and warmth, and instead of that there would be hunger and cold and more walking over the frozen ground. Somehow she would have to instill courage into these eleven people, most of them strangers, would have to feed them on hope and bright dreams of freedom instead of the fried pork and corn bread and milk she had promised them.

They stumbled along behind her, half dead for sleep, and she urged them on, though she was as tired and as discouraged as they were. She had never been in Canada, but she kept painting wondrous word pictures of what it would be like. She managed to dispel their fear of pursuit, so that they would not become hysterical, panic-stricken. Then she had to bring some of the fear back, so that they would stay awake and keep walking though they drooped with sleep.

Yet during the day, when they lay down deep in a thicket, they never really slept, because if a twig snapped or the wind sighed in the branches of a pine tree, they jumped to their feet, afraid of their own shadows, shivering and shaking. It was very cold, but they dared not make fires because someone would see the smoke and wonder about it.

She kept thinking, eleven of them. Eleven thousand dollars' worth of slaves. And she had to take them all the way to Canada. Sometimes she told them about Thomas Garrett, in Wil-mington. She said he was their friend even though he did not know them. He was the friend of all fugitives. He called them God's poor. He was a Quaker and his speech was a little different from that of other people. His clothing was different, too. He wore the wide-brimmed hat that the Quakers wear.

She said that he had thick white hair, soft, almost like a baby's, and the kindest eyes she had ever seen. He was a big man and strong, but he had never used his strength to harm anyone, always to help people. He would give all of them a new pair of shoes. Everybody. He always did. Once they reached his house in Wilmington, they would be safe. He would see to it that they were.

She described the house where he lived, told them about the store where he sold shoes. She said he kept a pail of milk and a loaf of bread in the drawer of his desk so that he would have food ready at hand for any of God's poor who should suddenly appear before him, fainting with hunger. There was a hidden room in the store. A whole wall swung open, and behind it was a room where he could hide fugitives. On the wall there were shelves filled with small boxes—boxes of shoes—so that you would never guess that the wall actually opened.

While she talked, she kept watching them. They did not believe her. She could tell by their expressions. They were thinking, New shoes, Thomas Garrett, Quaker, Wilmington—what foolishness was this? Who knew if she told the truth? Where was she taking them anyway?

That night they reached the next stop—a farm that belonged to a German. She made the runaways take shelter behind trees at the edge of the fields before she knocked at the door. She hesitated before she approached the door, thinking, suppose that he, too, should refuse shelter, suppose— Then she thought, Lord, I'm going to hold steady on to You and You've got to see me through—and knocked softly.

She heard the familiar guttural[3] voice say, "Who's there?"

She answered quickly, "A friend with friends."

He opened the door and greeted her warmly. "How many this time?" he asked.

"Eleven," she said and waited, doubting, wondering.

He said, "Good. Bring them in."

He and his wife fed them in the lamplit kitchen, their faces glowing, as they offered food and more food, urging them to eat, saying there was plenty for everybody, have more milk, have more bread, have more meat.

They spent the night in the warm kitchen. They really slept, all that night and until dusk the next day. When they left, it was with reluctance. They had all been warm and safe and well-fed. It was hard to exchange the security offered by that clean, warm kitchen for the darkness and the cold of a December night.

Harriet had found it hard to leave the warmth and friendliness, too. But she urged them on. For a while, as they walked, they seemed to carry in them a measure of contentment; some of the serenity and the cleanliness of that big, warm kitchen lingered on inside them. But as they walked farther and farther away from the warmth and light, the cold and the darkness entered into them. They fell silent, sullen, suspicious. She waited for the moment when some one of them would turn mutinous. It did not happen that night.

Two nights later she was aware that the feet behind her were moving slower and slower. She heard the irritability in their voices, knew that soon someone would refuse to go on.

She started talking about William Still and the Philadelphia Vigilance Committee.[4] No one commented. No one asked any questions. She told them the story of William and Ellen Craft and how they escaped from Georgia. Ellen was so fair that she looked as though she were white, and so she dressed up in a man's clothing and she looked like a wealthy young planter. Her husband, William, who was dark, played the role of her slave. Thus they traveled from Macon, Georgia, to Philadelphia, riding on the trains, staying at the finest hotels. Ellen pretended to be very ill—her right arm was in a sling, and her right hand was bandaged, because she was supposed to have rheumatism. Thus she avoided having to sign the register at the hotels, for she could not read or write. They finally arrived safely in Philadelphia, and then went on to Boston.

No one said anything. Not one of them seemed to have heard her.

She told them about Frederick Douglass, the most famous of the escaped slaves, of his eloquence, of his magnificent appearance. Then she told them of her own first vain effort at running away, evoking the memory of that miserable life she had led as a child, reliving it for a moment in the telling.

But they had been tired too long, hungry too long, afraid too long, footsore too long. One of them suddenly cried out in despair, "Let me go back. It is better to be a slave than to suffer like this in order to be free."

She carried a gun with her on these trips. She had never used it—except as a threat. Now as she aimed it, she experienced a feeling of guilt, remembering that time, years ago, when she had prayed for the death of Edward Brodas, the Master, and then not too long afterward had heard that great wailing cry that

---

3. **guttural** (gŭt'ər-əl): a reference to the man's German language, which uses many guttural sounds—that is, sounds produced in the back of the throat.

4. **Philadelphia Vigilance Committee:** a committee of citizens who offered assistance to slaves who had escaped. William Still, a free black man, was secretary of the Committee.

came from the throats of the field hands, and knew from the sound that the Master was dead.

One of the runaways said, again, "Let me go back. Let me go back," and stood still, and then turned around and said, over his shoulder, "I am going back."

She lifted the gun, aimed it at the despairing slave. She said, "Go on with us or die." The husky low-pitched voice was grim.

He hesitated for a moment and then he joined the others. They started walking again. She tried to explain to them why none of them could go back to the plantation. If a runaway returned, he would turn traitor, the master and the overseer would force him to turn traitor. The returned slave would disclose the stopping places, the hiding places, the corn-stacks they had used with the full knowledge of the owner of the farm, the name of the German farmer who had fed them and sheltered them. These people who had risked their own security to help runaways would be ruined, fined, imprisoned.

She said, "We got to go free or die. And freedom's not bought with dust."

This time she told them about the long agony of the Middle Passage on the old slave ships, about the black horror of the holds, about the chains and the whips. They too knew these stories. But she wanted to remind them of the long, hard way they had come, about the long hard way they had yet to go. She told them about Thomas Sims, the boy picked up on the streets of Boston and sent back to Georgia. She said when they got him back to Savannah, got him in prison there, they whipped him until a doctor who was standing by watching said, "You will kill him if you strike him again!" His master said, "Let him die!"

Thus she forced them to go on. Sometimes she thought she had become nothing but a voice speaking in the darkness, cajoling, urg-ing, threatening. Sometimes she told them things to make them laugh, sometime she sang to them, and heard the eleven voices behind her blending softly with hers, and then she knew that for the moment all was well with them.

She gave the impression of being a short, muscular, indomitable woman who could never be defeated. Yet at any moment she was liable to be seized by one of those curious fits of sleep, which might last for a few minutes or for hours.[5]

Even on this trip, she suddenly fell asleep in the woods. The runaways, ragged, dirty, hungry, cold, did not steal the gun, as they might have, and set off by themselves, or turn back. They sat on the ground near her and waited patiently until she awakened. They had come to trust her implicitly, totally. They, too, had come to believe her repeated statement, "We got to go free or die." She was leading them into freedom, and so they waited until she was ready to go on.

Finally, they reached Thomas Garrett's house in Wilmington, Delaware. Just as Harriet had promised, Garrett gave them all new shoes, and provided carriages to take them on to the next stop.

By slow stages they reached Philadelphia, where William Still hastily recorded their names, and the plantations whence they had come, and something of the life they had led in slavery. Then he carefully hid what he had written, for fear it might be discovered. In 1872 he published this record in book form and called it *The Underground Railroad*. In the foreword to his book he said: "While I knew the danger of keeping strict records, and while

5. **sleep . . . hours:** When Harriet was about thirteen, she accidentally received a severe blow on the head from a two-pound weight that an overseer was hurling at a man trying to escape. After the accident, Harriet frequently lost consciousness. When this happened, she could not be roused until the episode passed of its own accord.

Twenty-Eight Fugitives Escaping from the Eastern Shore of Maryland.
Illustration from *Underground Railroad* by William Still (1872).

I did not then dream that in my day slavery would be blotted out, or that the time would come when I could publish these records, it used to afford me great satisfaction to take them down, fresh from the lips of fugitives on the way to freedom, and to preserve them as they had given them."

William Still, who was familiar with all the station stops on the Underground Railroad, supplied Harriet with money and sent her and her eleven fugitives on to Burlington, New Jersey.

Harriet felt safer now, though there were danger spots ahead. But the biggest part of her job was over. As they went farther and farther north, it grew colder; she was aware of the wind on the Jersey ferry and aware of the cold damp in New York. From New York they went on to Syracuse, where the temperature was even lower.

In Syracuse she met the Reverend J. W. Loguen, known as "Jarm" Loguen. This was the beginning of a lifelong friendship. Both Harriet and Jarm Loguen were to become friends and supporters of Old John Brown.[6]

From Syracuse they went north again, into a colder, snowier city—Rochester. Here they almost certainly stayed with Frederick Douglass, for he wrote in his autobiography: "On one occasion I had eleven fugitives at the same time under my roof, and it was necessary for them to remain with me until I could collect sufficient money to get them to Canada. It was the largest number I ever had at any one time, and I had some difficulty in providing so many with food and shelter, but, as may well be imag-

6. **John Brown:** a famous white abolitionist (1800–1859). He was hanged for leading an attack on the federal arsenal at Harper's Ferry, Virginia, in order to get arms to start a slave uprising.

They Called Her Moses **425**

ined, they were not very fastidious in either direction, and were well content with very plain food, and a strip of carpet on the floor for a bed, or a place on the straw in the barnloft."

Late in December, 1851, Harriet arrived in St. Catharines, Canada West (now Ontario), with the eleven fugitives. It had taken almost a month to complete this journey; most of the time had been spent getting out of Maryland.

That first winter in St. Catharines was a terrible one. Canada was a strange, frozen land, snow everywhere, ice everywhere, and a bone-biting cold the like of which none of them had ever experienced before. Harriet rented a small frame house in the town and set to work to make a home. The fugitives boarded with her. They worked in the forests, felling trees, and so did she. Sometimes she took other jobs, cooking or cleaning house for people in the town. She cheered on these newly arrived fugitives, working herself, finding work for them, finding food for them, praying for them, sometimes begging for them.

Often she found herself thinking of the beauty of Maryland, the mellowness of the soil, the richness of the plant life there. The climate itself made for an ease of living that could never be duplicated in this bleak, barren countryside.

In spite of the severe cold, the hard work, she came to love St. Catharines, and the other towns and cities in Canada where black men lived. She discovered that freedom meant more than the right to change jobs at will, more than the right to keep the money that one earned. It was the right to be elected to office. In Canada there were black men who were country officials and members of school boards. St. Catharines had a large colony of ex-slaves, and they owned their own homes. They lived in whatever part of town they chose and sent their children to the schools.

When spring came she decided that she would make this small Canadian city her home—as much as any place could be said to be home to a woman who traveled from Canada to the Eastern Shore of Maryland as often as she did.

In the spring of 1852, she went back to Cape May, New Jersey. She spent the summer there, cooking in a hotel. That fall she returned, as usual, to Dorchester County, and brought out nine more slaves, conducting them all the way to St. Catharines, in Canada West, to the bone-biting cold, the snow-covered forests—and freedom.

She continued to live in this fashion, spending the winter in Canada, and the spring and summer working in Cape May, New Jersey, or in Philadelphia. She made two trips a year into slave territory, one in the fall and another in the spring. She now had a definite crystallized purpose, and in carrying it out, her life fell into a pattern which remained unchanged for the next six years.

Reading Check

1. On what day of the week did the slave owners usually discover that slaves were missing?
2. How long did it take the slaves to make the trip from Maryland to Canada?
3. How many trips between Maryland and Canada did Harriet Tubman make each year?
4. Why wouldn't she allow a slave to go back after starting the trip?
5. What was the name of the book in which the stories of the escaping slaves were recorded?

Analyzing and Interpreting the Selection

1. Moses was the great Biblical hero who led the Israelites out of slavery in Egypt. Moses took his people on a long, perilous journey and brought them to the "Promised Land." How was Harriet Tubman another Moses?

2. The forbidden spiritual "Go Down, Moses" was a code song used by Harriet to announce her presence. What other signals did Harriet use to announce that she had returned?

3a. In what ways did Harriet keep hope alive in her group and instill courage in them? **b.** Why did she have to tell them, "Go on with us or die"?

4. The Underground Railroad, of course, was really not a railroad at all, and it was not literally "underground." Railroad terminology was part of the code. **a.** From what you've read here, tell what a "station" on the railroad was. **b.** In what sense was Harriet a "conductor" on the railroad?

5. "Freedom's not bought with dust," Harriet told her band of fugitives. What price did all these people, including Harriet, pay in order to purchase freedom?

Descriptive Writing

Using Specific Details in Description

The selection you have just read is from a book about Harriet Tubman's life. Earlier in that book, Harriet is described in this way:

> She worked from dawn to dusk, worked in the rain, in the heat of the sun. Her muscles hardened. She sang when she was in the fields or working in the nearby woods. Her voice was unusual because of the faint huskiness. Once having heard it, people remembered it. The low notes were rich and deep. The high notes were sweet and true. . . .

In 1831, Harriet started wearing a bandanna. It was made from a piece of brilliantly colored cotton cloth. She wound it around her head, deftly, smoothly, and then tied it in place, pulling the knots tight and hard. This new headgear was an indication that she was no longer regarded as a child. These colorful bandannas were worn by young women: they were a symbol of maturity. . . .

Sometimes this short, straight-backed young girl hummed under her breath, or sang, while she hoed the corn or tugged on the reins when a refractory mule refused to budge. True, work in the fields had calloused her hands, but it had given her a strong, erect body. She carried her head proudly as she sang.

One characteristic emphasized here is Harriet's beautiful voice. What specific details help you picture what Harriet looked like, and what she wore?

Write a paragraph or two describing a person you know well. Try to include a few specific details that will give your reader a picture of what this person looks like, and perhaps of the clothing he or she usually wears.

About the Author

Ann Petry   (1911–   )

Ann Petry graduated from the University of Connecticut. She has been a pharmacist and a salesperson in addition to being a reporter, novelist, short-story writer, and biographer. Her novels include *The Narrows,* which is about racial conflict in a New England town, and *The Street,* which concerns black poor in a ghetto. Petry says her aim is "to show how simply and easily the environment can change the course of a person's life."

Cub Pilot on the Mississippi

MARK TWAIN

A hundred years ago many boys living along the Mississippi dreamed of becoming steamboat pilots. One of them was the famous American writer, Mark Twain, who realized his ambition. In this excerpt from Life on the Mississippi, *Twain recalls events from his days as an apprentice to a riverboat pilot. What impression do you get of Twain from his attitude toward these events?*

When I was a boy, there was but one permanent ambition among my comrades in our village on the west bank of the Mississippi River. That was to be a steamboatman. We had transient[1] ambitions of other sorts, but they were only transient. When a circus came and went, it left us all burning to become clowns; the first minstrel show that ever came to our section left us all suffering to try that kind of life; now and then we had a hope that, if we lived and were good, God would permit us to be pirates. These ambitions faded out, each in its turn; but the ambition to be a steamboatman always remained.

I first wanted to be a cabin boy, so that I could come out with a white apron on and shake a tablecloth over the side, where all my old comrades could see me; later I thought I would rather be the deckhand who stood on the end of the stage plank with the coil of rope in his hand, because he was particularly conspicuous.

Boy after boy managed to get on the river. The minister's son became an engineer. The

1. **transient** (trăn′shənt): temporary; passing.

doctor's and the postmaster's sons became "mud clerks";[2] the wholesale liquor dealer's son became a barkeeper on a boat; four sons of the chief merchant, and two sons of the county judge, became pilots. Pilot was the grandest position of all. The pilot, even in those days of trivial wages, had a princely salary—from a hundred and fifty to two hundred and fifty dollars a month, and no board to pay. Two

2. **mud clerks:** the lowest of several clerks who assisted the purser, the officer in charge of financial accounts. A mud clerk was paid very little.

Rounding a Bend on the Mississippi,
The Parting Salute (1866) by
Currier and Ives. Lithograph.

months of his wages would pay a preacher's salary for a year. Now some of us were left disconsolate. We could not get on the river—at least our parents would not let us.

So, by and by, I ran away. I said I would never come home again until I was a pilot and could come in glory.

During the two or two and a half years of my apprenticeship I served under many pilots, and had experience of many kinds of steamboatmen and many varieties of steamboats. I am to this day profiting somewhat by that experience; for in that brief, sharp schooling, I got personally and familiarly acquainted with about all the different types of human nature

that are to be found in fiction, biography, or history.

The figure that comes before me oftenest, out of the shadows of that vanished time, is that of Brown, of the steamer *Pennsylvania*. He was a middle-aged, long, slim, bony, smooth-shaven, horsefaced, ignorant, stingy, malicious, snarling, fault-hunting, mote[3]-magnifying tyrant. I early got the habit of coming on watch with dread at my heart. No matter how good a time I might have been having with the off-watch below, and no matter how high my spirits might be when I started aloft, my soul became lead in my body the moment I approached the pilothouse.

I still remember the first time I ever entered the presence of that man. The boat had backed out from St. Louis and was "straightening down." I ascended to the pilothouse in high feather, and very proud to be semiofficially a member of the executive family of so fast and famous a boat. Brown was at the wheel. I paused in the middle of the room, all fixed to make my bow, but Brown did not look around. I thought he took a furtive glance at me out of the corner of his eye, but as not even this notice was repeated, I judged I had been mistaken. By this time he was picking his way among some dangerous "breaks" abreast the wood-yards; therefore it would not be proper to interrupt him; so I stepped softly to the high bench and took a seat.

There was silence for ten minutes; then my new boss turned and inspected me deliberately and painstakingly from head to heel for about—as it seemed to me—a quarter of an hour. After which he removed his countenance, and I saw it no more for some seconds; then it came around once more, and this question greeted me: "Are you Horace Bixby's cub?"

"Yes, sir."

After this time there was a pause and another inspection. Then: "What's your name?"

I told him. He repeated it after me. It was probably the only thing he ever forgot; for although I was with him many months he never addressed himself to me in any other way than "Here!" and then his command followed.

"Where was you born?"

"In Florida, Missouri."

A pause. Then: "Dern sight better stayed there!"

By means of a dozen or so of pretty direct questions, he pumped my family history out of me.

The leads[4] were going now in the first crossing. This interrupted the inquest.

It must have been all of fifteen minutes—fifteen minutes of dull, homesick silence—before that long horseface swung round upon me again—and then what a change! It was as red as fire, and every muscle in it was working. Now came this shriek: "Here! You going to set there all day?"

I lit in the middle of the floor, shot there by the electric suddenness of the surprise. As soon as I could get my voice I said apologetically: "I have had no orders, sir."

"You've had no *orders!* My, what a fine bird we are! We must have *orders!* Our father was a *gentleman*—and *we've* been to *school*. Yes, *we* are a gentleman, *too*, and got to have *orders!* ORDERS, is it? ORDERS is what you want! Dod dern my skin, *I'll* learn you to swell yourself up and blow around *here* about your dod-derned *orders!* G'way from the wheel!" (I had approached it without knowing it.)

I moved back a step or two and stood as in a

---

3. **mote:** a small particle, such as a speck of dust.

4. **leads** (lĕdz): weights lowered to test the depth of the river.

The Pilothouse of a Mississippi Steamboat (1875). Illustration by Edward W. King.

dream, all my senses stupefied by this frantic assault.

"What you standing there for? Take that ice pitcher down to the texas tender![5] Come, move along, and don't you be all day about it!"

The moment I got back to the pilothouse Brown said:

"Here! What was you doing down there all this time?"

"I couldn't find the texas tender; I had to go all the way to the pantry."

"Derned likely story! Fill up the stove."

5. **texas tender:** the waiter in the officers' quarters. The rooms on Mississippi steamboats were named after the states. Since the officers' area was the largest, and since Texas was the largest state at this time, it was called the *texas*.

I proceeded to do so. He watched me like a cat. Presently he shouted: "Put down that shovel! Derndest numskull I ever saw—ain't even got sense enough to load up a stove."

All through the watch this sort of thing went on. Yes, and the subsequent watches were much like it during a stretch of months. As I have said, I soon got the habit of coming on duty with dread. The moment I was in the presence, even in the darkest night, I could feel those yellow eyes upon me and knew their owner was watching for a pretext to spit out some venom on me. Preliminarily he would say: "Here! Take the wheel."

Two minutes later: "*Where* in the nation you going to? Pull her down! Pull her down!"

After another moment: "Say! You going to hold her all day? Let her go—meet her! Meet her!"

Then he would jump from the bench, snatch the wheel from me, and meet her himself, pouring out wrath upon me all the time.

George Ritchie was the other pilot's cub. He was having good times now, for his boss, George Ealer, was as kindhearted as Brown wasn't. Ritchie had steered for Brown the season before; consequently, he knew exactly how to entertain himself and plague me, all by the one operation. Whenever I took the wheel for a moment on Ealer's watch, Ritchie would sit back on the bench and play Brown, with continual ejaculations of "Snatch her! Snatch her! Derndest mudcat I ever saw!" "Here! Where are you going *now*? Going to run over that snag?" "Pull her *down!* Don't you hear me? Pull her *down!*" "There she goes! *Just* as I expected! I told you not to cramp that reef. G'way from the wheel!"

So I always had a rough time of it, no matter whose watch it was; and sometimes it seemed to me that Ritchie's good-natured badgering was pretty nearly as aggravating as Brown's dead-earnest nagging.

I often wanted to kill Brown, but this would not answer. A cub had to take everything his boss gave, in the way of vigorous comment and criticism; and we all believed that there was a United States law making it a penitentiary offense to strike or threaten a pilot who was on duty.

Two trips later, I got into serious trouble. Brown was steering; I was "pulling down." My younger brother [Henry] appeared on the hurricane deck, and shouted to Brown to stop at some landing or other, a mile or so below. Brown gave no intimation that he had heard anything. But that was his way: he never condescended to take notice of an underclerk. The

wind was blowing; Brown was deaf (although he always pretended he wasn't), and I very much doubted if he had heard the order. If I had had two heads, I would have spoken; but as I had only one, it seemed judicious to take care of it; so I kept still.

Presently, sure enough, we went sailing by that plantation. Captain Klinefelter appeared on the deck, and said: "Let her come around, sir, let her come around. Didn't Henry tell you to land here?"

"*No,* sir!"

"I sent him up to do it."

"He *did* come up; and that's all the good it done, the dod-derned fool. He never said anything."

"Didn't *you* hear him?" asked the captain of me.

Of course I didn't want to be mixed up in this business, but there was no way to avoid it; so I said: "Yes, sir."

I knew what Brown's next remark would be, before he uttered it. It was: "Shut your mouth! You never heard anything of the kind."

I closed my mouth, according to instructions. An hour later Henry entered the pilothouse, unaware of what had been going on. He was a thoroughly inoffensive boy, and I was sorry to see him come for I knew Brown would have no pity on him. Brown began, straightway. "Here! Why didn't you tell me we'd got to land at that plantation?"

"I did tell you, Mr. Brown."

"It's a lie!"

I said: "You lie, yourself. He did tell you."

Brown glared at me in unaffected surprise; and for as much as a moment he was entirely speechless; then he shouted to me: "I'll attend to your case in a half a minute!"; then to Henry, "And you leave the pilothouse; out with you!"

It was pilot law, and must be obeyed. The boy started out, and even had his foot on the

Mark Twain's steamboat pilot certificate (1859).
The Mariners Museum

upper step outside the door, when Brown, with a sudden access of fury, picked up a ten-pound lump of coal and sprang after him; but I was between, with a heavy stool, and I hit Brown a good honest blow which stretched him out.

I had committed the crime of crimes—I had lifted my hand against a pilot on duty! I supposed I was booked for the penitentiary sure, and couldn't be booked any surer if I went on and squared my long account with this person while I had the chance; consequently I stuck to him and pounded him with my fists a consider-

able time. I do not know how long; the pleasure of it probably made it seem longer than it really was; but in the end he struggled free and jumped up and sprang to the wheel: a very natural solicitude, for, all this time, here was this steamboat tearing down the river at the rate of fifteen miles an hour and nobody at the helm! However, Eagle Bend was two miles wide at this bank-full stage, and correspondingly long and deep; and the boat was steering herself straight down the middle and taking no chances. Still, that was only luck—a body *might* have found her charging into the woods.

Perceiving at a glance that the *Pennsylvania* was in no danger, Brown gathered up the big spyglass, war-club fashion, and ordered me out of the pilothouse with more than bluster. But I was not afraid of him now; so, instead of going, I tarried and criticized his grammar. I reformed his ferocious speeches for him and put them into good English, calling his attention to the advantages of pure English over the dialect of the Pennsylvania collieries[6] whence he was extracted. He could have done his part to admiration in a crossfire of mere vituperation,[7] of course; but he was not equipped for this species of controversy; so he presently laid aside his glass and took the wheel, muttering and shaking his head; and I retired to the bench. The racket had brought everybody to the hurricane deck, and I trembled when I saw the old captain looking up from amid the crowd. I said to myself, "Now I *am* done for!" for although, as a rule, he was so fatherly and indulgent toward the boat's family, and so patient of minor shortcomings, he could be stern enough when the fault was worth it.

I tried to imagine what he *would* do to a cub pilot who had been guilty of such a crime as mine, committed on a boat that was guard-

6. **collieries** (kŏl′yər-ēz): coal mines.
7. **vituperation** (vī-tōō′pə-rā′shən): abusive language.

deep[8] with costly freight and alive with passengers. Our watch was nearly ended. I thought I would go and hide somewhere till I got a chance to slide ashore. So I slipped out of the pilothouse, and down the steps, and around to the texas door, and I was in the act of gliding within, when the captain confronted me! I dropped my head, and he stood over me in silence a moment or two, then said impressively: "Follow me."

I dropped into his wake; he led the way to his parlor in the forward end of the texas. We were alone now. He closed the afterdoor, then moved slowly to the forward one and closed that. He sat down; I stood before him. He looked at me some little time, then said: "So you have been fighting Mr. Brown?"

I answered meekly: "Yes, sir."

"Do you know that that is a very serious matter?"

"Yes, sir."

"Are you aware that this boat was plowing down the river fully five minutes with no one at the wheel?"

"Yes, sir."

"Did you strike him first?"

"Yes, sir."

"What with?"

"A stool, sir."

"Hard?"

"Middling, sir."

"Did it knock him down?"

"He—he fell, sir."

"Did you follow it up? Did you do anything further?"

"Yes, sir."

"What did you do?"

"Pounded him, sir."

"Pounded him?"

"Yes, sir."

"Did you pound him much? That is, severely?"

"One might call it that, sir, maybe."

"I'm deuced glad of it! Hark ye, never mention that I said that. You have been guilty of a great crime; and don't you ever be guilty of it again, on this boat. *But*—lay for him ashore! Give him a good sound thrashing, do you hear? I'll pay the expenses. Now go—and mind you, not a word of this to anybody. Clear out with you! You've been guilty of a great crime, you whelp!"[9]

I slid out, happy with the sense of a close shave and a mighty deliverance, and I heard him laughing to himself and slapping his fat thighs after I had closed his door.

When Brown came off watch he went straight to the captain, who was talking with some passengers on the boiler deck, and demanded that I be put ashore in New Orleans—and added: "I'll never turn a wheel on this boat again while that cub stays."

The captain said: "But he needn't come round when you are on watch, Mr. Brown."

"I won't even stay on the same boat with him. *One* of us has got to go ashore."

"Very well," said the captain, "let it be yourself," and resumed his talk with the passengers.

During the brief remainder of the trip I knew how an emancipated slave feels, for I was an emancipated slave myself.

---

8. **guard-deep:** The *guard* of a ship is an extension of the deck. In this case, it refers to a wooden frame protecting the paddle wheel.

9. **whelp:** a puppy or cub; here, a disrespectful young man.

1. Why did Twain want to be the cabin boy or the deckhand on a steamboat?
2. Which position on a steamboat was considered to be the grandest of all?
3. Why was it essential for Twain to obey Brown's orders?
4. What was considered the most serious crime on a steamboat?
5. What advice did the captain give Twain?

For Study and Discussion

Analyzing and Interpreting the Selection

1. Twain tells a story in this part of his recollections. At the heart of the story is a conflict between two very different people. **a.** What was the conflict? **b.** How did the captain settle it?

2. Brown seemed to be furious at Twain the first time they met. Why do you think the old pilot disliked the young cub so much?

3. Why did Twain finally attack Brown?

4. People seem to enjoy reading about a conflict between an underdog and a bully—when the underdog wins. **a.** Were your sympathies with the cub or with Brown? **b.** With whom did the captain sympathize?

Literary Elements

Recognizing the Writer's Tone

Tone is the attitude a writer takes toward a subject. Tone can be serious, humorous, sarcastic, affectionate, and so on.

The events that Twain narrates here are certainly unpleasant. Yet the overall effect is not heavy and tragic because of the tone of the writing—the attitude that Twain takes toward these events.

Twain begins by itemizing the ambitions of his childhood comrades on page 428. What details here would make a reader smile?

Brown is clearly a bully and a villain. Yet a reader has to smile at his conflict with the cub. Look again at the first description of Brown on page 430. The sentence has twelve adjectives and one noun describing Brown. The first few adjectives seem unbiased; *middle-aged, long, slim, smooth-shaven*. Even *bony* and *horsefaced* might be considered neutral. But then the list builds to a comic crescendo: *ignorant, stingy, malicious, snarling, fault-hunting, mote-magnifying*. The final noun, *tyrant*, finishes the list off perfectly. Part of the fun is the exaggeration. We are used to the term *fault-finding*. How does *fault-hunting* differ from that?

A *mote* is a tiny speck, a bit of dust. What would a *mote-magnifying* person be like?

What is unusual about the way in which the cub humiliates the bully after attacking him? (Have you ever heard of a person using grammar to win a battle?)

How would you describe this story's tone?

Language and Vocabulary

Recognizing Jargon

Throughout this selection, Mark Twain uses words drawn from his experiences on a Mississippi steamboat. He refers to mud clerks, pilots, and texas tenders, and to "straightening down" and "pulling down." These words and phrases are examples of *jargon,* the specialized vocabulary of an occupation or field of knowledge. What other examples of jargon can you find in the selection? How do they contribute to the feeling Twain creates about his experiences as a cub pilot?

Descriptive Writing

Describing an Imaginary Character

Twain creates a vivid picture of the pilot, Mr. Brown, by describing him as a "middle-aged, long, slim, bony, smooth-shaven, horsefaced, ignorant, stingy, malicious, snarling, fault-hunting, mote-magnifying tyrant." Notice how Twain describes both the physical appearance and the personality of this unpleasant man. Write a paragraph in which you describe an imaginary character. Be sure to use vivid and specific words that convey the character's appearance and personality. You might want to share your description with your classmates by reading it in a small group.

About the Author

Mark Twain   (1835–1910)

Mark Twain is the pen name of Samuel Langhorne Clemens. The name came from the steamboatmen's cry: "By the mark, twain!" This cry meant that by their *mark* (measure), the river was *twain* (two) fathoms deep, which was a safe depth.

Twain was born in Missouri and lived an adventuresome boyhood, which he later made use of in his novels *The Adventures of Tom Sawyer* and *Adventures of Huckleberry Finn*. For a while, he worked for a newspaper, but he gave up this occupation to apprentice himself to a steamboat pilot on the Mississippi. He stayed on the river until the Civil War brought the steamboats nearly to a standstill. After the war, Twain started his career as a traveler and journalistic humorist in the frontier style. He was soon one of the most popular writers and lecturers in America, perhaps because he showed typical American irreverence for stuffiness and tradition.

Financial difficulties and the deaths of his wife and two daughters caused Twain great unhappiness. This is reflected in the bitter tone of some of his later writings. But he is remembered chiefly for his earlier, comic writings—his Western tales and his two great novels of American boyhood. One of his famous Western tales is "The Celebrated Jumping Frog of Calaveras County."

I Know Why the Caged Bird Sings

MAYA ANGELOU

In this part of her true story, Maya Angelou and her older brother, Bailey, lived with their grandmother in the small rural town of Stamps, Arkansas. As you read the selection, note how Maya as a young girl felt lonely and unloved until she met an unusual woman who threw her a "lifeline."

We lived with our grandmother and uncle in the rear of the Store (it was always spoken of with a capital *s*), which she had owned some twenty-five years.

Early in the century, Momma (we soon stopped calling her Grandmother) sold lunches to the sawmen in the lumberyard (east Stamps) and the seedmen at the cotton gin (west Stamps). Her crisp meat pies and cool lemonade, when joined to her miraculous ability to be in two places at the same time, assured her business success. From being a mobile lunch counter, she set up a stand between the two points of fiscal[1] interest and supplied the workers' needs for a few years. Then she had the Store built in the heart of the Negro area. Over the years it became the lay[2] center of activities in town. On Saturdays, barbers sat their customers in the shade on the porch of the Store, and troubadours on their ceaseless crawlings through the South leaned across its benches and sang their sad songs of the Brazos[3] while they played juice harps[4] and cigar-box guitars.

The formal name of the Store was the Wm. Johnson General Merchandise Store. Customers could find food staples, a good variety of colored thread, mash for hogs, corn for chickens, coal oil for lamps, light bulbs for the wealthy, shoestrings, hair dressing, balloons, and flower seeds. Anything not visible had only to be ordered.

Until we became familiar enough to belong to the Store and it to us, we were locked up in a Fun House of Things where the attendant had gone home for life.

Weighing the half-pounds of flour, excluding the scoop, and depositing them dust-free into the thin paper sacks held a simple kind of adventure for me. I developed an eye for measuring how full a silver-looking ladle of flour, mash, meal, sugar or corn had to be to push the scale indicator over to eight ounces or one pound. When I was absolutely accurate our appreciative customers used to admire: "Sister Henderson sure got some smart grandchildrens." If I was off in the Store's favor, the eagle-eyed women would say, "Put some more in that sack, child. Don't you try to make your profit offa me."

Then I would quietly but persistently punish myself. For every bad judgment, the fine was no silver-wrapped kisses, the sweet chocolate drops that I loved more than anything in the world, except Bailey. And maybe canned pineapples. My obsession with pineapples nearly drove me mad. I dreamt of the days when I would be grown and able to buy a whole carton for myself alone.

Although the syrupy golden rings sat in their exotic cans on the shelves year round, we only tasted them during Christmas. Momma used the juice to make almost-black fruit cakes. Then she lined heavy soot-encrusted iron skillets with the pineapple rings for rich upside-down cakes. Bailey and I received one slice each, and I carried mine around for hours, shredding off the fruit until nothing was left except the perfume on my fingers. I'd like to think that my desire for pineapples was so sacred that I wouldn't allow myself to steal a can (which was possible) and eat it alone out in the garden, but I'm certain that I must have weighed the possibility of the scent exposing me and didn't have the nerve to attempt it.

Until I was thirteen and left Arkansas for good, the Store was my favorite place to be. Alone and empty in the mornings, it looked like an unopened present from a stranger.

---

1. **fiscal:** financial.
2. **lay:** not religious. The religious center would be the church.
3. **the Brazos** (brăz'əs): a district in central Texas around the Brazos River.
4. **juice harps:** the author's misunderstanding, as a child, of *jew's-harps*, musical instruments held in the mouth and plucked.

Opening the front doors was pulling the ribbon off the unexpected gift. The light would come in softly (we faced north), easing itself over the shelves of mackerel, salmon, tobacco, thread. It fell flat on the big vat of lard and by noontime during the summer the grease had softened to a thick soup. Whenever I walked into the Store in the afternoon, I sensed that it was tired. I alone could hear the slow pulse of its job half done. But just before bedtime, after numerous people had walked in and out, had argued over their bills, or joked about their neighbors, or just dropped in "to give Sister Henderson a 'Hi y'all,'" the promise of magic mornings returned to the Store and spread itself over the family in washed life waves.

At this point in her story, Maya was about ten years old and had returned to Stamps from a visit to St. Louis with her mother. She had become very unhappy and withdrawn.

For nearly a year, I sopped around the house, the Store, the school and the church, like an old biscuit. Then I met, or rather got to know, the lady who threw me my first lifeline.

Mrs. Bertha Flowers was the aristocrat of Black Stamps. She had the grace of control to appear warm in the coldest weather, and on the Arkansas summer days it seemed she had a private breeze which swirled around, cooling her. She was thin without the taut look of wiry people, and her printed voile dresses and flowered hats were as right for her as denim overalls for a farmer.

Her skin was a rich black that would have peeled like a plum if snagged, but then no one would have thought of getting close enough to Mrs. Flowers to ruffle her dress, let alone snag her skin. She didn't encourage familiarity. She wore gloves too.

I don't think I ever saw Mrs. Flowers laugh, but she smiled often. A slow widening of her thin black lips to show even, small white teeth, then the slow effortless closing. When she chose to smile on me, I always wanted to thank her. The action was so graceful and inclusively benign.[5]

She was one of the few gentlewomen I have ever known, and has remained throughout my life the measure of what a human being can be.

One summer afternoon, sweet-milk fresh in my memory, she stopped at the Store to buy provisions. Another woman of her health and age would have been expected to carry the paper sacks home in one hand, but Momma said, "Sister Flowers, I'll send Bailey up to your house with these things."

She smiled that slow dragging smile, "Thank you, Mrs. Henderson. I'd prefer Marguerite, though." My name was beautiful when she said it. "I've been meaning to talk to her, anyway." They gave each other age-group looks.

There was a little path beside the rocky road, and Mrs. Flowers walked in front swinging her arms and picking her way over the stones.

She said, without turning her head, to me, "I hear you're doing very good schoolwork, Marguerite, but that it's all written. The teachers report that they have trouble getting you to talk in class." We passed the triangular farm on our left and the path widened to allow us to walk together. I hung back in the separate unasked and unanswerable questions.

"Come and walk along with me, Marguerite." I couldn't have refused even if I wanted to. She pronounced my name so nicely. Or more correctly, she spoke each word with such clarity that I was certain a foreigner who didn't understand English could have understood her.

"Now no one is going to make you talk—pos-

5. **benign** (bǐ-nīn′): kind.

sibly no one can. But bear in mind, language is man's way of communicating with his fellow-man and it is language alone which separates him from the lower animals." That was a totally new idea to me, and I would need time to think about it.

"Your grandmother says you read a lot. Every chance you get. That's good, but not good enough. Words mean more than what is set down on paper. It takes the human voice to infuse them with the shades of deeper meaning."

I memorized the part about the human voice infusing words. It seemed so valid and poetic.

She said she was going to give me some books and that I not only must read them, I must read them aloud. She suggested that I try to make a sentence sound in as many different ways as possible.

"I'll accept no excuse if you return a book to me that has been badly handled." My imagination boggled at the punishment I would deserve if in fact I did abuse a book of Mrs. Flowers'. Death would be too kind and brief.

The odors in the house surprised me. Somehow I had never connected Mrs. Flowers with food or eating or any other common experience of common people. There must have been an outhouse, too, but my mind never recorded it.

The sweet scent of vanilla had met us as she opened the door.

"I made tea cookies this morning. You see, I had planned to invite you for cookies and lemonade so we could have this little chat. The lemonade is in the icebox."

It followed that Mrs. Flowers would have ice on an ordinary day, when most families in our town bought ice late on Saturdays only a few times during the summer to be used in the wooden ice cream freezers.

She took the bags from me and disappeared through the kitchen door. I looked around the room that I had never in my wildest fantasies imagined I would see. Browned photographs leered or threatened from the walls and the white, freshly done curtains pushed against themselves and against the wind. I wanted to gobble up the room entire and take it to Bailey, who would help me analyze and enjoy it.

"Have a seat, Marguerite. Over there by the table." She carried a platter covered with a tea towel. Although she warned that she hadn't tried her hand at baking sweets for some time, I was certain that like everything else about her the cookies would be perfect.

They were flat round wafers, slightly browned on the edges and butter-yellow in the center. With the cold lemonade they were sufficient for childhood's lifelong diet. Remembering my manners, I took nice little ladylike bites off the edges. She said she had made them expressly for me and that she had a few in the kitchen that I could take home to my brother. So I jammed one whole cake in my mouth and the rough crumbs scratched the insides of my jaws, and if I hadn't had to swallow, it would have been a dream come true.

As I ate she began the first of what we later called "my lessons in living." She said that I must always be intolerant of ignorance but understanding of illiteracy. That some people, unable to go to school, were more educated and even more intelligent than college professors. She encouraged me to listen carefully to what country people called mother wit. That in those homely[6] sayings was couched the collective wisdom of generations.

When I finished the cookies she brushed off the table and brought a thick, small book from the bookcase. I had read *A Tale of Two Cities* and found it up to my standards as a romantic novel. She opened the first page and I heard poetry for the first time in my life.

6. **homely:** ordinary; everyday.

"It was the best of times, it was the worst of times . . . ." Her voice slid in and curved down through and over the words. She was nearly singing. I wanted to look at the pages. Were they the same that I had read? Or were there notes, music, lined on the pages, as in a hymnbook? Her sounds began cascading gently. I knew from listening to a thousand preachers that she was nearing the end of her reading, and I hadn't really heard, heard to understand, a single word.

"How do you like that?"

It occurred to me that she expected a response. The sweet vanilla flavor was still on my tongue and her reading was a wonder in my ears. I had to speak.

I said, "Yes, ma'am." It was the least I could do, but it was the most also.

"There's one more thing. Take this book of poems and memorize one for me. Next time you pay me a visit, I want you to recite."

I have tried often to search behind the sophistication of years for the enchantment I so easily found in those gifts. The essence escapes but its aura[7] remains. To be allowed, no, invited, into the private lives of strangers, and to share their joys and fears, was a chance to exchange bitter wormwood[8] for a cup of mead with Beowulf[9] or a hot cup of tea and milk with Oliver Twist. When I said aloud, "It is a far, far better thing that I do, than I have ever done . . . "[10] tears of love filled my eyes at my selflessness.

On that first day, I ran down the hill and into the road (few cars ever came along it) and had

the good sense to stop running before I reached the Store.

I was liked, and what a difference it made. I was respected not as Mrs. Henderson's grandchild or Bailey's sister but for just being Marguerite Johnson.

Childhood's logic never asks to be proved (all conclusions are absolute). I didn't question why Mrs. Flowers had singled me out for attention, nor did it occur to me that Momma might have asked her to give me a little talking to. All I cared about was that she had made tea cookies for *me* and read to *me* from her favorite book. It was enough to prove that she liked me.

7. **aura** (ôr′ ə): an atmosphere; a general feeling or quality.
8. **wormwood:** a bitter-tasting plant.
9. **Beowulf:** the hero of an old Anglo-Saxon epic. In this epic, people drink mead, a sweet drink made with honey.
10. **"It is . . . than I have ever done":** The speech is from *A Tale of Two Cities* by Charles Dickens. The narrator of this novel imagines that the hero says these words as he heroically goes to die on the guillotine so that another man can live.

I Know Why the Caged Bird Sings   **441**

Reading Check

1. What work did the narrator do in her grandmother's store?
2. How did she punish herself for errors in judgment?
3. What food did the family have only at Christmas?
4. What complaint did teachers have about the narrator's schoolwork?
5. What "assignment" did Mrs. Flowers give her before she left?

For Study and Discussion

Analyzing and Interpreting the Selection

1. In this part of her autobiography, Maya Angelou tells about a place and a person that were important in her childhood. The place was the Store. She compares the Store to a "Fun House of Things." **a.** What does she say the Store looked like in the morning? **b.** What do these descriptions tell you about her feelings for the Store?

2. The important person in Maya's childhood was Mrs. Flowers. How did Mrs. Flowers teach her to have compassion for other people in her first "lesson in living"?

3. How did Mrs. Flowers show that she "liked" and "respected" Maya?

4. Maya eventually grew up to become a well-known writer. What details in this story show that Mrs. Flowers probably awakened her love of language?

5. Maya compares herself to an old biscuit. **a.** What beautiful fruit does she compare Mrs. Flowers' skin to? **b.** What do these two comparisons tell you of Maya's feelings about herself and Mrs. Flowers?

Descriptive Writing

Describing a Setting

Note how Maya Angelou uses specific details and precise words to evoke the character of the Store. Choose a favorite place of your own and describe it in one or two paragraphs.

About the Author

Maya Angelou (1928–)

Maya Angelou eventually moved away from Stamps, Arkansas. She lived in San Francisco for a while and studied to become a professional dancer and an actress. She toured Europe and Africa in a production of *Porgy and Bess* for the State Department. She also worked in the civil-rights movement for Dr. Martin Luther King, Jr., and wrote for newspapers in Egypt and Ghana.

Angelou has written about her own life and feelings as a black American woman in the twentieth century in four autobiographical books, beginning with *I Know Why the Caged Bird Sings* in 1970. She took the title of that work from a poem called "Sympathy" by the black poet Paul Laurence Dunbar. Like the poet, Maya Angelou identified with the songbird that sings because it wants to be free. She has written a number of books, plays, screenplays, television productions, and magazine articles. She also has made several recordings, including *The Poetry of Maya Angelou.*

A Time of Beginnings

JADE SNOW WONG

In this excerpt from No Chinese Stranger, *Jade Snow Wong tells about her struggle to become a ceramic artist. Because she had no money to rent a studio, Jade Snow Wong persuaded one of the merchants in the community to let her use part of his shop for her work. She set up her potter's wheel in a store window.*

Although this story is an autobiography, the author writes about her experiences in the third person.

After Jade Snow began working in Mr. Fong's window, which confined her clay spatters, her activity revealed for the first time to Chinatown residents an art which had distinguished Chinese culture. Ironically, it was not until she was at college that she became fascinated with Tang and Sung Dynasty[1] achievements in clay, a thousand years ago.

Her ability to master pottery made her father happy, for Grandfather Wong believed that a person who could work with his hands would never starve. When Father Wong was young, Grandfather made him learn how to hand-pierce and stitch slipper soles, and how to knot Chinese button heads, both indispensable in clothing. But to Mother Wong, the merits of making pottery escaped her—to see her college-educated daughter up to her elbows in clay, and more clay flying around as she worked in public view, was strangely unladylike. As for Chinatown merchants, they laughed openly at her, "Here comes the girl who plays with mud. How many bowls could

you sell today?" Probably they thought: Here is a college graduate foolish enough to dirty her hands.

It has been the traditional belief from Asia to the Middle East, with Japan the exception, that scholars do not soil their hands and that a person studies literature in order to escape hard work. This attitude is still prevalent in most Asian countries outside of the People's Republic of China and Japan.

From the first, the local Chinese were not Jade Snow's patrons. The thinness and whiteness of porcelains imported from China and ornate decorations which came into vogue during the late Ching Dynasty[2] satisfied their tastes. They could not understand why "silly Americans" paid dollars for a hand-thrown bowl utilizing crude California colored clays, not much different from the inexpensive peasant ware of China. That the Jade Snow Wong bowl went back to an older tradition of understated beauty was not apparent. They could see only that she wouldn't apply a dragon or a hundred flowers.

1. **Tang and Sung Dynasty:** The Tang Dynasty lasted from 618 to 906; the Sung Dynasty, from 960 to 1279.

2. **Ching Dynasty:** the period from 1644 to 1912.

Many years later when Jade Snow met another atypical artist, a scholar and calligrapher[3] born and educated in China, he was to say to her, "I shudder if the majority of people look at my brush work and say it is pretty, for then I know it is ordinary and I have failed. If they say they do not understand it, or even that it is ugly, I am happy, for I have succeeded."

However, there were enough numbers of the American public who bought Jade Snow's pottery to support her modestly. The store window was a temporary experiment which proved what she needed to know. In the meantime, her aging father, who was fearful that their home and factory might be in a redevelopment area, made a down payment with lifetime savings to purchase a small white wooden building with six rentable apartments at the perimeter of Chinatown. Jade Snow agreed to rent the two tiny empty storefronts which he did not yet need, one for a display room, with supplies and packing center at its rear, the other for the potter's wheel, kiln, glazing booth, compressor, and other equipment. Now, instead of paying Mr. Fong a commission on gross sales, she had bills to pay. Instead of sitting in a window, she worked with doors thrown open to the street.

Creativeness was 90 percent hard work and 10 percent inspiration. It was learning from errors, either from her lack of foresight or because of the errors of others. The first firing in an unfamiliar new gas kiln brought crushing disappointment when the wares blew up into tiny pieces. In another firing, glaze results were uneven black and dark green, for the chemical supply house had mistakenly labeled five pounds of black copper oxide as black iron oxide. One morning there was a personal catastrophe. Unaware of a slow leak all night

from the partially opened gas cock, she lit a match at the kiln. An explosion injured both hands, which took weeks to heal.

The day-to-day work of pottery making tested her deepest discipline. A "wedged" ball of clay (prepared by kneading) would be "thrown" (shaped) on the potter's wheel, then dried overnight and trimmed, sometimes decorated with Chinese brush or bamboo tools. It took about a hundred thoroughly dried pieces to fill a kiln for the first firing that transformed fragile mud walls into hard bisque[4] ware. Glazes, like clays the results of countless experiments, were then applied to each piece. A second twelve-hour firing followed, with the temperatures raised hour by hour up to the final maturing point of somewhere around 2,000 degrees Fahrenheit. Then the kiln was turned off for twenty-four hours of cooling. Breakage was a potential hazard at every stage; each step might measure short in technical and artistic accomplishment. A piece she worked on diligently could disappoint. Another made casually had been enhanced successively until it delighted. One piece in ten might be of exhibition quality, half might be salable, and others would be flawed "seconds" she would discard.

Yet Jade Snow never wavered from her belief that if moments in time could result in a thing of beauty that others could share, those moments were immeasurably satisfying. She owned two perfect Sung tea bowls. Without copying, she tried to make her pottery "stand up" in strength and grace to that standard.

It became routine to work past midnight without days off. Handwork could not be rushed; failures had to be replaced, and a host of other unanticipated business chores suddenly manifested themselves. She had kept comparable hours when she worked all

3. **calligrapher** (kə-lĭg′rə-fər): an expert in the art of beautiful and decorative handwriting.

4. **bisque** (bĭsk) **ware**: pottery that is left unglazed.

through college to meet her expenses. Again, the hope of reaching valued goals was her spur. If she should fail, then she could accept what tradition dictated for most Chinese daughters—to be a wife, daughter-in-law, and mother. But unlike her college, the American business world was not dedicated to helping her. Because she was pioneering in a new venture, her identity was a liability. Her brains and hands were her only assets. How could she convert that liability? How could she differ from other struggling potters?

To enlarge her production base, she experimented with enamels on copper forms conceived in the fluid shapes of her pottery, layering jewel tones for brilliant effects. They differed from the earth tints of clay and attracted a new clientele. With another kiln and new equipment she made functional forms, believing that fine things should become part of the user's everyday life. The best results were submitted to exhibitions. Some juries rejected them, some accepted, and others awarded prizes.

To reach a market larger than San Francisco, she wrote to store buyers around the country, and, encouraged, she called on them. Traveling to strange cities far across the United States, as a rare Oriental woman alone in hotel dining rooms, she developed strong nerves against curious stares. That trip produced orders. Stipulated delivery and cancellation dates made it necessary to hire first one and then more helpers who had to be trained, checked, kept busy and happy.

The strains increased. So did the bills, and she borrowed in small amounts from her sympathetic father, who said, "A hundred dollars is easy to come by, but the first thousand is very, very tricky. Look at the ideograph[5] for hun-

---

5. **ideograph** (ĭd′ē-ə-grăf′): a written symbol that represents an idea or a thing in the form of a picture.

---

dred—solidly square. Look at it for thousand

(hundred)   (thousand)

—pointed, slippery. The ancients knew this long ago." When hundreds were not enough, tactful Western friends offered help. Oldest Brother, noticing her worries and struggles, sniffed scornfully, "You'll be out of business in a year."

She had learned to accept family criticism in silence, but she was too deeply involved to give up. Money was a worry, but creating was exciting and satisfying. These were lonely years. Jade Snow's single-minded pursuit did not allow her pleasant interludes with friends. To start a kiln at dawn, then watch till its critical maturing moment, which could happen any time between early evening and midnight or later (when gas pressure was low it took until the next dawn), kept her from social engagements.

Then, gradually, signs indicated that she was working in the right direction. The first was a letter from the Metropolitan Museum of Art in New York, where the Eleventh Ceramic National Syracuse Show had been sent. The curator wrote, "We think the green, gold, and ivory enamel bowl a skillful piece of workmanship and are anxious to add it to our collections." They referred to a ten-inch shallow bowl which Jade Snow had made.

A reviewer in *Art Digest* wrote, "In plain enamels without applied design, Jade Snow Wong of San Francisco seemed to this critic to top the list."

Recognition brought further recognition. National decorating magazines featured her enamels, and in the same year, 1947, the Museum of Modern Art installed an exhibit by

Mies van der Rohe[6] which displayed 100 objects of fine design costing less than $100. A note introducing this exhibit read, "Every so often the Museum of Modern Art selects and exhibits soundly designed objects available to American purchasers in the belief that this will encourage more people to use beautiful things in their everyday life. . . ." Two of Jade Snow's enamels, a dinner plate in Chinese red and a dessert plate in grayish-gold, were included in the exhibition, which subsequently went to Europe.

So it did not seem unusual to receive an interviewer from *Mademoiselle,* but it was indeed unexpected to receive one of the magazine's ten awards for 1948 to women outstanding in ten different fields. They invited Jade Snow to fly to New York to claim her silver medal.

The more deeply one delves into a field, the more one realizes limitations. When Bernard Leach, the famous English potter, accepted an invitation from Mills College to teach a special course, Jade Snow attended. Another summer, Charles Merritt came from Alfred University's staff to give a course in precise glaze chemistry. Again, she commuted to Oakland. She became friends with these two unusual teachers. Both agreed that in potterymaking, one never found a final answer. A mass-produced bathtub may be a technical triumph; yet a chemically balanced glaze on a pot can be aesthetically dull. Some of the most pleasing glaze effects could never be duplicated, for they were the combination of scrapings from the glaze booth. Like the waves of the sea, no two pieces of pottery art can be identical.

After three years of downs, then ups, the business promised to survive. Debts had been cleared. A small staff could handle routine duties. A steady clientele of San Franciscans came to her out-of-the-way shop. A beginning had been made.

---

6. **Mies van der Rohe** (mēs′ vän dər rō′ə): Ludwig Mies van der Rohe (1886–1969), a famous American architect and industrial designer, born in Germany.

Reading Check

1. Why was Jade Snow's father happy that she was working with her hands?
2. Why did her mother disapprove of her work?
3. Who became Jade Snow's patrons?
4. What award did Jade Snow receive?

For Study and Discussion

Analyzing and Interpreting the Selection

1. In striving to become an artist, Jade Snow Wong had her father's support. However, she had to overcome the prejudices of other people in her family and in her community. Why was her behavior considered unladylike and foolish?

2. In the work that she had chosen for herself, Jade Snow Wong felt that "her identity was a liability. Her brains and hands were her only assets" (page 445). How was her identity a disadvantage to her?

3a. What steps did Jade Snow Wong take to build up her business?   **b.** What sacrifices did she have to make in order to devote herself to her art?   **c.** How was she encouraged to continue with her work?

4. In order to achieve her goal, Jade Snow Wong had to overcome many obstacles. What qualities of character enabled her to do this?

Language and Vocabulary

Tracing Word Histories

You can learn a good deal about the history of a word by consulting a dictionary. Most dictionaries use abbreviations to indicate the origin and development of words. Some of these abbreviations are *L.* (for Latin), *F.* or *Fr.* (for French), *Sp.* (for Spanish), and *Gk.* (for Greek). You will generally find information about the origin of a word given in parentheses or brackets.

The word *ceramic* comes from Greek. A dictionary will show you the history of the word in this way:

[<Gk. *keramikos* <*keramos,* potter's clay]

The symbol < means "derived from." The word *ceramic* comes from the Greek word *keramikos,* which in turns comes from another Greek word, *keramos,* meaning "potter's clay."

Use a dictionary to find the history of each of the following words from the selection:

    hazard   interlude   kiln   vogue

About the Author

Jade Snow Wong (1922–   )

Jade Snow Wong wrote about her upbringing in San Francisco's Chinatown in *Fifth Chinese Daughter. No Chinese Stranger,* written more than twenty-five years later, is a sequel to that story. In this second of her memoirs, Jade Snow Wong describes the changes that have taken place in Chinese-American life as old customs have weakened and new problems have arisen. "A Time of Beginnings," which tells of her career as a ceramist, is part of the first chapter of this book.

DEVELOPING SKILLS
IN CRITICAL THINKING

Distinguishing Between Facts and Opinions

A *fact* is something that has happened or is true. An *opinion* is a statement that represents a belief or judgment and that cannot be proved. This statement is a fact: *As a steamboat pilot, Mark Twain had to become familiar with 1,200 miles of the Mississippi River.* This statement is an opinion: *Mark Twain knew the Mississippi River better than anyone else.* The second statement is an assertion that cannot be proved. There is nothing wrong with opinions as long as they are not presented as or mistaken for facts.

As a reader and as a listener, you need to know whether you are being presented with facts or opinions. In the following passage, which statements would you consider fact and which would you consider opinion or hearsay?

In our own American annals, no individual member of the zoological world can rival Old Abe, the Wisconsin Civil War eagle, in the nation's affections, although one might get an argument in favor of Jumbo, P. T. Barnum's celebrated elephant, or of a magnificent, shaggy, American bull bison whose name may or may not have been Black Diamond and whose home was probably, but not certainly, New York's Central Park Zoo. The bison was real, all right, but the high regard in which he was held was due in part to an unfair advantage: he represented money since his profile appeared on the reverse of the "buffalo" nickel.

But on to our eagle, who was, after all, designated our national bird in 1782. Early in 1861, at sugar-making time, a Chippewa Indian called Chief Sky captured a young bald eagle at the headwaters of the Flambeau River near the line between Wisconsin's Ashland and Pierce counties. Finding a large, tublike nest of mud and sticks in a tall pine, the Indian felled the tree amid the screams and menaces of the parent birds.

PRACTICE IN
READING AND WRITING

Nonfiction

Nonfiction is not invented; it is "true" or "factual." Examples of nonfiction in this unit include an informative article, an informal essay, an excerpt from a biography, and selections from autobiographies. Other examples of nonfiction are news articles, articles on science or history, movie reviews, how-to-do-it books, letters, and speeches.

Here are some questions you should ask yourself as you read nonfiction:

1. What is the topic?
2. What details develop the topic?
3. Does the writer state any conclusions about the topic?
4. What is the writer's purpose?

Suggestions for Writing

Write a factual paragraph on one of these topics or on one of your own choosing:

How to raise a hamster
The origin of soccer
The disappearance of Pompeii
Famous monster movies
An accidental scientific discovery

Here are some guidelines to follow in planning and writing your report.

Prewriting

- Choose a topic you are interested in or know something about. Be sure that it is one on which you can find information in reference sources such as encyclopedias and magazines.
- Gather information from your sources. Keep a record of each source you use.
- Use note cards to take notes as you read material about your topic. Be sure to identify the source, including the page number, from which you take each note.
- Decide what general divisions or subtopics you will cover under the main topic of your report. Use these divisions or subtopics as headings for your note cards.
- Organize your note cards in stacks according to the headings, and use them to develop an informal outline for your report.

Writing

As you write the first draft of your report, remember that you will need an introduction, a body, and a conclusion. Use your own words most of the time. When it is necessary to quote directly, be sure to use quotation marks.

Evaluating and Revising

Evaluate the draft of your report by answering the following questions. Then revise your draft by adding, cutting, reordering, or replacing words or ideas.

- Is there enough factual information to develop the topic?

- Have you used your own words whenever possible?
- Are all the details in the report related to the topic?
- Are the details arranged in a logical order? Have you used transitional expressions such as *however*, *then*, and *finally* to make clear the relationships among the facts?
- Does the report have an interesting introduction and a conclusion that gives your reader a sense of completion?

Proofreading

Reread your revised draft to locate and correct any errors in usage, punctuation, capitalization, or spelling. Be sure that you have used quotation marks correctly for any direct quotations. Then prepare a clean copy of your report by following correct manuscript form.

For Further Reading

Anderson, Marian, *My Lord, What a Morning: An Autobiography* (Viking, 1956)
  One of America's greatest singers tells her own story, including the time she delivered an unforgettable concert before 75,000 people on the steps of the Lincoln Memorial in Washington, D.C.

Barth, Edna, *I'm Nobody! Who Are You?: The Story of Emily Dickinson* (Seabury, 1971)
  This easy-to-read biography of the secluded life of the New England poet includes some of her poems and passages from her letters.

Branley, Franklyn M., *The Mystery of Stonehenge* (Thomas Y. Crowell, 1969)
  The author presents several theories about the origins of the mysterious ring of massive stones set up in England about 1800 B.C.

Buckmaster, Henrietta, *Women Who Shaped History* (Macmillan, 1966; paperback, Collier)
  These six nineteenth-century women succeeded in changing the future.

Butler, Hal, *Sports Heroes Who Wouldn't Quit* (Messner, 1973)
  Here are stories about men and women who overcame handicaps to succeed in baseball, swimming, hockey, track, golf, and other sports.

Clemens, Samuel L., *Autobiography of Mark Twain* (Harper & Row, 1959; paperback, Harper)
  America's greatest humorist tells about his life. This is a big book that is worth sampling.

Day, Clarence, *Life with Father* (Knopf, 1946; paperback, Washington Square Press)
  The author writes humorously about his stubborn father and their family life in New York City in the 1890s.

Hersey, John, *Hiroshima* (Knopf, 1946; paperback, Bantam)
  This famous and unforgettable report follows six people who survived the atomic blast in Hiroshima, Japan, in 1945.

Lindbergh, Charles A., *The Spirit of St. Louis* (Scribner, 1953; paperback, Avon, 1985)
  Lindbergh tells his own exciting story of the first nonstop solo transatlantic flight from New York to Paris.

Ogg, Oscar, *The Twenty-Six Letters* (Thomas Y. Crowell, 1971)
  When did people begin to write—and why? This illustrated book traces the history of writing from ancient to present times.

Place, Marian T., *On the Track of Bigfoot* (Dodd, Mead, 1974)
  Monstrous hairy creatures are said to roam the mountains of the Pacific Northwest. Do they really exist? The author presents the evidence and lets you decide.

Robertson, Dougal, *Survive the Savage Sea* (Praeger, 1973; paperback, Sheridan, 1984)
  This is a true account of a family's struggle to survive thirty-eight days on a raft, adrift in the Pacific Ocean, after their boat had been destroyed by killer whales. The incredible story is told by the father.

Roueché, Berton, *Eleven Blue Men* (Little, Brown, 1954; paperback, Berkley)
  These are stories about health workers who investigate mysterious killer diseases.

Steinbeck, John, *Travels with Charley in Search of America* (Viking, 1962; paperback, Penguin, 1980)
  Accompanied by a comical old poodle named Charley, Steinbeck travels in a camper across America in the hopes of "rediscovering" a country he has known all his life.

Sullivan, George, *Marathon—The Longest Race* (Westminster Press, 1980)
  This an account of running from the marathon in ancient Greece to the Boston marathon.

POETRY

Detail from *A Field of Poppies* (1873)
by Claude Monet (1840–1926). Oil.
Musée D'Orsay

Long before there was writing, there was poetry. When people wanted to commemorate a battle or a birth, they did it in the rhythmic language we call poetry. When they told the history of their society, they did it in a form of poetry. Many of their most important laws, rituals, and beliefs were passed on from generation to generation in the form of poetry.

Poetry is a rhythmic use of language that seems to come naturally to people. Children use poetry. They recite nursery rhymes and nonsense jingles. They play games to the swing of rhythmic chants. Perhaps you recall using poetry to aid your memory. Remember the rhyme about the days of the months beginning "Thirty days hath September . . . "?

Poetry packs a good deal of meaning into a small space. It can help us see the world in an entirely fresh, new way. It can make us use our emotions. Robert Frost, himself a poet, said that poetry helped him remember things he didn't know ne knew. Perhaps some of the poems in this unit will have a special effect on you.

CLOSE READING
OF A POEM

Developing Skills in Critical Thinking

Poets make use of many elements to communicate experience. They rely on the suggestive power of language and choose words for their emotional effect as well as for their literal meaning. They appeal to both the mind and the senses through images and figures of speech. Poets also make use of patterns, such as rhyme and rhythm, and special forms, such as the ballad.

It is a good idea to read a poem several times, and aloud at least once. Often it is helpful to write a prose paraphrase of a poem, restating all its ideas in plain language (see pages 456 and 513).

Read the following poem several times. Then read the *explication,* a line-by-line examination of the poem's content and technique.

The Dark Hills

E. A. ROBINSON

Dark hills at evening in the west,
Where sunset hovers like a sound
Of golden horns that sang to rest
Old bones of warriors under ground,
Far now from all the bannered ways
Where flash the legions of the sun,
You fade—as if the last of days
Were fading, and all wars were done.

Explication

The speaker is watching a sunset. As the light fades, the hills grow dark. The real subject of the poem, however, is not the sunset but the thoughts and feelings that are set into motion by the dying day.

The poem is made up of a single sentence. In the opening line the speaker addresses the dark hills, but the subject and verb—"You fade"—do not appear until line 7. All the word groups in the first four lines modify the dark hills; all the word groups in lines 5–8 modify the verb *fade*.

The first four lines are devoted to a description of the hills at sunset. The poet describes the sunset in musical terms, drawing his simile from the fanfare of ancient warfare. The "golden horns" are trumpets that were played at a military cemetery to honor the "Old bones of warriors" laid to rest. The golden light of the setting sun seems to hover, or linger, over the scene the way the mellow sound of those "golden horns" once seemed to linger over the dead. Thus the reader is made to associate the final phase of the day with the calm of the grave.

Lines 5–6 also evoke military scenes from the past. The phrase "bannered ways" makes one think of roads or streets lined with flags. The "legions" refer to armies. The rays of the sun flashing across the sky during the day are the soldiers marching to battle. By drawing upon martial spectacles of the past, the speaker seems to be saying that throughout history human beings have made an elaborate and showy drama of war. At sunset, the dark hills seem remote from the heroics of battle.

In the final simile of lines 7–8, the speaker associates the peaceful mood of dusk with the "last of days." The speaker finds in the fading hills a symbol for the end of time and the end of human strife. What is not stated in the poem, but is clearly felt, is a longing on the part of the speaker for a world without war.

Guidelines for Reading a Poem

1. *Read the poem several times, and aloud at least once, following the author's clues for phrasing.* Punctuation marks tell you where to pause. Robinson does not expect the reader to pause at the end of each line. Lines 2 and 3, for example, are run-on lines, signifying that the author wishes no break in thought.

2. *Look up key words and references.* If you did not know the meaning of *legions* in line 6, you might miss the meaning of lines 5–6.

3. *Write a paraphrase of any lines that need clarification or simplification.* A paraphrase helps a reader understand imagery and figurative language. A paraphrase also puts into normal word order any inverted constructions. A paraphrase of lines 2–4 might read: "Where the glow of sunset lingers in the sky the way the mellow notes of trumpets, blown at the ceremonious burial of old soldiers, seemed to linger in the air."

4. *Arrive at the central idea or meaning of the poem.* Try to state this theme in one or two sentences: *In "The Dark Hills," watching the sun set in the west leads the speaker to reflect on the desire for peace and the inevitability of war.*

Language and Meaning

THE SPEAKER

Who is the *speaker* in a poem? The speaker may be the poet, but often the speaker will be someone or something entirely different. The speaker of a poem may be an animal, a building, or a child. There may even be more than one speaker in a poem. As you read "Southbound on the Freeway," ask yourself who is speaking. Then think about how the speaker affects the meaning of the poem.

Southbound on the Freeway

MAY SWENSON

A tourist came in from
Orbitville, parked in the air, and said:

The creatures of this star
are made of metal and glass.

Through the transparent parts   5
you can see their guts.

Their feet are round and roll
on diagrams or long

measuring tapes, dark
with white lines.   10

They have four eyes.
The two in back are red.

Sometimes you can see a five-eyed
one, with a red eye turning

on the top of his head.   15
He must be special—

the others respect him
and go slow

when he passes, winding
among them from behind.   20

They all hiss as they glide,
like inches, down the marked

tapes. Those soft shapes,
shadowy inside

the hard bodies—are they   25
their guts or their brains?

For Study and Discussion

Analyzing and Interpreting the Poem

1. What clues in the first four lines tell you that the tourist is from outer space?

2. The tourist describes creatures that are made of metal and glass (lines 3–4). **a.** In what other ways does this tourist describe the creatures? **b.** What are they?

3a. What are the soft shapes (line 23) that the tourist sees inside the creatures? **b.** How do they puzzle the tourist?

4. This poem describes a part of our world from an unusual point of view. The poet may be suggesting that human beings have become so dependent on mechanical devices that they have lost part of their human identity. Do the tourist's conclusions force you to think about this idea? Why or why not?

5. What does the tourist fail to see on our planet?

Creative Writing

Using an Unusual Point of View

In Swenson's poem a speaker looks down at cars on the freeway and describes them as if they were living creatures. Imagine that you are a visitor from outer space. How would you describe the mechanical things you see around you? A radio might be a small, rigid creature that talks and sings in different voices. A subway might be a serpent that screams. A bicycle and its rider might be a creature that moves on two round feet.

Choose an ordinary object or device. Try to think of something that moves or makes noise. In two or three sentences, describe it as though you were a tourist from another planet.

About the Author

May Swenson (1919–)

May Swenson was born in Logan, Utah, but has lived mostly in or near New York City. She frequently arranges her poems in shapes that suggest animals or ordinary objects. Some of her poems are riddles. Swenson has said, "The poet works (and plays) with the elements of language, forming and transforming his material to the point where a new perception emerges." Swenson has written eight volumes of poetry and received numerous awards. She also has taught poetry at universities.

Literary Elements

Identifying the Speaker

Identifying the speaker is an important step in understanding a poem's meaning. For example, May Swenson's poem would be difficult to understand if you didn't know that the "tourist" is a visitor from outer space. Who is the speaker in "Paul Revere's Ride" (page 136)? What characteristics has Longfellow given his speaker?

DICTION

Diction refers to a writer's choice of words. Poets choose words for precise effects. They depend on the associations, or *connotations,* of words as well as on their literal meanings, or *denotations.* Consider the phrases "three little pigs" and "three diminutive mammals with long, broad snouts." What is your reaction to the diction in each phrase?

The diction of a poem may be formal or informal. In "Southbound on the Freeway," the speaker refers to "their guts" in line 6. More formal usage would be *entrails.*

Poets may make up words, use unusual word order, or run words together. In "old age sticks" (page 98), E. E. Cummings achieves interesting effects by stretching out words. This freedom with language is called *poetic license.*

Mother to Son

LANGSTON HUGHES

Well, son, I'll tell you:
Life for me ain't been no crystal stair.
It's had tacks in it,
And splinters,
And boards torn up,   5
And places with no carpet on the floor—
Bare.
But all the time
I'se been a-climbin' on,
And reachin' landin's   10
And turnin' corners,
And sometimes goin' in the dark
Where there ain't been no light.
So boy, don't you turn back.
Don't set you down on the steps   15
'Cause you finds it's kinder hard.
Don't you fall now—
For I'se still goin', honey,
I'se still climbin',
And life for me ain't been no crystal stair.   20

Analyzing and Interpreting the Poem

1. In this poem, a mother talks to her son about her life. What does she compare her life to?

2. What images does the mother use to describe the difficulties she has faced?

3. Although the mother has often been "Where there ain't been no light" (line 13), she is "still climbin' " (line 19). What advice does she give her son?

Understanding Diction

The language that we use in conversation has a rhythm and a music of its own. "Mother to Son" is an example of how plain speech can be made into poetry.

Langston Hughes uses the natural rhythms of everyday speech to create a poetic effect:

> It's had tacks in it,
> And splinters,
> And boards torn up,
> And places with no carpet on the floor—
> Bare.

The poet uses these ordinary speech patterns in a careful, deliberate way. How does the repetition of *and* suggest the climb up a long, winding staircase?

The poet puts the word *bare* on a line by itself. What does he want to emphasize? How would you say this line aloud?

Plain speech can be used to suggest strong emotions. Which lines of this poem do you think should be spoken softly and tenderly?

Using Clues to Interpretation

Present an oral reading of "Mother to Son," using a conversational tone. Before reading aloud, look carefully at the clues for phrasing within the poem. In the first line, for example, the two commas and the colon indicate pauses. Which of these pauses would you give greater emphasis? Which words in the poem do you think should be stressed? Where would you lower your voice to reflect the speaker's sadness or tenderness?

The First Spring Day

CHRISTINA ROSSETTI

How is the language in this poem different from that in "Mother to Son"?

I wonder if the sap is stirring yet,
If wintry birds are dreaming of a mate,
If frozen snowdrops feel as yet the sun
And crocus fires are kindling one by one:
    Sing, robin, sing;   5
I still am sore in doubt concerning Spring.

I wonder if the Springtide of this year
Will bring another Spring both lost and dear;
If heart and spirit will find out their spring,
Or if the world alone will bud and sing: 10
    Sing, hope, to me;
Sweet notes, my hope, soft notes for memory.

The sap will surely quicken soon or late,
The tardiest bird will twitter to a mate;
So Spring must dawn again with warmth and bloom,   15
Or in this world, or° in the world to come:
    Sing, voice of Spring,
Till I too blossom and rejoice and sing.

16. **Or . . . or:** either or.

For Study and Discussion

Analyzing and Interpreting the Poem

1a. In the first stanza, what are five signs of spring that the speaker is waiting for? **b.** Why is she in doubt?

2. Springtime often stands for rebirth. What personal experience do you think the speaker refers to in lines 7–9?

3. How are the speaker's doubts resolved in the last stanza?

4. Rossetti has chosen words with precision. **a.** What happens to the effectiveness of line 1 if you substitute the word *moving* for *stirring*? **b.** Is the word *revive* as good a choice as the word *quicken* in line 13? **c.** What other words in the poem lose their effectiveness if you change them?

About the Authors

Langston Hughes   (1902–1967)

For a biography of Hughes, see page 234.

Christina Rossetti   (1830–1894)

 Christina Rossetti is considered one of the finest lyrical poets of the nineteenth century. She was born in London. Her distinguished family included her brothers, Dante Gabriel Rossetti, a poet and painter, and William Michael Rossetti, a biographer and editor, both of whom were leading spirits of an artistic group know as the Pre-Raphaelite Brotherhood. Her first volume of poetry was printed privately when she was twelve. She was extremely devout and on two separate occasions refused to marry because of religious differences. In later life she became quite ill and was preoccupied with the idea of death. Her principal works include *Goblin Market and Other Poems*, *The Prince's Progress and Other Poems*, and *Sing Song*, a book of poems for children.

IMAGERY

We learn about the world through our senses—sight, touch, smell, taste, and hearing. *Imagery* is language that appeals to the senses. Poets use imagery to involve the reader and to convey meaning.

Although imagery can appeal to any of the five senses, it is most often visual. Swenson (page 457) uses visual imagery when she describes the police car as "a five-eyed / one, with a red eye turning / on the top of his head." In a later line she uses the imagery of sound: "They all hiss as they glide." As you read the following poem by Alice Walker, note how she uses imagery to appeal to your senses.

For My Sister Molly Who in the Fifties

ALICE WALKER

You have to read the title of this poem as its first line. Fifties *refers to the 1950s.*

Once made a fairy rooster from
Mashed potatoes
Whose eyes I forget
But green onions were his tail
And his two legs were carrot sticks   5
A tomato slice his crown.
Who came home on vacation
When the sun was hot
and cooked
and cleaned   10
And minded least of all
The children's questions
A million or more
Pouring in on her
Who had been to school   15
And knew (and told us too) that certain
Words were no longer good

And taught me not to say us for we
No matter what "Sonny said" up the
road.   20

FOR MY SISTER MOLLY WHO IN THE FIFTIES
Knew Hamlet well and read into the night
And coached me in my songs of Africa
A continent I never knew
But learned to love   25
Because "they" she said could carry
A tune
And spoke in accents never heard
In Eatonton.
Who read from *Prose and Poetry*   30
And loved to read "Sam McGee from Tennessee"
On nights the fire was burning low
And Christmas wrapped in angel hair
And I for one prayed for snow.

WHO IN THE FIFTIES   35
Knew all the written things that made
Us laugh and stories by
The hour   Waking up the story buds
Like fruit. Who walked among the flowers
And brought them inside the house   40
And smelled as good as they
And looked as bright.
Who made dresses, braided
Hair. Moved chairs about
Hung things from walls   45
Ordered baths
Frowned on wasp bites
And seemed to know the endings
Of all the tales
I had forgot.   50

For Study and Discussion

Analyzing and Interpreting the Poem

1. The speaker in this poem wants you to know her sister Molly. What details in the first part of the poem help you see what Molly created with vegetables?

2. According to the second part of the poem, what new experiences did Molly bring into the speaker's life in Eatonton?

3. In lines 38–39, the speaker tells of Molly's "Waking up the story buds/Like fruit." What picture does this comparison put in your mind's eye?

4. In what ways was Molly like the flowers she brought into the house?

5. The speaker never states directly how she feels about her sister Molly. How would you describe her feelings for Molly?

Literary Elements

Responding to Imagery

Alice Walker uses imagery that appeals to different senses. One of her most vivid images occurs in lines 1–6, where she describes the rooster made of vegetables. How does she use both color and shape to help you imagine what she saw? Find another vivid visual image in the poem.

Where does the poet appeal to your sense of smell? hearing? Are there any images that appeal to your sense of touch?

What do all the images associated with Molly suggest about her as a person? How do the images help reveal the importance of Molly to her sister?

About the Author

Alice Walker (1944–   )

Alice Walker's roots are rural Georgia. She graduated from Sarah Lawrence College in 1965. The following year she won *The American Scholar* essay contest with a work called "The Civil Rights Movement: How Good Was It?" *Once,* her first collection of poems, appeared in 1968. In 1983 she won the Pulitzer Prize for *The Color Purple,* a novel about a black girl growing up in the South. She now teaches writing and literature at Wellesley College and the University of Massachusetts.

In an interview Walker talked about her sister as a brilliant girl "who collected scholarship like trading stamps and wandered all over the world." Walker worked on "For My Sister Molly" over a period of five years and says that the poem went through at least fifty drafts.

FIGURATIVE LANGUAGE

Figurative language is language that is not intended to be understood as factually or literally true. When we say, "March came in like a lion and went out like a lamb," we are speaking figuratively. What we are referring to is a change in weather. Many expressions in everyday language are figurative.

The term *figure of speech* refers to a particular kind of figurative language. Two figures of speech commonly used in poetry are *simile* and *metaphor*. Each figure expresses a likeness between two different things. However, a simile uses a word such as *like* or *as* to express the comparison. In "The Dark Hills" (page 455), Robinson says that "sunset hovers like a sound / Of golden horns." A metaphor identifies two things. Robinson uses a metaphor when he refers to the rays of the sun as *legions*, soldiers marching to battle.

As you read the following poems, look for the figures of speech. Think about how they appeal to your imagination and how they add to your understanding of the poems.

I Like to See It Lap the Miles

EMILY DICKINSON

This poem describes a train. Yet the speaker never mentions the word train, *and, in fact, seems to be describing an animal. She appears to be looking at this great noisy train from above, watching it as it goes through the New England mountains.*

I like to see it lap the miles,
And lick the valleys up,
And stop to feed itself at tanks;
And then, prodigious,° step

Around a pile of mountains   5
And, supercilious,° peer
In shanties by the sides of roads;
And then a quarry pare°

4. **prodigious** (prə-dĭj′əs): huge.

6. **supercilious** (so͞o′pər-sĭl′ē-əs): proud and scornful.

8. **pare**: trim or peel away.

To fit its sides, and crawl between,
Complaining all the while   10
In horrid, hooting stanza;
Then chase itself down hill

And neigh like Boanerges;°
Then, punctual as a star,
Stop—docile and omnipotent°—   15
At its own stable door.

13. **Boanerges** (bō'ə-nûr'jēz): any
loud, thunderous public speaker.

15. **omnipotent** (ŏm-nĭp'ə-tənt):
all-powerful.

For Study and Discussion

Analyzing and Interpreting the Poem

1. The speaker in this poem uses images that seem to describe an animal. What words and phrases help you picture this animal's activities as it moves along?

2. What words and phrases help you picture the animal as something huge and powerful?

3a. What words in the last stanza identify the animal with a horse? **b.** Could it be a horse in the other stanzas? Why or why not?

4. The poet never names what she is describing. What reveals that her subject is a train?

5. This train is both "docile" (manageable) and "omnipotent" (all-powerful) at the same time. What other things can be both docile and omnipotent at the same time?

6. How does the speaker feel about this train?

Literary Elements

Recognizing Metaphors

When you compare two different things by using a word such as *like* or *as*, you are using a **simile:** "Russell is like a lamb"; "Her eyes are like stars"; "The dog is like a devil." When you identify two different things, without using a word such as *like* or *as,* you are using a **metaphor**: "Russell is a lamb"; "Her eyes are stars"; "The dog is a devil."

Metaphors, of course, are not literally, or factually, true. Russell is not really a lamb; her eyes are not really stars; the dog is not really a devil. However, metaphors are very powerful. Like similes, they help us use our imagination to see surprising likenesses between things that are basically different.

In its simplest form, a metaphor says directly that one thing *is* another, different thing. In "Mother to Son" (page 461), the speaker says, "Life for me ain't been no crystal stair." This is a metaphor, even though it is expressed negatively. What kind of stairway would you say the mother's life has been? In what ways are life and a stairway alike? What do you think the mother means when she says her stairway has had "bare" spots in it? What is "the dark"?

Emily Dickinson's poem is built around a metaphor. How would you state the metaphor in her poem?

The Grinder (1924) by Diego M. Rivera (1886–1957) Encaustic on canvas.

Food

VICTOR M. VALLE

One eats
the moon in a tortilla
Eat frijoles°
and you eat the earth
Eat chile
and you eat the sun and fire
Drink water
and you drink sky

3. **frijoles** (frē-hōl′ĕs): beans.

For Study and Discussion

Analyzing and Interpreting the Poem

1. The poet makes a comparison between things that one eats or drinks and elements of nature. **a.** What is the similarity in shape between the moon and a tortilla? **b.** What is the similarity in color?

2. What is the similarity in the color of beans and of the earth?

3. Chile is compared to both the sun and fire. What similarities are there?

4. In what way is water like the sky?

The Road Not Taken

ROBERT FROST

Many readers feel that the roads in this poem have a significance that applies to life. What meaning do you see in them?

Two roads diverged° in a yellow wood,
And sorry I could not travel both
And be one traveler, long I stood
And looked down one as far as I could
To where it bent in the undergrowth;   5

Then took the other, as just as fair,
And having perhaps the better claim,
Because it was grassy and wanted wear;
Though as for that the passing there
Had worn them really about the same,   10

And both that morning equally lay
In leaves no step had trodden black.
Oh, I kept the first for another day!
Yet knowing how way leads on to way,
I doubted if I should ever come back.   15

I shall be telling this with a sigh
Somewhere ages and ages hence:
Two roads diverged in a wood, and I—
I took the one less traveled by,
And that has made all the difference.   20

1. **diverged** (dĭ-vûrjd′): branched off.

For Study and Discussion

Analyzing and Interpreting the Poem

1. How does this speaker feel when he has to choose one road instead of the other?

2. Why does the second road seem to be a better choice?

3. The speaker hopes to take the first road on "another day." Yet why does he doubt that he will ever be able to do this?

4a. What larger choices in life do you think the poet could be talking about here? **b.** Name some choices that could "make all the difference" in a person's life.

5. How would you describe the mood, or feeling, of this poem?

Literary Elements

Recognizing Symbols

When you see the colors red, white, and blue together, you probably think of the United States. These colors stand for the United States, just as a dove stands for peace and a red rose stands for love or beauty. These are examples of **symbols.** A **symbol** is anything that represents, or stands for, something else.

A road is a common symbol for life. What would we mean, for example, if we said, "It's the end of the road for him"? The forked road in this poem is a symbol for a choice that the speaker has to make. Why is a forked road a good symbol for choices in life?

The speaker says that "way leads on to way."

How does this suggest that life is a maze of roads that cannot be retraveled?

If a road is a symbol for life, what kind of life does the speaker choose when he takes a road "less traveled by"?

The title of the poem is "The Road *Not* Taken." How do you think the speaker feels about the road he did *not* take and can never find again?

Writing About Literature

Interpreting a Poem's Title

What do you think is Frost's attitude toward the road he did *not* take? Does he have any regrets? Write a paragraph in which you interpret the meaning of the poem's title. Refer to specific lines in the poem to support your statements. For assistance in writing your paper, see the section called *Writing About Literature* at the back of this textbook.

About the Authors

Emily Dickinson   (1830–1886)

A seventh-generation New Englander, Emily Dickinson lived and died in the house in which she was born, in Amherst, Massachusetts. For most of her adult life, she traveled no farther than her own garden. She wrote her poems in the rhythms she found in her Bible and hymnbook. A few friends knew that she had written some poems, but after her death, even her sister was amazed to discover almost eighteen hundred poems tied in bundles in her bedroom. Emily Dickinson might have lacked worldly experience, but she lived an intense inner life. In her imagination, the smallest, most ordinary object or scene could be a sign of something deep and mysterious.

Victor M. Valle   (1950–   )

Victor M. Valle is a native of California, where he has been a part-time instructor in folklore and mythology at California State University, Long-Beach. He has also been a California Arts Council artist in residence and Director of the Los Angeles Latino Writers' Workshop. His poetry has been published in several literary magazines, and he received the *Caracol* Poetry Prize in 1979.

Robert Frost   (1874–1963)

After working as a country schoolteacher, a newspaper editor, and a cobbler, Robert Frost tended a small chicken farm in New Hampshire. In 1912, having had little success as a farmer, he sold the farm and moved to England with his family. There he devoted all his time to writing. He soon published his first two volumes of poems. These books were so highly praised that when Frost returned to America in 1915, he was recognized as a major poet. The rest of his long and productive life was spent living quietly on a small farm in Vermont, writing poetry and occasionally lecturing and teaching. Though Robert Frost's poems reflect the quiet dignity and simplicity of the countryside, they often give us a glimpse into the tragic and puzzling sides of life.

Sound and Meaning

REPETITION AND RHYME

In addition to such elements as diction, imagery, and figurative language, poets use devices of sound to convey meaning. One important sound device is *repetition*. Repetition may occur in different forms. It may occur in the form of *rhyme*, in which similar sounds are repeated within or at the end of lines. Repetition may also occur with a single letter or group of letters, as in these lines from Emily Dickinson's poem (page 468): "I *l*ike to see it *l*ap the miles, / And *l*ick the valleys up." This kind of repetition is known as *alliteration* (ə-lĭt′ə-rā′shən). Poets may also choose to repeat a single word, a phrase, or an entire line. In the short poem "Food" (page 470), Victor Valle repeats the word *eat* five times. Repetition is a way of emphasizing and communicating meaning as well as giving pleasure.

The Raven

EDGAR ALLAN POE

This poem is famous for its mood and for its dazzling musical effects. How does Poe use sound to create a mood of mystery?

Once upon a midnight dreary, while I pondered, weak and weary,
Over many a quaint and curious volume of forgotten lore°—
While I nodded, nearly napping, suddenly there came a tapping,
As of someone gently rapping, rapping at my chamber door.
" 'Tis some visitor," I muttered, "tapping at my chamber door—   5
                Only this and nothing more."

2. **lore:** knowledge.

Ah, distinctly I remember it was in the bleak December;
And each separate dying ember wrought its ghost upon the floor.
Eagerly I wished the morrow—vainly I had sought to borrow
From my books surcease° of sorrow—sorrow for the lost Lenore—   10
For the rare and radiant maiden whom the angels name Lenore—
       Nameless *here* forevermore.

And the silken, sad, uncertain rustling of each purple curtain
Thrilled me—filled me with fantastic terrors never felt before;
So that now, to still the beating of my heart, I stood repeating,   15
" 'Tis some visitor entreating entrance at my chamber door—
Some late visitor entreating entrance at my chamber door—
       That it is and nothing more."

Presently my soul grew stronger; hesitating then no longer,
"Sir," said I, "or Madam, truly your forgiveness I implore;   20
But the fact is I was napping, and so gently you came rapping,
And so faintly you came tapping, tapping at my chamber door,
That I scarce was sure I heard you"—here I opened wide the door—
       Darkness there and nothing more.

10. **surcease:** an end.

Illustrations on pages 475,
476, 477, and 479
by W.L. Taylor for an 1883
edition of *The Raven*.

General Research Division, The
New York Public Library, Astor,
Lenox and Tilden Foundations

Deep into that darkness peering, long I stood there wondering, fearing,   25
    fearing,
Doubting, dreaming dreams no mortal ever dared to dream before;
But the silence was unbroken, and the stillness gave no token,
And the only word there spoken was the whispered word, "Lenore?"
This I whispered, and an echo murmured back the word "Lenore!"—
                    Merely this and nothing more.   30

Back into the chamber turning, all my soul within me burning,
Soon again I heard a tapping somewhat louder than before.
"Surely," said I, "surely that is something at my window lattice;
Let me see, then, what threat is, and this mystery explore—
Let my heart be still a moment and this mystery explore—   35
                  'Tis the wind and nothing more!"

Open here I flung the shutter, when, with many a flirt and flutter,
In there stepped a stately Raven of the saintly days of yore;
Not the least obeisance° made he; not a minute stopped or stayed he;
But, with mien° of lord or lady, perched above my chamber door—   40
Perched upon a bust of Pallas° just above my chamber door—
                    Perched, and sat, and nothing more.

Then this ebony bird beguiling my sad fancy into smiling,
By the grave and stern decorum of the countenance it wore,
"Though thy crest be shorn and shaven, thou," I said, "art sure no
        craven,°   45
Ghastly, grim, and ancient Raven wandering from the Nightly
        shore—
Tell me what thy lordly name is on the Night's Plutonian shore!"°
                    Quoth the Raven, "Nevermore."

Much I marveled this ungainly fowl to hear discourse so plainly,
Though its answer little meaning—little relevancy bore;   50
For we cannot help agreeing that no living human being
Ever yet was blessed with seeing bird above his chamber door—
Bird or beast upon the sculptured bust above his chamber door,
                    With such name as "Nevermore."

But the Raven, sitting lonely on the placid bust, spoke only   55
That one word, as if his soul in that one word he did outpour.
Nothing further then he uttered, not a feather then he fluttered—
Till I scarcely more than muttered, "Other friends have flown
        before—
On the morrow *he* will leave me, as my Hopes have flown before."
                    Then the bird said, "Nevermore."   60

Startled at the stillness broken by reply so aptly spoken,
"Doubtless," said I, "what it utters is its only stock and store
Caught from some unhappy master whom unmerciful Disaster
Followed fast and followed faster till his songs one burden° bore—
Till the dirges of his Hope that melancholy burden bore   65
                    Of 'Never—nevermore.'"

---

39. **obeisance** (ō-bā′səns): a gesture of respect; a bow. 40. **mien** (mēn): manner. 41. **bust of Pallas:** a statue of the head of Pallas Athena, the Greek goddess of wisdom. 45. **craven:** coward. 47. **Plutonian shore:** the shore of the river leading to the underworld, ruled by Pluto. 64. **burden:** here, a repeated word or phrase in a song.

But the Raven still beguiling all my fancy° into smiling,
Straight I wheeled a cushioned seat in front of bird and bust and
    door;
Then, upon the velvet sinking, I betook myself to linking
Fancy unto fancy, thinking what this ominous° bird of yore—   70
What this grim, ungainly, ghastly, gaunt, and ominous bird of yore
                        Meant in croaking, "Nevermore."

This I sat engaged in guessing, but no syllable expressing
To the fowl, whose fiery eyes now burned into my bosom's core;
This and more I sat divining, with my head at ease reclining   75
On the cushion's velvet lining that the lamplight gloated o'er,
But whose velvet violet lining with the lamplight gloating o'er,
                   She shall press, ah, nevermore!

Then, methought, the air grew denser, perfumed from an unseen
    censer°
Swung by seraphim° whose footfalls tinkled on the tufted floor.   80
"Wretch," I cried, "thy God hath lent thee—by these angels he hath
    sent thee
Respite°—respite and nepenthe° from thy memories of Lenore!
Quaff,° oh, quaff this kind nepenthe and forget this lost Lenore!"
                   Quoth the Raven, "Nevermore."

"Prophet!" said I, "thing of evil—prophet still, if bird or devil!—   85
Whether Tempter° sent, or whether tempest tossed thee here ashore,
Desolate yet all undaunted, on this desert land enchanted—
On this home by Horror haunted—tell me truly, I implore—
Is there—*is* there balm in Gilead?°—tell me—tell me, I implore!"
                   Quoth the Raven, "Nevermore."   90

"Prophet!" said I, "thing of evil!—prophet still, if bird or devil!
By that Heaven that bends above us—by that God we both adore—
Tell this soul with sorrow laden if, within the distant Aidenn,°
It shall clasp a sainted maiden whom the angels name Lenore—
Clasp a rare and radiant maiden whom the angels name Lenore."   95
                   Quoth the Raven, "Nevermore."

---

67. **fancy:** imagination. 70. **ominous** (ŏm′ə-nəs): threatening. 79. **censer:** a container for incense. 80. **seraphim** (sĕr′ə-fĭm): angels. 82. **Respite** (rĕs′pĭt): relief or rest. **nepenthe** (nĭ-pĕn′thē): a drug thought to banish sorrow. 83. **Quaff** (kwŏf): drink. 86. **Tempter:** Satan. 89. **Is there...Gilead** (gĭl′ē-əd): This line is from the Bible, where it means "Is there any relief from pain?" 93. **Aidenn** (ā′dən): Paradise.

"Be that word our sign of parting, bird or fiend!" I shrieked,
    upstarting—
"Get thee back into the tempest and the Night's Plutonian shore!
Leave no black plume as a token of that lie thy soul hath spoken!
Leave my loneliness unbroken!—quit the bust above my door!   100
Take thy beak from out my heart, and take thy form from off my
    door!"
                    Quoth the Raven, "Nevermore."

And the Raven, never flitting, still is sitting, *still* is sitting
On the pallid° bust of Pallas just above my chamber door;
And his eyes have all the seeming of a demon's that is dreaming,   105
And the lamplight o'er him streaming throws his shadow on the floor;
And my soul from out that shadow that lies floating on the floor
                    Shall be lifted—nevermore!

104. **pallid:** pale.

For Study and Discussion

Analyzing and Interpreting the Poem

1. In this mysterious poem, a man is driven to hysteria by a Raven that enters his room and refuses to leave. **a.** What is the poem's setting, or the time and place of the action? **b.** How does the setting create a mood of mystery?

2a. What tragic loss has the speaker suffered? **b.** How does this create a mood of loneliness?

3. The mystery increases when the Raven enters the room (line 38). Ravens are often associated with death and evil. What evidence in the poem tells you that the speaker thinks this bird is a visitor from the land of the dead?

4a. What three questions does the speaker ask the Raven (see lines 47, 89, and 93–95)? **b.** How does the Raven answer?

5a. What is the speaker's final, shrieking demand in the next-to-last stanza? **b.** How do you know that the Raven will never leave the speaker's chamber?

6. Some people say that this poem describes a nightmare. Others say it tells of a man going insane. What do you think?

Literary Elements

Responding to Sounds in a Poem

The speaker talks about a woman named Lenore. The name *Lenore* is repeated throughout the poem. Each stanza also has words that rhyme with *Lenore*. Identify these rhyming words in each stanza. How does the echoing of the dead woman's name suggest what is going on in the speaker's mind?

Rhymes are heard in every line of this poem. Poe even rhymes words within the same line. In the first line, the word *weary* rhymes with *dreary*. Find another example of this **internal rhyme** in line 3. Read aloud the first and third lines of every stanza to hear the internal rhymes.

Poe creates other musical effects by using alliteration:

And the silken, sad, uncertain rustling of each purple curtain

Read this line aloud so that the repeated **s** sounds suggest the faint "rustling" of the curtains. If you look closely at each stanza of this poem, you will find other lines that use alliteration. Read some of these lines aloud.

In addition to alliteration and rhyme, Poe uses words that suggest or echo mysterious and frightening sounds. Here are some from the first stanza alone:

tapping   rapping   muttered

Add words from other stanzas to this list.

In the first stanza of "The Raven," Poe describes the sounds of *rapping* and *tapping* at the speaker's chamber door. These words to some degree imitate the actual sounds made. Poe is making use of **onomatopoeia** (ŏn′ə-măt′ə-pē′ə). Find other examples of this technique in "The Raven."

Understanding Allusions

In Greek and Roman mythology, the underworld—the land of the dead—was ruled by a god known as Pluto. It was believed that the spirits of the dead reached the underworld by being ferried across the River Styx. When Poe refers to "Night's Plutonian shore" (line 47), he has in mind the shore of the river leading to the underworld. Such a reference to a place, a character, or an event is called an **allusion**.

In line 89 the speaker cries out, "Is there—*is* there balm in Gilead?" This line is an allusion to the Bible, in which the prophet Jeremiah, in his sorrow, asks the same question. Gilead was a region of ancient Palestine where balm, a soothing ointment, was made. You will find the source of this allusion in Jeremiah 8:22.

In Dickinson's poem "I Like to See It Lap the Miles" (page 468) there is another allusion to the Bible. Look in Mark 3:17. How does this Biblical passage explain the allusion in line 13?

For Oral Reading

Avoiding Singsong

In order to stress the rhyme of a poem, people sometimes read in a monotonous pattern called *singsong*. One way to avoid singsong is to read a poem in a natural voice. Do not stress rhyme words by pausing mechanically at the end of each line. Follow the punctuation and phrasing of the poem.

Plan to read "The Raven" aloud, either as a solo performance or in an ensemble. Practice reading the poem aloud, paying attention to meaning as well as to sound.

About the Author

Edgar Allan Poe   (1809–1849)

For a biography of Poe, see page 279.

RHYTHM

Rhythm is the pattern of stressed and unstressed sounds in a line of poetry. Rhythm not only contributes to the musical quality of a poem, but also gives emphasis to important words and ideas. Sometimes the rhythm of a poem actually suggests its subject matter. This is the case with the poem you are about to read.

Lochinvar

SIR WALTER SCOTT

This story takes place in the fifteenth century, when "Border" wars raged between England and Scotland. Lochinvar had gone off to battle. But shocking news brings him home . . .

Oh, young Lochinvar is come out of the west,
Through all the wide Border his steed was the best;
And, save his good broadsword, he weapons had none,
He rode all unarmed, and he rode all alone.
So faithful in love, and so dauntless in war,   5
There never was knight like the young Lochinvar.

He stayed not for brake,° and he stopped not for stone,
He swam the Eske River where ford there was none;
But ere he alighted at Netherby gate,
The bride had consented, the gallant came late: 10
For a laggard° in love, and a dastard° in war,
Was to wed the fair Ellen of brave Lochinvar.

So boldly he entered the Netherby Hall,
Among bridesmen, and kinsmen, and brothers, and all.
Then spoke the bride's father, his hand on his sword   15
(For the poor craven° bridegroom said never a word),
"Oh, come ye in peace here, or come ye in war,
Or to dance at our bridal, young Lord Lochinvar?"

7. **brake:** a clump of bushes or trees.

11. **laggard:** a slow person.
dastard: a sneak.

16. **craven:** cowardly.

"I long wooed your daughter, my suit you denied—
Love swells like the Solway,° but ebbs like its tide—
And now I am come, with this lost love of mine,
To lead but one measure,° drink one cup of wine.
There are maidens in Scotland more lovely by far,
That would gladly be bride to the young Lochinvar."

The bride kissed the goblet; the knight took it up;
He quaffed off° the wine, and he threw down the cup.
She looked down to blush, and she looked up to sigh,
With a smile on her lips, and a tear in her eye.
He took her soft hand, ere her mother could bar—
"Now tread we a measure!" said young Lochinvar.

20

25

30

20. **Solway:** an inlet between England and Scotland.

22. **measure:** a movement of the dance.

26. **quaffed** (kwŏft) **off:** drank deeply.

So stately his form, and so lovely her face,
That never a hall such a galliard° did grace;
While her mother did fret, and her father did fume,
And the bridegroom stood dangling his bonnet and plume,
And the bridesmaidens whispered, "Twere better by far,   35
To have matched our fair cousin with young Lochinvar."

One touch to her hand, and one word to her ear,
When they reached the hall door, and the charger° stood near,
So light to the croup° the fair lady he swung.
So light to the saddle before her he sprung!   40
"She is won! we are gone, over bank, brush, and scaur;°
They'll have fleet steeds that follow," quoth young Lochinvar.

There was mounting 'mong Graemes of the Netherby clan;
Forsters, Fenwicks, and Musgraves, they rode and they ran.
There was racing and chasing on Cannobie Lee,°   45
But the lost bride of Netherby ne'er did they see.
So daring in love, and so dauntless in war,
Have ye e'er heard of gallant like young Lochinvar?

32. **galliard** (găl'yərd): a lively dance.

38. **charger:** a horse.

39. **croup** (kro͞op): the horse's back, behind the saddle area.

41. **scaur** (skär): a rocky hillside.

45. **Cannobie Lee:** a meadow.

For Study and Discussion

Analyzing and Interpreting the Poem

1. When Lochinvar arrives at Netherby Hall, Ellen is about to marry another man. How does the brideroom contrast with Lochinvar?

2a. What does Ellen's father fear when Lochinvar arrives? **b.** What answer does Lochinvar give to reassure him?

3a. What are Ellen's reactions when Lochinvar drinks the goblet of wine? **b.** What do her reactions tell about her feelings for Lochinvar?

4. How do Lochinvar and Ellen trick everyone?

Literary Elements

Responding to Rhythm

All spoken language has rhythm. When you speak, your voice rises and falls naturally in ways that help communicate meaning. In a poem, rhythm often follows a pattern. Read the following lines from "Lochinvar" aloud, and listen to the rhythm. The symbol (′) indicates a stressed syllable. The symbol (˘) indicates an unstressed syllable.

> He stayed nŏt fŏr bráke, aňd hĕ stoppĕd nŏt
>   fŏr stóne,
> He swám thĕ Eské Rívĕr whĕre fŏrd thĕre
>   wăs nóne;
> But erĕ hĕ ălíghtĕd ăt Néthĕrbў gáte,
> Thĕ brídĕ hăd cŏnséntĕd, thĕ gállaňt cáme
>   láte:

Sometimes the rhythm of a poem suggests what the poem is about. "Lochinvar" is about a knight who gallops over the countryside. Reread the lines above and tap out the rhythm gently on your desk. Does the rhythm sound like the galloping of a horse?

Recognizing Inverted Word Order

Poets, like other writers, sometimes reverse the usual order of words in their sentences. When they do, they are using **inverted word order.** For example, in line 3 Scott says, ". . . he weapons had none." A standard English sentence would use subject-verb-object order: "he had no weapons." But what happens to Scott's swinging, regular rhythm when "he had no weapons" is substituted for "he weapons had none"?

Rewrite the following inverted lines from the poem so that they reflect standard English word order:

> . . . where ford there was none;   (line 8)
> Now tread we a measure!   (line 30)
> That never a hall such a galliard did grace;
>   (line 32)
> So light to the croup the fair lady he swung.
>   (line 39)
> But the lost bride of Netherby ne'er did they see.
>   (line 46)

Paraphrasing a Stanza

To **paraphrase** a line or passage of poetry is to restate its ideas in your own words. A paraphrase puts inverted constructions into normal order. It also restates images and figures of speech in plain language.

Paraphrase the first stanza of "Lochinvar." Then check your paraphrase to see if you have included all of Scott's details.

About the Author

Sir Walter Scott   (1771–1832)

As a boy, Sir Walter Scott was fascinated by the tales of Scotland's past that his mother and grandfather told him. When he grew older, he traveled throughout the countryside on ballad "raids," writing down the songs he heard. At the age of thirty-one, he published a collection of these old Scottish folk ballads. He then wrote three long narrative poems, of which *The Lady of the Lake* is the most famous. Scott was the best-loved poet in England when he began publishing a series of historical novels, which were filled with adventure and romance. *Ivanhoe* is one of the most famous of these novels.

Types of Poetry

NARRATIVE POETRY

Like a short story, a *narrative* poem tells a story. A narrative poem has characters, a setting, and action. "Paul Revere's Ride" (page 136), "The Raven" (page 474), and "Lochinvar" (page 482) are well-known narrative poems.

A special kind of narrative poem is the *ballad.* Folk ballads were not written down, but were transmitted over the centuries by word of mouth. "John Henry" (page 185) is an example of a folk ballad.

Another kind of narrative poem is the *epic,* a long poem about heroic figures and events. *The Song of Hiawatha* is a *literary epic,* written to imitate characteristics of ancient epics. A portion of that poem is included here.

Illustrations on pages 486, 489, 490, and 491 by Frederic Remington (1861–1909) for *The Song of Hiawatha* (1890).
Rare Books and Manuscripts Division, The New York Public Library, Astor, Lenox and Tilden Foundations

The Song of Hiawatha

HENRY WADSWORTH LONGFELLOW

Longfellow's Song of Hiawatha *was an immediate success when it appeared in 1855 and sold 10,000 copies in the first four weeks after publication. Hiawatha, the hero of the poem, grows up among the Ojibwas. Longfellow described the scene of the poem as "the southern shore of Lake Superior, in the region between the Pictured Rocks and the Grand Sable."*

Hiawatha's mother is Wenonah, the daughter of Nokomis. His father is the West Wind, Mudjekeewis. After his mother is deserted by Mudjekeewis and dies of a broken heart, Hiawatha is brought up by his grandmother, Nokomis.

Two well-known episodes from the poem are included here. The first tells how Hiawatha is educated by animals and how he grows into a fine hunter. The second tells of his great battle with his father, Mudjekeewis.

FROM
Hiawatha's Childhood

By the shores of Gitche Gumee,
By the shining Big-Sea-Water,
Stood the wigwam of Nokomis.
Daughter of the Moon, Nokomis.
Dark behind it rose the forest,　　　　5
Rose the black and gloomy pine-trees,
Rose the firs with cones upon them;
Bright before it beat the water,
Beat the clear and sunny water,
Beat the shining Big-Sea Water.　　　　10
　There the wrinkled old Nokomis
Nursed the little Hiawatha,
Rocked him in his linden cradle,
Bedded soft in moss and rushes,
Safely bound with reindeer sinews;　　　　15
Stilled his fretful wail by saying,
"Hush! the Naked Bear will hear thee!"
Lulled him into slumber, singing,
"Ewa-yea! my little owlet!
Who is this, that lights the wigwam?　　　　20

With his great eyes lights the wigwam?
Ewa-yea! my little owlet!"
　Many things Nokomis taught him
Of the stars that shine in heaven;
Showed him Ishkoodah, the comet,　　　　25
Ishkoodah, with fiery tresses;
Showed the Death-Dance of the spirits,
Warriors with their plumes and war-clubs,
Flaring far away to northward
In the frosty nights of Winter;　　　　30
Showed the broad white road in heaven,
Pathway of the ghosts, the shadows,
Running straight across the heavens,
Crowded with the ghosts, the shadows.
　At the door on summer evenings　　　　35
Sat the little Hiawatha;
Heard the whispering of the pine-trees,
Heard the lapping of the waters,
Sounds of music, words of wonder;
"Minne-wawa!" said the pine-trees,　　　　40
"Mudway-aushka!" said the water.
　Saw the fire-fly, Wah-wah-taysee,
Flitting through the dusk of evening,

With the twinkle of its candle
Lighting up the brakes and bushes, 45
And he sang the song of children,
Sang the song Nokomis taught him:
"Wah-wah-taysee, little fire-fly,
Little, flitting, white-fire insect,
Little, dancing, white-fire creature, 50
Light me with your little candle,
Ere upon my bed I lay me,
Ere in sleep I close my eyelids!"
    Saw the moon rise from the water
Rippling, rounding from the water, 55
Saw the flecks and shadows on it,
Whispered, "What is that, Nokomis?"
And the good Nokomis answered:
"Once a warrior, very angry,
Seized his grandmother, and threw her 60
Up into the sky at midnight;
Right against the moon he threw her;
'Tis her body that you see there."
    Saw the rainbow in the heaven,
In the eastern sky, the rainbow, 65
Whispered, "What is that, Nokomis?"
And the good Nokomis answered:
" 'Tis the heaven of flowers you see there;
All the wild-flowers of the forest,
All the lilies of the prairie, 70
When on earth they fade and perish,
Blossom in that heaven above us."
    When he heard the owls at midnight,
Hooting, laughing in the forest,
"What is that?" he cried in terror, 75
"What is that," he said, "Nokomis?"
And the good Nokomis answered:
"That is but the owl and owlet,
Talking in their native language,
Talking, scolding at each other." 80
    Then the little Hiawatha
Learned of every bird its language,
Learned their names and all their secrets,
How they built their nests in Summer,
Where they hid themselves in Winter, 85
Talked with them whene'er he met them,

Called them "Hiawatha's Chickens."
    Of all the beasts he learned the language,
Learned their names and all their secrets,
How the beavers built their lodges, 90
Where the squirrels hid their acorns,
How the reindeer ran so swiftly,
Why the rabbit was so timid,
Talked with them whene'er he met them,
Called them "Hiawatha's Brothers." 95
    Then Iagoo, the great boaster,
He the marvellous story-teller,
He the traveller and the talker,
He the friend of old Nokomis,
Made a bow for Hiawatha; 100
From a branch of ash he made it,
From an oak-bough made the arrows,
Tipped with flint, and winged with feathers,
And the cord he made of deer-skin.
    Then he said to Hiawatha: 105
"Go, my son, into the forest,
Where the red deer herd together,
Kill for us a famous roebuck,
Kill for us a deer with antlers!"
    Forth into the forest straightway 110
All alone walked Hiawatha
Proudly, with his bow and arrows;
And the birds sang round him, o'er him,
"Do not shoot us, Hiawatha!"
Sang the robin, the Opechee, 115
Sang the bluebird, the Owaissa,
"Do not shoot us, Hiawatha!"
    Up the oak-tree, close beside him,
Sprang the squirrel, Adjidaumo,
In and out among the branches, 120
Coughed and chattered from the oak-tree,
Laughed, and said between his laughing,
"Do not shoot me, Hiawatha!"
    And the rabbit from his pathway
Leaped aside, and at a distance 125
Sat erect upon his haunches,
Half in fear and half in frolic,
Saying to the little hunter,
"Do not shoot me, Hiawatha!"

But he heeded not, nor heard them,   130
For his thoughts were with the red deer;
On their tracks his eyes were fastened,
Leading downward to the river,
To the ford across the river,
And as one in slumber walked he.   135
   Hidden in the alder-bushes,
There he waited till the deer came,
Till he saw two antlers lifted,
Saw two eyes look from the thicket,
Saw two nostrils point to windward,   140
And a deer came down the pathway,
Flecked with leafy light and shadow.
And his heart within him fluttered,
Trembled like the leaves above him,
Like the birch-leaf palpitated,   145
As the deer came down the pathway.
   Then, upon one knee uprising,
Hiawatha aimed an arrow;
Scarce a twig moved with his motion,
Scarce a leaf was stirred or rustled,   150
But the wary roebuck started,
Stamped with all his hoofs together,
Listened with one foot uplifted,
Leaped as if to meet the arrow;
Ah! the singing, fatal arrow,   155
Like a wasp it buzzed and stung him!
   Dead he lay there in the forest,
By the ford across the river;
Beat his timid heart no longer,
But the heart of Hiawatha   160
Throbbed and shouted and exulted,
As he bore the red deer homeward,
And Iagoo and Nokomis
Hailed his coming with applauses.
   From the red deer's hide Nokomis   165
Made a cloak for Hiawatha,
From the red deer's flesh Nokomis
Made a banquet to his honor.
All the village came and feasted,
All the guests praised Hiawatha,   170
Called him Strong-Heart, Soan-ge-taha!
Called him Loon-Heart, Mahn-go-taysee!

Hiawatha and Mudjekeewis

Out of childhood into manhood
Now had grown my Hiawatha,
Skilled in all the craft of hunters,   175
Learned in all the lore of old men,
In all youthful sports and pastimes,
In all manly arts and labors.

   Swift of foot was Hiawatha;
He could shoot an arrow from him,   180
And run forward with such fleetness,
That the arrow fell behind him!
Strong of arm was Hiawatha;
He could shoot ten arrows upward,
Shoot them with such strength and
    swiftness,   185
That the tenth had left the bow-string
Ere the first to earth had fallen!

   He had mittens, Minjekahwun,

Magic mittens made of deer-skin;
When upon his hands he wore them,   190
He could smite the rocks asunder,
He could grind them into powder.
He had moccasins enchanted,
Magic moccasins of deer-skin;
When he bound them round his ankles,   195
When upon his feet he tied them,
At each stride a mile he measured!

   Much he questioned old Nokomis
Of his father Mudjekeewis;
Learned from her the fatal secret   200
Of the beauty of his mother,
Of the falsehood of his father;
And his heart was hot within him,
Like a living coal his heart was.

   Then he said to old Nokomis,   205
"I will go to Mudjekeewis,
See how fares it with my father,

At the doorways of the West-Wind,
At the portals of the Sunset!"

From his lodge went Hiawatha,   210
Dressed for travel, armed for hunting;
Dressed in deer-skin shirt and leggings,
Richly wrought with quills and wampum;
On his head his eagle-feathers,
Round his waist his belt of wampum,   215
In his hand his bow of ash-wood,
Strung with sinews of the reindeer;
In his quiver oaken arrows,
Tipped with jasper, winged with feathers;
With his mittens, Minjekahwun,   220
With his moccasins enchanted.

Warning said the old Nokomis,
"Go not forth, O Hiawatha!
To the kingdom of the West-Wind,
To the realms of Mudjekeewis,   225
Lest he harm you with his magic,
Lest he kill you with his cunning!"

But the fearless Hiawatha
Heeded not her woman's warning;
Forth he strode into the forest,   230
At each stride a mile he measured;
Lurid seemed the sky above him,

Lurid seemed the earth beneath him,
Hot and close the air around him,
Filled with smoke and fiery vapors,   235
As of burning woods and prairies,
For his heart was hot within him,
Like a living coal his heart was.

So he journeyed westward, westward,
Left the fleetest deer behind him,   240
Left the antelope and bison;
Crossed the rushing Esconaba,
Crossed the mighty Mississippi,
Passed the Mountains of the Prairie,
Passed the land of Crows and Foxes,   245
Passed the dwellings of the Blackfeet,
Came unto the Rocky Mountains,
To the kingdom of the West-Wind,
Where upon the gusty summits
Sat the ancient Mudjekeewis,   250
Ruler of the winds of heaven.

Filled with awe was Hiawatha
At the aspect of his father.
On the air about him wildly
Tossed and streamed his cloudy tresses,   255
Gleamed like drifting snow his tresses,
Glared like Ishkoodah, the comet,

Like the star with fiery tresses.
  Filled with joy was Mudjekeewis
When he looked on Hiawatha,   260
Saw his youth rise up before him
In the face of Hiawatha,
Saw the beauty of Wenonah
From the grave rise up before him.
  "Welcome!" said he, "Hiawatha,   265
To the kingdom of the West-Wind!
Long have I been waiting for you!
Youth is lovely, age is lonely,
Youth is fiery, age is frosty;
You bring back the days departed,   270
You bring back my youth of passion,
And the beautiful Wenonah!"
  Many days they talked together,
Questioned, listened, waited, answered;
Much the mighty Mudjekeewis   275
Boasted of his ancient prowess,
Of his perilous adventures,
His indomitable courage,
His invulnerable body.
  Patiently sat Hiawatha,   280
Listening to his father's boasting;
With a smile he sat and listened,
Uttered neither threat nor menace,
Neither word nor look betrayed him,
But his heart was hot within him,   285
Like a living coal his heart was.
  Then he said, "O Mudjekeewis,
Is there nothing that can harm you?
Nothing that you are afraid of?"
And the mighty Mudjekeewis,   290
Grand and gracious in his boasting,
Answered, saying, "There is nothing,
Nothing but the black rock yonder,
Nothing but the fatal Wawbeek!"
  And he looked at Hiawatha   295
With a wise look and benignant,
With a countenance paternal,
Looked with pride upon the beauty
Of his tall and graceful figure,
Saying, "O my Hiawatha!   300

Is there anything can harm you?
Anything you are afraid of?"
  But the wary Hiawatha
Paused awhile, as if uncertain,
Held his peace, as if resolving,   305
And then answered, "There is nothing,
Nothing but the bulrush yonder,
Nothing but the great Apukwa!"
  And as Mudjekeewis, rising,
Stretched his hand to pluck the bulrush,   310
Hiawatha cried in terror,
Cried in well-dissembled terror,
"Kago! kago! do not touch it!"
"Ah, kaween!" said Mudjekeewis,
"No indeed, I will not touch it!"   315
  Then they talked of other matters;
First of Hiawatha's brothers,
First of Wabun, of the East-Wind,
Of the South-Wind, Shawondasee,
Of the North, Kabibonokka;   320
Then of Hiawatha's mother,
Of the beautiful Wenonah,
Of her birth upon the meadow,
Of her death, as old Nokomis
Had remembered and related.   325
  And he cried, "O Mudjekeewis,
It was you who killed Wenonah,
Took her young life and her beauty,
Broke the Lily of the Prairie,
Trampled it beneath your footsteps;   330
You confess it! you confess it!"
And the mighty Mudjekeewis
Tossed upon the wind his tresses,
Bowed his hoary head in anguish,
With a silent nod assented.   335
  Then up started Hiawatha,
And with threatening look and gesture
Laid his hand upon the black rock,
On the fatal Wawbeek laid it,
With his mittens, Minjekahwun,   340
Rent the jutting crag asunder,
Smote and crushed it into fragments,
Hurled them madly at his father,

The remorseful Mudjekeewis,
For his heart was hot within him, 345
Like a living coal his heart was.

 But the ruler of the West-Wind
Blew the fragments backward from him,
With the breathing of his nostrils,
With the tempest of his anger, 350
Blew them back at his assailant;
Seized the bulrush, the Apukwa,
Dragged it with its roots and fibers
From the margin of the meadow,
From its ooze the giant bulrush; 355
Long and loud laughed Hiawatha!

 Then began the deadly conflict,
Hand to hand among the mountains;
From his eyry screamed the eagle,
The Keneu, the great war-eagle, 360
Sat upon the crags around them,
Wheeling flapped his wings above them.

 Like a tall tree in the tempest
Bent and lashed the giant bulrush;
And in masses huge and heavy 365
Crashing fell the fatal Wawbeek;
Till the earth shook with the tumult
And confusion of the battle,
And the air was full of shoutings,
And the thunder of the mountains, 370
Starting, answered, "Baim-wawa!"

 Back retreated Mudjekeewis,
Rushing westward o'er the mountains,
Stumbling westward down the mountains,
Three whole days retreated fighting, 375
Still pursued by Hiawatha
To the doorways of the West-Wind,
To the portals of the Sunset,
To the earth's remotest border,
Where into the empty spaces 380
Sinks the sun, as a flamingo
Drops into her nest at nightfall
In the melancholy marshes.

 "Hold!" at length cried Mudjekeewis,
"Hold, my son, my Hiawatha! 385
'Tis impossible to kill me,

For you cannot kill the immortal!
I have put you to this trial,
But to know and prove your courage;
Now receive the prize of valor! 390
 "Go back to your home and people,
Live among them, toil among them,
Cleanse the earth from all that harms it,
Clear the fishing-grounds and rivers,
Slay all monsters and magicians, 395
All the Wendigoes, the giants,
All the serpents, the Kenabeeks,
As I slew the Mishe-Mokwa,
Slew the Great Bear of the mountains.

 "And at last when Death draws near you, 400
When the awful eyes of Pauguk
Glare upon you in the darkness,
I will share my kingdom with you,
Ruler shall you be thenceforward
Of the Northwest-Wind, Keewaydin, 405
Of the home-wind, the Keewaydin."

 Thus was fought that famous battle
In the dreadful days of Shah-shah,
In the days long since departed,
In the kingdom of the West-Wind. 410
Still the hunter sees its traces
Scattered far o'er hill and valley;
Sees the giant bulrush growing
By the ponds and water-courses,
Sees the masses of the Wawbeek 415
Lying still in every valley.

 Homeward now went Hiawatha;
Pleasant was the landscape round him,
Pleasant was the air above him,
For the bitterness of anger 420
Had departed wholly from him,
From his brain the thought of vengeance,
From his heart the burning fever.

 Only once his pace he slackened,
Only once he paused or halted, 425
Paused to purchase heads of arrows
Of the ancient Arrow-maker,
In the land of the Dacotahs,
Where the Falls of Minnehaha

Flash and gleam among the oak-trees,   430
Laugh and leap into the valley.
    There the ancient Arrow-maker
Made his arrow-heads of sandstone,
Arrow-heads of chalcedony,
Arrow-heads of flint and jasper,   435
Smoothed and sharpened at the edges,
Hard and polished, keen and costly.
    With him dwelt his dark-eyed daughter,
Wayward as the Minnehaha,
With her moods of shade and sunshine,   440
Eyes that smiled and frowned alternate,
Feet as rapid as the river,
Tresses flowing like the water,
And as musical a laughter:
And he named her from the river,   445
From the water-fall he named her,
Minnehaha, Laughing Water.
    Was it then for heads of arrows,
Arrow-heads of chalcedony,
Arrow-heads of flint and jasper,   450
That my Hiawatha halted
In the land of the Dacotahs?
    Was it not to see the maiden,
See the face of Laughing Water
Peeping from behind the curtain,   455
Hear the rustling of her garments
From behind the waving curtain,
As one sees the Minnehaha
Gleaming, glancing through the branches,
As one hears the Laughing Water   460
From behind its screen of branches?
    Who shall say what thoughts and visions
Fill the fiery brains of young men?
Who shall say what dreams of beauty
Filled the heart of Hiawatha?   465
All he told to old Nokomis,
When he reached the lodge at sunset,
Was the meeting with his father,
Was his fight with Mudjekeewis;
Not a word he said of arrows,   470
Not a word of Laughing Water.

Reading Check

1. What name does Hiawatha give to the birds?
2. Why is Hiawatha honored at a village banquet?
3. What magic can Hiawatha perform with his mittens?
4. What special powers do his moccasins give him?
5. What does Mudjekeewis claim to be afraid of?
6. What does Hiawatha pretend to be frightened of?
7. How does Mudjekeewis repel the rock fragments that Hiawatha hurls at him?
8. How does the hand-to-hand conflict between father and son end?
9. Why does Hiawatha stop in the land of the Dacotahs?
10. What does the name Minnehaha mean?

For Study and Discussion

Analyzing and Interpreting the Poem

1. In lines 176–178 Longfellow describes Hiawatha as

Learned in all the lore of old men,
In all youthful sports and pastimes,
In all manly arts and labors.

Find examples in the poem where Hiawatha proves himself to be a skillful hunter and a great hero.

2. Throughout the poem, Longfellow gives hints about Hiawatha's feelings toward his father, Mudjekeewis. Although the poet never says what Hiawatha plans to do when he reaches the kingdom of the West-Wind, the reader is led to believe that Hiawatha is seeking revenge. Describe Hiawatha's feelings toward Mudjekeewis and tell why he feels this way.

3. Do you think Hiawatha's need for revenge is satisfied by the outcome of the conflict with his father? Explain your answer.

4. Returning home from battle, Hiawatha stops only once, in the land of the Dacotahs. What does the poet suggest happens when Hiawatha sees the maiden, Laughing Water?

5. An **epic** is a long narrative poem about a great hero. Epics often include supernatural forces, descriptions of battles and weapons, and acts of great physical strength and courage. Find examples of these characteristics in the excerpts you have read.

6. Choose twenty lines from *The Song of Hiawatha* to read aloud. **a.** What mood or feeling does the sound of the poem convey? **b.** Although Longfellow does not use rhyme, what devices of sound does he depend upon?

Language and Vocabulary

Finding the Origins of Words

The history of a word is called its **etymology** (ĕt′ə-mŏl′ə-jē). An etymology tells the origin of a word and traces its transmission from one language to another. In a dictionary, the etymology of a word is often given in brackets at the beginning or at the end of an entry.

A number of words in our language come from American Indian languages. For example, the word *opossum* comes from the Algonquian language. The Algonquian name for *opossum* was *apasum,* which means "white beast." Because its color made it visible to its enemies, the opossum developed the defense of faking death, or "playing possum."

Use a dictionary to find the etymology of each of the following words:

raccoon	moose	persimmon
caribou	moccasin	squash
hominy	pecan	squaw

Creative Writing

Creating a Mythical Character

Write a short story about a mythical character. Give your character human and superhuman characteristics. You might consider using a familiar setting, such as your community, school, or home. Plan your story so that it includes a beginning, middle, and end. Be sure to include descriptive details and heroic deeds. You and your classmates might enjoy reading your stories in a small group.

About the Author

Henry Wadsworth Longfellow (1807–1882)

For a biography of Longfellow, see page 141.

LYRIC POETRY

Lyric poetry is generally used to express personal thoughts and feelings. In many lyrics the poet is felt to be speaking in his or her own voice. Some lyrics, like the song from Shakespeare's *Love's Labor's Lost,* were intended to be sung.

When Icicles Hang by the Wall

WILLIAM SHAKESPEARE

One of William Shakespeare's comedies, Love's Labor's Lost, *ends with two songs—the first is Spring's song and the second is Winter's. This is the song of Winter.*

When icicles hang by the wall,
  And Dick the shepherd blows his nail,°
And Tom bears logs into the hall,
  And milk comes frozen home in pail,
When blood is nipped, and ways be foul,°   5
Then nightly sings the staring owl,
  Tu-whit,
Tu-who, a merry note,
While greasy Joan doth keel° the pot.

When all aloud the wind doth blow,   10
  And coughing drowns the parson's saw,°
And birds sit brooding in the snow,
  And Marian's nose looks red and raw,
When roasted crabs° hiss in the bowl,
Then nightly sings the staring owl,   15
  Tu-whit,
Tu-who, a merry note,
While greasy Joan doth keel the pot.

2. **blows his nail:** blows on his fingernails to warm his hands.

5. **ways be foul:** roads are muddy.

9. **keel:** cool by stirring.

11. **saw:** wise saying.

14. **crabs:** crab apples.

For Study and Discussion

Analyzing and Interpreting the Poem

1. This poem uses images to help you imagine a cold winter scene in sixteenth-century England. For example, line 2 pictures a shepherd blowing on his fingernails to warm his hands. **a.** What other images in the poem help you picture this cold winter scene? **b.** What sounds do you hear?

2. Although the images in the poem emphasize the harshness of winter, some of them suggest warmth and comfort. Tom's logs (line 3) must be for a fire. **a.** What do you think Joan is stirring in the pot? **b.** Which image suggests that something tasty is being cooked?

3. Many poems about autumn or winter give the reader a sense of sadness or loneliness. How does this "Winter's song" affect you?

Calling in the Cat

ELIZABETH COATSWORTH

Now from the dark, a deeper dark,
The cat slides,
Furtive and aware,
His eyes still shine with meteor spark
The cold dew weights his hair.   5
Suspicious,
Hesitant, he comes
Stepping morosely from the night,
Held but repelled,
Repelled but held,   10
By lamp and firelight.

Now call your blandest,
Offer up
The sacrifice of meat,
And snare the wandering soul with greeds,   15
Give him to drink and eat,
And he shall walk fastidiously
Into the trap of old
On feet that still smell delicately
Of withered ferns and mould.   20

For Study and Discussion

Analyzing and Interpreting the Poem

1. What characteristics of the cat are emphasized in this poem? Refer to specific lines in formulating your answer.

2. Why is the cat both held and repelled?

3. What words and phrases in the second stanza emphasize that the cat must be lured indoors?

Writing About Literature

Discussing Elements of Mystery

From earliest times the cat has been associated with magic. One superstition, for example, claimed that witches were attended by cats that were spirits in animal form. Discuss the elements in the poem that give the cat a fascinating and mysterious character.

Stars

SARA TEASDALE

Alone in the night
  On a dark hill
With pines around me
  Spicy and still,

And a heaven full of stars   5
  Over my head,
White and topaz
  And misty red;

Myriads° with beating
  Hearts of fire   10
That aeons°
  Cannot vex or tire;

Up the dome of heaven
  Like a great hill,
I watch them marching   15
  Stately and still,

And I know that I
  Am honored to be
Witness
  Of so much majesty.   20

9. **myriads** (mîr′ē-ədz): very large numbers.

11. **aeons** (ē′ŏnz′): eons, very long periods of time.

For Study and Discussion

Analyzing and Interpreting the Poem

1. What is the setting of the poem?

2. Describe the poet's feelings as she looks up at the stars.

3. What are the "beating/Hearts of fire" (lines 9–10)?

4. Which lines suggest a royal procession?

5. Lines 15–16 seem to be contradictory. What is the poet's meaning?

About the Authors

William Shakespeare (1564–1616)

William Shakespeare was born in the town of Stratford-on-Avon in England. In his twenties he went to London, and after a time he joined a well-known company of actors there. For this acting company he wrote a great series of comedies, tragedies, and historic dramas.

Shakespeare's plays were especially popular for various reasons. For one thing, he wrote in magnificent language. He also had the power to create living characters of all kinds and classes. Moreover, his plays have a unique kind of vitality; at each rereading they reveal new depth and meanings.

Elizabeth Coatsworth (1893–1986)

Elizabeth Coatsworth was born in Buffalo. Her work is known for blending the natural and supernatural. She first achieved recognition with *The Cat Who Went to Heaven* (1930), a story based on Japanese folklore. This book was awarded the Newberry Medal for 1931. She wrote many books for children.

Sara Teasdale (1884–1933)

Sara Teasdale was born in St. Louis, Missouri. Her childhood was sheltered. She was sent to private schools, and she was not allowed to travel without a guardian. Her family encouraged her to write. After Harriet Monroe took an interest in her work, Teasdale became successful. Her collections of poetry include *Flame and Shadow* (1920), *Dark of the Moon* (1926), and *Strange Victory* (1933).

DRAMATIC POETRY

A *dramatic* poem resembles a play in some ways. Sometimes a dramatic poem is in the form of a dialogue between two speakers. Sometimes the speaker is addressing someone who does not respond but whose presence is understood. Narrative poems may also be dramatic, and dramatic poems may contain narrative elements.

Incident of the French Camp

ROBERT BROWNING

This poem is based upon an actual incident which occurred during Napoleon's Austrian campaign in 1809. Marshal Lannes, one of Napoleon's most trusted commanders, stormed the fortified city of Ratisbon in a battle which was crucial for the French.

You know, we French stormed Ratisbon.
   A mile or so away,
On a little mound, Napoleon
   Stood on our storming-day;
With neck out-thrust, you fancy how,   5
   Legs wide, arms locked behind,
As if to balance the prone brow
   Oppressive with its mind.

Just as perhaps he mused "My plans
   That soar, to earth may fall,   10
Let once my army leader Lannes
   Waver at yonder wall"—
Out 'twixt the battery smokes there flew
   A rider, bound on bound
Full galloping; nor bridle drew   15
   Until he reached the mound.

Then off there flung in smiling joy,
    And held himself erect
By just his horse's mane, a boy:
    You hardly could suspect—   20
(So tight he kept his lips compressed,
    Scarce any blood came through)
You looked twice ere you saw his breast
    Was all but shot in two.

"Well," cried he, "Emperor, by God's grace   25
    We've got you Ratisbon!
The Marshal's in the market-place,
    And you'll be there anon°
To see your flag-bird flap his vans°
    Where I, to heart's desire,   30
Perched him!" The chief's eye flashed; his plans
    Soared up again like fire.

The chief's eye flashed; but presently
    Softened itself, as sheathes
A film the mother-eagle's eye   35
    When her bruised eaglet breathes;
"You're wounded!" "Nay," the soldier's pride
    Touched to the quick, he said:
"I'm killed, Sire!" And, his chief beside,
    Smiling, the boy fell dead.   40

28. **anon:** right away.

29. **vans:** wings.
The emblem on Napoleon's banner was an eagle.

For Study and Discussion

Analyzing and interpreting the Poem

1a. Who is the speaker in this poem? **b.** To whom might he be telling this incident of the French camp?

2. Many dramatic poems are also narrative poems. Show that this poem contains the three basic elements of a short story: characters, setting, and plot.

3a. According to lines 27–31, what part did the boy play in the battle? **b.** Some historians say that a man, not a boy, performed the act of bravery. Why is Browning's choice of a boy more effective in arousing the reader's sympathy?

4. Look again at the description of the boy's ride (lines 14–24). **a.** In which line do we realize that the rider is a boy? **b.** Why would an observer see him at first as simply "a rider"? **c.** Does the information that he is a boy come at the best dramatic moment?

5. What special qualities does the narrator see in Napoleon that might inspire devotion such as that of the wounded boy?

Literary Elements

Understanding Simile

To describe Napoleon's reaction to the boy's injury, the poet uses a **simile** (lines 34–36). As you have seen, a simile is a figure of speech that compares one thing to another, using the word *like* or *as* to suggest the similarity the poet sees between two things. In "Incident of the French Camp," Napoleon's eye softens *as* a mother eagle's eye is sheathed by a membranous film. What is Napoleon compared to in this simile? What does this comparison suggest about his reaction to the boy's wound? Can you find another effective simile in this poem?

Language and Vocabulary

Recognizing Multiple Meanings of Words

What is the meaning of the word *oppressive* in line 8? What is another common meaning of this word? Look up the root of the word *oppress* in a dictionary. What is the meaning of the Latin word from which it came? Does this original meaning of the word give you a more vivid sense of what it means to be oppressed? How is the oppression of a dictator, for instance, different from that of Napoleon's mind? How are the two similar?

Creative Writing

Using Similes in Description

Suppose you wanted to describe to someone what it was like on an oppressively hot day in the middle of summer. One way to make your description vivid would be to use a simile. You might start thinking about it this way: what else is as heavy and stifling as a hot, humid day? When you have thought of something similar, express the comparison in a simile. (Be sure to use either *like* or *as* in your simile.) After you have described a summer day, try to describe a winter day by using simile.

About the Author

Robert Browning   (1812–1889)

Robert Browning, one of England's greatest poets, is noted for the dramatic situations and vivid characters in his poems. Fascinated by history, he frequently drew upon the past of other countries, especially Italy and France, for his subjects. His elopement with the English poet Elizabeth Barrett, one of the world's famous love stories, has been told by numerous biographers and dramatized by Rudolf Besier in the play *The Barretts of Wimpole Street.*

Anonymous Limericks

A limerick *is a short humorous poem with a characteristic form. What is its rhythm and rhyme pattern?*

There was a young man of Bengal
Who went to a fancy-dress ball.
  He went just for fun
  Dressed up as a bun,
And a dog ate him up in the hall.

I sat next the Duchess at tea.
It was just as I feared it would be:
  Her rumblings abdominal
  Were simply abominable,
And everyone thought it was me.

There was a young fellow of Perth,
Who was born on the day of his birth;
  He was married, they say,
  On his wife's wedding day,
And he died when he quitted the earth.

A gentleman dining at Crewe
Found quite a large mouse in his stew.
  Said the waiter, "Don't shout,
  And wave it about,
Or the rest will be wanting one too!"

Creative Writing

Writing Limericks

No one knows who invented this funny five-line verse form. Some say limericks began in Limerick, Ireland, but most people there refuse to take responsibility for them. Wherever they came from, limericks seem here to stay. Some groups hold limerick contests. Great poets write limericks for fun. A former President of the United States wrote limericks.

Try writing some limericks of your own. Often limericks include the name of some town or country, or the name of a person. You could start out with a line like one of these:

There was a young lady from York
There once was a fellow named Hank

Private Zoo

OGDEN NASH

The Octopus

Tell me, O Octopus, I begs,
Is those things arms, or is they legs?
I marvel at thee, Octopus;
If I were thou, I'd call me Us.

The Panther

The panther is like a leopard,
Except it hasn't been peppered.
Should you behold a panther crouch,
Prepare to say Ouch.
Better yet, if called by a panther,
Don't anther.

The Rhinoceros

The rhino is a homely beast,
For human eyes he's not a feast.
Farewell, farewell, you old rhinoceros.
I'll stare at something less prepocerous.

On the Vanity of Earthly Greatness

ARTHUR GUITERMAN

The word vanity *in this title means "uselessness." The title has a serious ring to it, but don't let it fool you.*

The tusks that clashed in mighty brawls
Of mastodons, are billiard balls.

The sword of Charlemagne the Just
Is ferric oxide, known as rust.

The grizzly bear whose potent hug
Was feared by all, is now a rug.

Great Caesar's bust is on the shelf,
And I don't feel so well myself.

Literary Elements

Recognizing the Techniques of Comic Verse

Many writers over the ages have written seriously about the passage of time and the worthlessness of earthly success. But this poem is meant to be comical. Part of its humor comes from the way in which the poet links very mighty things with very ordinary things. For example, when he thinks of the mastodon's gigantic tusks, he thinks of billiard balls, which are all that he imagines is left of them today.

What other mighty things from the past does he think of? What does he say is left of them today? Is it any wonder that the poet doesn't feel well himself?

This verse is also comical because of its strong rhymes and rhythms. Notice how the poet never skips a beat, even though he probably had to do some thinking to match up "potent hug" with "now a rug."

Perhaps you can add to the poet's comical complaint. What other great and glorious things are now gone, remaining only as leather shoes, note paper, or old portraits?

Casey at the Bat

ERNEST LAWRENCE THAYER

This is one of the most famous poems ever written about baseball. When it was first recited to a group of baseball fans, the audience went wild. As you read, see if you can find reasons for the poem's enormous popularity.

The outlook wasn't brilliant for the Mudville nine that day;
The score stood four to two, with but one inning more to play;
And so, when Cooney died at first, and Burrows did the same,
A sickly silence fell upon the patrons of the game.

A straggling few got up to go in deep despair. The rest   5
Clung to the hope which springs eternal in the human breast;
They thought, if only Casey could but get a whack, at that,
They'd put up even money now, with Casey at the bat.

But Flynn preceded Casey, as did also Jimmy Blake,
And the former was a pudding, and the latter was a fake;   10
So upon that stricken multitude grim melancholy sat,
For there seemed but little chance of Casey's getting to the bat.

But Flynn let drive a single, to the wonderment of all,
And Blake, the much-despised, tore the cover off the ball;
And when the dust had lifted, and they saw what had occurred,   15
There was Jimmy safe on second, and Flynn a-hugging third.

Then from the gladdened multitude went up a joyous yell;
It bounded from the mountaintop, and rattled in the dell;
It struck upon the hillside, and recoiled upon the flat;
For Casey, mighty Casey, was advancing to the bat.   20

There was ease in Casey's manner as he stepped into his place;
There was pride in Casey's bearing, and a smile on Casey's face;
And when, responding to the cheers, he lightly doffed his hat,
No stranger in the crowd could doubt 'twas Casey at the bat.

Ten thousand eyes were on him as he rubbed his hands with dirt;   25
Five thousand tongues applauded when he wiped them on his shirt;
Then while the writhing pitcher ground the ball into his hip,
Defiance gleamed in Casey's eye, a sneer curled Casey's lip.

And now the leather-covered sphere came hurtling through the air,
And Casey stood a-watching it in haughty grandeur there;   30
Close by the sturdy batsman the ball unheeded sped.
"That ain't my style," said Casey. "Strike one," the umpire said.

From the benches, black with people, there went up a muffled roar,
Like the beating of the storm waves on a stern and distant shore;
"Kill him! Kill the umpire!" shouted someone on the stand;   35
And it's likely they'd have killed him had not Casey raised his hand.

With a smile of Christian charity great Casey's visage shone;
He stilled the rising tumult; he bade the game go on;
He signaled to the pitcher, and once more the spheroid flew;
But Casey still ignored it, and the umpire said, "Strike two."   40

Mighty Casey Has Struck Out by Albert Dorne (1904–1965). Watercolor. The National Baseball Hall of Fame and Museum, Inc.

"Fraud!" cried the maddened thousands, and the echo
     answered, "Fraud!"
But a scornful look from Casey, and the audience was awed;
They saw his face grow stern and cold, they saw his muscles strain,
And they knew that Casey wouldn't let that ball go by again.

The sneer is gone from Casey's lips, his teeth are clenched in hate,   45
He pounds with cruel violence his bat upon the plate;
And now the pitcher holds the ball, and now he lets it go,
And now the air is shattered by the force of Casey's blow.

Oh! somewhere in this favored land the sun is shining bright;
The band is playing somewhere, and somewhere hearts are light;   50
And somewhere men are laughing, and somewhere children shout,
But there is no joy in Mudville—mighty Casey has struck out!

For Study and Discussion

Analyzing and Interpreting the Poem

1. Ernest Lawrence Thayer creates a humorous effect by using high-flown, or fancy, language to describe an ordinary event—a baseball game played in a town called Mudville. For example, in line 29, the poet doesn't say "baseball"; instead, he says "leather-covered sphere." What does the poet say instead of "baseball" in line 39?

2. Casey, Mudville's hero, is also described in high-flown, heroic language. **a.** What words and phrases in lines 20–30 describe him? **b.** How does Casey's own speech in line 32 differ from the heroic language used to describe him?

3a. What image, or picture, is created in line 11? **b.** How is this image funny if you take it literally? **c.** What fancy simile is used in lines 33–34 to describe the crowd's roar?

Creative Writing

Writing a Humorous Poem

Try your hand at writing a humorous poem similar to the story of Casey. Perhaps you can describe another sport (basketball, hockey, football, soccer) in elegant-sounding, heroic language. Perhaps you'll want to imitate the rhythm of Thayer's poem. Create a good title for your own sports saga.

For Dramatization

Using Pantomime

Present a dramatization of "Casey at the Bat." While you recite the poem, other students can pantomime the actions of the players and umpire. Remember that pantomime is using gestures without words. You might ask the rest of the class to pantomime the part of the spectators in the stands, moving their heads to follow the action of the players and ball. You might also have the pitcher, Casey, the umpire, and some of the spectators take the brief speaking parts in the poem.

Jabberwocky

LEWIS CARROLL

In a book called Through the Looking Glass, *Alice steps through a mirror and into a world of reversals. She finds this poem in a "mirror-book," written backward. As you read the poem, note how the poet manages to tell a story with some very unusual words.*

'Twas brillig, and the slithy toves
   Did gyre and gimble in the wabe;
All mimsy were the borogoves,
   And the mome raths outgrabe.

"Beware the Jabberwock, my son!   5
   The jaws that bite, the claws that catch!
Beware the Jubjub bird, and shun
   The frumious Bandersnatch!"

He took his vorpal sword in hand;
   Long time the manxome foe he sought—   10
So rested he by the Tumtum tree,
   And stood awhile in thought.

And, as in uffish thought he stood,
   The Jabberwock, with eyes of flame,
Came whiffling through the tulgey wood,   15
   And burbled as it came!

One, two! One, two! And through and through
   The vorpal blade went snicker-snack!
He left it dead, and with its head
   He went galumphing back.   20

"And hast thou slain the Jabberwock?
   Come to my arms, my beamish boy!
O frabjous day! Callooh! Callay!"
   He chortled in his joy.

Illustration by Sir John Tenniel (1820–1914) for
Through the Looking-Glass (1870).

'Twas brillig and the slithy toves   25
   Did gyre and gimble in the wabe;
All mimsy were the borogoves,
   And the mome raths outgrabe.

Language and Vocabulary

Explaining Portmanteau Words

Alice asks Humpty Dumpty to explain "Jabberwocky." Here is their conversation.

"*Brillig* means four o'clock in the afternoon—the time when you begin *broiling* things for dinner."

"That'll do very well," said Alice; "and *slithy?*"

"Well, *slithy* means 'lithe and slimy.' *Lithe* is the same as 'active.' You see it's like a portmanteau—there are two meanings packed up into one word."

"I see it now," Alice remarked thoughtfully; "and what are *toves?*"

"Well, *toves* are something like badgers—they're something like lizards—and they're something like corkscrews."

"They must be very curious-looking creatures."

"They are that," said Humpty Dumpty; "also they make their nests under sundials—also they live on cheese."

"And what's to *gyre* and to *gimble?*"

"To *gyre* is to go round and round like a gyroscope. To *gimble* is to make holes like a gimlet."

"And *the wabe* is the grass plot round a sundial, I suppose?" said Alice, surprised at her own ingenuity.

"Of course it is. It's called *wabe,* you know, because it goes a long way before it, and a long way behind it——"

"And a long way beyond it on each side," Alice added.

"Exactly so. Well then, *mimsy* is 'flimsy and miserable' (there's another portmanteau for you). And a *borogove* is a thin, shabby-looking bird with its feathers sticking out all round—something like a live mop."

"And then *mome raths?*" said Alice. "I'm afraid I'm giving you a great deal of trouble."

"Well, a *rath* is a sort of green pig; but *mome* I'm not certain about. I think it's short for 'from home'—meaning that they'd lost their way, you know."

"And what does *outgrabe* mean?"

"Well, *outgribing* is something between bellowing and whistling, with a kind of sneeze in the middle; however, you'll hear it done, maybe—down in the wood yonder—and, when you've once heard it, you'll be *quite* content. Who's been repeating all that hard stuff to you?"

"I read it in a book," said Alice.

A *portmanteau* is a suitcase that opens into two parts. What does Humpty Dumpty say a *portmanteau word* is?

Try to explain the two meanings "packed up into" these common portmanteau words. Check your answers in your dictionary.

brunch   motel   smog   transistor

Ogden Nash   (1902–1971)

Ogden Nash is America's most famous writer of comic verse. He was admired greatly during his lifetime, and his whimsical poems for adults and children still are extremely popular. Some of his lines—such as "If called by a panther, / Don't anther"—have become part of modern American folk culture. He once described himself as a "worsifier." Nash was born in Rye, New York. He worked as a teacher and a bond salesman, and then as an advertising copy writer before he could support his family with his verse. His first book of humorous verse, *Hard Lines,* was published in 1931. In addition to many books of poetry, Nash wrote three screenplays, lyrics for the successful Broadway musical *One Touch of Venus,* and lyrics for several television specials. He also made regular radio and television appearances.

Ernest Lawrence Thayer   (1863–1940)

Ernest Lawrence Thayer, a native of Lawrence, Massachusetts, was an American journalist and poet. He was a graduate of Harvard University and president of the *Harvard Lampoon* during his senior year. In 1886 he joined the staff of the *San Francisco Examiner,* where he wrote a humorous column and ballads for the Sunday editions. The newspaper printed "Casey at the Bat" in 1888. The poem became a nationwide favorite when recited all over the country by touring actor De Wolfe Hopper. Thayer devoted his later years to traveling, studying philosophy, and writing.

Lewis Carroll   (1832–1898)

Lewis Carroll, whose real name was Charles Lutwidge Dodgson, was a mathematics teacher at Oxford University in England. He was friendly with a little girl named Alice Liddell, to whom he told stories. Out of this friendship came two of the most popular fantasies ever written, *Alice's Adventures in Wonderland* and *Through the Looking Glass.* Some of the other famous characters in these two books are the Mad Hatter, the March Hare, the Cheshire Cat, and Tweedledum and Tweedledee. Carroll once claimed that mathematics is the true wonderland, for "nothing is impossible" there.

DEVELOPING SKILLS IN CRITICAL THINKING

Analyzing Poetry

When you use the critical thinking skill of analysis, you divide something into its parts and examine the relationships among the parts. Analysis can help you better understand how a poet uses different elements to convey a particular meaning or feeling. Here is a short poem for analysis. Follow the suggestions below.

A Choice of Weapons

Phyllis McGinley

Sticks and stones are hard on bones.
Aimed with angry art,
Words can sting like anything.
But silence breaks the heart.

1. *Look for complete thoughts.* The end of a complete thought in most poems is indicated by a period or semicolon. Sometimes these punctuation marks will come in the middle of a line. Sometimes you will have to read several lines before a thought is completed. How many sentences are contained in this poem? Where should you pause when you read these lines?

2. *Be aware of inverted (reversed) word order.* Poets sometimes put words in an order that is not normal in English sentences. They do this for emphasis or to make their rhymes and rhythms work out. Look at line 39 from "The Raven" (page 477):

Not the least obeisance made he; not a minute
stopped or stayed he;

In normal word order, the line would read this way:

He did not make the least obeisance; he did not
stop or stay a minute;

Recite this line as part of the poem. What happens to the rhythm and rhyme? Put line 49 of "The Raven" in normal word order. How does the emphasis change?

3. *Interpret the figurative language.* When the speaker in "Casey at the Bat" (page 507) says that Cooney "died at first," he is using a common figure of speech. Cooney, of course, didn't really fall over dead on first base. The speaker means that the possible run "died" at first base. Where is the figure of speech in these lines (9-10) from "Casey at the Bat"?

But Flynn preceded Casey, as did also Jimmy
Blake,
And the former was a pudding, and the latter was
a fake;

What picture does the figure of speech create? Do you think it is a good comparison?

4. *Paraphrase the poem or difficult lines in the poem.* To paraphrase is to restate a line or a passage in your own words. Here are lines 1–2 of "On the Vanity of Earthly Greatness" (page 506) and a paraphrase:

The tusks that clashed in mighty brawls
Of mastodons, are billiard balls.

Mastodon tusks, once used in battles of these
great beasts, are now made into billiard balls.

5. *Be aware of sound effects in the poem.* Ask how sound reinforces meaning.

PRACTICE IN
READING AND WRITING

Writing Poetry

Write four or more lines of poetry in which you use a figure of speech to describe a feeling or an idea about something. Do not worry about using rhyme and regular rhythm. (You might imitate the style used by Alice Walker on page 465.) Here are some suggestions:

The feeling you have when you run (or swim, or hike)
The way the earth smells after a rainfall
The way the streets look at night
What a dog sounds like when it eats
What a dripping faucet sounds like when you are trying to sleep

Prewriting

- Search your memory for a special person, event, experience, or feeling you would like to write about in your poem.
- List details that describe or tell about the subject you are going to write about.
- Use details that come from all of your senses: sight, hearing, touch, smell, and taste.
- Decide which details make the strongest impression on you.
- Organize the details so they best convey the main impression and meaning you would like your readers to grasp. You can use chronological, or time, order; spatial order, or the order in which things are placed; or details of one sense, then another, and so on.

- Decide where you can use figures of speech to surprise or delight your readers.

Writing
As you write your poem, concentrate on using vivid and fresh figures of speech that will make the main impression and meaning come alive for your readers.

Evaluating and Revising
Evaluate your poem by answering the following questions. Then revise your draft by adding, cutting, reordering, or replacing words.
- Does the poem convey a main impression about the subject?
- Have you included vivid descriptions and sensory details to tell about the subject?
- Do the figures of speech create fresh and lively images for your readers?
- Do the punctuation and capitalization in the poem help to make the meaning clear?

Proofreading
Reread your revised poem to locate and correct any errors that might confuse your readers. Then make a clean copy and proofread again to catch any errors or omissions made in recopying. You and your classmates might enjoy either reading your poems in a small group or collecting them into a class anthology.

For Further Reading

Adoff, Arnold, *Sports Pages* (Lippincott, 1986)
These poems are written in the voices of teen-age athletes who express their feelings and experiences.

Baron, Virginia, *Here I Am!: An Anthology of Poems Written by Young People in Some of America's Minority Groups* (Dutton, 1969)
Students from all over the United States write poems on things they care about most.

Benét, Rosemary, and Stephen Vincent Benét, *A Book of Americans* (Holt, Rinehart and Winston, 1933)
These easy-to-read poems create "portraits" of fifty-six unusual Americans.

Bontemps, Arna, editor, *Golden Slippers: An Anthology of Negro Poetry for Young Readers* (Harper & Row, 1941)
Arna Bontemps, a poet himself, chose these appealing poems from the works of America's black poets.

Brooks, Gwendolyn, *Selected Poems* (Harper & Row, 1963; paperback, Harper)
The poet has selected these poems from her earlier books: *A Street in Bronzeville, Annie Allen,* and *The Bean Eaters.*

Browning, Robert, *The Pied Piper of Hamelin* (Coward-McCann & Geoghegan, 1971)
This illustrated edition presents the funny story of the piper who has his revenge on the adults of Hamelin for breaking their promise.

Carroll, Lewis, *The Walrus and the Carpenter and Other Poems* (Dutton, 1969)
Eleven of Lewis Carroll's best nonsense poems are illustrated here.

Dunning, Steven, Edward Lueders, and Hugh Smith, editors, *Reflections on a Gift of Watermelon Pickle and Other Modern Verse* (Lothrop, Lee & Shepard, 1967)
If you think poetry is hard to understand, or only about "poetic" subjects, you should look into these modern poems especially chosen for young people. *Some Haystacks Don't Even Have Any Needle and Other Complete Modern Poems* (Lothrop, Lee & Shepard, 1969) is another gathering of poems, by the same editors, that are fun to read.

Frost, Robert, *You Come Too: Favorite Poems for Young Readers* (Holt, Rinehart and Winston, 1959)
Frost chose these fifty poems of his to please young people.

Janeczko, Paul, *Pocket Poems* (Bradbury Press, 1985)
These short modern poems deal with daily life and cover such topics as food, cars, pets, love, and friendship.

Jordan, June, *Who Look at Me* (Thomas Y. Crowell, 1969)
Twenty-seven poems accompany paintings of black people by prominent American artists.

Koch, Kenneth, editor, *Sleeping in the Wing: An Anthology of Modern Poetry* (Random House, 1981)
Here are selections by twenty-three poets.

Lear, Edward, *Complete Nonsense Book* (Dodd, Mead, 1948; paperback, Dover)
Here are limericks, nonsense rhymes, and silly poems designed to make you laugh.

Livingston, Myra Cohn, editor, *A Tune Beyond Us* (Harcourt Brace Jovanovich, 1968)
These poems from all over the world were chosen by a writer of books for young people.

Merriam, Eve, *Independent Voices* (Atheneum, 1968)
Read aloud these poems about Frederick Douglass, Henry David Thoreau, Lucretia Mott, and other famous Americans.

Peck, Richard, editor, *Sounds and Silences: Poetry for Now* (Delacorte, 1970; paperback, Dell)
Song lyrics are included in this collection of contemporary poems on such themes as isolation, illusion, communication, realities, and identity.

Poems of the Unknowable (Atheneum, 1982)
This is a collection of poems by men and women who have tried to explain the mysteries of the universe.

Swenson, May, *Poems to Solve* (Scribner, 1966; paperback, Scribner)
Try to solve these thirty-five riddle poems and puzzling poems with hidden meanings.

THE
NOVEL

The term *novel* comes from the Italian *novella*, a short realistic tale popular in medieval times. The first American novel written and published in America appeared in 1789. Since then the novel has become the most widely read form of literature in America.

The novel is a type of imaginative literature and shares many of the same literary elements as short stories, epics, and myths. A novel may be defined as *a fictional narrative in prose, generally longer than a short story.* The novel allows for greater complexity of character and plot development than the short story. The forms the novel may take cover a wide range. For example, there are the *historical novel*, in which historical characters, settings, and periods are drawn in detail; the *picaresque novel*, presenting the adventures of a rogue; and the *psychological novel*, which focuses on characters' emotions and thoughts. Other forms of the novel include the detective story, the spy thriller, the Western, and the science-fiction novel.

In this unit, you will read Jack Schaefer's Western novel *Shane*, the story of a mysterious hero who enters the lives of the Starretts, a family of homesteaders struggling to establish their roots in the Wyoming frontier during the late 1880s. The story is narrated from the point of view of young Bob Starrett, who sees Shane as a noble, heroic figure dealing out violent justice. This novel has won great acclaim as a notable work of fiction and has been translated into thirty-one languages. It has been selected by a British committee of readers as one of the hundred best novels of the twentieth century.

When you read a novel, it is important to develop as complete an understanding as possible. This requires the process of studying and reviewing what you have read. The following guidelines will help you to understand the uses of literary elements found in the novel.

Guidelines for Reading a Novel

1. *Define all unfamiliar words.* Use a dictionary to define any unfamiliar words that might cause difficulty in understanding a passage. Be sure to locate the correct definition as it applies to the word and its use in context.

2. *Read actively, asking questions as you read.* For example, as you read, try to predict how a conflict or event will turn out. Try to determine the author's purpose for using specific events or conflicts.

3. *Become aware of information that establishes the setting or background of the novel.* The language of characters, for example, can help to set the time and place of the action.

4. *Look for clues that reveal what characters are like: dialogue, important actions, or descriptive details.* Discover how characters develop and change as the novel progresses.

5. *Determine the major action of the novel.* As you read, consider how individual episodes are connected to the main plot.

6. *Note the point of view of the novel.* Seek to understand the author's reason for selecting a particular point of view.

7. *Consider how all the elements of the novel contribute to its theme.* Try to identify the various elements and how they contribute to the overall theme of the novel.

Shane

JACK SCHAEFER

1

He rode into our valley in the summer of '89. I was a kid then, barely topping the backboard of father's old chuck-wagon.[1] I was on the upper rail of our small corral, soaking in the late afternoon sun, when I saw him far down the road where it swung into the valley from the open plain beyond.

In that clear Wyoming air I could see him plainly, though he was still several miles away. There seemed nothing remarkable about him, just another stray horseman riding up the road toward the cluster of frame buildings that was our town. Then I saw a pair of cowhands, loping past him, stop and stare after him with a curious intentness.

He came steadily on, straight through the town without slackening pace, until he reached the fork a half-mile below our place. One branch turned left across the river ford and on to Luke Fletcher's big spread. The other bore ahead along the right bank where we homesteaders had pegged our claims in a row up the valley. He hesitated briefly, studying the choice, and moved again steadily on our side.

As he came near, what impressed me first was his clothes. He wore dark trousers of some serge material tucked into tall boots and held at the waist by a wide belt, both of a soft black leather tooled[2] in intricate design. A coat of the same dark material as the trousers was neatly folded and strapped to his saddle-roll. His shirt was finespun linen, rich brown in color. The handkerchief knotted loosely around his throat was black silk. His hat was not the familiar Stetson, not the familiar gray or muddy tan. It was a plain black, soft in texture, unlike any hat I had ever seen, with a creased crown and a wide curling brim swept down in front to shield the face.

All trace of newness was long since gone from these things. The dust of distance was beaten into them. They were worn and stained and several neat patches showed on the shirt. Yet a kind of magnificence remained and with it a hint of men and manners alien to my limited boy's experience.

Then I forgot the clothes in the impact of the man himself. He was not much above medium height, almost slight in build. He would have looked frail alongside father's square, solid bulk. But even I could read the endurance in the lines of that dark figure and the quiet power in its effortless, unthinking adjustment to every movement of the tired horse.

He was clean-shaven and his face was lean and hard and burned from high forehead to firm, tapering chin. His eyes seemed hooded in the shadow of the hat's brim. He came closer, and I could see that this was because the brows were drawn in a frown of fixed and ha-

---

1. **chuck-wagon:** a wagon used as a kitchen to feed outdoor workers.
2. **tooled:** stamped or impressed.

Scenes (pages 521, 523, 524, 535, 541, 548–549, 552, 554, 562, 566, 568, 571, 576–577, 584, 590 and 596) from the film *Shane* (1953).

bitual alertness. Beneath them the eyes were endlessly searching from side to side and forward, checking off every item in view, missing nothing. As I noticed this, a sudden chill, I could not have told why, struck through me there in the warm and open sun.

He rode easily, relaxed in the saddle, leaning his weight lazily into the stirrups. Yet even in this easiness was a suggestion of tension. It was the easiness of a coiled spring, of a trap set.

He drew rein not twenty feet from me. His glance hit me, dismissed me, flicked over our place. This was not much, if you were thinking in terms of size and scope. But what there was was good. You could trust father for that. The corral, big enough for about thirty head if you crowded them in, was railed right to true sunk posts. The pasture behind, taking in nearly half of our claim, was fenced tight. The barn was small, but it was solid, and we were raising a loft at one end for the alfalfa growing green in the north forty. We had a fair-sized field in potatoes that year and father was trying a new corn he had sent all the way to Washington for and they were showing properly in weedless rows.

Behind the house mother's kitchen garden was a brave sight. The house itself was three rooms—two really, the big kitchen where we spent most of our time indoors and the bedroom beside it. My little lean-to room was added back of the kitchen. Father was planning, when he could get around to it, to build mother the parlor she wanted.

We had wooden floors and a nice porch across the front. The house was painted too, white with green trim, rare thing in all that region, to remind her, mother said when she made father do it, of her native New England. Even rarer, the roof was shingled. I knew what that meant. I had helped father split those shingles. Few places so spruce and well worked

could be found so deep in the Territory[3] in those days.

The stranger took it all in, sitting there easily in the saddle. I saw his eyes slow on the flowers mother had planted by the porch steps, then come to rest on our shiny new pump and the trough beside it. They shifted back to me, and again, without knowing why, I felt that sudden chill. But his voice was gentle and he spoke like a man schooled to patience.

"I'd appreciate a chance at the pump for myself and the horse."

I was trying to frame a reply and choking on it, when I realized that he was not speaking to me but past me. Father had come up behind me and was leaning against the gate to the corral.

"Use all the water you want, stranger."

Father and I watched him dismount in a single flowing tilt of his body and lead the horse over to the trough. He pumped it almost full and let the horse sink its nose in the cool water before he picked up the dipper for himself.

He took off his hat and slapped the dust out of it and hung it on a corner of the trough. With his hands he brushed the dust from his clothes. With a piece of rag pulled from his saddle-roll he carefully wiped his boots. He untied the handkerchief from around his neck and rolled his sleeves and dipped his arms in the trough, rubbing thoroughly and splashing water over his face. He shook his hands dry and used the handkerchief to remove the last drops from his face. Taking a comb from his shirt pocket, he smoothed back his long dark hair. All his movements were deft and sure, and with a quick precision he flipped down his sleeves, reknotted the handkerchief, and picked up his hat.

Then, holding it in his hand, he spun about and strode directly toward the house. He bent

3. **Territory:** Wyoming was admitted to the Union in 1890.

low and snapped the stem of one of mother's petunias and tucked this into the hatband. In another moment the hat was on his head, brim swept down in swift, unconscious gesture, and he was swinging gracefully into the saddle and starting toward the road.

I was fascinated. None of the men I knew were proud like that about their appearance. In that short time the kind of magnificence I had noticed had emerged into plainer view. It was in the very air of him. Everything about him showed the effects of long use and hard use, but showed too the strength of quality and competence. There was no chill on me now.

Already I was imagining myself in hat and belt and boots like those.

He stopped the horse and looked down at us. He was refreshed and I would have sworn the tiny wrinkles around his eyes were what with him would be a smile. His eyes were not restless when he looked at you like this. They were still and steady and you knew the man's whole attention was concentrated on you even in the casual glance.

"Thank you," he said in his gentle voice and was turning into the road, back to us, before father spoke in his slow, deliberate way.

"Don't be in such a hurry, stranger."

Shane **523**

I had to hold tight to the rail or I would have fallen backwards into the corral. At the first sound of father's voice, the man and the horse, like a single being, had wheeled to face us, the man's eyes boring at father, bright and deep in the shadow of the hat's brim. I was shivering, struck through once more. Something intangible and cold and terrifying was there in the air between us.

I stared in wonder as father and the stranger looked at each other a long moment, measuring each other in an unspoken fraternity of adult knowledge beyond my reach. Then the warm sunlight was flooding over us, for father was smiling and he was speaking with the drawling emphasis that meant he had made up his mind.

"I said don't be in such a hurry, stranger. Food will be on the table soon and you can bed down here tonight."

The stranger nodded quietly as if he too had made up his mind. "That's mighty thoughtful of you," he said and swung down and came toward us, leading his horse. Father slipped into step beside him and we all headed for the barn.

"My name's Starrett," said father. "Joe Starrett. This here," waving at me, "is Robert MacPherson Starrett. Too much name for a boy. I make it Bob."

The stranger nodded again. "Call me Shane," he said. Then to me: "Bob it is. You were watching me for quite a spell coming up the road."

It was not a question. It was a simple statement. "Yes . . ." I stammered. "Yes. I was."

"Right," he said. "I like that. A man who watches what's going on around him will make his mark."

A man who watches . . . For all his dark appearance and lean, hard look, this Shane knew what would please a boy. The glow of it held me as he took care of his horse, and I fussed around, hanging up his saddle, forking over some hay, getting in his way and my own in my eagerness. He let me slip the bridle off and the horse, bigger and more powerful than I had thought now that I was close beside it, put its head down patiently for me and stood quietly while I helped him curry away the caked dust. Only once did he stop me. That was when I reached for his saddle-roll to put it to one side. In the instant my fingers touched it, he was taking it from me and he put it on a shelf with a finality that indicated no interference.

When the three of us went up to the house, mother was waiting and four places were set at the table. "I saw you through the window," she said and came to shake our visitor's hand. She was a slender, lively woman with a fair complexion even our weather never seemed to affect and a mass of light brown hair she wore piled high to bring her, she used to say, closer to father's size.

"Marian," father said, "I'd like you to meet Mr. Shane."

"Good evening, ma'am," said our visitor. He took her hand and bowed over it. Mother stepped back and, to my surprise, dropped in a dainty curtsy. I had never seen her do that before. She was an unpredictable woman. Father and I would have painted the house three times over and in rainbow colors to please her.

"And a good evening to you, Mr. Shane. If Joe hadn't called you back, I would have done it myself. You'd never find a decent meal up the valley."

She was proud of her cooking, was mother. That was one thing she learned back home, she would often say, that was of some use out in this raw land. As long as she could still prepare a proper dinner, she would tell father when things were not going right, she knew she was still civilized and there was hope of getting ahead. Then she would tighten her lips and whisk together her special most delicious biscuits and father would watch her bustling about and eat them to the last little crumb and stand up and wipe his eyes and stretch his big frame and stomp out to his always unfinished work like daring anything to stop him now.

We sat down to supper and a good one. Mother's eyes sparkled as our visitor kept pace with father and me. Then we all leaned back and while I listened the talk ran on almost like old friends around a familiar table. But I could sense that it was following a pattern. Father was trying, with mother helping and both of them avoiding direct questions, to get hold of facts about this Shane and he was dodging at every turn. He was aware of their purpose and not in the least annoyed by it. He was mild and courteous and spoke readily enough. But always he put them off with words that gave no real information.

He must have been riding many days, for he was full of news from towns along his back trail as far as Cheyenne and even Dodge City and others beyond I had never heard of before. But he had no news about himself. His past was fenced as tightly as our pasture. All they could learn was that he was riding through, taking each day as it came, with nothing particular in mind except maybe seeing a part of the country he had not been in before.

Afterwards mother washed the dishes and I dried and the two men sat on the porch, their voices carrying through the open door. Our visitor was guiding the conversation now and in no time at all he had father talking about his own plans. That was no trick. Father was ever one to argue his ideas whenever he could find a listener. This time he was going strong.

"Yes, Shane, the boys I used to ride with don't see it yet. They will some day. The open range can't last forever. The fence lines are closing in. Running cattle in big lots is good business only for the top ranchers and it's really a poor business at that. Poor in terms of the resources going into it. Too much space for too little results. It's certain to be crowded out."

"Well, now," said Shane, "that's mighty interesting. I've been hearing the same quite a lot lately from men with pretty clear heads. Maybe there's something to it."

"By Godfrey, there's plenty to it. Listen to me, Shane. The thing to do is pick your spot, get your land, your own land. Put in enough crops to carry you and make your money play with a small herd, not all horns and bone, but bred for meat and fenced in and fed right. I haven't been at it long, but already I've raised stock that averages three hundred pounds more than that long-legged stuff Fletcher runs on the other side of the river and it's better beef, and that's only a beginning.

"Sure, his outfit sprawls over most of this valley and it looks big. But he's got range rights on a lot more acres than he has cows and he won't even have those acres as more homesteaders move in. His way is wasteful. Too much land for what he gets out of it. He can't see that. He thinks we small fellows are nothing but nuisances."

"You are," said Shane mildly. "From his point of view, you are."

"Yes, I guess you're right. I'll have to admit that. Those of us here now would make it tough for him if he wanted to use the range behind us on this side of the river as he used to. Altogether we cut some pretty good slices out of it. Worse still, we block off part of the river, shut the range off from the water. He's been grumbling about that off and on ever since we've been here. He's worried that more of us will keep coming and settle on the other side too, and then he will be in a fix."

The dishes were done and I was edging to the door. Mother nailed me as she usually did and shunted me off to bed. After she had left me in my little back room and went to join the men on the porch, I tried to catch more of the words. The voices were too low. Then I must have dozed, for with a start I realized that father and mother were again in the kitchen. By now, I gathered, our visitor was out in the barn in the bunk father had built there for the hired man who had been with us for a few weeks in the spring.

"Wasn't it peculiar," I heard mother say, "how he wouldn't talk about himself?"

"Peculiar?" said father. "Well, yes. In a way."

"Everything about him is peculiar." Mother sounded as if she was stirred up and interested. "I never saw a man quite like him before."

"You wouldn't have. Not where you come from. He's a special brand we sometimes get out here in the grass country. I've come across a few. A bad one's poison. A good one's straight grain clear through."

"How can you be so sure about him? Why, he wouldn't even tell where he was raised."

"Born back east a ways would be my guess. And pretty far south. Tennessee maybe. But he's been around plenty."

"I like him." Mother's voice was serious. "He's so nice and polite and sort of gentle. Not like most men I've met out here. But there's something about him. Something underneath the gentleness . . . Something . . ." Her voice trailed away.

"Mysterious?" suggested father.

"Yes, of course. Mysterious. But more than that. Dangerous."

"He's dangerous all right." Father said it in a musing way. Then he chuckled. "But not to us, my dear." And then he said what seemed to me a curious thing. "In fact, I don't think you ever had a safer man in your house."

2

In the morning I slept late and stumbled into the kitchen to find father and our visitor working their way through piles of mother's flapjacks. She smiled at me from over by the stove. Father slapped my rump by way of greeting. Our visitor nodded at me gravely over his heaped-up plate.

"Good morning, Bob. You'd better dig in fast or I'll do away with your share too. There's magic in your mother's cooking. Eat enough of these flannel cakes and you'll grow a bigger man than your father."

"Flannel cakes! Did you hear that, Joe?" Mother came whisking over to tousle father's hair. "You must be right. Tennessee or some such place. I never heard them called that out here."

Our visitor looked up at her. "A good guess, ma'am. Mighty close to the mark. But you had a husband to help you. My folks came out of Mississippi and settled in Arkansas. Me, though—I was fiddle-footed and left home at fifteen. Haven't had anything worth being called a real flannel cake since." He put his hands on the table edge and leaned back and the little wrinkles at the corners of his eyes were plainer and deeper. "That is, ma'am, till now."

Mother gave what in a girl I would have called a giggle. "If I'm any judge of men," she said, "that means more." And she whisked back to the stove.

That was how it was often in our house, kind of jolly and warm with good feeling. It needed to be this morning because there was a cool grayness in the air and before I had even begun to slow on my second plate of flapjacks the wind was rushing down the valley with the rain of one of our sudden summer storms following fast.

Our visitor had finished his breakfast. He had eaten so many flapjacks that I had begun to wonder whether he really would cut into my share. Now he turned to look out the window and his lips tightened. But he pushed back from the table and started to rise. Mother's voice held him to his chair.

"You'll not be traveling in any such weather. Wait a bit and it'll clear. These rains don't last long. I've another pot of coffee on the stove."

Father was getting his pipe going. He kept his eyes carefully on the smoke drifting upward. "Marian's right. Only she doesn't go far enough. These rains are short. But they sure mess up the road. It's new. Hasn't settled much yet. Mighty soggy when wet. Won't be fit for traveling till it drains. You better stay over till tomorrow."

Our visitor stared down at his empty plate as if it was the most important object in the whole room. You could see he liked the idea. Yet he seemed somehow worried about it.

"Yes," said father. "That's the sensible dodge. That horse of yours was pretty much beat last night. If I was a horse doctor now, I'd order a day's rest right off. Hanged if I don't think the same prescription would do me good too. You stick here the day and I'll follow it. I'd like to take you around, show you what I'm doing with the place."

He looked pleadingly at mother. She was surprised and good reason. Father was usually so set on working every possible minute to catch up on his plans that she would have a tussle making him ease some once a week out of respect for the Sabbath. In bad weather like this he usually would fidget and stomp about the house as if he thought it was a personal insult to him, a trick to keep him from being out and doing things. And here he was talking of a whole day's rest. She was puzzled. But she played right up.

"You'd be doing us a favor, Mr. Shane. We don't get many visitors from outside the valley. It'd be real nice to have you stay. And besides—" She crinkled her nose at him the way she did when she would be teasing father into some new scheme of hers. "And besides—I've been waiting for an excuse to try a deep-dish apple pie I've heard tell of. It would just be wasted on these other two. They eat everything in sight and don't rightly know good from poor."

He was looking up, straight at her. She shook a finger at him. "And another thing. I'm fair bubbling with questions about what the women are wearing back in civilization. You know, hats and such. You're the kind of man would notice them. You're not getting away till you've told me."

Shane sat back in his chair. A faint quizzical expression softened the lean ridges of his face. "Ma'am, I'm not positive I appreciate how you've pegged me. No one else ever wrote me down an expert on ladies' millinery." He reached out and pushed his cup across the table toward her. "You said something about more coffee. But I draw the line on more flannel cakes. I'm plumb full. I'm starting in to conserve space for that pie."

"You'd better!" Father was mighty pleased about something. "When Marian puts her mind to cooking, she makes a man forget he's got any limits to his appetite. Only don't you go giving her fancy notions of new hats so she'll be sending off to the mail-order house and

throwing my money away on silly frippery. She's got a hat."

Mother did not even notice that. She knew father was just talking. She knew that whenever she wanted anything real much and said so, father would bust himself trying to get it for her. She whisked over to the table with the coffee pot, poured a fresh round, then set it down within easy reach and sat down herself.

I thought that business about hats was only a joke she made up to help father persuade our visitor to stay. But she began almost at once, pestering him to describe the ladies he had seen in Cheyenne and other towns where the new styles might be. He sat there, easy and friendly, telling her how they were wearing wide floppy-brimmed bonnets with lots of flowers in front on top and slits in the brims for scarves to come through and be tied in bows under their chins.

Talk like that seemed foolish to me to be coming from a grown man. Yet this Shane was not bothered at all. And father listened as if he thought it was all right, only not very interesting. He watched them most of the time in a good-natured quiet, trying every so often to break in with his own talk about crops and steers and giving up and trying again and giving up again with a smiling shake of his head at those two. And the rain outside was a far distance away and meaningless because the friendly feeling in our kitchen was enough to warm all our world.

Then Shane was telling about the annual stock show at Dodge City and father was interested and excited, and it was mother who said: "Look, the sun's shining."

It was, so clear and sweet you wanted to run out and breathe the brilliant freshness. Father must have felt that way because he jumped up and fairly shouted, "Come on, Shane. I'll show you what this hop-scotch climate does to my alfalfa. You can almost see the stuff growing."

Shane was only a step behind him, but I beat them to the door. Mother followed and stood watching awhile on the porch as we three started out, picking our path around the puddles and the taller clumps of grass bright with the raindrops. We covered the whole place pretty thoroughly, father talking all the time, more enthusiastic about his plans than he had been for many weeks. He really hit his stride when we were behind the barn where we could have a good view of our little herd spreading out through the pasture. Then he stopped short. He had noticed that Shane was not paying much attention. He was quiet as could be for a moment when he saw that Shane was looking at the stump.

That was the one bad spot on our place. It stuck out like an old scarred sore in the cleared space back of the barn—a big old stump, all jagged across the top, the legacy of some great tree that must have died long before we came into the valley and finally been snapped by a heavy windstorm. It was big enough, I used to think, so that if it was smooth on top you could have served supper to a good-sized family on it.

But you could not have done that because you could not have got them close around it. The huge old roots humped out in every direction, some as big about as my waist, pushing out and twisting down into the ground like they would hold there to eternity and past.

Father had been working at it off and on, gnawing at the roots with an axe, ever since he finished poling the corral. The going was slow, even for him. The wood was so hard that he could not sink the blade much more than a quarter inch at a time. I guess it had been an old burr oak. Not many of these grew that far up in the Territory, but the ones that did grew big and hard. Ironwood we called it.

Father had tried burning brushpiles against it. That old stump just jeered at fire. The scorching seemed to make the wood harder than ever. So he was fighting his way around root by root. He never thought he had much time to spare on it. The rare occasions he was real mad about something he would stomp out there and chew into another root.

He went over to the stump now and kicked the nearest root, a smart kick, the way he did every time he passed it. "Yes," he said. "That's the millstone round my neck.[1] That's the one fool thing about this place I haven't licked yet. But I will. There's no wood ever grew can stand up to a man that's got the strength and the will to keep hammering at it."

He stared at the stump like it might be a person sprouting in front of him. "You know, Shane, I've been feuding with this thing so long I've worked up a spot of affection for it. It's tough. I can admire toughness. The right kind."

He was running on again, full of words and sort of happy to be letting them out, when he noticed again that Shane was not paying much attention, was listening to some sound in the distance. Sure enough, a horse was coming up the road.

Father and I turned with him to look toward town. In a moment we saw it as it cleared the grove of trees and tall bushes about a quarter-mile away, a high-necked sorrel drawing a light buckboard wagon.[2] The mud was splattering from its hooves, but not bad, and it was stepping free and easy. Shane glanced sideways at father.

"Not fit for traveling," he said softly. "Starrett, you're poor shakes as a liar." Then his attention was on the wagon and he was tense and alert, studying the man upright on the swaying seat.

Father simply chuckled at Shane's remark.

1. **millstone . . . neck:** burden.
2. **buckboard wagon:** a four-wheeled open carriage.

"That's Jake Ledyard's outfit," he said, taking the lead toward our lane. "I thought maybe he'd get up this way this week. Hope he has that cultivator I've been wanting."

Ledyard was a small, thin-featured man, a peddler or trader who came through every couple of months with things you could not get at the general store in town. He would pack in his stock on a mule-team freighter driven by an old, white-haired Negro who acted like he was afraid even to speak without permission. Ledyard would make deliveries in his buckboard, claiming a hard bargain always and picking up orders for articles to bring on the next trip. I did not like him, and not just because he said nice things about me he did not mean for father's benefit. He smiled too much and there was no real friendliness in it.

By the time we were beside the porch, he had swung the horse into our lane and was pulling it to a stop. He jumped down, calling greetings. Father went to meet him. Shane stayed by the porch, leaning against the end post.

"It's here," said Ledyard. "The beauty I told you about." He yanked away the canvas covering from the body of the wagon and the sun was bright on a shiny new seven-pronged cultivator lying on its side on the floor boards. "That's the best buy I've toted this haul."

"Hm-m-m-m," said father. "You've hit it right. That's what I've been wanting. But when you start chattering about a best buy that always means big money. What's the tariff?"[3]

"Well, now." Ledyard was slow with his reply. "It cost me more than I figured when we was talking last time. You might think it a bit steep. I don't. Not for a new beauty like that there. You'll make up the difference in no time with the work you'll save with that. Handles so

3. **tariff:** charge.

easy even the boy here will be using it before long."

"Pin it down," said father. "I've asked you a question."

Ledyard was quick now. "Tell you what, I'll shave the price, take a loss to please a good customer. I'll let you have it for a hundred and ten."

I was startled to hear Shane's voice cutting in, quiet and even and plain. "Let you have it? I reckon he will. There was one like that in a store in Cheyenne. List price sixty dollars."

Ledyard shifted part way around. For the first time he looked closely at our visitor. The surface smile left his face. His voice held an ugly undertone. "Did anyone ask you to push in on this?"

"No," said Shane, quietly and evenly as before. "I reckon no one did." He was still leaning against the post. He did not move and he did not say anything more. Ledyard turned to father, speaking rapidly.

"Forget what he says, Starrett. I've spotted him now. Heard of him half a dozen times along the road up here. No one knows him. No one can figure him. I think I can. Just a stray wandering through, probably chased out of some town and hunting cover. I'm surprised you'd let him hang around."

"You might be surprised at a lot of things," said father, beginning to bite off his words. "Now give it to me straight on the price."

"It's what I said. A hundred and ten. I'll be out money on the deal anyway, so I'll shave it to a hundred if that'll make you feel any better." Ledyard hesitated, watching father. "Maybe he did see something in Cheyenne. But he's mixed up. Must have been one of those little makes—flimsy and barely half the size. That might match his price."

Father did not say anything. He was looking at Ledyard in a steady, unwavering way. He had not even glanced at Shane. You might have believed he had not even heard what Shane had said. But his lips were folding in to a tight line like he was thinking what was not pleasant to think. Ledyard waited and father did not say anything and the climbing anger in Ledyard broke free.

"Starrett! Are you going to stand there and let that—that tramp nobody knows about call me a liar? Are you going to take his word over mine? Look at him! Look at his clothes! He's just a cheap, tinhorn—"

Ledyard stopped, choking on whatever it was he had meant to say. He fell back a step with a sudden fear showing in his face. I knew why even as I turned my head to see Shane. That same chill I had felt the day before, intangible and terrifying, was in the air again. Shane was no longer leaning against the porch post. He was standing erect, his hands clenched at his sides, his eyes boring at Ledyard, his whole body alert and alive in the leaping instant.

You felt without knowing how that each teetering second could bring a burst of indescribable deadliness. Then the tension passed, fading in the empty silence. Shane's eyes lost their sharp focus on Ledyard and it seemed to me that reflected in them was some pain deep within him.

Father had pivoted so that he could see the two of them in the one sweep. He swung back to Ledyard alone.

"Yes, Ledyard, I'm taking his word. He's my guest. He's here at my invitation. But that's not the reason." Father straightened a little and his head went up and he gazed into the distance beyond the river. "I can figure men for myself. I'll take his word on anything he wants to say any day of God's whole year."

Father's head came down and his voice was flat and final. "Sixty is the price. Add ten for a fair profit, even though you probably got it wholesale. Another ten for hauling it here.

That tallies to eighty. Take that or leave that. Whatever you do, snap to it and get off my land."

Ledyard stared down at his hands, rubbing them together as if they were cold. "Where's your money?" he said.

Father went into the house, into the bedroom where he kept our money in a little leather bag on the closet shelf. He came back with the crumpled bills. All this while Shane stood there, not moving, his face hard, his eyes following father with a strange wildness in them that I could not understand.

Ledyard helped father heave the cultivator to the ground, then jumped to the wagon seat and drove off like he was glad to get away from our place. Father and I turned from watching him into the road. We looked around for Shane and he was not in sight. Father shook his head in wonderment. "Now where do you suppose—" he was saying, when we saw Shane coming out of the barn.

He was carrying an axe, the one father used for heavy kindling. He went directly around the corner of the building. We stared after him and we were still staring when we heard it, the clear ringing sound of steel biting into wood.

I never could have explained what that sound did to me. It struck through me as no single sound had ever done before. With it ran a warmth that erased at once and forever the feeling of sudden chill terror that our visitor had evoked in me. There were sharp hidden hardnesses in him. But these were not for us. He was dangerous as mother had said. But not to us as father too had said. And he was no longer a stranger. He was a man like father in whom a boy could believe in the simple knowing that what was beyond comprehension was still clean and solid and right.

I looked up at father to try to see what he was thinking, but he was starting toward the barn with strides so long that I had to run to stay close behind him. We went around the far corner and there was Shane squared away at the biggest uncut root of that big old stump. He was swinging the axe in steady rhythm. He was chewing into that root with bites almost as deep as father could drive.

Father halted, legs wide, hands on hips. "Now lookahere," he began, "there's no call for you—"

Shane broke his rhythm just long enough to level a straight look at us. "A man has to pay his debts," he said and was again swinging the axe. He was really slicing into that root.

He seemed so desperate in his determination that I had to speak. "You don't owe us anything," I said. "Lots of times we have folks in for meals and—"

Father's hand was on my shoulder. "No, Bob. He doesn't mean meals." Father was smiling, but he was having to blink several times together and I would have sworn that his eyes were misty. He stood in silence now, not moving, watching Shane.

It was something worth seeing. When father worked on that old stump, that was worth seeing too. He could handle an axe mighty well and what impressed you was the strength and will of him making it behave and fight for him against the tough old wood. This was different. What impressed you as Shane found what he was up against and settled to it was the easy way the power in him poured smoothly into each stroke. The man and the axe seemed to be partners in the work. The blade would sink into the parallel grooves almost as if it knew itself what to do and the chips from between would come out in firm and thin little blocks.

Father watched him and I watched the two of them and time passed over us, and then the axe sliced through the last strip and the root was cut. I was sure that Shane would stop. But he stepped right around to the next root and squared away again and the blade sank in once more.

As it hit this second root, father winced like it had hit him. Then he stiffened and looked away from Shane and stared at the old stump. He began to fidget, throwing his weight from one foot to the other. In a short while more he was walking around inspecting the stump from different angles as if it was something he had never seen before. Finally he gave the nearest root a kick and hurried away. In a moment he was back with the other axe, the big double-bladed one that I could hardly heft from the ground.

He picked a root on the opposite side from Shane. He was not angry the way he usually was when he confronted one of those roots. There was a kind of serene and contented look on his face. He whirled that big axe as if it was only a kid's tool. The striking blade sank in maybe a whole half-inch. At the sound Shane straightened on his side. Their eyes met over the top of the stump and held and neither one of them said a word. Then they swung up their axes and both of them said plenty to that old stump.

3

It was exciting at first watching them. They were hitting a fast pace, making the chips dance. I thought maybe each one would cut through a root now and stop. But Shane finished his and looked over at father working steadily away and with a grim little smile pulling at his mouth he moved on to another root. A few moments later father smashed through his with a blow that sent the axe head into the ground beneath. He wrestled with the handle to yank the head loose and he too tackled another root without even waiting to wipe off the dirt. This began to look like a long session, so I started to wander away. Just as I headed around the corner of the barn, mother came past the corner.

She was the freshest, prettiest thing I had ever seen. She had taken her hat and stripped the old ribbon from it and fixed it as Shane had told her. Some of the flowers by the house were in a small bouquet in front. She had cut slits in the brim and the sash from her best dress came around the crown and through the slits and was tied in a perky bow under her chin. She was stepping along daintily, mighty proud of herself.

She went up close to the stump. Those two choppers were so busy and intent that even if they were aware she was there they did not really notice her.

"Well," she said, "aren't you going to look at me?"

They both stopped and they both stared at her.

"Have I got it right?" she asked Shane. "Is this the way they do it?"

"Yes, ma'am," he said. "About like that. Only their brims are wider." And he swung back to his root.

"Joe Starrett," said mother, "aren't you at least going to tell me whether you like me in this hat?"

"Lookahere, Marian," said father, "you know right well that whether you have a hat on or whether you don't have a hat on, you're the nicest thing to me that ever happened on God's green earth. Now stop bothering us. Can't you see we're busy?" And he swung back to his root.

Mother's face was a deep pink. She pulled the bow out and the hat from her head. She held it swinging from her hand by the sash ends. Her hair was mussed and she was really mad.

"Humph," she said. "This is a funny kind of resting you're doing today."

Father set the axe head on the ground and leaned on the handle. "Maybe it seems funny to you, Marian. But this is the best resting I've had for about as long as I can remember."

"Humph," said mother again. "You'll have to quit your resting for a while anyhow and do what I suppose you'll call work. Dinner's hot on the stove and waiting to be served."

She flounced around and went straight back to the house. We all tagged her in and to an uncomfortable meal. Mother always believed you should be decent and polite at mealtime, particularly with company. She was polite enough now. She was being special sweet, talking enough for the whole table of us without once saying a word about her hat lying where she had thrown it on the chair by the stove. The trouble was that she was too polite. She was trying too hard to be sweet.

As far as you could tell, though, the two men were not worried by her at all. They listened absently to her talk, chiming in when she asked them direct questions, but otherwise keeping quiet. Their minds were on that old stump and whatever it was that old stump had come to mean to them and they were in a hurry to get at it again.

After they had gone out and I had been helping mother with the dishes awhile, she began humming low under her breath and I knew she was not mad any more. She was too curious and puzzled to have room for anything else.

"What went on out there, Bob?" she asked me. "What got into those two?"

I did not rightly know. All I could do was try to tell her about Ledyard and how our visitor had called him on the cultivator. I must have used the wrong words, because, when I told her about Ledyard talking mean and the way Shane acted, she got all flushed and excited.

"What do you say, Bob? You were afraid of him? He frightened you? Your father would never let him do that."

"I wasn't frightened of him," I said, struggling to make her see the difference. "I was—well, I was just frightened. I was scared of whatever it was that might happen."

She reached out and rumpled my hair. "I think I understand," she said softly. "He's made me feel a little that way too." She went to the window and stared toward the barn. The steady rhythm of double blows, so together they sounded almost as one, was faint yet clear in the kitchen. "I hope Joe knows what he's doing," she murmured to herself. Then she turned to me. "Skip along out, Bob. I'll finish myself."

It was no fun watching them now. They had eased down to a slow, dogged pace. Father sent me once for the hone, so they could sharpen the blades, and again for a spade so he could clear the dirt away from the lowest roots, and I realized he might keep me running as long as I was handy. I slipped off by myself to see how mother's garden was doing after the rain and maybe add to the population in the box of worms I was collecting for when I would go fishing with the boys in town.

I took my time about it. I played pretty far afield. But no matter where I went, always I could hear the chopping in the distance. You could not help beginning to feel tired just to hear it, to think how they were working and staying at it.

Along the middle of the afternoon, I wandered into the barn. There was mother by the rear stall, up on a box peering through the little window above it. She hopped down as soon as she heard me and put a finger to her lips.

"I declare," she whispered. "In some ways those two aren't even as old as you are, Bob. Just the same—" She frowned at me in such a funny, confiding manner that I felt all warm inside. "Don't you dare tell them I said so. But there's something splendid in the battle they're giving that old monster." She went past me and toward the house with such a brisk air that I followed to see what she was going to do.

She whisked about the kitchen and in almost no time at all she had a pan of biscuits in the oven. While they were baking, she took her hat and carefully sewed the old ribbon into its old place. "Humph," she said, more to herself than to me. "You'd think I'd learn. This isn't Dodge City. This isn't even a whistle stop.[1] It's Joe Starrett's farm. It's where I'm proud to be."

Out came the biscuits. She piled as many as she could on a plate, popping one of the leftovers into her mouth and giving me the rest. She picked up the plate and marched with it out behind the barn. She stepped over the cut roots and set the plate on a fairly smooth spot on top of the stump. She looked at the two men, first one and then the other. "You're a pair of fools," she said. "But there's no law against me being a fool too." Without looking at either of them again, she marched away, her head high, back toward the house.

The two of them stared after her till she was out of sight. They turned to stare at the biscuits. Father gave a deep sigh, so deep it seemed to come all the way from his heavy work shoes. There was nothing sad or sorrowful about it. There was just something in him too big to be held tight in comfort. He let his axe fall to the ground. He leaned forward and separated the biscuits into two piles beside the plate, counting them even. One was left on the plate. He set this by itself on the stump. He took up his axe and reached it out and let it drop gently on the lone biscuit exactly in the middle. He rested the axe against the stump and took the two halves of the biscuit and put one on each pile.

He did not say a word to Shane. He pitched into one pile and Shane did into the other, and

---

1. **whistle stop:** small town.

the two of them faced each other over the last uncut roots, munching at those biscuits as if eating them was the most serious business they had ever done.

Father finished his pile and dabbled his fingers on the plate for the last crumbs. He straightened and stretched his arms high and wide. He seemed to stretch and stretch until he was a tremendous tower of strength reaching up into the late afternoon sun. He swooped suddenly to grab the plate and toss it to me. Still in the same movement he seized his axe and swung it in a great arc into the root he was working on. Quick as he was, Shane was right with him, and together they were talking again to that old stump.

I took the plate in to mother. She was peeling apples in the kitchen, humming gaily to herself. "The woodbox, Bob," she said, and went on humming. I carried in stove-lengths till the box would not hold any more. Then I slipped out before she might think of more chores.

I tried to keep myself busy down by the river skipping flat stones across the current all muddy still from the rain. I was able to for a while. But that steady chopping had a peculiar fascination. It was always pulling me toward the barn. I simply could not grasp how they could stick at it hour after hour. It made no sense to me, why they should work so when routing out[2] that old stump was not really so important. I was wavering in front of the barn, when I noticed that the chopping was different. Only one axe was working.

I hurried around back. Shane was still swinging, cutting into the last root. Father was using the spade, was digging under one side of the stump, bringing the dirt out between the cut roots. As I watched, he laid the spade aside and put his shoulder to the stump. He heaved

2. **routing out:** digging or cutting away.

against it. Sweat started to pour down his face. There was a little sucking sound and the stump moved ever so slightly.

That did it. Of a sudden I was so excited that I could hear my own blood pounding past my eardrums. I wanted to dash to that stump and push it and feel it move. Only I knew father would think I was in the way.

Shane finished the root and came to help him. Together they heaved against the stump.

Shane **535**

It angled up nearly a whole inch. You could begin to see an open space in the dirt where it was ripping loose. But as soon as they released the pressure, it fell back.

Again and again they heaved at it. Each time it would angle up a bit farther. Each time it would fall back. They had it up once about a foot and a half, and that was the limit. They could not get past it.

They stopped, breathing hard, mighty streaked now from the sweat rivulets down their faces. Father peered underneath as best he could. "Must be a taproot," he said. That was the one time either of them had spoken to the other, as far as I knew, the whole afternoon through. Father did not say anything more. And Shane said nothing. He just picked up his axe and looked at father and waited.

Father began to shake his head. There was some unspoken thought between them that bothered him. He looked down at his own big hands and slowly the fingers curled until they were clenched into big fists. Then his head stopped shaking and he stood taller and he drew a deep breath. He turned and backed in between two cut root ends, pressing against the stump. He pushed his feet into the ground for firm footholds. He bent his knees and slid his shoulders down the stump and wrapped his big hands around the root ends. Slowly he began to straighten. Slowly that huge old stump began to rise. Up it came, inch by inch, until the side was all the way up to the limit they had reached before.

Shane stooped to peer under. He poked his axe into the opening and I heard it strike wood. But the only way he could get in position to swing the axe into the opening was to drop on his right knee and extend his left leg and thigh into the opening and lean his weight on them. Then he could bring the axe sweeping in at a low angle close to the ground.

He flashed one quick glance at father beside

and behind him, eyes closed, muscles locked in that great sustained effort, and he dropped into position with the whole terrible weight of the stump poised above nearly half of his body and sent the axe sweeping under in swift powerful strokes.

Suddenly father seemed to slip. Only he had not slipped. He had straightened even further. The stump had leaped up a few more inches. Shane jumped out and up and tossed his axe aside. He grabbed one of the root ends and helped father ease the stump down. They both were blowing like they had run a long way. But they would not stay more than a minute before they were heaving again at the stump. It came up more easily now and the dirt was tearing loose all around it.

I ran to the house fast as I could. I dashed into the kitchen and took hold of mother's hand. "Hurry!" I yelled. "You've got to come!" She did not seem to want to come at first and I pulled at her. "You've got to see it! They're getting it out!" Then she was excited as I was and was running right with me.

They had the stump way up at a high angle. They were down in the hole, one on each side of it, pushing up and forward with hands flat on the under part reared before them higher than their heads. You would have thought the stump was ready to topple over clear of its ancient foundation. But there it stuck. They could not quite push it the final inches.

Mother watched them battling with it. "Joe," she called, "why don't you use some sense? Hitch up the team. Horses will have it out in no time at all."

Father braced himself to hold the stump still. He turned his head to look at her. "Horses!" he shouted. All the pent silence of the two of them that long afternoon through was being shattered in the one wonderful shout. "Horses! Great jumping Jehosaphat! No! We started this with manpower and, by Godfrey, we'll finish it with manpower!"

He turned his head to face the stump once more and dropped it lower between his humped shoulders. Shane, opposite him, stiffened, and together they pushed in a fresh assault. The stump quivered and swayed a little—and hung fixed at its crazy high angle.

Father grunted in exasperation. You could see the strength building up in his legs and broad shoulders and big corded arms. His side of the upturned stump rocked forward and Shane's side moved back and the whole stump trembled like it would twist down and into the hole on them at a grotesque new angle.

I wanted to shout a warning. But I could not speak, for Shane had thrown his head in a quick sideways gesture to fling his hair from falling over his face and I had caught a glimpse of his eyes. They were aflame with a concentrated cold fire. Not another separate discernible movement did he make. It was all of him, the whole man, pulsing in the one incredible surge of power. You could fairly feel the fierce energy suddenly burning in him, pouring through him in the single coordinated drive. His side of the stump rocked forward even with father's and the whole mass of the stump tore loose from the last hold and toppled away to sprawl in ungainly defeat beyond them.

Father climbed slowly out of the hole. He walked to the stump and placed a hand on the rounded bole and patted it like it was an old friend and he was perhaps a little sorry for it. Shane was with him, across from him, laying a hand gently on the old hard wood. They both looked up and their eyes met and held as they had so long ago in the morning hours.

The silence should have been complete. It was not because someone was shouting, a high-pitched, wordless shout. I realized that the voice was mine and I closed my mouth. The silence was clean and wholesome, and this was one of the things you could never forget whatever time might do to you in the furrowing of the years, an old stump on its side with root ends making a strange pattern against the glow of the sun sinking behind the far mountains and two men looking over it into each other's eyes.

I thought they should join the hands so close on the bole of the stump. I thought they should at least say something to each other. They stood quiet and motionless. At last father turned and came toward mother. He was so tired that the weariness showed in his walk. But there was no weariness in his voice. "Marian," he said, "I'm rested now. I don't believe any man since the world began was ever more rested."

Shane too was coming toward us. He too spoke only to mother. "Ma'am, I've learned something today. Being a farmer has more to it than I ever thought. Now I'm about ready for some of that pie."

Mother had been watching them in a wide-eyed wonder. At his last words she let out a positive wail. "Oh-h-h—you—you—men! You made me forget about it! It's probably all burned!" And she was running for the house so fast she was tripping over her skirt.

The pie was burned all right. We could smell it when we were in front of the house and the men were scrubbing themselves at the pump-trough. Mother had the door open to let the kitchen air out. The noises from inside sounded as if she might be throwing things around. Kettles were banging and dishes were clattering. When we went in, we saw why. She had the table set and was putting supper on it and she was grabbing the things from their places and putting them down on the table with solid thumps. She would not look at one of us.

We sat down and waited for her to join us.

Shane   **537**

She put her back to us and stood by the low shelf near the stove staring at her big pie tin and the burned stuff in it. Finally father spoke kind of sharply. "Lookahere, Marian. Aren't you ever going to sit down?"

She whirled and glared at him. I thought maybe she had been crying. But there were no tears on her face. It was dry and pinched-looking and there was no color in it. Her voice was sharp like father's. "I was planning to have a deep-dish apple pie. Well, I will. None of your silly man foolishness is going to stop me."

She swept up the big tin and went out the door with it. We heard her on the steps, and a few seconds later the rattle of the cover of the garbage pail. We heard her on the steps again. She came in and went to the side bench where the dishpan was and began to scrub the pie tin. The way she acted, we might not have been in the room.

Father's face was getting red. He picked up his fork to begin eating and let it drop with a little clatter. He squirmed on his chair and kept taking quick side looks at her. She finished scrubbing the tin and went to the apple barrel and filled her wooden bowl with fat round ones. She sat by the stove and started peeling them. Father fished in a pocket and pulled out his old jackknife. He moved over to her, stepping softly. He reached out for an apple to help her.

She did not look up. But her voice caught him like she had flicked him with a whip. "Joe Starrett, don't you dare touch a one of these apples."

He was sheepish as he returned to his chair. Then he was downright mad. He grabbed his knife and fork and dug into the food on his plate, taking big bites and chewing vigorously. There was nothing for our visitor and me to do but follow his example. Maybe it was a good supper. I could not tell. The food was only something to put in your mouth. And when we

finished, there was nothing to do but wait because mother was sitting by the stove, arms folded, staring at the wall, waiting herself for her pie to bake.

We three watched her in a quiet so tight that it hurt. We could not help it. We would try to look away and always our eyes would turn back to her. She did not appear to notice us. You might have said she had forgotten we were there.

She had not forgotten because as soon as she sensed that the pie was done, she lifted it out, cut four wide pieces, and put them on plates. The first two she set in front of the two men. The third one she set down for me. The last one she laid at her own place and she sat down in her own chair at the table. Her voice was still sharp.

"I'm sorry to keep you men waiting so long. Your pie is ready now."

Father inspected his portion like he was afraid of it. He needed to make a real effort to take his fork and lift a piece. He chewed on it and swallowed and he flipped his eyes sidewise at mother and back again quickly to look across the table at Shane. "That's prime pie," he said.

Shane raised a piece on his fork. He considered it closely. He put it in his mouth and chewed on it gravely. "Yes," he said. The quizzical expression on his face was so plain you could not possibly miss it. "Yes. That's the best bit of stump I ever tasted."

What could a silly remark like that mean? I had no time to wonder, for father and mother were acting so queer. They both stared at Shane and their mouths were sagging open. Then father snapped his shut and he chuckled and chuckled till he was swaying in his chair.

"By Godfrey, Marian, he's right. You've done it, too."

Mother stared from one to the other of them. Her pinched look faded and her cheeks were flushed and her eyes were soft and warm as they should be, and she was laughing so that the tears came. And all of us were pitching into that pie, and the one thing wrong in the whole world was that there was not enough of it.

4

The sun was already well up the sky when I awakened the next morning. I had been a long time getting to sleep because my mind was full of the day's excitement and shifting moods. I could not straighten out in my mind the way the grown folks had behaved, the way things that did not really matter so much had become so important to them.

I had lain in my bed thinking of our visitor out in the bunk in the barn. It scarce seemed possible that he was the same man I had first seen, stern and chilling in his dark solitude, riding up our road. Something in father, something not of words or actions but of the essential substance of the human spirit, had reached out and spoken to him and he had replied to it and had unlocked a part of himself to us. He was far off and unapproachable at times even when he was right there with you. Yet somehow he was closer, too, than my uncle, mother's brother, had been when he visited us the summer before.

I had been thinking, too, of the effect he had on father and mother. They were more alive, more vibrant, like they wanted to show more what they were, when they were with him. I could appreciate that because I felt the same way myself. But it puzzled me that a man so deep and vital in his own being, so ready to respond to father, should be riding a lone trail out of a closed and guarded past.

I realized with a jolt how late it was. The door to my little room was closed. Mother must have closed it so I could sleep undisturbed. I

was frantic that the others might have finished breakfast and that our visitor was gone and I had missed him. I pulled on my clothes, not even bothering with buttons, and ran to the door.

They were still at the table. Father was fussing with his pipe. Mother and Shane were working on a last round of coffee. All three of them were subdued and quiet. They stared at me as I burst out of my room.

"My heavens," said mother. "You came in here like something was after you. What's the matter?"

"I just thought," I blurted out, nodding at our visitor, "that maybe he had ridden off and forgotten me."

Shane shook his head slightly, looking straight at me. "I wouldn't forget you, Bob." He pulled himself up a little in his chair. He turned to mother and his voice took on a bantering tone. "And I wouldn't forget your cooking, ma'am. If you begin having a special lot of people passing by at mealtimes, that'll be because a grateful man has been boasting of your flannel cakes all along the road."

"Now there's an idea," struck in father as if he was glad to find something safe to talk about. "We'll turn this place into a boarding house. Marian'll fill folks full of her meals and I'll fill my pockets full of their money. That hits me as a mighty convenient arrangement."

Mother sniffed at him. But she was pleased at their talk and she was smiling as they kept on playing with the idea while she stirred me up my breakfast. She came right back at them, threatening to take father at his word and make him spend all his time peeling potatoes and washing dishes. They were enjoying themselves even though I could feel a bit of constraint behind the easy joshing. It was remarkable, too, how natural it was to have this Shane sitting there and joining in almost like he was a member of the family. There was none of the awkwardness some visitors always brought with them. You did feel you ought to be on your good behavior with him, a mite extra careful about your manners and your speech. But not stiffly so. Just quiet and friendly about it.

He stood up at last and I knew he was going to ride away from us and I wanted desperately to stop him. Father did it for me.

"You certainly are a man for being in a hurry. Sit down, Shane. I've a question to ask you."

Father was suddenly very serious. Shane, standing there, was as suddenly withdrawn into a distant alertness. But he dropped back into his chair.

Father looked directly at him. "Are you running away from anything?"

Shane stared at the plate in front of him for a long moment. It seemed to me that a shade of sadness passed over him. Then he raised his eyes and looked directly at father.

"No. I'm not running away from anything. Not in the way you mean."

"Good." Father stooped forward and stabbed at the table with a forefinger for emphasis. "Look, Shane. I'm not a rancher. Now you've seen my place, you know that. I'm a farmer. Something of a stockman, maybe. But really a farmer. That's what I decided to be when I quit punching cattle for another man's money. That's what I want to be and I'm proud of it. I've made a fair start. This outfit isn't as big as I hope to have it some day. But there's more work here already than one man can handle if it's to be done right. The young fellow I had ran out on me after he tangled with a couple of Fletcher's boys in town one day." Father was talking fast and he paused to draw breath.

Shane had been watching him intently. He moved his head to look out the window over the valley to the mountains marching along the horizon. "It's always the same," he murmured. He was sort of talking to himself. "The old ways die hard." He looked at mother and then at me, and as his eyes came back to father he seemed to have decided something that had been troubling him. "So Fletcher's crowding you," he said gently.

Father snorted. "I don't crowd easy. But I've got a job to do here and it's too big for one man, even for me. And none of the strays that drift up this way are worth a hoot."

"Yes?" Shane said. His eyes were crinkling again, and he was one of us again and waiting.

"Will you stick here awhile and help me get things in shape for the winter?"

Shane rose to his feet. He loomed up taller across the table than I had thought him. "I never figured to be a farmer, Starrett. I would have laughed at the notion a few days ago. All the same, you've hired yourself a hand." He and father were looking at each other in a way that showed they were saying things words could never cover. Shane snapped it by swinging toward mother. "And I'll rate your cooking, ma'am, wages enough."

Father slapped his hands on his knees. "You'll get good wages and you'll earn 'em. First off, now, why don't you drop into town and get some work clothes. Try Sam Grafton's store. Tell him to put it on my bill."

Shane was already at the door. "I'll buy my own," he said, and was gone.

Father was so pleased he could not sit still. He jumped up and whirled mother around. "Marian, the sun's shining mighty bright at last. We've got ourselves a man."

"But, Joe, are you sure what you're doing? What kind of work can a man like that do? Oh, I know he stood right up to you with that stump. But that was something special. He's been used to good living and plenty of money.

You can tell that. He said himself he doesn't know anything about farming."

"Neither did I when I started here. What a man knows isn't important. It's what he is that counts. I'll bet you that one was a cowpuncher when he was younger and a tophand too. Anything he does will be done right. You watch. In a week he'll be making even me hump or he'll be bossing the place."

"Perhaps."

"No perhapsing about it. Did you notice how he took it when I told him about Fletcher's boys and young Morley? That's what fetched him. He knows I'm in a spot and he's not the man to leave me there. Nobody'll push him around or scare him away. He's my kind of a man."

"Why, Joe Starrett. He isn't like you at all. He's smaller and he looks different and his clothes are different and he talks different. I know he's lived different."

"Huh?" Father was surprised. "I wasn't talking about things like that."

Shane came back with a pair of dungaree pants, a flannel shirt, stout work shoes, and a good, serviceable Stetson. He disappeared into the barn and emerged a few moments later in his new clothes, leading his horse unsaddled.

At the pasture gate he slipped off the halter, turned the horse in with a hearty slap, and tossed the halter to me.

"Take care of a horse, Bob, and it will take care of you. This one now has brought me better than a thousand miles in the last few weeks." And he was striding away to join father, who was ditching the field out past the growing corn where the ground was rich but marshy and would not be worth much till it was properly drained. I watched him swinging through the rows of young corn, no longer a dark stranger but part of the place, a farmer like father and me.

Only he was not a farmer and never really could be. It was not three days before you saw that he could stay right beside father in any kind of work. Show him what needed to be done and he could do it, and like as not would figure out a better way of getting it done. He never shirked the meanest task. He was ever ready to take the hard end of any chore. Yet you always felt in some indefinable fashion that he was a man apart.

There were times when he would stop and look off at the mountains and then down at himself and any tool he happened to have in his hands as if in wry amusement at what he was doing. You had no impression that he thought himself too good for the work or did not like it. He was just different. He was shaped in some firm forging of past circumstance for other things.

For all his slim build he was plenty rugged. His slenderness could fool you at first. But when you saw him close in action, you saw that he was solid, compact, that there was no waste weight on his frame just as there was no waste effort in his smooth, flowing motion. What he lacked alongside father in size and strength, he made up in quickness of movement, in instinctive coordination of mind and muscle, and in that sudden fierce energy that had burned in

him when the old stump tried to topple back on him. Mostly this last slept in him, not needed while he went easily through the day's routine. But when a call came, it could flame forward with a driving intensity that never failed to frighten me.

I would be frightened, as I had tried to explain to mother, not at Shane himself, but at the suggestion it always gave me of things in the human equation beyond my comprehension. At such times there would be a concentration in him, a singleness of dedication to the instant need, that seemed to me at once wonderful and disturbing. And then he would be again the quiet, steady man who shared with father my boy's allegiance.

I was beginning to feel my oats about then, proud of myself for being able to lick Ollie Johnson at the next place down the road. Fighting, boy style, was much in my mind.

Once, when father and I were alone, I asked him: "Could you beat Shane? In a fight, I mean."

"Son, that's a tough question. If I had to, I might do it. But, by Godfrey, I'd hate to try it. Some men just plain have dynamite inside them, and he's one. I'll tell you, though. I've never met a man I'd rather have more on my side in any kind of trouble."

I could understand that and it satisfied me. But there were things about Shane I could not understand. When he came in to the first meal after he agreed to stay on with us, he went to the chair that had always been father's and stood beside it waiting for the rest of us to take the other places. Mother was surprised and somewhat annoyed. She started to say something. Father quieted her with a warning glance. He walked to the chair across from Shane and sat down like this was the right and natural spot for him and afterwards he and Shane always used these same places.

I could not see any reason for the shift until

the first time one of our homestead neighbors knocked on the door while we were eating and came straight on in as most of them usually did. Then I suddenly realized that Shane was sitting opposite the door where he could directly confront anyone coming through it. I could see that was the way he wanted it to be. But I could not understand why he wanted it that way.

In the evenings after supper when he was talking lazily with us, he would never sit by a window. Out on the porch he would always face the road. He liked to have a wall behind him and not just to lean against. No matter where he was, away from the table, before sitting down he would swing his chair into position, back to the nearest wall, not making any show, simply putting it there and bending into it in one easy motion. He did not even seem to be aware that this was unusual. It was part of his fixed alertness. He always wanted to know everything happening around him.

This alertness could be noted, too, in the watch he kept, without appearing to make any special effort, on every approach to our place. He knew first when anyone was moving along the road and he would stop whatever he was doing to study carefully any passing rider.

We often had company in the evenings, for the other homesteaders regarded father as their leader and would drop in to discuss their affairs with him. They were interesting men in their own fashions, a various assortment. But Shane was not anxious to meet people. He would share little in their talk. With us he spoke freely enough. We were, in some subtle way, his folks. Though we had taken him in, you had the feeling that he had adopted us. But with others he was reserved; courteous and soft-spoken, yet withdrawn beyond a line of his own making.

These things puzzled me and not me alone. The people in town and those who rode or drove in pretty regularly were all curious about him. It was a wonder how quickly everyone in the valley, and even on the ranches out in the open country, knew that he was working with father.

They were not sure they liked having him in their neighborhood. Ledyard had told some tall tale about what happened at our place that made them stare sharply at Shane whenever they had a chance. But they must have had their own measure of Ledyard, for they did not take his story too straight. They just could not really make up their minds about Shane and it seemed to worry them.

More than once, when I was with Ollie Johnson on the way to our favorite fishing hole the other side of town, I heard men arguing about him in front of Mr. Grafton's store. "He's like one of these here slow-burning fuses," I heard an old mule-skinner say one day. "Quiet and no sputtering. So quiet you forget it's burning. Then it sets off one mighty big blow-off of trouble when it touches powder. That's him. And there's been trouble brewing in this valley for a long spell now. Maybe it'll be good when it comes. Maybe it'll be bad. You just can't tell." And that puzzled me too.

What puzzled me most, though, was something it took me nearly two weeks to appreciate. And yet it was the most striking thing of all. Shane carried no gun.

In those days guns were as familiar all through the Territory as boots and saddles. They were not used much in the valley except for occasional hunting. But they were always in evidence. Most men did not feel fully dressed without one.

We homesteaders went in mostly for rifles and shotguns when we had any shooting to do. A pistol slapping on the hip was a nuisance for a farmer. Still every man had his cartridge belt and holstered Colt to be worn when he was not working or loafing around the house. Father buckled his on whenever he rode off on any trip, even just into town, as much out of habit, I guess, as anything else.

But this Shane never carried a gun. And that was a peculiar thing because he had a gun.

I saw it once. I saw it when I was alone in the barn one day and I spotted his saddle-roll lying on his bunk. Usually he kept it carefully put away underneath. He must have forgotten it this time, for it was there in the open by the pillow. I reached to sort of feel it—and I felt the gun inside. No one was near, so I unfastened the straps and unrolled the blankets. There it was, the most beautiful-looking weapon I ever saw. Beautiful and deadly-looking.

The holster and filled cartridge belt were of the same soft black leather as the boots tucked under the bunk, tooled in the same intricate design. I knew enough to know that the gun was a single-action Colt, the same model as the Regular Army issue that was the favorite of all men in those days and that oldtimers used to say was the finest pistol ever made.

This was the same model. But this was no Army gun. It was black, almost due black, with the darkness not in any enamel but in the metal itself. The grip was clear on the outer curve, shaped to the fingers on the inner curve, and two ivory plates were set into it with exquisite skill, one on each side.

The smooth invitation of it tempted your grasp. I took hold and pulled the gun out of the holster. It came so easily that I could hardly believe it was there in my hand. Heavy like father's, it was somehow much easier to handle. You held it up to aiming level and it seemed to balance itself into your hand.

It was clean and polished and oiled. The empty cylinder, when I released the catch and flicked it, spun swiftly and noiselessly. I was surprised to see that the front sight was gone, the barrel smooth right down to the end, and that the hammer had been filed to a sharp point.

Why should a man do that to a gun? Why should a man with a gun like that refuse to wear it and show it off? And then, staring at that dark and deadly efficiency, I was again suddenly chilled, and I quickly put everything back exactly as before and hurried out into the sun.

The first chance I tried to tell father about it. "Father," I said, all excited, "do you know what Shane has rolled up in his blankets?"

"Probably a gun."

"But—but how did you know? Have you seen it?"

"No. That's what he would have."

I was all mixed up. "Well, why doesn't he ever carry it? Do you suppose maybe it's because he doesn't know how to use it very well?"

Father chuckled like I had made a joke. "Son, I wouldn't be surprised if he could take that gun and shoot the buttons off your shirt with you awearing it and all you'd feel would be a breeze."

"Gosh agorry! Why does he keep it hidden in the barn then?"

"I don't know. Not exactly."

"Why don't you ask him?"

Father looked straight at me, very serious. "That's one question I'll never ask him. And don't you ever say anything to him about it. There are some things you don't ask a man. Not if you respect him. He's entitled to stake his claim to what he considers private to himself alone. But you can take my word for it, Bob, that when a man like Shane doesn't want to tote a gun you can bet your shirt, buttons and all, he's got a mighty good reason."

That was that. I was still mixed up. But whenever father gave you his word on something, there was nothing more to be said. He never did that except when he knew he was right. I started to wander off.

"Bob."

"Yes, father."

"Listen to me, son. Don't get to liking Shane too much."

"Why not? Is there anything wrong with him?"

"No-o-o-o. There's nothing wrong about Shane. Nothing you could put that way. There's more right about him than most any man you're ever likely to meet. But—" Father was throwing around for what to say. "But he's fiddle-footed. Remember. He said so himself. He'll be moving on one of these days and then you'll be all upset if you get to liking him too much."

That was not what father really meant. But that was what he wanted me to think. So I did not ask any more questions.

5

The weeks went rocking past, and soon it did not seem possible that there ever had been a time when Shane was not with us. He and father worked together more like partners than boss and hired man. The amount they could get through in a day was a marvel. The ditching father had reckoned would take him most of the summer was done in less than a month. The loft was finished and the first cutting of alfalfa stowed away.

We would have enough fodder to carry a few more young steers through the winter for fattening next summer, so father rode out of the valley and all the way to the ranch where he worked once and came back herding a half-dozen more. He was gone two days. He came back to find that Shane, while he was gone, had knocked out the end of the corral and posted a new section making it half again as big.

"Now we can really get going next year," Shane said as father sat on his horse staring at the corral like he could not quite believe what he saw. "We ought to get enough hay off that new field to help us carry forty head."

"Oho!" said father. "So we can get going. And we ought to get enough hay." He was pleased as could be because he was scowling at Shane the way he did at me when he was tickled silly over something I had done and did not want to let on that he was. He jumped off his horse and hurried up to the house where mother was standing on the porch.

"Marian," he demanded right off, waving at the corral, "whose idea was that?"

"Well-l-l," she said, "Shane suggested it." Then she added slyly, "But I told him to go ahead."

"That's right." Shane had come up beside him. "She rode me like she had spurs to get it done by today. Kind of a present. It's your wedding anniversary."

"Well, I'll be blowed," said father. "So it is." He stared foolishly at one and then the other of them. With Shane there watching, he hopped on the porch and gave mother a kiss. I was embarrassed for him and I turned away— and hopped about a foot myself.

"Hey! Those steers are running away!"

The grown folks had forgotten about them. All six were wandering up the road, straggling and separating. Shane, that soft-spoken man, let out a whoop you might have heard halfway to town and ran to father's horse, putting his hands on the saddle and vaulting into it. He fairly lifted the horse into a gallop in one leap and that old cowpony of father's lit out after those steers like this was fun. By the time father reached the corral gate, Shane had the run-aways in a compact bunch and padding back at a trot. He dropped them through the gateway neat as pie.

He was tall and straight in the saddle the few seconds it took father to close the gate. He and the horse were blowing a bit and both of them were perky and proud.

"It's been ten years," he said, "since I did anything like that."

Father grinned at him. "Shane, if I didn't know better, I'd say you were a faker. There's still a lot of kid in you."

The first real smile I had seen yet flashed across Shane's face. "Maybe. Maybe there is at that."

I think that was the happiest summer of my life.

The only shadow over our valley, the recurrent trouble between Fletcher and us homesteaders, seemed to have faded away. Fletcher himself was gone most of those months. He had gone to Fort Bennett in Dakota and even on East to Washington, so we heard, trying to get a contract to supply beef to the Indian agent at Standing Rock, the big Sioux reservation over beyond the Black Hills. Except for his foreman, Morgan, and several surly older men, his hands were young, easy-going cowboys who made a lot of noise in town once in a while but rarely did any harm and even then only in high spirits. We liked them—when Fletcher was not there driving them into harassing us in constant shrewd ways. Now, with him away, they kept to the other side of the river and did not bother us. Sometimes, riding in sight on the other bank, they might even wave to us in their rollicking fashion.

Until Shane came, they had been my heroes. Father, of course, was special all to himself. There could never be anyone quite to match him. I wanted to be like him, just as he was. But first I wanted, as he had done, to ride the range, to have my own string of ponies and take part in an all brand round-up and in a big cattle drive and dash into strange towns with just such a rollicking crew and with a season's pay jingling in my pockets.

Now I was not so sure. I wanted more and more to be like Shane, like the man I imagined he was in the past fenced off so surely. I had to imagine most of it. He would never speak of it, not in any way at all. Even his name remained mysterious. Just Shane. Nothing else. We never knew whether that was his first name or last name or, indeed, any name that came from his family. "Call me Shane," he said, and that was all he ever said. But I conjured up all manner of adventures for him, not tied to any particular time or place, seeing him as a slim and dark and dashing figure coolly passing through perils that would overcome a lesser man.

I would listen in what was closely akin to worship while my two men, father and Shane, argued long and amiably about the cattle business. They would wrangle over methods of feeding and bringing steers up to top weight. But they were agreed that controlled breeding was better than open range running and that improvement of stock was needed even if that meant spending big money on imported bulls. And they would speculate about the chances of a railroad spur[1] ever reaching the valley, so you could ship direct without thinning good meat off your cattle driving them to market.

It was plain that Shane was beginning to enjoy living with us and working the place. Little by little the tension in him was fading out. He was still alert and watchful, instinct with that unfailing awareness of everything about him. I came to realize that this was inherent in him, not learned or acquired, simply a part of his natural being. But the sharp extra edge of conscious alertness, almost of expectancy of some unknown trouble always waiting, was wearing away.

Yet why was he sometimes so strange and stricken in his own secret bitterness? Like the time I was playing with a gun Mr. Grafton gave me, an old frontier model Colt with a cracked barrel someone had turned in at the store.

1. **railroad spur:** a side track connecting with the main track of a railroad system.

I had rigged a holster out of a torn chunk of oilcloth and a belt of rope. I was stalking around near the barn, whirling every few steps to pick off a skulking Indian, when I saw Shane watching me from the barn door. I stopped short, thinking of that beautiful gun under his bunk and afraid he would make fun of me and my sorry old broken pistol. Instead he looked gravely at me.

"How many you knocked over so far, Bob?"

Could I ever repay the man? My gun was a shining new weapon, my hand steady as a rock as I drew a bead on another one.

"That makes seven."

"Indians or timber wolves?"

"Indians. Big ones."

"Better leave a few for the other scouts," he said gently. "It wouldn't do to make them jealous. And look here, Bob. You're not doing that quite right."

He sat down on an upturned crate and beckoned me over. "Your holster's too low. Don't let it drag full arm's length. Have it just below the hip, so the grip is about halfway between your wrist and elbow when the arm's hanging limp. You can take the gun then as your hand's coming up and there's still room to clear the holster without having to lift the gun too high."

"Gosh agorry! Is that the way the real gunfighters do?"

A queer light flickered in his eyes and was gone. "No. Not all of them. Most have their own tricks. One likes a shoulder holster; another packs his gun in his pants belt. Some carry two guns, but that's a show-off stunt and a waste of weight. One's enough, if you know how to use it. I've even seen a man have a tight holster with an open end and fastened on a little swivel to the belt. He didn't have to pull the gun then. Just swung up the barrel and blazed away from the hip. That's mighty fast for close work and a big target. But it's not certain past ten or fifteen paces and no good at all for putting your shot right where you want it. The way I'm telling you is as good as any and better than most. And another thing—"

He reached and took the gun. Suddenly, as for the first time, I was aware of his hands. They were broad and strong, but not heavy and fleshy like father's. The fingers were long and square on the ends. It was funny how, touching the gun, the hands seemed to have an intelligence all their own, a sure movement that needed no guidance of thought.

His right hand closed around the grip and you knew at once it was doing what it had been created for. He hefted the old gun, letting it lie loosely in the hand. Then the fingers tightened and the thumb toyed with the hammer, testing the play of it.

While I gaped at him, he tossed it swiftly in the air and caught it in his left hand and in the instant of catching, it nestled snugly into this hand too. He tossed it again, high this time and spinning end over end, and as it came down, his right hand flicked forward and took it. The forefinger slipped through the trigger guard and the gun spun, coming up into firing position in the one unbroken motion. With him that old pistol seemed alive, not an inanimate and rusting metal object, but an extension of the man himself.

"If it's speed you're after, Bob, don't split the move into parts. Don't pull, cock, aim, and fire. Slip back the hammer as you bring the gun up and squeeze the trigger the second it's up level."

"How do you aim it, then? How do you get a sight on it?"

"No need to. Learn to hold it so the barrel's right in line with the fingers if they were out straight. You won't have to waste time bringing it high to take a sight. Just point it, low and quick and easy, like pointing a finger."

Like pointing a finger. As the words came, he was doing it. The old gun was bearing on some target over by the corral and the hammer was clicking at the empty cylinder. Then the hand around the gun whitened and the fingers slowly opened and the gun fell to the ground. The hand sank to his side, stiff and awkward. He raised his head and the mouth was a bitter gash in his face. His eyes were fastened on the mountains climbing in the distance.

"Shane! Shane! What's the matter?"

He did not hear me. He was back somewhere along the dark trail of the past.

He took a deep breath, and I could see the effort run through him as he dragged himself into the present and a realization of a boy staring at him. He beckoned to me to pick up the gun. When I did, he leaned forward and spoke earnestly.

"Listen, Bob. A gun is just a tool. No better and no worse than any other tool, a shovel—or an axe or a saddle or a stove or anything. Think of it always that way. A gun is as good—and as bad—as the man who carries it. Remember that."

He stood up and strode off into the fields and I knew he wanted to be alone. I remembered what he said all right, tucked away unforgettably in my mind. But in those days I remembered more the way he handled the gun and the advice he gave me about using it. I would practice with it and think of the time when I could have one that would really shoot.

And then the summer was over. School began again and the days were growing shorter and the first cutting edge of cold was creeping down from the mountains.

6

More than the summer was over. The season of friendship in our valley was fading with the

sun's warmth. Fletcher was back and he had his contract. He was talking in town that he would need the whole range again. The homesteaders would have to go.

He was a reasonable man, he was saying in his smooth way, and he would pay a fair price for any improvements they had put in. But we knew what Luke Fletcher would call a fair price. And we had no intention of leaving. The land was ours by right of settlement, guaranteed by the government. Only we knew, too, how faraway the government was from our valley way up there in the Territory.

The nearest marshal was a good hundred miles away. We did not even have a sheriff in our town. There never had been any reason for one. When folks had any lawing to do, they would head for Sheridan, nearly a full day's ride away. Our town was small, not even organized as a town. It was growing, but it was still not much more than a roadside settlement.

The first people there were three or four miners who had come prospecting after the blow-up of the Big Horn Mining Association about twenty years before, and had found gold traces leading to a moderate vein in the jutting rocks that partially closed off the valley where it edged into the plain. You could not have called it a strike, for others that followed were soon disappointed. Those first few, however, had done fairly well and had brought in their families and a number of helpers.

Then a stage and freighting line had picked the site for a relay post. That meant a place where you could get drinks as well as horses, and before long the cowboys from the ranches out on the plain and Fletcher's spread in the valley were drifting in of an evening. With us homesteaders coming now, one or two more almost every season, the town was taking shape. Already there were several stores, a harness and blacksmith shop, and nearly a dozen houses. Just the year before, the men had put together a one-room schoolhouse.

Sam Grafton's place was the biggest. He had a general store with several rooms for living quarters back of it in one half of his rambling building, a saloon with a long bar and tables for cards and the like in the other half. Upstairs he had some rooms he rented to stray drummers[1] or anyone else stranded overnight. He acted as our postmaster, an elderly man, a close bargainer but honest in all his dealings. Sometimes he served as a sort of magistrate in minor disputes. His wife was dead. His daughter Jane kept house for him and was our schoolteacher when school was in session.

Even if we had had a sheriff, he would have been Fletcher's man. Fletcher was the power in the valley in those days. We homesteaders had been around only a few years and the other people still thought of us as there by his sufferance. He had been running cattle through the whole valley at the time the miners arrived, having bought or bulldozed out the few small ranchers there ahead of him. A series of bad years working up to the dry summer and terrible winter of '86 had cut his herds about the time the first of the homesteaders moved in and he had not objected too much. But now there were seven of us in all and the number rising each year.

It was a certain thing, father used to say, that the town would grow and swing our way. Mr. Grafton knew that too, I guess, but he was a careful man who never let thoughts about the future interfere with present business. The others were the kind to veer with the prevailing wind. Fletcher was the big man in the valley, so they looked up to him and tolerated us. Led to it, they probably would have helped him run us out. With him out of the way, they would just as willingly accept us. And Fletcher

1. **drummers:** traveling salesmen.

was back, with a contract in his pocket, wanting his full range again.

There was a hurried counsel in our house soon as the news was around. Our neighbor toward town, Lew Johnson, who heard it in Grafton's store, spread the word and arrived first. He was followed by Henry Shipstead, who had the place next to him, the closest to town. These two had been the original homesteaders, staking out their hundred and eighties two years before the drought and riding out Fletcher's annoyance until the cut in his herds gave him other worries. They were solid, dependable men, old-line farmers who had come West from Iowa.

You could not say quite as much for the rest, straggling in at intervals. James Lewis and Ed Howells were two middle-aged cowhands who had grown dissatisfied and tagged father into the valley, coming pretty much on his example. Lacking his energy and drive, they had not done too well and could be easily discouraged.

Frank Torrey from farther up the valley was a nervous, fidgety man with a querulous[2] wife and a string of dirty kids growing longer every year. He was always talking about pulling up stakes and heading for California. But he had a stubborn streak in him, and he was always saying, too, that he'd be damned if he'd make tracks just because some big-hatted rancher wanted him to.

Ernie Wright, who had the last stand up the valley butting out into the range still used by Fletcher, was probably the weakest of the lot. Not in any physical way. He was a husky, likable man, so dark-complected[3] that there were rumors he was part Indian. He was always singing and telling tall stories. But he would be off hunting when he should be working and he

had a quick temper that would trap him into doing fool things without taking thought.

He was as serious as the rest of them that night. Mr. Grafton had said that this time Fletcher meant business. His contract called for all the beef he could drive in the next five years and he was determined to push the chance to the limit.

"But what can he do?" asked Frank Torrey. "The land's ours as long as we live on it and we get title in three years. Some of you fellows have already proved up."

"He won't really make trouble," chimed in James Lewis. "Fletcher's never been the shooting kind. He's a good talker, but talk can't hurt us." Several of the others nodded. Johnson and Shipstead did not seem to be so sure. Father had not said anything yet and they all looked at him.

"Jim's right," he admitted. "Fletcher hasn't ever let his boys get careless thataway. Not yet anyhow. That ain't saying he wouldn't, if there wasn't any other way. There's a hard streak in him. But he won't get real tough for a while. I don't figure he'll start moving cattle in now till spring. My guess is he'll try putting pressure on us this fall and winter, see if he can wear us down. He'll probably start right here. He doesn't like any of us. But he doesn't like me most."

"That's true." Ed Howells was expressing the unspoken verdict that father was their leader. "How do you figure he'll go about it?"

"My guess on that," father said—drawling now and smiling a grim little smile like he knew he was holding a good hole card in a tight game—"my guess on that is that he'll begin by trying to convince Shane here that it isn't healthy to be working with me."

"You mean the way he—" began Ernie Wright.

"Yes." Father cut him short. "I mean the way he did with young Morley."

2. **querulous** (kwĕr′ə-ləs, kwĕr′yə-): complaining.
3. **complected** (kəm-plĕk′ tĭd): complexioned.

I was peeping around the door of my little room. I saw Shane sitting off to one side, listening quietly as he had been right along. He did not seem the least bit surprised. He did not seem the least bit interested in finding out what had happened to young Morley. I knew what had. I had seen Morley come back from town, bruised and a beaten man, and gather his things and curse father for hiring him and ride away without once looking back.

Yet Shane sat there quietly as if what had happened to Morley had nothing to do with him. He simply did not care what it was. And then I understood why. It was because he was not Morley. He was Shane.

Father was right. In some strange fashion the feeling was abroad that Shane was a marked man. Attention was on him as a sort of symbol. By taking him on father had accepted in a way a challenge from the big ranch across the river. What had happened to Morley had been a warning and father had deliberately answered it. The long unpleasantness was sharpened now after the summer lull. The issue in our valley was plain and would in time have to be pushed to a showdown. If Shane could be driven out, there would be a break in the homestead ranks, a defeat going beyond the loss of a man into the realm of prestige and morale. It could be the crack in the dam that weakens the whole structure and finally lets through the flood.

The people in town were more curious than ever, not now so much about Shane's past as about what he might do if Fletcher tried any move against him. They would stop me and ask me questions when I was hurrying to and from school. I knew that father would not want me to say anything and I pretended that I did not know what they were talking about. But I used to watch Shane closely myself and wonder how all the slow-climbing tenseness in our valley could be so focused on one man and he seem to be so indifferent to it.

For of course he was aware of it. He never missed anything. Yet he went about his work as usual, smiling frequently now at me, bantering mother at mealtimes in his courteous manner, arguing amiably as before with father on plans for next year. The only thing that was different was that there appeared to be a lot of new activity across the river. It was surprising how often Fletcher's cowboys were finding jobs to do within view of our place.

Then one afternoon, when we were stowing away the second and last cutting of hay, one fork of the big tongs we were using to haul it up to the loft broke loose. "Have to get it welded in town," father said in disgust and began to hitch up the team.

Shane stared over the river where a cowboy was riding lazily back and forth by a bunch of cattle. "I'll take it in," he said.

Father looked at Shane and he looked across the way and he grinned. "All right. It's as good a time as any." He slapped down the final buckle and started for the house. "Just a minute and I'll be ready."

"Take it easy, Joe." Shane's voice was gentle, but it stopped father in his tracks. "I said I'll take it in."

Father whirled to face him. "Damn it all, man. Do you think I'd let you go alone? Suppose they —" He bit down his own words. He wiped a hand slowly across his face and he said what I had never heard him say to any man. "I'm sorry," he said. "I should have known bet-

ter." He stood there silently watching as Shane gathered up the reins and jumped to the wagon seat.

I was afraid father would stop me, so I waited till Shane was driving out of the lane. I ducked behind the barn, around the end of the corral, and hopped into the wagon going past. As I did, I saw the cowboy across the river spin his horse and ride rapidly off in the direction of the ranchhouse.

Shane saw it, too, and it seemed to give him a grim amusement. He reached backwards and hauled me over the seat and sat me beside him.

"You Starretts like to mix into things." For a moment I thought he might send me back. Instead he grinned at me. "I'll buy you a jackknife when we hit town."

He did, a dandy big one with two blades and a corkscrew. After we left the tongs with the blacksmith and found the welding would take nearly an hour, I squatted on the steps on the long porch across the front of Grafton's building, busy whittling, while Shane stepped into the saloon side and ordered a drink. Will Atkey, Grafton's thin, sad-faced clerk and bartender, was behind the bar and several other men were loafing at one of the tables.

It was only a few moments before two cowboys came galloping down the road. They slowed to a walk about fifty yards off and with a show of nonchalance ambled the rest of the way to Grafton's, dismounting and looping their reins over the rail in front. One of them I had seen often, a young fellow everyone called Chris, who had worked with Fletcher several years and was known for a gay manner and reckless courage. The other was new to me, a sallow, pinch-cheek man, not much older, who looked like he had crowded a lot of hard living into his years. He must have been one of the new hands Fletcher had been bringing into the valley since he got his contract.

They paid no attention to me. They stepped

softly up on the porch and to the window of the saloon part of the building. As they peered through, Chris nodded and jerked his head toward the inside. The new man stiffened. He leaned closer for a better look. Abruptly he turned clear about and came right down past me and went over to his horse.

Chris was startled and hurried after him. They were both so intent they did not realize I was there. The new man was lifting the reins back over his horse's head when Chris caught his arm.

"What's got into you?"

"I'm leaving."

"Huh? I don't get it."

"I'm leaving. Now. For good."

"Hey, listen. Do you know that guy?"

"I didn't say that. There ain't nobody can claim I said that. I'm leaving, that's all. You can tell Fletcher. This is a rotten kind of a country up here anyhow."

Chris was getting mad. "I might have known," he said. "Scared, eh. Yellow."

Color rushed into the new man's sallow face. But he climbed on his horse and swung out from the rail. "You can call it that," he said flatly and started down the road, out of town, out of the valley.

Chris was standing still by the rail, shaking his head in wonderment. "Well," he said to himself, "I'll brace him myself." He stalked up on the porch, into the saloon.

I dashed into the store side, over to the opening between the two big rooms. I crouched on a box just inside the store where I

could hear everything and see most of the other room. It was long and fairly wide. The bar curved out from the opening and ran all the way along the inner wall to the back wall, which closed off a room Grafton used as an office. There was a row of windows on the far side, too high for anyone to look in from outside. A small stairway behind them led up to a balcony-like across the back with doors opening into several little rooms.

Shane was leaning easily with one arm on the bar, his drink in his other hand, when Chris came to perhaps six feet away and called for a whiskey bottle and a glass. Chris pretended he did not notice Shane at first and bobbed his head in greeting to the men at the table. They were a pair of mule-skinners who made regular trips into the valley freighting in goods for Grafton and the other shops. I could have sworn that Shane, studying Chris in his effortless way, was somehow disappointed.

Chris waited until he had his whiskey and had gulped a stiff shot. Then he deliberately looked over like he had just spotted him.

"Hello, farmer," he said. He said it as if he did not like farmers.

Shane regarded him with grave attention. "Speaking to me?" he asked mildly and finished his drink.

"Don't see anybody else standing there. Here, have a drink of this." Chris shoved his bottle along the bar. Shane poured himself a generous slug and raised it to his lips.

"Well, look at that," flipped Chris. "So you drink whiskey."

Shane tossed off the rest in his glass and set it down. "I've had better," he said, as friendly as could be. "But this will do."

Chris slapped his leather chaps[4] with a loud smack. He turned to take in the other men. "Did you hear that? This farmer drinks whis-

4. **chaps:** trousers without a seat, worn over other trousers to protect a cowhand's legs.

key! I didn't think these plow-pushing dirt-grubbers drank anything stronger than soda pop!"

"Some of us do," said Shane, friendly as before. Then he was no longer friendly and his voice was like winter frost. "You've had your fun and it's mighty young fun. Now run home and tell Fletcher to send a grown-up man next time." He turned away and sang out to Will Atkey. "Do you have any soda pop? I'd like a bottle."

Will hesitated, looked kind of funny, and scuttled past me into the store room. He came back right away with a bottle of the pop Grafton kept there for us school kids. Chris was standing quiet, not so much mad, I would have said, as puzzled. It was as though they were playing some queer game and he was not sure of the next move. He sucked on his lower lip for a while. Then he snapped his mouth and began to look elaborately around the room, sniffing loudly.

"Hey, Will!" he called. "What's been happening in here? It smells. That ain't no clean cattleman smell. That's plain dirty barnyard." He stared at Shane. "You, farmer. What are you and Starrett raising out there? Pigs?"

Shane was just taking hold of the bottle Will had fetched him. His hand closed on it and the knuckles showed white. He moved slowly, almost unwillingly, to face Chris. Every line of his body was as taut as stretched whipcord, was alive and somehow rich with an immense eagerness. There was that fierce concentration in him, filling him, blazing in his eyes. In that moment there was nothing in the room for him but that mocking man only a few feet away.

The big room was so quiet the stillness fairly hurt. Chris stepped back involuntarily, one pace, two, then pulled up erect. And still nothing happened. The lean muscles along the sides of Shane's jaw were ridged like rock.

Then the breath, pent in him, broke the stillness with a soft sound as it left his lungs. He looked away from Chris, past him, over the tops of the swinging doors beyond, over the roof of the shed across the road, on into the distance where the mountains loomed in their own unending loneliness. Quietly he walked, the bottle forgotten in his hand, so close by Chris as almost to brush him yet apparently not even seeing him, through the doors and was gone.

I heard a sigh of relief near me. Mr. Grafton had come up from somewhere behind me. He was watching Chris with a strange, ironic quirk at his mouth corners. Chris was trying not to look pleased with himself. But he swaggered as he went to the doors and peered over them.

"You saw it, Will," he called over his shoulder. "He walked out on me." Chris pushed up his hat and rolled back on his heels and laughed. "With a bottle of soda pop too!" He was still laughing as he went out and we heard him ride away.

"That boy's a fool," Mr. Grafton muttered.

Will Atkey came sidling over to Mr. Grafton. "I never pegged Shane for a play like that," he said.

"He was afraid, Will."

"Yeah. That's what was so funny. I would've guessed he could take Chris."

Mr. Grafton looked at Will as he did often, like he was a little sorry for him. "No, Will. He wasn't afraid of Chris. He was afraid of himself." Mr. Grafton was thoughtful and perhaps sad too. "There's trouble ahead, Will. The worst trouble we've ever had."

He noticed me, realizing my presence. "Better skip along, Bob, and find your friend. Do you think he got that bottle for himself?"

True enough, Shane had it waiting for me at the blacksmith shop. Cherry pop, the kind I favored most. But I could not enjoy it much. Shane was so silent and stern. He had slipped back into the dark mood that was on him when he first came riding up our road. I did not dare say anything. Only once did he speak to me and I knew he did not expect me to understand or to answer.

"Why should a man be smashed because he has courage and does what he's told? Life's a dirty business, Bob. I could like that boy." And he turned inward again to his own thoughts and stayed the same until we had loaded the tongs in the wagon and were well started home. Then the closer we came, the more cheerful he was. By the time we swung in toward the barn, he was the way I wanted him again, crinkling his eyes at me and gravely joshing me about the Indians I would scalp with my new knife.

Father popped out the barn door so quick you could tell he had been itching for us to return. He was busting with curiosity, but he would not come straight out with a question to Shane. He tackled me instead.

"See any of your cowboy heroes in town?"

Shane cut in ahead of me. "One of Fletcher's crew chased us in to pay his respects."

"No," I said, proud of my information. "There was two of them."

"Two?" Shane said it. Father was the one who was not surprised. "What did the other one do?"

"He went up on the porch and looked in the window where you were and came right back down and rode off."

"Back to the ranch?"

"The other way. He said he was leaving for good."

Father and Shane looked at each other. Father was smiling. "One down and you didn't even know it. What did you do to the other?"

"Nothing. He passed a few remarks about farmers. I went back to the blacksmith shop."

Father repeated it, spacing the words like there might be meanings between them. "You—went—back—to—the—black-smith—shop."

I was worried that he must be thinking what Will Atkey did. Then I knew nothing like that had even entered his head. He switched to me. "Who was it?"

Father was smiling again. He had not been there but he had the whole thing clear. "Fletcher was right to send two. Young ones like Chris need to hunt in pairs or they might get hurt." He chuckled in a sort of wry amusement. "Chris must have been considerable surprised when the other fellow skipped. And more when you walked out. It was too bad the other one didn't stick around."

"Yes," Shane said, "it was."

The way he said it sobered father. "I hadn't thought of that. Chris is just cocky enough to take it wrong. That can make things plenty unpleasant."

"Yes," Shane said again, "it can."

7

It was just as father and Shane had said. The story Chris told was common knowledge all through the valley before the sun set the next day and the story grew in the telling. Fletcher had an advantage now and he was quick to push it. He and his foreman, Morgan, a broad slab of a man with flattened face and head small in proportion to great sloping shoulders, were shrewd at things like this and they kept their men primed to rowel[1] us homesteaders at every chance.

They took to using the upper ford, up above Ernie Wright's stand, and riding down the road past our places every time they had an excuse for going to town. They would go by slowly, looking everything over with insolent

1. **rowel** (rou′əl): to spur or incite.

interest and passing remarks for our benefit.

The same week, maybe three days later, a covey of them came riding by while father was putting a new hinge on the corral gate. They acted like they were too busy staring over our land to see him there close.

"Wonder where Starrett keeps the critters," said one of them. "I don't see a pig in sight."

"But I can smell 'em!" shouted another one. With that they all began to laugh and whoop and holler and went tearing off, kicking up a lot of dust and leaving father with a tightness around his mouth that was not there before.

They were impartial with attentions like that. They would hand them out anywhere along the line an opportunity offered. But they liked best to catch father within earshot and burn him with their sarcasm.

It was crude. It was coarse. I thought it silly for grown men to act that way. But it was effective. Shane, as self-sufficient as the mountains, could ignore it. Father, while it galled him, could keep it from getting him. The other homesteaders, though, could not help being irritated and showing they felt insulted. It roughed their nerves and made them angry and restless. They did not know Shane as father and I did. They were not sure there might not be some truth in the big talk Chris was making.

Things became so bad they could not go into Grafton's store without someone singing out for soda pop. And wherever they went, the conversation near by always snuck around somehow to pigs. You could sense the contempt building up in town, in people who used to be neutral, not taking sides.

The effect showed, too, in the attitude our neighbors now had toward Shane. They were constrained when they called to see father and Shane was there. They resented that he was linked to them. And as a result their opinion of father was changing.

That was what finally drove Shane. He did not mind what they thought of him. Since his session with Chris he seemed to have won a kind of inner peace. He was as alert and watchful as ever, but there was a serenity in him that had erased entirely the old tension. I think he did not care what anyone anywhere thought of him. Except us, his folks. And he knew that with us he was one of us, unchangeable and always.

But he did care what they thought of father. He was standing silently on the porch the night Ernie Wright and Henry Shipstead were arguing with father in the kitchen.

"I can't stomach much more," Ernie Wright was saying. "You know the trouble I've had with those blasted cowboys cutting my fence. Today a couple of them rode over and helped me repair a piece. Helped me, blast them! Waited till we were through, then said Fletcher didn't want any of my pigs getting loose and mixing with his cattle. My pigs! There ain't a pig in this whole valley and they know it. I'm sick of the word."

Father made it worse by chuckling. Grim, maybe, yet still a chuckle. "Sounds like one of Morgan's ideas. He's smart. Mean, but—"

Henry Shipstead would not let him finish. "This is nothing to laugh at, Joe. You least of all. Man, I'm beginning to doubt your judgment. None of us can keep our heads up around here any more. Just a while ago I was in Grafton's and Chris was there blowing high about your Shane must be thirsty because he's so scared he hasn't been in town lately for his soda pop."

Both of them were hammering at father now. He was sitting back, saying nothing, his face clouding.

"You can't dodge it, Joe." This was Wright. "Your man's responsible. You can try explaining all night, but you can't change the facts. Chris braced him for a fight and he ducked out—and left us stuck with those stinking pigs."

"You know as well as I do what Fletcher's doing," growled Henry Shipstead. "He's pushing us with this and he won't let up till one of us gets enough and makes a fool play and starts something so he can move in and finish it."

"Fool play or not," said Ernie Wright. "I've had all I can take. The next time one of those—"

Father stopped him with a hand up for silence. "Listen. What's that?"

It was a horse, picking up speed and tearing down our lane into the road. Father was at the door in a single jump, peering out.

The others were close behind him. "Shane?"

Father nodded. He was muttering under his breath. As I watched from the doorway of my little room, I could see that his eyes were bright and dancing. He was calling Shane names, cursing him, softly, fluently. He came back to his chair and grinned at the other two. "That's Shane," he told them and the words meant more than they seemed to say. "All we can do now is wait."

They were a silent crew waiting. Mother got up from her sewing in the bedroom where she had been listening as she always did and came into the kitchen and made up a pot of coffee and they all sat there sipping at the hot stuff and waiting.

It could not have been much more than twenty minutes before we heard the horse again, coming swiftly and slewing around to make the lane without slowing. There were quick steps on the porch and Shane stood in the doorway. He was breathing strongly and his face was hard. His mouth was a thin line in the bleakness of his face and his eyes were deep and dark. He looked at Shipstead and Wright and he made no effort to hide the disgust in his voice.

"Your pigs are dead and buried."

As his gaze shifted to father, his face softened. But the voice was still bitter. "There's another one down. Chris won't be bothering anybody for quite a spell." He turned and disappeared and we could hear him leading the horse into the barn.

In the quiet following, hoofbeats like an echo sounded in the distance. They swelled louder and this second horse galloped into our lane and pulled to a stop. Ed Howells jumped to the porch and hurried in.

"Where's Shane?"

"Out in the barn," father said.

"Did he tell you what happened?"

"Not much," father said mildly. "Something about burying pigs."

Ed Howells slumped into a chair. He seemed a bit dazed. The words came out of him slowly at first as he tried to make the others grasp just how he felt. "I never saw anything like it," he said, and he told about it.

He had been in Grafton's store buying a few things, not caring about going into the saloon because Chris and Red Marlin, another of Fletcher's cowboys, had hands in the evening poker game, when he noticed how still the place was. He went over to sneak a look and there was Shane just moving to the bar, cool and easy as if the room was empty and he the only one in it. Neither Chris nor Red Marlin was saying a word, though you might have thought this was a good chance for them to cut loose with some of their raw sarcasm. One look at Shane was enough to tell why. He was cool and easy, right enough. But there was a curious kind of smooth flow to his movements that made you realize without being conscious of thinking about it that being quiet was a mighty sensible way to be at the moment.

"Two bottles of soda pop," he called to Will Atkey. He leaned his back to the bar and looked the poker game over with what seemed a friendly interest while Will fetched the bottles from the store. Not another person even twitched a muscle. They were all watching him and wondering what the play was. He took the two bottles and walked to the table and set them down, reaching over to put one in front of Chris.

"The last time I was in here you bought me a drink. Now it's my turn."

The words sort of lingered in the stillness. He got the impression, Ed Howells said, that Shane meant just what the words said. He wanted to buy Chris a drink. He wanted Chris to take that bottle and grin at him and drink with him.

You could have heard a bug crawl, I guess, while Chris carefully laid down the cards in his right hand and stretched it to the bottle. He lifted it in a sudden jerk and flung it across the table at Shane.

So fast Shane moved, Ed Howells said, that the bottle was still in the air when he had dodged, lunged forward, grabbed Chris by the shirtfront and hauled him right out of his chair and over the table. As Chris struggled to get his feet under him, Shane let go the shirt and slapped him, sharp and stinging, three times, the hand flicking back and forth so quick you could hardly see it, the slaps sounding like pistol shots.

Shane stepped back and Chris stood swaying a little and shaking his head to clear it. He was a game one and mad down to his boots. He plunged in, fists smashing, and Shane let him come, slipping inside the flailing arms and jolting a powerful blow low into his stomach. As Chris gasped and his head came down, Shane brought his right hand up, open, and with the heel of it caught Chris full on the mouth, snapping his head back and raking up over the nose and eyes.

The force of it knocked Chris off balance and he staggered badly. His lips were crushed.

Blood was dripping over them from his battered nose. His eyes were red and watery and he was having trouble seeing with them. His face, Ed Howells said, and shook a little as he said it, looked like a horse had stomped it. But he drove in again, swinging wildly.

Shane ducked under, caught one of the flying wrists, twisted the arm to lock it and keep it from bending, and swung his shoulder into the armpit. He yanked hard on the wrist and Chris went up and over him. As the body hurtled over, Shane kept hold of the arm and wrenched it sideways and let the weight bear on it and you could hear the bone crack as Chris crashed to the floor.

A long sobbing sigh came from Chris and that died away and there was not a sound in the room. Shane never looked at the crumpled figure. He was straight and deadly and still. Every line of him was alive and eager. But he stood motionless. Only his eyes shifted to search the faces of the others at the table. They stopped on Red Marlin and Red seemed to dwindle lower in his chair.

"Perhaps," Shane said softly, and the very softness of his voice sent shivers through Ed Howells, "perhaps you have something to say about soda pop or pigs."

Red Marlin sat quiet like he was trying not even to breathe. Tiny drops of sweat appeared on his forehead. He was frightened, maybe for the first time in his life, and the others knew it and he knew they knew and he did not care. And none of them blamed him at all.

Then, as they watched, the fire in Shane smouldered down and out. He seemed to withdraw back within himself. He forgot them all and turned toward Chris unconscious on the floor, and a sort of sadness, Ed Howells said, crept over him and held him. He bent and scooped the sprawling figure up in his arms and carried it to one of the other tables. Gently he set it down, the legs falling limp over the edge. He crossed to the bar and took the rag Will used to wipe it and returned to the table and tenderly cleared the blood from the face. He felt carefully along the broken arm and nodded to himself at what he felt.

All this while no one said a word. Not a one of them would have interfered with that man for a year's top wages. He spoke and his voice rang across the room at Red Marlin. "You'd better tote him home and get that arm fixed. Take right good care of him. He has the makings of a good man." Then he forgot them all again and looked at Chris and went on speaking as if to that limp figure that could not hear him. "There's only one thing really wrong with you. You're young. That's the one thing time can always cure."

The thought hurt him and he strode to the swinging doors and through them into the night.

That was what Ed Howells told. "The whole business," he finished, "didn't take five minutes. It was maybe thirty seconds from the time he grabbed holt of Chris till Chris was out cold on the floor. In my opinion that Shane is the most dangerous man I've ever seen. I'm glad he's working for Joe here and not for Fletcher."

Father leveled a triumphant look at Henry Shipstead. "So I've made a mistake, have I?"

Before anyone else could push in a word, mother was speaking. I was surprised, because she was upset and her voice was a little shrill. "I wouldn't be too sure about that, Joe Starrett. I think you've made a bad mistake."

"Marian, what's got into you?"

"Look what you've done just because you got him to stay on here and get mixed up in this trouble with Fletcher!"

Father was edging toward being peeved himself. "Women never do understand these things. Lookahere, Marian. Chris will be all right. He's young and he's healthy. Soon as that arm is mended, he'll be in as good shape as he ever was."

"Oh, Joe, can't you see what I'm talking about? I don't mean what you've done to Chris. I mean what you've done to Shane."

8

This time mother was right. Shane was changed. He tried to keep things as they had been with us and on the surface nothing was different. But he had lost the serenity that had seeped into him through the summer. He would no longer sit around and talk with us as much as he had. He was restless with some far hidden desperation.

At times, when it rode him worst, he would wander alone about our place, and this was the one thing that seemed to soothe him. I used to see him, when he thought no one was watching, run his hands along the rails of the corral he had fastened, test with a tug the posts he had set, pace out past the barn looking up at the bulging loft and stride out where the tall corn was standing in big shocks to dig his hands in the loose soil and lift some of it and let it run through his fingers.

He would lean on the pasture fence and study our little herd like it meant more to him than lazy steers to be fattened for market. Sometimes he would whistle softly, and his horse, filled out now so you could see the quality of him and moving with a quiet sureness and power that made you think of Shane himself, would trot to the fence and nuzzle at him.

Often he would disappear from the house in the early evening after supper. More than once, the dishes done, when I managed to slip past mother, I found him far back in the pasture alone with the horse. He would be standing there, one arm on the smooth arch of the horse's neck, the fingers gently rubbing around the ears, and he would be looking out over our land where the last light of the sun, now out of sight, would be flaring up the far side of the mountains, capping them with a deep glow and leaving a mystic gloaming[1] in the valley.

Some of the assurance that was in him when he came was gone now. He seemed to feel that he needed to justify himself, even to me, to a boy tagging his heels.

"Could you teach me," I asked him, "to throw somebody the way you threw Chris?"

He waited so long I thought he would not answer. "A man doesn't learn things like that," he said at last. "You know them and that's all." Then he was talking rapidly to me, as close to pleading as he could ever come. "I tried. You can see that, can't you, Bob? I let him ride me and I gave him his chance. A man can keep his self-respect without having to cram it down another man's throat. Surely you can see that, Bob?"

I could not see it. What he was trying to explain to me was beyond my comprehension then. And I could think of nothing to say.

"I left it up to him. He didn't have to jump me that second time. He could have called it off without crawling. He could have if he was man enough. Can't you see that, Bob?"

And still I could not. But I said I could. He was so earnest and he wanted me to so badly. It was a long, long time before I did see it and then I was a man myself and Shane was not there for me to tell. . . .

I was not sure whether father and mother were aware of the change in him. They did not talk about it, not while I was around anyway. But one afternoon I overheard something that showed mother knew.

I had hurried home from school and put on

1. **mystic gloaming:** magical twilight.

my old clothes and started out to see what father and Shane were doing in the cornfield, when I thought of a trick that had worked several times. Mother was firm set against eating between meals. That was a silly notion. I had my mind set on the cookies she kept in a tin box on a shelf by the stove. She was settled on the porch with a batch of potatoes to peel, so I slipped up to the back of the house, through the window of my little room, and tiptoed into the kitchen. Just as I was carefully putting a chair under the shelf, I heard her call to Shane.

He must have come to the barn on some errand, for he was there by the porch in only a moment. I peeped out the front window and saw him standing close in, his hat in his hand, his face tilted up slightly to look at her leaning forward in her chair.

"I've been wanting to talk to you when Joe wasn't around."

"Yes, Marian." He called her that the same as father did, familiar yet respectful, just as he always regarded her with a tenderness in his eyes he had for no one else.

"You've been worrying, haven't you, about what may happen in this Fletcher business? You thought it would just be a case of not letting him scare you away and of helping us through a hard time. You didn't know it would come to what it has. And now you're worried about what you might do if there's any more fighting."

"You're a discerning woman, Marian."

"You've been worrying about something else too."

"You're a mighty discerning woman, Marian."

"And you've been thinking that maybe you'll be moving on."

"And how did you know that?"

"Because it's what you ought to do. For your own sake. But I'm asking you not to." Mother

was intense and serious, as lovely there with the light striking through her hair as I had ever seen her. "Don't go, Shane. Joe needs you. More than ever now. More than he would ever say."

"And you?" Shane's lips barely moved and I was not sure of the words.

Mother hesitated. Then her head went up. "Yes. It's only fair to say it. I need you too."

"So-o-o," he said softly, the word lingering on his lips. He considered her gravely. "Do you know what you're asking, Marian?"

"I know. And I know that you're the man to stand up to it. In some ways it would be easier for me, too, if you rode out of this valley and never came back. But we can't let Joe down. I'm counting on you not ever to make me do that. Because you've got to stay, Shane, no matter how hard it is for us. Joe can't keep this place without you. He can't buck Fletcher alone."

Shane was silent, and it seemed to me that he was troubled and hard pressed in his mind. Mother was talking straight to him, slow and feeling for the words, and her voice was beginning to tremble.

"It would just about kill Joe to lose this place. He's too old to start in again somewhere else. Oh, we would get along and might even do real well. After all, he's Joe Starrett. He's all man and he can do what has to be done. But he promised me this place when we were married. He had it in his mind for all the first years. He did two men's work to get the extra money for the things we would need. When Bob was big enough to walk and help some and he could leave us, he came on here and filed his claim and built this house with his own hands, and when he brought us here it was home. Nothing else would ever be the same."

Shane drew a deep breath and let it ease out slowly. He smiled at her and yet, somehow, as I watched him, my heart ached for him. "Joe should be proud of a wife like you. Don't fret any more, Marian. You'll not lose this place."

Mother dropped back in her chair. Her face, the side I could see from the window, was radiant. Then, woman like, she was talking against herself. "But that Fletcher is a mean and tricky man. Are you sure it will work out all right?"

Shane was already starting toward the barn. He stopped and turned to look at her again. "I said you won't lose this place." You knew he was right because of the way he said it and because he said it.

Reading Check

1. Where does the story take place?
2. Who narrates the story?
3. Identify the stranger who rides into the valley and becomes a part of the Starretts' lives.
4. What is the "one bad spot" on the Starretts' place?
5. Why does Shane try to prevent Joe from buying the new seven-pronged cultivator from Ledyard?
6. Who is the rancher that is trying to take the homesteaders' land from them?
7. What does Bob discover in Shane's saddle-roll?
8. According to Shane, what is the one thing that is wrong with Chris?
9. When Marian realizes that Shane is thinking of moving on, what reason does she give Shane for wanting him to stay?
10. Marian is a skillful homemaker. In what special skill does she pride herself?

For Study and Discussion

Analyzing and Interpreting the Novel

1. Shane is described as a mysterious character. According to Joe Starrett, men such as Shane can be as bad as poison or "straight grain clear through." In spite of this, why do the Starretts decide to ask Shane to stay on at the farm?

2a. Why does the act of cutting out the old stump join Joe and Shane in friendship?
b. When Marian suggests that Shane and Joe use horses to pull the stump from the ground, why do they refuse?

3. Joe tells Bob not to like Shane too much because he is "fiddle-footed." Bob knows this is not what his father really means. What do you think his father really means?

4a. Why does Luke Fletcher stand between the homesteaders and the rights to their land claims? **b.** What did Fletcher do to Morley, Joe's first hired hand? **c.** In what way is Shane Joe's answer to Fletcher's threat?

5a. What reason does Shane give Bob for refusing to fight with Fletcher's man the first time he is insulted? **b.** Why do you think Shane changes his mind and decides to go back to Grafton's to set things straight with Chris?

Literary Elements

Understanding the Novel

Setting
1. The setting plays a significant part in this novel. Much of the action which takes place in the story concerns disputes over territory. The land also represents a binding force among the homesteaders. Tell how the setting creates both conflict and unity.

Character
2. A **dynamic character** is one that is capable of growth and change. This type of character can be a hero or heroine and is usually developed in detail by the author. **a.** In what ways are Shane and Bob Starrett dynamic characters? Give examples of how they change or grow throughout the novel. **b.** As you read, look for passages in the novel that describe Shane in such a way that he seems to take on extraordinary or superhuman characteristics.

3. A **static character** is usually a minor character that is not central to the plot. Static characters do not grow or change but are useful in providing information necessary to the development of the story. Name two static charac-

ters and explain their role in the development of the story.

Plot
4. Plot can be defined as the series of interrelated actions within a novel. The plot is made up of the actions of the characters and what happens to them. The most important element of plot is **conflict**. There are three types of major conflicts: conflict with environment, conflict with self, and conflict with others. Give an example of each type of conflict in the novel.

Foreshadowing
5. Foreshadowing is the author's method of giving hints about what is to happen later in the novel. Explain how the author of *Shane* uses foreshadowing to give clues about Shane's hidden character.

Point of View
6. *Shane* is narrated in the **first person**; the story is told from a young boy's point of view. **a.** Give three examples in the story which reflect a young boy's impression of the events that take place in the story. **b.** Explain why you think the author chose the voice of a young boy to tell the story.

Language and Vocabulary

Identifying the Meanings of Colloquialisms

Colloquial English is the language you use in informal conversation. It is not the language you would use to write a formal paper or to give a speech. It differs from conventional usage in grammar and vocabulary. Expressions of colloquial speech can be imaginative. They result from the flexibility of language and imply or connote special meanings.

Many words or expressions grow out of widespread use in a particular region. You might call them the language of "Land." For example, in *Shane*, Marian finds Shane's description of pancakes interesting. He refers to them as "flannel cakes" and the Starretts call them "flapjacks." Marian guesses, with the help of Joe, that Shane comes from Tennessee because she has never heard anyone from the valley call flapjacks "flannel cakes." Shane reveals that he grew up in Arkansas and that his folks were from Mississippi.

Define the following expressions and words in *Shane* and tell what you think they mean. You may use a dictionary, keeping in mind that the words used in these colloquialisms connote meanings which differ from their **denotations**—dictionary meanings.

quite a spell   (p. 524)
be in a fix   (p. 526)
straight grain clear through   (p. 526)
fiddle-footed   (p. 527)
pegged   (p. 528)
plumb full   (p. 528)
tariff   (p. 530)
heft   (p. 532)
a mite   (p. 540)

Writing About Literature

Illustrating How Imagery Is Used

When you read, your mind forms pictures of the scenes and descriptions of what you are reading. Sometimes the pictures are very clear and sharp, and you can imagine the scene as if you were right there inside it. When a writer is able to make the reader see, touch, taste, smell, or hear what he is writing about, he or she is using imagery to its fullest extent.

Imagery is often connected to setting. For example, in *Shane* you find the author has used imagery to bring you into the Starretts' home and their surrounding farmland. There are also many fine descriptions of landscape throughout the novel. Take a few minutes and review the novel for examples of imagery that you particularly enjoyed.

Write two paragraphs using examples from the novel to show how the author of *Shane* has used imagery in the novel to appeal to the senses of sight, sound, smell, taste, and touch in the reader. You do not have to use direct quotations from the story in this exercise, but using your textbook as a reference may prove to be helpful.

Descriptive Writing

Describing a Character

You have learned that one way an author can provide information about a character is through physical description. *Shane* provides many examples of the use of descriptive language. The main characters in the novel are presented in a manner that allows you to form mental pictures of their size, mannerisms, and facial features. Particular attention is paid to details of these characters to give you a sense of seeing them in person. Actions and dialogue are also important means of revealing a character's true nature. Joe and Shane are both admirable characters in the novel. Through their actions, words, and physical descriptions you come to know these characters in a personal way.

Using the first person point of view, write a short description about an admirable character that you have met. Include your impressions and responses to this character. Be sure to include a physical description, paying particular attention to significant details. Try to bring the character to life in your description by using the elements discussed above to show the unusual characteristics of your subject.

9

Another period of peace had settled over our valley. Since the night Shane rode into town, Fletcher's cowboys had quit using the road past the homesteads. They were not annoying us at all and only once in a while was there a rider in view across the river. They had a good excuse to let us be. They were busy fixing the ranch buildings and poling a big new corral in preparation for the spring drive of new cattle Fletcher was planning.

Just the same, I noticed that father was as watchful as Shane now. The two of them worked always together. They did not split any more to do separate jobs in different parts of the farm. They worked together, rode into town together when anything was needed. And father took to wearing his gun all the time, even in the fields. He strapped it on after breakfast the first morning following the fight with Chris, and I saw him catch Shane's eye with a questioning glance as he buckled the belt. But Shane shook his head and father nodded, accepting the decision, and they went out together without saying a word.

Those were beautiful fall days, clear and stirring, with the coolness in the air just enough to set one atingling, not yet mounting to the bitter cold that soon would come sweeping down out of the mountains. It did not seem possible that in such a harvest season, giving a lift to the spirit to match the well-being of the body, violence could flare so suddenly and swiftly.

Saturday evenings all of us would pile into the light work wagon, father and mother on the seat, Shane and I swinging legs at the rear, and go into town. It was the break in routine we looked forward to all week.

There was always a bustle in Grafton's store with people we knew coming and going.

Mother would lay in her supplies for the week ahead, taking a long time about it and chatting with the womenfolk. She and the wives of the other homesteaders were great ones for swapping recipes and this was their bartering ground. Father would give Mr. Grafton his order for what he wanted and go direct for the mail. He was always getting catalogues of farm equipment and pamphlets from Washington. He would flip through their pages and skim through any letters, then settle on a barrel and spread out his newspaper. But like as not he would soon be bogged down in an argument with almost any man handy about the best crops for the Territory and it would be Shane who would really work his way into the newspaper.

I used to explore the store, filling myself with crackers from the open barrel at the end of the main counter, playing hide and seek with Mr. Grafton's big and knowing old cat that was a whiz of a mouser. Many a time, turning up boxes, I chased out fat furry ones for her to pounce on. If mother was in the right mood, I would have a bag of candy in my pocket.

This time we had a special reason for staying longer than usual, a reason I did not like. Our schoolteacher, Jane Grafton, had made me take a note home to mother asking her to stop in for a talk. About me. I never was too smart at formal schooling to begin with. Being all excited over the doings at the big ranch and what they might mean to us had not helped any. Miss Grafton, I guess, just sort of endured me under the best of conditions. But what tipped her into being downright annoyed and writing to mother was the weather. No one could expect a boy with any spirit in him to be shut up in a schoolroom in weather like we had been having. Twice that week I had persuaded Ollie Johnson to sneak away with me after the lunch hour to see if the fish were still biting in our favorite pool below town.

Mother finished the last item on her list, looked around at me, sighed a little, and stiffened her shoulders. I knew she was going to the living quarters behind the store and talk to Miss Grafton. I squirmed and pretended I did not notice her. Only a few people were left in the store, though the saloon in the adjoining big room was doing fair business. She went over to where father was leafing through a catalogue and tapped him.

"Come along, Joe. You should hear this, too. I declare, that boy is getting too big for me to handle."

Father glanced quickly over the store and paused, listening to the voices from the next room. We had not seen any of Fletcher's men all evening and he seemed satisfied. He looked at Shane, who was folding the newspaper.

"This won't take long. We'll be out in a moment."

As they passed through the door at the rear of the store, Shane strolled to the saloon opening. He took in the whole room in his easy, alert way and stepped inside. I followed. But I was supposed not ever to go in there, so I stopped at the entrance. Shane was at the bar, joshing Will Atkey with a grave face that he didn't think he'd have soda pop tonight. It was a scattered group in the room, most of them from around town and familiar to me by sight at least. Those close to Shane moved a little away, eyeing him curiously. He did not appear to notice.

He picked up his drink and savored it, one elbow on the bar, not shoving himself forward into the room's companionship and not withdrawing either, just ready to be friendly if anyone wanted that and unfriendly if anyone wanted that too.

I was letting my eyes wander about, trying to tag names to faces, when I saw that one of the swinging doors was partly open and Red Marlin was peeking in. Shane saw it too. But he could not see that more men were out on the porch, for they were close by the building wall and on the store side. I could sense them through the window near me, hulking shapes in the darkness. I was so frightened I could scarcely move.

But I had to. I had to go against mother's rule. I scrambled into the saloon and to Shane and I gasped: "Shane! There's a lot of them out front!"

I was too late. Red Marlin was inside and the others were hurrying in and fanning out to close off the store opening. Morgan was one of them, his flat face sour and determined, his huge shoulders almost filling the doorway as he came through. Behind him was the cowboy they called Curly because of his shock of unruly hair. He was stupid and slow-moving, but he was thick and powerful, and he had worked in harness with Chris for several years. Two others followed them, new men to me, with the tough, experienced look of old herd hands.

There was still the back office with its outside door opening on a side stoop and the rear alley. My knees were shaking and I tugged at Shane and tried to say something about it. He stopped me with a sharp gesture. His face was clear, his eyes bright. He was somehow happy, not in the pleased and laughing way, but happy that the waiting was over and what had been ahead was here and seen and realized and he was ready for it. He put one hand on my head and rocked it gently, the fingers feeling through my hair.

"Bobby boy, would you have me run away?"

Love for that man raced through me and the warmth ran down and stiffened my legs and I was so proud of being there with him that I could not keep the tears from my eyes. I could see the rightness of it and I was ready to do as he told me when he said: "Get out of here, Bob. This isn't going to be pretty."

But I would go no farther than my perch just inside the store where I could watch most of the big room. I was so bound in the moment that I did not even think of running for father.

Morgan was in the lead now with his men

spread out behind him. He came about half the way to Shane and stopped. The room was quiet except for the shuffling of feet as the men by the bar and the nearest tables hastened over to the far wall and some of them ducked out the front doors. Neither Shane nor Morgan gave any attention to them. They had attention only for each other. They did not look aside even when Mr. Grafton, who could smell trouble in his place from any distance, stalked in from the store, planting his feet down firmly, and pushed past Will Atkey behind the bar. He had a resigned expression on his face and he reached under the counter, his hands reappearing with a short-barreled shotgun. He laid it before him on the bar and he said in a dry, disgusted voice: "There will be no gunplay, gentlemen. And all damages will be paid for."

Morgan nodded curtly, not taking his eyes from Shane. He came closer and stopped again little more than an arm's length away. His head was thrust forward. His big fists were clenched at his sides.

"No one messes up one of my boys and gets away with it. We're riding you out of this valley on a rail, Shane. We're going to rough you a bit and ride you out and you'll stay out."

"So you have it all planned," Shane said softly. Even as he was speaking, he was moving. He flowed into action so swift you could hardly believe what was happening. He scooped up his half-filled glass from the bar, whipped it and its contents into Morgan's face, and when Morgan's hands came up reaching or striking for him, he grasped the wrists and flung himself backwards, dragging Morgan with him. His body rolled to meet the floor and his legs doubled and his feet, catching Morgan just below the belt, sent him flying on and over to fall flat in a grotesque spraddle and slide along the boards in a tangle of chairs and a table.

The other four were on Shane in a rush. As they came, he whirled to his hands and knees and leaped up and behind the nearest table, tipping it in a strong heave among them. They scattered, dodging, and he stepped, fast and light, around the end and drove into the tail man, one of the new men, now nearest to him. He took the blows at him straight on to get in close and I saw his knee surge up and into the man's groin. A high scream was literally torn from the man and he collapsed to the floor and dragged himself toward the doors.

Morgan was on his feet, wavering, rubbing a hand across his face, staring hard as if trying to focus again on the room about him. The other three were battering at Shane, seeking to box him between them. They were piling blows into him, crowding in. Through that blur of movement he was weaving, quick and confident. It was incredible, but they could not hurt him. You could see the blows hit, hear the solid chunk of knuckles on flesh. But they had no effect. They seemed only to feed that fierce energy. He moved like a flame among them. He would burst out of the mêlée[1] and whirl and plunge back, the one man actually pressing the three. He had picked the second new man and was driving always directly at him.

Curly, slow and clumsy, grunting in exasperation, grabbed at Shane to grapple with him and hold down his arms. Shane dropped one shoulder and as Curly hugged tighter brought it up under his jaw with a jolt that knocked him loose and away.

They were wary now and none too eager to let him get close to any one of them. Then Red Marlin came at him from one side, forcing him to turn that way, and at the same time the second new man did a strange thing. He jumped high in the air, like a jack rabbit in a spy hop, and lashed out viciously with one boot at

1. **mêlée** (mā′lā′, mā-lā′): skirmish; fight.

Shane's head. Shane saw it coming, but could not avoid it, so he rolled his head with the kick, taking it along the side. It shook him badly. But it did not block the instant response. His hands shot up and seized the foot and the man crashed down to land on the small of his back. As he hit, Shane twisted the whole leg and threw his weight on it. The man buckled on the floor like a snake when you hit it and groaned sharply and hitched himself away, the leg dragging, the fight gone out of him.

But the swing to bend down on the leg had put Shane's back to Curly and the big man was plowing at him. Curly's arms clamped around him, pinning his arms to his body. Red Marlin leaped to help and the two of them had Shane caught tight between them.

"Hold him!" That was Morgan, coming forward with the hate plain in his eyes. Even then, Shane would have broke away. He stomped one heavy work shoe, heel edged and with all the strength he could get in quick leverage, on Curly's near foot. As Curly winced and pulled it back and was unsteady, Shane strained with his whole body in a powerful arch and you could see their arms slipping and loosening. Morgan, circling in, saw it too. He swept a bottle off the bar and brought it smashing down from behind on Shane's head.

Shane slumped and would have fallen if they had not been holding him. Then, as Morgan stepped around in front of him and watched, the vitality pumped through him and his head came up.

"Hold him!" Morgan said again. He deliberately flung a huge fist to Shane's face. Shane tried to jerk aside and the fist missed the jaw, tearing along the cheek, the heavy ring on one finger slicing deep. Morgan pulled back for another blow. He never made it.

Nothing, I would have said, could have drawn my attention from those men. But I heard a kind of choking sob beside me and it was queer and yet familiar and it turned me instantly.

Father was there in the entranceway!

He was big and terrible and he was looking across the overturned table and scattered chairs at Shane, at the dark purplish bruise along the side of Shane's head and the blood running down his cheek. I had never seen father like this. He was past anger. He was filled with a fury that was shaking him almost beyond endurance.

I never thought he could move so fast. He was on them before they even knew he was in the room. He hurtled into Morgan with ruthless force, sending that huge man reeling across the room. He reached out one broad hand and grabbed Curly by the shoulder and you could see the fingers sink into the flesh. He took hold of Curly's belt with the other hand and ripped him loose from Shane and his own shirt shredded down the back and the great muscles there knotted and bulged as he lifted Curly right up over his head and hurled the threshing body from him. Curly spun through the air, his limbs waving wildly, and crashed on the top of a table way over by the wall. It cracked under him, collapsing in splintered pieces, and the man and the wreckage smacked against the wall. Curly tried to rise, pushing himself with hands on the floor, and fell back and was still.

Shane must have exploded into action the second father yanked Curly away, for now there was another noise. It was Red Marlin, his face contorted, flung against the bar and catching at it to keep himself from falling. He staggered and caught his balance and ran for the front doorway. His flight was frantic, headlong. He tore through the swinging doors without slowing to push them. They flapped with a swishing sound and my eyes shifted quickly to Shane, for he was laughing.

He was standing there, straight and superb,

the blood on his face bright like a badge, and he was laughing.

It was a soft laugh, soft and gentle, not in amusement at Red Marlin or any single thing, but in the joy of being alive and released from long discipline and answering the urge in mind and body. The lithe power in him, so different from father's sheer strength, was singing in every fiber of him.

Morgan was in the rear corner, his face clouded and uncertain. Father, his fury eased by the mighty effort of throwing Curly, had looked around to watch Red Marlin's run and now was starting toward Morgan. Shane's voice stopped him.

"Wait, Joe. The man's mine." He was at father's side and he put a hand on father's arm. "You'd better get them out of here." He nodded in my direction and I noticed with surprise that mother was near and watching. She must

have followed father and have been there all this while. Her lips were parted. Her eyes were glowing, looking at the whole room, not at anyone or anything in particular, but at the whole room.

Father was disappointed. "Morgan's more my size," he said, grumbling fashion. He was not worried about Shane. He was thinking of an excuse to take Morgan himself. But he went no further. He looked at the men over by the wall. "This is Shane's play. If a one of you tries to interfere, he'll have me to reckon with." His tone showed that he was not mad at them, that he was not even really warning them. He was simply making the play plain. Then he came to us and looked down at mother. "You wait out at the wagon, Marian. Morgan's had this coming to him for quite a long time now and it's not for a woman to see."

Mother shook her head without moving her

eyes now from Shane. "No, Joe. He's one of us. I'll see this through." And the three of us stayed there together and that was right, for he was Shane.

He advanced toward Morgan, as flowing and graceful as the old mouser in the store. He had forgotten us and the battered men on the floor and those withdrawn by the wall and Mr. Grafton and Will Atkey crouched behind the bar. His whole being was concentrated on the big man before him.

Morgan was taller, half again as broad, with a long reputation as a bullying fighter in the valley. But he did not like this and he was desperate. He knew better than to wait. He rushed at Shane to overwhelm the smaller man with his weight. Shane faded from in front of him and as Morgan went past hooked a sharp blow to his stomach and another to the side of his jaw. They were short and quick, flicking in so fast they were just a blur of movement. Yet each time at the instant of impact Morgan's big frame shook and halted in its rush for a fraction of a second before the momentum carried him forward. Again and again he rushed, driving his big fists ahead. Always Shane slipped away, sending in those swift hard punches.

Breathing heavily, Morgan stopped, grasping the futility of straight fighting. He plunged at Shane now, arms wide, trying to get hold of him and wrestle him down. Shane was ready and let him come without dodging, disregarding the arms stretching to encircle him. He brought up his right hand, open, just as Ed Howells had told us, and the force of Morgan's own lunge as the hand met his mouth and raked upwards snapped back his head and sent him staggering.

Morgan's face was puffy and red-mottled. He bellowed some insane sound and swung up a chair. Holding it in front of him, legs forward, he rushed again at Shane, who side-stepped neatly. Morgan was expecting this and halted suddenly, swinging the chair in a swift arc to strike Shane with it full on the side. The chair shattered and Shane faltered, and then, queerly for a man usually so sure on his feet, he seemed to slip and fall to the floor.

Forgetting all caution, Morgan dove at him—and Shane's legs bent and he caught Morgan on his heavy work shoes and sent him flying back and against the bar with a crash that shook the whole length of it.

Shane was up and leaping at Morgan as if there had been springs under him there on the floor. His left hand, palm out, smacked against Morgan's forehead, pushing the head back, and his right fist drove straight to Morgan's throat. You could see the agony twist the man's face and the fear widen his eyes. And Shane, using his right fist now like a club and lining his whole body behind it, struck him on the neck below and back of the ear. It made a sickening, dull sound and Morgan's eyes rolled white and he went limp all over, sagging slowly and forward to the floor.

10

In the hush that followed Morgan's fall, the big barroom was so quiet again that the rustle of Will Atkey straightening from below the bar level was loud and clear and Will stopped moving, embarrassed and a little frightened.

Shane looked neither at him nor at any of the other men staring from the wall. He looked only at us, at father and mother and me, and it seemed to me that it hurt him to see us there.

He breathed deeply and his chest filled and he held it, held it long and achingly, and released it slowly and sighing. Suddenly you were impressed by the fact that he was quiet, that he was still. You saw how battered and bloody he was. In the moments before you saw only the splendor of movement, the flowing brute beauty of line and power in action. The man, you felt, was tireless and indestructible. Now that he was still and the fire in him banked and subsided, you saw, and in the seeing remembered, that he had taken bitter punishment.

His shirt collar was dark and sodden. Blood was soaking into it, and this came only in part from the cut on his cheek. More was oozing from the matted hair where Morgan's bottle had hit. Unconsciously he put up one hand and it came away smeared and sticky. He regarded it grimly and wiped it clean on his shirt. He swayed slightly and when he started toward us, his feet dragged and he almost fell forward.

One of the townsmen, Mr. Weir, a friendly man who kept the stage post, pushed out from the wall, clucking sympathy, as though to help him. Shane pulled himself erect. His eyes blazed refusal. Straight and superb, not a tremor in him, he came to us and you knew that the spirit in him would sustain him thus alone for the farthest distance and forever.

But there was no need. The one man in our valley, the one man, I believe, in all the world whose help he would take, not to whom he would turn but whose help he would take, was there and ready. Father stepped to meet him and put out a big arm reaching for his shoulders. "All right, Joe," Shane said, so softly I doubt whether the others in the room heard. His eyes closed and he leaned against father's arm, his body relaxing and his head dropping sideways. Father bent and fitted his other arm under Shane's knees and picked him up like he did me when I stayed up too late and got all drowsy and had to be carried to bed.

Father held Shane in his arms and looked over him at Mr. Grafton. "I'd consider it a favor, Sam, if you'd figure the damage and put it on my bill."

For a man strict about bills and keen for a bargain, Mr. Grafton surprised me. "I'm marking this to Fletcher's account. I'm seeing that he pays."

Mr. Weir surprised me even more. He spoke promptly and he was emphatic about it. "Listen to me, Starrett. It's about time this town worked up a little pride. Maybe it's time, too, we got to be more neighborly with you homesteaders. I'll take a collection to cover this. I've been ashamed of myself ever since it started tonight, standing here and letting five of them jump that man of yours." ˙

Father was pleased. But he knew what he wanted to do. "That's mighty nice of you, Weir. But this ain't your fight. I wouldn't worry, was I you, about keeping out of it." He looked down at Shane and the pride was plain busting out of him. "Matter of fact, I'd say the odds tonight, without me butting in, too, was mighty close to even." He looked again at Mr. Grafton. "Fletcher ain't getting in on this with a nickel. I'm paying." He tossed back his head. "No, by Godfrey! We're paying. Me and Shane."

He went to the swinging doors, turning sideways to push them open. Mother took my hand and we followed. She always knew when to talk and when not to talk, and she said no word while we watched father lift Shane to the wagon seat, climb beside him, hoist him to sitting position with one arm around him and take the reins in the other hand. Will Atkey trotted out with our things and stowed them away. Mother and I perched on the back of the wagon, father chirruped to the team, and we were started home.

There was not a sound for quite a stretch except the clop of hooves and the little creakings of the wheels. Then I heard a chuckle up front. It was Shane. The cool air was reviving him and he was sitting straight, swaying with the wagon's motion.

"What did you do with the thick one, Joe? I was busy with the redhead."

"Oh, I just kind of tucked him out of the way." Father wanted to let it go at that. Not mother.

"He picked him up like—like a bag of potatoes and threw him clear across the room." She did not say it to Shane, not to any person. She said it to the night, to the sweet darkness around us, and her eyes were shining in the starlight.

We turned in at our place and father shooed the rest of us into the house while he unhitched the team. In the kitchen mother set some water to heat on the stove and chased me to bed. Her back was barely to me after she tucked me in before I was peering around the door jamb. She got several clean rags, took the water from the stove, and went to work on Shane's head. She was tender as could be, crooning like to herself under her breath the while. It pained him plenty as the warm water soaked into the gash under the matted hair and as she washed the clotted blood from his cheek. But it seemed to pain her more, for her hand shook at the worst moments, and she was the one who flinched while he sat there quietly and smiled reassuringly at her.

Father came in and sat by the stove, watching them. He pulled out his pipe and made a very careful business of packing it and lighting it.

She finished. Shane would not let her try a bandage. "This air is the best medicine," he said. She had to be content with cleaning the cuts thoroughly and making certain all bleeding had stopped. Then it was father's turn.

"Get that shirt off, Joe. It's torn all down the back. Let me see what I can do with it." Before he could rise, she had changed her mind. "No. We'll keep it just like it is. To remember tonight by. You were magnificent, Joe, tearing that man away and—"

"Shucks," said father. "I was just peeved.

Him holding Shane so Morgan could pound him."

"And you, Shane." Mother was in the middle of the kitchen, looking from one to the other. "You were magnificent, too. Morgan was so big and horrible and yet he didn't have even a chance. You were so cool and quick and—and dangerous and—"

"A woman shouldn't have to see things like that." Shane interrupted her, and he meant it. But she was talking right ahead.

"You think I shouldn't because it's brutal and nasty and not just fighting to see who is better at it, but mean and vicious and to win by any way, but to win. Of course it is. But you didn't start it. You didn't want to do it. Not until they made you anyway. You did it because you had to."

Her voice was climbing and she was looking back and forth and losing control of herself. "Did ever a woman have two such men?" And she turned from them and reached out blindly for a chair and sank into it and dropped her face into her hands and the tears came.

The two men stared at her and then at each other in that adult knowledge beyond my understanding. Shane rose and stepped over by mother. He put a hand gently on her head and I felt again his fingers in my hair and the affection flooding through me. He walked quietly out the door and into the night.

Father drew on his pipe. It was out and absently he lit it. He rose and went to the door and out on the porch. I could see him there dimly in the darkness, gazing across the river.

Gradually mother's sobs died down. She raised her head and wiped away the tears.

"Joe."

He turned and started in and waited then by the door. She stood up. She stretched her hands toward him and he was there and had her in his arms.

"Do you think I don't know, Marian?"

"But you don't. Not really. You can't. Because I don't know myself."

Father was staring over her head at the kitchen wall, not seeing anything there. "Don't fret yourself, Marian. I'm man enough to know a better when his trail meets mine. Whatever happens will be all right."

"Oh, Joe . . . Joe! Kiss me. Hold me tight and don't ever let go."

11

What happened in our kitchen that night was beyond me in those days. But it did not worry me because father had said it would be all right, and how could anyone, knowing him, doubt that he would make it so.

And we were not bothered by Fletcher's men any more at all. There might not have been a big ranch on the other side of the river, sprawling up the valley and over on our side above Ernie Wright's place, for all you could tell from our house. They left us strictly alone and were hardly ever seen now even in town. Fletcher himself, I heard from kids at school, was gone again. He went on the stage to Cheyenne and maybe farther, and nobody seemed to know why he went.

Yet father and Shane were more wary than they had been before. They stayed even closer together and they spent no more time than they had to in the fields. There was no more talking on the porch in the evenings, though the nights were so cool and lovely they called you to be out and under the winking stars. We kept to the house, and father insisted on having the lamps well shaded and he polished his rifle and hung it, ready loaded, on a couple of nails by the kitchen door.

All this caution failed to make sense to me. So at dinner about a week later I asked: "Is

there something new that's wrong? That stuff about Fletcher is finished, isn't it?"

"Finished?" said Shane, looking at me over his coffee cup. "Bobby boy, it's only begun."

"That's right," said father. "Fletcher's gone too far to back out now. It's a case of now or never with him. If he can make us run, he'll be setting pretty for a long stretch. If he can't, it'll be only a matter o' time before he's shoved smack out of this valley. There's three or four of the men who looked through here last year ready right now to sharpen stakes and move in soon as they think it's safe. I'll bet Fletcher feels he got ahold of a bear by the tail and it'd be nice to be able to let go."

"Why doesn't he do something, then?" I asked. "Seems to me mighty quiet around here lately."

"Seems to you, eh?" said father. "Seems to me you're mighty young to be doing much seemsing. Don't you worry, son. Fletcher is fixing to do something. The grass that grows under his feet won't feed any cow. I'd be easier in my mind if I knew what he's up to."

"You see, Bob"—Shane was speaking to me the way I liked, as if maybe I was a man and could understand all he said—"by talking big and playing it rough, Fletcher has made this a straight win or lose deal. It's the same as if he'd kicked loose a stone that starts a rockslide and all he can do is hope to ride it down and hit bottom safe. Maybe he doesn't realize that yet. I think he does. And don't let things being quiet fool you. When there's noise, you know where to look and what's happening. When things are quiet, you've got to be most careful."

Mother sighed. She was looking at Shane's cheek where the cut was healing into a scar like a thin line running back from near the mouth corner. "I suppose you two are right. But does there have to be any more fighting?"

"Like the other night?" asked father. "No,

Marian. I don't think so. Fletcher knows better now."

"He knows better," Shane said, "because he knows it won't work. If he's the man I think he is, he's known that since the first time he sicced Chris on me. I doubt that was his move the other night. That was Morgan's. Fletcher'll be watching for some way that has more finesse—and will be more final."

"Hm-m-m," said father, a little surprised. "Some legal trick, eh?"

"Could be. If he can find one. If not—" Shane shrugged and gazed out the window. "There are other ways. You can't call a man like Fletcher on things like that. Depends on how far he's willing to go. But whatever he does, once he's ready, he'll do it speedy and sure."

"Hm-m-m," said father again. "Now you put it thataway, I see you're right. That's Fletcher's way. Bet you've bumped against someone like him before." When Shane did not answer, just kept staring out the window, he went on. "Wish I could be as patient about it as you. I don't like this waiting."

But we did not have to wait long. It was the next day, a Friday, when we were finishing supper, that Lew Johnson and Henry Shipstead brought us the news. Fletcher was back and he had not come back alone. There was another man with him.

Lew Johnson saw them as they got off the stage. He had a good chance to look the stranger over while they waited in front of the post for horses to be brought in from the ranch. Since it was beginning to get dark, he had not been able to make out the stranger's face too well. The light striking through the post window, however, was enough for him to see what kind of man he was.

He was tall, rather broad in the shoulders and slim in the waist. He carried himself with a sort of swagger. He had a mustache that he favored and his eyes, when Johnson saw them reflecting the light from the window, were cold and had a glitter that bothered Johnson.

This stranger was something of a dude about his clothes. Still, that did not mean anything. When he turned, the coat he wore matching his pants flapped open and Johnson could see what had been half-hidden before. He was carrying two guns, big capable forty-fives, in holsters hung fairly low and forward. Those holsters were pegged down at the tips with thin straps fastened around the man's legs. Johnson said he saw the tiny buckles when the light flashed on them.

Wilson was the man's name. That was what Fletcher called him when a cowboy rode up leading a couple of horses. A funny other name. Stark. Stark Wilson. And that was not all.

Lew Johnson was worried and went into Grafton's to find Will Atkey, who always knew more than anyone else about people apt to be coming along the road because he was constantly picking up information from the talk of men drifting in to the bar. Will would not believe it at first when Johnson told him the name. What would he be doing up here, Will kept saying. Then Will blurted out that this Wilson was a bad one, a killer. He was a gunfighter said to be just as good with either hand and as fast on the draw as the best of them. He came to Cheyenne from Kansas, Will claimed he had heard, with a reputation for killing three men there and nobody knew how many more down in the southwest territories where he used to be.

Lew Johnson was rattling on, adding details as he could think of them. Henry Shipstead was slumped in a chair by the stove. Father was frowning at his pipe, absently fishing in a pocket for a match. It was Shane who shut off Johnson with a suddenness that startled the rest of us. His voice was sharp and clear and it seemed to crackle in the air. You could feel him taking charge of that room and all of us in it.

"When did they hit town?"

"Last night."

"And you waited till now to tell it!" There was disgust in Shane's voice. "You're a farmer all right, Johnson. That's all you ever will be." He whirled on father. "Quick, Joe. Which one has the hottest head? Which one's the easiest to prod into being a fool? Torrey is it? Or Wright?"

"Ernie Wright," father said slowly.

"Get moving, Johnson. Get out there on your horse and make it to Wright's in a hurry. Bring him here. Pick up Torrey, too. But get Wright first."

"He'll have to go into town for that," Henry Shipstead said heavily. "We passed them both down the road riding in."

Shane jumped to his feet. Lew Johnson was shuffling reluctantly toward the door. Shane brushed him aside. He strode to the door himself, yanked it open, started out. He stopped, leaning forward and listening.

"Easy, man," Henry Shipstead was grumbling, "what's your hurry? We told them about Wilson. They'll stop here on their way back." His voice ceased. All of us could hear it now, a horse pounding up the road at full gallop.

Shane turned back into the room. "There's your answer," he said bitterly. He swung the nearest chair to the wall and sat down. The fire blazing in him a moment before was gone. He was withdrawn into his own thoughts, and they were dark and not pleasant.

We heard the horse sliding to a stop out front. The sound was so plain you could fairly see the forelegs bracing and the hooves digging into the ground. Frank Torrey burst into the doorway. His hat was gone, his hair blowing wild. His chest heaved like he had been running as hard as the horse. He put his hands on the doorposts to hold himself steady and his voice was a hoarse whisper, though he was trying to shout across the room at father.

"Ernie's shot! They've killed him!"

The words jerked us to our feet and we stood staring. All but Shane. He did not move. You might have thought he was not even interested in what Torrey had said.

Father was the one who took hold of the scene. "Come in, Frank," he said quietly. "I take it we're too late to help Ernie now. Sit down and talk and don't leave anything out." He led Frank Torrey to a chair and pushed him into it. He closed the door and returned to his own chair. He looked older and tired.

It took Frank Torrey quite a while to pull himself together and tell his story straight. He was frightened. The fear was bedded deep in him and he was ashamed of himself for it.

He and Ernie Wright, he told us, had been to the stage office asking for a parcel Ernie was expecting. They dropped into Grafton's for a freshener before starting back. Since things had been so quiet lately, they were not thinking of any trouble even though Fletcher and the new man, Stark Wilson, were in the poker game at the big table. But Fletcher and Wilson must have been watching for a chance like that. They chucked in their hands and came over to the bar.

Fletcher was nice and polite as could be, nodding to Torrey and singling out Ernie for talk. He said he was sorry about it, but he really needed the land Ernie had filed on. It was the right place to put up winter windshelters for the new herd he was bringing in soon. He knew Ernie had not proved up on it yet. Just the same, he was willing to pay a fair price.

"I'll give you three hundred dollars," he said, "and that's more than the lumber in your buildings will be worth to me."

Ernie had more than that of his money in the place already. He had turned Fletcher down three or four times before. He was mad, the way he always was when Fletcher started his smooth talk.

"No," he said shortly. "I'm not selling. Not now or ever."

Fletcher shrugged like he had done all he could and slipped a quick nod at Stark Wilson. This Wilson was half-smiling at Ernie. But his eyes, Frank Torrey said, had nothing like a smile in them.

"I'd change my mind if I were you," he said to Ernie. "That is, if you have a mind to change."

"Keep out of this," snapped Ernie. "It's none of your business."

"I see you haven't heard," Wilson said softly. "I'm Mr. Fletcher's new business agent. I'm handling his business affairs for him. His business with stubborn jackasses like you." Then he said what showed Fletcher had coaxed him to it. "You're a fool, Wright. But what can you expect from a breed?"

"That's a lie!" shouted Ernie. "My mother wasn't no Indian!"

"Why, you crossbred squatter," Wilson said, quick and sharp, "are you telling me I'm wrong?"

"I'm telling you you're a low-crawling liar!"

The silence that shut down over the saloon was so complete, Frank Torrey told us, that he could hear the ticking of the old alarm clock on the shelf behind the bar. Even Ernie, in the second his voice stopped, saw what he had done. But he was mad clear through and he glared at Wilson, his eyes reckless.

"So-o-o-o," said Wilson, satisfied now and stretching out the word with ominous softness. He flipped back his coat on the right side in front and the holster there was free with the gun grip ready for his hand.

"You'll back that, Wright. Or you'll crawl out of here on your belly."

Ernie moved out a step from the bar, his arms stiff at his sides. The anger in him held him erect as he beat down the terror tearing at him. He knew what this meant, but he met it straight. His hand was firm on his gun and pulling up when Wilson's first bullet hit him and staggered him. The second spun him half-way around and a faint froth appeared on his lips and all expression died from his face and he sagged to the floor.

While Frank Torrey was talking, Jim Lewis and a few minutes later Ed Howells had come in. Bad news travels fast and they seemed to know something was wrong. Perhaps they had heard that frantic galloping, the sound carrying far in the still night air. They were all in our kitchen now and they were more shaken and sober than I had ever seen them.

I was pressed close to mother, grateful for her arms around me. I noticed that she had little attention for the other men. She was watching Shane, bitter and silent across the room.

"So that's it," father said grimly. "We'll have to face it. We sell and at his price or he slips the leash on his hired killer. Did Wilson make a move toward you, Frank?"

"He looked at me." Simply recalling that made Torrey shiver through. "He looked at me and he said, 'Too bad, isn't it, mister, that Wright didn't change his mind?'"

"Then what?"

"I got out of there quick as I could and came here."

Jim Lewis had been fidgeting on his seat, more nervous every minute. Now he jumped up, almost shouting. "Joe! A man can't just go around shooting people!"

"Shut up, Jim," growled Henry Shipstead. "Don't you see the setup? Wilson badgered Ernie into getting himself in a spot where he had to go for his gun. Wilson can claim he shot in self-defense. He'll try the same thing on us."

"That's right, Jim," put in Lew Johnson. "Even if we tried to get a marshal in here, he couldn't hold Wilson. It was an even break and the faster man won is the way most people will figure it and plenty of them saw it. A marshal couldn't get here in time anyway."

"But we've got to stop it!" Lewis was really shouting now. "What chance have any of us got against Wilson? We're not gunmen. We're just a bunch of old cowhands and farmers. Call it anything you want. I call it murder."

"Yes!"

The word sliced through the room. Shane was up and his face was hard with the rock ridges running along his jaw. "Yes. It's murder. Trick it out as self-defense or with fancy words about an even break for a fair draw and it's still murder." He looked at father and the pain was deep in his eyes. But there was only contempt in his voice as he turned to the others.

"You five can crawl back in your burrows. You don't have to worry—yet. If the time comes, you can always sell and run. Fletcher won't bother with the likes of you now. He's going the limit and he knows the game. He picked Wright to make the play plain. That's done. Now he'll head straight for the one real man in this valley, the man who's held you here and will go on trying to hold you and keep for you what's yours as long as there's life in him. He's standing between you and Fletcher and Wilson this minute and you ought to be thankful that once in a while this country turns out a man like Joe Starrett."

And a man like Shane. . . . Were those words only in my mind or did I hear mother whisper them? She was looking at him and then at father and she was both frightened and proud at once. Father was fumbling with his pipe, packing it and making a fuss with it like it needed his whole attention.

The others stirred uneasily. They were reassured by what Shane said and yet shamed that they should be. And they did not like the way he said it.

"You seem to know a lot about that kind of dirty business," Ed Howells said, with maybe an edge of malice to his voice.

"I do."

Shane let the words lie there, plain and short and ugly. His face was stern and behind the hard front of his features was a sadness that fought to break through. But he stared levelly at Howells and it was the other man who dropped his eyes and turned away.

Father had his pipe going. "Maybe it's a lucky break for the rest of us," he said mildly, "that Shane here has been around a bit. He can call the cards for us plain. Ernie might still be alive, Johnson, if you had had the sense to tell us about Wilson right off. It's a good thing Ernie wasn't a family man." He turned to Shane. "How do you rate Fletcher now he's shown his hand?"

You could see that the chance to do something, even just to talk at the problem pressing us, eased the bitterness in Shane.

"He'll move in on Wright's place first thing tomorrow. He'll have a lot of men busy on this side of the river from now on, probably push some cattle around behind the homesteads, to keep the pressure plain on all of you. How quick he'll try you, Joe, depends on how he reads you. If he thinks you might crack, he'll wait and let knowing what happened to Wright work on you. If he really knows you, he'll not wait more than a day or two to make sure you've had time to think it over and then he'll grab the first chance to throw Wilson at you. He'll want it, like with Wright, in a public place where there'll be plenty of witnesses. If you don't give him a chance, he'll try to make one."

"Hm-m-m," father said soberly. "I was sure you'd give it to me straight and that rings right." He pulled on his pipe for a moment. "I reckon, boys, this will be a matter of waiting for the next few days. There's no immediate danger right off anyway. Grafton will take care of Ernie's body tonight. We can meet in town in the morning to fix him a funeral. After that, we'd better stay out of town and stick close home as much as possible. I'd suggest you all study on this and drop in again tomorrow night. Maybe we can figure out something. I'd like to see how the town's taking it before I make up my mind on anything."

They were ready to leave it at that. They were ready to leave it to father. They were decent men and good neighbors. But not a one of them, were the decision his, would have stood up to Fletcher now. They would stay as long as father was there. With him gone, Fletcher would have things his way. That was how they felt as they muttered their goodnights and bunched out to scatter up and down the road.

Father stood in the doorway and watched them go. When he came back to his chair, he walked slowly and he seemed haggard and worn. "Somebody will have to go to Ernie's place tomorrow," he said, "and gather up his things. He's got relatives somewhere in Iowa."

"No." There was finality in Shane's tone. "You'll not go near the place. Fletcher might be counting on that. Grafton can do it."

"But Ernie was my friend," father said simply.

"Ernie's past friendship. Your debt is to the living."

Father looked at Shane and this brought him again into the immediate moment and cheered him. He nodded assent and turned to mother, who was hurrying to argue with him.

"Don't you see, Joe? If you can stay away from any place where you might meet Fletcher and—and that Wilson, things will work out. He can't keep a man like Wilson in this little valley forever."

She was talking rapidly and I knew why. She was not really trying to convince father as much as she was trying to convince herself. Father knew it, too.

"No, Marian. A man can't crawl into a hole somewhere and hide like a rabbit. Not if he has any pride."

"All right, then. But can't you keep quiet and not let him ride you and drive you into any fight?"

"That won't work either." Father was grim, but he was better and facing up to it. "A man can stand for a lot of pushing if he has to. 'Specially when he has his reasons." His glance shifted briefly to me. "But there are some things a man can't take. Not if he's to go on living with himself."

I was startled as Shane suddenly sucked in his breath with a long breaking intake. He was battling something within him, that old hidden desperation, and his eyes were dark and tormented against the paleness of his face. He seemed unable to look at us. He strode to the door and went out. We heard his footsteps fading toward the barn.

I was startled now at father. His breath, too, was coming in long, broken sweeps. He was up and pacing back and forth. When he swung on mother and his voice battered at her, almost fierce in its intensity, I realized that he knew about the change in Shane and that the knowing had been cankering in him all the past weeks.

"That's the one thing I can't stand, Marian. What we're doing to him. What happens to me doesn't matter too much. I talk big and I don't belittle myself. But my weight in any kind of a scale won't match his and I know it. If I understood him then as I do now, I'd never have got him to stay on here. But I didn't figure Fletcher would go this far. Shane won his fight before ever he came riding into this valley. It's been tough enough on him already. Should we let him lose just because of us? Fletcher can have his way. We'll sell out and move on."

I was not thinking. I was only feeling. For some strange reason I was feeling Shane's fingers in my hair, gently rocking my head. I could not help what I was saying, shouting across the room. "Father! Shane wouldn't run away! He wouldn't run away from anything!"

Father stopped pacing, his eyes narrowed in surprise. He stared at me without really seeing me. He was listening to mother.

"Bob's right, Joe. We can't let Shane down." It was queer, hearing her say the same thing to father she had said to Shane, the same thing with only the name different. "He'd never forgive us if we ran away from this. That's what we'd be doing. This isn't just a case of bucking Fletcher any more. It isn't just a case of keeping a piece of ground Fletcher wants for his range. We've got to be the kind of people Shane thinks we are. Bob's right. He wouldn't run away from anything like that. And that's the reason we can't."

"Lookahere, Marian, you don't think I want to do any running? No. You know me better than that. It'd go against everything in me. But what's my fool pride and this place and any plans we've had alongside of a man like that?"

"I know, Joe. But you don't see far enough." They were both talking earnestly, not breaking in, hearing each other out and sort of groping to put their meaning plain. "I can't really explain it, Joe. But I just know that we're bound up in something bigger than any one of us, and that running away is the one thing that would be worse than whatever might happen to us. There wouldn't be anything real ahead for us, any of us, maybe even for Bob, all the rest of our lives."

"Humph," said father. "Torrey could do it. And Johnson. All the rest of them. And it wouldn't bother them too much."

"Joe! Joe Starrett! Are you trying to make me mad? I'm not talking about them. I'm talking about us."

"Hm-m-m," said father softly, musing like to himself. "The salt would be gone. There just wouldn't be any flavor. There wouldn't be much meaning left."

"Oh, Joe! Joe! That's what I've been trying to say. And I know this will work out some way. I don't know how. But it will, if we face it and stand up to it and have faith in each other. It'll work out. Because it's got to."

"That's a woman's reason, Marian. But you're part right anyway. We'll play this game through. It'll need careful watching and close figuring. But maybe we can wait Fletcher out and make him overplay his hand. The town won't take much to this Wilson deal. Men like that fellow Weir have minds of their own."

Father was more cheerful now that he was beginning to get his thoughts straightened out. He and mother talked low in the kitchen for a long time after they sent me to bed, and I lay in my little room and saw through the window the stars wheeling distantly in the far outer darkness until I fell asleep at last.

12

The morning sun brightened our house and everything in the world outside. We had a good breakfast, father and Shane taking their time because they had routed out early to get the chores done and were waiting to go to town. They saddled up presently and rode off, and I moped in front of the house, not able to settle to any kind of playing.

After she bustled through the dishes, mother saw me standing and staring down the road and called me to the porch. She got our tattered old parchesi[1] board and she kept me

1. **parchesi** (pär-chē′zē): a game for two players, in which the moves are determined by throws of the dice.

humping to beat her. She was a grand one for games like that. She would be as excited as a kid, squealing at the big numbers and doubles and counting proudly out loud as she moved her markers ahead.

When I had won three games running, she put the board away and brought out two fat apples and my favorite of the books she had from the time she taught school. Munching on her apple, she read to me and before I knew it the shadows were mighty short and she had to skip in to get dinner and father and Shane were riding up to the barn.

They came in while she was putting the food on the table. We sat down and it was almost like a holiday, not just because it was not a work day, but because the grown folks were talking lightly, were determined not to let this Fletcher business spoil our good times. Father was pleased at what had happened in town.

"Yes, sir," he was saying as we were finishing dinner. "Ernie had a right good funeral. He would have appreciated it. Grafton made a nice speech and, by Godfrey, I believe he meant it. That fellow Weir had his clerk put together a really fine coffin. Wouldn't take a cent for it. And Sims over at the mine is knocking out a good stone. He wouldn't take a cent either. I was surprised at the crowd, too. Not a good word for Fletcher among them. And there must have been thirty people there."

"Thirty-four," said Shane. "I counted 'em. They weren't just paying their respects to Wright, Marian. That wouldn't have brought in some of those I checked. They were showing their opinion of a certain man named Starrett, who made a pretty fair speech himself. This husband of yours is becoming quite a respected citizen in these parts. Soon as the town gets grown up and organized, he's likely to start going places. Give him time and he'll be mayor."

Mother caught her breath with a little sob.

"Give . . . him . . . time," she said slowly. She looked at Shane and there was panic in her eyes. The lightness was gone and before anyone could say more, we heard the horses turning into our yard.

I dashed to the window to peer out. It struck me strange that Shane, usually so alert, was not there ahead of me. Instead he pushed back his chair and spoke gently, still sitting in it. "That will be Fletcher, Joe. He's heard how the town is taking this and knows he has to move fast. You take it easy. He's playing against time now, but he won't push anything here."

Father nodded at Shane and went to the door. He had taken off his gunbelt when he came in and now passed it to lift the rifle from its nails on the wall. Holding it in his right hand, barrel down, he opened the door and stepped out on the porch, clear to the front edge. Shane followed quietly and leaned in the doorway, relaxed and watchful. Mother was beside me at the window, staring out, crumpling her apron in her hand.

There were four of them, Fletcher and Wilson in the lead, two cowboys tagging. They had pulled up about twenty feet from the porch. This was the first time I had seen Fletcher for nearly a year. He was a tall man who must once have been a handsome figure in the fine clothes he always wore and with his arrogant air and his finely chiseled face set off by his short-cropped black beard and brilliant eyes.

Now a heaviness was setting in about his features and a fatty softness was beginning to show in his body. His face had a shrewd cast and a kind of reckless determination was on him that I did not remember ever noticing before.

Stark Wilson, for all the dude look Frank Torrey had mentioned, seemed lean and fit. He was sitting idly in his saddle, but the pose did not fool you. He was wearing no coat and the two guns were swinging free. He was sure of himself, serene and deadly. The curl of his lip beneath his mustache was a combination of confidence in himself and contempt for us.

Fletcher was smiling and affable. He was certain he held the cards and was going to deal them as he wanted. "Sorry to bother you, Starrett, so soon after that unfortunate affair last night. I wish it could have been avoided. I really do. Shooting is so unnecessary in these things, if only people would show sense. But Wright never should have called Mr. Wilson here a liar. That was a mistake."

"It was," father said curtly. "But then Ernie always did believe in telling the truth." I could see Wilson stiffen and his lips tighten. Father did not look at him. "Speak your piece, Fletcher, and get off my land."

Fletcher was still smiling. "There's no call for us to quarrel, Starrett. What's done is done. Let's hope there's no need for anything like it to be done again. You've worked cattle on a big ranch and you can understand my position. I'll be wanting all the range I can get from now on. Even without that, I can't let a bunch of nesters keep coming in here and choke me off from my water rights."

"We've been over that before," father said. "You know where I stand. If you have more to say, speak up and be done with it."

"All right, Starrett. Here's my proposition. I like the way you do things. You've got some queer notions about the cattle business, but when you tackle a job, you take hold and do it thoroughly. You and that man of yours are a combination I could use. I want you on my side of the fence. I'm getting rid of Morgan and I want you to take over as foreman. From what I hear your man would make a top-rank driving trail boss. The spot's his. Since you've proved up on this place, I'll buy it from you. If you want to go on living here, that can be arranged. If you want to play around with that little herd of yours, that can be arranged too. But I want you working for me."

Father was surprised. He had not expected anything quite like this. He spoke softly to Shane behind him. He did not turn or look away from Fletcher, but his voice carried clearly.

"Can I call the turn for you, Shane?"

"Yes, Joe." Shane's voice was just as soft, but it, too, carried clearly and there was a little note of pride in it.

Father stood taller there on the edge of the porch. He stared straight at Fletcher. "And the others," he said slowly. "Johnson, Shipstead, and the rest. What about them?"

"They'll have to go."

Father did not hesitate. "No."

"I'll give you a thousand dollars for this place as it stands and that's my top offer."

"No."

The fury in Fletcher broke over his face and he started to turn in the saddle toward Wilson. He caught himself and forced again that shrewd smile. "There's no percentage in being hasty, Starrett. I'll boost the ante to twelve hundred. That's a lot better than what might happen if you stick to being stubborn. I'll not take an answer now. I'll give you till tonight to think it over. I'll be waiting at Grafton's to hear you talk sense."

He swung his horse and started away. The two cowboys turned to join him by the road. Wilson did not follow at once. He leaned forward in his saddle and drove a sneering look at father.

"Yes, Starrett. Think it over. You wouldn't like someone else to be enjoying this place of yours—and that woman there in the window."

He was lifting his reins with one hand to pull his horse around and suddenly he dropped them and froze to attention. It must have been what he saw in father's face. We could not see it, mother and I, because father's back was to us. But we could see his hand tightening on the rifle at his side.

"Don't, Joe!"

Shane was beside father. He slipped past, moving smooth and steady, down the steps and over to one side to come at Wilson on his right hand and stop not six feet from him. Wilson was puzzled and his right hand twitched and then was still as Shane stopped and as he saw that Shane carried no gun.

Shane looked up at him and Shane's voice flicked in a whiplash of contempt. "You talk like a man because of that flashy hardware you're wearing. Strip it away and you'd shrivel down to boy size."

The very daring of it held Wilson motionless for an instant and father's voice cut into it. "Shane! Stop it!"

The blackness faded from Wilson's face. He smiled grimly at Shane. "You do need someone to look after you." He whirled his horse and put it to a run to join Fletcher and the others in the road.

It was only then that I realized mother was gripping my shoulders so that they hurt. She dropped on a chair and held me to her. We could hear father and Shane on the porch.

"He'd have drilled you, Joe, before you could have brought the gun up and pumped in a shell."

"But you, you crazy fool!" Father was covering his feelings with a show of exasperation.

"You'd have made him plug you just so I'd have a chance to get him."

Mother jumped up. She pushed me aside. She flared at them from the doorway. "And both of you would have acted like fools just because he said that about me. I'll have you two know that if it's got to be done, I can take being insulted just as much as you can."

Peering around her, I saw them gaping at her in astonishment. "But, Marian," father objected mildly, coming to her. "What better reason could a man have?"

"Yes," said Shane gently. "What better reason?" He was not looking just at mother. He was looking at the two of them.

13

I do not know how long they would have stood there on the porch in the warmth of that moment. I shattered it by asking what seemed to me a simple question until after I had asked it and the significance hit me.

"Father, what are you going to tell Fletcher tonight?"

There was no answer. There was no need for one. I guess I was growing up. I knew what he would tell Fletcher. I knew what he would say. I knew, too, that because he was father he would have to go to Grafton's and say it. And I understood why they could no longer bear to look at one another, and the breeze blowing in from the sun-washed fields was suddenly so chill and cheerless.

They did not look at each other. They did not say a word to each other. Yet somehow I realized that they were closer together in the stillness there on the porch than they had ever been. They knew themselves and each of them knew that the other grasped the situation whole. They knew that Fletcher had dealt himself a winning hand, had caught father in the one play that he could not avoid because he would not avoid it. They knew that talk is meaningless when a common knowledge is already there. The silence bound them as no words ever could.

Father sat on the top porch step. He took out his pipe and drew on it as the match flamed and fixed his eyes on the horizon, on the mountains far across the river. Shane took the chair I had used for the games with mother. He swung it to the house wall and bent into it in that familiar unconscious gesture and he, too, looked into the distance. Mother turned into the kitchen and went about clearing the table as if she was not really aware of what she was doing. I helped her with the dishes and the old joy of sharing with her in the work was gone and there was no sound in the kitchen except the drop of the water and the chink of dish on dish.

When we were done, she went to father. She sat beside him on the step, her hand on the wood between them, and his covered hers and the moments merged in the slow, dwindling procession of time.

Loneliness gripped me. I wandered through the house, finding nothing there to do, and out on the porch and past those three and to the barn. I searched around and found an old shovel handle and started to whittle me a play saber with my knife. I had been thinking of this for days. Now the idea held no interest. The wood curls dropped to the barn floor, and after a while I let the shovel handle drop among them. Everything that had happened before seemed far off, almost like another existence. All that mattered was the length of the shadows creeping across the yard as the sun drove down the afternoon sky.

I took a hoe and went into mother's garden where the ground was caked around the turnips, the only things left unharvested. But there was scant work in me. I kept at it for a couple of rows, then the hoe dropped and I let it lie. I went to the front of the house, and there they were sitting, just as before.

I sat on the step below father and mother, between them, and their legs on each side of me made it seem better. I felt father's hand on my head.

"This is kind of tough on you, Bob." He could talk to me because I was only a kid. He was really talking to himself.

"I can't see the full finish. But I can see this. Wilson down and there'll be an end to it. Fletcher'll be done. The town will see to that. I can't beat Wilson on the draw. But there's strength enough in this clumsy body of mine to keep me on my feet till I get him, too." Mother stirred and was still, and his voice went on. "Things could be worse. It helps a man to know that if anything happens to him, his family will be in better hands than his own."

There was a sharp sound behind us on the porch. Shane had risen so swiftly that his chair had knocked against the wall. His hands were clenched tightly and his arms were quivering. His face was pale with the effort shaking him. He was desperate with an inner torment, his eyes tortured by thoughts that he could not escape, and the marks were obvious on him and he did not care. He strode to the steps, down past us and around the corner of the house.

Mother was up and after him, running headlong. She stopped abruptly at the house corner, clutching at the wood, panting and irresolute. Slowly she came back, her hands outstretched as if to keep from falling. She sank again on the step, close against father, and he gathered her to him with one great arm.

The silence spread and filled the whole valley and the shadows crept across the yard. They touched the road and began to merge in the deeper shading that meant the sun was dipping below the mountains far behind the house. Mother straightened, and as she stood up, father rose, too. He took hold of her two arms and held her in front of him. "I'm counting on you, Marian, to help him win again. You can do it, if anyone can." He smiled a strange little sad smile and he loomed up there above me the biggest man in all the world. "No supper for me now, Marian. A cup of your coffee is all I want." They passed through the doorway together.

Where was Shane? I hurried toward the barn. I was almost to it when I saw him out by the pasture. He was staring over it and the grazing steers at the great lonely mountains tipped with the gold of the sun now rushing down behind them. As I watched, he stretched his arms up, the fingers reaching to their utmost limits, grasping and grasping, it seemed, at the glory glowing in the sky.

He whirled and came straight back, striding with long steady steps, his head held high. There was some subtle, new, unchangeable certainty in him. He came close and I saw that his face was quiet and untroubled and that little lights danced in his eyes.

"Skip into the house, Bobby boy. Put on a smile. Everything is going to be all right." He was past me, without slowing, swinging into the barn.

But I could not go into the house. And I did not dare follow him, not after he had told me to go. A wild excitement was building up in me while I waited by the porch, watching the barn door.

The minutes ticked past and the twilight deepened and a patch of light sprang from the house as the lamp in the kitchen was lit. And still I waited. Then he was coming swiftly toward me and I stared and stared and broke and ran into the house with the blood pounding in my head.

"Father! Father! Shane's got his gun!"

He was close back of me. Father and mother barely had time to look up from the table before he was framed in the doorway. He was dressed as he was that first day when he rode into our lives, in that dark and worn magnificence from the black hat with its wide curling brim to the soft black boots. But what caught your eye was the single flash of white, the outer ivory plate on the grip of the gun, showing sharp and distinct against the dark material of the trousers. The tooled cartridge belt nestled around him, riding above the hip on the left, sweeping down on the right to hold the holster snug along the thigh, just as he had said, the gun handle about halfway between the wrist and elbow of his right arm hanging there relaxed and ready.

Belt and holster and gun . . . These were no things he was wearing or carrying. They were part of him, part of the man, of the full sum of the integrate[1] force that was Shane. You could see now that for the first time this man who had been living with us, who was one of us, was complete, was himself in the final effect of his being.

Now that he was no longer in his crude work clothes, he seemed again slender, almost slight, as he did that first day. The change was more than that. What had been seeming iron was again steel. The slenderness was that of a tempered blade and a razor edge was there. Slim and dark in the doorway, he seemed somehow to fill the whole frame.

This was not our Shane. And yet it was. I remembered Ed Howells' saying that this was the most dangerous man he had ever seen. I remembered in the same rush that father had said he was the safest man we ever had in our house. I realized that both were right and that this, this at last, was Shane.

He was in the room now and he was speaking to them both in that bantering tone he used

---

1. **integrate** (ĭn′tĕ-grāt): whole or complete.

to have only for mother. "A fine pair of parents you are. Haven't even fed Bob yet. Stack him full of a good supper. Yourselves, too. I have a little business to tend to in town."

Father was looking fixedly at him. The sudden hope that had sprung in his face had as quickly gone. "No, Shane. It won't do. Even your thinking of it is the finest thing any man ever did for me. But I won't let you. It's my stand. Fletcher's making his play against me. There's no dodging. It's my business."

"There's where you're wrong, Joe," Shane said gently. "This is my business. My kind of business. I've had fun being a farmer. You've shown me new meaning in the word, and I'm proud that for a while maybe I qualified. But there are a few things a farmer can't handle."

The strain of the long afternoon was telling on father. He pushed up from the table. "Great Godfrey, Shane, be sensible. Don't make it harder for me. You can't do this."

Shane stepped near, to the side of the table, facing father across a corner. "Easy does it, Joe. I'm making this my business."

"No. I won't let you. Suppose you do put Wilson out of the way. That won't finish anything. It'll only even the score and swing things back worse than ever. Think what it'll mean to you. And where will it leave me? I couldn't hold my head up around here any more. They'd say I ducked and they'd be right. You can't do it and that's that."

"No?" Shane's voice was even more gentle, but it had a quiet, inflexible quality that had never been there before. "There's no man living can tell me what I can't do. Not even you, Joe. You forget there is still a way."

He was talking to hold father's attention. As he spoke the gun was in his hand and before father could move he swung it, swift and sharp, so the barrel lined flush along the side of father's head, back of the temple, above the ear. Strength was in the blow and it thudded dully on the bone and father folded over the table and as it tipped with his weight slid toward the floor. Shane's arm was under him before he hit and Shane pivoted father's loose body up into his chair and righted the table while the coffee cups rattled on the floor boards. Father's head lolled back and Shane caught it and eased it and the big shoulders forward till they rested on the table, the face down and cradled in the limp arms.

Shane stood erect and looked across the table at mother. She had not moved since he appeared in the doorway, not even when father fell and the table teetered under her hands on its edge. She was watching Shane, her throat curving in a lovely proud line, her eyes wide with a sweet warmth shining in them.

Darkness had shut down over the valley as they looked at each other across the table and the only light now was from the lamp swinging ever so slightly above them, circling them with its steady glow. They were alone in a moment that was all their own. Yet, when they spoke, it was of father.

"I was afraid," Shane murmured, "that he would take it that way. He couldn't do otherwise and be Joe Starrett."

"I know."

"He'll rest easy and come out maybe a little groggy but all right. Tell him, Marian. Tell him no man need be ashamed of being beat by Shane."

The name sounded queer like that, the man speaking of himself. It was the closest he ever came to boasting. And then you understood that there was not the least hint of a boast. He was stating a fact, simple and elemental as the power that dwelled in him.

"I know," she said again. "I don't need to tell him. He knows, too." She was rising, earnest and intent. "But there is something else I must know. We have battered down words that might have been spoken between us and that was as it should be. But I have a right to know now. I am part of this, too. And what I do depends on what you tell me now. Are you doing this just for me?"

Shane hesitated for a long, long moment. "No, Marian." His gaze seemed to widen and encompass us all, mother and the still figure of father and me huddled on a chair by the window, and somehow the room and the house and the whole place. Then he was looking only at mother and she was all that he could see.

"No, Marian. Could I separate you in my mind and afterwards be a man?"

He pulled his eyes from her and stared into the night beyond the open door. His face hardened, his thoughts leaping to what lay ahead in town. So quiet and easy you were scarce aware that he was moving, he was gone into the outer darkness.

14

Nothing could have kept me there in the house that night. My mind held nothing but the driving desire to follow Shane. I waited, hardly daring to breathe, while mother watched him go. I waited until she turned to father, bending over him, then I slipped around the doorpost out to the porch. I thought for a moment she had noticed me, but I could not be sure and she did not call to me. I went softly down the steps and into the freedom of the night.

Shane was nowhere in sight. I stayed in the darker shadows, looking about, and at last I saw him emerging once more from the barn. The moon was rising low over the mountains, a clean, bright crescent. Its light was enough for me to see him plainly in outline. He was

carrying his saddle and a sudden pain stabbed through me as I saw that with it was his saddle-roll. He went toward the pasture gate, not slow, not fast, just firm and steady. There was a catlike certainty in his every movement, a silent, inevitable[1] deadliness. I heard him, there by the gate, give his low whistle and the horse came out of the shadows at the far end of the pasture, its hooves making no noise in the deep grass, a dark and powerful shape etched in the moonlight drifting across the field straight to the man.

I knew what I would have to do. I crept along the corral fence, keeping tight to it, until I reached the road. As soon as I was around the corner of the corral with it and the barn between me and the pasture, I started to run as rapidly as I could toward town, my feet plumping softly in the thick dust of the road. I walked this every school day and it had never seemed long before. Now the distance stretched ahead, lengthening in my mind as if to mock me.

I could not let him see me. I kept looking back over my shoulder as I ran. When I saw him swinging into the road, I was well past Johnson's, almost past Shipstead's, striking into the last open stretch to the edge of town. I scurried to the side of the road and behind a clump of bulberry bushes. Panting to get my breath, I crouched there and waited for him to pass. The hoofbeats swelled in my ears, mingled with the pounding beat of my own blood. In my imagination he was galloping furiously and I was positive he was already rushing past me. But when I parted the bushes and pushed forward to peer out, he was moving at a moderate pace and was only almost abreast of me.

He was tall and terrible there in the road, looming up gigantic in the mystic half-light. He was the man I saw that first day, a stranger, dark and forbidding, forging his lone way out of an unknown past in the utter loneliness of his own immovable and instinctive defiance. He was the symbol of all the dim, formless imaginings of danger and terror in the untested realm of human potentialities beyond my understanding. The impact of the menace that marked him was like a physical blow.

I could not help it. I cried out and stumbled and fell. He was off his horse and over me before I could right myself, picking me up, his grasp strong and reassuring. I looked at him, tearful and afraid, and the fear faded from me. He was no stranger. That was some trick of the shadows. He was Shane. He was shaking me gently and smiling at me.

"Bobby boy, this is no time for you to be out. Skip along home and help your mother. I told you everything would be all right."

He let go of me and turned slowly, gazing out across the far sweep of the valley silvered in the moon's glow. "Look at it, Bob. Hold it in your mind like this. It's a lovely land, Bob. A good place to be a boy and grow straight inside as a man should."

My gaze followed his, and I saw our valley as though for the first time and the emotion in me was more than I could stand. I choked and reached out for him and he was not there.

He was rising into the saddle and the two shapes, the man and the horse, became one and moved down the road toward the yellow squares that were the patches of light from the windows of Grafton's building a quarter of a mile away. I wavered a moment, but the call was too strong. I started after him, running frantic in the middle of the road.

Whether he heard me or not, he kept right on. There were several men on the long porch of the building by the saloon doors. Red Marlin's hair made him easy to spot. They were scanning the road intently. As Shane hit the panel of light from the near big front window, the store window, they stiffened to attention.

---

1. **inevitable** (ĭn-ĕv′ə-tə-bəl): unable to be avoided.

Red Marlin, a startled expression on his face, dived quickly through the doors.

Shane stopped, not by the rail but by the steps on the store side. When he dismounted, he did not slip the reins over the horse's head as the cowboys always did. He left them looped over the pommel of the saddle and the horse seemed to know what this meant. It stood motionless, close by the steps, head up, waiting, ready for whatever swift need.

Shane went along the porch and halted briefly, fronting the two men still there.

"Where's Fletcher?"

They looked at each other and at Shane. One of them started to speak. "He doesn't want—" Shane's voice stopped him. It slapped at them, low and with an edge that cut right into your mind. "Where's Fletcher?"

One of them jerked a hand toward the doors and then, as they moved to shift out of his way, his voice caught them.

"Get inside. Go clear to the bar before you turn."

They stared at him and stirred uneasily and swung together to push through the doors. As the doors came back, Shane grabbed them, one with each hand, and pulled them out and wide open and he disappeared between them.

Clumsy and tripping in my haste, I scrambled up the steps and into the store. Sam Grafton and Mr. Weir were the only persons there and they were both hurrying to the entrance to the saloon, so intent that they failed to notice me. They stopped in the opening. I crept behind them to my familiar perch on my box where I could see past them.

The big room was crowded. Almost everyone who could be seen regularly around town was there, everyone but our homestead neighbors. There were many others who were new to me. They were lined up elbow to elbow nearly the entire length of the bar. The tables were full and more men were lounging along the far wall. The big round poker table at the back between the stairway to the little balcony and the door to Grafton's office was littered with glasses and chips. It seemed strange, for all the men standing, that there should be an empty chair at the far curve of the table. Someone must have been in that chair, because chips were at the place and a half-smoked cigar, a whisp of smoke curling up from it, was by them on the table.

Red Marlin was leaning against the back wall, behind the chair. As I looked, he saw the smoke and appeared to start a little. With a careful show of casualness he slid into the chair and picked up the cigar.

A haze of thinning smoke was by the ceiling over them all, floating in involved streamers around the hanging lamps. This was Grafton's saloon in the flush of a banner evening's business. But something was wrong, was missing. The hum of activity, the whirr of voices, that should have risen from the scene, been part of it, was stilled in a hush more impressive than any noise could be. The attention of everyone in the room, like a single sense, was centered on that dark figure just inside the swinging doors, back to them and touching them.

This was the Shane of the adventures I had dreamed for him, cool and competent, facing that room full of men in the simple solitude of his own invincible completeness.

His eyes searched the room. They halted on a man sitting at a small table in the front corner with his hat on low over his forehead. With a thump of surprise I recognized it was Stark Wilson and he was studying Shane with a puzzled look on his face. Shane's eyes swept on, checking off each person. They stopped again on a figure over by the wall and the beginnings of a smile showed in them and he nodded almost imperceptibly. It was Chris, tall and lanky, his arm in a sling, and as he caught the nod he flushed a little and shifted his weight from one foot to the other. Then he straightened his shoulders and over his face came a slow smile, warm and friendly, the smile of a man who knows his own mind at last.

But Shane's eyes were already moving on. They narrowed as they rested on Red Marlin. Then they jumped to Will Atkey trying to make himself small behind the bar.

"Where's Fletcher?"

Will fumbled with the cloth in his hands. "I—I don't know. He was here awhile ago." Frightened at the sound of his own voice in the stillness, Will dropped the cloth, started to stoop for it, and checked himself, putting his hands to the inside rim of the bar to hold himself steady.

Shane tilted his head slightly so his eyes could clear his hatbrim. He was scanning the balcony across the rear of the room. It was empty and the doors there were closed. He stepped forward, disregarding the men by the bar, and walked quietly past them the long length of the room. He went through the doorway to Grafton's office and into the semidarkness beyond.

And still the hush held. Then he was in the office doorway again and his eyes bored toward Red Marlin.

"Where's Fletcher?"

The silence was taut and unendurable. It had to break. The sound was that of Stark Wilson coming to his feet in the far front corner. His voice, lazy and insolent, floated down the room.

"Where's Starrett?"

While the words yet seemed to hang in the air, Shane was moving toward the front of the room. But Wilson was moving, too. He was crossing toward the swinging doors and he took his stand just to the left of them, a few feet out from the wall. The position gave him command of the wide aisle running back between the bar and the tables and Shane coming forward in it.

Shane stopped about three quarters of the way forward, about five yards from Wilson. He cocked his head for one quick sidewise glance again at the balcony and then he was looking only at Wilson. He did not like the setup. Wilson had the front wall and he was left in the open of the room. He understood the fact, assessed it, accepted it.

They faced each other in the aisle and the men along the bar jostled one another in their hurry to get to the opposite side of the room. A reckless arrogance was on Wilson, certain of himself and his control of the situation. He was not one to miss the significance of the slim deadliness that was Shane. But even now, I think, he did not believe that anyone in our valley would deliberately stand up to him.

"Where's Starrett?" he said once more, still mocking Shane but making it this time a real question.

The words went past Shane as if they had not been spoken. "I had a few things to say to Fletcher," he said gently. "That can wait. You're a pushing man, Wilson, so I reckon I had better accommodate you."

Wilson's face sobered and his eyes glinted coldly. "I've no quarrel with you," he said flatly, "even if you are Starrett's man. Walk out of here without any fuss and I'll let you go. It's Starrett I want."

"What you want, Wilson, and what you'll get are two different things. Your killing days are done."

Wilson had it now. You could see him grasp the meaning. This quiet man was pushing him just as he had pushed Ernie Wright. As he measured Shane, it was not to his liking. Something that was not fear but a kind of wondering and baffled reluctance showed in his face. And then there was no escape, for that gentle voice was pegging him to the immediate and implacable[2] moment.

"I'm waiting, Wilson. Do I have to crowd you into slapping leather?"

Time stopped and there was nothing in all the world but two men looking into eternity in each other's eyes. And the room rocked in the sudden blur of action indistinct in its incredible swiftness and the roar of their guns was a single sustained blast. And Shane stood, solid on his feet as a rooted oak, and Wilson swayed, his right arm hanging useless, blood beginning to show in a small stream from under the sleeve over the hand, the gun slipping from the numbing fingers.

He backed against the wall, a bitter disbelief twisting his features. His left arm hooked and the second gun was showing and Shane's bullet smashed into his chest and his knees buckled, sliding him slowly down the wall till the lifeless weight of the body toppled it sideways to the floor.

Shane gazed across the space between and he seemed to have forgotten all else as he let his gun ease into the holster. "I gave him his chance," he murmured out of the depths of a great sadness. But the words had no meaning for me, because I noticed on the dark brown of his shirt, low and just above the belt to one side of the buckle, the darker spot gradually widening. Then others noticed, too, and there was a stir in the air and the room was coming to life.

Voices were starting, but no one focused on them. They were snapped short by the roar of a shot from the rear of the room. A wind seemed to whip Shane's shirt at the shoulder and the glass of the front window beyond shattered near the bottom.

Then I saw it.

It was mine alone. The others were turning to stare at the back of the room. My eyes were fixed on Shane and I saw it. I saw the whole man move, all of him, in the single flashing instant. I saw the head lead and the body swing and the driving power of the legs beneath. I saw the arm leap and the hand take the gun in the lightning sweep. I saw the barrel line up like—like a finger pointing—and the flame spurt even as the man himself was still in motion.

And there on the balcony Fletcher, impaled[3] in the act of aiming for a second shot, rocked on his heels and fell back into the open doorway behind him. He clawed at the jambs and pulled himself forward. He staggered to the rail and tried to raise the gun. But the strength was draining out of him and he collapsed over the rail, jarring it loose and falling with it.

Across the stunned and barren silence of the room Shane's voice seemed to come from a great distance. "I expect that finishes it," he said. Unconsciously, without looking down, he broke out the cylinder of his gun and reloaded it. The stain on his shirt was bigger now, spreading fanlike above the belt, but he did not appear to know or care. Only his movements were slow, retarded by an unutterable weariness. The hands were sure and steady, but they moved slowly and the gun dropped into the holster of its own weight.

He backed with dragging steps toward the swinging doors until his shoulders touched them. The light in his eyes was unsteady like the flickering of a candle guttering toward darkness. And then, as he stood there, a strange thing happened.

How could one describe it, the change that came over him? Out of the mysterious resources of his will the vitality came. It came creeping, a tide of strength that crept through him and fought and shook off the weakness. It

2. **implacable** (ĭm-plā′-kə-bəl): unable to be stopped or changed.

3. **impaled** (ĭm-pāld′): caught helplessly, as if pierced through by a stake.

shone in his eyes and they were alive again and alert. It welled up in him, sending that familiar power surging through him again until it was singing again in every vibrant line of him.

He faced that room full of men and read them all with the one sweeping glance and spoke to them in that gentle voice with that quiet, inflexible quality.

"I'll be riding on now. And there's not a one of you that will follow."

He turned his back on them in the indifference of absolute knowledge they would do as he said. Straight and superb, he was silhouetted against the doors and the patch of night above them. The next moment they were closing with a soft swish of sound.

The room was crowded with action now. Men were clustering around the bodies of Wilson and Fletcher, pressing to the bar, talking excitedly. Not a one of them, though, approached too close to the doors. There was a cleared space by the doorway as if someone had drawn a line marking it off.

I did not care what they were doing or what they were saying. I had to get to Shane. I had to get to him in time. I had to know, and he was the only one who could ever tell me.

I dashed out the store door and I was in time. He was on his horse, already starting away from the steps.

"Shane," I whispered desperately, loud as I dared without the men inside hearing me. "Oh, Shane!"

He heard me and reined around and I hurried to him, standing by a stirrup and looking up.

"Bobby! Bobby boy! What are you doing here?"

"I've been here all along," I blurted out. "You've got to tell me. Was that Wilson—"

He knew what was troubling me. He always knew. "Wilson," he said, "was mighty fast. As fast as I've ever seen."

"I don't care," I said, the tears starting. "I don't care if he was the fastest that ever was. He'd never have been able to shoot you, would he? You'd have got him straight, wouldn't you—if you had been in practice?"

He hesitated a moment. He gazed down at me and into me and he knew. He knew what goes on in a boy's mind and what can help him stay clean inside through the muddled, dirtied years of growing up.

"Sure. Sure, Bob. He'd never even have cleared the holster."

He started to bend down toward me, his hand reaching for my head. But the pain struck him like a whiplash and the hand jumped to his shirt front by the belt, pressing hard, and he reeled a little in the saddle.

The ache in me was more than I could bear. I stared dumbly at him, and because I was just a boy and helpless I turned away and hid my face against the firm, warm flank of the horse.

"Bob."

"Yes, Shane."

"A man is what he is, Bob, and there's no breaking the mold. I tried that and I've lost. But I reckon it was in the cards from the moment I saw a freckled kid on a rail up the road there and a real man behind him, the kind that could back him for the chance another kid never had."

"But—but, Shane, you—"

"There's no going back from a killing, Bob. Right or wrong, the brand sticks and there's no going back. It's up to you now. Go home to your mother and father. Grow strong and straight and take care of them. Both of them."

"Yes, Shane."

"There's only one thing more I can do for them now."

I felt the horse move away from me. Shane was looking down the road and on to the open plain and the horse was obeying the silent command of the reins. He was riding away and I knew that no word or thought could hold him. The big horse, patient and powerful, was already settling into the steady pace that had brought him into our valley, and the two, the man and the horse, were a single dark shape in the road as they passed beyond the reach of the light from the windows.

I strained my eyes after him, and then in the moonlight I could make out the inalienable outline of his figure[4] receding into the distance. Lost in my loneliness, I watched him go, out of town, far down the road where it curved out to the level country beyond the valley. There were men on the porch behind me, but I was aware only of that dark shape growing small and indistinct along the far reach of the road. A cloud passed over the moon and he merged into the general shadow and I could not see him and the cloud passed on and the road was a plain thin ribbon to the horizon and he was gone.

I stumbled back to fall on the steps, my head in my arms to hide the tears. The voices of the men around me were meaningless noises in a bleak and empty world. It was Mr. Weir who took me home.

15

Father and mother were in the kitchen, almost as I had left them. Mother had hitched her chair close to father's. He was sitting up, his face tired and haggard, the ugly red mark standing out plain along the side of his head. They did not come to meet us. They sat still and watched us move into the doorway.

4. **inalienable** (īn-āl′yə-nə-bəl) **. . . figure:** In other words, the figure clearly belongs to Shane and to no one else.

They did not even scold me. Mother reached and pulled me to her and let me crawl into her lap as I had not done for three years or more. Father just stared at Mr. Weir. He could not trust himself to speak first.

"Your troubles are over, Starrett."

Father nodded. "You've come to tell me," he said wearily, "that he killed Wilson before they got him. I know. He was Shane."

"Wilson," said Mr. Weir. "And Fletcher."

Father started. "Fletcher, too? By Godfrey, yes. He would do it right." Then father sighed and ran a finger along the bruise on his head. "He let me know this was one thing he wanted to handle by himself. I can tell you, Weir, waiting here is the hardest job I ever had."

Mr. Weir looked at the bruise. "I thought so. Listen, Starrett. There's not a man in town doesn't know you didn't stay here of your own will. And there's mighty few that aren't glad it was Shane came into the saloon tonight."

The words broke from me. "You should have seen him, father. He was—he was—" I could not find it at first. "He was—beautiful, father. And Wilson wouldn't even have hit him if he'd been in practice. He told me so."

"He told you!" The table was banging over as father drove to his feet. He grabbed Mr. Weir by the coat front. "My God, man! Why didn't you tell me? He's alive?"

"Yes," said Mr. Weir. "He's alive all right. Wilson got to him. But no bullet can kill that man." A puzzled, faraway sort of look flitted across Mr. Weir's face. "Sometimes I wonder whether anything ever could."

Father was shaking him. "Where is he?"

"He's gone," said Mr. Weir. "He's gone, alone and unfollowed as he wanted it. Out of the valley and no one knows where."

Father's hands dropped. He slumped again into his chair. He picked up his pipe and it broke in his fingers. He let the pieces fall and stared at them on the floor. He was still staring at them when new footsteps sounded on the porch and a man pushed into our kitchen.

It was Chris. His right arm was tight in the sling, his eyes unnaturally bright and the color high in his face. In his left hand he was carrying a bottle, a bottle of red cherry soda pop. He came straight in and righted the table with the hand holding the bottle. He smacked the bottle on the top boards and seemed startled at the noise he made. He was embarrassed and he was having trouble with his voice. But he spoke up firmly.

"I brought that for Bob. I'm a poor substitute, Starrett. But as soon as this arm's healed, I'm asking you to let me work for you."

Father's face twisted and his lips moved, but no words came. Mother was the one who said it. "Shane would like that, Chris."

And still father said nothing. What Chris and Mr. Weir saw as they looked at him must have shown them that nothing they could do or say would help at all. They turned and went out together, walking with long, quick steps.

Mother and I sat there watching father. There was nothing we could do either. This was something he had to wrestle alone. He was so still that he seemed even to have stopped breathing. Then a sudden restlessness hit him and he was up and pacing aimlessly about. He glared at the walls as if they stifled him and strode out of the door into the yard. We heard his steps around the house and heading into the fields and then we could hear nothing.

I do not know how long we sat there. I know that the wick in the lamp burned low and sputtered awhile and went out and the darkness was a relief and a comfort. At last mother rose, still holding me, the big boy bulk of me, in her arms. I was surprised at the strength in her. She was holding me tightly to her and she carried me into my little room and helped me undress in the dim shadows of the moonlight through the window. She tucked me in and sat on the edge of the bed, and then, only then, she whispered to me: "Now, Bob. Tell me everything. Just as you saw it happen."

I told her, and when I was done, all she said in a soft little murmur was "Thank you." She looked out the window and murmured the words again and they were not for me and she was still looking out over the land to the great gray mountains when finally I fell asleep.

She must have been there the whole night through, for when I woke with a start, the first streaks of dawn were showing through the window and the bed was warm where she had been. The movement of her leaving must have wakened me. I crept out of bed and peeked into the kitchen. She was standing in the open outside doorway.

I fumbled into my clothes and tiptoed through the kitchen to her. She took my hand and I clung to hers and it was right that we should be together and that together we should go find father.

We found him out by the corral, by the far end where Shane had added to it. The sun was beginning to rise through the cleft in the mountains across the river, not the brilliant glory of midday but the fresh and renewed reddish radiance of early morning. Father's arms were folded on the top rail, his head bowed on them. When he turned to face us, he leaned back against the rail as if he needed the support. His eyes were rimmed and a little wild.

"Marian, I'm sick of the sight of this valley and all that's in it. If I tried to stay here now, my heart wouldn't be in it any more. I know it's hard on you and the boy, but we'll have to pull up stakes and move on. Montana, maybe. I've heard there's good land for the claiming up that way."

Mother heard him through. She had let go my hand and stood erect, so angry that her eyes snapped and her chin quivered. But she heard him through.

"Joe! Joe Starrett!" Her voice fairly crackled and was rich with emotion that was more than anger. "So you'd run out on Shane just when he's really here to stay!"

"But, Marian. You don't understand. He's gone."

"He's not gone. He's here, in this place, in this place he gave us. He's all around us and in us, and he always will be."

She ran to the tall corner post, to the one Shane had set. She beat at it with her hands. "Here, Joe. Quick. Take hold. Pull it down."

Father stared at her in amazement. But he did as she said. No one could have denied her in that moment. He took hold of the post and pulled at it. He shook his head and braced his feet and strained at it with all his strength. The big muscles of his shoulders and back knotted and bulged till I thought this shirt, too, would shred. Creakings ran along the rails and the post moved ever so slightly and the ground at the base showed little cracks fanning out. But the rails held and the post stood.

Father turned from it, beads of sweat breaking on his face, a light creeping up his drawn cheeks.

"See, Joe. See what I mean. We have roots here now that we can never tear loose."

And the morning was in father's face, shining in his eyes, giving him new color and hope and understanding.

16

I guess that is all there is to tell. The folks in town and the kids at school liked to talk about Shane, to spin tales and speculate about him. I never did. Those nights at Grafton's became legends in the valley and countless details were added as they grew and spread just as the town, too, grew and spread up the river banks. But I never bothered, no matter how strange the tales became in the constant retelling. He belonged to me, to father and mother and me, and nothing could ever spoil that.

For mother was right. He was there. He was there in our place and in us. Whenever I needed him, he was there. I could close my eyes and he would be with me and I would see him plain and hear again that gentle voice.

I would think of him in each of the moments that revealed him to me. I would think of him most vividly in that single flashing instant when he whirled to shoot Fletcher on the balcony at Grafton's saloon. I would see again the power and grace of a coordinate force beautiful beyond comprehension. I would see the man and the weapon wedded in the one indivisible deadliness. I would see the man and the tool, a good man and a good tool, doing what had to be done.

And always my mind would go back at the last to that moment when I saw him from the bushes by the roadside just on the edge of town. I would see him there in the road, tall and terrible in the moonlight, going down to kill or be killed, and stopping to help a stumbling boy and to look out over the land, the lovely land, where that boy had a chance to live out his boyhood and grow straight inside as a man should.

And when I would hear the men in town talking among themselves and trying to pin him down to a definite past, I would smile quietly to myself. For a time they inclined to the notion, spurred by the talk of a passing stranger, that he was a certain Shannon who was famous as a gunman and gambler way down in Arkansas and Texas and dropped from sight without anyone knowing why or where. When that notion dwindled, others followed, pieced together in turn from scraps of information gleaned from stray travelers. But when they talked like that, I simply smiled because I knew he could have been none of these.

He was the man who rode into our little valley out of the heart of the great glowing West and when his work was done rode back whence he had come and he was Shane.

Reading Check

1. What happens to Shane when he and the Starretts go into town to Grafton's store on Saturday evening?

2. Whom does Fletcher bring back with him on the stagecoach?

3. According to Shane, why do the homesteaders make a point of attending Ernie Wright's funeral?

4. When Fletcher comes to talk to Joe about buying his farm, he makes Joe a cash offer for the land. How do Fletcher's plans include Joe and Shane?

5. How do Shane and Joe respond to Fletcher's offer?

6. Why does Fletcher want Joe to meet him at Grafton's store?

7. Why does Shane stop Joe from going into town to meet Fletcher?

8. What is the outcome of the confrontation at Grafton's between Shane and Fletcher and his hired man, Wilson?

9. Who offers to take Shane's place as Joe's hired hand after Shane leaves the valley?

10. Why does Joe want to leave the valley?

For Study and Discussion

Analyzing and Interpreting the Novel

1a. When Shane and Joe are forced into a fight with Fletcher's men in Grafton's store, why does Joe insist on paying for the damages that have resulted from the brawl? **b.** When Mr. Weir offers to take up a collection to pay for the damages, why do you think Joe refuses?

2a. What plan does Stark Wilson use to lure Ernie Wright into a fight with him? **b.** How do you think Shane knows what Fletcher and Wilson are planning?

3. When Shane finally puts on his gun to go to town, he seems to be a different man to Bob. How is Shane different?

4. Shane leaves the message for Joe that "no man need be ashamed of being beat by Shane." What conclusions can you draw from this statement?

5. When Shane is about to leave the valley after the gunfight with Wilson and Fletcher, he tells Bob "But I reckon it was in the cards from the moment I saw a freckled kid on a rail up the road there and a real man behind him, the kind that could back him for the chance another kid never had." **a.** Who is the "other kid" to whom Shane is referring? **b.** What might this comment tell you about Shane's past? **c.** How do you think this affected Shane's decision to stay and help the Starretts?

6. Shane knows that Bob admires him and his ability to handle a gun, but he doesn't want Bob to imitate him. **a.** Why does Shane think it would be wrong for Bob to become a gunfighter? **b.** What kind of person does Shane want Bob to become?

7. What reasons can you give for the popularity of Western books, movies, and television shows?

Literary Elements

Understanding the Novel

Theme

1. Theme is the central idea or insight about life or human nature expressed in a literary work. Plot, setting, characterization, and figurative language all contribute to the development of its theme. Here is one way to state the theme of *Shane*: In order for a small community to survive and grow, it may be necessary for one individual to willingly risk his life for the community, suffer wounds, and even lose the opportunity to continue living in the community. Give examples that illustrate or support this statement of theme.

Crisis

2. The crisis can be considered the **turning point** of a story. It involves the actions or the decisions the major characters make to resolve the conflict. There may be more than one crisis in a novel leading up to the final outcome or resolution. The crisis comes before the climax of events in the story. **a.** Describe the major crisis that occurs in *Shane*. **b.** List the significant events that lead up to this crisis.

Climax

3. The **climax** of a story marks the point of greatest emotional intensity, interest, action, or suspense. The events leading up to this point reach their fullest development, and the sequence of events following the climax become inescapable. In which part of *Shane* does the climax occur?

Resolution

4. The actions which bring a story to its conclusion form the **resolution**. The resolution in a novel follows the climax. **a.** When does the resolution begin in *Shane*? **b.** List the resolutions of conflicts in the novel.

Language and Vocabulary

Recognizing Concrete Terms

The writer's choice of words is part of his or her overall style. Skillful writers use specific language to describe characters, actions, attitudes, and qualities. Specific language can pin down an object so that it is easily identified. Further, writers use concrete terms to help you experience an object, person, or place through your senses. In the opening paragraph of *Shane*, the setting is described as having clear air, a small corral, and a swinging road which led "into the valley from the open plain beyond."

Find one example of the author's use of concrete language in *Shane* for each of the following: a place, a person, and an object. Identify the sense or senses (sight, sound, taste, touch, and smell) to which each of your examples appeal.

Writing About Literature

Discussing Shane as Tragic Figure

In *Shane*, Fletcher is the land-hungry villain who tries to crowd out the homesteaders, and Shane is the avenging hero who saves the homesteaders from the loss of their land and their lives.

Some of the characteristics of a hero in a Western might include sacrifice, loyalty, physical strength, courage, and honor. The Western hero also meets the problems and struggles which arise from survival in a dangerous territory on his own terms. He is a survivor and endures hardship with rugged determination.

Shane is portrayed as a tragic hero in the novel. Although he risks death and suffers wounds, he is unable to stay and enjoy the peace and safety he provides for the homesteaders. Shane tells Bob "A man is what he is, Bob, and there's no breaking the mold."

Write a brief essay, using any of the qualities listed above to explain why Shane is truly a hero. Give examples, using your own words, of how Shane demonstrates these characteristics. Tell how these qualities lead him to become a tragic figure in the novel.

Creative Writing

Inventing Another Outcome

The set of actions that form the ending or conclusion of a short story or novel is called the **resolution**. Usually the resolution ties together the actions and circumstances which have made up the plot. Sometimes an author will choose to leave some aspect of the resolution unfinished to allow the reader to speculate upon its outcome.

In the conclusion of *Shane*, the author resolves all of the conflicts presented in the story except one. He leaves the fate of the hero, Shane, to the imagination of the reader. The final act of riding away, injured, tells the reader that Shane has left the valley but does not reveal what his fate may be.

Write a short essay in which you speculate upon Shane's fate. Use your imaginative skills in creating a future or end for the hero. The final chapter provides some speculative ideas which the townspeople in the story have imagined. You might want to include a brief description of the life you think Shane had led before arriving in the valley to help you explain your conclusion.

Extending Your Study

Reporting on the Background of the Novel

Jack Schaefer re-created the life and times of the settlers of the West. Although Schaefer never lived in the West, his studies and interest in history provided a foundation for the creation of his first novel, *Shane*.

Write a short report on the settlement of the Wyoming Territory. Include any information which you think might be important in understanding the nature of the conflict over land in *Shane*, such as the Homestead Act of 1862, the Sioux Indian Reservation, the range wars, and the Johnson County War of 1892.

About the Author

Jack Schaefer   (1907–   )

Jack Schaefer was born in Cleveland, Ohio, on November 19, 1907. He attended Oberlin College. He pursued a career in journalism and wrote for the United Press and held other editorial positions on newspapers in Connecticut, Maryland, and Virginia. Dissatisfied with journalism, Schaefer turned to fiction writing. His first published work, originally a novella, was published in *Argosy* in three parts. The work was entitled *Rider from Nowhere* and was later revised and is now entitled *Shane*. Schaefer's literary accomplishments include the novels *The Canyon, First Blood, Stubby Pringle's Christmas, Old Ramon,* as well as his published articles on the West.

DEVELOPING SKILLS IN CRITICAL THINKING

Drawing Inferences

In *Shane,* Bob Starrett, the narrator, usually describes scenes directly, leaving little for the reader to guess about. But in some scenes, you must draw inferences, or conclusions, about what is happening, based on clues that you are given. For example, just after Shane has entered Grafton's crowded saloon looking for Fletcher, Bob gives you this description:

> It seemed strange, for all the men standing, that there should be an empty chair at the far curve of the table. Someone must have been in that chair, because chips were at the place and a half-smoked cigar, a whisp of smoke curling up from it, was by them on the table.
>
> Red Marlin was leaning against the back wall, behind the chair. As I looked, he saw the smoke and appeared to start a little. With a careful show of casualness he slid into the chair and picked up the cigar.

Bob does not say that Fletcher has been sitting in the chair, that he has left to hide, and that Red Marlin is trying to cover up for him. Did you realize that this is what has happened? What evidence can you find to support this inference?

In an earlier scene, Bob sees Shane going for his horse and says:

> He was carrying his saddle and a sudden pain stabbed through me as I saw that with it was his saddle-roll.

Bob does not say directly that he realizes that Shane is going to leave them after the showdown with Fletcher. What clue in this sentence tells you that Shane will be taking off on a journey? (You have to know what a saddle-roll is.)

After the gunfight, Shane tells Bob to go back home to his parents. He says: "There's only one thing more I can do for them now." What is the "one thing more" that Shane can do for the Starretts?

PRACTICE IN READING AND WRITING

Writing a Précis

The word *précis* is a French word meaning a precise summary. The purpose of writing a précis is to give a shortened version of a longer piece of writing such as a novel, short story, article, passage, or report. The précis condenses a longer work to its bare essentials.

Précis-writing eliminates such details as illustrations, quotations, and examples and includes only those details which highlight the main points of a story or other work.

The methods used to write a précis can help you in reporting on a piece of literature, note taking, preparing for exams, and summarizing any material for study. In writing a précis you develop comprehension skills as well as writing skills. You must be able to select the most important ideas and express them in writing clearly and accurately.

The following rules should be observed when writing a précis:

- Be brief. A précis is short. It is always much shorter than the original material.
- Include only the central points of the material. Avoid using unnecessary information.
- Use your own words. Tell the main points by writing your own account of the necessary information.
- Use the author's ideas and viewpoints. Stay away from inserting your own opinions about the material. Report on the author's account of details and events.
- Arrange the events in the order of the original story.
- Avoid short, choppy sentences. Present the information so that the ideas and details flow together.

Read the following précis of Chapter 1 of *Shane*:

Shane, a mysterious stranger, rides onto the Starretts' ranch in the Wyoming Territory in the summer of 1889. He stops to get water for his horse and himself, and Joe Starrett invites him to stay for dinner. Mrs. Starrett, Marian, cooks dinner for Joe, Bob, their son, and Shane. They share friendly conversation during dinner, but the Starretts find out very little about their guest. Shane is guarded and avoids talking about himself. He leaves a distinct impression upon the Starretts before retiring to the bunkhouse to spend the night on the Starrett farm. Joe, Bob, and Marian Starrett are all intrigued by Shane's dual personality—he is a curious combination of kindness and caution.

Use the following guidelines to write your précis:

- Carefully read the material you are about to summarize. Be sure you know what it says.
- Write down the important points. Write a brief statement for each point.
- Write a rough draft by using your statements. Develop each statement so that the précis begins to read smoothly.
- After you have established the main points, check your work by going back through the material.
- Revise your draft. Be sure that it is readable and states the information clearly.

Use these guidelines to write a précis of any chapter other than Chapter 1 in *Shane*.

For Further Reading

Bloch, Louis M., *Overland to California in 1859; a guide for wagon train travelers* (Bloch, 1983)
This book is a guide for wagon train travelers, which includes advice on how to survive from day to day on a wagon train.

Durham, Philip, and Everett L. Jones, *The Negro Cowboy* (Dodd, Mead, 1965)
Would you like to break wild horses for ten cents apiece? Well, read this book and find out what "Deadwood Dick," "Bronco Sam," and "One Horse Charley" did to get their names.

Fletcher, Sydney E., *The Cowboy and His Horse* (Grosset & Dunlap, 1951)
Cowboy life and equipment is described in excellent stories and pictures. Learn about different kinds of spurs, boots, and how angora chaps are different from batwing chaps. Learn what a "Hoodlum" does and why a "fall back" is dangerous.

Forbis, William H., *The Cowboys* (Time-Life Books, 1973)
Everything you need to know about the life of cowboys. Pictures and drawings show how to rope cows, identify brands, and break broncos. Other interesting tales explain why a man who could read and write was paid four times more than a regular cowboy. Also included are stories of six famous women of the Old West.

Freedman, Russell, *Cowboys of the Wild West* (Clarion Books, 1985)
This book tells of adventures and hardships of cowboys on a trail ride, special clothes and equipment they needed to survive, and how they lived on the open range.

Keith, Harold, *The Obstinate Land* (Thomas Y. Crowell, 1977)
Fritz, a fourteen-year-old boy, travels with his family from Texas to take part in the Oklahoma land rush. After the family has to settle on a poor plot of land and his father freezes to death in a blizzard, Fritz has to become head of the family and learns how to work with the other ranchers while keeping the family's land productive.

Lyons, Grant, *Mustangs, Six-Shooters, and Barbed Wire, How the West Was Really Won* (Messner, 1981)
Exciting stories about how barbed wire was used to divide the open plains for private ownership, the way the introduction of the horse changed the lives of Indians, and the importance of the buffalo.

McDowell, Bart, *The American Cowboy in Life and Legend* (National Geographic Society, 1972)
Stories and pictures show the life of a cowboy from tumbleweeds and longhorns, to cattle drives and rodeos, leading up to the working ranches of today.

Moody, Ralph, *Riders of the Pony Express* (Houghton Mifflin, 1958)
The creation of the Pony Express shortened delivery of a letter across the country from two months to twenty days, but it was a dangerous and hard ride for the pony express rider. This book tells of Johnny Frey, the first pony express rider, Kit Carson, and others who had to brave flash floods, Indian attacks, and other hardships to deliver the mail.

Portis, Charles, *True Grit* (Simon & Schuster, 1968)
Courageous, fourteen-year-old Mattie Ross sets out with a rough, wild, one-eyed gunfighter to avenge her father's murder.

Ross, Nancy Wilson, *Heroines of the Early West* (Random House, 1960)
Six exciting stories of women of the Western frontier. Find out why Nancy Walker had eight people on her honeymoon, and why Abigail Scott Duniway was a prophet, and how she became one of the first suffragettes and a fighter for equal rights for women.

Wormer, Richard, *The Black Mustanger* (Morrow, 1971)
After his father is injured, young Dan Riker earns money to help support his family by working for a mustanger who is part black man and part Apache Indian. A great friendship develops while Dan learns how to survive in the Wild West.

PART III

LITERARY HERITAGE

Unit Nine   THE EPIC

Selections from

THE EPIC OF GILGAMESH
612

THE ILIAD
624

BEOWULF
645

THE SONG OF ROLAND
656

THE EPIC

Greeks and Trojans in battle from *The Ambrosiana Iliad*. Illustrated manuscript (third to fifth centuries A.D.).

Biblioteca Ambrosiana, Milan

An *epic* is a long narrative poem about heroic people and events. The characters in epics are depicted as larger than life and possessing great strength and dignity. Because of these qualities, the word *epic,* in our day, has come to stand for something that is grand or colossal in size.

There are two general types of epics. One is the *folk epic,* which develops out of an oral tradition of songs and legends, and which does not have a known author. The other type is the *literary epic,* which is written by a known author and which imitates the characteristics of the folk epic.

The earliest of the ancient epics is *Gilgamesh* (gĭl'gə-mĕsh), composed in the Near East more than four thousand years ago. There are three outstanding epics from classical antiquity. The *Iliad* (ĭl'ē-əd) and the *Odyssey* (ŏdə-sē), attributed to the Greek poet Homer, were composed about the eighth century B.C. The *Aeneid* (ĭ-nē'ĭd) was composed by the Roman poet Virgil in the first century B.C. It is called a literary epic because it was written in imitation of the Homeric poems. The longest poem in the world is the *Mahabharata* (mə-hä'bä'rə-tə), an ancient Indian epic, which consists of eighteen volumes. It is fifteen times as long as the Bible.

The Middle Ages produced several great epics, including *Beowulf* (bā'ə-wo͝olf'), set down in Old English, or Anglo-Saxon; *The Song of Roland,* the national epic of France; *The Poem of the Cid* (sĭd), the national epic of Spain; and *The Divine Comedy,* by the Italian poet Dante, considered by some readers to be the greatest poem ever written. The most celebrated epic in the English language is John Milton's *Paradise Lost,* written in the seventeenth century. Some readers believe that Milton's work is the last great epic in world literature.

In addition to those reading skills that you bring to any literary work, reading an epic requires that you understand certain characteristics of the form. For example, it is customary for an epic to be written in a dignified style. When you read an ancient epic that has been translated into Modern English, you will find that the language of the modern version is often formal and stately, to convey the flavor of the original.

An epic tends to draw upon many sources: myths, legends, folk tales, and historical events. While Charles the Great was a real figure, the events recounted in *The Song of Roland* are largely invented, the accumulation of many stories told over several centuries.

Although the characters in epics experience very much the same emotions that we do, their actions are extraordinary, superhuman, or fantastic. Beowulf, for instance, can wage an underwater battle against a monster while wearing a suit of armor.

The hero of an epic is often a *demigod;* that is, one of his parents is divine. Thus, in the *Iliad,* Achilles is the son of Thetis, a sea goddess, and a mortal father. It is also common for the gods and goddesses to intervene in the lives of human characters and to take sides. In *Gilgamesh,* the fate of the hero and his friend is determined by a council of gods and goddesses.

Some epics are part of a *cycle* of poems developed around a hero or event. *The Song of Roland,* for example, is one of a cycle of poems about the life of Charles the Great.

In some epics it is customary for the narrative to open in the middle of the action. This is the case in the Homeric epics and in the *Aeneid.*

An epic generally reflects the values of the society from which it originates. Thus, we are able to understand a great deal about the ideals of medieval Germanic society by reading the epic of *Beowulf* or the traditions of chivalry by reading *The Song of Roland.*

In this unit you will be in introduced to some of the greatest epics in world literature. Here are some guidelines to assist you in reading these works.

Guidelines for Reading an Epic

1. *Become familiar with the names of characters and places.* The names in these epics may seem strange at first. Refer to the list provided at the opening of each selection as often as necessary. The individual entries identify the people and places mentioned in the epic.

2. *Take note of the heroic characteristics of the central figure or figures.* The qualities attributed to the hero reveal the underlying beliefs and values of the society that produced the epic.

3. *Determine the role played by gods, goddesses, and other supernatural agents.* In particular, consider their responsibility for the destiny of human beings.

4. *Look for common elements in different epics.* For example, in many epics the hero undertakes a perilous journey or is involved in dangerous adventures. Watch for recurrent patterns and themes.

THE EPIC OF GILGAMESH

The Epic of Gilgamesh is a very old work. The story was known throughout the Near East for centuries before it was written down and preserved by the Assyrians in the seventh century B.C. What we have of the poem survives on clay tablets that were discovered in the nineteenth century. A great deal of the story is missing, but even in its incomplete form, the poem is one of the masterpieces of world literature.

Gilgamesh may have been a real king in the land of Uruk in Mesopotamia (měs′ə-pə-tä′mē-ə), in southwestern Asia. In the poem, Gilgamesh is the son of a goddess and a high priest. Although he is two parts god, Gilgamesh is mortal. Because of his many gifts, especially his great beauty and strength, he grows proud and arrogant. He becomes a tyrant and oppresses his people, who pray to the gods for relief. The gods decide to create a rival for Gilgamesh, the wild man Enkidu, so that Gilgamesh will be forced to compete with him. However, after a wrestling bout, Gilgamesh and Enkidu become fast friends and companions in adventure. One of their adventures takes them into the Land of the Cedars, guarded by an evil giant named Humbaba.

The eleventh tablet of the *Epic of Gilgamesh* (seventh century B.C.). This clay tablet, which shows cuneiform writing, gives the Babylonian account of the Flood.

Names and Places in *Gilgamesh*

Cylinder seal impression from a region in Babylonia (c. 2300 B.C.). The Sun God Shamash is rising between two mountains. Center right is Ea, God of the Waters. Center left is the Goddess Ishtar with wings and arrows.

Annunaki: the judges of the dead, who live in the underworld.

Anshan: a district in southwest Persia, the source of wood for bows.

Dilmun: the garden of the gods, a paradise where Utnapishtim and his wife live.

Ea: the god of drinking water.

Egalmah: the palace of Ninsun, in Uruk.

Enkidu: a natural man, raised in the wild, who becomes the friend of Gilgamesh.

Enlil: the god of earth and sky.

Euphrates: a river in southwestern Asia.

Gilgamesh: the fifth king of Uruk, son of the goddess Ninsun and a priest of Uruk, and hero of the epic.

Humbaba: a giant who guards the Cedar Forest.

Ishtar: the goddess of love and war, whose chief temple is in Uruk.

Ninsun: a goddess, the mother of Gilgamesh.

Shamash: the sun god.

Siduri: a winemaker who lives by the sea.

Urshanabi: the boatman who ferries Gilgamesh across the Waters of the Dead.

Uruk: a city state in southern Babylonia, known as Erech in the Bible. It was an important city in ancient times.

Utnapishtim: a wise man who was granted eternal life.

A relief showing Gilgamesh as a tamer of wild beasts. Assyrian (eighth century B.C.). Louvre, Paris

FROM
Gilgamesh

Retold by
JENNIFER WESTWOOD

The Slaying of Humbaba

Gilgamesh sat in Uruk and was sad, pondering the life of men, and death. He fell asleep at last and dreamed a dream of his own dying, because he was one third a mortal man and shared their bitter fate. He woke to sorrow, and he told his dream to Enkidu, his dear friend.

"Do not grieve," said Enkidu. "You will not live forever, yet still yours is the kingship, yours the power to rule. Deal justly by your people, win their love, and leave behind you an everlasting name."

"My name will not endure without brave deeds," said Gilgamesh, "and therefore let us go into the Cedar Forest to win fame."

Enkidu sighed bitterly.

"Why set your heart on this?"

"In that forest dwells Humbaba, the great giant, set there by Enlil to safeguard the trees, but he has grown too proud. So let us go and fell him, cut him down, uproot the evil that is in that land."

"When I was as a beast and roamed the plains, I saw that land. The Cedar Forest runs a full ten thousand leagues from side to side, and if some creature stirs within its depths, Humbaba hears though sixty leagues away. What man would venture into his dark realm, would choose to meet the keeper of the trees, whose breath is hot as fire, whose mighty roar is like the fearful thunder of the storm? No man on earth can equal *him* in strength, for Enlil made him perilous to men. Weakness takes hold of those who enter in his dark dominions. We shall not return."

"What man can live forever, Enkidu? Our days are numbered and our time runs fast, and all our deeds are but a breath of wind. Already, in the city, you fear death—what has become of all your manly strength? I will walk before you. You may call: 'Gilgamesh, go on! Be not afraid!' from where you stand in safety. If I fall, my name will live forever. They will say: 'Gilgamesh has fallen in fight with the terrible Humbaba,' and sons as yet unborn will speak my name with pride in days to come. Your fearfulness afflicts my heart with grief, but I shall still go on, still put my hand to this great task and cut the cedar down. I shall give orders to my armorers; they will forge for us weapons fit for gods, so come with me."

Gilgamesh set his armorers to work. Great swords they cast, and made them sheaths of gold; forged monstrous axes for a giant's bane.[1] When all was ready, each of them would arm with massive weapons of ten talents' weight.[2]

Gilgamesh called the elders of Uruk and said: "O elders, listen to your King. I wish to see him of whom all men talk, him with whose dread name the lands are filled. In the Cedar

---

1. **bane** (bān): destruction.
2. **ten talents' weight:** A talent was a unit of weight or money.

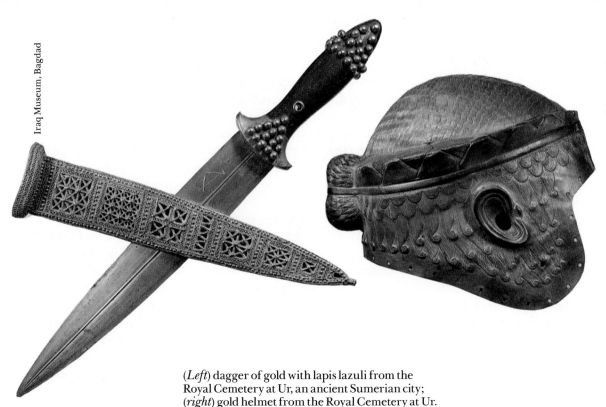

(*Left*) dagger of gold with lapis lazuli from the Royal Cemetery at Ur, an ancient Sumerian city; (*right*) gold helmet from the Royal Cemetery at Ur.

Forest I will vanquish him and cause the lands to hear of Gilgamesh."

The elders of Uruk said to their King: "You are young, O Gilgamesh. Your heart is rash. You do not know what you propose to do. Humbaba is no man like other men! Who is there that can stand against his might? His roar is like the storm, his mouth holds fire, and he breathes out death to all mankind. Why must you do this thing? For you must fail."

Gilgamesh looked at Enkidu, and laughed.

"What shall I tell them? That I am afraid? Would you have us sit here all our days, each growing old in fear and idleness?"

The elders said: "If you must go, then may your patron god protect you; may he bring you safely home; to the quay[3] of Uruk cause you to return."

3. **quay** (kē): a wharf, or landing place, for ships to dock.

Gilgamesh bowed himself down to the ground before the sun god, Shamash, and he prayed: "I go, O Shamash, and I raise my hands to you in prayer. Let it be well with me. Bring me back to Uruk. Keep me safe."

Gilgamesh called his friend to go with him and in the temple have the omens read. He came out weeping, tears ran down his face, for the omens spelled disaster.

"Must I walk alone, down a road which I have never gone before without your guidance, Shamash?" cried the King.

His workmen brought the weapons, the massive swords and axes, and placed a bow of Anshan in his hand. The elders gave their blessing once again, and for the journey counseled Gilgamesh.

"Do not trust in your strength! Let Enkidu go on before you. He has seen the way, has walked the road that leads up to the Gate. He who goes before will save his friend. May Shamash grant you victory. May he cause your eyes to see the fulfillment of the vows that you have made. May he open up closed paths, and send propitious[4] dreams, and cause you to slay Humbaba like a child. In the river of the forest, wash your feet. Every evening dig a well and let there be pure water always in your waterskin for an offering to Shamash."

Enkidu said: "Come, friend. Let us set out on our way. Let your heart be not afraid, but follow me."

Gilgamesh said: "First, we must take farewell of Ninsun, my wise mother. Let us go into the temple Egalmah, her home."

The friends went hand in hand to Egalmah, the palace of the goddess.

"Hear me, Mother," said King Gilgamesh, "for I must tread a strange road from today, and from today face dangers unforeseen, until the day when I return again. I must slay the keeper of the trees to win myself an everlasting name, so pray for me to Shamash that I may uproot the evil that is in his land."

Ninsun the Queen put on her finest robes, and on her head the royal diadem. She mounted to the roof of Egalmah, where stood the Sun Lord's altar, nearest Heaven, and throwing incense on the sacred fire, she sent her prayers up with the winding smoke.

"Why did you give my son a restless heart? Now that you have touched him and he walks a strange road, facing dangers unforeseen, guard him until the day that he returns. When you have turned your eye away from earth, entrust him to the Watchmen of the Night till you come back with Aya, Bride of Dawn, and your bright glances watch the world again."

Ninsun put out the incense and went down to where her son still stood with Enkidu.

"Enkidu," she said, "from this day on, you are my child. I have adopted you. Here is my amulet;[5] it is a pledge that I have taken you to be my son. Into your keeping I give Gilgamesh, your brother; keep him safe, and bring him back to me when all is done."

The friends bade her farewell. They set out now, and as they left the gates, the elders cried: "In our assembly we have paid heed to your words; pay heed to ours in turn, O Gilgamesh! Let Enkidu protect the friend he loves."

"Fear not," said Enkidu. "All will be well."

For twenty leagues they walked before they ate; and thirty more before they stopped for sleep. A journey of six weeks was made by them in just three days, and after they had crossed the seventh mountain in their path, they saw ahead the Gate into the Forest. It was shut, and guarded by a watchman, set there by Humbaba, the great giant; less in size, but as terrible of aspect as it seemed the giant could be, and Gilgamesh fell back.

"Remember the vows you made!" cried Enkidu. "Stand forth and slay this watchman!"

At his words, the King took heart and said: "We must be quick. He is used to put on seven coats of mail when he goes into battle. One is on. If we delay, he will be fully armed, and how then shall we take his life from him?"

Like a furious wild ox, the watchman roared, and cried out: "Go! You may not enter in! This is the Cedar Forest, and the realm of Humbaba the giant. Mortal men may not pass by these gates."

"Yet we shall pass," said Gilgamesh the King.

The two advanced and struck the watchman down. As yet he had put on but one mail coat, and so his life was taken, though he was the servant of the giant, great of strength and towering of stature. Enkidu stepped forward to the Gate, when once its keeper lay dead on the ground. Such was its beauty and its craftsman-

---

4. **propitious** (prə-pĭsh′əs): favorable.

5. **amulet** (ăm′yə-lĭt): a charm worn around the neck.

ship that he could not bear to strike it with his ax, but pushed it open with his outstretched hand. He sprang back with a cry, for on the Gate lay deep enchantments.

Enkidu cried out: "O let us not go down into the Forest; see my hand! When I touched the Gate, my hand lost all its strength and now it hangs down lifeless at my side. Some deep enchantment lies about this Gate. Let us not pass inside!"

"Should we turn back, now we have come so far?" asked Gilgamesh. "Would you remain behind? No, stay with me. The weakness will soon pass. Together we will go into the depths of this great Forest and perform the task for which we came. Forget your thoughts of death."

They passed inside the Gate and caught their breath. Their words were stilled to silence. They were still, and gazed upon the Forest, the green mountain. They beheld the height of the cedars and the broad path through the trees where the giant was used to walk in the cool and pleasant shade. Greener were the shadows of the Mountain of the Cedar than of any other place, and Gilgamesh the King dug a well at sunset there, to offer up to Shamash waters from the earth. He poured out meal and prayed: "Mountain of the Cedar, send me a dream to show me if my fate be good or bad."

The two lay down to sleep. When midnight came, Gilgamesh awoke and roused his friend: "Enkidu, I dreamed that we two stood within deep gorges, when a mountain fell and by its side we seemed as small as flies. I dreamed again; again the mountain fell. It struck me down; the mountain caught my foot. Then light blazed out and in it was a form more beautiful than any in the land. He took the mountain off me, pulled me out, and giving me water, set me on my feet."

Enkidu said: "This dream was fortunate.

The mountain was Humbaba. It must mean that we shall likewise bring about his fall, and by the help of Shamash, Lord of Light."

They traveled on next day, and once again Gilgamesh, at evening, dug a well in honor of the Sun God, and again he scattered meal upon the ground. This time he prayed: "Mountain, bring a dream for Enkidu, to show him if his fate be good or bad."

The Mountain sent a dream to Enkidu. He thought that in his dream a cold rain fell, but he kept silent, for he was afraid. Then Gilgamesh awoke. He said: "My friend, did you not call me? Did you not touch me, or has some god now passed this way? I have dreamed a third dream. In it lightning filled the air. Heaven thundered, earth resounded, daylight failed and darkness fell. The brightness vanished and the fire went out. Then death rained down and turned the world to ashes and to dust."

"My friend, be not afraid," said Enkidu. "For this dream too, may mean that we shall slay Humbaba, and his fall will be as dreadful as the storms that you have seen."

Though he spoke cheerful words, his heart was cold. The two resolved to go on with their task. Gilgamesh took an ax up in his hand and he cut down a cedar. Far away, the giant Humbaba heard the noise. He grew enraged: "Who has come among my trees? Who is cutting down my cedar?"

Then from Heaven the Sun God Shamash called: "Be not afraid! Go forward without fear—you have my help."

The two advanced. With great strides from his house the giant Humbaba came and horror fell upon the two friends' hearts, for he was huger than the tales had made him and more terrible. He fastened on the King the eye of death. The strength of Gilgamesh began to fail and, with his one sound hand, Enkidu his friend could not hope to defend him.

Gilgamesh the King called out to heavenly Shamash: "Help me, Lord! I have honored you! I have pursued the road decreed by fate which brought me to this place, here to cut down Humbaba, who is evil in your sight, to root out all the evil in your land."

The Sun God heard, and called from their far caves the Great Wind, and the Whirlwind, the Tempest and the Storm, the North, the South, the Freezing Wind, the Burning Wind—all eight rose up against Humbaba and beat against his evil eyes. He was unable to go forward, unable to turn back. He was helpless, and he pleaded: "Let me go, O Gilgamesh. You shall be my master if you spare me, I your slave. I will cut down the cedars which I have tended on the Mountain, and build a palace for you. Have mercy, Gilgamesh!"

The King was moved by his strong pleas. He said: "Is it not right for us to set the prisoner free, for us to send the captive back to his mother's house, and to return the caught bird to his nest?"

"It is not right to set *this* prisoner free, and send *this* captive back to his mother's house, and to return *this* caught bird to his nest, if you would see *your* mother once again. Where is your judgment? What use is your strength if wisdom does not guide it? If we do not slay him, then he will turn on us. Do not listen to his pleading. He is evil and must die."

"It will be as in the dream," said Gilgamesh, "the brightness of our fame will be eclipsed and all our deeds as ash, if we kill him."

"It is not so. Our fame will be as great. The giant must die or us, and you must choose."

Gilgamesh struck first; next Enkidu; and at the third blow Humbaba lay still.

But he was the keeper of the cedar trees, whose power made forests tremble; now his death caused the whole world to shudder, mountains move, and hills and valleys be put from their place. Yet Gilgamesh still cut the cedars down and Enkidu hacked out the twining roots as far as the Euphrates. Then they turned their faces from the Forest and went home.

Gilgamesh and Enkidu destroy the Bull of Heaven, sent by the angry goddess Ishtar after she is rejected by Gilgamesh. Ishtar demands that the two heroes die, but the council of gods decides to spare Gilgamesh. Enkidu grows sick and dies. After a period of mourning for his friend, Gilgamesh undertakes a journey in search of immortality. He seeks out Utnapishtim, a man who lives in the Garden of the Gods and who enjoys everlasting life. In his wanderings, Gilgamesh finds his way barred by the Scorpion man, who guards the gate of the Underworld; Shamash, the sun god; and Siduri, the winemaker, who guards the shore of the sea. Finally, he reaches Urshanabi, the boatman. Gilgamesh shatters the Images of Stone that protect Urshanabi. Then the two launch a boat and cross the Waters of Death to the Garden of the Gods.

The Flower of Youth

Utnapishtim, called the Faraway, was sitting at his ease upon the slopes of Dilmun, in the Garden of the Gods, and when he saw the boat come in to land, he took counsel with himself, and in his heart said: "Who has destroyed the Images of Stone that used to guard the ship? Who is this man who comes here with my boatman on the sea? He is none of mine!"

As they approached, he called: "Who are you, and what is it you seek, that you have crossed such waters on your way?"

"Do you not know that I am Gilgamesh, who killed Humbaba, cut the cedar down, and seized and slew the Bull that came from Heaven?"

Utnapishtim said: "If *you* are he, who killed Humbaba, cut the cedar down, and seized and slew the Bull that came from Heaven, why are your cheeks so thin, why are they burnt with cold and heat, why do you wander in the desert and the plain? Why is despair within your heart and on your face the look of one who travels without hope?"

He answered him: "Why should these things not be? My friend, my younger brother who once ran with the wild ass and the panther of the plain, who ascended mountains with me, killed the Bull and slew Humbaba, keeper of the trees; my friend whom I loved dearly, and who went beside me through all hardships—he is dead. The fate of man has overtaken him. For seven days and seven nights I wept, and would not give him up for burial, thinking: 'My friend will rise at my lament.' But the Annunaki, Judges of the Dead, seized him. He is gone, and now my life is empty, so I roam the grassy plains and deserts, far and wide. How can I be silent when my friend, my younger brother whom I loved, has turned to clay? And I, shall I not like him soon lie down and never rise again? I am afraid."

"Gilgamesh, where are you running? You will never find what you are looking for while this world lasts, because the gods decreed that darkness be the end of mortal life. For do we build a house to last forever, make a law to last forever—from the days of old there is no permanence. The river brings a flood but then it falls; the sun comes out then hides behind a cloud; the gods allotted life but also death. How like they are—the sleeping and the dead; both picture death, a lesser and a great. Sleep is the sign of your mortality."

"I have crossed mountains, I have crossed the seas and never had my fill of restful sleep. I was wearied out with walking and my clothing hung in rags before I reached Siduri of the Vine. I have killed the lion and tiger, the bear, the panther and the stag, the ibex and hyena, and the creatures of the plain, to eat their flesh and wear their skins, since I set out to find you. For you alone can tell me how to win immortal life, life everlasting. *You* look like a man, you are no different from myself, and yet you live. In my heart I thought that you would seem a god, a mighty man of battle—here you lie idly on your side out in the sun! Tell me how you got the precious gift of everlasting life and entered into the company of the gods."

Utnapishtim said: "I will reveal a hidden thing, a secret of the gods, and tell how Ea saved me from the Flood."

He told him how the gods had drowned the world, but for his piety had taken him to live for ever in fair Dilmun.

"As for you," he said, "what can we do to help you win this life for which you seek? First, we must see if you can pass the test and overcome the little death of sleep. Six days and seven nights you must not sleep."

But Gilgamesh had walked the desert waste and he was weary; sleep came falling down, sleep like a rainstorm blew on him; he slept.

Utnapishtim said: "Look at the man who thought that he could win eternal life! Sleep like a rainstorm blows on him; he sleeps, and sleeping proves he is no more than man. Did I not say the sleeping and the dead both picture death? Wife, see him where he lies! If Gilgamesh cannot even conquer sleep, a little dying, how much less shall he withstand its image, true death, when it comes."

Utnapishtim's wife said: "Touch the man that he may awake, that he may return upon the road by which he came, to his own land."

"Deceitful is mankind! This man will try to deceive us by denying he slept. We must give him proof. Therefore bake loaves of bread and each day stand a fresh one by his head to mark the passing time as he sleeps on."

So she baked loaves of bread and every day stood one beside the King, till the day came when the first was hard as stone, the third still

Gilgamesh strangling two lions. Iranian textile (tenth to eleventh centuries A.D.).

moist, the sixth one freshly baked, the seventh unmade. Then Utnapishtim touched the sleeping man and he awoke.

"I hardly slept," he said.

"Count up the loaves and see how many days."

"Where shall I go now, and what shall I do? Wherever I set my foot, death comes behind! For if I cannot even conquer sleep, a little dying, how much less shall I be able to withstand its image, death?"

Utnapishtim told his Boatman that he must take the King down to the washing place to bathe him and to cleanse his matted hair.

"And I will give him garments such that they will show no sign of wear until he comes into Uruk again. You must go with him; since you brought him here, across the boundaries of life and death, and broke the rule established by the gods, you cannot stay, you can no longer be my Boatman. Urshanabi, you must leave."

Urshanabi did as he was told and when the King was washed and clothed anew, they launched the boat to make the journey back. But Utnapishtim's wife said: "Gilgamesh was weary when he came and weary goes. What will you give him now for all his pains, to take back to his land?"

So Utnapishtim called to them; the King took up a pole and brought the boat back in towards the bank.

"Gilgamesh, you were weary when you came

and weary go. What would you have of me for all your pains, to take back to your land? I will reveal to you a hidden thing, a secret of the gods, so listen well. Beneath the waters in a certain place there grows a little plant with spines as sharp as any thorn or rose. If you can pluck it, then your hands will hold the Flower of Youth, to make you young again."

Utnapishtim told him where to look and, with the Boatman, Gilgamesh set out. When they reached the place that they were looking for, Gilgamesh tied stones upon his feet and leaped into the waters. Down and down, into the deepest channels of the sea he sank, and there he saw the plant. He grasped its stem; although it pricked his hands, he plucked it from its roots, cut off the stones, and let the waters bear him to the light.

He said to Urshanabi: "See this plant. It is the Flower of Youth, and by its power old men grow young again. I will return to Uruk and there give this magic plant to all the old to eat and at the last, when I have reached old age, I too shall eat and have back all my strength."

So Gilgamesh and Urshanabi sailed over the sea towards Uruk again, and after fifty leagues they stopped to rest because the night had come. They pulled to shore. There was a pool of cool, clean water near, and Gilgamesh the King went down to bathe, leaving the Flower of Youth upon the bank. But deep down in the pool, a serpent lay that smelled the Flower. It rose up, seized it, ate. It sloughed[6] its skin, becoming young again.

Then Gilgamesh sat down and wept aloud: "Was it for this I have labored? Has the life-blood of my heart been spent all for a serpent? This my prize? Though everlasting life could not be mine, yet in my hand I held the Flower of Youth. Now I have lost it there is nothing left.

6. **sloughed** (slŭf): shed.

"Come with me, Urshanabi, to Uruk; let us leave the boat and make our way by land. I will show you my great city. There at least, my toil has not been fruitless. Its high walls and the ramparts I have raised—these things will be all there is left of me when I am dead."

So Gilgamesh the golden, King of Kings, resigned himself to death, the fate of men. He came back weary from his wandering and wrote on brick this tale of ancient days. Though he was mortal man, he set his name where great men's names were set, and where no names were, there he built an altar to the gods.

Reading Check

1. Why does Gilgamesh undertake a journey into the Cedar Forest?
2. Identify Gilgamesh's patron god.
3. Why does Enkidu lose the strength of one hand?
4. How does Utnapishtim prove that Gilgamesh has failed the test?
5. What happens to the snake when it eats the Flower of Youth?

For Study and Discussion

Analyzing and Interpreting the Epic

1. In the opening episode we learn that Gilgamesh is preoccupied with thoughts of his own death. Examine the dialogue between Gilgamesh and Enkidu. **a.** How does Gilgamesh hope to achieve immortality? **b.** Why does Enkidu object to Gilgamesh's plan? **c.** How does Gilgamesh overcome the objections of Enkidu and the elders of Uruk?

2. Dreams and omens are often of great importance in epics since they show the

influence of divine forces controlling human destiny. Gilgamesh has several dreams before he vanquishes Humbaba. How does Enkidu interpret those dreams?

3a. How do the gods assist Gilgamesh in slaying Humbaba? **b.** What does he do to win the favor of the gods?

4a. How does Enkidu's advice contrast with the ambitions of Gilgamesh? **b.** In what way does Enkidu represent the voice of reason or common sense?

5. After the death of Enkidu, Gilgamesh undergoes great hardships to win the secret of eternal life. **a.** What test must he pass? **b.** What significance is there in his failure to overcome "the little death of sleep"?

6. Gilgamesh is given a second chance to obtain eternal life. How does he lose this opportunity?

7a. How does Gilgamesh finally become reconciled to his fate? **b.** In what way does he gain wisdom as a result of his trials?

Literary Elements

Understanding the Epic Hero

Gilgamesh is often cited as the first tragic hero in literature. Although he is two parts god, he is mortal, and his search for everlasting life leads to the tragic fact that there is no escape from death.

The different episodes of the story are unified by the search for permanence. In the early episodes, Gilgamesh wishes to gain eternal fame by heroic actions. After the death of his faithful companion, Enkidu, Gilgamesh becomes obsessed with his own mortality. He undertakes a futile journey in search of everlasting life. What he gains is wisdom and resignation to the common fate of all human beings.

One writer has noted that the tragedy in the epic is "the conflict between the desires of the god and the destiny of the man." What evidence can you offer to support this conclusion?

Writing About Literature

Interpreting the Quest of Gilgamesh

Scholars have pointed out that the journey to the Cedar Forest may be interpreted on several levels. On one level we may interpret Gilgamesh's quest as rooted in some historical fact. In order to build the walls and temples of his city, the king needed the timber of the forest and set out to take the trees by conquering the forest tribes. On another level, the journey may be seen as a dangerous adventure involving magic powers and supernatural forces. On a third level, the episode may be viewed as a moral conflict between the forces of good, represented by Gilgamesh and Enkidu, and the forces of evil, represented by the monster Humbaba.

Choose one level of interpretation, and in a brief essay give details that best support that interpretation.

Discussing Changes in Character

How does the character of Gilgamesh change in the course of these episodes? In your essay refer to specific evidence in the selection.

The Judgment of Paris by Cecchino Da Verona (fifteenth century).
Museo Nazionale del Bargello, Florence

THE ILIAD

Two great classical epics, the *Iliad* and the *Odyssey*, are attributed to Homer. According to tradition, he was a blind poet who lived around the eighth century B.C. The events recounted in both epics were legendary even in Homer's time. The background for both poems was the Trojan War, a long conflict between Greeks and Trojans, which had taken place around 1200 B.C.

Historians believe that the reasons for the Trojan War were economic. However, according to legend, the war began over a woman, who became known as Helen of Troy. The story goes that all the gods and goddesses were invited to the wedding of Peleus and Thetis except Eris, the goddess of discord. She was determined to be revenged for this insult. She threw a golden apple among the wedding guests, which was inscribed "For the Fairest." The apple was immediately claimed by three goddesses: Hera, queen of the gods; Athena, goddess of wisdom and the arts; and Aphrodite, queen of love and beauty. Zeus, the king of the gods, left the judgment of the contest to a mortal named Paris, who was a Trojan prince. Each of the goddesses attempted to bribe Paris. Hera promised him wealth and power; Athena assured him of great glory in war; Aphrodite offered him the most beautiful woman in the world as his wife. Paris gave the apple to Aphrodite, a decision which infuriated the other goddesses.

In the kingdom of Sparta, in Greece, lived King Menelaus and his beautiful wife, Helen. Helen had been much sought after as a bride, and before she chose a husband, all her suitors took an oath to defend her if it ever became necessary. Paris sailed to Sparta, and with the assistance of Aphrodite, persuaded Helen to elope with him. He took her to Troy, a great fortified city across the Aegean Sea. Menelaus called together the Greek chieftains who had pledged to protect Helen. After two years of preparation, the Greek armies sailed to Troy to recover Helen.

Thus began the Trojan War, which lasted for ten years. In the end, the Greeks won and Helen was returned to her husband. One of the Greek soldiers who fought in the war was Odysseus, whose adventures are the subject of Homer's *Odyssey*.

The *Iliad* is named for Ilium, or Troy, which is the setting of the first epic. It opens in the last year of the Trojan War. Things have not been going well in the Greek camp. Then, a quarrel erupts between Achilles, the greatest of the Greek warriors, and Agamemnon, leader of the Greek forces. Ironically, this quarrel, too, is over a woman.

The Abduction of Helen by Paris by a follower of Fra Angelico (fifteenth century). Wood, irregular octagon, painted surface. The National Gallery, London

NAMES AND PLACES
IN THE *ILIAD*

Greeks

Achaian (ə-kī′ən, ə-kā′ə n): a Greek.

Achilles (ə-kĭl′ēz): leader of the Myrmidons and hero of the *Iliad*.

Agamemnon (ăg′ə-mĕm′nŏn′): king of Mycenae (mī-sēn′nē) and leader of the Greeks.

Automedon (ô-tŏm′ə-dŏn): Achilles' charioteer.

Calchas (kăl′kəs): a soothsayer, or prophet, in the Greek camp.

Helen: the wife of Menelaus, abducted by Paris.

Menelaus (mĕn′ə-lā′əs): king of Sparta, husband of Helen, and brother of Agamemnon.

Myrmidon (mûr′mə-dŏn′, dən): a warrior from Thessaly; a follower of Achilles.

Nestor (nĕs′tər, tôr′): a wise old man, counselor to the Greeks.

Odysseus (ō-dĭs′yōōs′, ō-dĭs′ē-əs): king of Ithaca and shrewdest of the Greeks.

Patroclus (pə-trō′kləs): the close friend of Achilles.

Menelaus
Vatican Museums

Six Myrmidons. Attic,
black-figured amphora
(vase) (575–550 B.C.) by
the Camtar Painter
J. M. Rodocanachi Fund, Courtesy,
Museum of Fine Arts, Boston

Trojans

Andromache (ăn-drŏm′ə-kē): Hector's wife.

Astyanax (ə-stī′ə-năks′): son of Hector and Andromache.

Cassandra (kə-săn′drə): a daughter of King Priam, who has the gift of prophecy.

Hector (hĕk′tər): a Trojan prince and greatest warrior in Troy.

Hecuba (hĕk′yŏŏ-bə): queen of Troy.

Idaeus (ī-dē′-əs): the herald of the Trojans.

Paris (păr′ĭs): a Trojan prince who abducted Helen.

Pergamus (pəŭr′gə-məs, -mŏs′): the citadel, or fortress, of Troy.

Priam (prī′əm): king of Troy.

Scaean (sē′ăn) **Gate:** the gateway to the city of Troy.

Gods and Goddesses

Aphrodite (ăf′rə-dī′tē): goddess of love and beauty. She sides with the Trojans.

Apollo (ə-pŏl′ō): god of youth, music, prophecy, archery, and the sun. He is called **Phoebus** (fē′bəs) **Apollo,** from the Greek word for "shining." He helps the Trojans.

Ares (âr′ēz): god of war. He takes sides with Aphrodite.

Artemis (är′tə-mĭs): goddess of hunting, wild animals, and the moon. She helps the Trojans.

Athena (ə-thē′nə): goddess of wisdom, arts, crafts, and war. She is called **Pallas** (păl′əs) **Athena.** She sides with the Greeks.

Hades (hā′dēz): god of the underworld.

Hephaestus (hĭ-fĕs′təs): god of fire and metalworking.

Hera (hîr′ə): goddess of marriage, Zeus's wife, and queen of the gods. She sides with the Greeks.

Hermes (hûr′mēz): god of travelers, thieves, and messenger of the gods.

Olympus (ō-lĭm′pəs): the highest mountain in Greece, the home of the gods and goddesses.

Poseidon (pō-sī′dən): god of the sea. He favors the Greeks, who are a seafaring people.

Thetis (thē′tĭs): a sea goddess, the mother of Achilles.

Zeus (zōōs): god of the sky and weather, and king of the gods. He favors the Trojans but has to be neutral in order to pacify Hera, his wife.

Bronze statue (c. 465 B.C.) identified as Poseidon or Zeus.

National Archaeological Museum, Athens

FROM

The Iliad

Retold by
BARBARA LEONIE PICARD

The Quarrel

Chryses,[1] a priest of Apollo, comes to the Greek camp to ransom his daughter, Chryseïs,[2] who is a captive. When Agamemnon refuses to release the girl, Apollo sends a pestilence to punish the Greeks. For nine days he rains his arrows on the Greeks. Then Achilles calls a conference, which leads to a bitter quarrel.

For nine days did the plague rage, and on the tenth day, Achilles from Phthia,[3] who was the youngest of all the kings and princes of the Greeks, called the other leaders to an assembly. When they were all gathered together, he stood up and spoke. "My friends, without a doubt one of the gods is angry with us, else would this plague not have come upon us. Let us with no more delay ask a priest, or one who is skilled in such matters, to tell us which of the gods we have displeased by our neglect, that we may speedily offer sacrifices to appease his wrath. For otherwise, or so it seems to me, we shall never live to take Troy. We shall all of us die here, on the shore, and the theft of Helen will go unavenged."

Achilles sat down, and immediately Calchas the prophet arose. "Lord Achilles, son of King Peleus, I can tell you which of the gods is angered with us, and why. But first, swear to me that you will protect me, whatever I may say, for I fear that my words will displease one amongst us, who is the best of all the Greeks. Promise me your protection, and I will speak."

"Have no fear, Calchas," replied Achilles, "but speak the truth to us, for while I live no man of all the Greeks shall harm you." He paused a moment and glanced across to where Agamemnon sat, before adding, "Not even great King Agamemnon himself, whom I have often heard declare himself to be the best of all the Greeks, shall do you ill, I promise it."

"Then," said Calchas, reassured, "I will tell you why this plague has come upon us. It comes from immortal Apollo, and not because we have forgotten to sacrifice to him, but because King Agamemnon would not heed the pleas of old Chryses, who is Apollo's priest. Until the maiden Chryseïs is given back to her father, freely and unransomed, the god will not lift his wrath from us."

Agamemnon frowned at his words, and, when Calchas had done, the great king sat silent, glowering, knowing that the eyes of everyone were upon him. Then he rose. "Your words always make ill hearing, Calchas. Never

1. **Chryses** (krī′sēz).
2. **Chryseïs** (krī-sē′ĭs).
3. **Phthia** (thī′ə): a town in Thessaly, a section of Greece on the Aegean Sea.

have I heard you prophesy good fortune or the favor of the gods, but warnings and bad omens come always easily to your tongue. Now you choose to blame me for Apollo's wrath and this plague, and say that in my hands alone lies the remedy." He paused, remembering how all the other kings and princes had been for accepting the ransom and restoring Chryseïs to her father. He flung out his arm in an angry gesture. "Very well, the priest shall have his daughter back. I do not want to let her go, but I would rather lose her than be the death of all the Greeks. Odysseus shall make ready a ship and take the girl to Thebe."

There was a murmur of approval from the assembled Greeks, but Agamemnon looked about him sullenly. He had been at fault and he had been set down before them all, and he was not minded to be the only one to suffer. He caught sight of Achilles, with his friend Patroclus sitting at his side. They were smiling at each other, now that it seemed likely that Apollo's wrath would soon be ended. Agamemnon thought how it was young Achilles who had called the assembly, and so caused his discomfiture. Suddenly he shouted out, "I am the leader of you all, and the greatest king amongst you. It is not fitting that I alone should be without my chosen spoils. I shall send away Chryseïs because I must, but I will have instead a share of the booty of some other man—yours, perhaps, Achilles."

Achilles sprang to his feet, his eyes blazing. "You are our leader, King Agamemnon, but in this you presume too much. I have no quarrel with the Trojans. They have never stolen my father's cattle or his horses, nor have they harvested our fields of grain in Phthia. The mountains are too high and the sea too wide that lie between Troy and my father's land. No, I have led the Myrmidons to battle against the Trojans for the sake of your brother's quarrel, that he might win back his wife; though, since I was

Achilles. Detail from Attic, red-figured amphora (c. 450–440 B.C.).
Vatican Museums

never a suitor for Helen's hand—being too young by far—I was bound by no oath to do so. Remember that, before you talk shamelessly of sharing my booty." He paused for a moment, and then went on hotly, "And what is my share of the booty compared with all that you have taken from the towns that we have sacked? Because I am accounted a good warrior, and because my father's men are brave, to me falls more than my fair share of the fighting, so long as the battle lasts. But when the fighting is over, do I get a like share of the spoils? No. After you, King Agamemmon, have taken your pick, I get some small thing of little worth from whatever is left over, and I have to be content with that. What have I gained from this war with Troy? A little gold and silver and a few slaves—not many, since, unlike you, I am always ready to take a ransom for my captives." He paused again, and then said, "By all the gods, it would be better if I were to set sail with my father's men and return to Phthia, rather than stay here, slighted, to win more wealth for you to carry home to Mycenae."

Agamemnon laughed. "Go if you will," he sneered. "We shall do well enough without you. You may be brave, and a fine warrior, but of all the kings and princes of the Greeks, you, with your arrogance and your hot temper that you have not yet learned to curb, you are the one whom I could best do without. Go home. Take your ships and your Myrmidons. Lord it over your own men, show your temper to your friends and rail at them and not at me. Go home; but part, at least, of your booty you shall leave behind. When we sacked the city of Lyrnessus, you chose as your share of the spoils the girl Briseïs,[4] to be your slave. I must give up Chryseïs to her father, since it is the will of Apollo; but you shall give up Briseïs to me, since that is my will." He laughed again, shortly. "And when she is gone from your hut and dwells in mine, perhaps you will have learned at last that I am indeed the leader of all the Greeks, and a greater king than your father Peleus."

For a moment Achilles was too angry to speak or even move, and then he laid his hand upon the silver hilt of his sword, for in his rage he would have leaped upon Agamemnon and killed him there, in sight of all the other Greeks; but before even Patroclus could restrain him, prudent Athene, goddess of wisdom, who had been watching from high Olympus, came swiftly down amongst them, unseen of any, and standing behind Achilles, she took hold of his long yellow hair. He looked round and knew at once that it was one of the immortal gods who held him back, and he thrust his sword again into its scabbard, and immediately Athene left him.

Achilles, furious, but obedient to the divine injunction,[5] said, "Your wits must be befuddled with wine, Agamemnon, that you speak so to one who is braver than yourself. One day you will regret those words which have cost you my help and the help of my father's men, for neither I nor they, nor the friends who came with me to Troy, will fight any longer against the Trojans for your sake." He sat down, flushed and still angry, beside Patroclus.

Agamemnon would have scoffed further at him, but old Nestor rose. He was the king of Pylos,[6] and had come with ninety ships to fight against the Trojans with Antilochus[7] his son, who had been one of Helen's suitors. He was the oldest of all the kings and princes of the Greeks, and his counsel was valued amongst them and his words were always heard with respect.

"Shame upon you both!" he exclaimed. "How King Priam and his sons would rejoice to hear you now. I can chide you both, since I am older by far than either of you. In my time

4. **Briseïs** (brī-sē′ĭs).

5. **injunction:** command.
6. **Pylos** (pī′lŏs).
7. **Antilochus** (ăn-tĭl′ə -kəs).

I have known greater warriors than any here today, and called them my comrades in battle. I fought beside Peirithoüs[8] and great Theseus[9] himself, against the Centaurs[10] who dwelt in the mountain caves. No such grim fighting as that shall we see before the walls of Troy, yet we destroyed the Centaurs utterly. Even Theseus did not scorn my counsel, so why should you? Cease your quarreling, my friends. Let Achilles keep the girl he won, King Agamemnon, she is his by right. And, as you have said yourself, he is a fine warrior, and the Trojans fear him. As for you, Achilles, you are yet very young; you should show more respect to a great king whose lands are far wider than any you will ever rule."

"What you say is true, good Nestor," said Agamemnon, "but I am weary of Achilles' arrogance, his flouting of my authority, and his quick temper, which we see far too often."

Before he could speak further, Achilles broke in, "Your authority, King Agamemnon, do I no longer acknowledge. If you will, come and take the girl from me. I shall not prevent you. For I chose her by your favor: and what a man has given, that may he take away. Yet I warn you, lay but a finger on any of the goods I brought with me from Phthia, and it will not be Trojan blood which will be red upon my sword." He rose abruptly, flung his cloak about him, and gestured to his friend. "Come, Patroclus." And without another glance at Agamemnon, he left the assembly, and Patroclus went with him.

Achilles withdraws to his tent and refuses to fight. The war rages on. The Trojans are led by Hector, son of King Priam and the greatest warrior in Troy. He returns home from battle to spend a few moments with his wife, Andromache, and their child, Astyanax.

Hector and Andromache

Hector turned and hurried from his house, down the broad street from the Pergamus towards the Scaean Gate; and as he neared the gateway, Andromache saw him and came running to him from the watchtower beside the gate, followed by the nurse who carried Astyanax.

Hector smiled when he saw the child, but Andromache was weeping. She took hold of his hand. "Your courage will be the end of you, dear husband. Must you go again to battle? Think of me, if you will not consider yourself. My mother is dead, my father died when the town of Thebe was taken, and my seven brothers Achilles slew. I have no one left but you, Hector. To me you are not only husband, but father and mother and brother as well. If I lose you, what have I left? Have pity on me, Hector, and on our son. Stay with me on the wall today. Call the Trojans together and let them take their stand by the wild fig tree. For opposite the old fig tree the wall is weakest, and three times today have I watched the Greeks attack it at that place." She held his hand in both of hers and clasped it close to her.

He put his other arm about her. "My dearest wife, if I stayed with you and kept from battle, how could I face our people ever again? Indeed, I think that I could not keep from the fighting even if I would; for, all my life, I have learned only to be valiant and first in danger, to lead other men where they should follow, and to earn honor for my father and myself." He sighed. "I think that we cannot win this

8. **Peirithoüs** (pī-rĭth'ō-əs): At his wedding, a quarrel erupted between his people, the Lapiths, and the Centaurs.
9. **Theseus** (thē'sē-əs): a hero who killed the Minotaur, a monster half man and half bull.
10. **Centaurs** (sĕn'tôrz'): monsters that were half man and half horse.

war, Andromache, and that there must come a day when Troy will fall to the Greeks. My heart is torn when I think of all who will suffer then, my mother, my father, my brothers and sisters, our people; but for none of them do I grieve as I grieve for you, my wife, whom some Greek will take as the spoils of battle. Then, far away over the sea, in Greece, in the house of a harsh master, someone, someday, will see you weeping as you work at the loom or fetch water from the spring, and he will say, "She was the wife of Hector, the greatest warrior among the Trojans." And, hearing, your tears will flow yet faster for the husband who was not able to save you." He paused and then broke out, "Oh, may I be dead and the earth heaped high above me, before I hear your cries as they carry you off into slavery."

Andromache wept; and Hector turned from her and, leaning forward, stretched out his hands to take Astyanax from the nurse. But the child was afraid of the great horsehair crest on his father's helmet, and shrank back into his nurse's arms, so that Hector and Andromache, for all their grief, had to smile, and even laugh a little, as Hector took off his helmet and laid it on the ground, and Astyanax, reassured, came willingly into his arms.

Hector's Farewell (c. 1815) Drawing by Felice Giani (1758–1823).
Cooper-Hewitt Museum, the Smithsonian's National Museum of Design

Then Hector kissed his son, and holding him, prayed for him. "Great Zeus and all you immortal gods, grant that my child shall be brave and prove to be, even as I am, the greatest warrior amongst the Trojans, and grant that he shall rule mightily, here in Troy. And let there be a day, when, coming back from battle, it will be said of him, 'He is a far better man than his father,' so that he may gladden his mother's heart."

He put Astyanax in Andromache's arms, and she smiled at him through her tears. He held her and the child close to him, and said, "Do not torment yourself too much, dearest wife, for no man can send me down to the land of Hades before the time allotted by the immortal gods. Now go home and busy yourself with the household tasks, that you may forget to fret for me. War is not for women, but for men. And of the men in Troy, for me above all others, who should one day rule here."

He kissed her, and put on his helmet, while she went up the street towards the Pergamus, turning back time after time to see him, though her eyes were all but blinded by her tears.

Achilles' close friend, Patroclus, asks to borrow Achilles' armor and to lead his men, the Myrmidons, into battle. Patroclus is slain by Hector, who then strips Achilles' armor from his body. Grief for his dead friend rouses Achilles' desire for vengeance. Wearing new armor forged by the god Hephaestus, Achilles mounts his chariot and rides to battle. He pursues Hector to the gates of Troy.

The Vengeance

King Priam came upon the walls of Troy, and from the watchtower beside the Scaean Gate, he saw his people driven in rout before the spears of the Greeks and he called down to the

Thetis watching Hephaestus as he makes the armor of Achilles. Attic, red-figured amphora (c. 460–450 B.C.) by the Dutuit Painter.

gatekeepers, bidding them fling wide the gates, that the fleeing Trojans might win through to safety.

Through the Scaean Gate the Trojans poured, with the Greeks coming after them across the plain. But their fear gave them speed, and of those Trojans who had lived to cross the river all passed safely through the gates. All save Hector. He stood before the gateway, watching the oncoming Greeks, and wondering what it were best to do: to save his

The Iliad **633**

life and live to fight again, or to stay and face Achilles.

It was Priam, from the watchtower, who first saw Achilles as he drew near, his god-given armor shining in the afternoon sun, and in fear the old king called down to Hector, "My son, I beg of you, come within the walls. Do not stay to meet with Achilles. Many of my people has he slain since he first came against Troy, and many sons have I lost to his pitiless spear. Today Lycaon[11] went forth and, against my will, young Polydorus,[12] and I have not seen either return. Oh, my dearest and my best and eldest son, who should be king in my place when I am gone, do not let me have to mourn the death of a third son in a single day."

Hector looked up at him, and his heart was filled with pity, but he shook his head and set his heavy shield against the wall, and remained where he was, before the gates, alone.

King Priam tore his gray hair and pleaded with his son, and, while he spoke, those who stood near him on the wall moved aside to let Queen Hecuba come by. When she came to the watchtower, to her husband's side, and looked down and saw Hector standing there alone, she gave a great cry.

"If you are slain, my son," said Priam, "who will be left to guard the men and women of Troy? For you are our strong shield and our safety, and if you are killed we shall be left defenseless. Troy will fall to Achilles and the Greeks, and I, your old father, shall be slain, my naked body left for the dogs and the vultures, as though I had not been a king."

So Priam spoke with tears, yet he could not persuade his son. Nor could Hecuba prevail with him, though she, too, wept and said, "Have pity on me, my child, if on no other. I gave you life: must I now see that life taken from you with my own eyes?"

But Hector, torn between two duties, stood where he was until he, too, could see Achilles coming, in the forefront of the Greeks. Then he almost turned and fled in through the gates, but checked himself, thinking, "If I go within the walls to safety now, I must face Polydamas,[13] who gave me such good counsel, bidding me order the Trojans back to the city when he knew that Achilles was to fight again: and I would not hear him. He will reproach me, that by my folly so many men have died who did not need to die. How can I go into the city now, to hear some wretch of no account say of me, 'Hector, in his pride, has brought ruin on his people'? No, I would rather stay and meet Achilles and either kill him or die gloriously."

Then he thought how, perhaps for the Greeks as well as for the Trojans, the war had lasted long enough. "What if I were to lay down my weapons and strip off my armor and go all unarmed to meet Achilles, offer him Helen for Menelaus, and half of the great wealth of Troy, that the war between us might be over and our two peoples be at peace?" For a moment he was eager and hopeful; and then he remembered that it was he who had killed Patroclus, and that there could be no mercy for him from Achilles, though he offered him the whole of Troy and all its riches, for himself alone. "He would kill me as I stood unarmed before him. For between Achilles and myself there can be no pretty speeches, such as loving youths and maidens toss lightly to one another—fool that I was to think it." He shrugged his shoulders and took up his shield again.

Moving forward from the Scaean Gate, he saw Achilles running towards him, brandish-

11. **Lycaon** (lī-kā′ŏn).
12. **Polydorus** (pŏl-ĭ-dō′rəs): Priam's youngest son.

13. **Polydamas** (pō-lĭd′ə-məs): Hector's brother-in-law.

Hector prepares for battle.
Franco–Flemish wool and silk
tapestry (1472–1474).
(*Above*) Hector being armed,
surrounded by Andromache,
Astyanax, Hecuba, Helen,
and Polyxene. (*Below*) Hector
detained by Priam.

The Iliad **635**

ing his father's long spear, and knew that the time was very close when Patroclus might be avenged.

Then suddenly he thought, "By all the immortal gods, I do not want to die," and a great fear came upon him, and he turned and fled along the walls; and with a shout, Achilles was after him, signing to his men to keep away, for Hector was for him alone.

Past the watchtower Hector fled, and by the old figtree, and on to the smoother surface of the wagon track, a short distance from the walls, where the going was easier; and close after him came Achilles. They reached, and passed, the two springs and the washing troughs of stone, where, in the days of peace, before the Greek ships had come, the wives and women of Troy had brought their clothes to wash. On, on, they ran, as though it were a race that they were running, and for a prize. A prize there was indeed, and it was Hector's life.

Right around the city they ran; and ever Hector sought to run close in beneath the walls, so that the watchers might drop stones and weapons down on Achilles. But Achilles saw his intention, and always contrived to keep between him and the walls, to prevent him. Three times about the city they ran, and each time, as they passed the Scaean Gate, Hector tried to turn aside to escape within; and each time Achilles was there to intercept him and drive him back again on to the track.

But when they came for the fourth time to the springs and the washing troughs, the immortal gods, beguiling him—for he was doomed—sent Hector's fear from him, and he stood and turned to face Achilles. And in that moment, bright Apollo, till then his constant protector, abandoned him, leaving him, at last, to stand alone.

Breathlessly Hector called out to Achilles, "I will fly from you no longer, son of Peleus. Here let one of us make an end of the other. But first let us take an oath together that whichever is the victor will respect the other's body. I swear to you, Achilles, that if the gods are with me today and let me take your life, your armor I shall keep for myself, but your body I shall give to the Greeks, that they may burn it as befits the son of a king. Give me your oath to do likewise for me."

Achilles stood a short way off and leaned upon his spear, his breast heaving underneath the shining armor. When he had breath enough to speak, he said, "You must be mad to talk to me of oaths. There are no oaths made between men and beasts of prey. Wolves do not swear oaths with the sheep within the fold. There can be no oaths between us, Hector." He straightened up and moved his hand along the spear shaft. "Now show if you have courage, son of Priam, or whether all your great fame is undeserved, for the time has come for you to pay me for the death of Patroclus." He raised his spear and flung it; but Hector, watching carefully, crouched down, so that it passed over him and lodged, transfixed and quivering, in the ground behind him.

"Your aim was poor, Achilles. Now may the gods speed my spear and may it find its mark, for all Troy's enemies, you are the one most to be feared." Hector cast his spear and his aim was true, for the bronze head struck, ringing, full upon Achilles' shield; but the shield made by immortal Hephaestus held and was not pierced, and the spear fell harmlessly to the ground.

Hector stood dismayed, for he had no second spear; then he drew his sword and stepped aside, ready to fall upon Achilles, who leaped forward to snatch up once again his father's spear: and Athene herself, unseen, put it into his hand. And so the two of them stood close and faced each other, Achilles in the armor which a god had made for him, and Hector in Achilles' armor which the gods had given to

Peleus; and each watched the other warily to see where he should strike, for on that next blow would hang the outcome of the combat.

But Achilles knew the weak place in his own armor that he had brought from his father's house and worn so many times: a gap between the breastplate and the cheekpiece of the helmet. And there he thrust his spear, into Hector's neck, and Hector fell to the ground, gasping out his life.

Achilles laughed to see him. "Fool that you were, Hector. You forgot me when you killed Patroclus. Did you think that I would not remember you?"

Weakly, with fast ebbing breath, Hector whispered, "I beg of you, Achilles, accept a ransom for my body, that my people may burn it fittingly. Do not leave me for the vultures."

Angrily and bitterly Achilles answered him,

"Ask me no favors, Hector. Was it not you who would have set the head of Patroclus upon the walls of Troy? By all the gods, I wish that in my hatred I might tear and devour your flesh myself, for the grief that you have brought to me. There does not live the man who could pay me ransom enough for your body. Let your father offer your weight in gold. He shall never look upon your face again, nor shall your mother lay you on a bier and weep for you."

The blood dripped from the wound in Hector's neck, and his voice was no more than a murmur. "Your heart is hard as iron, Achilles, how could I have hoped to move you?" His voice rattled in his throat, his head sank down, and he was dead.

Exulting, Achilles raised the triumph cry and bent to strip his armor from Hector's body; and the Greeks ran forward, rejoicing

Achilles Kills Hector by Peter Paul Rubens (1577–1640). Museum Boymans–Van Beuningen, Rotterdam

Women working wool on loom. Attic, black–figured lekythos (vase),
sixth century B.C.

that the Trojans had lost their greatest warrior.
And there were many, seeing Hector lying
there defenseless, thrust their sharp spears
into his body, who would not have dared to
face him while he lived.

Watching, helplessly and with horror, from
the walls, the Trojans cried aloud and
lamented that their best protection against the
enemy was lost. Queen Hecuba shrieked and
tore her veil; and it was all that they could do
to hold back old Priam, who would have run
out through the Scaean Gate in frenzy to reach
his son.

Hector's wife, Andromache, was in her husband's house, working at her loom on a strip of
purple cloth, adorning it with flowers of every
color. She had just called to her women to set
the great tripod and cauldron upon the fire, so
that there should be hot water ready for a bath
for Hector when he came from the battlefield,
for it was nearing evening.

They were hastening to do her bidding at
that very moment when she heard the sounds
of lamentation from the walls. Her cheeks
grew pale and her hand shook, so that the
shuttle fell to the floor, and she ran out from

the house and through the streets to the wall, and the people made way for her. She looked down upon the plain, gave one cry, and fell senseless into the arms of those about her.

When she came to herself again, she wept and exclaimed, "To what an ill fate were we born, you and I, Hector. And to what an ill fate has our little son been born, that he is left fatherless while yet a babe." And so she wept, and her women wept with her.

There were some amongst the triumphant Greeks who were for attacking the city at that very moment, sure that it would fall easily to them while the Trojans were all confounded by the calamity that they had seen and crushed by their great loss.

And though at first Achilles agreed with them, he then said, "Let Troy be. I have done what I came out to do. Let us return to the ships, for we have had a great victory today. Shall Patroclus lie longer unburied, unmourned and forgotten? I shall not forget him so long as I still live; and even if, in the land of Hades, men forget their dead, yet I shall remember Patroclus, even there. Come, let us go."

And Achilles, in his hatred, pierced the sinews[14] of Hector's feet from heel to ankle and bound them together with a thong, and made fast the body to the back rail of his chariot, so that the head lay along the ground. He flung in Hector's weapons and his own armor, then leaped himself into the chariot, and snatching the reins and the whip from Automedon, he turned the horses' heads for the shore. He lashed them to a gallop, and Xanthus and Balius[15] went like the West Wind, who was their sire; and so Hector's body was dragged behind the chariot all across the Trojan plain, with his dark hair trailing in the dust.

14. **sinews** (sĭn′yo͞oz): tendons.
15. **Xanthus:** (zăn′thəs); **Balius** (bā′lĭ-əs): twin horses.

Achilles dragging Hector's body. Attic, black–figured lekythos (early fifth century B.C.). Attributed to the Diosphos Painter.

The Greeks hold a funeral feast and games to honor the memory of Patroclus. After twelve days, King Priam goes to Achilles to ransom the body of his son, Hector. Achilles, who is moved by the old man's grief, relents and returns Hector's body so that he can be mourned by the people of Troy. The poem ends when the remains of Hector's body are laid to rest in a burial mound.

The Ransom

Priam came down from his chariot, and leaving Idaeus to hold the horses and the mules, he went alone into the hut of Achilles.

Achilles, having at that moment finished his meal, was sitting, unsmiling, apart from his companions, and only Automedon was near him, to pour more wine for him, or fetch more meat, should he demand it. Straight to Achilles old Priam went, unhesitatingly; and before he could be prevented, knelt in front of him and clasped his knees in supplication, and kissed the hands which had slain his son.

Achilles looked at him with amazement; whilst all his companions in the hut fell silent, watching the stranger who had come amongst them, and wondering who he might be.

"Great Achilles, I beseech your mercy in the name of King Peleus, your father, whose years equal mine, and who, even as I, stands now on the sad threshold of old age. Yet, unlike me, he lives with hope, hope that one day soon he will see his dear son return to him, victorious after many battles. But I, I have no hope to lighten my remaining days. The dearest and the best of all my sons is gone, and I shall never speak with him or hear his voice again. Nor will he ever return victorious to his father's house. Yet one little grain of comfort would it bring to me, in my last years, if I might look upon his face once more and touch him with my hands; and a great solace would it be to me if, in the sad and

lonely, unprotected days which yet remain to me, I could remember how his body had been burnt with all honor as befitted the son of a king, and if I could look upon the burial mound which his mourning comrades had raised for him. In the name of your own father and in the name of immortal Thetis,[16] your mother, have mercy, great Achilles, and give back to Priam, that most wretched king, the body of Hector, his son. A great ransom have I brought you for him; do not refuse it." The tears streamed down his cheeks and he could hardly speak for weeping. He clasped Achilles' hands and said, "I implore you, have pity on an old man who must humble himself and kneel to one who has slain so many of his sons."

Achilles, much moved, gently loosed the old king's clasp and put him from him. His eyes were filled with tears and he turned his head away, thinking how his father Peleus would wait in vain for his homecoming. "I shall never see my father or my own land again," he thought. Then he thought how he would never again see Patroclus, a far greater grief than any other, and the tears would not be denied. And so they wept together: Achilles for his father and his friend, with the old king crouched at his feet, weeping for his son.

But at last, as Achilles' tears grew less, he was once again aware of Priam, and immediately he stood and raised the old man kindly, saying, "Your courage is indeed great, King Priam, that you ventured alone amongst your enemies to seek me out. But, come, sit here upon this seat and let us put aside our sorrowing. For of what avail are tears? They cannot bring back the dead. That is a thing which I have learnt." And he led him to a chair.

But Priam shook his head sternly. "Should I sit and take my ease, son of Peleus, while Hector lies in the dust amongst his enemies? No. Give

16. **Thetis** (thē′tĭs).

him back to me and let me see him. Take the ransom I have brought you, it is a fitting price for the son of a great king."

For a moment Achilles frowned, then with an effort he forced down his rising anger and answered, "Do not provoke me with ill-chosen words, good king. I shall give you Hector's body, as you ask, for I think that you came here today by the will of the gods, else could you not have reached my hut unharmed." He signed to Automedon to follow him, and quickly left the hut.

Outside, he called Idaeus, bidding him go in to his master and rest himself; then he ordered Automedon to unharness the mules and the horses from the wagon and the chariot, and to carry the ransom into his hut. "But leave a tunic and two cloaks to wrap the body in," he said, "lest Priam, seeing his son's wounds, should reproach me, and I should grow angry at his words and do what I would afterwards regret. For I would not dishonor the gods by mistreating a suppliant, and he a gray-haired king."

He bade the captive women take Hector's body from where it lay, and, in some place apart, where Priam could not see them, to wash it and anoint it with oil and wrap it in the tunic and the cloaks. And when all had been done as he commanded, he himself helped to lay Hector's body on the wagon; and as he did so, in his heart he cried out, "Do not be angry, Patroclus, if, even in the land of Hades, you hear that I have given Hector's body to the father who loved him. Do not be angry with me, but understand why I have done it, even as you would have understood while you yet lived."

Then Achilles returned once more into his hut. "I have done as you asked, King Priam. Your son lies on your wagon. Tomorrow you shall bear him back to Troy. But now you shall eat and drink with me, and for tonight you shall lie safely beneath my roof."

Priam sat, and Achilles gave him roasted meat upon a platter, and Automedon brought bread to him in a basket; and in silence they ate and drank together peaceably, the old king and the young warrior who had slain his son.

When the meal was finished, it had grown dark, and a slave set torches on the walls, and Priam, rested and refreshed, looked well for the first time at Achilles, all golden in the flaring torchlight, and saw how all that he had heard of his peerless beauty was true, and he thought, "Truly, rumor has not lied. He is like one of the immortal gods to look upon."

Achilles, watching, marked how Priam gazed at him, but he said nothing; and it was Priam who broke their silence.

"This is the first time in twelve long days," he said, "that I have sat to eat and drink with other men, for I have cared nothing for food or wine since Hector died. As little as I have tasted, so little have I slept for grief. But this evening, son of Peleus, I have eaten and drunk with you, and now I am weary and would sleep."

At once Achilles ordered beds to be prepared for Priam and Idaeus in the outer porch. "Forgive it, good king," he said, "that I put an honored guest to sleep outside. But if any leader of the Greeks should come here through the darkness to speak with me tonight—as well might be—he would see you, should you be lying near the hearth, and know you for the king of Troy. And if word reached Agamemnon that you were here, no doubt, to spite me, he would try to make it difficult for you to take with you the body of your son, which I have given you leave to take. But now, before we part tonight, tell me, how many days do you need to celebrate the funeral rites of Hector? For I doubt, with matters as they are, that the Greeks will go out to fight unless I go with them; and I shall keep from battle for as many days as you need."

Priam, touched by his offer, said "I am grateful for your kindness, son of Peleus. May the gods reward you for it. You must know that it is not easy for us, pent up in our city as we are, to venture far from the walls to fetch wood. Give us eleven days, good Achilles. Nine days to mourn for Hector and to gather the wood we shall need for his pyre; on the tenth day we shall burn him and keep his funeral feast, and on the eleventh we shall raise the burial mound above him." He paused, then added, "On the twelfth day, if need be, we shall fight again."

Achilles smiled a little. "You shall have your twelve days' truce, King Priam, I give you my word on it." He laid his hand for a moment upon the old king's arm in reassurance, saying to him, "Now lie down and sleep, you and your herald, and have no fear, for you will be safe beneath my roof."

And so, amongst his enemies, Priam slept calmly and in peace; but long before dawn Hermes, once again in the likeness of a Greek youth, woke him, saying, "You came to Achilles as a suppliant, and as a guest he has received you. Him you can trust, for you sleep beneath his roof; yet you can trust no other amongst the Greeks. Do not delay here, close by the ships. A great ransom you have given for your son, but it would be a ransom three times as great that the people of Troy would need to pay to buy your freedom, once Agamemnon knew that you were here."

Hastily, and in fear, Priam roused Idaeus, and they hurried from Achilles' hut, while Hermes himself harnessed the mules and the horses and, once again, led them safely past the ships across the plain. At the ford of the Scamander[17] he left them and returned to high Olympus.

As the sun was rising, the wagon and the chariot came slowly along the track towards the Scaean Gate. Cassandra, Hector's sister, watching from the walls, beheld, in the first light of day, her father and Idaeus, and saw that they had returned with him whom they had gone to fetch, and with a loud cry she roused all the people. "Come, all you men and women of Troy. If ever you welcomed back Hector, living, from the battle, come now and welcome him, dead. For he died to save our city and us all."

Out from their houses and out from Priam's palace came the people of Troy, crowding about the gates as Priam brought home his son, and with tears and wailing they welcomed him, following the wagon up the wide street to the Pergamus.

In the palace Hector was laid upon a bier, and about him stood the singers to sing his dirge; and one by one the noble women of the household made lament for him.

First spoke Andromache, his wife, with her arms clasped about her husband's head. "Oh, Hector, ill-fated are we whom you have left defenseless, and ill-fated is your little son, but most ill-fated of all am I, your unlucky wife; for you did not stretch out your arms to me when you were dying, nor speak to me in words which I might have remembered with tears and treasured in my heart for all my life."

Beside her stood Queen Hecuba. "You were the eldest and the dearest to me of all my children, Hector," she said. "And while you lived divine Apollo, the Bright One, cared well for you. Yet even in your death the immortal gods did not utterly forsake you; for, though I dared not hope to do so, I have seen your dear face once again, and in all honor do you lie in your father's house, and in all honor shall we celebrate your funeral." But, after that, she could say no more for weeping.

Then Helen came to them, and the women drew aside as she passed and would not look at her, walking slowly until she stood beside the bier, looking down on Hector. "Kind Hector," she said quietly, "of all the brothers of Paris, you alone never reproached me for the trouble that I brought on Troy, and always would you

17. **Scamander** (skă-măn′dər): river of Troy.

defend me against the harsh words of others. Now that you are gone, in all Troy I have no man to speak for me, save your father, who, with you, alone was kind." And she drew her veil across her face to hide her tears.

For nine days was Hector mourned; and on the tenth day, when dawn was come, they laid him on a tall pyre and fired it. All day it burnt, and through the night the ashes smoldered; but on the morning of the eleventh day they poured wine upon the ashes and gathered up the dead man's bones and laid them in a golden urn and set upon it stones and earth, raising a high burial mound.

And so, by the compassion of Achilles, was Hector buried, who had slain Patroclus and brought Achilles so much grief. *10*

Reading Check

1. Why does Calchas ask for Achilles' protection?
2. How has Agamemnon angered the god Apollo?
3. How does Agamemnon make an enemy of Achilles?
4. Why is Patroclus mistaken for Achilles during battle?
5. What prevents the Greeks from attacking Troy?
6. What oath does Hector ask Achilles to swear before their combat?
7. How does Achilles know which is the weakest place in the armor Hector is wearing?
8. What is Hector's dying request?
9. Why does Priam go to Achilles' hut?
10. What truce do Achilles and Priam agree upon?

For Study and Discussion

Analyzing and Interpreting the Epic

1. Achilles, the greatest of the Greek warriors, is the hero of the *Iliad*. He is depicted as having intense emotions. **a.** How does he show that he is quick to anger in his quarrel with Agamemnon? **b.** How is his anger shown later in the story? **c.** Where does he admit that he cannot control his rages? **d.** How does this human failing make Achilles a more believable figure?

2. Hector is the greatest warrior among the Trojans. **a.** What impression do you receive of him in the scene with his family? **b.** How does Homer evoke sympathy for him in the combat with Achilles? **c.** Do you find him more or less admirable than Achilles? Explain.

3. In the *Iliad* the outcome of battles is often decided by the Olympian gods and goddesses. Where else do they intervene to affect the action?

4. **a.** What aspect of Achilles' nature is revealed in the scene with Priam? **b.** How does this scene make a nobler figure of Achilles?

5. Women play an important role in this epic. Identify each of these figures and explain her role in the events: Helen, Hecuba, Andromache, Cassandra.

Writing About Literature

Comparing Heroic Figures

Write an essay comparing Achilles and Hector. What do you learn about each hero from his words, his actions, and his thoughts, as well as from the reactions of others? How are they alike and how are they different?

BEOWULF

Although *Beowulf* was composed around the eighth century, its legendary adventures are much older and were probably known for centuries before the poem was written. The poem reveals a great deal about the customs and values of the Germanic people who invaded the British Isles and established settlements there in the Middle Ages. Important in this society was the relationship of the lord and his thanes, or followers. In return for loyalty and military service, the lord rewarded his followers with treasure and feasts.

The poem focuses on the adventures of Beowulf, a great warrior with superhuman powers. In his youth, Beowulf battles with two terrible monsters, Grendel and Grendel's mother. In his old age, he fights his last battle against a fire dragon. The only surviving manuscript of the poem is in Anglo-Saxon, or Old English. The excerpts you will read are from a verse translation in Modern English by Ian Serraillier.

Names and Places in *Beowulf*

Beowulf (bā'ə-woolf'): hero of the epic. He is from the land of the Geats, in Sweden.

Breca (brĕk'ə): Beowulf's opponent in a swimming match.

Geats (yă'əts, yā'əts): a people in Sweden. Beowulf becomes their king and rules them for fifty years.

Grendel (grĕn'dəl): a troll-like monster who lives in the fens and attacks the warriors of Hrothgar's court.

Heorot (hā'ō-rŏt): the mead hall built by King Hrothgar to feast his followers.

Hrothgar (hrŏth'gär): the Danish king who builds Heorot.

Unferth (ŭn'fârth): a jealous noble who attacks Beowulf as a braggart.

Wulfgar (woolf'gär): herald of King Hrothgar.

Statue of Rurik, a Viking chief who settled in Russia in A.D. 862.

Beowulf the Warrior

Translated by
IAN SERRAILLIER°

Silver arm ring from
Hornelund, Denmark
(tenth century).
National Museum, Denmark

The Battle with Grendel

Hrothgar, King of the Danes, glorious in battle,
Built him a huge hall—its gleaming roof
Towering high to heaven—strong to withstand
The buffet of war. He called it Heorot
And lived there with his Queen. At time of feasting   5
He gave to his followers rings and ornaments
And bracelets of bright gold, cunningly wrought,°
Graved with runes° and deeds of dead heroes.
Here they enjoyed feasts and high fellowship,
Story and song and the pride of armed peace.   10
But away in the treacherous fens, beyond the moor,
A hideous monster lurked, fiend from hell,
Misbegotten son of a foul mother,
Grendel his name, hating the sound of the harp,
The minstrel's song, the bold merriment of men   15
In whose distorted likeness he was shaped
Twice six feet tall, with arms of hairy gorilla
And red ferocious eyes and ravening jaws.
He, one night, when the warriors of Hrothgar lay
Slumbering after banquet, came to Heorot,   20
Broke down the door, seized in his fell grip
A score and more of the sleeping sons of men
And carried them home for meat. At break of day
The hall of Heorot rang loud and long
With woe of warriors and grief of the great King.   25
Thereafter, from dark lake and dripping caves
Night after night over the misty moor
Came Grendel, gross and grim, famished for flesh.
Empty the beds, no man dared sleep at Heorot,

Three—ringed gold collar
with filigree and carved
figures from Gotland,
Sweden (sixth century A.D.).
This is an example of
fine Viking craftsmanship.
Statens Historiska Museet,
Stockholm

°**Serraillier** (sə-rāl′yər).   7. **cunningly wrought:** skillfully made.   8. **runes:** characters in an ancient alphabet.

But Grendel smelt them out of their hiding place, And many a meal he made of warriors.
For twelve years he waged war with Hrothgar,
Piling grief upon grief. For twelve years
He haunted great Heorot.

30

University Museum of National Antiquities, Oslo, Norway

A Viking ship discovered in Gokstad, Norway, in 1880.

When Beowulf, the young Swedish warrior, heard of Hrothgar's plight, he was determined to help him. With fourteen of his bravest men he sailed away over the Baltic Sea to Denmark. They left their boat at anchor and climbed up the white cliff.

Thus came the warriors   35
To Heorot and, heavy with weariness, halted by the door.
They propped their spears by a pillar; from blistered hands
Their shields slid clattering to the floor. Then Wulfgar,
Herald of the King, having demanded their errand,
Ran to his royal master and quick returning   40
Urged them within. The long hall lay before them,
The floor paved with stone, the roof high-raftered.
In mournful state upon his throne sat brooding
Aged Hrothgar, gray-haired and bowed with grief.
Slowly he raised his eyes, leaden, lusterless,   45
And gazed upon the youth as with ringing step
Boldly he strode forth till he stood at his feet.
    "O noble Hrothgar, giver of treasure,
Lord of the rousing war song, we bring you greeting.
Because we grieve deep for your desolation,   50
Over the long paths of the ocean have we labored,
I and my warriors, to rid you of the brute
That nightly robs you of rest. I am no weakling.
With my trusty blade I have slain a monster brood
And blindly at night many a foul sea-beast   55
That writhed and twisted in the bounding wave.
I beg you to grant my wish. I shall not fail."
    Then Hrothgar stretched out his arms in welcome
And took him by the hand and said, "Beowulf,
I knew you as a child, and who has not exulted   60
In your fame as a fighter? It is a triumph song
That ocean thunders to her farthest shore,
It is a whisper in the frailest seashell.
Now, like your princely father long ago,
In the brimming kindness of your heart you have come   65
To deliver us."

But Unferth bristled at these words—
Unferth, who sat always at the feet of Hrothgar,
A groveling, jealous man who could not bear
That anyone should win more fame than he.
    "Braggart!" he cried. "Are you not that Beowulf   70
Who failed against Breca in the swimming match?

Viking ship with sea monster. Ms. Ashmole 1511, f.86v (late twelfth century).
Bodleian Library, Oxford

648 THE EPIC

Seven nights you wallowed in the wintry sea—
Some sport that was!—sport for jeering waves
That jollied you like spindrift° from crest to crest
Till, sick with cold, you shrieked for mercy. Who heard?   75
Not Breca, who long since had battled to land,
But the sea, tired at last of its puny plaything,
Spewed you ashore."

                Angrily Beowulf answered:
"That's a drunkard's tale! True, Breca was first
Ashore, but I could have raced him had I wished.   80
We were boys then, with our full share of folly,
Plunging—sword in hand—giddily to battle
With monster whales, when a storm came sweeping down
And gruesome waves ground and trampled us under.
It was Breca that cried for help—I fought to save him,   85
But a fierce northeaster whipped us apart
And I saw him no more. In the dark and bitter cold,
The icy brine° was heaving murkily with monsters.
Glad was I of my sword and mailcoat—for a serpent
Had wound his sinewy coils about my waist,   90
And squeezing, dragged me below. But before he could break me,
I slew him—nine others too before the raging floodtide
Rolled me to land. . . . . .
I am not aware that you, brave Unferth, can boast
Such a record. If you be as bold as you proclaim,   95
Tell me, how comes it that Grendel is still alive?
Ha, I know a coward when I see one! Soon,
If the King be willing, I shall grapple with Grendel
And show you what courage means." . . . . .

                Over the misty moor   100
From the dark and dripping caves of his grim lair,
Grendel with fierce ravenous stride came stepping.
A shadow under the pale moon he moved,
That fiend from hell, foul enemy of God,
Toward Heorot. He beheld it from afar, the gleaming roof   105
Towering high to heaven. His tremendous hands
Struck the studded door, wrenched it from the hinges
Till the wood splintered and the bolts burst apart.
Angrily he prowled over the polished floor,

---

74. **spindrift:** spray from the waves. 88. **brine** (brīn): ocean.

A terrible light in his eyes—a torch flaming!   110
As he scanned the warriors, deep-drugged in sleep,
Loud loud he laughed, and pouncing on the nearest
Tore him limb from limb and swallowed him whole,
Sucking the blood in streams, crunching the bones.
Half-gorged, his gross appetite still unslaked,°   115
Greedily he reached his hand for the next—little reckoning
For Beowulf. The youth clutched it and firmly grappled.

Such torture as this the fiend had never known.
In mortal fear, he was minded to flee to his lair,
But Beowulf prisoned him fast. Spilling the benches,   120
They tugged and heaved, from wall to wall they hurtled.
And the roof rang to their shouting, the huge hall
Rocked, the strong foundations groaned and trembled.
Then Grendel wailed from his wound, his shriek of pain
Roused the Danes in their hiding and shivered to the stars.   125
The warriors in the hall spun reeling from their couches,
In dull stupor they fumbled for their swords, forgetting
No man-made weapon might avail. Alone, Beowulf
Tore Grendel's arm from his shoulder asunder,°
Wrenched it from the root while the tough sinews cracked.   130
And the monster roared in anguish, well knowing
That deadly was the wound and his mortal days ended.
Wildly lamenting, away into the darkness he limped,
Over the misty moor to his gloomy home.
But the hero rejoiced in his triumph and wildly waved   135
In the air his blood-soaked trophy.

                              And the sun,
God's beacon of brightness, banishing night,
Made glad the sky of morning. From near and far
The Danes came flocking to Heorot to behold
The grisly trophy—Grendel's giant arm   140
Nailed to the wall, the fingertips outspread,
With nails of sharpened steel and murderous spikes
Clawing the roof. Having drunk their fill of wonder,
Eagerly they followed his track to the lake, and there
Spellbound they stared at the water welling with blood,   145
Still smoking hot where down to the joyless deep

115. **unslaked:** unsatisfied.   129. **asunder:** apart.

He had dived, downward to death. And they praised Beowulf
And swore that of all men under the sun, beyond measure
Mightiest was he and fittest to govern his people.

    Meanwhile, in the hall at Heorot the grateful King,   150
All glooming gone, his countenance clear and cloudless
As the sky in open radiance of the climbing sun,
Gave thanks to God for deliverance. "Beowulf," he said,
"Bravest of men, I shall love you now as my son.
All I have is yours for the asking. Take   155
What treasure you will. But first let us feast and be merry."

    Straightway they washed the blood from the floor, propped up
The battered door; the drooping walls they draped
With embroidery, bright hangings of woven gold.
There was drinking and feasting again, revelry of heroes,   160
And the jeweled goblets clashed. At last the King,
Aged Hrothgar, gray-haired giver of treasure,
Ordered gifts to be brought. To Beowulf he gave
A sword and mailcoat and banner of gleaming gold;
A plated helmet so tough no steel might cleave it;   165
Eight prancing horses with golden harness
And bridles of silver, the proudest saddled with his own
Battle-seat, all set with splendid jewels,
Most cunningly inlaid; to each of the warriors
A sword and bountiful recompense of gold   170
For their friend that Grendel slew.
                Then the minstrel sang
Of rousing deeds of old. Like flames in the firelight
The heart leapt to hear them. And when he had done
And the harp lay silent, the Queen of the Danes spoke out:
"Beowulf, dearest youth, son of most favored   175
And fortunate of mothers, this your deed is matchless.
Greater than all these. In the farthest corners
Of the earth your name shall be known. Wherever the ocean
Laps the windy shore and the wave-worn headland,
Your praise shall be sung."

              And now the feast was ended.   180
With final clarion of trumpets they left the hall,
Hrothgar and his gracious Queen, leading Beowulf
To a stately chamber to rest. But the Danes remained.
Clearing the banquet, they brought couches spread
With pillows and warm coverlets, and lay down,   185

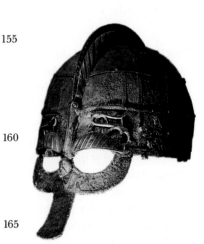

Helmet from Vendel,
Sweden (seventh century).
Statens Historiska Museet,
Stockholm

Viking sword from
Steinsvik, Lodingen,
Nordland [Norway]
(tenth century).

University Museum of National Antiquities,
Oslo, Norway

Each with his broad shield at his head, his mailcoat,
His spear and shining helmet—as was the custom
Long ere Grendel came. Now fearless of monster,
Their minds were at ease, quiet as the summer sea,
The sparkling water, unmurmuring and serene   190
Under the moon. In comfort of spirit, in blessed
Trust and tranquillity they sank to rest.

Grendel's mother, a she-monster as horrible as her son, comes out of her lair to avenge the death of Grendel. She snatches up one of the Danes and carries him off, along with Grendel's arm and claw. Beowulf follows her to her den and plunges into the lake in full armor. There is a fierce struggle. Finally, Beowulf finds a magic sword and kills the monster.

Beowulf becomes king of the Geats and rules over them for fifty years. Then a dragon begins to ravage the land, and Beowulf goes out to fight his final battle. He overcomes the dragon, but receives his death wound. His final request is that his followers raise a funeral pyre and build a mound upon his ashes, to serve as a beacon to sailors.

Beowulf's final battle
with the dragon.
Illustrated by Rockwell
Kent (1882–1971) for
Beowulf (1932).

Beowulf the Warrior **653**

For Study and Discussion

Analyzing and Interpreting the Epic

1a. What indications are there in the opening lines that this poem is about a warrior society? **b.** How are Hrothgar's followers rewarded in times of "armed peace"?

2a. What motives for Grendel's savagery are given in lines 11–18? **b.** Why are Hrothgar and his warriors powerless to stop Grendel?

3. Why does Beowulf believe that he can destroy Grendel? See lines 53–57.

4a. How does Unferth attempt to cast doubt on Beowulf's reputation as a fighter? **b.** How does Beowulf defend himself against Unferth's charge?

5. Beowulf defeats Grendel in hand-to-hand combat, without the help of any weapons. **a.** How does this episode emphasize the hero's superhuman prowess? **b.** Where else in the selection are we told that Beowulf has performed extraordinary feats?

6. What customs are restored at Heorot after Grendel's death?

7a. What heroic characteristics are celebrated in the epic of Beowulf? **b.** What is the importance of such qualities as loyalty, fame, and glory?

Literary Elements

Recognizing Characteristics of Old English Poetry

Old English poems like *Beowulf* were memorized and recited at banquets in the halls of kings and rulers by wandering poets (see lines 171–180). Eventually the poems came to be written down.

The translation in your textbook retains certain features of the oral tradition of Old English poetry. One important characteristic of this verse was **alliteration,** the repetition of similar consonant sounds, usually at the beginning of words. In Old English poetry, alliteration usually occurs on three or more accented syllables in a line. Ian Serraillier creates a similar effect in line 36:

> To *Heorot* and, *h*eavy with weariness, *h*alted by the door

Find at least two places in the poem where alliteration is used for emphasis.

Another characteristic in Old English poetry is the use of a descriptive phrase as an indirect way of identifying a person or thing. The term for this device is **kenning.** The sun, for example, is called "God's beacon of brightness" in line 137. What kennings are used for Hrothgar?

Viking Ship Museum, Bygdoy, Norway

Dragon head, a popular motif in Viking art, found in a burial ship discovered in Oseberg, Norway, in 1904.

About the Translator

Ian Serraillier

Ian Serraillier, who lives in England, is a poet and a translator. His books include *Escape from Warsaw* and *Silver Sword*.

When asked about the pronunciation of his name, he responded with the following limerick and note:

If in Doubt

Just call me Ian SerRAILlier
Of Sussex, U.K. (not Australia).
   This is not my best verse
   But I have written worse
So it's neither a hit nor a failure.

The Christian name is easy—just ignore the first nine letters in antediluvIAN.

Extending Your Study

Comparing Famous Monsters

In many heroic stories, the enemy is as repulsive as the hero is admirable. Like Grendel, the monsters often live in darkness and hate light. Often they are cannibals.

Using a mythology book or an encyclopedia for reference, write a brief description of each of the following famous monsters. How does each one compare with Grendel?

Cyclops
Medusa
Minotaur

THE SONG OF ROLAND

The Song of Roland (pronounced rô-läɴ′ in French) belongs to a cycle of epics dealing with the reign of Charlemagne (shär′lə-mān′), "Charles the Great," also known as Charles I (742–814). He was king of the Franks and emperor of the Romans. The poem is based on an historical event. In the year 778, Charlemagne had fought against Moslem Saracens in Spain. While he was returning to France through

Charlemagne with Roland and Oliver. Stained glass window (c. 1200), from Strasbourg Cathedral, Strasbourg.

Musée de l'Oeuvre Notre-Dame, Strasbourg

the Pass of Roncesvalles (rôNs-vō′) in the Pyrenees Mountains, his army was attacked and his rear guard destroyed by inhabitants of the region called Basques (băsks). This incident became the subject of songs, and over the course of centuries, the historical facts were greatly altered. By the time *The Song of Roland* was composed, around 1100, Roland, one of Charlemagne's leaders, had become a nephew of the king; the Basque attackers had become Saracens; and a traitorous villain was introduced, Roland's stepfather, Ganelon.

The Song of Roland reflects the ideal of knighthood that flowered during the Middle Ages. Knights were sworn to uphold a code of honor and service known as *chivalry* (shĭv′əl-rē). The story of Roland tells us a great deal about the code of chivalry. A knight took vows to defend his king and his Christian faith. He considered his duty and his honor more important than his own life.

As the poem opens, Charlemagne has conquered all of Spain except Saragossa. Marsile, King of the Saracens, pretends to renounce his faith, and offers to follow Charles to Aix (ĕks) to be baptized a Christian. Charlemagne's knights caution him against trusting the Saracens, but Ganelon, Roland's stepfather, persuades the king to trust Marsile. When he is sent as an ambassador to negotiate for peace, he betrays Charlemagne and Roland, for whom he feels jealous hatred. Ganelon counsels Marsile to attack Charlemagne's rear guard, and then arranges to have the command of the rear guard assigned to Roland.

Names and Places
in *The Song of Roland*

Aix: a city in southern France.

Charlemagne: "Charles the Great," the king of the Franks and emperor of the Romans.

Durendal: Roland's sword.

Ganelon: Roland's stepfather, who betrays the Franks.

Marsile: the Saracen king.

Oliver: a French count; Roland's trusted friend.

Roland: hero of the epic; nephew of Charlemagne.

Roncesvalles: the pass in the Pyrenees Mountains where Roland and the Franks are attacked by the Saracens.

Saracens: Moslems at the time of the Crusades.

Turpin: the archbishop who fights beside Roland.

The Song of Roland

Translated by
<u>HILDA CUMINGS PRICE</u>

The Enemy Approaches

Resplendent shines the sun upon that host,
That moves like some strange brightly colored snake
Along the valley in unending line.
A hundred thousand Saracens are there,
Each rider filled with pride and lust for blood.   5
The steel of sabers flashes in the light.
The flaunting banners ripple in the breeze
And wake the darkened scene to vivid life.
Behold these hundred thousand marching men;
A wondrous sight they make, a deadly too!   10
For how can Roland with his few stand firm
Against such overwhelming odds as this?
The bugles sound a carillon° of notes
And from the hills a thousand echoes ring.
The air is vibrant like a restless sea;   15
It seems the heavens and earth reverberate
To this defiant call from pagan throats.
It travels high upon the air as far
As Roncevaux° where Roland and his French
Stand guard against their Emperor's retreat.   20
Count Oliver is quick to note the sound
And turns to Roland standing by his side.
"My dearest friend, the enemy is near."

13. **carillon** (kăr′ə-lŏn,′ kə-rĭl′yən): melody.

19. **Roncevaux:** Roncesvalles (rôns-vō′), a pass in the Pyrenees Mountains.

Roland riding on horseback through the Pyrénées.
Miniature from *Karl de Grosse* by der Stricker.
Ms. Germ. fol.623, f 21v (c. 1300).
Staatsbibliothek Preussischer Kulturbesitz, West Berlin

"If that be so," is Roland's firm reply,
"May God defend our arms and grant us strength   25
To beat the Saracens and at the end
Be counted worthy to be men of Charles.
Our cause is just and for myself I pray
That I may fight as well becomes a knight,
And when the minstrels sing in years to come   30
The story of this day at Roncevaux,
Then would I have them tell of those who fell,
And if I fall in battle with the rest,
Of Roland may they say: ''Twas here the earth
Was stained with valiant blood.' 'Tis all I ask."   35
No answer comes from Oliver to this,
But running in impetuous haste he climbs
A little hill to view the scene from there.
He scarce believes his eyes that now behold
The valley filled with Marsile's Saracens.   40
"Such numbers have I never seen," he cries
To Roland in alarm. "Ours are too few.
Outnumbered thus we cannot hope to bring
This foe to earth. I swear this is the work
Of Ganelon, vile Ganelon, whose heart   45
Is full of hate. By foul deceit he plans
That you and all the French shall be destroyed."
But Roland stops him as he speaks in wrath.
Hold thou thy tongue, my friend. This Ganelon
Is one of us, the Emperor's man, our peer.°   50
You charge him with an act of treachery
But cannot prove the truth of what you fear,
Wherefore no word of it will I believe,
Nor hear it said of Ganelon that he
In mood of violent spleen° betrayed his own."   55

But Oliver heeds not these gentle words;
He turns from Roland to address the French.
"The enemy is near and plans attack.
Brave men of France, stand firm and with God's help
We'll triumph yet against these pagan hordes."   60
And with one voice the French to this reply:
"Let evil fall on him who flees the fight.
Stand firm we will, unconquered save by death!"
Yet Oliver is sad although he knows
Each man will do as he has vowed to do,   65

Ganelon before the kings of
Saragossa. Miniature from
Les Grandes Chroniques de France,
Ms. Fr. 20350, f 109v (fourteenth
century).
Bibliothèque Nationale, Paris

50. **peer:** There were Twelve Peers,
chosen by Charlemagne as companions.

55. **spleen:** ill will and bad temper.

But few they are. How few against this foe!
Again he climbs the hill and looks beyond
And sees Marsile's advancing line of men,
And overcome with dread he seeks to plead
With Roland, his most dear and cherished friend.   70
"This heathen host is more than we can count.
To pit our strength against these many spears
Can only bring disaster and defeat.
Oh Roland, sweet companion of my youth,
I pray you for the sake of these brave French   75
Blow now upon your horn and Charles will hear
And with his army turn from his retreat
To come and help us in our hour of need."
But Roland will not hearken to his friend.
"Not e'en at your desire can I do this.   80
Such action on my part doth seem to me
To forfeit my good name, upon which name
Has Charles entrusted me with his command.
The moment soon will come when I may strike
For France and for our glorious Emperor.   85
Strike hard I will with this, my trusty sword.
Good Durendal shall reddened be with blood,
With heathen blood for not a Saracen
But to his cost shall learn he cannot spring
Attack on Roland and keep safe his life."   90

Brave words are these, but Oliver is sad.
Upon his heart there lies the awful dread
Of courage wasted and endeavor lost.
With fervent pleading yet again he speaks:
"Most noble Roland, none could ever doubt   95
Your valor as a knight, but comes a time
That calls for wisdom. Now is such a time.
I beg you sound your horn that Charles may come
To aid us in the fight lest we should fail."
But Roland shakes his head. "It cannot be   100
That I should bring disgrace upon sweet France
Or on my father's name; enough for me
To face the foe with my good Durendal.
Together we will dare and it shall be
That not a pagan shall escape our might."   105
Most urgently does Oliver reply:
"Oh Roland, Roland hearken now or fall

A prey to Marsile and his hungry hordes.
Blow, blow your horn that Charles may turn about
And share this fight with you and Durendal." 110
As urgently does Roland answer him:
"May God forbid that living man shall say
That Roland feared to stand alone and fight.
No, no, my friend, I will not blow my horn.
A hundred thousand Saracens I defy: 115
They shall not raise their swords 'gainst France and live."
With harder pleading still does Oliver
Entreat his friend. "As far as eye can reach
The valleys and the hills are thick with men,
As swarming bees upon an apple bough. 120
Let go your pride before it is too late."
But Roland will not hear. "Better to die
By sword of Saracen than shame my birth.
For France and for the Emperor forthwith°   124. **forthwith:** immediately.
I go and God's good angels be my stay, 125
And evil be to him who shrinks for fear."

Now bold as any lion Roland calls
To all the French and Oliver, his friend:
"For us it is to guard this mountain pass.
From glorious Charles have we received the charge, 130
And Charles knows well that cowards do not thrive
Within his hardy ranks. Then rise, brave men,
And set your faces t'wards the crafty foe.
Behold this shining sword, my uncle's gift;
Full hard my Durendal shall strike, and if 135
This day 'tis death awaits me at the end,
I pray it may be said: 'This was the sword
Of one who served his king right manfully.'"

Roland Sounds His Horn

*The Franks gallantly hurl themselves on the Saracens. The battle rages
furiously all day. The Franks, greatly outnumbered, foresee defeat.
Roland, reluctant to confess his error, finally agrees to sound his horn.
Charles hears the notes in his far distant camp and realizes that Roland
needs his help. The wicked Ganelon attempts to keep the king from turn-*

ing back, but Charles soon concludes that Ganelon has betrayed him. He has the traitor seized and then leads his army back toward Spain in hopes of saving Roland.

While Charles rides to their aid, the Franks defend the pass to the last man. Roland wounds Marsile, who retreats from the field, and then kills Marsile's son. Oliver is fatally wounded. Before he dies, he makes his peace with Roland.

Roland sounds his horn once more, and Charles has his bugler blow a clarion call so that Roland and his Franks will know that help is on the way. Alarmed by their fear of the Emperor's warlike skill, the pagans turn and flee.

The Death of Roland

The fighting is no more, the foe is gone,
And slowly, in great weariness of soul,   140
Count Roland seeks for Turpin whom he saw
Long since in fiercest combat on the field.
He finds the faithful priest in deadly pain,
All crumpled in a heap upon the ground.
He tries to ease him of his agony   145
By taking off his helm° and coat of mail;
This done, he goes to bring the other knights
Who lie in lonely death upon the field,
For he would have them lie together here.
He brings them one by one and at the sight   150
Of his most noble peers, their lives cut short
By swords of heathen Saracens, he mourns;
His spirit fails him and he faints from grief.
The good archbishop strives to help the count,
Though weak from loss of blood he scarce can move;   155
He takes the horn that hangs at Roland's side,
And edges inch by inch to reach a stream
That flows in rippling coolness near at hand.
To fill the horn with water is his will,
But Turpin's will is greater than his strength;   160
His body is too feeble to obey;
The distance is too far for him to go;
Ere half of it is traveled, Turpin dies.

Count Roland wakens from his faint and sees
The dead Archbishop. "Gentle priest," he cries   165

> 146. **helm:** an archaic word for helmet.

Scenes from the Battle of Roncevaux: (*above*) Roland and Turpin are
surrounded by the enemy and Roland sounds his horn; (*below*) Roland
bids farewell to Turpin; Roland strikes the pagan who has stolen his
sword. Miniature from *Karl de Grosse* by der Stricker, Ms. 302, f50v.
(c. 1300).

"Oh knight of fair renown, thou too art gone?
Now truly am I left in loneliness.
To God in Heaven do I commend thy soul;
None ever was more worthy to be praised,
Nor fought more nobly for the Christian faith.   170
I pray the gates of Paradise this day
Stand wide that you may enter into rest."

664 THE EPIC

In sadness Roland turns away, his eyes
Brimful of tears. With slow dejected steps
He climbs a little hill to lie alone   175
And there await his end which he feels near.
His right hand grasps firm hold of Durendal;
His horn he carries with his left: these two
The only friends that still remain of all
That glorious company that rode with him   180
To guard the pass for Charles at Roncevaux.
But walking even those few steps is more
Than he can do without his strength gives out;
He stumbles blindly then he faints again.
Oh woeful thought, he lies there not alone!   185

A Saracen lurks near in wait for him.
With cunning devilry the man has smeared
His face with blood from others' wounds and so
Feigns death. Fair Roland is deceived and thinks
This enemy's beyond an evil act;   190
But as he falls the pagan springs to life
And laughs aloud in fiendish glee to see
His prostrate foe. "At last!" he shouts. "At last,
Proud nephew of a prouder king, thou'rt mine!
Thou'lt trouble Spain no more. Thy day is done.   195
This sword of thine I take now for my own."
The sword lies close by Roland's mailéd hand,
And as the Arab crouches at his side
To steal from him his precious Durendal,
Does Roland wake to consciousness most clear.   200
He sees the pagan's dark-browed face o'er his,
And instantly he seeks for Durendal.
His sword is gone! Then savagely his horn
He lifts and with a sudden heav'n-sent strength
He strikes the man and cleaves his skull in two.   205
Good Durendal he clasps close to his breast.
"Thou fool," he cries. "How durst thou think to steal
My Durendal? 'Tis well that thou art dead."

His weakness now is very great, yet not
Content is he to lie and wait for death.   210
His sword he will not leave upon the field
For some uncaring wanderer to find.
"Ah, Durendal, my trusty friend, thy work
For me is done. My life is ebbing fast.

How oft have thou and I together fought,   215
Not seeking glory for ourselves but Charles,
On whose white hairs let brightest honor rest.
Oh, none shall call good Durendal his own
Save Roland who received thee as a gift."
So Roland takes his sword and strikes it hard   220
Against a stone to break it at the hilt;
The quivering steel rings out a thin clear note
But will not break. Again does Roland strike
With all the strength at his command and still
That finely tempered blade stays keen and straight.   225
A third time Roland strikes and Durendal
Escapes his hold and rises in the air;
Rebounding then, it falls at Roland's side.
No longer can the Count hold death at bay;
He feels its icy hand upon his heart.   230
Beneath a pine he lies and close beside
He lays his ivory horn and Durendal;
His face he turns t'wards Spain that Charles may know
The fight brought no retreat save for the foe.
Resigned to death and contrite for his sins,   235
Good Roland beats his chest before he prays:
"Oh just and gracious God, forgive me now
For every wrong that ever I have done."
Then quietly he lies remembering
The past and how he fought and won fair lands   240
For France and for the honor of his lord;
But as he thinks of Charles he cannot hold
The falling tears, for that the love that binds
These two has always been so strong. He prays
Again: "Oh Father true, Who once did save   245
The Prophet Daniel° from the lion's mouth
And Lazarus° from the grave, receive my soul,
And from death's perils now deliver me."
He lifts his glove and offers it to heaven
In token that he dies a Christian knight,   250
And then he sees, although his eyes are dim,
A host of God's bright cherubim° appear.
They hover over him, and Gabriel,
The brightest of them all, bends low to take
From him the mailéd glove, and Roland's heart   255
Wells up with joy to know that heaven accepts
The deeds which he has done for love of Charles.

246–247. Daniel's faith saved him when he was sent into a den of lions (Daniel 6:16-23); Lazarus was raised from the dead (John 11:1–44).

252. **cherubim** (chĕr'ə-bĭm'): angels.

Scenes from the death of Roland: (*top left*) Roland tries to break his sword; (*top right*) he delivers his glove to Heaven; (*bottom left*) Charlemagne takes Durendal from the dead Roland. Miniature from *Karl de Grosse* by der Stricker, Ms. 302, f52v. (c. 1300).

Content to die he clasps his hands in prayer;
So Roland's soul is borne on angels' wings
From this dark world to those empyrean° heights   260
Where faithful spirits dwell in Paradise.

260. **empyrean** (ĕm′pī-rē′ən): heavenly.

Charlemagne avenges the deaths of his knights by pursuing the Saracens, who plunge into the Ebro River and are drowned. Marsile joins forces with the Emir of Egypt, who arrives in Spain to battle Charlemagne. After a furious battle, Charlemagne defeats his enemies. In Aix, the French knights hold court to judge Ganelon. They pronounce him a traitor and sentence him to death. Thus Roland's death is avenged.

Reading Check

1. What order has Roland received from Charles?
2. How does Oliver know the Saracens are approaching before he sees them?
3. What does Oliver ask Roland to do before the battle begins?
4. Identify Durendal.
5. Why does Roland turn his face toward Spain before he dies?

For Study and Discussion

Analyzing and Interpreting the Epic

1. Both Oliver and Roland know that they are outnumbered by the Saracens. **a.** Contrast their reactions. **b.** What are Roland's reasons for refusing to call for help?

2. At first Roland will not believe that Ganelon is a traitor. What does this show about his own ideals of honor and loyalty?

3. In line 121, Oliver pleads with Roland to let go his pride. **a.** Do you believe Roland is motivated by pride? **b.** According to Roland, what are his responsibilities to his emperor and to his country?

4. As Roland lies dying on the battlefield, an enemy soldier tries to steal his sword. **a.** Why is his sword so important to Roland? **b.** Why does he try to destroy it?

5. Roland is considered to be a model of the ideal Christian knight. Where does he exhibit the following characteristics: heroic valor, love of glory and personal honor, compassion, religious faith?

Writing About Literature

Analyzing Values and Beliefs

An epic embodies a society's most significant values and beliefs. *The Song of Roland* reveals a great deal about the code of chivalry that governed the lives of knights in the Middle Ages. Using the selection in your textbook, what conclusions can you draw about the standards of chivalry and the qualities of the ideal warrior? What importance is given to courage, skill in combat, honorable behavior, kindness, and Christian faith? Write an essay analyzing the values and beliefs that have emerged from your study of *The Song of Roland.*

DEVELOPING SKILLS
IN CRITICAL THINKING

Using Methods of Comparison and Contrast

You can often gain insight into a particular work by comparing some aspect of it with that of another, similar work. In this unit you have been introduced to four representative epics. By examining their similarities and differences, you can gain a better idea of what an epic is.

1. *An epic deals with the adventures of a great hero or warrior.* How is the hero depicted in each of the epics you have read? What extraordinary or superhuman deeds does he perform? Does the hero defend his people from some enemy or monster?

2. *An epic embodies the values and beliefs of a particular society or people.* What are the heroic ideals represented in the *Iliad*? Are these the same ideals represented in *Beowulf* and in *The Song of Roland*?

3. *The hero of an epic often undertakes a perilous journey.* How does this theme appear in *The Epic of Gilgamesh* and *Beowulf*?

4. *Supernatural forces often play an important role in the action.* What supernatural agents affect the action in *The Epic of Gilgamesh* and the *Iliad*?

PRACTICE IN READING AND WRITING

Writing an Informal Research Report

The following steps will help you to plan and write an informal report:

Prewriting

- Choose a topic which is interesting to you and others as well. Be sure there is enough information on the topic you have selected. Have your teacher approve your selection.
- After you have selected a broad topic, brainstorm or cluster to limit your topic to a narrow subject. A broad topic can make your job difficult. Focus your attention on one aspect of the topic. For example, you might choose the following broad topic and then limit it to a more specific subject:

  > BROAD TOPIC: *Beowulf*
  > LIMITED TOPIC: *The Background of Beowulf*

- Write a statement of purpose. This is your topic sentence. This statement will tell your audience what your report is about. Your statement of purpose is very important and should be the first sentence in your report. The following thesis sentence can serve as an example:

  > PURPOSE: *Beowulf* is the first heroic poem in English literature.

- Gather information on your topic from the library or other places which might offer information needed in writing your report. Use magazines, television, and newspapers to find information. Keep notes and list the names of books, articles, and television shows from which you draw information. Record the names of authors of books or articles and document your sources.
- Make an outline. An outline will help you to achieve your goal; it will guide you in your writing. Use your notes: organize them, and list your findings in a logical order. Be sure to choose ideas and facts that you find interesting.

Writing and Evaluating

- Begin writing a rough draft by using your outline to guide you. You may want your teacher to check your draft before you make your revisions. Your teacher can help you evaluate your writing. Eliminate any unnecessary information.
- After evaluating your paper, prepare a clean, final draft. Have a friend edit your final copy. If all errors are eliminated, your paper is complete.

In your study of the epics in this unit, you have been introduced to many different customs, places, and characters. Choose one of the epics you enjoyed reading. Write a research report about an aspect of the epic which you find interesting. Select one of the general topics listed below as your starting point in your research or choose a topic of your own pertaining to one of the epics.

Cultural customs
Weapons and armor used in battle
Geographical locations
Myths and supernatural forces in epics
Origin of names for gods and goddesses
Historical background of the epic

For Further Reading

Asimov, Isaac, *Words from the Myths* (Houghton Mifflin, 1961)

This book includes stories of gods and monsters—who they were, what happened to them (and how to say their names). The stories also show how ancient words and expressions are used in daily conversation.

Colum, Padraic, *The Children of Odin; The Book of Northern Myths* (Macmillan, 1984)

Here are easy-to-read stories of the Norse gods.

Colum, Padraic, *The Frenzied Prince* (David McKay, 1943)

This is a collection of heroic stories of ancient Ireland.

Curtis, Edward S., *The Girl Who Married a Ghost and Other Tales from the North American Indians* (Four Winds, 1978)

Here are haunting stories of nine different Indian tribes.

Homer, *The Iliad*. Retold by Barbara Leonie Picard (Walck, 1960)

Marriott, Alice Lee, *The Black Stone Knife* (Crowell, 1957)

This is the exciting story of five Kiowa boys, their adventures through the lands of the enemy Apache, and their first encounter with white men.

Miquel, Pierre, *The Days of Knights and Castles* (Silver Burdett, 1980)

Here is a story in pictures of daily life and events of the Middle Ages from 1066 through 1485.

Sargent, Sarah, *Lure of the Dark* (Four Winds, 1984)

This is a story of what happens when the troublesome Norse god, Loki, enters the life of a modern girl.

Song of Roland, Translated by Merriam Sherwood. Illustrations by Edith Emerson (David McKay, 1967)

Exciting stories and drawings of the battles and adventures of the Emperor Charlemagne.

Sutcliff, Rosemary, *Beowulf* (Dutton, 1962)

A prose retelling of the epic.

Williams, Ursula Moray, *The Earl's Falconer* (Morrow, 1961)

This is the story of a boy whose only interest in life is falconry and who, because of his talent with falcons, is permitted to study with a great falcon master.

WRITING
ABOUT
LITERATURE

Developing Skills
in Critical Thinking

Many of the compositions you will be asked to write in English class will be about the literature you read. The writing may be in response to an examination question, a homework assignment, or a research project. At times you may be assigned a topic to work on; at other times you may be instructed to choose your own subject.

In writing about literature, you generally focus on some aspect of a work or group of works. For example, you may compare two characters in a story; you may discuss the conflict that is developed in a play; you may analyze the imagery in a poem. Such writing assignments are an important part of literary study, which aims at greater understanding and appreciation of the works you read.

Writing about a literary work brings you closer to it. Before you write a composition about a story, a poem, or a play, you must read and reread the selection carefully. You must sort out your thoughts and reach conclusions. In putting your thoughts down on paper, you become more fully involved with the work.

Throughout your studies you will become familiar with a great many elements that are useful in analyzing literary works. When you refer to the techniques a writer uses to create suspense, for instance, you may use the term *foreshadowing*. In discussing the attitude a writer takes toward a subject, you may concern yourself with *tone*. In examining the musical effects of a poem, you may point to patterns of *rhyme* and *rhythm*. These words are part of a common vocabulary used in writing about literature. You can assume that your readers will understand what you mean when you write about such elements. (See the *Guide to Literary Terms and Techniques,* page 696.)

The material on the following pages offers help in planning and writing papers about literature. Here you will find suggestions for answering examination questions, choosing topics, gathering evidence, organizing essays, and writing, evaluating, and revising papers. Also included are several model essays.

The Writing Process

We often refer to writing an essay as a *process*, which consists of six key stages: **prewriting, writing, evaluating, revising, proofreading,** and **making a final copy.** In this process, much of the important work—the thinking and planning—comes before writing the first draft.

In the **prewriting** stage, the writer must decide what to say and how to say it. Prewriting includes choosing a topic, gathering ideas and organizing them into a plan, and developing a *thesis*—the main idea for the paper. In the **writing** stage, the writer uses the plan to write a first draft of the essay. In the **evaluating** stage, the writer judges the first draft to identify strengths and weaknesses in content, organization, and style. **Revising,** the fourth stage, involves making changes to improve the weaknesses in the draft. The writer can revise by adding, cutting, reordering, or replacing words. In the **proofreading** stage, the writer reads the draft to locate and correct any mistakes in grammar, usage, and mechanics. The last stage, **making a final copy,** involves preparing a clean copy and then proofreading it to catch any mistakes made in copying.

The stages of the writing process are related. For this reason, there is usually a "back and forth" movement among the stages. Few writers finish one stage completely before they move on to the next one. At the same time, few writers move in a straight line from one stage to the next. For example, the writer might think up new ideas as he or she is writing a first draft. This would probably require going "back" to prewriting to restate the thesis or to locate new supporting evidence. This movement among the stages of the writing process is a natural part of writing—for all writers.

The amount of time devoted to each stage will vary with individual assignments. During a classroom examination, you will have limited time to plan your essay and to proofread your paper. For a term paper, you may have weeks or months to prepare your essay.

On the following pages the steps in this process are illustrated through the development of several model essays.

Answering Examination Questions

Often you may be asked to show your understanding of a literary work or topic by writing a short essay in class. Usually, your teacher will give you a specific question to answer. How well you do will depend not only on how carefully you have read and mastered the material, but on how carefully you read and interpret the essay question.

Before you begin to write, be sure you understand what the question calls for. If a question requires that you give *three* reasons for a character's actions, your answer will be incomplete if you supply only *two* reasons. If a question specifies that you deal with the *theme* of a work, take care not to give a summary of action or your answer will be unacceptable. Always take some time to read the essay question carefully in order to determine how it should be answered.

Remember that you are expected to demonstrate specific knowledge of the literature. Any general statement should be supported by evidence. If you wish to show that a character changes, for example, you should refer to specific actions, dialogue, thoughts and feelings, or direct comments by the author, in order to illustrate your point. If you are allowed to use your textbook during the examination, you may occasionally quote short passages or refer to a specific page in order to provide supporting evidence.

At the start, it may be helpful to jot down some notes to guide you in writing your essay. If you have four main points to make, you may then decide what the most effective order of presentation will be. You might build up to your strongest point, or you might present your points to develop a striking contrast. Aim for a logical organization.

Remember that length alone is not satisfactory. Your answer must be clearly related to the question, and it must be presented in acceptable, correct English. Always take some time to proofread your paper, checking for mistakes in spelling, punctuation, and usage.

Let us look briefly at some common instructions used in examinations.

ANALYSIS   A question may ask you to *analyze* some aspect of a literary work. When you analyze something, you take it apart to see how each part works. In literary analysis you generally focus on some limited aspect of a work in order to better understand and appreciate the work as a whole. For example, you might analyze the technique of suspense in "The Sea Devil" (page 30); you might analyze O. Henry's use of irony in "A Retrieved Reformation" (page 210); you might analyze Twain's tone in "Cub Pilot on the Mississippi" (page 428).

COMPARISON
CONTRAST   A question may ask that you *compare* (or *contrast*) two characters, two settings, two ideas. When you *compare*, you point out likenesses; when you *contrast*, you point out differences. Sometimes you will be asked to *compare and contrast*. In that event, you will be expected to deal with similarities and differences. You might, for instance, compare and contrast the two fathers in "A Cap for Steve" (page 78); you might compare the characters of the folk heroes in "Paul Bunyan's Been There" (page 173) and "Pecos Bill, Coyote Cowboy" (page 177). Sometimes the word *compare* is used to include both comparison and contrast. Always check with your teacher to make sure that you understand what the question calls for.

DEFINITION   A question may ask you to *define* a literary term—to answer the question "What is it?" To define a term first assign it to a general class or large group. Then discuss the features or characteristics that make it different from other members of the same class or group. You should also provide a specific example to illustrate the term. For example, if asked to define the term *metaphor,* you would first say it is a figure of speech (large group) in which two unlike things are compared (feature). You might use Emily Dickinson's poem, "I Like to See It Lap the Miles" (page 468) as an example of metaphor. Here the metaphor compares a train to a horse.

DESCRIPTION   If a question asks you to *describe* a setting or a character, you are expected to give a picture in words. In describing a setting, remember to include not only features of the physical locale, but those features that establish the historical period or evoke a mood. In describing a character, you should deal with both direct characterization and indirect characterization (see page 234). You might describe the setting in "The Parachutist" (page 235); you might describe the hawk in the same story.

DISCUSSION   The word *discuss* in a question is much more general than the other words we've looked at. When you are asked to discuss something, you are expected to examine it in detail. If you are asked to discuss the images in a poem, for example, you must deal with all major images; if asked to discuss the use of dialect in a story or poem, you must be sure to cover all significant examples. You might be asked to discuss humorous elements in a group of poems (pages 504–510).

EVALUATION If a question asks you to *evaluate* a literary work or some aspect of one or more works, you are expected to determine whether an author has achieved his or her purpose. To evaluate, you must apply standards of judgment that may relate to both literary content and form. For example, you might be asked to evaluate the use of rhyme to reveal the speaker's state of mind in "The Raven" (page 474). You might be asked to evaluate O. Henry's use of the surprise ending in "A Retrieved Reformation" (page 210).

EXPLANATION A question may ask you to *explain* something. When you explain, you give the reasons for something being the way it is. You make clear a character's actions, or you show how something has come about. For example, you might explain what the talents are of "The No-Talent Kid"(page 10); you might explain the mystery of identity in "The Rule of Names" (page 220); you might explain how the author gives the appearance of authenticity to the story of "The Man Without a Country" (page 142).

ILLUSTRATION The word *illustration, demonstrate,* or *show* asks that you provide examples to support a point. You might be asked for examples of Harriet Tubman's courage illustrated in "They Called Her Moses" (page 419). You might be asked to demonstrate exaggerated characteristics of heroes in the American folk tales about Paul Bunyan, Pecos Bill, and Davy Crockett (pages 173–184).

INTERPRETATION The word *interpret* in a question asks that you give the meaning or significance of something. You might, for example, be asked to interpret "The Road Not Taken" (page 471), a poem that is famous for its symbolism.

At times it will be useful to combine approaches. In discussing a subject, you may draw upon illustration, explanation, or analysis. In comparing or contrasting two works, you may rely on description or interpretation. However, an examination question generally will have a central purpose, and you should focus on this purpose in preparing your answer.

Using the Writing Process to Answer an Essay Question

Even if you are well prepared for an examination, you may not develop your essay effectively unless you manage your time well. Although you may have to work quickly, you should nevertheless devote some time to each stage of the writing process. The following suggestions indicate how you can use the writing process to develop an answer to an essay question. Once you become familiar with this pattern, you will have a plan that enables you to work quickly and efficiently.

PREWRITING   In an essay examination, the question itself gives a narrow topic. Its key verb also suggests a way to answer the question. Several prewriting steps remain:

1. *Write a thesis statement.* A thesis statement gives the main idea of your essay. It should appear at the beginning of your essay.

2. *Develop points to support, or explain, the thesis.* The main idea should be supported by at least two main points. In a short essay all the points may be discussed in a single paragraph. In a longer essay each point may be discussed in a separate paragraph. Each point must clearly support the main idea of the essay.

3. *Locate supporting evidence from the literary work(s).* Evidence can include specific details, direct quotations, incidents, or images. This evidence should support or explain each main point you are discussing.

4. *Organize the main points and evidence.* You should arrange your ideas and details into a logical order—one that your reader can follow easily. By arranging your ideas, you will develop a plan that you can use to write your essay. This plan should include an introduction, a body, and a conclusion for your essay.

WRITING   Write your essay, following the plan you made in prewriting. In the introduction, state the title of the literary work and your thesis. In the body, present the main points and the supporting evidence. In the conclusion, state your thesis again or summarize your main points. Be sure to use language that is serious enough for your purpose (to convey ideas) and for your audience (your teacher, in most cases). Also use transitional expressions (words or phrases that connect ideas, such as *first, then,* and *finally*) to make it clear how ideas are related.

EVALUATING   Quickly evaluate, or judge, your essay by answering the following questions:

Purpose	1. Have I answered the specific question given?
Introduction	2. Have I included a thesis statement that expresses the main idea of my essay?
Body	3. Have I included at least two main points that support the thesis statement?
	4. Have I included evidence from the literary work to support each main point?
	5. Is the order of ideas clear and logical?
Conclusion	6. Have I included a conclusion that states the main idea again or that summarizes the main points?

REVISING   Using your evaluation, improve your essay by *adding, cutting, reordering,* or *replacing* words.

PROOFREADING   Read your essay to locate and correct any mistakes in grammar, usage, and mechanics. You can make a clean copy of your essay if your teacher says you have time to do so. If so, proofread again to catch any mistakes made in copying.

Sample Examination Questions and Answers

On the following pages you will find some sample examination questions and answers for study and discussion. Note that the assignments (shown in italics) may be phrased as direct questions or as essay topics.

I

QUESTION   *The conflict in the myth of "Antigone" (page 68) involves two strong wills. In a single paragraph, explain the struggle between Antigone and Creon.*

DEVELOPING AN ANSWER   Before writing, jot down some prewriting notes to guide you:

Both characters are obstinate and unyielding in their beliefs.
As king, Creon makes it a penalty for anyone to bury Polynices.
Antigone defies Creon's laws and buries her brother.
Creon holds the established laws of the country uppermost.
Antigone claims that the laws of the gods have a prior claim over the laws made by men.

In the opening sentence of your answer, state your *thesis,* your main point, wording it in such a way that you restate the key words of the question.

Here is a model answer based on the writer's notes.

The struggle between Antigone and her uncle centers on the matter of law. As king, Creon makes it a penalty for anyone to bury Polynices, whom he considers a traitor. Antigone feels obligated to perform the burial rites for her brother Polynices; otherwise his soul will be unable to find rest. Creon accuses her of breaking the laws of the kingdom in disobeying his will. In defending her actions, Antigone claims that the laws of pity and mercy must be obeyed first, for those are the laws of the gods.

Length: 90 words

II

Discuss the clues that point to the true identity of Mr. Underhill in "The Rule of Names" (page 220). Refer to your textbook.

Before writing, go through the story and jot down all the clues that point to Mr. Underhill's identity. Use these prewriting notes to guide your writing.

Here is a model answer for the question.

Mr. Underhill, in "The Rule of Names," is really a powerful dragon named Yevaud that has come to Sattins Island in disguise. Through the story there are clues that indicate Mr. Underhill is not what he seems to be. When he first appears in the story he is breathing hard. The breath comes out of his nostrils "as a double puff of steam" (page 220). According to legend, dragons are fire-breathing. Mr. Underhill has come to Sattins Island as a wizard, but he is not a great success. His magic remedies are weak, and his enchantments are a failure. Whenever a strange ship comes to the island, Mr. Underhill stays out of sight. Another indication that he has something to hide is that he does not allow people to visit his cave. Dragons keep their treasures in caves. When the boys try to pry open the door, they are greeted by a terrific roar and a "cloud of purple steam" (page 221), a further clue to the wizard's true identity. We learn that Mr. Underhill has an enormous appetite. After visiting Palani, the schoolteacher, and the children, he becomes very hungry. Dragons are known for devouring maidens. When we put these clues together, we are prepared for Mr. Underhill's transformation into a dragon.

Clue 1

Clue 2

Clue 3

Clue 4
Clue 5

Clue 6

Conclusion

Length: 213 words

III

QUESTION *Is the narrator of Poe's "The Tell-Tale Heart" (page 273) mad or sane? Give your interpretation, referring to specific details in the story. You may use your textbook.*

DEVELOPING AN ANSWER Begin by deciding whether the narrator in the story is mad or sane. Then list details from the story that support your viewpoint. The following set of notes supports the opinion that the narrator is mad.

> **Notes**
> The narrator is mad.
> He claims to hear sounds in hell, the insects in the wall, the dead man's heart beating.
> He is nervous; his broken speech shows he is in a state of excitement.
> He has no rational motive for killing the old man.
> He is obsessed by the old man's eye, which he calls the Evil Eye.
> He has contradictory emotions: he pities the old man, but chuckles at the thought of murder; after he kills the old man, he smiles gaily.
> He is unable to control himself, working himself up to an hysterical pitch in the presence of the police.
> He keeps insisting on his sanity.

There is a considerable amount of information to organize here. You might try grouping the notes so that you can present the evidence under a few categories, perhaps 1) his sense of hearing; 2) his lack of motive for the murder; 3) his inability to control his emotions.

WRITING AN ANSWER Here is a model essay that uses the writer's notes.

Main Idea *The narrator in Poe's "The Tell-Tale Heart" is incapable of distinguishing between reality and fantasy.* Although he tries to convince his audience that he is sane, pointing to examples of his cleverness and cunning, his behavior throughout the story reveals a diseased mind.

Point 1 **One significant piece of evidence is his claim that his sense of hearing is acute.** In his very first speech, he says that he can hear "many things in hell' (page 273). A little later he says he has been in the habit of listening to the deathwatches in the wall (page 274). Be-

Supporting Statements fore he suffocates the old man, he claims to hear the man's heart beating, and again, after the old man has been murdered and his body dismembered, the narrator claims to hear the heart beating in ever-increasing loudness.

Point 2

Supporting Statements

Another indication of his insanity is his admission that he has no rational motive for killing the old man. In fact, he loves the old man, but he is obsessed by the old man's blue eye, an "Evil Eye" which vexes him. For eight nights he postpones the murder, until the sight of the eye incites him to fury.

Point 3

Supporting Statements

Furthermore, the narrator is unable to control his emotions, and he seems to be constantly on the verge of hysteria. He admits to being "very dreadfully nervous" (page 273); his speech is broken, showing his state of excitement and tension. His emotions also are contradictory. He pities the old man, yet chuckles inwardly (page 274). After he smothers the old man, he smiles gaily (page 275). His behavior after murdering the old man also shows that he is emotionally unbalanced. He brings the police officers into the room where he has buried the body and places his own chair on the very spot where the dismembered corpse is concealed. He soon works himself up into a frenzy, foaming at the mouth, raving, swearing, and scraping his chair upon the boards. His confession is brought on by his delusion that the police actually know of the crime and hear the heart beating, but deliberately wish to mock him.

Length: 357 words

Writing on a Topic of Your Own

Choosing a Topic

At times you may be asked to choose a topic of your own. Often it will be necessary to read a work more than once before a suitable topic presents itself.

A topic may focus on one element or technique in a work. If you are writing about fiction, you might concentrate on some aspect of a plot, such as conflict. Or you might concentrate on a character, setting, or theme. If you are writing about poetry, you might choose to analyze imagery or figurative language. A topic may deal with more than one aspect of a work. You might, for example, discuss several elements of a short story in order to show how an idea or theme is developed.

Above all, be sure to limit a broad subject to a manageable topic—one that is sufficiently narrow. A narrow topic is one you can discuss in the time and space you have for the essay. Once you have a topic in mind, your object is to form it into a *thesis*, a controlling idea that represents the conclusion of your findings. You would then need to present the evidence supporting your position. It may be necessary to read a work several times before you can formulate a thesis. Here are some examples:

Shane (page 520)

Topic   Analyzing the character of Shane
Thesis   Shane is a noble, heroic figure who cannot overcome some tragedy in his past.

The Epic of Gilgamesh (page 615) and *Beowulf* (page 646)

Topic   Comparing characters of Gilgamesh and Beowulf
Thesis   Both characters, who have superhuman attributes, value courage, friendship, and honor above all else.

"Flowers for Algernon" (page 240)

Topic   Explaining the effect of increasing intelligence on Charlie's life
Thesis   As Charlie becomes more intelligent, he finds himself becoming more isolated from other people.

"The Dog That Bit People" (page 413)

Topic   Describing Muggs
Thesis   Muggs was a big, irritable, moody dog, who intimidated everyone with whom he came into contact.

"The Road Not Taken" (page 471)

Topic Explaining significance of title
Thesis The speaker emphasizes the choice he made in life by not taking the easier and more conventional path.

"The Raven" (page 474)

Topic Discussing the responses of the speaker to the raven
Thesis The speaker, at first seemingly assured, becomes increasingly distracted and loses emotional control.

"The Land and the Water" (page 265)

Topic Interpreting the theme of the story
Thesis When some of her neighbors are lost at sea, a young girl learns for the first time that death can touch young people like her.

Gathering Evidence/ Developing Major Points

It is a good idea to take notes as you read, even if you do not yet have a topic in mind. Later on, when you have settled on a topic, you can discard any notes that are not relevant. Some people prefer a worksheet, others index cards. In the beginning, you should record all your reactions. A topic may emerge during this early stage. As you continue to read, you will shape your topic into a rough thesis.

When you take notes, make an effort to state ideas in your own words. If a specific phrase or line is so important that it deserves to be quoted directly, be sure to enclose the words in quotation marks. When you transfer your notes to your final paper, be sure to copy quotations exactly.

In working with a short poem, you may cite phrases and lines without identifying the quotations by line numbers. If you cite lines in a long poem, you should enclose the line numbers in parentheses following the quotation. The following note, which is for "Casey at the Bat" (page 507), shows you how to do this:

When the narrator describes the final pitch, he says: "And now the pitcher holds the ball, and now he lets it go,/And now the air is shattered by the force of Casey's blow" (lines 47–48).

The slash (/) shows the reader where line 47 ends and line 48 begins.

If you cite three or more lines, you should separate the quotation from your own text. The following note, which is for "Paul Revere's Ride" (page 136), shows you how to do this:

After he climbs the North Church tower, Revere's friend looks into the distance and sees the British crossing by water:

> Where the river widens to meet the bay—
> A line of black that bends and floats
> On the rising tide, like a bridge of boats.
> (lines 54–56)

Let us suppose that you have chosen to contrast the characters of the narrator and his Uncle Wash in the following story.

Thanksgiving Hunter
JESSE STUART

"Hold your rifle like this," Uncle Wash said, changing the position of my rifle. "When I throw this marble into the air, follow it with your bead;[1] at the right time gently squeeze the trigger!"

Uncle Wash threw the marble high into the air and I lined my sights with the tiny moving marble, gently squeezing the trigger, timing the speed of my object until it slowed in the air ready to drop to earth again. Just as it reached its height, my rifle cracked and the marble was broken into tiny pieces.

Uncle Wash was a tall man with a hard leathery face, dark discolored teeth and blue eyes that had a faraway look in them. He hunted the year round; he violated all the hunting laws. He knew every path, creek, river and rock cliff within a radius of ten miles. Since he was a great hunter, he wanted to make a great hunter out of me. And tomorrow, Thanksgiving Day, would be the day for Uncle Wash to take me on my first hunt.

Uncle Wash woke me long before daylight.

"Oil your double-barrel," he said. "Oil it just like I've showed you."

I had to clean the barrel with an oily rag tied to a long string with a knot in the end. I dropped the heavy knot down the barrel and

---

1. **bead:** the sight at the muzzle end of a gun barrel.

pulled the oily rag through the barrel. I did this many times to each barrel. Then I rubbed a meat-rind over both barrels and shined them with a dry rag. After this was done I polished the gunstock.

"Love the feel of your gun," Uncle Wash had often told me. "There's nothing like the feel of a gun. Know how far it will shoot. Know your gun better than you know your own self; know it and love it."

Before the sun had melted the frost from the multicolored trees and from the fields of stubble and dead grasses, we had cleaned our guns, had eaten our breakfasts and were on our way. Uncle Wash, Dave Pratt, Steve Blevins walked ahead of me along the path and talked about the great hunts they had taken and the game they had killed. And while they talked, words that Uncle Wash had told me about loving the feel of a gun kept going through my head. Maybe it is because Uncle Wash speaks of a gun like it was a living person is why he is such a good marksman, I thought.

"This is the dove country," Uncle Wash said soon as we had reached the cattle barn on the west side of our farm. "Doves are feeding here. They nest in these pines and feed around this barn fall and winter. Plenty of wheat grains, rye grains, and timothy seed here for doves."

Uncle Wash is right about the doves, I thought. I had seen them fly in pairs all summer long into the pine grove that covered the knoll east of our barn. I had heard their mournful songs. I had seen them in early April carrying straws in their bills to build their nests; I had seen them flying through the blue spring air after each other; I had seen them in the summer carrying food in their bills for their tiny young. I had heard their young ones crying for more food from the nests among the pines when the winds didn't sough[2] among the pine boughs to drown their sounds. And when the leaves started turning brown I had seen whole flocks of doves, young and old ones, fly down from the tall pines to our barnyard to pick up the wasted grain. I had seen them often and been so close to them that they were no longer afraid of me.

"Doves are fat now," Uncle Wash said to Dave Pratt.

"Doves are wonderful to eat," Dave said.

And then I remembered when I had watched them in the spring and summer, I had never thought about killing and eating them. I had thought of them as birds that lived in the tops of pine trees and that hunted their food from the earth. I remembered their mournful songs that often made me feel lonely when I worked in the cornfield near the barn. I had thought of them as flying over the deep hollows

2. **sough** (sŭf, sou): make a murmuring sound; sigh.

in pairs in the bright sunlight air chasing each other as they flew toward their nests in pines.

"Now we must get good shooting into this flock of doves," Uncle Wash said to us, "before they get wild. They've not been shot among this season."

Then Uncle Wash, to show his skill in hunting, sent us in different directions so that when the doves flew up from our barn lot, they would have to fly over one of our guns. He gave us orders to close in toward the barn, and when the doves saw us, they would take to the air and we would do our shooting.

"And if they get away," Uncle Wash said, "follow them up and talk to them in their own language."

Each of us went his separate way. I walked toward the pine grove, carrying my gun just as Uncle Wash had instructed me. I was ready to start shooting as soon as I heard the flutter of dove wings. I walked over the frosted white grass and the wheat stubble until I came to the fringe of pine woods. And when I walked slowly over the needles of pines that covered the autumn earth, I heard the flutter of many wings and the barking of guns. The doves didn't come my way. I saw many fall from the bright autumn air to the brown crab-grass-colored earth.

I saw these hunters pick up the doves they had killed and cram their limp, lifeless, bleeding bodies with tousled feathers into their brown hunting coats. They picked them up as fast as they could, trying to watch the way the doves went.

"Which way did they go, Wash?" Dave asked as soon as he had picked up his kill.

"That way," Uncle Wash pointed to the low hill on the west.

"Let's be after 'em, men," Steve said.

The seasoned hunters hurried after their prey while I stood under a tall pine and kicked the toe of my brogan[3] shoe against the brown pine needles that had carpeted the ground. I saw these men hurry over the hill, cross the ravine and climb the hill over which the doves had flown.

I watched them reach the summit of the hill, stop and call to the doves in tones not unlike the doves' own calling. I saw them with guns poised against the sky. Soon they had disappeared the way the doves had gone.

I sat down on the edge of a lichened[4] rock that emerged from the rugged hill. I laid my double-barrel down beside me, and sunlight fin-

3. **brogan** (brō′gən): a heavy work shoe, fitting ankle-high.
4. **lichened** (lī′kənd): covered with lichen, a type of plant that grows in colored patches on wood or rock.

gered through the pine boughs above me in pencil-sized streaks of light. And when one of these shifting pencil-sized streaks of light touched my gun barrels, they shone brightly in the light. My gun was cleaned and oiled and the little pine needles stuck to its meat-rind-greased barrels. Over my head the wind soughed lonely among the pine needles. And from under these pines I could see the vast open fields where the corn stubble stood knee-high, where the wheat stubble would have shown plainly had it not been for the great growth of crab grass after we had cut the wheat; crab grass that had been blighted by autumn frost and shone brilliantly brown in the sun.

Even the air was cool to breathe into the lungs; I could feel it deep down when I breathed and it tasted of the green pine boughs that flavored it as it seethed through their thick tops. This was a clean cool autumn earth that both men and birds loved. And as I sat on the lichened rock with pine needles at my feet, with the soughing pine boughs above me, I thought the doves had chosen a fine place to find food, to nest and raise their young. But while I sat looking at the earth about me, I heard the thunder of the seasoned hunters' guns beyond the low ridge. I knew that they had talked to the doves until they had got close enough to shoot again.

As I sat on the rock, listening to the guns in the distance, I thought Uncle Wash might be right after all. It was better to shoot and kill with a gun than to kill with one's hands or with a club. I remembered the time I went over the hill to see how our young corn was growing after we had plowed it the last time. And while I stood looking over the corn whose long ears were in tender blisters, I watched a groundhog come from the edge of the woods, ride down a stalk of corn, and start eating a blister-ear. I found a dead sassafras[5] stick near me, tiptoed quietly behind the groundhog and hit him over the head. I didn't finish him with that lick. It took many licks.

When I left the cornfield, I left the groundhog dead beside his ear of corn. I couldn't forget killing the groundhog over an ear of corn and leaving him dead, his gray-furred clean body to waste on the lonely hill.

I can't disappoint Uncle Wash, I thought. He has trained me to shoot. He says that I will make a great hunter. He wants me to hunt like my father, cousins and uncles. He says that I will be the greatest marksman among them.

I thought about the way my people had hunted and how they had loved their guns. I thought about how Uncle Wash had taken care of his gun, how he had treated it like a living thing and how he had told

---

5. **sassafras** (săs′ə-frăs′): a type of tree having a fragrant bark.

me to love the feel of it. And now my gun lay beside me with pine needles sticking to it. If Uncle Wash were near he would make me pick the gun up, brush away the pine needles and wipe the gun barrels with my handkerchief. If I had lost my handkerchief as I had seen Uncle Wash often do, he would make me pull out my shirttail to wipe my gun with it. Uncle Wash didn't object to wearing dirty clothes or to wiping his face with a dirty bandanna; he didn't mind living in a dirty house—but never, never would he allow a speck of rust or dirt on his gun.

It was comfortable to sit on the rock since the sun was directly above me. It warmed with a glow of autumn. I felt the sun's rays against my face and the sun was good to feel. But the good fresh autumn air was no longer cool as the frost that covered the autumn grass that morning, nor could I feel it go deep into my lungs; the autumn air was warmer and it was flavored more with the scent of pines.

Now that the shooting had long been over near our cattle barn, I heard the lazy murmur of the woodcock in the pine woods nearby. Uncle Wash said that the woodcocks were game birds and he killed them wherever he found them. Once I thought I would follow the sound and kill the woodcock. I picked up my gun but laid it aside again. I wanted to kill something to show Uncle Wash. I didn't want him to be disappointed in me.

Instead of trying to find a rabbit sitting behind a broom-sedge[6] cluster or in a briar thicket as Uncle Wash had trained me to do, I felt relaxed and lazy in the autumn sun that had now penetrated the pine boughs from directly overhead. I looked over the brown, vast autumn earth about me where I had worked when everything was green and growing, where birds sang in the spring air as they built their nests. I looked at the tops of barren trees and thought how a few months ago they were waving clouds of green. And now it was a sad world, a dying world. There was so much death in the world that I had known: flowers were dead, leaves were dead, and the frosted grass was lifeless in the wind. Everything was dead and dying but a few wild birds and rabbits. I had almost grown into the rock where I sat but I didn't want to stir. I wanted to glimpse the life about me before it was covered with winter snows. I hated to think of killing in this autumn world. When I picked up my gun, I didn't see life in it—I felt death.

I didn't hear the old hunters' guns now but I knew that wherever they were, they were hunting for something to shoot. I thought they would return to the barn if the doves came back, as they surely would, for the pine grove where I sat was one place in this autumn world that

6. **broom sedge:** a type of beard grass, also known as broom grass.

was a home to the doves. And while I sat on the rock, I thought I would practice the dove whistle that Uncle Wash had taught me. I thought a dove would come close and I would shoot the dove so that I could go home with something in my hunting coat.

As I sat whistling a dove call, I heard the distant thunder of their guns beyond the low ridge. Then I knew they were coming back toward the cattle barn.

And, as I sat whistling my dove call, I heard a dove answer me. I called gently to the dove. Again it answered. This time it was closer to me. I picked up my gun from the rock and gently brushed the pine needles from its stock and barrels. And as I did this, I called pensively to the dove, and it answered plaintively.

I aimed my gun soon as I saw the dove walking toward me. When it walked toward my gun so unafraid, I thought it was a pet dove. I lowered my gun; laid it across my lap. Never had a dove come this close to me. When I called again, it answered at my feet. Then it fanned its wings and flew upon the rock beside me trying to reach the sound of my voice. It called, but I didn't answer. I looked at the dove when it turned its head to one side to try to see me. Its eye was gone, with the mark of a shot across its face. Then it turned the other side of its head toward me to try to see. The other eye was gone.

As I looked at the dove the shooting grew louder; the hunters were getting closer. I heard the fanning of dove wings above the pines. And I heard doves batting their wings against the pine boughs. And the dove beside me called to them. It knew the sounds of their wings. Maybe it knows each dove by the sound of his wings, I thought. And then the dove spoke beside me. I was afraid to answer. I could have reached out my hand and picked this dove up from the rock. Though it was blind, I couldn't kill it, and yet I knew it would have a hard time to live.

When the dove beside me called again, I heard an answer from a pine bough nearby. The dove beside me spoke, and the dove in the pine bough answered. Soon they were talking to each other as the guns grew louder. Suddenly, the blind dove fluttered through the treetops, chirruping its plaintive melancholy notes, toward the sound of its mate's voice. I heard its wings batting the wind-shaken pine boughs as it ascended, struggling, toward the beckoning voice.

Contrast, as you recall, focuses on differences. However, you must be selective about the differences you choose to point out. There wouldn't be much point, for example, in noting that Uncle Wash is older than the narrator, since age is not an essential feature in the story. If you have read the story carefully, you have no doubt concluded that the story points out a difference in attitudes toward hunting and killing. In other words, the story makes you, the reader, look closely at different *values*.

You might work out a chart of this kind for taking notes:

Uncle Wash	*The Narrator*
He is described as a "tall man with a hard leathery face." He is a seasoned sportsman, used to the outdoors.	He is a beginner. This is to be his first hunt.
He is a "great hunter" and wants his nephew to follow in his footsteps.	He doesn't want to disappoint his uncle. He has never openly questioned his uncle's ideas. He has followed his uncle's advice in cleaning his rifle, in shooting at targets.
He takes better care of his guns than of his person or home. He never allows his gun to be dirty or rusty. He tells the narrator to know and love his gun. He speaks of his weapon "like it was a living person."	He has a sensitivity to nature that the others lack. He has observed the doves all summer. He talks about their "mournful songs." He has watched them building nests and feeding their young. They are not afraid of him. He had never thought about killing and eating them.
He has no respect for hunting laws. He hunts all year round. He has no attachment to the things he kills. He talks about the doves being fat and making "good shooting."	He loves the feel of the cool autumn earth. He prefers enjoying nature to joining the hunt.
He likes to show his skill as a hunter. He teaches his nephew how to shoot. He shows others how to close in around the doves, how to follow them, and how to call to them.	He once killed a groundhog, and the memory of the killing has haunted him.
	There is so much death in the autumn world that he hates the thought of killing.
	The dove, blinded by a hunter, becomes a symbol for nature misused by people. The narrator's decision not to kill the bird shows that he has rejected the code of the hunters.

You might find at this point that a thesis statement has begun to emerge: *Uncle Wash views nature as a challenge to the hunter's skill, while the narrator feels protective toward the natural world and its creatures.* You would continue to study the story, gathering additional evidence and refining your ideas. The next step is organizing your ideas.

Organizing Ideas

Before you begin writing, organize your main ideas to provide for an introduction, a body, and a conclusion. The introduction should identify the author (or authors, if you are dealing with two or more works), the work (or works), or the problem that is under study. It should contain a statement of your thesis as well. The body of your paper should present the evidence supporting your thesis. The conclusion should bring together your main ideas.

This is one kind of plan you might use for a short paper. It indicates the main idea of each paragraph.

INTRODUCTION

Paragraph 1   *Thesis*   Uncle Wash views nature as a challenge to the hunter's skill, while the narrator feels protective toward the natural world and its creatures.

BODY

Paragraph 2   Uncle Wash, whose skill as a hunter is greatly admired, has no qualms about hunting and killing wildlife.

Paragraph 3   The narrator, who is sensitive to the mystery and beauty of nature, finds hunting and killing distasteful.

CONCLUSION

Paragraph 4   In making the decision not to kill the blind dove, in fact—not to kill any of the creatures in the woods, the narrator resists the pressures of the hunters and listens to his own, inner sense of right and wrong.

Writing the Essay

As you write your essay, you should use language that is serious enough for your purpose and audience. Remember that your purpose is to convey ideas clearly, and that you are writing for your teacher or, occasionally, for your classmates. Use transitional expressions (words like *then, second,* and *therefore*) to make the order of ideas clear.

Here is a model essay based on the prewriting plan. Notice how the essay follows the writer's plan.

TITLE

INTRODUCTION

Identify the selection and the subject.

Thesis

CONTRASTING ATTITUDES TOWARD NATURE IN
"THANKSGIVING HUNTER"

In Jesse Stuart's "Thanksgiving Hunter," the two main characters, Uncle Wash and the narrator, represent contrasting attitudes toward nature. *Uncle Wash views nature as a challenge to the hunter's skill, while the narrator feels protective toward the natural world and its creatures.* The situation that the story presents, the narrator's first hunt, brings these two attitudes into conflict.

BODY

Topic Sentence

Supporting Evidence

Uncle Wash, whose skill as a hunter is greatly admired, has no qualms about hunting and killing wildlife. His "hard leathery face" shows that he is a seasoned sportsman, used to the outdoors. He does not allow anything to interfere with his pleasure in hunting. He has no respect for hunting laws and violates them by hunting out of season. To him, doves are not gentle creatures but fat birds that make "good shooting." He enjoys hunting and enjoys teaching others how to close in around the doves and how to call to them. He considers his weapon to be a living thing and tells the narrator to know and love his gun.

Topic Sentence

Show evidence of close reading.

The narrator, by contrast, is sensitive to the mystery and beauty of nature, and finds hunting and killing distasteful. This Thanksgiving hunt is an important occasion. It is his first hunt, and a great deal is expected of him. Although he doesn't want to disappoint his uncle, he cannot bring himself to use his gun to inflict pain and death. There is so much death in autumn that he hates the thought of killing. He has observed the doves all summer; he has listened to their songs and watched them building their nests and feeding their young. He feels he cannot betray their trust. Moreover, he remembers killing a groundhog once, and the memory of that killing has haunted him.

CONCLUSION

Stuart presents these characters without drawing moral judgments about them. The resolution of the conflict, however, seems to say that Stuart's sympathies lie with the narrator. The dove that has been blinded by a hunter becomes a symbol for nature misused by people. In its innocence the dove answers the narrator's call. He knows that the dove will have a hard time trying to survive, yet he cannot kill it. His decision not to kill—to face Uncle Wash with his hunting coat empty—shows that the narrator has resisted the pressures of the hunters and has trust in his own sense of right and wrong.

Length: 397 words

Evaluating and Revising Papers

When you write an essay in class, you have a limited amount of time to plan and develop your essay. Nevertheless, you should save a few minutes to read over your work and make necessary corrections.

When an essay is assigned as homework, you have more time to prepare it carefully. Get into the habit of revising your work. A first draft of an essay should be treated as a rough copy of your manuscript. Chances are that reworking your first draft will result in a clearer and stronger paper.

To evaluate an essay, you judge its content, organization, and style. Your aim is to decide what the strong points and weak points are in your essay. Knowing this, you will be able to revise, or make the changes that will improve your essay. To evaluate your essay, answer the following questions:

Guidelines for Evaluating a Paper

Introduction
1. Have I included an introduction that identifies the title and author of the literary work(s)?
2. Have I included a thesis statement that gives the main idea of the essay?

Body
3. Have I included at least two main points that support the thesis statement?
4. Have I included evidence from the literary work to support each main point?

Conclusion
5. Have I included a conclusion that brings together the main points?

Coherence
6. Does the order of ideas make sense?

Style
7. Do the sentences differ in length and in the way they begin?
8. Is the language serious enough for the purpose and audience?

Word Choice
9. Have I defined unfamiliar words for the audience?
10. Have I used vivid and specific words?

Using your evaluation, you can revise your essay. Writers revise by using four basic techniques: *adding, cutting, reordering,* or *replacing.* For example, if the order of ideas is not clear, you can *add* words like *first, second,* and *finally.* If your language is not serious enough, you can *replace* slang and contractions with formal language. You can *cut* evidence that does not explain a main point, and you can *reorder* ideas that are difficult to follow.

On the following pages you will find a revised draft of the essay that appears on page 692. The notes in the margin show which revision technique the writer used. Study the two versions of the essay. As you do so, notice how the writer has revised for greater clarity, accuracy, and conciseness.

cut; reorder	In Jesse Stuart's ~~short story~~ "Thanksgiving Hunter," Uncle Wash
cut; add; cut	and the narrator ~~are~~ (the **two** main characters.) ~~They~~ represent contrasting
	attitudes toward nature. Uncle Wash views nature as a challenge to
	the hunter's skill, while the narrator feels protective toward the
add; cut	*The situation that the story presents, the narrator's first hunt, brings* natural world and its creatures. These two attitudes ~~are brought~~
cut	into conflict ~~during the hunt.~~
	Uncle Wash, whose skill as a hunter is greatly admired, has no
cut	qualms about hunting and killing wildlife. ~~We are told that he has~~
replace; cut	*His* ~~a~~ "hard leathery face," ~~which~~ shows that he is a seasoned sportsman,
replace; cut	*He does not allow anything to* used to the outdoors. ~~Nothing~~ interferes with his pleasure in hunting.
cut	~~He is a "great hunter" and wants his nephew to follow in his footsteps.~~
add; cut	He considers his weapon to be a living thing and tells the narrator to know and love his gun. He has no respect for hunting laws. ~~He~~ *and*
replace; add	*them* violates ~~the laws~~ by hunting out of season. *To him,* Doves are not gentle
	creatures but fat birds that make "good shooting." He enjoys hunting
add; replace	*enjoys* *ing* and ~~teaches~~ others how to close in around the doves and how to call
reorder	to them.
replace	*by contrast,* The narrator, ~~who~~ is sensitive to the mystery and beauty of
add; add	*and* nature, finds hunting and killing distasteful. This hunt is an *Thanksgiving*

694   WRITING ABOUT LITERATURE

important occasion. It is his first hunt, and a great deal is

expected of him. Although he doesn't want to disappoint his uncle. He cannot bring himself

never openly questioned his uncle's ideas. to use his gun to inflict pain and death. There is so much death in

autumn that he hates the thought of killing. He has observed the doves he has listened to their songs and watched them building their nests and feeding their young.

all summer, and he feels he cannot betray their trust. He once killed

Moreover, he remembers killing a groundhog, and once the memory of that killing has haunted him.

Stuart presents these characters in the story without drawing

moral judgments about them. The resolution of the conflict, however, seems to say that

Stuart's sympathies lie with the narrator. The dove that has been blinded by a hunter becomes a

symbol for nature misused by people. In its innocence The dove answers the

narrator's call. He knows that the dove will have a hard time trying

to survive, yet he cannot kill it. His decision not to

kill to face Uncle Wash with his hunting coat empty—shows that the narrator has ed resists the

pressures of the hunters and has trust in his own sense of right

and wrong.

Proofreading and Making a Final Copy

After you revise, you should proofread your essay to correct any mistakes in grammar, usage, and mechanics. Pay special attention to the correct capitalization and punctuation of any quotations you use as supporting evidence. Then make a final copy of your essay by using correct manuscript form or your teacher's instructions. After writing this clean copy, proofread again to catch mistakes made in copying.

GUIDE TO LITERARY TERMS AND TECHNIQUES

ALLITERATION *The repetition of a sound in a group of words.* Alliteration is used in many common expressions: "safe and sound," "over and out," "do or die." Most alliteration occurs at the beginning of words, but sometimes we also find alliteration in the middle or at the end of words, as in "tickled pink" and "dribs and drabs."

Two uses of alliteration seem to be to gain emphasis and to aid our memory. This is why many advertising jingles depend on alliteration and why so many products are given names that are alliterated.

Politicians often use alliteration. When we are asked to put up with hardship, we are asked to "tighten our belts" or to "bite the bullet." A famous political slogan during a presidential campaign went "Tippecanoe and Tyler too!"

Poets use alliteration to the most obvious and memorable effect. Here are some examples of alliteration in poetry:

Mere prattle, without practice,
Is all his soldiership.
William Shakespeare
Othello

Open here I flung the shutter, when, with
many a flirt and flutter,
In there stepped a stately Raven of the
saintly days of yore.
Edgar Allan Poe
"The Raven"

I like to see it lap the miles,
And lick the valleys up,
Emily Dickinson

Sometimes alliteration is used simply for the fun of it. One poet, Algernon Charles Swinburne, wrote a poem that made fun of his own style. He had been criticized for using too much alliteration. So he composed "Nephelidia" (little clouds), which is complicated and funny nonsense. It starts this way:

From the depth of the dreamy decline of the
dawn through a notable nimbus of nebulous
noonshine,
Pallid and pink as the palm of the flagflower that
flickers with fear of the flies as they float,

Swinburne makes the amusing point that heavily alliterated poetry can seem to mean more than it does.

Prose writers use alliteration, too, but they have to be careful not to sound too artificial. Mary O'Hara's story "My Friend Flicka" uses alliteration in its title. Some of the most memorable expressions from the King James translation of the Bible are alliterated: "Let there be light: and there was light" (Genesis), and "There is no new thing under the sun" (Ecclesiastes).

See pages 474, 480.

ALLUSION *A reference to a work of literature or to an actual event, person, or place, which the speaker expects the audience to recognize.* Allusions are used in everyday conversation, as well as in prose and poetry. The great danger with an allusion is that the reader or listener won't understand it. People can seem snobbish if they allude to very obscure works or events.

Writers often allude to other works of literature. In titling one of his plays *The Ugly Duckling*, A. A. Milne alludes to the fairy tale by Hans Christian Andersen.

Literature contains many allusions to the Bible. Emily Dickinson expects us to recognize her allusion to a thunderous speaker in the New Testament when she says that a train "roared like Boanerges." The title of a section of a biography about Harriet Tubman is "They Called Her Moses," which alludes to the Biblical leader Moses. In that case, we are expected to make the connection between Moses and Harriet Tubman, both deliverers of their people.

Allusions to the myths of ancient Greece and Rome are also common in literature. The great writers used to be carefully trained to read both Latin and Greek. We do not study these languages as intensely nowadays, so we miss many of the allusions that writers like William Shakespeare, John Milton, William Wordsworth, and Alfred, Lord Tennyson took for granted. When the speaker in Edgar Allan Poe's poem "The Raven" thinks that the Raven came from "Night's Plutonian shore," he expects us to know that he is alluding to the shore of the underworld ruled by Pluto, a Roman god identified with night and darkness.

Allusions to the media are growing more and more common, though these are not as lasting as allusions to the Bible and classical literature. Squeaky, in the story "Raymond's Run" by Toni Cade Bambara, describes an encounter with some unfriendly girls as "one of those Dodge City scenes." This is an allusion to the television series "Gunsmoke," a Western that was popular in the 1950s and 1960s.

See page 481.

ANECDOTE *A very short story which is told to make a point.* Many anecdotes are funny; some are jokes. Originally, anecdotes were little-known, entertaining facts about a person or about a historical event. Anecdotes are used in nearly all kinds of literature. Mark Twain uses several anecdotes in his tale "The Celebrated Jumping Frog of Calaveras County." Twain tells this anecdote to prove that a man named Jim Smiley would bet on *anything*:

> Why, it never made no difference to *him*—he'd bet on *anything*—the dangdest feller. Parson Walker's wife laid very sick once, for a good while, and it seemed as if they warn't going to save her; but one morning he come in, and Smiley up and asked him how she was, and he said she was considerable better—thank the Lord for his inf'nite mercy—and coming on so smart that with the blessing of Prov'dence she'd get well yet; and Smiley, before he thought, says, "Well, I'll resk two and a half she don't anyway."

See page 417.

ATMOSPHERE *The general mood or feeling established in a piece of literature.* Atmosphere can be gloomy, peaceful, frightful, tense, etc. Atmosphere is usually achieved through description. Landscapes, such as dark, dank moors that ooze a steaming mist, often lend themselves to creating atmosphere. Poe is famous for the creation of gloomy atmospheres, as in this opening passage of his story "The Fall of the House of Usher." Notice how the italicized words make us sense the atmosphere:

> During the whole of a *dull, dark* and soundless day in the *autumn* of the year, when the clouds *hung oppressively low* in the heavens, I had been passing alone, on horseback, through a singularly *dreary* tract of country, and at length found myself, as the *shades of the evening* drew on, within view of the *melancholy* House of Usher.

Atmosphere doesn't always have to be spooky and frightening. Notice how the italicized words create an atmosphere of comfort and well-being in this passage from Washington Irving's "The Legend of Sleepy Hollow":

> His stronghold was situated on the banks of the Hudson, in one of those *green, sheltered, fertile*

nooks in which the Dutch farmers are so fond of *nestling.* A great elm tree spread its broad branches over it. At the foot of the tree *bubbled* up a *spring* of the *softest* and *sweetest water,* in a little well formed of a barrel. The spring then stole *sparkling* away through the *grass* to a neighboring *brook* that *bubbled* along among alders and dwarf willows. Close by the farmhouse was a vast barn, which might have served for a church, every window and crevice of which seemed *bursting* forth with the *treasures* of the farm.

See page 278.

BALLAD *A storytelling poem that uses regular patterns of rhythm and strong rhymes. Most ballads are meant to be sung.* **Folk ballads**, in fact, are sung long before they are written down. Others, the so-called **"literary" ballads,** are composed by writers and are not specifically intended for singing. Most ballads are full of adventure, action, and romance, such as you find in Sir Walter Scott's rousing "Lochinvar." Many ballads tell stories of famous villains, like Jesse James and Billy the Kid. One very famous folk ballad, "John Henry," celebrates the heroic railroad worker who raced a machine. There are often several versions of folk ballads, since they change a bit as people sing them and pass them on.

See page 185.

BIOGRAPHY *The life story of a person written by someone else.* When a person writes his or her own biography, it is called an *autobiography.* Ann Petry wrote a biography called *Harriet Tubman: Conductor on the Underground Railroad.* Richard Wright wrote his own life story in an autobiography called *Black Boy.* Biography and autobiography are two of the most popular forms of nonfiction, and most libraries have a section set aside for them. Almost every famous person has been the subject of a biography. Some famous people have had three or four biographies written about them, by different people.

CHARACTERIZATION *The methods used to present the personality of a character in a narrative.* A writer can create a character by: (1) giving a physical description of the character; (2) showing the character's actions and letting the character speak; (3) revealing the character's thoughts; (4) revealing what others think of the character; and (5) commenting directly on the character. Characterization can be sketchy, particularly if the character does not take an important role in a story. Or, characterization can be extraordinarily full, as when the character is the main focus of a story.

Washington Irving describes Ichabod Crane in "The Legend of Sleepy Hollow" in many ways to reveal his character. Here is a physical description:

> The name of Crane was not inapplicable to his person. He was tall, but exceedingly lank, with narrow shoulders, long arms and legs, hands that dangled a mile out of his sleeves, feet that might have served for shovels, and his whole frame most loosely hung together.

Here Irving tells about Ichabod's thoughts and fears:

> How often did he shrink with curdling awe at the sound of his own steps on the frosty crust beneath his feet, and dread to look over his shoulder, lest he should behold some uncouth being tramping close behind him!

Here he reveals what others think of Ichabod:

> He was, moreover, esteemed by the women as a man of great learning, for he had read several books quite through. . . .

And here Irving gives his own evaluation of his hero:

> He was, in fact, an odd mixture of small shrewdness and simple credulity.

Sometimes animals can be characterized, using the same techniques. Rudyard Kipling's famous story "Rikki-tikki-tavi" has as its hero a little mongoose, who is characterized as if he were a person.

See pages 28, 86, 234, 317, 394.

COMEDY *A literary work with a generally happy ending. A comedy can be funny and, sometimes, rather serious under it all.* Any narrative can be a comedy—a short story, novel, play, or narrative poem, though the term is most often applied to plays. One of the typical plots of comedies is the one involving young lovers who almost don't get together. The plot of such a comedy always ends happily, often with a marriage, and the theme usually has something to do with the power of love. A comedy that has these characteristics is A. A. Milne's play *The Ugly Duckling.* Many movies and novels are also based on this kind of plot.

Television features a great many situation comedies—weekly episodes about funny complications that take place in the lives of the same group of characters. Slapstick comedy, with a lot of roughhousing and knockabout humor, was popular in early movies. The films of Abbott and Costello, Laurel and Hardy, and the Three Stooges are examples.

See page 317.

CONFLICT *The struggle that takes place between two opposing forces.* A conflict can take place between a character and a natural force, like a bear or a hurricane; between two characters; or between opposing views held by separate characters or groups of characters. Such conflicts are **external** conflicts. Conflict can also be **internal**—it can exist within the mind of a character who must make a difficult decision or overcome a fear.

Usually, a conflict arises when a character's wishes or desires are blocked. In Sir Walter Scott's poem "Lochinvar," Ellen's father is marrying her to someone else, and so Lochinvar is blocked from wedding the maiden he loves. Lochinvar resolves this conflict by stealing Ellen away from her own bridal feast. We might expect this to produce new conflict, but as the poem tells us, Lochinvar and Ellen escape and are never seen again.

In Arthur Gordon's story "The Sea Devil," a man struggles with a manta ray which nearly drowns him. In Dorothy Canfield's story "The Apprentice," a girl's views on how she should behave clash with her parents' views. In Langston Hughes's story "Thank You, M'am," the character Roger has an internal conflict: he must decide whether to respect someone's trust in him, or do the easy thing and run away.

In many types of literature, especially in novels and dramas, there are two or more kinds of conflict. In the play *The Diary of Anne Frank,* for example, there is the conflict between the "family" in hiding and the hostile outside world which seeks to destroy them; there is the conflict of views between Anne and the adults; there is also the internal conflict within Anne's mind, between her feelings of love for her parents and her desire to please them, and her need to grow up and be herself.

See **Plot.**
See also page 218.

CONNOTATION *All the emotions and associations that a word or phrase arouses.* Connotation is different from **denotation,** which is the strict literal (or "dictionary") definition of a word. For example, the word *springtime* literally means "the season of the year between the vernal equinox and the summer solstice." But *springtime* usually makes most people think of love, rebirth, youth, and romance.

Poets are especially sensitive to the connotations of words. For example, Poe uses the word *midnight* in "The Raven." *Midnight* literally means "the middle of the night." But the word *midnight* has certain connotations associated with death, remorse, and gloom that help create the poem's atmosphere of foreboding. You can imagine how different the poem would be if you were to substitute the phrase "high noon" for *midnight.*

DESCRIPTION *The kind of writing that creates pictures of persons, places, things, or actions. Description may also tell how something sounds, smells, tastes, or feels.* Washington Irving, a master of description, gives us this picture of Ichabod Crane's route homeward. Notice how he uses words like *barking, crowing, chirp,* and *twang,* which help us hear certain sounds.

> The hour was as dismal as himself. Far below him, the Tappan Zee spread its dusky and indistinct waste of waters, with here and there the tall mast of a sloop riding quietly at anchor under the land. In the dead hush of midnight he could even hear the barking of the watchdog from the opposite shore of the Hudson, but it was so vague and faint as only to give an idea of his distance from this faithful companion of man. Now and then, too, the long-drawn crowing of a cock, accidentally awakened, would sound far, far off, from some farmhouse away among the hills—but it was like a dreaming sound in his ear. No signs of life occurred near him, but occasionally the melancholy chirp of a cricket or, perhaps, the guttural twang of a bullfrog from a neighboring marsh, as if sleeping uncomfortably and turning suddenly in his bed.

See **Atmosphere, Imagery.**
See also page 73.

DIALECT *A representation of the speech patterns of a particular region or social group.* Dialect is often used to make a character or place seem authentic. Some of the regional dialects in the United States are the Down-East dialect of Maine, the Cajun dialect of Louisiana, and the dialects of the South and West.

Hosea Bigelow was one of the great American humorists who used dialect simply for the fun of it—and sometimes to make a point. Here is a letter he wrote to the editor of a Down-East newspaper about a debate in the United States Senate:

To Mr. Buckenam.

Mr. Editer, As i wuz kinder prunin round, in a little nussry sot out a year or 2 a go, the Dbait in the sennit cum inter my mine. An so i took & Sot it to wut I call a nussry rime. I hev made sum onnable Gentlemun speak that dident speak in a Kin uv Poetikul lie sense the seeson is dreffle backerd up This way.

ewers as ushul
Hosea Bigelow.

DIALOGUE *Talk or conversation between two or more characters.* Dialogue usually attempts to present the speech of characters in a realistic fashion. It is used in almost all literary forms: biography, essays, fiction and nonfiction, poetry, and drama. Dialogue is especially important in drama, where it forwards *all* the action of the play. Dialogue must move the plot of a play, reveal the characters, and even help establish some of the mood. When dialogue appears in a play, there are no quotation marks to set it apart, since—besides stage directions—a play is nothing but dialogue.

When dialogue appears in a prose work, or in a poem, it is usually set apart with quotation marks. Since actual life is conducted almost entirely in dialogue, a short story that uses a lot of dialogue will not only move fast, but it will also seem realistic.

See **Dialect.**
See also pages 87, 394, 397.

DRAMA *A story written to be acted out on a stage, with actors and actresses taking the parts of specific characters.* The word *drama* comes from a Greek word meaning "act," so it is important to stress the idea of action in a drama. While reading a drama, we have to try to imagine real people as they would play the parts on stage.

We usually think of two main kinds of drama. **Tragedies** are serious plays in which a hero or heroine suffers defeat or death. William Shakespeare's *Hamlet* and *Macbeth* are tragedies, as is *The Diary of Anne Frank.* **Comedies** are lighter plays, which usually end happily and are often funny. A. A. Milne's play *The Ugly Duckling* is a comedy.

Drama involves the use of **plot,** the series of related events that make up the story.

Conflict, the most important element in the plot, pits the characters in a play against one another, or against forces that are powerful and sometimes greater than they are. The characters carry forward the plot of a play by means of **dialogue.**

Most playwrights include **stage directions,** which tell the actors and actresses what to do or what feelings to project when certain lines are spoken. The stage directions are useful to the director, who must help the actors and actresses interpret their lines. The director decides things like the timing of a line, the speed of delivery, the way the actors and actresses stand or move when speaking their lines, and what they do when they are not speaking their lines. The director really interprets the way the whole play should go. In many productions, the director is as important as the author of the play.

Most plays are presented on stages with **sets.** The set is a representation of the room, landscape, or other locale in which the play takes place. **Props** are important items used in the drama, such as a telephone, a sword, a book, a glass of water, or any other item that figures in the action. **Lighting** helps to establish the desired moods, or the time of day or the season.

Each act of a play is usually composed of several scenes. The end of each act often includes a **climax,** which is an emotional or suspenseful moment, designed to keep the audience interested so it will come back after the intermission. The final act of the drama usually builds to a final climax or **crisis,** which is greater than any that went before. The end of the drama involves the **resolution** of the conflict: usually by death in a tragedy, or by marriage in a comedy.

See **Dialogue.**
See also pages 317, 394, 397.

ELEGY *A mournful poem or lament, usually a meditation on the death of someone famous or of someone important to the writer.* Elegies may also be laments on the nature of death itself, or on the loss of youth and beauty. The most famous elegy is probably "Elegy Written in a Country Churchyard," by the English poet Thomas Gray. One of its frequently quoted stanzas is

The boast of heraldry, the pomp of power,
And all that beauty, all that wealth e'er gave,
Awaits alike the inevitable hour.
The paths of glory lead but to the grave.

Walt Whitman's poem "O Captain! My Captain!" is one of several elegies he wrote mourning the death of Abraham Lincoln.

EPIC *A long narrative poem that relates the deeds of a hero.* Epics incorporate myth, legend, folk tale, and history, and usually reflect the values of the societies from which they originate. The tone is generally grand, and the heroes and their adventures appear larger than life.

Many epics were drawn from an oral tradition and are known as **primary epics.** These were transmitted by song and recitation before they were written down. Two of the most famous primary epics of Western civilization are Homer's *Iliad* and *Odyssey.* Another primary epic is one of the earliest works in history, the *Epic of Gilgamesh,* from ancient Mesopotamia.

A second type of epic is the **literary** or **secondary epic.** These were written down from the start. Examples include the *Aeneid,* Rome's national epic written by the poet Virgil to give the ancient Romans a sense of their own destiny; the *Divine Comedy,* the great epic of the Middle Ages written by the Italian poet Dante; and *Paradise Lost* and *Paradise Regained,* two great epics written by the seventeenth-century English poet John Milton.

See **Narrative Poetry.**
See also pages 610, 612, 624, 645, 656.

ESSAY *A short piece of prose writing which discusses a subject in a limited way and which usually expresses a particular point of view.* The word *essay* means "an evaluation or consideration of something." Most essays tend to be thoughtful considerations about a subject of interest to the writer. Most essays are *expository* in nature, which simply means that they do not tell a story, but explain or give information about a situation, an event, or a process.

See **Exposition.**

EXPOSITION *The kind of writing that explains something or gives information about something.* Exposition can be used in fiction and nonfiction, but its most familiar form is the **essay.** A typical example of exposition is this passage from Henry David Thoreau's *Walden,* in which Thoreau explains why he decided to spend some time alone in a cabin in the woods:

I went to the woods because I wished to live deliberately, to front only the essential facts of life, and see if I could not learn what it had to teach, and not, when I came to die, discover that I had not lived. I did not wish to live what was not life, living is so dear; nor did I wish to practice resignation, unless it was quite necessary. I wanted to live deep and suck out all the marrow of life, to live so sturdily and Spartan-like as to put to rout all that was not life. . . .

Exposition is also that part of a play or other narrative that helps the reader understand important background information. For example, in *The Diary of Anne Frank* the authors provide background information, or exposition, in the first scene. Here the audience is told how the Frank family and others were forced to go into hiding in a warehouse in Amsterdam, to escape the Nazis.

See **Essay.**
See also page 197.

FABLE *A brief story with a moral, written in either prose or poetry.* The characters in fables are often animals who speak and act like human beings. The most famous fables are those of Aesop, who was said to be a Greek slave living in the sixth century B.C. Almost as famous are the fables of the seventeenth-century French writer, La Fontaine.

A typical fable is Aesop's "Belling the Cat," the story of the mice who decided to put a bell around a cat's neck so they'd hear it coming. It was a wonderful solution that every mouse applauded. Then came the obvious problem: Who would actually put the bell on the cat? Their solution had merely gotten them another problem. The moral of the story is "It is easy to propose impossible remedies."

FICTION *A prose account which is invented and not a record of things as they actually happened.* Much fiction is based on real personal experience, but it almost always involves invented characters, or invented actions or settings, or other details which are made up for the sake of the story itself. Fiction can be brief, as a fable or short story is, or it can be book length, as a novel is.

FIGURATIVE LANGUAGE *Any language that is not intended to be interpreted in a strict literal sense.*

When we call a car a "lemon," we use figurative language. We do not mean that the car is really a citrus fruit, but that its performance is "sour"—it will cause its owner to lose money. When we refer to someone as a lamb, or a peach, or a rock, or an angel, we know that the person is none of those things. Instead, we mean simply that the person shares some quality with those other things.

The main form of figurative language used in literature is **metaphor.** Metaphor makes a comparison between two different things. The father in Mary O'Hara's story "My Friend Flicka" uses metaphors when he says that the mares are hellions and the stallions outlaws. He is comparing the mares to ghastly creatures from hell. They are not *really* from hell, as we know, but the comparison makes us realize how troublesome they can be. To say the stallions are outlaws is also a metaphor, because it compares the horses to human outlaws. Horses do not have legal institutions: that's reserved for humankind. By comparing the stallions to human outlaws, this speaker shows how bad they are and how hard they are to control.

These metaphors are stated clearly: "The mares *are* hellions." But sometimes a metaphor does not state the comparison so directly. We also use a metaphor when we say something like: "Kate's sunny smile enchanted us." We are actually comparing her smile to the brightness and the welcoming warmth of the sun.

Similes are another form of figurative language. Similes are easy to recognize because they always use special words to state their comparisons. When the poet Robert Burns says "My luve is like a red, red rose," he uses a simile. It is a comparison and it is, indeed, like a metaphor. But it's different because it uses a special word to state the comparison. That word is *like.* Other words and phrases used in similes are *as, as if, than, such as,* and *resembles*—all of which state a comparison directly. Just as with metaphor, the simile does not use *all* the points of comparison for its force. It uses only some. For instance, the comparison of "my luve" to "a rose" does not necessarily mean that the loved one is thorny, nor that she lives in a garden, nor that she has a green neck. Rather, it means that "my luve" is delicate, fragrant, rare, and beautiful, as the flower is.

Emily Dickinson uses a simile in "I Like to See It Lap the Miles" when she says that the train is "punctual as a star." But she also uses a metaphor in this poem, since she makes other comparisons between the train and an animal, which seems to be a horse. The verbs in particular suggest this metaphor: she tells us that the train *laps, licks, feeds itself, steps, peers, crawls, chases,* and *neighs at its own stable door.* All of these verbs describe actions that we know a train cannot perform, but an animal can.

Similes in everyday language are common. "He was madder than a hornet." "She roared like a bull." "Louie laughed like a hyena." "Float like a butterfly, sting like a bee." "Be as firm as Gibraltar and as cool as a cucumber." "She resembles Wonder Woman."

See **Metaphor, Simile, Symbol.**
See also pages 45, 50, 176, 468, 514.

FLASHBACK *An interruption of the action in a story to tell about something that happened earlier in time.* The usual plot moves in chronological order: it starts at a given moment, progresses through time, and ends at some later moment. A flashback interrupts that flow by suddenly shifting to past time and narrating important incidents that make the present action

Guide to Literary Terms and Techniques   **701**

more understandable. Usually there is a signal to indicate the flashback, but occasionally a writer will leave out the signal. The reader must pay very close attention to find the point where the narrative picks up the action again.

The play *The Diary of Anne Frank* is almost entirely a flashback. In the opening scene, when Mr. Frank enters the warehouse, it is 1945. The play then flashes back to 1942, and not until the final scene are we brought back to 1945 again.

See page 394.

FOLK TALE *A story that was not originally written down, but was passed on orally from one storyteller to another.* Folk tales often exist in several forms because they are carried by storytellers to different parts of the world. Over the years, and according to changing local customs, the same tale can take on slightly different qualities. Many fairy tales, such as the story of Cinderella and the story of Jack and the Beanstalk, are folk tales that originated in Europe, and versions of them later appeared in the Appalachian Mountains of the New World. Folk tales often involve unreal creatures, like dragons, cannibalistic giants, and chatty animals.

In the United States, folk tales have grown up about such figures as the frontiersman Davy Crockett, the steel-drivin' man John Henry, and the original cowhand Pecos Bill.

See pages 173, 177, 184, 185.

FORESHADOWING *The use of hints or clues in a narrative to suggest action that is to come.* Foreshadowing helps to build suspense in a story because it alerts the reader to what is about to happen. It also helps the reader enjoy all the details of the buildup. Lewis Carroll uses a bit of foreshadowing in his poem "Jabberwocky" when he has the old man warn: "Beware the Jabberwock, my son! / The jaws that bite, the claws that catch!" But foreshadowing is more common in short stories, longer fiction, and drama. It is often said that if a loaded gun is presented in Act One of a play, it should go off before Act Five. In other words, the gun in the first act usually foreshadows some danger to come.

See page 229.

HERO/HEROINE *The chief character in a story or drama.* In older heroic stories, the heroes and heroines often embody qualities that their society thought were best and most desirable. The heroines and heroes in such stories are often of noble blood and are usually physically strong, courageous, and intelligent, characteristics that are shown by the great Sumerian hero, Gilgamesh. Often the conflict involves the hero or heroine with a monster or with a force that threatens the entire social group. For example, Beowulf must kill the monster Grendel, who has nearly destroyed the Danes. Folk heroes like Daniel Boone and John Henry, and the heroes of tall tales, like Paul Bunyan and Pecos Bill, share most of these heroic qualities with their counterparts in myth.

Nowadays, we use the term **hero** or **heroine** to mean the main character in any narrative. At times, this person might be admirable, as in "Thank You, M'am" by Langston Hughes, in which Mrs. Jones rewards a boy with kindness instead of punishment. At times, however, the hero or heroine in modern stories is not entirely admirable. Some of them might even show ordinary human weaknesses, such as fear or poor judgment. For example, in Mary O'Hara's story "My Friend Flicka," the hero, Kennie, seems to be a failure in everything but his devotion to his horse. In some stories, the hero or heroine might even be "unheroic" and not admirable at all. In Washington Irving's "The Legend of Sleepy Hollow," the hero, Ichabod, is cowardly and superstitious, just the opposite of the noble, strong intelligent heroes of old.

IMAGERY *Words and phrases that describe something in a way that creates pictures, or images, that appeal to the reader's senses.* Most images tend to be visual, though many times a writer will also use words that suggest the way things sound, smell, taste, or feel to the touch. Images appear in all kinds of writing: poetry, nonfiction, fiction, and drama. Not all writers use imagery extensively. But those who do, use it in an effort to make an experience in literature more intense for us. Because good images involve our sensory awareness, they help us to be more responsive readers.

Washington Irving, in "The Legend of Sleepy Hollow," describes something (a phantom?) as if it were a wind that could be felt and heard: "some rushing blast, howling among the trees." Katrina Van Tassel is described in images that appeal to our sense of taste: "a blooming lass of fresh eighteen, plump as a partridge, ripe and melting and rosy cheeked as one of her father's peaches." The Van Tassel barnyard is described in visual images that also make our mouths water: "he pictured to himself every roasting-pig running about with an apple in his mouth. The pigeons were snugly put to bed in a comfortable pie, and tucked in with a coverlet of crust; the geese were swimming in their own gravy."

See **Description.**
See also pages 465, 467.

INFERENCE *A reasonable conclusion made about something based on certain clues or facts.* Often the writer of a piece of literature will not tell us everything there is to tell. At times, we have the pleasure of drawing an inference about a scene, a character, or an action. The process of drawing an inference is pleasurable, because we are actually making a discovery on our own.

In her poem "I Like to See It Lap the Miles," Emily Dickinson never tells us that she is describing a train. Yet readers have inferred that she is talking about a train from clues given in the poem: it speeds over the miles, goes around mountains and through passages hewn out of rocks, hoots and makes other noises, "chases itself" downhill, and when it stops, it is quiet.

In "Casey at the Bat," Ernest Lawrence Thayer never tells us directly that Casey is a fellow who is very sure of himself. He lets us infer that his character is enormously confident—perhaps even overconfident—when Casey lets a perfectly good ball go by and says, "That ain't my style." By that point in the poem, we also infer that Casey's pride and confidence are going to do him in.

See page 603.

INVERSION *A reversal of the normal order of words in a sentence, usually for some kind of emphasis.* The normal word order in an English sentence is subject-verb-complement. When writers and speakers invert, or reverse, this pattern, the word or phrase that is placed out of order usually receives more emphasis. The device often appears in poetry, but it occurs in prose and in speech as well. In poetry, inversion is often used to make a line's rhythm beat out in a certain way, or to achieve a certain end-rhyme.

Edgar Allan Poe used inversion in many of his poems. In these lines from "The Raven," we find inversion in the clause in the second line. Poe probably used inversion here so that he could get a word to rhyme with *nevermore*:

But the Raven, sitting lonely on the placid bust, spoke only
That one word, as if his soul in that one word he did outpour.

The normal word order of the last clause would be:

. . . as if he did outpour his soul in that one word.

At times, inversion can make a passage sound too literary or poetical, or even old-fashioned. Its use must be cautious, since too much inversion makes a passage seem artificial.

See pages 485, 513.

IRONY *A contrast between what is stated and what is really meant, or between what is expected to happen and what actually does happen.* Irony is used in everyday conversation. When we say, "It's not at all warm here," when we're standing in the desert in July, we are using irony.

There are three kinds of irony used in literature: (1) **Verbal irony** occurs when a writer or speaker says one thing and means something entirely different; (2) **Irony of situation** occurs when a situation turns out to be completely different from what we expect; (3) **Dramatic irony** occurs when a reader or an audience knows something that a character in a play or story does not know. Irony is used in literature for all kinds of effects, from humor to serious comments on the unpredictable nature of life.

A humorous example of *verbal irony* is found in this short verse by Lewis Carroll:

The Crocodile

How doth the little crocodile
  Improve his shining tail,
And pour the waters of the Nile
  On every shining scale!

How cheerfully he seems to grin,
  How neatly spread his claws
And welcomes little fishes in
  With gently smiling jaws!

This speaker says one thing but really means something else. He says that the crocodile "welcomes" little fish into his "gently" smiling jaws. He really means that the crocodile is eating the fish and that his massive, toothy jaws are anything but gentle.

One of the most famous examples of *irony of situation* is the ending of William Shakespeare's tragedy *King Lear*. After a terrible struggle and a mighty battle, King Lear is saved by his faithful daughter, Cordelia. We expect her to be able to enjoy her victory, but just the reverse happens: she is executed after the battle is won. She lies dead in Lear's arms, and, instead of enjoying his new-found freedom and safety, Lear dies too. This unpleasant ending is so ironic that throughout the eighteenth century, people insisted that the play be performed with a happy ending.

A good example of *dramatic irony* is found in the play *The Diary of Anne Frank.* We, the audience, are told at the beginning of the play that no one but Mr. Frank survives the Nazi prison camps. Thus, we watch the play knowing what the main characters themselves don't know: that only one of them will survive the war.

See page 218.

LEGEND   *A story handed down from the past. Legends seem to have some basis in history.* A legend usually centers on some historical incident, such as a battle or a journey in search of a treasure or the founding of a city or nation. A legend usually features a great hero or heroine who struggles against some powerful force to achieve the desired goal. Most legends were passed on orally long before they were written down, so the characters became larger than life, and their actions became fantastic and unbelievable. An example of a famous legend is the story of the Trojan War, which figures in three classical epics.

See page 624.

LIMERICK   *A comic poem written in five lines, rhymed in the pattern a a b b a, and having a definite pattern of rhythm.* Writing limericks is a great popular pastime. Much of the fun comes in finding rhymes to match the name of a person or place. A typical limerick begins like this: "There was a young girl from St. Paul." What comes later is up to the writer.

Sometimes writers of limericks twist the spellings of the rhyming words to build more humor. The following limerick plays on the Irish spelling of a town south of Dublin, *Dun Laoghaire,* pronounced "dun leery."

> An ancient old man of Dun Laoghaire
> Said, "Of pleasure and joy I've grown
>   waoghaire.
>   The life that is pure,
>   Will suit me I'm sure,
> It's healthy and noble though draghaire."

You can see that the pattern of rhythm for lines 1, 2, and 5 is the same and that the pattern for lines 3 and 4 is the same.

See page 504.

LYRIC POEM   *A brief poem which expresses an emotion and which usually represents the poet as "I."* (A lyric poem does *not* tell a story. A poem that tells a story is called a **narrative poem.**) The word *lyric* is derived from the word *lyre,* a musical instrument. The lyre is a stringed instrument remotely related to our guitar. It was struck in chords by the ancient Greek lyric poets, who sang their poems in a chant-like fashion. The lyre was used to help build up the emotional effects and to help the listener respond to the poem. Today we do not necessarily associate the lyric poem with music, although we do call the words to songs "lyrics."

English poet Leigh Hunt expresses a number of emotions in this lyric poem:

Jenny Kissed Me

> Jenny kissed me when we met,
>   Jumping from the chair she sat in;
> Time, you thief, who love to get
>   Sweets into your list, put that in!
> Say I'm weary, say I'm sad,
>   Say that health and wealth have missed
>   me,
> Say I'm growing old, but add,
>   Jenny kissed me.

METAMORPHOSIS   *In literature, a fantastic change, mainly of shape or form.* Myths often use metamorphosis to suggest a close relationship among gods, humans, and the world of nature. The Greek goddess Aphrodite, for instance, sprang from the foam of the sea. The goddess Athena appeared to the Greek hero Odysseus in the form of a mist. She also assumed the form of an owl when it suited her. Such metamorphoses reflected the ancient Greeks' wonder about the nature of the world, by suggesting that the shapes of things were not necessarily true indications of what the things really were. If an owl could be a goddess, then it was only wise for a Greek to be cautious of the owl and to respect it.

In A.D. 8, a Roman poet named Ovid collected the Greek and Roman myths of shape-changing into a book called *The Metamorphoses.* One of the famous stories from Ovid's collection is "Midas," in which a king is given the power to change everything he touches into gold. *The Metamorphoses* influenced many later writers to introduce sudden changes of form or shape into their works. Metamorphoses are found in many popular European folk tales, in which handsome princes are often reduced to ugly and repellent creatures. In "The Princess and the Frog," a frog is transformed back into a beautiful prince, and in "Beauty and the Beast," a prince is transformed into a beast and then returned to his original form.

Metamorphoses are used in modern literature as well. In "Flowers for Algernon," Daniel Keyes writes about a scientifically induced metamorphosis, in which a retarded man is transformed into a mental giant as a result of a surgical procedure. In fact, metamorphoses are found in many works of science fiction.

METAPHOR *A comparison made between two different things, as in the saying "Life is a dream," "You are my sunshine," or "He is a peach."* The intention of a metaphor is to give added meaning to one of the things being compared. A metaphor is one of the most important forms of **figurative language.** It is used in virtually all forms of language, including everyday speech, formal prose, and all forms of fiction and poetry.

If we say, "He was a gem to help me out," we use a metaphor, because we say a person is a gem. Gems are stones; they are hard; they glisten; they are often quite small. But these are *not* the qualities which the metaphor wants us to consider. We rely on our listener to understand that the metaphor is comparing the person's *value* to a gem's value.

If we say, "Misers have hearts of flint," we do not mean that their hearts are small dark stones that are bloodless and nonfunctioning. Rather, we mean that misers cannot show sympathy and kindness, just as the piece of stone cannot.

Metaphors are not always stated directly. In "Paul Revere's Ride" (page 136), Longfellow says that the spark struck out by Revere's horse "kindled the land into flame with its heat." Longfellow expects us to understand that the "fire" refers to the American Revolution.

A poet will sometimes **extend** a metaphor throughout a poem. Langston Hughes does this in his poem "Mother to Son." In the second line, the mother compares life to a stairway, and throughout the poem she talks of life as if it *were* a stairway. A metaphor is also extended throughout the following poem by Emily Dickinson. In the first line, the poet compares hope to a bird. Throughout the poem, she continues to describe hope as if it were a bird:

Hope is the thing with feathers
That perches in the soul,
And sings the tune without the words,
And never stops at all,

And sweetest in the gale is heard;
And sore must be the storm

That could abash the little bird
That kept so many warm.

I've heard it in the chillest land,
And on the strangest sea;
Yet, never, in extremity,
It asked a crumb of me.

See **Figurative Language, Simile.**
See also pages 45, 468, 469.

MYTH *A story, often about gods and goddesses, that attempts to give meaning to the world.* Almost every society has myths which explain the beginnings of the world, the beginnings of the human race, and the origins of evil. Myths tell people other things that they are concerned about: who their gods are, what their most sacred beliefs are, who their heroes are, and what their purpose in life is.

The term "classical mythology" refers to the myths told by the ancient Greeks and Romans. Most of the classical myths have to do with divinities who lived on Olympus, such as Zeus, Aphrodite, Apollo, Athena, and many others. Some of the classical myths have to do with the histories of great families. The myth "Antigone" is one of several stories told about the family of a king named Oedipus.

See page 71.

NARRATION *The kind of writing or speaking that relates a story (a narrative).* Narration tells about a series of connected events, explaining what happened, when it happened, and to whom it happened. Narration can be fictional, or it can be based on actual events. Narration can take the form of prose or poetry. It can be as long as a novel, or it can be as brief as an anecdote, which may be only a paragraph. Short stories, narrative poems, myths, fables, and legends are all examples of narration.

See **Point of View.**
See also page 123.

NARRATIVE POETRY *Poetry that tells a story.* A narrative poem is usually longer than a lyric poem, though it need not be extensive. For instance, Lewis Carroll's poem "Jabberwocky" tells a story about a young man who slays a monster, but the poem is only twenty-eight lines long. In "Casey at the Bat," Ernest Lawrence Thayer tells; in fifty-two lines, the entire saga of Mudville's hero and his humiliating strikeout.

In Edgar Allan Poe's "The Raven," a narrator uses 108 lines to tell the story of a strange bird that flew into his study, an event which seems to have driven him to madness. Other famous narrative poems are Henry Wadsworth Longfellow's "Paul Revere's Ride" and Sir Walter Scott's "Lochinvar."

See **Ballad, Narration, Point of View.**
See also pages 140, 486.

NONFICTION *Any prose account that tells about something that actually happened or that presents factual information about something.* Fiction is invented; nonfiction is *not* invented. One of the chief kinds of nonfiction is the history of someone's life. When a person writes his or her own personal life history, we call it **autobiography** (such as Richard Wright's *Black Boy*). When someone else writes a person's life history, we call it **biography** (such as Ann Petry's book called *Harriet Tubman: Conductor on the Underground Railroad*). Another kind of nonfiction is the **essay.**

Essays are among the most common forms of nonfiction, and they appear in most of the magazines we see on newsstands. Another kind of nonfiction is also found on newsstands: in the newspaper itself. News stories, editorials, letters to the editor, and features of all kinds are forms of nonfiction. Travel accounts, personal journals, and diaries are also forms of nonfiction.

See **Biography, Essay.**
See also pages 402, 449.

NOVEL *A fictional narrative in prose, generally longer than a short story.* The novel allows for greater complexity of character and plot development than the short story. The forms the novel may take cover a wide range. For example, there are the **historical novel,** in which historical characters, settings, and periods are drawn in detail; the **picaresque novel,** presenting the adventures of a rogue; and the **psychological novel,** which focuses on characters' emotions and thoughts. Other forms of the novel include the **detective story,** the **spy thriller,** the **Western,** and the **science-fiction novel.**

See pages 518, 564, 601.

ONOMATOPOEIA *The use of a word whose sound in some degree imitates or suggests its meaning.* The names of some birds are onomatopoetic, imitating the cries of the birds named: *cuckoo, whippoorwill, owl, crow, towhee, bobwhite.* Some onomatopoetic words are *hiss, clang, rustle,* and *snap.* In these lines from Edgar Allan Poe's poem "The Bells," the word *tintinnabulation* is onomatopoetic:

> Keeping time, time, time
> In a sort of Runic rhyme,
> To the *tintinnabulation* that so musically wells
> From the bells, bells, bells, bells,
>   Bells, bells, bells—

See page 480.

PARAPHRASE *A summary or restatement of a piece of writing, which expresses its meaning in other words.* A paraphrase of Ernest Lawrence Thayer's poem "Casey at the Bat" might go this way:

> The Mudville baseball team was behind in the last inning, and it looked as if Casey would not even get a chance at bat. But, when some batters before him actually got on base, everyone had high hopes that Casey could win the game with one of his famous home runs. But Casey showed off, did not swing at the first two good pitches, and struck out on the third one.

It is clear that such a paraphrase takes all the fun out of the original poem. The purpose of the paraphrase is to see that we understand just what really did happen in the poem.

See pages 485, 513.

PARODY *The humorous imitation of a serious piece of literature, or of some other art form, for the sake of amusement or ridicule.* In literature, a parody can be made of a character, a plot, a writer's style, or a theme.

Casey, in Ernest Lawrence Thayer's "Casey at the Bat," is a parody of the great heroes of old, like King Arthur, who never fail to come to the rescue of their people. The last and highest hopes of the home-team crowd are focused on Casey, their conquering hero. But all hopes die, and the hero fails the home team after all.

The following verse is a parody of the style of Edgar Allan Poe's "The Raven," a poem which has been often parodied over the years:

> Once upon a midnight dreary, while I shivered
>   eerie, bleary,
>   Full of teary leer-y, fear-y
> Thinking of my lost Lenore, my lost Len-
>   ore. . . .
> Lenore and nothing more!
> Not the oaken door, the grocery store, the dreadful bore, the apple core, the golf fore, the
>   marine corps, or the Lakers' score:
> My lost Lenore and nothing more.
> While I shivered nearly freezing, in my thin pajamas sneezing,

Who should wing right in a-breezing but a bris-
tling Raven wheezing,
Wheezing, wheezing right above my chamber
door.

Such parodies are fun and harmless, even if they do
make us laugh a bit at some of the techniques used
by a respected poet like Poe.

See page 332.

PERSONIFICATION *A figure of speech in which
something nonhuman is given human qualities.* In these
lines from "Blow, Blow, Thou Winter Wind," William Shakespeare personifies the wind. He addresses it as if it were a person who could
consciously act with kindness or unkindness. He
also gives it teeth and breath.

Blow, blow, thou winter wind,
Thou art not so unkind
　　As man's ingratitude.
Thy tooth is not so keen,
Because thou are not seen,
　　Although thy breath be rude.

PLOT *The sequence of events that take place in a story.*
Short stories, novels, dramas, and narrative poems
all have plots.

The major element in a plot is a **conflict,** or a struggle of some kind that takes place between the characters and their environment, or between warring
desires in the characters' own minds. A plot will introduce the characters, reveal the nature of their
conflict, and show us how the conflict is resolved.

Many times, especially in novels and plays, there will
be more than one plot. In *The Diary of Anne Frank,*
the main plot tells what happens as the "family"
hides from their enemies; the **subplot** tells what
happens to Anne and her growing love for Peter.

See **Conflict.**
See also pages 218, 317, 394.

POETRY *Traditional poetry is language arranged in
lines, with a regular rhythm and often with a definite
rhyme scheme. Nontraditional poetry does away with regular rhythm and rhyme, though it usually is set up in lines.*
There is no satisfactory way of defining poetry, although most people have little trouble knowing
when they read it. Some definitions offered by those
concerned with poetry may help us. The English
poet William Wordsworth called it "the spontaneous
overflow of powerful feelings." Matthew Arnold, an
English writer and poet of the nineteenth century,
defined it in this way: "Poetry is simply the most
beautiful, impressive and widely effective mode of
saying things."

Poetry uses **figurative language** and **imagery** extensively. It is often divided into **stanzas.** Poetry often
uses **rhyme** in order to create a kind of music or to
emphasize certain moods or effects. Poetry depends
heavily on strong **rhythms,** even when the rhythms
are not regular. Techniques like **alliteration** and **inversion** are often considered especially poetic.

There are two general categories of poetry: **narrative poetry,** which tells a story, and **lyric poetry,**
which does not tell a story but expresses some personal emotion. Some of the well-known poetic
forms are the **ballad,** the **elegy,** and the **limerick.**

See **Figurative Language, Rhyme, Rhythm.**
See also pages 99, 140, 480, 506, 513, 654.

POINT OF VIEW *The vantage point from which a
story is told.* Every story has to have a point of view,
since it has to be told to us by some "voice." Writers
may tell their stories from a third-person point of
view, or they may use a first-person point of view.

(1) The **third-person point of view** is one of the
most common in literature. In this point of view, a
story is told by someone not in the story at all. The
following paragraph is an example of the third-
person point of view. We are told here that a character, Hester Martin, has made a decision. She is
referred to in the third person ("she"), which is how
this point of view gets its name:

Hester Martin could let the insult get her down.
She could reply rudely or call for the manager
and make a formal complaint. But she decided
against both courses. Instead she took the man
aside and explained to him what it felt like to have
a total stranger say something cruel, even if the
man did not intend to be insulting. The man did
not intend to be insulting at all, and once Hester
told him how she felt, he changed his manner entirely. Hester had done the right thing. She had
educated someone.

This is an example of an **omniscient,** or **all-
knowing, third-person point of view.** The narrator
tells us things that Hester Martin does not directly
think or observe. The narrator tells us also that
Hester made the right decision.

A third-person point of view might *not* be all-
knowing. A **limited third-person point of view** tells
us what only one character sees, feels, and thinks.

This same scene written from a limited third-person point of view might go this way:

Hester Martin felt her face flush. Did he notice, too? Should she go to his manager? Should she insult him back? She took a moment to bring her emotions back under control, but when she collected herself she drew the man aside and lectured him carefully and patiently on the subject of insulting a patron. His apologies and his extraordinary politeness and caution gave her a small measure of satisfaction.

This limited third-person point of view tells the story from the point of view of one character only. The narrator does not tell us what other characters are thinking or feeling.

(2) The **first-person point of view** tells everything from the vantage point of a narrator who is usually a character in the story. We can be told only what this narrator knows and feels. We cannot be told what any other character thinks, except when the narrator may guess about that character's feelings or thoughts. The first-person is a very limited point of view, but its popularity is secure since we all identify with "I" in a story. The passage about Hester Martin's decision might be told like this by a first-person narrator:

I felt my face burn with the insult. I wondered if he noticed it. Should I go to his manager? No, I thought. And I won't stoop to his level and return the comment. When I thought I could control myself, I took the man aside and I told him in no uncertain terms that I did not like being insulted by a stranger. The only satisfaction I got was watching him try to squirm out of it, telling me he didn't mean it as an insult. But at least I got him to admit he was wrong. Maybe he learned a lesson.

The first-person point of view is much like our own view of life. It is limited to what one person knows and is controlled by that one person's thoughts and feelings.

See page 262.

PROSE *All literature which is not written as poetry.* Essays, short stories, novels, biographies, and most dramas are written in prose. Prose styles differ widely, from the simple and direct style of a story like Mary O'Hara's "My Friend Flicka," to the tense, nervous style of Poe's "The Tell-Tale Heart." One of the most remarkable pieces of prose is Abraham Lincoln's "Gettysburg Address," which was so short

that very few people who were present when Lincoln spoke actually remembered hearing it.

REFRAIN *A word, phrase, line, or group of lines that is repeated regularly in a poem or song, usually at the end of each stanza.* Refrains are sometimes used to emphasize a particularly important idea. In Poe's "The Raven," for example, the sentence "Quoth the Raven, 'Nevermore'" is a refrain. It helps to build up the mood of despair, and it reminds us continually of the sound of the name of the dead Lenore.

Sometimes the refrain in a poem or song is repeated exactly the same way, and sometimes it is varied slightly for effect. One of the delights in refrains is in anticipating their return.

RHYME *The repetition of sounds in words that appear close to each other in a poem.* One of the primary uses of rhyme seems to be as an aid to memory. You may have used some of the simpler rhymes for this purpose yourself, such as the one about months, beginning: "Thirty days hath September, April, June, and November." A rhyme that might help you remember a spelling rule is the one beginning: "*I* before *e* except after *c*."

The most familiar form of rhyme is **end rhyme.** This simply means that the rhymes come at the ends of the lines. The following lines are from a long poem on music, by the English poet Alexander Pope. In this part of the poem, Pope is trying to recreate the sounds of the underworld when Orpheus sings there in an attempt to rescue his beloved Eurydice:

What sounds are heard,
What scenes appeared,
　　O'er all the dreary coasts!
　　　Dreadful gleams,
　　　Dismal screams,
　　　Fires that glow,
　　　Shrieks of woe,
　　　Sullen moans,
　　　Hollow groans,
And cries of tortured ghosts!

Each of these rhymes is an exact rhyme, although we would now pronounce *heard* differently from *appeared.*

Rhyme that occurs within a line is called **internal rhyme.** One of the masters of internal rhyme is Edgar Allan Poe, who uses it in the first line of "The Raven": "Once upon a midnight *dreary*, while I pondered, weak and *weary*." One of Poe's clever internal rhymes is "lattice" and "thereat is" (lines 33–34).

Clearly, in poetry, rhymes are used for more than an aid to memory. Rhymes in the works of Pope or Poe, or any other careful poet, serve many purposes. One is to increase the musicality of the poem. (Songwriters also do this.) Another purpose of rhyme is to give delight by rewarding our anticipation of a returning sound, as in Pope's "coasts"/ "ghosts" rhyme. Rhyme is also used for humor. *Limericks,* for instance, would not be half so funny if they did not rhyme. The English poet George Gordon, Lord Byron invented one of the funniest rhymes in English when he rhymed "intellectual" with "hen-pecked you all."

See **Poetry.**
See also pages 474, 480, 505.

RHYTHM *The pattern of stressed and unstressed sounds in a line of poetry.* All language has rhythm of some sort or another, but rhythm is most important in poetry, where it is carefully controlled for effect.

There are several effects of rhythm in poetry. Rhythm lends poetry a musical quality, which gives the reader or listener pleasure. Rhythm can also be used to imitate the action being described in a poem. For example, in Robert Browning's poem "How They Brought the Good News from Ghent to Aix," the rhythm actually imitates the galloping rhythm of horses' hoofs.

And there was my Roland to bear the whole weight

Of the news which alone could save Aix from her fate,

With his nostrils like pits full of blood to the brim,

And with circles of red for his eye sockets' rim.

One thing to remember is that good poets usually put the stress on the most important words in the line. If you say a line to yourself in a natural voice, you will hear that the most important words demand stress.

In addition to using a pattern of stressed and unstressed syllables, a poet has another powerful means of building rhythm. This is by the use of **repetition.** In this passage from "The Bells," Edgar Allan Poe repeats the word *bells* eighteen times. He echoes the word three more times with the repetition of the rhyming word *knells.* He also repeats the word *time* six times, and echoes it twice more with the rhyming word *rhyme.* All of this repetition builds

up a kind of pounding rhythm, which might remind us of the repeated ringing of bells themselves.

Keeping time, time, time,
In a sort of runic rhyme,
   To the throbbing of the bells,
Of the bells, bells, bells—
   To the sobbing of the bells;
Keeping time, time, time,
   As he knells, knells, knells,
In a happy runic rhyme,
   To the rolling of the bells,
Of the bells, bells, bells:
   To the tolling of the bells,
Of the bells, bells, bells, bells,
   Bells, bells, bells—
To the moaning and the groaning of the bells.

See **Alliteration, Rhyme.**
See also pages 482, 484.

SETTING *The time and place in which the events of a story take place.* In short stories, novels, poems, and nonfiction, setting is established by **description.** In dramas, setting is usually established by **stage directions,** but since dramas normally have **sets** which appear before the audience, elaborate descriptions of setting are unnecessary.

In some stories, setting is not important at all, but in other stories setting is very significant. Washington Irving's story "The Legend of Sleepy Hollow," for example, could happen in only one setting—a "spellbound" region, where people believe in ghosts:

A drowsy, dreamy influence seems to hang over the land. The whole neighborhood abounds with local tales, haunted spots, and twilight superstitions; and the nightmare seems to make it the favorite scene of her gambols.

Setting can serve simply as the physical background of a story, or it can be used to establish atmosphere. In his poem "The Raven," Edgar Allan Poe uses setting to establish an atmosphere of gloom and mystery. He does this by telling us what time it is (a "midnight dreary"), what month it is ("bleak December"), what the study looks like ("each separate dying ember wrought its ghost upon the floor"), and what sounds are heard ("the silken, sad, uncertain rustling of each purple curtain").

See **Atmosphere.**
See also page 239.

SIMILE *A comparison made between two different things, using a word such as* like *or* as. Similes are *figures of speech* and are common in everyday language and in most forms of literature. We use similes when we say, "He fought like a tiger"; "He was as mild as a dove"; "She was as cool as a cucumber." A more poetic use of simile is this, from George Gordon, Lord Byron's "Stanzas for Music":

There will be none of Beauty's daughters
  With a magic like to thee;
And like music on the waters
  Is thy sweet voice to me.

See **Figurative Language.**
See also pages 45, 468, 503.

STANZA *A group of lines forming a unit in a poem.* Some poems, such as limericks, consist of a single stanza. "Lochinvar" by Sir Walter Scott is divided into eight stanzas, each of which has six lines and the same rhyme scheme.

See **Poetry.**

SUSPENSE *That quality in a literary work that makes the reader or audience uncertain or tense about what is to come next.* Suspense is a kind of "suspending" of our emotions. We know something is about to happen, and the longer the writer can keep us guessing, the greater the suspense. Suspense is popular in any kind of literature that involves **plot,** whether it be nonfiction, drama, short stories, novels, or narrative poems.

Every reader of Ernest Lawrence Thayer's "Casey at the Bat," for example, wants to find out if the hero of the poem will come to the rescue of the Mudville Nine. Holding the reader off for as long as possible is part of the poet's strategy of building suspense.

Suspense is possible even when the reader *knows* what to expect. Even though we know in Edward Everett Hale's "The Man Without a Country" that Philip Nolan has died in exile, we want to keep on reading to find out what his life at sea was like. We also are kept in suspense over Nolan's feelings; we want to know if he changed his mind about his country during his exile.

See **Foreshadowing, Plot.**
See also page 229.

SYMBOL *Any person, place, or thing which has meaning in itself but which is made to represent, or stand for, something else as well.* A symbol can be an object, a person, an action, a place, or a situation. Writers sometimes rely on commonly used symbols: most people know, for example, that an old man with a scythe usually is a symbol for time, that a dove is a symbol for peace, that a snake is often a symbol for evil, that ice is often a symbol for hatred, and that red is often a symbol for passion. But often we have to be on our toes in order to understand what something in literature is supposed to symbolize.

Symbols are often personal. In Robert Frost's poem "The Road Not Taken," we know that the road symbolizes a choice, but we do not know exactly what choice the poet has in mind. Frost purposely leaves its full meaning indefinite, so that the road can take on any number of symbolic meanings. For Frost, it may have symbolized a choice of careers—should he be a schoolteacher or a poet, for example. For us, it may symbolize other choices. Frost's road works well as a symbol because everybody has choices to make and nobody can make all of them. There has to be "a road not taken" in everyone's life.

A symbol is like a rock thrown in a pond: we see the splash right away, but then we notice that the ripples go much further than we expected. As we reflect on a symbol, its suggested meanings move out like the ripples, slowly and ever more widely.

See page 472.

TALL TALE *A highly improbable, humorous story that stretches facts beyond any hope of belief.* Tall tales feature things like people as high as mountains, pancake griddles two city blocks wide, and lakes used for boiling vegetables. Tall tales seem to have been extremely popular in the American West, where even nature seemed to assume gigantic proportions. The tales of Mike Fink, the keelboatman, John Henry, the railroad man, and Paul Bunyan, the logger, were the delight of the evening campfire. Some tall tales continue to become taller as generations of new storytellers add to them.

See pages 176, 183.

THEME *The main idea expressed in a literary work.* Many stories, such as some murder mysteries and sports stories, seem to have little to say about life or about human nature. Such stories are told chiefly for entertainment, and theme is of little or no importance in them. But other stories do try to make a comment on the human condition, and in those stories, theme is of great importance.

Because themes are rarely expressed directly, they are not always obvious to the reader. Theme is one of those qualities which must be dug out and thought about. One of the rewards of reading is the pleasure of coming upon the theme of a literary work on our own.

Usually, however, careful writers plan their stories so that readers can pick out sentences or events that point toward the theme. Such "key passages" are recognizable because they seem to speak directly to us as readers. They make direct, thoughtful statements, discussing the meaning of an action or a lesson the characters may have learned.

For example, Dorothy Canfield's story "The Apprentice" is a story with a strong theme. Its theme has to do with a young person's coming-of-age, or achieving adult status. A key passage in this story explicitly tells us that when the young heroine realizes what unendurable tragedy is, she becomes a mature adult.

Often the title of a story will also help us arrive at its theme. This is the case with "The Apprentice." The title reminds us of the old custom of apprenticeship, where young people learn a particular skill that prepares them to earn their living as adults.

Some simple themes can be stated in a single sentence. But sometimes a literary work is so rich and complex that a paragraph or essay is needed to state the theme satisfactorily.

See pages 38, 96, 271, 317, 394.

TONE *The attitude the writer takes toward his or her subject.* A writer may approach a subject with absolute seriousness, as Abraham Lincoln approached the subject of the war dead in his speech "The Gettysburg Address." Or, a writer can approach a subject with humor and mockery, as Ernest Lawrence Thayer approaches Casey in "Casey at the Bat." We get the feeling that Thayer is mocking Casey because he presents him as a proud and vain hero whose overconfidence prevents him from winning the ball game.

Tone is present in all kinds of writing. It is very important for a reader to recognize the tone of a biography. A biographer who loves his or her subject may not be completely objective or truthful. The same is true of a biographer who does *not* think well of his or her subject. In poetry, tone can sometimes change our entire view of a subject. Arthur Guiterman has written a poem called "The Vanity of Earthly Greatness," which is a very serious topic. But Guiterman only pretends to be solemn about this "deep" subject. His tone makes us laugh at something that most people treat very seriously. On

the other hand, Edgar Allan Poe's "The Raven" is totally serious in tone. If we make fun of the poem (see the example under **Parody**), we can see how tone can change our entire view of a situation.

See pages 103, 435.

TRAGEDY *A serious literary work which portrays a heroic, dignified, or courageous character who comes to a terrible end, such as death or exile.* Any narrative can be a tragedy—short stories, novels, narrative poems, and plays, though the term is most often applied to plays. Some famous tragedies are the dramas of ancient Greece, such as *Agamemnon, Oedipus Rex,* and *Antigone.* The tragedies written by William Shakespeare are also famous. They include such plays as *Romeo and Juliet, Julius Caesar, Hamlet,* and *Macbeth.* All of these titles are the names of people, and this is appropriate, since tragedies usually tell of the downfall of one person. In older tragedies (such as the Greek tragedies and Shakespeare's tragedies), this person is usually a noble character, perhaps a king, queen, prince, or princess. This tragic hero or heroine often falls because of a defect in character, which gives way under the stress of events. Or, a tragic hero or heroine might fall because a series of outside events just cannot be controlled. The outcome of the action in a tragedy is always terrible. Tragedies are not usually depressing, however, because they show us how human dignity and courage can be maintained, even in the face of defeat.

See page 393.

YARN *An exaggerated story that seems to go on and on, like a ball of yarn.* A yarn is a story told in the tradition of the **folk tale,** often handed down orally from teller to listener. A yarn seems to be built out of many episodes, which gradually are added on to the central core of a story. The origins of the yarn are connected to the sea and to stories told by sailors.

GLOSSARY

The words listed in the glossary in the following pages are found in the selections in this textbook. You can use this glossary to look up words that are unfamiliar to you. Strictly speaking, the word *glossary* means a collection of technical, obscure, or foreign words found in a certain field of work. Of course, the words in this glossary are not "technical, obscure, or foreign," but are those that might present difficulty as you read the selections in this textbook.

Many words in the English language have several meanings. This glossary does not give all the meanings of a word. The meanings given here are the ones that apply to the words as they are used in the selections in the textbook. Words closely related in form and meaning are frequently listed together in one entry (**afflict** and **afflicted**), and the definition is given for the first form. Regular adverbs (ending in -*ly*) are defined in their adjective form, with the adverb form shown at the end of the definition.

The following abbreviations are used:

adj., adjective   *n.*, noun
adv., adverb   *v.*, verb

For more information about the words in this glossary, consult a dictionary.

A

abate (ə-bāt′) *v.* To lessen.

abdominal (ăb-dŏm′ə-nəl) *adj.* In the abdomen, the part of the body between the chest and the hips.

abominable (ə-bŏm′ə-nə-bəl) *adj.* Hateful.

abound (ə-bound′) *v.* To have a plentiful supply of.

abrupt (ə-brŭpt′) *adj.* Sudden.—**abruptly** *adv.*—**abruptness** *n.*

absorption (ăb-sôrp′shən, ăb-zôrp′-) *n.* The passing of matter into the bloodstream.

abundance (ə-bŭn′dəns) *n.* A great supply.

abyss (ə-bĭs′) *n.* Any great depth or void.

accelerate (ăk-sĕl′ə-rāt′) *v.* To make something happen more quickly than usual.

accentuation (ăk-sĕn′chŏŏ-ā′shən) *n.* Stress; emphasis.

access (ăk′sĕs′) *n.* **1.** A way of approaching or getting something. **2.** An outburst.

acclaim (ə-klām′) *n.* General approval.

acclimate (ə-klī′mĭt, ăk′lə-māt′) *v.* To become accustomed to a foreign climate or to a new environment.

accommodate (ə-kŏm′ə-dāt′) *v.* To oblige.

account (ə-kount′) *v.* To consider.

acute (ə-kyŏŏt′) *adj.* Severe.

adjacent (ə-jā′sənt) *adj.* Next to.

adjourn (ə-jûrn′) *v.* To end a meeting.

adversary (ăd′vər-sĕr′ē) *n.* An enemy.

adobe (ə-dō′bē) *n.* sun-dried brick.

adorn (ə-dôrn′) *v.* To decorate; add ornaments.

aesthetic (ĕs-thĕt′ĭk) *adj.* Relating to principles of beauty.—**aesthetically** *adv.*

affable (ăf′ə-bəl) *adj.* Friendly; agreeable.

affect (ə-fĕkt′) *v.* To pretend.

affinity (ə-fĭn′ə-tē) *n.* **1.** A close relationship. **2.** An attraction.

affirm (ə-fûrm′) *v.* To declare something to be true.

afflict (ə-flĭkt′) *v.* To cause to suffer.—**afflicted** *adj.*

aggravate (ăg′rə-vāt′) *v.* To annoy; irritate.—**aggravating** *adj.*

aggressive (ə-grĕs′ĭv) *adj.* **1.** Hostile. **2.** Bold.

aghast (ə-găst′, ə-gäst′) *adj.* Shocked.

agitated (aj′ə-tāt′əd) *adj.* Upset; disturbed.—**agitation** *n.*

agony (ăg′ə-nē) *n.* Intense suffering.

alien (ā′lē-ən, āl′yən) *adj.* **1.** Foreign. **2.** Strange and unfriendly.

alight (ə-līt′) *v.* To settle; come down.

align (ə-līn′) *v.* To ally with; to line up with.

allot (ə-lŏt′) *v.* To give out; assign.

allure (ə-lŏŏr′) *v.* To tempt; attract.

allusion (ə-lŏŏ′zhən) *n.* A reference; mention.

aloof (ə-lŏŏf′) *adv.* Apart; separate.

altitude (ăl′tə-tŏŏd′, -tyŏŏd′) *n.* Height above sea level.

amble (ăm′bəl) *v.* To walk in a slow, relaxed way.

amiable (ā′mē-ə-bəl) *adj.* Friendly.—**amiably** *adv.*

amnesia (ăm-nē′zhə) *n.* A loss of memory.

ample (ăm′pəl) *adj.* Plentiful.

amputate (ăm′pyŏŏ-tāt′) *v.* To cut off.—**amputation** *n.*

anatomical (ăn′ə-tŏm′ĭ-kəl) adj. Referring to the structure of the body.

anatomy (ə-năt′ə-mē) *n.* The study of the shape and structure of animals and plants.

anecdote (ăn′ĭk-dōt′) *n.* A brief story.

anguish (ăng′gwĭsh) *n.* Great suffering.

animated (ăn′ə-mā′tĭd) *adj.* Lively.

annals (ăn′əlz) *n. p.* Records; history.

antagonist (ăn-tăg′ə-nĭst) *n.* Enemy; opponent; adversary.

ante (ăn′tē) *n.* **1.** An amount of money that a player in a card game must put in the pot. **2.** The amount a person pays as his or her share.

anteroom (ăn′tĭ-rōōm′, -rŏŏm′) *n.* A small room that leads into a larger room.

anticipation (ăn-tĭs′ə-pā′shən) *n.* An expectation.

apologetic (ə-pŏl′ə-jĕt′ĭk) *adj.* Showing or expressing regret for a wrong.—**apologetically** *adv.*

appall (ə-pôl′) *v.* To shock; horrify.—**appalling** *adj.*

apparatus (ăp′ə-rā′təs, -răt′əs) *n.* Equipment.

apparition (ăp′ə-rĭsh′ən) *n.* A ghostly shape or figure.

appease (ə-pēz′) *v.* To satisfy; soothe.

appendix (ə-pĕn′dĭks) *n.* Additional material at the end of a book or article.

appraise (ə-prāz′) *v.* To judge the quality or value of.—**appraisingly** *adv.*

apprehensive (ăp′rĭ-hĕn′sĭv) *adj.* Fearful.—**apprehensively** *adv.*

appropriation (ə-prō′prē-ā′shən) *n.* Money given for a certain purpose.

apt (ăpt) *adj.* Suitable.—**aptly** *adv.*

ardent (är′dənt) *adj.* Passionate.—**ardently** *adv.*

arduous (är′jōō-əs) *adj.* Difficult; laborious.

arid (ăr′ĭd) *adj.* Very dry.

arrogance (ăr′ə-gəns) *n.* Overbearing pride.—**arrogant** *adj.*

ascend (ə-sĕnd′) *v.* To move upward.—**ascending** *adj.*

ascent (ə-sĕnt′) *n.* Upward climb.

askew (ə-skyōō′) *adv.* Crookedly.

aspect (ăs′pĕkt) *n.* Appearance.

assailant (ə-sā′lənt) *n.* A person who attacks another.

assassin (ə-săs′ĭn) *n.* Murderer.

assault (ə-sôlt′) *n.* An attack.

assent (ə-sĕnt′) *v.* To agree.

assess (ə-sĕs′) *v.* To judge the importance or value of.

asset (ăs′ĕt′) *n.* An advantage.

assiduous (ə-sĭj′ōō-əs) *adj.* Hardworking.—**assiduously** *adv.*

attire (ə-tīr′) *n.* Clothing.

atypical (ā-tĭp′ĭ-kəl) *adj.* Unusual.

audacious (ô-dā′shəs) *adj.* Showing no fear; daring; bold.

auspicious (ô-spĭsh′əs) *adj.* Favorable.

authoritative (ə-thôr′ə-tā′tĭv, ə-thŏr′-) *adj.* Official; reliable.

avail (ə-vāl′) *v.* To make use of.

avenge (ə-vĕnj′) *v.* To get revenge for.

avert (ə-vûrt′) *v.* To turn away.

awed (ôd) *adj.* Filled with respect and wonder.

B

badger (băj′ər) *v.* To nag.—**badgering** *n.*

baffle (băf′əl) *v.* To puzzle.

balk (bôk) *v.* To refuse.

banner (băn′ər) *adj.* Outstanding.

banter (băn′tər) *v.* To tease; make gentle fun of.

bar (bär) *v.* To prevent.

barometer (bə-rŏm′ə-tər) *n.* An instrument that measures air pressure and is used to predict change in the weather.

barren (băr′ən) *adj.* **1.** Empty. **2.** Without plant life.

barter (bär′tər) *v.* To trade.

bayou (bī′ōō, bī′ō) *n.* A swamp.

beacon (bē′kən) *n.* A warning signal.

bearing (bâr′ĭng) *n.* A determination of someone's or something's position.

befit (bĭ-fĭt′) *v.* To be suitable.

befuddle (bĭ-fŭd′l) *v.* To confuse.

beguile (bĭ-gīl′) *v.* To charm or amuse.

behoove (bĭ-hōōv′) *v.* To be necessary or right for.

belfry (bĕl′frē) *n.* A tower in which a bell is hung.

belligerent (bə-lĭj′ər-ənt) *adj.* Ready to fight.—**belligerently** *adv.*

benignant (bĭ-nĭg′nənt) *adj.* Kind.

bereft (bĭ-rĕft′) *adj.* Deprived of something.

beseech (bĭ-sēch′) *v.* To beg.

besiege (bĭ-sēj′) *v.* To surround in order to attack and capture.—**besieged** *adj.*

betray (bĭ-trā′) *v.* **1.** To be disloyal to. **2.** To reveal.—**betraying** *adj.*

bevy (bĕv′ē) *n.* A large group.

bier (bîr) *n.* A stand for holding a body or coffin.

ă pat/ā pay/âr care/ä father/b bib/ch church/d deed/ĕ pet/ē be/f fife/g gag/h hat/hw which/ĭ pit/ī pie/îr pier/j judge/k kick/ l lid, needle/m mum/n no, sudden/ng thing/ŏ pot/ō toe/ô paw, for/oi noise/ou out/ŏŏ took/ōō boot/p pop/r roar/s sauce/ sh ship, dish/t tight/th thin, path/th this, bathe/ŭ cut/ûr urge/v valve/w with/y yes/z zebra, size/zh vision/ə about, item, edible, gallop, circus/à *Fr.* ami/œ *Fr.* feu, *Ger.* schön/ü *Fr.* tu, *Ger.* über/ΚΗ *Ger.* ich, *Scot.* loch/Ν *Fr.* bon.

bilk (bĭlk) *v.* To cheat.

billow (bĭl′ō) *v.* To cause to swell out.

blackjack (blăk′jăk′) *n.* A kind of oak tree with a black bark.

bleak (blēk) *adj.* Barren.

blunt (blŭnt) *adj.* Abrupt.—**bluntly** *adv.*

blurt (blûrt) *v.* To speak suddenly without thought.

bluster (blŭs′tər) *n.* **1.** Empty threats. **2.** Loud, noisy talk.

bolt (bōlt) *v.* To run away.

booty (boo′tē) *n.* Prey or plunder taken in war.

breach (brēch) *n.* An opening.

brimful (brĭm′fool′) *adj.* Completely full.

bristle (brĭs′əl) *v.* To show anger.

broach (brōch) *v.* To bring up a topic for discussion.

brood (brood) *v.* To hover.

buffet (bŭf′ĭt) *v.* To strike repeatedly; knock about.

bulrush (bool′rŭsh′) *n.* A cattail.

buoyant (boi′ənt, boo′yənt) *adj.* **1.** Having buoyancy, the ability to keep afloat. **2.** Cheery.

burnish (bûr′nĭsh) *v.* To make shiny.—**burnished** *adj.*

C

cache (kăsh) *n.* A hiding place or storage place; also the things stored.

cajole (kə-jōl′) *v.* To coax.

candid (kăn′dĭd) *adj.* Honest.

canker (kăng′kər) *v.* To become infected.

canopy (kăn′ə-pē) *n.* A cloth that serves as a roof or cover.

caper (kā′pər) *v.* To jump about playfully.

capitulate (kə-pĭch′oo-lāt′) *v.* To give up.

captor (kăp′tər, -tôr′) *n.* Someone or something that holds a person or animal prisoner.

carillon (kăr′ə-lŏn′, kə-rĭl′yən) *n.* A set of bells that can be played from a keyboard.

carp (kärp) *n.* A kind of fish.

cascade (kăs-kād′) *v.* To fall in great amounts.

causeway (kôz′wā′) *n.* A raised road, often above water.

cavernous (kăv′ər-nəs) *adj.* Like a cave.

cavort (kə-vôrt′) *v.* To run and jump in a playful manner.

celebrity (sə-lĕb′rə-tē) *n.* A famous figure.

centennial (sĕn-tĕn′ē-əl) *n.* One-hundredth anniversary celebration.

chaos (kā′ŏs′) *n.* Complete disorder.

charger (chär′jər) *n.* A horse trained for battle.

chasm (kăz′əm) *n.* A deep crack in the earth's surface.

chastise (chăs-tīz′) *v.* To punish.—**chastisement** *n.*

chide (chīd) *v.* To scold.

chortle (chôrt′l) *n.* A laugh, midway between a chuckle and a snort.

chronicle (krŏn′ĭ-kəl) *v.* To record; list.

circumference (sər-kŭm′fər-əns) *n.* The measurement of the outer edge of a circular object.

clarion (klăr′ē-ən) *n.* Sound of a trumpet.

cleave (klēv) *v.* To split.

clemency (klĕm′ən-sē) *n.* Mercy.

clientele (klī′ən-tĕl′) *n.* Customers.

coax (kōks) *v.* To persuade by using soothing words and an agreeable manner.

colossal (kə-lŏs′əl) *adj.* Gigantic.

commemorate (kə-mĕm′ə-rāt′) *v.* To honor the memory of someone or some event.

commend (kə-mĕnd′) *v.* To recommend.

commission (kə-mĭsh′ən) *v.* To give someone a job to do.—*n.* A fee or percentage paid to another for doing something.

common (kŏm′ən) *n.* A public park in a village or town.

commute (kə-myoot′) *v.* To travel back and forth regularly, as from one city to another.

compassion (kəm-păsh′ən) *n.* Pity.

competent (kŏm′pə-tənt) *adj.* Able; capable.

compliance (kəm-plī′əns) *n.* The act of following a request.

compressor (kəm-pres′ər) *n.* A machine for increasing the pressure of gases.

compromise (kŏm′prə-mīz′) *v.* **1.** To settle by concessions from both sides. **2.** To put someone's good reputation in danger.

compulsory (kəm-pŭl′sə-rē) *adj.* Required.

con (kŏn) *v.* To study.

conceive (kən-sēv′) *v.* To think of.

condense (kən-dĕns′) *v.* To put in a briefer form.

condescend (kŏn′dĭ-sĕnd′) *v.* **1.** To lower oneself willingly. **2.** To deal with others in a proud or overbearing way.

confront (kən-frŭnt′) *v.* To stand or to put face to face with; to oppose.

congeal (kən-jēl′) *v.* To solidify.

conical (kŏn′ĭ-kəl) *adj.* Shaped like a cone.

conjure (kŏn′jər, kən-joor′) *v.* To summon or call upon.—**conjure up** To evoke or call to mind.

conscientious (kŏn′shē-ĕn′shəs) *adj.* Careful; painstaking.

consciousness (kŏn′shəs-nĭs) *n.* An awareness of one's thoughts, feelings, and sensory impressions.

consecrate (kŏn′sə-krāt′) *v.* To dedicate as something sacred.

consolidate (kən-sŏl′ə-dāt′) *v.* To stengthen; establish firmly.

conspicuous (kən-spĭk′yoo-əs) *adj.* Easily seen; noticeable.

constancy (kŏn′stən-sē) *n.* Steadfastness; firmness of purpose.

constitution (kŏn′stə-too′shən, -tyoo′shən) *n.* One's state of health.

constrained (kən-strānd′) *adj.* Forced; unnatural.

constraint (kən-strānt′) *n.* Lack of ease; unnaturalness in manner.

consul (kŏn′səl) *n.* An official representative of a government.

consume (kən-soom′, -syoom′) *v.* To use up.

contagion (kən-tā′jən) *n.* A tendency to spread by contact.

contemplate (kŏn′təm-plāt′) *v.* **1.** To look at thoughtfully. **2.** To think about intently.

contend (kən-tĕnd′) *v.* **1.** To compete. **2.** To hold to be a fact.

contort (kən-tôrt′) *v.* To twist into unusual shapes.—**contorted** *adj.*

contrite (kən-trīt′, kŏn′trīt′) *adj.* Repentant.

convene (kən-vēn′) *v.* To come together, as for a meeting.—**convened** *adj.*

converge (kən-vûrj′) *v.* To come together at a point; meet.

convey (kən-vā′) *v.* **1.** To carry from one place to another. **2.** To make known.

conviction (kən-vĭk′shən) *n.* A belief.

convoy (kŏn′voi′, kən-voi′) *v.* To accompany in order to protect.

convulsion (kən-vŭl′shən) *n.* A violent muscle spasm; a fit.

convulsive (kən-vŭl′sĭv) *adj.* Like a convulsion.—**convulsively** *adv.*

coordination (kō-ôr′də-nā′shən) *n.* The ability of the muscles to act together and result in a smooth action.—**coordinate** *adj.* Having all parts working together harmoniously.

countenance (koun′tə-nəns) *n.* A face.

counteract (koun′tər-ăkt′) *v.* To act against.

courtier (kôr′tē-ər, kōr′-, -tyər) *n.* One who serves a king or queen at court.

cove (kōv) *n.* A bay.

covet (kŭv′ĭt) *v.* To envy.

covey (kŭv′ē) *n.* A small group.

cower (kou′ər) *v.* To shrink back, as in fear.

crag (krăg) *n.* A projecting rock.

cranium krā′nē-əm) *n.* The skull.

cranny (krăn′ē) *n.* A crevice or small opening.

craven (krā′vən) *adj.* Cowardly.—**cravenly** *adv.*

credible (krĕd′ə-bəl) *adj.* Believable.

creed (krēd) *n.* A statement of belief.

crescent (krĕs′ənt) *n.* The moon in its first or last quarter, when its shape is thin and not rounded.

crest (krĕst) *n.* **1.** A crownlike growth on the head of some birds. **2.** Summit.

crystallize (krĭs′tə-līz′) *v.* To take definite shape.—**crystallized** *adj.*

cudgel (kŭj′əl) *v.* To strike, as with a club.

cunning (kŭn′ĭng) *adj.* Clever in a tricky way. *n.* Cleverness; trickery.–**cunningly** *adv.*

curative (kyoo′-ə-tĭv) *adj.* Something that cures; a remedy.

curator (kyoo-rā′tər, kyoor′ə-tər) *n.* A person in charge of a museum, library, or exhibit.

curb (kûrb) *v.* To control or hold back.

curry (kûr′ē) *v.* To groom a horse.

curt (kûrt) *adj.* Rude and abrupt.—**curtly** *adv.*

curvaceous (kûr-vā′shəs) *adj.* Pleasingly curved.

D

dauntless (dônt′lĭs, dänt′-) *adj.* Fearless; courageous.

dawdle (dôd′l) *v.* To spend time aimlessly.

daybed (dā′bĕd′) *n.* A couch that can also be used as a bed.

decorum (dĭ-kôr′əm, dĭ-kōr′əm) *n.* Proper appearance.

decree (dĭ-krē′) *v.* To establish or decide.

deem (dēm) *v.* To judge.

default (dĭ-fôlt′) *n.* Failure to do something.

deft (dĕft) *adj.* Skillful.

deign (dān) *v.* To stoop to do something beneath one's dignity.

dejection (dĭ-jĕk′shən) *n.* Sadness.

delectable (dĭ-lĕk′tə-bəl) *adj.* Delicious.

ă pat/ā pay/âr care/ä father/b bib/ch church/d deed/ĕ pet/ē be/f fife/g gag/h hat/hw which/ĭ pit/ī pie/îr pier/j judge/k kick/ l lid, needle/m mum/n no, sudden/ng thing/ŏ pot/ō toe/ô paw, for/oi noise/ou out/oo took/oo boot/p pop/r roar/s sauce/ sh ship, dish/t tight/th thin, path/th this, bathe/ŭ cut/ûr urge/v valve/w with/y yes/z zebra, size/zh vision/ə about, item, edible, gallop, circus/à *Fr.* ami/œ *Fr.* feu, *Ger.* schön/ü *Fr.* tu, *Ger.* über/KH *Ger.* ich, *Scot.* loch/N *Fr.* bon.

delve (dĕlv) *v.* To study something deeply.

denizen (dĕn′ə-zən) *n.* One who lives in a certain place.

deprive (dĭ-prīv′) *v.* To take something away from; dispossess.

depute (dĭ-pyo͞ot′) *v.* To assign.

derelict (dĕr′ə-lĭkt) *adj.* Something or someone abandoned or deserted.

descend (dĭ-sĕnd′) *v.* To go down.

desolation (dĕs′ə-lā′shən) *n.* Wretchedness.

deteriorate (dĭ-tîr′ē-ə-rāt′) *v.* To become worse.—**deterioration** *n.*

detract (dĭ-trăkt′) *v.* To take away; subtract.

devise (dĭ-vīz′) *v.* To plan.

dexterity (dĕk-stĕr′ə-tē) *n.* Skill.

diadem (dī′ə-dĕm′) *n.* Crown.

diameter (dī-ăm′ə-tər) *n.* Width; the distance across the center of a circular object.

dilapidated (dĭ-lăp′ə-dā′tĭd) *adj.* In very bad condition.

dilate (dī-lāt′, dī′lāt′, dĭ-lāt′) *v.* To expand.

diligent (dĭl′-ə-jənt) *adj.* Careful.

din (dĭn) *v.* To stun with deafening noise.

dinghy (dĭng′ē) *n.* A small rowboat.

direful (dīr′fəl) *adj.* Fearful; terrible.

dirge dûrj) *n.* **1.** A funeral song. **2.** Any sad piece of music.

discard (dĭs-kärd′) *v.* To remove from use.—**discarded** *adj.*

discernible (dĭ-sûr′nə-bəl, dĭ-zûr′-) *adj.* Capable of being seen or detected.

discerning (dĭ-šûr′nĭng, dĭ-zûr′-) *adj.* Keen; showing good understanding.

disciple (dĭ-sī′pəl) *n.* A pupil.

discomfiture (dĭs-kŭm′fĭ-cho͝or) *n.* Discomfort.

disconcert (dĭs′kən-sûrt′) *v.* To confuse; upset.—**disconcerted** *adj.*

disconsolate (dĭs-kŏn′sə-lĭt) *adj.* Very sad.

discord (dĭs′kôrd′) *n.* **1.** A disagreement. **2.** In music, a lack of harmony.

discourse (dĭs′kôrs′, -kōrs′) *v.* To speak.

discrimination (dĭs-krĭm′ə-nā′shən) *n.* Prejudice.

disdain (dĭs-dān′) *n.* Scorn.—**disdainful** *adj.*

disheveled (dĭ-shĕv′əld) *adj.* Disorderly in appearance.

dislodge (dĭs-lŏj′) *v.* To force from a position.

dismay (dĭs-mā′) *v.* To trouble; fill with fear.

dismember (dĭs-mĕm′bər) *v.* To cut the arms and legs off.

dispassionate (dĭs-păsh′ən-ĭt) *adj.* Fair; not partial.

dispel (dĭs-pĕl′) *v.* To get rid of.

dispirit (dĭs-pĭr′ĭt) *v.* To make unhappy; depress.—**dispirited** *adj.*

displace (dĭs-plās′) *v.* To take the place of.

display (dĭs-plā′) *v.* To show.

dispose (dĭs-pōz′) *v.* To arrange.—**dispose of** To get rid of.

disposition (dĭs′pə-zĭsh′ən) *n.* Management.

dispute (dĭs-pyo͞ot′) *n.* An argument.

dissemble (dĭ-sĕm′bəl) *v.* To pretend; feign.

dissolution (dĭs′-ə-lo͞o′shən) *n.* The process of dissolving into nothingness.

distort (dĭs-tôrt′) *v.* To twist out of shape.

divine (dĭ-vīn′) *v.* To guess; figure out.

docile (dŏs′əl) *adj.* Tame; easily handled.

doff (dôf, dŏf) *v.* To take off.

dogged (dô′gĭd, dŏg′ĭd) *adj.* Persistent; stubborn.—**doggedly** *adv.*

doleful (dōl′fəl) *adj.* Sad.

dominion (də-mĭn′yən) *n.* Territory of control.

drab (drăb) *adj.* Dull; colorless.

dread (drĕd) *adj.* Terrifying.

drone (drōn) *n.* **1.** A lazy person. **2.** A low, continuing sound.—*v.* To make a low, continuing sound. —**droning** *adj.*

drudgery (drŭj′ə-rē) *n.* Hard work.

E

ebb (ĕb) *v.* **1.** To become less. **2.** To recede; flow back.

ebony (ĕb′ə-nē) *adj.* Black.

eclipse (ĭ-klĭps′) *v.* To reduce in importance.

ecstasy (ĕk′stə-sē) *n.* Great joy.

eddy (ĕd′ē) *n.* Circular motion.

ejaculation (ĭ-jăk′yə-lā′shən) *n.* A sudden shout.

elation (ĭ-lā′shən) *n.* Great joy.

elemental (ĕl′ə-mĕnt′l) *adj.* Basic; fundamental.

eloquence (ĕl′ə-kwəns) *n.* Forceful and graceful speech.

elude (ĭ-lo͞od′) *v.* To escape from being noticed.

elusive (ĭ-lo͞o′sĭv) *adj.* Hard to find or catch.

emancipate (ĭ-măn′sə-pāt′) *v.* To free someone.—**emancipation** *n.*—**emancipated** *adj.*

emerge (ĭ-mûrj′) *v.* To come out.

emigrate (ĕm′ĭ-grāt′) *v.* To leave one's country to live elsewhere.—**emigration** *n.*

eminent (ĕm′ə-nənt) *adj.* Outstanding.

encompass (ĕn-kŭm′pəs, ĭn-) *v.* To include.

endeavor (ĕn-dĕv′ər) *v.* To try.

engulf (ĕn-gŭlf′, ĭn-) *v.* To cover completely.

enrapture (ĕn-răp′chər, ĭn-) *v.* To fill with joy.—**enraptured** *adj.*

enterprising (ĕn′tər-prī′zĭng) *adj.* Ambitious and imaginative.

entrance (ĕn-trăns′, -träns′, ĭn-) *v.* To fill with delight.—**entranced** *adj.*

entreat (ĕn-trēt′, ĭn-) *v.* To plead; beg.

enumerate (ĭ-nōō′mə-rāt′, ĭ-nyōō′-) *v.* To list.

envelop (ĕn-vĕl′əp, ĭn-) *v.* To cover completely.

envision (ĕn-vĭzh′ən) *v.* To picture in the imagination.

epilogue (ĕp′ə-lôg′) *n.* A short portion added to a work of literature to complete or conclude the story.

epitaph (ĕp′ə-tăf, -täf′) *n.* The writing on a tombstone.

era (îr′ə, ĕr′ə) *n.* An important period of time.

erratic (ĭ-răt′ĭk) *adj.* Straying; wandering.

esteem (ĕ-stēm′, ĭ-stēm′) *v.* To hold in high regard. —**esteem** *n.*

etch (ĕch) *v.* **1.** To draw; outline. **2.** To make a clear impression.

etiquette (ĕt′ə-kĕt′, -kĭt′) *n.* Proper social or official behavior.

evoke (ĭ-vōk′) *v.* To call forth; draw out.

evolve (ĭ-vŏlv′) *v.* To develop.

exact (ĕg-zăkt′, ĭg-) *v.* To demand.

exalt (ĕg-zôlt′, ĭg-) *v.* To raise in importance.— **exalted** *adj.*

exasperate (ĕg-zăs′pə-rāt′, ĭg-) *v.* to annoy greatly. —**exasperating** *adj.*

exasperation (ĕg-zăs′pə-rā′shən, ĭg-) *n.* A feeling of great annoyance.

exertion (ĕg-zûr′shən, ĭg-) *n.* Effort.

exhilaration (ĕg-zĭl′ə-rā′shən, ĭg-) *n.* Excitement.

exotic (ĕg-zŏt′ĭk, ĭg-) *adj.* **1.** Interestingly different. **2.** Foreign.

expire (ĕk-spīr′, ĭk-) *v.* To die.

exposition (ĕk′spə-zĭsh′ən) *n.* Public exhibition.

exquisite (ĕks′kwĭ-zĭt′) *adj.* Of great beauty.

extinguish (ĕk-stĭng′gwĭsh, ĭk-) *v.* To put out.

extract (ĕk-străkt′, ĭk-) *v.* To draw out or pull out.

exult (ĕg-zŭlt′, ĭg-) *v.* To rejoice.

F

fanatical (fə-năt′ĭ-kəl) *adj.* Enthusiastic beyond reason.

farce (färs) *n.* Something ridiculous and laughable.

fastidious (fă-stĭd′ē-əs, fə-) *adj.* Fussy; not easily pleased.

felicitous (fĭ-lĭs′ə-təs) *adj.* Fit; well-chosen.

fell (fĕl) *v.* To cut down.—*adj.* Cruel.

fen (fĕn) *n.* Swamp; marsh.

ferment (fər-mĕnt′) *v.* To undergo a chemical reaction that changes sugar into other compounds.— **fermented** *adj.*

ferocity (fə-rŏs′ə-tē) *n.* Fierceness; cruelty.

fervent (fûr′vənt) *adj.* Showing great warmth of feeling; intense.—**fervently** *adv.*

fervor (fûr′vər) *n.* Intense feeling.

fester (fĕs′tər) *v.* To produce pus.—**festering** *adj.*

festoon (fĕs-tōōn′) *n.* A wreath.—*v.* To decorate with wreathes of flowers or leaves.

fetch (fĕch) *v.* To get or bring.

finesse (fĭ-nĕs′) *n.* Subtlety or artfulness.

finicky (fĭn′ĭ-kē) *adj.* Hard to please.

flank (flăngk) *n.* Side.

flaunt (flônt) *v.* To wave with pride.

flay (flā) *v.* To beat wildly, without aim.

fleck (flĕk) *n.* A tiny mark or spot.

flinch (flĭnch) *v.* To draw back or make a face, as if in pain.

flog (flŏg, flôg) *v.* To whip.—**flogger** *n.*

florid (flôr′ĭd) *adj.* Red-faced; ruddy.

flotsam (flŏt′səm) *n.* Wreckage.

flounder (floun′dər) *v.* To move clumsily.— **floundering** *adj.*

flout (flout) *v.* To be scornful.

fluent (flōō′ənt) *adj.* Flowing easily.—**fluently** *adv.*

foray (fôr′ā′) *n.* A raid.

ford (fôrd, fōrd) *n.* A place in the river that is shallow enough to be crossed on foot.

forefront (fôr′frŭnt′) *n.* The very front.

forfeit (fôr′fĭt) *v.* To surrender.

forlorn (fôr-lôrn′, fər-) *adj.* Wretched.

formidable (fôr′mə-də-bəl) *adj.* **1.** Causing fear or wonder. **2.** Commanding respect and admiration.

formula (fôr′myə-lə) *n.* A statement expressed in symbols and numbers.

fortify (fôr′tə-fī′) *v.* To build up strength.—**fortified** *adj.*

frantic (frăn′tĭk) *adj.* Wild with fear or pain; desperate.—**frantically** *adv.*

ă pat/ā pay/âr care/ä father/b bib/ch church/d deed/ĕ pet/ē be/f fife/g gag/h hat/hw which/ĭ pit/ī pie/îr pier/j judge/k kick/ l lid, needle/m mum/n no, sudden/ng thing/ŏ pot/ō toe/ô paw, for/oi noise/ou out/ōō took/ōō boot/p pop/r roar/s sauce/ sh ship, dish/t tight/th thin, path/*th* this, bathe/ŭ cut/ûr urge/v valve/w with/y yes/z zebra, size/zh vision/ə about, item, edible, gallop, circus/à *Fr.* ami/œ *Fr.* feu, *Ger.* schön/ü *Fr.* tu, *Ger.* über/КН *Ger.* ich, *Scot.* loch/N *Fr.* bon.

fraternity (frə-tûr′nə-tē) *n.* Fellowship.

frenzied (frĕn′zēd) *adj.* Frantic.

frenzy (frĕn′zē) *n.* Wild excitement.

fretful (frĕt′fəl) *adj.* Peevish; plaintive.

front (frŭnt) *v.* To face.

fruitless (froot′lĭs) *adj.* Unsuccessful.

fumigate (fyoo′mĭ-gāt′) *v.* To disinfect.—**fumigated** *adj.*

functional (fŭngk′shən-əl) *adj.* Practical; usable.

furrow (fûr′ō) *n.* A groove.

G

gait (gāt) *n.* Step; way of walking.

gallant (gə-lănt′, -länt′, găl′ənt) *n.* An attentive, courteous man.

gape (gāp, găp) *v.* To be wide open.—**gaping** *adj.*

gaunt (gônt) *adj.* Thin; underfed-looking.—**gauntly** *adv.*

genial (jēn′yəl, jē′nē-əl) *adj.* Friendly.—**genially** *adv.*

gesticulate (jĕ-stĭk′yə-lāt′) *v.* To make gestures; use motions with or instead of speech.

ghastly (găst′lē, gäst′-) *adj.* 1. Like a ghost. 2. Horrible.

giddy (gĭd′ē) *adj.* Dizzy; dazed.—**giddily** *adv.*

gilt (gĭlt) *n.* Gold applied in a thin layer.

girth (gûrth) *n.* The measurement around something.

glacial (glā′shəl) *adj.* Produced by glaciers—huge masses of ice and snow.

gland (glănd) *n.* One of many organs, cells, or groups of cells that produce a secretion.

glandular (glăn′jə-lər) *adj.* Referring to the activity of the glands.

glare (glâr) *v.* To stare angrily.

glaze (glāz) *v.* To apply a shiny coating.—**glazing** *n.*

glean (glēn) *v.* To find out bit by bit.

glib (glĭb) *adj.* Speaking easily and smoothly, often in a way that is not convincing.—**glibly** *adv.*

gloat (glōt) *v.* To take great pleasure in.

glower (glou′ər) *v.* To stare angrily.

glut (glŭt) *v.* To supply or fill to excess.

gluttonous (glŭt′n-əs) *adj.* Given to eating greedily and excessively.

gorge (gôrj) *n.* A deep narrow passage with steep rocky sides and enclosed between mountains.

gourmet (goor-mā′) *n.* One who is a fine judge of food and drink.

grapple (grăp′əl) *v.* To struggle.

grate (grāt) *v.* To rub something noisily against another object.

grave (grāv) *adj.* Serious; dignified.—**gravely** *adv.*

grenadier (grĕn′ə-dîr′) *n.* Originally, a soldier trained to use grenades.

grille (grĭl) *n.* A metal grating.

grisly (grĭz′lē) *adj.* Horrifying.

grope (grōp) *v.* To search in an uncertain way.

gross (grōs) *adj.* Referring to total income before deductions are made.

grotesque (grō-tĕsk′) *adj.* Strangely misshapen.—**grotesquely** *adv.*

grovel (grŭv′əl, grŏv′-) *v.* To assume a humble position; cringe.

grueling (groo′ə-ling) *adj.* Exhausting; causing extreme fatigue.

gullible (gŭl′ə-bəl) *adj.* Easily fooled or cheated.

gully (gŭl′lē) *n.* A deep ditch.—*v.* To cut a deep ditch in the earth.

gutter (gŭt′ər) *v.* To melt quickly and run off in a stream as the wax of a burning candle does.

guttural (gŭt′ər-əl) *adj.* Coming from the throat.

gyrate (jī′rāt′) *v.* To circle.

H

haggard (hăg′ərd) *adj.* Worn-out looking; exhausted.

hallow (hăl′ō) *v.* To make holy.

hamlet (hăm′lĭt) *n.* A small village.

hardy (här′dē) *adj.* Strong and healthy.

harken (här′kən) *v.* To listen carefully.

harass (hăr′əs, hə-răs′) *v.* To worry; trouble.—**harassed** *adj.*

harry (hăr′ē) *v.* To torment.

hassock (hăs′ək) *n.* A large, padded footstool.

haughty (hô′tē) *adj.* Proud.

haunch (hônch, hänch) *n.* The hip and upper thigh.

haunt (hônt, hänt) *n.* A favorite place.

heathen (hē′thən) *adj.* Unbelieving; pagan.

heed (hēd) *v.* To pay attention to.

herald (hĕr′əld) *n.* Messenger.

herculean (hûr′kyə-lē′ən, -kyoo′lē-ən) *adj.* Very difficult.

hew (hyoo) *v.* To carve or shape.

hoist (hoist) *v.* To lift; raise.

homestead (hōm′stĕd′) *n.* Farm property.

horde (hôrd, hōrd) *n.* A large, disorderly group.

host (hōst) *n.* An army.

hostile (hŏs′təl) *adj.* Unfriendly.

hover (hŭv′ər, hŏv′-) *v.* To stay suspended in one place.

hoyden (hoid′n) *n.* A tomboy.

hull (hŭl) *n.* The frame of a ship.

hussy (hŭz′ē, hŭs′ē) *n.* A bold, immoral woman.

hybrid (hī′brĭd) *adj.* Produced from a mixture of parent plants.

hypocrite (hĭp′ə-krĭt′) *n.* One who pretends to have qualities he or she does not have.—**hypocritical** *adj.*

hypodermic syringe (hī′pə-dûr′mĭk sə-rĭnj′, sîr′ĭnj) *n.* A glass tube with attached needle, used for giving injections.

hypothesis (hī-pŏth′ə-sĭs) *n.* A theory; a possible explanation.

I

illiteracy (ĭ-lĭt′ər-ə-sē) *n.* The inability to read and write.

immanent (ĭm′ə-nənt) *adj.* Existing or remaining within; inherent.

immemorial (ĭm′ə-môr′ē-l, -mōr′ē-əl) *adj.* Extending beyond recorded history.

imminent (ĭm′ə-nənt) *adj.* About to happen.

immortal (ĭ-môrt′l) *adj.* One who lives forever.

impact (ĭm′păkt′) *n.* Force.

impair (ĭm-pâr′) *v.* To weaken; damage.

impartial (ĭm-pär′shəl) *adj.* Not prejudiced; evenhanded.

impassioned (ĭm-păsh′ənd) *adj.* Very emotional.

impede (ĭm-pēd′) *v.* To interfere with.

impend (ĭm-pĕnd′) *v.* To be about to happen.—**impending** *adj.*

imperceptible (ĭm′pər-sĕp′tə-bəl) *adj.* Barely noticeable.—**imperceptibly** *adv.*

imperial (ĭm-pîr′ē-əl) *adj.* Referring to an emperor.

imperious (ĭm-pîr′ē-əs) *adj.* Domineering; arrogant (like an emperor).

impersonation (ĭm-pûr′sə-nā′shən) *n.* The embodiment or representation in physical form of some idea.

impetuous (ĭm-pĕch′o̅o̅-əs) *adj.* Eager to act; impatient.

implement (ĭm′plə-mənt) *n.* A tool.

implicit (ĭm-plĭs′ĭt) *adj.* without doubt; absolute.—**implicitly** *adv.*

implore (ĭm-plôr′, -plōr′) *v.* To beg; ask.—**imploring** *adj.*—**imploringly** *adv.*

imply (ĭm-plī′) *v.* To suggest; hint.

inanimate (ĭn-ăn′ə-mĭt) *adj.* Lifeless.

inarticulate (ĭn′är-tĭk′yə-lĭt) *adj.* **1.** Unable to speak. **2.** Not clearly spoken.

inaudible (ĭn-ô′də-bəl) *adj.* Not able to be heard.

incentive (ĭn-sĕn′tĭv) *n.* Something that stimulates one to action.

incision (ĭn-sĭzh′ən) *n.* A cut.

incisor (ĭn-sī′zər) *n.* A tooth shaped for cutting—the middle four upper and middle four lower teeth.

inclination (ĭn′klə-nā′shən) *n.* A desire to do something.

incompetent (ĭn-kŏm′pə-tənt) *adj.* Not capable.

incomprehensible (ĭn′kŏm-prĭ-hĕn′sə-bəl) *adj.* Not able to be understood.

incredible (ĭn-krĕd′ə-bəl) *adj.* Unbelievable.

indecorous (ĭn-dĕk′ər-əs) *adj.* Not proper.

indelible (ĭn-dĕl′ə-bəl) *adj.* Not able to be erased.

indignant (ĭn-dĭg′nənt) *adj.* Very angry.—**indignantly** *adv.*

indignation (ĭn′dĭg-nā′shən) *n.* Great anger; outrage.

indispensable (ĭn′dĭs-pĕn′sə-bəl) *adj.* Necessary.

indistinct (ĭn′dĭs-tĭngkt′) *adj.* Not clear.

indomitable (ĭn-dŏm′ə-tə-bəl) *adj.* Not easily defeated or discouraged.

indubitable (ĭn-do̅o̅′bə-tə-bəl, ĭn-dyo̅o̅′-) *adj.* Definite; without a doubt.—**indubitably** *adv.*

induce (ĭn-do̅o̅s′, -dyo̅o̅s′) *v.* To persuade.

indulgent (ĭn-dŭl′jənt) *adj.* Overly considerate or generous.—**indulgently** *adv.*—**indulge** *v.*

inert (ĭn-ûrt′) *adj.* Without power to move; inactive.

inevitable (ĭn-ĕv′ə-tə-bəl) *adj.* Sure to happen.—**inevitability** *n.*

infallible (ĭn-făl′ə-bəl) *adj.* Never wrong.—**infallibly** *adv.*

infamous (ĭn′fə-məs) *adj.* Having a bad reputation.

infectious (ĭn-fĕk′shəs) *adj.* Catching.

infernal (ĭn-fûr′nəl) *adj.* Evil.

infinite (ĭn′fə-nĭt) *adj.* Limitless; endless (like infinity).

inflexible (ĭn-flĕk′sə-bəl) *adj.* Unchanging; firm.

inflict (ĭn-flĭkt′) *v.* To force something unpleasant on someone.—**inflicted** *adj.*

infuse (ĭn-fyo̅o̅z′) *v.* To fill with.

ingenious (ĭn-jēn′yəs) *adj.* Very clever.

ă pat/ā pay/âr care/ä father/b bib/ch church/d deed/ĕ pet/ē be/f fife/g gag/h hat/hw which/ĭ pit/ī pie/îr pier/j judge/k kick/ l lid, needle/m mum/n no, sudden/ng thing/ŏ pot/ō toe/ô paw, for/oi noise/ou out/o̅o̅ took/o̅o̅ boot/p pop/r roar/s sauce/ sh ship, dish/t tight/th thin, path/*th* this, bathe/ŭ cut/ûr urge/v valve/w with/y yes/z zebra, size/zh vision/ə about, item, edible, gallop, circus/à *Fr.* ami/œ *Fr.* feu, *Ger.* schön/ü *Fr.* tu, *Ger.* über/KH *Ger.* ich, *Scot.* loch/N *Fr.* bon.

inherent (ĭn-hîr′ənt, hĕr′ənt) *adj.* Essential.

inimitable (ĭn-ĭm′ĭ-tə-bəl) *adj.* Not able to be imitated; matchless.

inquest (ĭn′kwĕst′) *n.* An investigation.

insignia (ĭn-sĭg′nē-ə) *n.* A badge; emblem.

insinuate (ĭn-sĭn′yo͞o-āt′) *v.* To hint at or suggest something in an indirect way.—**insinuating** *adj.*

insistent (ĭn-sĭs′tənt) *adj.* Demanding.

insolent (ĭn′sə-lənt) *adj.* Disrespectful.—**insolently** *adv.*

instinctive (ĭn-stĭngk′tĭv) *adj.* Inborn; not learned.

insufferable (ĭn-sŭf′ər-ə-bəl) *adj.* Impossible to put up with.

insuperable (ĭn-so͞o′pər-ə-bəl) *adj.* Not to be surmounted or overcome.

insupportable (ĭn′sə-pôr′tə-bəl, -pōr′) *adj.* Not capable of giving support.

intangible (ĭn-tăn′jə-bəl) *adj.* Not capable of being precisely identified.

intercept (ĭn′tər-sĕpt′) *v.* To stop or cut off.

intercourse (ĭn′tər-kôrs′, -kōrs′) *n.* Association with others, as in conversation.

interlude (ĭn′tər-lo͞od′) *n.* An intervening period of time.

interminable (ĭn-tûr′mə-nə-bəl) *adj.* Endless.

intervene (ĭn′tər-vēn′) *v.* **1.** To interfere. **2.** To be located between.

intimate (ĭn′tə-mĭt) *adj.* **1.** Close in affection; very friendly. **2.** Essential; innermost.—**intimately** *adv.*

intimate (ĭn′tə-māt′) *v.* To hint.—**intimation** *n.*

intolerable (ĭn-tŏl′ər-ə-bəl) *adj.* Unbearable.

intolerant (ĭn-tŏl′ər-ənt) *adj.* Unwilling to put up with.

introspective (ĭn′trə-spĕk′tĭv) *adj.* Given to private thought; contemplative.

invariable (ĭn-vâr′ē-ə-bəl) *adj.* Unchanging; constant.—**invariably** *adv.*

inventory (ĭn′vən-tôr′ē, -tōr′ē) *n.* A list of supplies on hand.

invincible (ĭn-vĭn′sə-bəl) *adj.* Unbeatable.

involuntary (ĭn-vŏl′ən-tĕr′ē) *adj.* Done without conscious thought.

invulnerable (ĭn-vŭl′nər-ə-bəl) *adj.* Not able to be harmed.

irk (ûrk) *v.* To annoy or tire; vex.

ironic (ī-rŏn′ĭk) *adj.* Opposite to what might be expected.—**ironically** *adv.*

irresistible (ĭr′ĭ-zĭs′tə-bəl) *adj.* Strongly appealing.

irresolute (ĭ-rĕz′ə-lo͞ot′) *adj.* Undecided; uncertain.

isolate (ī′sə-lāt, ĭs′ə-) *v.* To separate; set apart.

itinerant (ī-tĭn′ər-ənt, ĭ-tĭn′-) *adj.* Going from place to place in order to work.

J

jaunt (jônt, jänt) *n.* A short trip.

jest (jĕst) *v.* To joke.—**jestingly** *adv.*

jolt (jōlt) *v.* To jar or shake up.

jostle (jŏs′əl) *v.* To push and shove.

jovial (jō′vē-əl) *adj.* Good-humored.—**jovially** *adv.*

jubilant (jo͞o′bə-lənt) *adj.* Joyful.

jubilation (jo͞o′bə-lā′shən) *n.* Rejoicing.

judicious (jo͞o-dĭsh′əs) *adj.* Wise (like a judge).

K

kiln (kĭl, kĭln) *n.* An oven for baking or firing substances.

kindle (kĭnd′l) *v.* To start (a fire).

knoll (nōl) *n.* A small hill.

L

lacerate (lăs′ə-rāt′) *v.* To tear or cut jaggedly.—**lacerated** *adj.*

lagoon (lə-go͞on′) *n.* Shallow pool of water.

lair (lâr) *n.* A wild animal's den.

lament (lə-mĕnt′) *v.* To grieve; mourn. —*n.* An expression of grief.

lamentation (lăm′ən-tā′shən) *n.* An expression of grief.

lank (lăngk) *adj.* Tall and thin.

lateral (lăt′ər-əl) *adj.* Sideways.

lattice (lăt′ĭs) *adj.* Woven like a screen.

leaden (lĕd′n) *adj.* Burdened; depressed.

league (lēg) *n.* A distance of about three miles.

leer (lîr) *v.* To look at slyly or evilly.

legacy (lĕg′ə-sē) *n.* Something handed down from an ancestor.

legend (lĕj′ənd) *n.* A caption or inscription.

legion (lē′jən) *n.* A large group; band.

lethargy (lĕth′ər-jē) *n.* A state of dullness or inaction; stupor; apathy.

liability (lī′ə-bĭl′ə-tē) *n.* A disadvantage.

liberality (lĭb′ə-răl′ə-tē) *n.* Generosity.

limber (lĭm′bər) *v.* To loosen up by exercise.

listless (lĭst′lĭs) *adj.* Showing a lack of energy or interest.—**listlessly** *adv.*

literate (lĭt′ər-ĭt) *adj.* Able to read and write.

lithe (līth) *adj.* Supple; nimble.

loathe (lōth) *v.* To hate intensely.

lob (lŏb) *v.* To move clumsily.

loll (lŏl) *v.* **1.** To lounge about in a relaxed way. **2.** To hang out loosely.

loom (lo͞om) *v.* **1.** To appear dimly or indistinctly, as through a mist. **2.** To appear to the mind as large or threatening.

lope (lōp) *v.* To run with a long stride.

low (lō) *v.* Moo.—**lowing** *n.*

ludicrous (lo͞o′dĭ-krəs) *adj.* Ridiculous; laughable.

lumber (lŭm′bər) *v.* To move slowly and clumsily.

luminous (lo͞o′mə-nəs) *adj.* **1.** Able to shine in the dark; glowing. **2.** Filled with light.

lurid (loor′ĭd) *adj.* Glowing or glaring through a haze.

lurk (lûrk) *v.* To wait in ambush; remain concealed.

lusterless (lŭs′tər-lĭs) *adj.* Dull.

lusty (lŭs′tē) *adj.* Vigorous; strong.

M

majestic (mə-jĕs′tĭk) *adj.* Grand; dignified.

makeshift (māk′shĭft′) *adj.* Made quickly and used as a substitute.

malice (măl′ĭs) *n.* A desire to hurt others.

malignant (mə-lĭg′nənt) *adj.* Harmful; malicious.

maneuver (mə-no͞o′vər, -nyo͞o′-) *v.* To move.

manifest (măn′ə fest′) *adv.* Plain; apparent; evident; obvious.—**manifestly** *adv.*

manifold (măn′ə-fōld) *adj.* Many and different.

mantle (măn′təl) *n.* A sleeveless cape or cloak.

massive (măs′ĭv) *adj.* Unusually large.

mast (măst, mäst) *n.* A pole used to support the sails and rigging of a ship.

mastodon (măs′tə-dŏn′) *n.* An extinct animal that resembled an elephant.

matron (mā′trən) *n.* A married woman, one mature in age and appearance.—**matronly** *adv.*

matted (măt′ĭd) *adj.* Tangled.

meager (mē′gər) *adj.* Scanty; insufficient.

melancholy (mĕl′ən-kŏl′ē) *n.* Great sadness.—*adj.* Very sad.

mellow (mĕl′ō) *adj.* Rich.—**mellowness** *n.*

menace (mĕn′ĭs) *n.* A threat.

mercurial (mər-kyoor′ē-əl) *adj.* Changing quickly (like mercury).

merge (mûrj) *v.* To blend in.

mesa (mā′sə) *n.* A hill or plateau having steep sides and a flat top, especially in the southwestern United States.

meticulous (mə-tĭk′yə-ləs) *adj.* Extremely precise about minor details; fussy.

midwifery (mĭd′wīf′rē, -wī′fər-ē) *n.* The practice of assisting in childbirth.

minstrel (mĭn′strəl) *n.* Poet-musician.

misbegotten (mĭs′bĭ-gŏt′n) *adj.* **1.** Abnormally conceived. **2.** Wretched.

mishap (mĭs′hăp′, mĭs-hăp′) *n.* An unfortunate accident.

mobile (mō′bəl, -bēl′, -bĭl′) *adj.* Movable.

mobilize (mō′bə-līz′) *v.* To move into action.

molest (mə-lĕst′) *v.* To bother or to harm.

momentum (mō-mĕn′təm) *n.* The driving force of a moving object.

monotony (mə-nŏt′n-ē) *n.* Sameness.

moor (moor) *n.* Wasteland.

mooring (moor′ĭng) *n.* The place where a boat is tied up.

morass (mə-răs′, mô-) *n.* A swamp.

mortal (môrt′l) *n.* A human being.

mottled (mŏt′ld) *adj.* Covered with spots of different colors and shapes.

murky (mûr′kē) *adj.* Dark and gloomy.—**murkily** *adv.*

muster (mŭs′tər) *v.* To assemble; gather together.

mutilate (myo͞ot′l-āt′) *v.* To cut off or otherwise destroy a part of the body.—**mutilated** *adj.*

mutinous (myo͞ot′n-əs) *adj.* Rebellious.

N

naiveté (nä′ēv-tā′) *n.* Simplicity; lack of worldliness.

nettle (nĕt′l) *n.* A stinging or prickly plant.

neurosurgeon (noor′ō-sûr′jən, nyo͞o′-) *n.* A doctor who specializes in surgery involving the nervous system.

nonchalant (nŏn′shə-länt′) *adj.* Unconcerned; casual.—**nonchalantly** *adv.*—**nonchalance** *n.*

nondescript (nŏn′dĭ-skrĭpt′) *adj.* Commonplace; uninteresting.

nontransferable (nŏn-trăns-fûr′ə-bəl) *adj.* Not usable by anyone else.

nostalgia (nŏ-stăl′jə, nə-) *adj.* A longing for something in the past or far away.

novelty (nŏv′əl-tē) *n.* Something new or unusual.

ă pat/ā pay/âr care/ä father/b bib/ch church/d deed/ĕ pet/ē be/f fife/g gag/h hat/hw which/ĭ pit/ī pie/îr pier/j judge/k kick/ l lid, needle/m mum/n no, sudden/ng thing/ŏ pot/ō toe/ô paw, for/oi noise/ou out/o͝o took/o͞o boot/p pop/r roar/s sauce/ sh ship, dish/t tight/th thin, path/*th* this, bathe/ŭ cut/ûr urge/v valve/w with/y yes/z zebra, size/zh vision/ə about, item, edible, gallop, circus/à *Fr.* ami/œ *Fr.* feu, *Ger.* schön/ü *Fr.* tu, *Ger.* über/KH *Ger.* ich, *Scot.* loch/N *Fr.* bon.

O

oblique (ō-blēk′) *adj.* Slanting; sloping.—**obliquely** *adv.*

oblivious (ə-blĭv′ē-əs) *adj.* Not aware.

obnoxious (ŏb-nŏk′shəs, əb-) *adj.* Highly unlikable; hateful.

obscure (ŏb-skyoor′, əb-) *adj.* Little known.

obsession (əb-sĕsh′ən, ŏb-) *n.* An idea or thought that is impossible to get rid of.

obstinate (ŏb′stə-nĭt) *adj.* Stubborn.—**obstinately** *adv.*

omen (ō′mən) *n.* A sign of something to come.

ominous (ŏm′ə-nəs) *adj.* Warning; threatening.

onslaught (ŏn′slôt′, ôn′-) *n.* An attack.

opportunist (ŏp′ər-too′nĭst, -tyoo′nĭst) *n.* One who takes unfair advantage of another or of a situation.

oppression (ə-prĕsh′ən) *n.* Power used to crush or to persecute.

orbit (ôr′bĭt) *n.* Path someone moves in.

ordeal (ôr-dēl′) *n.* A very unpleasant experience.

ornate (ôr-nāt′) *adj.* Very fancy.

orthodontist (ôr′thə-dŏn′tĭst) *n.* A dentist who specializes in straightening teeth.

ostentatious (ŏs′tĕn-tā′shəs, ŏs′tən-) *adj.* Showy.—**ostentatiously** *adv.*

overwhelming (o′vər-hwĕl′mĭng) *adj.* Overpowering.

P

pagan (pā′gən) *n.* **1.** A heathen. **2.** A non-Christian.

pandemonium (păn′də-mō′nē-əm) *n.* Noisy confusion.

paroxysm (păr′ək-sĭz′əm) *n.* A sudden outburst.

passionate (păsh′ən-ĭt) *adj.* Intense.—**passionately** *adv.*

paternal (pə-tûr′nəl) *adj.* Referring to a father.

patron (pā′trən) *n.* **1.** A customer. **2.** A person who supports an artist or musician.

peer (pîr) *n.* **1.** Nobleman. **2.** Equal.

peerless (pîr′lĭs) *adj.* Unmatched.

peeve (pēv) *v.* To annoy.

pensive (pĕn′sĭv) *adj.* Thoughtful.

pent (pĕnt) *adj.* Shut up.

perception (pər-sĕp′shən) *n.* Sensation; realization; knowledge.

percussion (pər-kŭsh′ən) *n.* A musical instrument, such as a drum, that is played by striking.

perilous (pĕr′əl-əs) *adj.* Risky.

perimeter (pə-rĭm′ə-tər) *n.* The outer boundary of something.

periscope (pĕr′ə-skōp′) *n.* A tubelike instrument with lenses and mirrors that enables one to see an area otherwise not viewable.

permeate (pûr′mē-āt′) *v.* To spread through.—**permeated** *adj.*

perpendicular (pûr′pən-dĭk′yə-lər) *adj.* At a right angle.—**perpendicularly** *adv.*

perpetuate (pər-pĕch′oo-āt′) *v.* To preserve the memory of someone or something.

perpetuity (pûr′pə-too′ə-tē, -tyoo′ə-tē) *n.* Eternity; an unlimited time.

perplexity (pər-plĕk′sə-tē) *n.* Confusion.

persistent (pər-sĭs′tənt) *adj.* Repeated; continued.—**persistently** *adv.*

perverse (pər-vûrs′) *adj.* Stubbornly difficult.

petition (pə-tĭsh′ən) *n.* A formal request signed by a number of people.

pewter (pyoo′tər) *n.* Objects made from pewter, a mixture of tin and other metals.

phobia (fō′bē-ə) *n.* An exaggerated fear.

phonetic (fə-nĕt′ĭk) *adj.* Referring to the sounds of language.

photostat (fō′tə-stăt′) *v.* To make a copy of something using a certain kind of machine.

piety (pī′ə-tē) *n.* Reverence; religious devotion.

pinion (pĭn′yən) *v.* To tie or bind.—**pinioned** *adj.*

pinnacle (pĭn′ə-kəl) *n.* The highest point; summit; peak.

piston (pĭs′tən) *n.* A disk or cylinder fitted into a tube and moved back and forth by pressure, as in an engine.

placid (plăs′ĭd) *adj.* Quiet; peaceful.

plague (plāg) *adj.* A pestilence or epidemic disease.

pliable (plī′ə-bəl) *adj.* Flexible.—**pliability** *n.*

pliant (plī′ənt) *adj.* Easily bent; flexible.

pluck (plŭk) *n.* Courage.

plumage (ploo′mĭj) *n.* Feathers of a bird.

plume (ploom) *n.* A large feather or cluster of feathers worn as decoration.

plummet (plŭm′ĭt) *n.* Something that drops straight down.

plunder (plŭn′dər) *v.* To rob.

poise (poiz) *v.* To be balanced in a certain position.—**poised** *adj.*

ponder (pŏn′dər) *v.* To think deeply about.

pore (pôr, pōr) *v.* To study or read with care; with *over.*

portal (pôrt′l, pōrt′l) *n.* An entrance; door.

posterity (pŏ-stĕr′ə-tē) *n.* All those yet to be born.

potent (pōt′nt) *adj.* Powerful; strong.—**potency** *n.*

potentiality (pə-těn′shē-ăl′ə-tē) *n.* A possible ability. —**potential** *adj.*

preamble (prē′ăm′bəl) *n.* An introductory statement.

precinct (prē′sĭngkt) *n.* District or area.

precipice (prĕs′ə-pĭs) *n.* A high vertical or overhanging face of rock; the brink of a cliff.

precipitous (prĭ-sĭp′ə-təs) *adj.* Extremely steep.

predecessor (prĕd′ə-sĕs′ər, prē′də-) *n.* One who comes before another, as in a job or a political office.

predicament (prĭ-dĭk′ə-mənt) *n.* A difficult situation.

predominant (prĭ-dŏm′ə-nənt) *adj.* Most important.—**predominantly** *adv.*

preeminence (prē-ĕm′ə-nəns) *n.* The condition of holding first place in a particular grouping.—**preeminently** *adv.*

preliminary (prĭ-lĭm′ə-nĕr′ē) *n.* Something that comes before or introduces something else.

prestige (prĕ-stēzh′, -stēj) *n.* High standing in the eyes of others.

presume (prĭ-zoom′) *v.* To dare.

presumption (prĭ-zŭmp′shən) *n.* The act of taking something for granted.

pretext (prē′tĕkst′) *n.* An excuse.

prevail (prĭ′vāl′) *v.* To win out.

prevailing (prĭ-vā′lĭng) *adj.* Predominant; widespread.

prevalence (prĕv′ə-ləns) *n.* The state of being widespread.—**prevalent** *adj.*

prim (prĭm) *adj.* Formal; stiff.—**primly** *adv.*

prime (prīm) *adj.* Excellent; of finest quality.—*v.* To prepare.

proclaim (prō-klām′, prə-) *v.* To announce or declare.

prodigious (prə-dĭj′əs) *adj.* **1.** Amazing. **2.** Huge.

prodigy (prŏd′ə-jē) *n.* An unusually gifted child.

profound (prə-found′, prō) *adj.* **1.** Deep. **2.** Wise.—**profoundly** *adv.*

progressive (prə-grĕs′ĭv) *adj.* Ever-increasing.

prophesy (prŏf′ə-sī′) *v.* To predict.

proposition (prŏp′ə-zĭsh′ən) *n.* **1.** A statement that something is true. **2.** Proposal or plan.

propound (prə-pound′) *v.* To offer for consideration.

prostrate (prŏs′trāt′) *adj.* Stretched out.

providential (prŏv′ə-dĕn′shəl) *adj.* Of or resulting from divine intervention.—**providentially** *adv.*

provocation (prŏv′ə-kā′shən) *n.* An action that annoys or irritates.

provoke (prə-vōk′) *v.* To make angry.

prowess (prou′ĭs) *n.* Superior strength or courage.

prudent (prood′ənt) *adj.* Cautious.

prune (proon) *v.* To cut off dead or live parts of a plant in order to improve growth or shape.

pry (prī) *v.* To examine in a nosy way.

pulsation (pŭl-sā′shən) *n.* Throbbing or rhythmical beating.

pungent (pŭn′jənt) *adj.* Sharp-smelling.

puny (pyoo′nē) *adj.* Weak.

Q

quarry (kwôr′ē, kwŏr′ē) *n.* **1.** A mine from which marble and other kinds of stone are taken. **2.** A hunted object or person.

quash (kwŏsh) *v.* To suppress or put down.

quaver (kwā′vər) *v.* To shake; tremble.—*n.* A vibration.—**quavering** *adj.*

quicksilver (kwĭk′sĭl′vər) *n.* Mercury, a metal that moves very quickly in its liquid form.

quizzical (kwĭz′ĭ-kəl) *adj.* Puzzled; questioning.—**quizzically** *adv.*

R

radius (rā′dē-əs) *n.* A measure of circular area or extent.

rail (rāl) *v.* To scold; abuse.

rampart (răm′pärt) *n.* A defense.

rapacious (rə-pā′shəs) *adj.* Greedy; plundering.—**rapaciously** *adv.*

raptor (răp′tər) *n.* Bird of prey.

rash (răsh) *adj.* Unthinking; reckless.—**rashly** *adv.*

rasp (răsp, räsp) *v.* To scrape with a harsh sound.

rational (răsh′ən-əl) *adj.* Reasonable; able to think clearly.

ravage (răv′ĭj) *v.* To destroy.

rave (rāv) *v.* To talk like an insane person.

ravening (răv′ən-ĭng) *adj.* Greedy.

ravenous (răv′ən-əs) *adj.* Extremely hungry.

ravine (rə-vēn′) *n.* A deep, narrow valley.

realm (rĕlm) *n.* A kingdom.

ă pat/ā pay/âr care/ä father/b bib/ch church/d deed/ĕ pet/ē be/f fife/g gag/h hat/hw which/ĭ pit/ī pie/îr pier/j judge/k kick/ l lid, needle/m mum/n no, sudden/ng thing/ŏ pot/ō toe/ô paw, for/oi noise/ou out/oo took/oo boot/p pop/r roar/s sauce/ sh ship, dish/t tight/th thin, path/*th* this, bathe/ŭ cut/ûr urge/v valve/w with/y yes/z zebra, size/zh vision/ə about, item, edible, gallop, circus/à *Fr.* ami/œ *Fr.* feu, *Ger.* schön/ü *Fr.* tu, *Ger.* über/KH *Ger.* ich, *Scot.* loch/N *Fr.* bon.

rear (rîr) *v.* To bring up (a child).

rebound (rē'bound', rĭ-) *v.* To spring back.

rebuke (rĭ-byook') *v.* To show disapproval.

recede (rĭ-sēd') *v.* To become farther away; withdraw.

recoil (rĭ-koil') *v.* To spring back.

recommence (rē'kə-mĕns') *v.* To begin again.

recompense (rĕk'əm-pĕns') *v.* To reward.

reconnaissance (rĭ-kŏn'ə-səns, zəns) *n.* An advance study made by exploring and surveying.

recurrent (rĭ-kûr'ənt) *adj.* Happening repeatedly.

reformation (rĕf'ər-mā'shən) *n.* A change to a better way of behaving.

refrain (rĭ-frān') *v.* To keep someone from doing something.

regal (rē'gəl) *adj.* Kingly.

regression (rĭ-grĕsh'ən) *n.* A return to an earlier, less-advanced state.

rehabilitate (rē'hə-bĭl'ə-tāt') *v.* To return someone or something to a useful condition.

relent (rĭ-lĕnt') *v.* To become less firm or strict about something.—**relenting** *adj.*

relentless (rĭ-lĕnt'lĭs) *adj.* 1. Continuous. 2. Pitiless; unmerciful; unfeeling.

relevant (rĕl'ə-vənt) *adj.* To the point.—**relevancy** *n.*

relic (rĕl'ĭk) *n.* A fragment of something that no longer exists.

reluctance (rĭ-lŭk'təns) *n.* Unwillingness.—**reluctant** *adj.*

reminiscence (rĕm'ə-nĭs'əns) *n.* A memory.

remorse (rĭ-môrs') *n.* Strong regret over something.—**remorseful** *adj.*

render (rĕn'dər) *v.* 1. To give or hand over. 2. To make.

rendezvous (rän'dā-voo', rän'də-) *n.* A meeting place.

renown (rĭ-noun') *n.* Fame.

repast (rĭ-păst', -päst') *n.* A feast; meal.

repercussion (rē'pər-kŭsh'ən) *n.* A result, often an unpleasant one.

repose (rĭ-pōz') *v.* To lie at rest.

reproach (rĭ-prōch') *v.* To blame; scold.—**reproachfully** *adv.*

resigned (rĭ-zīnd') *adj.* Giving in; accepting without complaint.—**resignedly** *adv.*—**resign** *v.*

resolute (rĕz'ə-loot) *adj.* Firm; determined.—**resolutely** *adv.*

resolution (rĕz'ə-loo'shən) *n.* Firmness; determination.

resonant (rĕz'ə-nənt) *adj.* Rich-sounding.

resound (rĭ-zound') *v.* To sound loudly.

resource (rē'sôrs') *n.* A source of support or help.

resourceful (rĭ-sôrs'fəl, rĭ-sōrs'-, rĭ-zôrs'-, rĭ-zōrs'-) *adj.* Able to deal effectively with a situation.

respirator (rĕs'pə-rā'tər) *n.* 1. A mask worn to keep substances in the air from being breathed in. 2. A machine that gives artificial respiration.

respite (rĕs'pĭt) *n.* Period of rest or relief.

resplendent (rĭ-splĕn'dənt) *adj.* Shining.

restrain (rĭ-strān') *v.* To control; limit.

restriction (rĭ-strĭk'shən) *n.* A limit.

resurrect (rĕz'ə-rĕkt') *v.* To bring back into life or into use.

retaliate (rĭ-tăl'ē-āt') *v.* To strike back.

retard (rĭ-tärd') *v.* To slow down.

revel (rĕv'əl) *n.* A celebration.

revelry (rĕv'əl-rē) *n.* A noisy celebration.

reverberate (rĭ-vûr'bə-rāt') *v.* To re-echo.

revere (rĭ-vîr') *v.* To respect.

rigid (rĭj'ĭd) *adj.* Not moving.

rosette (rō-zĕt') *n.* A decorative ornament resembling a rose, made of ribbon or silk.

rouse (rouz) *v.* To awaken.

rousing (rou'zĭng) *adj.* Stirring; exciting.

rout (rout) *v.* To defeat.

rucksack (rŭk'săk', rook'-) *n.* A backpack; knapsack.

ruffle (rŭf'əl) *v.* To make feathers stand out.

rupture (rŭp'chər) *n.* Bursting.

ruthless (rooth'lĭs) *adj.* Cruel.

S

sack (săk) *v.* To loot or plunder.

sacrilege (săk'-rə-lĭj) *n.* A lack of respect for a sacred person or object.

sage (sāj) *adj.* Wise.—**sagely** *adv.*

sallow (săl'ō) *adj.* Of a pale, sickly color.

sally (săl'ē) *v.* To come out.

salutary (săl'yə-tĕr'ē) *adj.* Doing good; wholesome; beneficial.

sarcastic (sär-kăs'tĭk) *adj.* Given to sharp, biting humor.—**sarcastically** *adv.*

saunter (sôn'tər) *v.* To walk in a leisurely way.

savor (sā'vər) *v.* To enjoy.

scabbard (skăb'ərd) *n.* A sheath for a sword.

scan (skăn) *v.* To look at carefully.

scant (skănt) *adj.* Meager; inadequate.

scoff (skôf, skŏf) *v.* To jeer at.

scour (skour) *v.* To search thoroughly.

scowl (skoul) *v.* To frown; show disapproval.

scrutinize (skroot' n-īz') *v.* To inspect carefully.

scuttle (skŭt′l) *v.* To run off in haste; hurry.

scythe (sī*th*) *n.* A long-handled blade used to cut grass.

sear (sîr) *v.* To burn.

securities (sĭ-kyŏŏr′ə-tēz) *n.* Stock certificates or bonds.

self-assurance (sĕlf′ə-shŏŏr′əns) *n.* Confidence.

semantic (sə-măn′tĭk) *adj.* Referring to the relationships between words and meanings.

senility (sĭ-nĭl′ə-tē) *n.* A condition, usually occurring in old people, in which the mental powers are weakened.

sensibility (sĕn′sə-bĭl′ə-tē) *n.* The ability to respond emotionally.

shake (shāk) *n.* A rough shingle.

shallow (shăl′ō) *adj.* Not deep.

shamble (shăm′bəl) *v.* To walk in an awkward way.

sheath (shēth) *n.* A case or covering, as for a sword.

sheer (shîr) *adj.* Nearly perpendicular; steep.

shimmer (shĭm′ər) *v.* To shine.—**shimmering** *adj.*

shirk (shûrk) *v.* To avoid doing something that should be done.—**shirker** *n.*

shrew (shrŏŏ) *n.* A woman who scolds a lot.

sidle (sīd′l) *v.* To move sideways, often in a sneaky way.

siege (sēj) *n.* An organized attack.

simultaneous (sī′məl-tā′nē-əs) *adj.* Happening at the same time.—**simultaneously** *adv.*

sinew (sĭn′yŏŏ) *n.* A tendon.

sinewy (sĭn′yŏŏ-ē) *adj.* Strong; tough.

singular (sĭng′gyə-lər) *adj.* Unusual; peculiar.—**singularly** *adv.*

sinister (sĭn′ĭ-stər) *adj.* Evil-seeming.

skiff (skĭf) *n.* A small boat.

skirmish (skûr′mĭsh) *n.* A minor conflict or battle.

skulk (skŭlk) *v.* To move stealthily.

slacken (slăk′ən) *v.* To slow up.

slack (slăk) *n.* Looseness.

slight (slīt) *v.* To treat rudely or scornfully.

smite (smīt) *v.* **1.** To hit. **2.** To attack.

smolder (smōl′dər) *v.* To burn without a flame.—**smoldering** *adj.*

sneer (snîr) *v.* To show contempt.

sodden (sŏd′n) *adj.* Thoroughly wet.

sojourn (sō′jûrn, sō-jûrn′) *v.* To stay for a short time.

solace (sŏl′ĭs) *n.* Comfort.

solicitous (sə-lĭs′ə-təs) *adj.* Attentive.

solicitude (sə-lĭs′ə-tŏŏd′, -tyŏŏd′) *n.* Care; concern.

solitude (sŏl′ə-tŏŏd′, -tyŏŏd′) *n.* Aloneness.

sovereignty (sŏv′ər-ən-tē) *n.* Independence.

span (spăn) *v.* To stretch completely across, as a bridge spans a body of water.

spar (spär) *n.* A pole used to support a ship's rigging.

spasm (spăz′əm) *n.* A sudden, short-lived burst of activity or energy.

specter (spĕk′tər) *n.* **1.** A ghost. **2.** Something that causes fear or terror.

spectral (spĕk′trəl) *adj.* Ghost-like.

speculation (spĕk′yə-lā′shən) *n.* An unproved explanation; thought; guess.—**speculate** *v.*

spell (spĕl) *n.* A short period of time.

spew (spyŏŏ) *v.* To cast out.

spontaneous (spŏn-tā′nē-əs) *adj.* Not planned.

spraddle (sprăd′l) *v.* To sprawl.—*n.* Sprawl.

spume (spyŏŏm) *n.* The foamy part of a wave.

staple (stā′pəl) *n.* A basic food, such as flour, sugar, or salt.

stark (stärk) *adj.* Unrelieved; complete.

starveling (stärv′lĭng) *adj.* Starving.

stately (stāt′lē) *adj.* Dignified.

stethoscope (stĕth′ə-skōp′) *n.* An instrument used to listen to pulse beats.

stifle (stī′fəl) *v.* **1.** To smother. **2.** To hold back.—**stifled** *adj.*

still (stĭl) *v.* To quiet; calm.

stilted (stĭl′tĭd) *adj.* Stiff; formal.

stimulant (stĭm′yə-lənt) *n.* A substance that speeds up bodily activity.

stipulate (stĭp′yə-lāt′) *v.* To state the conditions of an agreement.—**stipulated** *adj.*

stoical (stō-ĭ-kəl) *adj.* Not caring about either pain or pleasure.

stolid (stŏl′ĭd) *adj.* Dull; lacking in imagination.—**stolidly** *adv.*

stout (stout) *adj.* **1.** Brave. **2.** Thick.—**stoutly** *adv.*

strew (strŏŏ) *v.* To scatter.

stupendous (stŏŏ-pĕn′dəs, styŏŏ-) *adj.* **1.** Amazing. **2.** Huge.

stupor (stŏŏ′pər, styŏŏ′-) *n.* Daze.

subside (səb-sīd′) *v.* To sink or settle.

ă pat/ā pay/âr care/ä father/b **bib**/ch **church**/d **deed**/ĕ pet/ē be/f **fife**/g **gag**/h **hat**/hw **which**/ĭ pit/ī **pie**/îr **pier**/j **judge**/k **kick**/ l **lid**, **needle**/m **mum**/n **no**, **sudden**/ng **thing**/ŏ pot/ō **toe**/ô **paw**, **for**/oi **noise**/ou **out**/ŏŏ **took**/ōō **boot**/p **pop**/r **roar**/s **sauce**/ sh **ship**, **dish**/t **tight**/th **thin**, **path**/*th* **this**, **bathe**/ŭ **cut**/ûr **urge**/v **valve**/w **with**/y **yes**/z **zebra**, **size**/zh **vision**/ə **about**, **item**, **edi**ble, **gallop**, **circus**/à *Fr.* **ami**/œ *Fr.* **feu**, *Ger.* **schön**/ü *Fr.* **tu**, *Ger.* **über**/KH *Ger.* **ich**, *Scot.* **loch**/N *Fr.* **bon**.

succeed (sək-sēd′) v. **1.** To come after; follow. **2.** To have success.

succession (sək-sesh′ən) n. A series.

successor (sək-sĕs′ər) n. One who comes after another, as in a job or a political office.

sufferance (sŭf′ər-əns, sŭf′rəns) n. Tolerance; permission.

suite (swēt) n. A group of attendants.

sullen (sŭl′ən) adj. Glum; ill-humored.—**sullenly** adv.

sumptuous (sŭmp′chŏŏ-əs) adj. Magnificent.

sup (sŭp) v. To eat.

suppliant (sŭp′lĭ-ənt) n. Someone who begs humbly.

supplication (sŭp′lĭ-kā′shən) n. Petition; humble request.

supposition (sŭp′ə-zĭsh′ən) n. Something that is supposed, or considered to be true.

surly (sûr′lē) adj. Rude; ill-natured.

surmise (sər-mīz′) v. To guess; suppose.

surmount (sər-mount′) n. **1.** To overcome. **2.** To be on top of.

surreptitious (sûr′əp-tĭsh′əs) adj. Secret.—**surreptitiously** adv.

sustain (sə-stān′) v. **1.** To keep up; keep in effect. **2.** To experience; undergo.—**sustained** adj.

swagger (swăg′ər) v. To walk in a proud, self-important way.

symmetrical (sĭ-mĕt′rĭ-kəl) adj. Regular; well-proportioned; with corresponding parts; possessing balance and beauty of form.

syndrome (sĭn′drōm′) n. A group of symptoms that occur together in a particular illness.

T

tactful (tăkt′fəl) adj. Considerate of another's feelings.—**tactfully** adv.

talon (tāl′ən) n. A sharp claw.

tangible (tăn′jə-bəl) adj. Real; definite.

tantalization (tăn′tə-lĭ-zā′shən) n. Teasing or torment.

tarry (tăr′ē) v. To stay longer than planned; linger.

taunt (tônt) v. To make fun of; mock.

taut (tôt) adj. **1.** Tight. **2.** Tense.

tawny (tô′nē) adj. Golden brown in color.

taxidermy (tăk′sə-dûr′mē) n. The art of stuffing and mounting the skins of dead animals to make them seem lifelike.

tedious (tē′dē-əs) adj. Boring.

teem (tēm) v. To be crowded or full of.—**teeming** adj.

teeter (tē′tər) v. To move unsteadily.

temper (tĕm′pər) v. To treat steel to make it hard and flexible.—**tempered** adj.

tempest (tĕm′pĭst) n. A severe storm.

tenacious (tə-nā′shəs) adj. **1.** Hard to get rid of. **2.** Stubborn.—**tenaciously** adv.

tend (tĕnd) v. To look after.

tentative (tĕn′tə-tĭv) adj. Not definite.

terse (tûrs) adj. Brief and to the point.

theory (thē′ə-rē, thîr′ē) n. An idea offered to explain a happening.

thrash (thrăsh) v. To move about wildly.

threshold (thrĕsh′ōld′, thrĕsh′hōld′) n. A doorway.

thrive (thrīv) v. To flourish; prosper.

tiller (tĭl′ər) n. A part of a boat used in steering.

tolerable (tŏl′ər-ə-bəl) adj. Fairly good.—**tolerably** adv.

totem (tō′təm) n. Image or emblem that serves as the symbol of a family or clan.

tourniquet (tŏŏr′nĭ-kĭt, -kā′, tûr′-) n. Any device tied around a part of the body (over an artery) to stop bleeding.

tousle (tou′zəl) v. To make untidy.—**tousled** adj.

towering (tou′ər-ĭng) adj. Of great height.

tranquil (trăn′kwəl) adj. Peaceful.

transfix (trăns-fĭks′) v. **1.** To make motionless, as with amazement or awe. **2.** To pierce through.

transfusion (trăns-fyŏŏ′zhən) n. The injection of large amounts of blood into the body.

transgression (trăns-grĕsh′ən, trănz-) n. The breaking of a law.

transparent (trăns-pâr′ənt, -păr′ənt) adj. Clear; able to be seen through.

traverse (trăv′ərs, trə-vûrs′) v. To cross; travel.

tread (trĕd) n. Step; to walk on.

tresses (trĕs′əz) n. Hair.

tribute (trĭb′yŏŏt) n. Money paid (out of fear) by one nation to another.

troubadour (trŏŏ′bə-dôr′, -dōr′, -dŏŏr′) n. A traveling poet-musician.

trough (trôf, trŏf) n. A long narrow container used for water or feed for animals.

tumbler (tŭm′blər) n. **1.** An acrobat. **2.** A drinking glass. **3.** A part of a lock.

tumult (tŏŏ′məlt, tyŏŏ′-) n. A noisy disturbance.

tyranny (tĭr′ə-nē) n. Power that is used cruelly or unjustly.

U

ultimate (ŭl′tə-mĭt) *adj.* Final.

unabashed (ŭn′ə-băsht′) *adj.* Not embarrassed.

unapproachable (ŭn-ə-prō′chə-bəl) *adj.* Distant; not friendly.

unassuming (ŭn′ə-soo′mĭng) *adj.* Humble; modest.

uncanny (ŭn′kăn′ē) *adj.* Strange; weird.

uncouth (ŭn′kooth′) *adj.* **1.** *Archaic* Unfamiliar. **2.** Not refined; crude.

undaunted (ŭn′dôn′tĭd) *adj.* Not discouraged; not giving up.

understate (ŭn′dər-stāt′) *v.* To express in a restrained way.—**understated** *adj.*

ungainly (ŭn′gān′lē) *adj.* Awkward; clumsy.

unhygienic (ŭn′hī′jē-ĕn′ĭk) *adj.* Not healthful.

unperceived (ŭn′pər-sēvd′) *adj.* Unseen; not noticed.

unwavering (ŭn′wā′vər-ĭng) *adj.* Steady; sure.

uproot (ŭp-root′, -root′) *v.* To remove completely.

urchin (ûr′chĭn) *n.* a mischievous youngster.

urn (ûrn) *n.* A vase containing the ashes of a cremated body.

V

vacuous (văk′yoo-əs) *adj.* **1.** Empty. **2.** Showing lack of intelligence or interest. **3.** Meaningless.

vagabond (văg′ə-bŏnd′) *n.* A tramp.

vain (vān) *adj.* Not successful.—**in vain.** To no use.

valiant (văl′yənt) *adj.* Brave.

valid (văl′ĭd) *adj.* True.

validate (văl′ə-dāt′) *v.* To declare something legal.

vanity (văn′ə-tē) *n.* **1.** The state of being overly proud and concerned about oneself. **2.** Uselessness.

variant (vâr′ē-ənt) *adj.* Differing.

vault (vôlt) *v.* To leap.

vaulted (vôlt′əd) *adj.* Having an arched ceiling.

veer (vîr) *v.* To turn.

vehement (vē′ə-mənt) *adj.* Very emotional; intense.—**vehemently** *adv.*

venerable (vĕn′ər-ə-bəl) *adj.* Old and respected.

venture (vĕn′chər) *v.* **1.** To say at the risk of another's disapproval. **2.** To dare.

verify (vĕr′ə-fī) *v.* To prove that something is true.

verse (vûrs) *v.* To make familiar with.

vex (vĕks) *v.* To annoy.

vibrant (vī′brənt) *adj.* Full of life.

vigilant (vĭj′ə-lənt) *adj.* Watchful.

virtuosity (vûr′choo-ŏs′ə-tē) *n.* Skill.

visage (vĭz′ĭj) *n.* The face.

vocation (vō-kā′shən) *n.* A type of work.

vogue (vōg) *n.* Fashion.

void (void) *adj.* Not usable.—*n.* Total emptiness; nothingness.

voracious (vô-rā′shəs, vō-, və-) *adj.* Greedy; ravenous.—**voraciously** *adv.*

W

wallow (wŏl′ō) *v.* To flounder.

wampum (wŏm′pəm) *n.* Beads made from polished shells.

wane (wān) *v.* To dwindle.

wanton (wŏn′tən) *adj.* Without cause; reckless.—**wantonly** *adv.*

warrant (wôr′ənt, wŏr′-) *v.* To state; declare.

wary (wâr′ē) *adj.* Cautious.—**warily** *adv.*

waver (wā′vər) *v.* To become unsteady.

wayward (wā′wərd) *adj.* Not able to be controlled.—**waywardness** *n.*

wedge (wĕj) *n.* Anything that separates people or things.

well (wĕl) *v.* To pour forth.

wigwam (wĭg′wŏm′) *n.* An American Indian dwelling, usually having an arched framework covered with hides or bark.

wily (wī′lē) *adj.* Tricky.

wince (wĭns) *v.* To shrink back or make a face, as if in pain.

windbreak (wĭnd′brāk′) *n.* A row of trees planted as a shelter from the wind.

winsome (wĭn′səm) *adj.* Pleasing; attractive.

wiry (wīr′ē) *adj.* Lean and strong.

wistful (wĭst′fəl) *adj.* Sad with longing.—**wistfully** *adv.*

wont (wônt, wōnt, wŭnt) *adj.* Used; accustomed.

woolgathering (wool′găth′ər-ĭng) *n.* Daydreaming.

wrangle (răng′gəl) *v.* To argue.

wrath (răth, räth) *n.* Great anger.

writhe (rīth) *v.* To squirm.—**writhing** *adj.*

wrought (rôt) *v.* Formed.

wry (rī) *adj.* Ironic.

ă pat/ā pay/âr care/ä father/b bib/ch church/d deed/ĕ pet/ē be/f fife/g gag/h hat/hw which/ĭ pit/ī pie/îr pier/j judge/k kick/ l lid, needle/m mum/n no, sudden/ng thing/ŏ pot/ō toe/ô paw, for/oi noise/ou out/oo took/oo boot/p pop/r roar/s sauce/ sh ship, dish/t tight/th thin, path/th this, bathe/ŭ cut/ûr urge/v valve/w with/y yes/z zebra, size/zh vision/ə about, item, edible, gallop, circus/à *Fr.* ami/œ *Fr.* feu, *Ger.* schön/ü *Fr.* tu, *Ger.* über/KH *Ger.* ich, *Scot.* loch/N *Fr.* bon.

OUTLINE OF SKILLS

Page numbers in italics refer to entries in the Guide to Literary Terms and Techniques

READING/LITERARY SKILLS

LANGUAGE/VOCABULARY SKILLS

WRITING

Writing an Informal Research Report (Practice in
Reading and Writing) 670

SPEAKING AND LISTENING

Preparing a Presentation 141
Reading a Story Aloud 279
Presenting a Scene 318
Using Clues to Interpretation 462
Avoiding Singsong 481
Using Pantomime 509

EXTENDING YOUR STUDY

Finding the Historical Facts 141
Reporting on American Tall-Tale Heroes 183
Reporting on the Background of the Novel 602
Comparing Famous Monsters 655

DEVELOPING SKILLS IN CRITICAL THINKING

Close Reading of a Selection 2
Analyzing a Literary Work 72
Making Generalizations About Theme 122
Predicting Probable Future Actions and
   Outcomes 196
Close Reading of a Short Story 204
Establishing Criteria for Evaluation 280
Close Reading of a Play 286
Using Methods of Comparison and Contrast 396
Close Reading of an Essay 402
Distinguishing Between Facts and Opinions 448
Close Reading of a Poem 454
Analyzing Poetry 513
Drawing Inferences 603
Using Methods of Comparison and Contrast 669

PRACTICE IN READING AND WRITING

The Writing Process 73
Descriptive Writing 73
Narrative Writing 123
Writing Dialogue 124
Expository Writing 197
Writing Stories 281
Writing a Play 397
Writing Nonfiction 449
Writing Poetry 514
Writing a Précis 604
Writing an Informal Research Report 670

INDEX OF CONTENTS BY TYPES

INDEX OF FINE ART AND ILLUSTRATIONS

PHOTO CREDITS

Abbr.: AR — Art Resource; BA — The Bettmann Archive; BC — Bruce Coleman, Inc.; BS — Black Star; CP — Culver Pictures; GC — Granger Collection; IB — Image Bank; MS — Memory Shop; MSA — Movie Still Archive; NPG — National Portrait Gallery, London; PR — Photo Researchers, Inc.; S —Scala; SM — The Stock Market; WCA —Woodfin Camp & Associates; WFA — Werner Forman Archive, Ltd., London

Page 1 (top left) 8–9, Allsport/Vandystadt/WCA; 13, Lawrence Migdale/PR; 18, Photo by Bob Daemmrich; 20, BA; 21, 26–27, Photos by David Madison; 29, © Nikky Finney/ courtesy Random House; 31, Roy Morsch/SM; 34, Pechter Photo/SM; 37, Photo by Howard Hall; 39, Courtesy Fleming H. Revell Co.; 43, Stephen Krasemann/PR; 45, Black Star; 46, Photo by Harald Sund; 49, Gordon/Traub/ Wheeler Pictures; 50, GC; 51, Gordon Wiltsie/BC; 53, nevada wier/IB; 56, Art Twomey/PR; 59, Wolfgang Steinmetz/IB; 62–63, Gordon Wiltsie/BC; 69, Photo by Jerry Bauer; 79, Charles Krebs/SM; 81, James Foote/PR; 87, Pictorial Parade; 88–95 Photos by John Kelly; 97, Historical Pictures Service, Chicago; 99, Photo by Rollie McKenna; 106, Dan Budnik/WCA; 111, MSA; 113, 115, CP; 118, Springer/Bettmann Film Archive; 131 (top) Photo courtesy Kennedy Galleries, Inc., NY; 132 (top) NASA; 133 (top) Anthony Suau/BS, (bottom left) Flip Schulke/BS, (bottom right) Sal di Marco/BS; 134–135, Photo by Steve Elmore; 135, Photo by Thomas Victor; 139, Estate of Grant Wood/VAGA New York; 141, BA;/144–154, From *The Man Without a Country* by Edward Everett Hale, illustrated by Everett Shinn. Copyright 1940 by Random House, Inc. Reprinted by permission of the publisher; Photos by Robert D. Rubic; 157, BA; 159, Library of Congress, Courtesy American Heritage Picture Collection; 160–161, BA; 164, CP; 166, Mountain Press Publishing Company, Missoula, Montana; 168–169, Courtesy of the General Services Administration's Public Buildings Service; on loan to the National Gallery of Art, Washington; 172, BA; 177, Photo by Mark Haynes; 190–191, Photos by R.C. Rogers; 193, Photo by Jess Ramirez; 194, Photo by Francis Miller, LIFE Magazine © 1963 Time, Inc.; 201, (top right) Photo by Dave Brookman; (bottom right) Timothy Egan/WCA; (center left) Magnum Photos; 212, Photo courtesy Kennedy Galleries, Inc., New York; 214, 217, Apeda Studio; 219, GC; 221, First published in the United States of America in 1979 by HARPER & ROW PUBLISHERS, INC., by arrangement with Pierrot Publishing Limited U.K.; 227, SCALA/Art Resource; 229, Photo by Jeff Levin, The Berkley Publ. Group; 234, Photo by Edward Weston/NPG/ Center for Creative Photography; 235, Ernst Haas/ Magnum; 236, Laura Riley/BC; 243, 246, Springer/ Bettmann Film Archive; 250, Movie Star News; 253, 260, MSA; 263, Photo by Harry Snavely, Bantam; 264, A. Upitis/Shostal Associates; 267, Frank Siteman/STOCK/ BOSTON; 272, Photo by Carol Lazar, Avon Books; 279, GC; 284–285, Photo by Dave Brookman/Courtesy Oregon Shakespeare Festival, Ashland; 301–315, Photos by Roger Vernon; 318, GC; 326, Martha Swope Associates/ Carol Rosegg; 334 BA/© by ANNE FRANK-Fonds/ COSMOPRESS, Genève; 335, CP; 336, 344, 347, 381, 387, 388 Photos by Fred Fehl; 342, 351, 360, 379 Photos by Gjon Mili, LIFE Magazine © Time Inc.; 353, 364, 371, 391, 392 Photos by Fred Fehl/Billy Rose Theater Collection, The New York Public Library at Lincoln Center; 395, CP; 400–401, Magnum Photos; 416, From *The Dog That Bit People* by James Thurber; 418, Henri Cartier-Bresson; 425, Published by Porter & Coates, Philadelphia. Picture Collection, New York Public Library; 427, Courtesy The Beacon Press; 428–429, Frederic Lewis; 431, Illustration from *The Great South,* Published by American Publishing Company, Hartford, Connecticut. Photo courtesy The Metropolitan Museum of Art, New York; 436, Library of Congress; 437, Photo by James Carroll; 441, Charles Harbutt/Archive Pictures, Inc.; 442, Mary Ellen Mark/ Archive Pictures, Inc.; 452–453, S/AR; 458–459, Ted Russell/IB; 459, Photo by Thomas Victor; 460, David Plowden/PR; 464, The Mansell Collection Limited; 467, UPI Bettmann Newsphotos; 470–471, Photo by Dirk Bakker, Courtesy of Founders Society, Detroit Institute of Arts; 473, (left) GC (right) Kosti Rudhomaa/BS; 474, (right) Rollie McKenna; 475, 476, 477, 479, Photos by Robert D. Rubic; 482–483, N. Habgood/PR; 485, BA; 486, 489, 490, 491, Photos by Robert D. Rubic; 497, Susan Sawade/SM; 498, Junebug Clark/PR; 500, (left) NPG, (right) Pictorial Parade; 503 (bottom right) NPG; 512, (top right) National Baseball Library, Cooperstown, New York, (top left) CP, (bottom right) GC; 516–517, Timothy Egan/ WCA; 521, Kobal Collection; 523, MS; 524, MSA; 535, Phototeque; 541, 547–548, MSA; 552, MS; 554, 562, MSA; 566, MS; 568, MSA; 571, Phototeque; 576–577, MSA; 584, MS; 590, 596, MSA. All stills from "SHANE" (1953). A Paramount Pictures Corporation Production; 602, Photo by Andy Gregg, 607, (top left) © Phedon Salou Artephot, Paris, (bottom right) from Rudolf Von Ems: *Chronique Mondiale* der Stricker: *Charlemagne* (1982)/ courtesy Editions Faksimile-Verlag Lucerne, (top right) *Two warriors,* Attic, black-figured amphora, c. 535, B.C., H. L. Pierce Fund, Courtesy Museum of Fine Arts, Boston, (bottom right) Jim Brandenburg/WCA; 612–613, Michael Holford, Essex, Eng.; 614, © Phedon Salou/Artephot, Paris; 616, (both) Hirmer Photo Archive, Munich; 621, © Artephot, Paris/Candelier-Brumaire; 624, 626, (top) S/AR; 627, M. Tzovaras/AR; 629, S/AR; 632, Photo by Ken Pelka, NY/AR; 637, Kavaler/AR; 644, Jim Brandenburg/WCA; 646, (both) WFA; 647, Copyright University Museum of National Antiquities, Oslo, Norway; 652, (top) WFA; 652, (bottom) Copyright University Museum of National Antiquities, Oslo, Norway; 653, Copyright 1932 and renewed 1960 by Random House, Inc. Reprinted from *Beowulf,* by permission of Random House, Inc./Photo by Robert D. Rubic; 655, WFA: 656, Giraudon/AR; 664, 667, from Rudolf Von Ems: *Chronique Mondiale* der Stricker: *Charlemagne* (1982)/Courtesy Editions Faksimile-Verlag Lucerne.

INDEX OF AUTHORS AND TITLES

The page numbers in italics indicate where a brief biography of the author is located.

0
1
2
F 3
G 4
H 5
I 6
J 7